Of Mists and Monsoons

ADELE SMITH

ISBN 10-1645502864
ISBN 13-9781645502869

God help the poor! Behold yon famished lad,
No shoes, nor hose, his wounded feet protect,
With limping gait, and looks so dreary sad,
He wanders onward, stopping to inspect
Each window, stored with articles of food.
He yearns but to enjoy one cheering meal;
Oh! To the hungry palate viands rude,
Would yield a zest the famished only feel!
He now devours a crust of mouldy bread;
With teeth and hands the precious boon is torn;
Unmindful of the storm that round his head
Impetuous sweeps. God help thee, child forlorn!
God help the poor.

From a poem by Bamford

Chapter 1

The sky was a clear cerulean blue. Daniel O'Malley squinted at the sun as he tried to spot the lark that was pouring out its song, dipping and rising in the overheated air. He used his kerchief wound round his neck to mop his streaming brow, as he seated himself on a handy boulder by the side of his field. In that year of 1831, the weather had been good for the potato crop; spring rains followed by warm summer days, and Daniel gazed sideways at the neat rows of potato haulms standing up above the rich earth, promising a harvest that would keep his family fed throughout the long winter. Daniel's face was a medley of lines and creases; for all that he had passed his fortieth year not too long ago. Years of working out in all weathers had taken their toll. But it was a kindly face, with a slightly pointed chin and warm hazel eyes, enlivened by a sparkle and edged by spreading creases that spoke of a man much given to laughter.

His gaze shifted towards the west where the verdant land fell away and leveled into a lush valley. High above him a spring bubbled out of the ground, and cascaded down the hillside as a stream, debouching into a lough as the slope leveled out. At the far end of the lough, the stream enriched an endless stretch of bog land, where the efforts of turf cutters could be seen in the long lines of exposed brown scars, in sharp contrast to the emerald green of the marshes. To the east, far beyond his gaze tumbled the grey, green waters of the Irish Sea, for his village of Clonarty was but five miles from that rocky coastline.

It was a sight that always gladdened his eyes, but a low rumble in his belly reminded him that he was hungry, and that his lunch was long overdue! The sound of a girl's high pitched giggle reached his ears, and turning his gaze to the village below, he saw a young maid, teetering on the brink of womanhood, and surrounded by a group of four or five young men. Daniel's forehead creased into a frown as he beheld his eldest child, the apple of his eye, his daughter Kate. She was sixteen years old and as slender as a wand, with her budding breasts just beginning to strain the front of her dress. Her skirts were short, testimony to a spurt of growth during the last year, and slender ankles and calves peeped from below the hem. Red gold hair cascaded down her back, and she tossed it back over her slight shoulders as she threw her head back again to laugh, the sound trilling through the air to where her father sat. Daniel frowned again as he gazed; where had his baby daughter gone? Impatiently he shouted,

'Kate, Kate, where are my victuals. Haven't I worked hard enough to feed you that you cannot be bothered to do the same for me?'

Kate looked up and waved cheerfully. 'Coming Pa', and with another wave to the circle of youths, she started to run up the hill to where her father sat fuming. She reached him and dropped a kiss in his upturned face, and plopped down beside him on the boulder.

'Oh Pa, I was just talking to..'

'So I saw' her father growled, 'and here am I dying for lack of food!'

Kate chuckled, and handed over a bundle of potatoes, still in their skins and tossed in buttermilk. She also handed him an earthenware crock of buttermilk, kept cool in the stream which trickled by their shebeen. She gazed at her father adoringly as he ate in silence, knowing that he couldn't stay angry with her for long. He studied her heart shaped face, with its brilliant blue eyes, and outlined by the cascading red gold hair. She was so like his own Eileen, whom he had courted and won when she was not much older than this one. But then they had waited four, long anxious years before she had quickened with their firstborn, his Kate. And now she was sixteen, and ready to be courted in her turn. He sighed deeply, prompting a quizzical look from Kate

'What ails you Pa? It is such a beautiful day, and you are such a grouch!'

'I was just wondering where the years have flown, a cara, you have such a look of your Ma', Daniel replied seriously.

Kate laughed again, and began to tease him out of his megrims, recounting some of the ridiculous things the youths said to her to as she had made her way up the hill to him.

The pair sat in comfortable companionship, until a shadow fell across them. They both looked up, startled, for they had heard no sound of approach. A young man, with intense brown eyes, stood gazing down at them. His sun browned face had a brooding look, but strong planes and angles topped by a shock of dark, almost black hair, one lock of which fell onto his forehead, gave him a romantic Byronic look.

'Oh it's you, Pat' noted Kate, 'I didn't hear you'.

Pat O'Hara just stood and gazed down at her intently, until Kate shifted uncomfortably on her stone seat.

'What ails you lad', said Daniel, impatiently, anxious to be rid of the dour youth and enjoy the company of his daughter.

'Sure, I was wonderin'' stammered the lad 'would Kate walk aways with me'. Daniel smiled inwardly at the young man's anguish, but took pity on him.

'You'd better ask her yourself', he answered gruffly; 'she no longer listens to her Pa!' 'Oh Pa', put in Kate, but surprising herself, said, 'I would like to walk with you, Pat.'

She jumped up from the rock, and swiftly kissing her father's cheek, stood waiting for Pat to move. But he just stood still, apparently stunned by her acquiescence.

'Ah, ah, yes', was all he managed to stammer, and began to move away, angling up the hillside to follow the course of the stream.

Daniel watched them go, a worried frown creasing his forehead.

'What could Kate possibly see in yon miserable face?' He asked himself, 'and her so full of life and fun. Ah well, she must've taken pity on the young man just like her Mam in that an' all'.

So saying, he rose from his stone seat, and went back to the row of potatoes he had been tending when he had stopped to eat. His trusty 'spud', his trench digging tool, was useful in so many ways, and he made short work of the row. By the time he had finished, and hefted his spud onto his shoulder, he had forgotten about his forebodings about Kate, and Pat, and all the other young men who were taking more than a little, unhealthy interest in her.

As Kate and Pat climbed the hill, listening to the gentle burble of the water as it slipped and slid over the pebbly bottom, Kate wondered if Pat was actually going to speak. She had known him all her life, and knew him to be taciturn to the point of rudeness. Like her father, she wondered why she had agreed to walk with him, but as she had looked up into his face, she had caught a glimpse of a pleading look he had given, and thought 'why, he is only shy'!

'It is so peaceful up here' Kate ventured.

'Aye' came back.

'Do you often come up here?'

'Aye'.

'If that is all you have to say, why did you ask me to walk with you?' Kate asked, tartly.

Pat stopped, and turned to look down into her tip tilted face, taking in the clear blue eyes, broad, intelligent brow, and cascading red gold hair.

'I…I…think you are beautiful, Kate'.

Kate was stunned for a moment, but suppressing an urge to giggle she replied 'thank you Pat, that is a lovely thing to say!'

They continued on with their walk, reaching the top of the hill, and came across a wall that surrounded an estate. Their absentee landlord owned the mansion, its high walls and turrets hidden in the depths of extensive grounds, and forbidden to his tenant farmers. In his absence, the estate was run by his agent, O'Leary, who carried out his duties with ruthless efficiency. Suddenly, as if a damn had burst, Pat spoke eloquently and bitterly about the system of absentee, Protestant landlords, who took their wealth from the backs of their subsistence farmers. Kate listened fascinated as he waxed lyrical as to how one day all the Catholic farmers would rise up as one and drive away their oppressors, and take back that which was stolen by the hated conquerors at the time of Cromwell and the Battle of the Boyne. Kate was fascinated, having had no inkling that Pat harboured such thoughts, and had no idea where had he gleaned all his information. They had halted by a spreading oak tree that had spread so much in girth that it had encroached on the six foot high wall that surrounded the estate. He smiled down into Kate's enthralled eyes, and her heart lurched as she saw for the first time how handsome he was when he smiled.

'Don't you feel the same' he queried.

'I haven't thought on it' she truthfully replied.

'Come' he said, and held his hand out to her.' She took it trustingly and allowed him to help her clamber into the lower branches of the oak, and thence onto the top of the wall. He jumped down the other side, and held his arms up to her. She dropped into his waiting arms, and for a moment, he held her close, but at the growing alarm in her eyes, released her.

'We shouldn't be in here' said Kate worriedly.

'It's alright; I often come up her when I want to be alone. O'Leary is too busy checking that we are all working to keep him and his master in the state they believe they are entitled'. The plants and animals in here are very different to the ones we see over there' tossing his head towards the wall.

Pat then showed Kate all of his favourite places, smiling at her 'oohs' and 'aahs'. They spied a small herd of roe deer, grazing under some trees, and so tame that they did not take fright and speed away. Kate was enthralled, but still anxious about their trespassing, so finally, Pat led her back to the wall, and helped her over. They wandered back down, again following the stream until they reached the lough close by to Kate's home. Pat turned to her,

'Will you walk with me again?' he whispered.

'Yes …. Yes I will' Kate whispered in response, and then she was gone, disappearing under the low doorway of the shebeen where she lived with her parents and siblings. Pat stood gazing at the doorway, as if hoping she would reappear, but eventually he turned away towards his own home, where his father and three brothers waited, a home devoid of a woman's touch, or any joy and laughter.

Chapter 2

Throughout that long, hot summer Pat courted Kate, in the face of opposition from her former admirers, notably Conor Murphy, who considered Kate to be his personal property. They had grown up together, and he had watched the enchanting child, with gangly legs, wild hair and pert tongue grow into a beautiful young woman. But Conor had a roving eye, and he was not yet ready to commit himself. He was aware that Kate was attracted to him, as she hung on his words, and gave him sly glances from beneath her sweeping lashes. But suddenly she was snatched away by, of all people, the dour Pat O'Hara. Conor couldn't believe that his fun loving, vibrant Kate would even spare a glance at such a miserable specimen as Pat, and concluded that she was simply teasing him with her apparent interest in the surly youth. So Conor did not waste an opportunity to mock Pat in Kate's presence, and to flirt outrageously with her whenever Pat was nearby, noting delightedly that it drew scowls from the long suffering Pat.

Towards the end of that long summer, on a day when the heat seemed to hang in the air, Kate sat herself by the lough, dangling her feet in the water in an attempt to keep cool. Conor threw himself down beside her, and started to pay her outrageous compliments. Glancing up, Conor noticed Pat approaching from the hillside. Full of devilment, Conor leaned forward to whisper in Kate's ear, nuzzling her and making her giggle. Pat stiffened, and then with a roar of rage, hurled himself at Conor, pushing Kate onto the grass as he passed. Kate sat up indignantly, and watched the two young men wrestling in the water.

'Stop it' she cried, her hand to her heart, but in time honoured fashion, she secretly enjoyed the sight of two lusty young men fighting over her!

Very soon, attracted by the noise, others from the village rushed to the lough, and shouted encouragement to Conor to 'show him what he was made of!' Children shrieked with laughter, and even the older members of the village came to see what the hubbub was about! The battle raged, with both contestants trying to gain the upper hand. They had locked their arms around each others waists, as they heaved and strained, trying to throw their opponent into the water. Conor was the taller of the two, but Pat was stockier, and had desperation on his side. And Conor's heart was not engaged, as was his, and he fought with a red mist before his eyes. It seemed for a while that Conor was gradually gaining the upper hand, when suddenly Pat loosened his hold on Conor's waist, slid a step sideways, and hooked his leg behind Conor's ankle. Conor, thrown off balance, fell on his back in the water, and immediately Pat threw himself on top of him, pushing his head back until his mouth was covered. The audience, thoroughly enjoying the skirmish, cheered and shouted for Conor to turn the tables on the unpopular Pat. It seemed to Kate that she was the only one aware that the situation had suddenly become fraught with danger, and Pat was close to herself at Pat, screaming at him to let go. Daniel saw too, what was happening, and came to her aid, alarmed by the look in Pat's eyes. As suddenly as he had thrown Conor, Pat released him, and stood back, head down and chest heaving.

Kate shook his arm, and screamed at him, 'you could have killed him; how could you, he was only talking to me!'

Pat looked up then, and into her eyes, seeing the anger there. Without a word, or a glance at Conor, sitting up now, and drawing ragged breaths, he strode out of the lough and disappeared up the hill; seeking refuge in the only place he could find peace; running from the look in Kate's eyes.

For several days, Pat was not seen in Clonarty, and rumours abounded that he had taken himself off to Dublin to find work, leaving his father and brothers to tend to their fields. But late in August, as harvesting of the potato crop was about to begin, Kate was waylaid by a contrite and anguished Pat.

'Walk with me, let me explain' he whispered.

'You could have killed him' Kate retorted.

'I know. I don't know what came over me. I saw him.....'

'You saw him talking to me; he was doing nothing to deserve what you did.'

'Please forgive me, it will never happen again'.

Kate was ready to walk away, still angry at the fright she had had. But she looked at Pat properly for the first time, and saw the torment in his eyes as he believed he had lost her forever. She relented, and agreed to walk with him, up the hill to their favourite trysting place. Once there, Pat leaned against the mighty oak and spoke of his hopes and fears, and that his life would not be worth living if she turned from him.

'I have never loved anyone as I love you, Kate, and will never again; you are my life!'

'Hush' said Kate, 'you must not say such things. You have a family, a father, brothers...'

Pat shook his head. He had never spoken of his home life, of the sombre, brooding man who had fathered him, and caused the death of his mother many years before. He could not tell Kate of these things; she would likely not believe him. He could only hope against hope.

Finally Kate looked into his tortured brown eyes, and said, 'Pat, if you ever lose your temper again like that, I don't believe we can go on. You frightened me sorely. You must promise me that it will never happen again.'

Pat could only mutely nod, and gathering Kate to his chest, mumbled into her hair that he promised on all that he held dear that he would never lose his temper again.

So Pat resumed his courtship, taking care to keep a tight rein on his temper. He sought Conor out soon after making his peace with Kate, and apologised. Conor generously accepted the olive branch, even extending his hand to shake. In truth, he knew he had provoked the man, not realising the depth of his feelings. The young men would never be friends, but they agreed to call a truce.

For the rest of the summer, and well into autumn, he took Kate up to the estate on the hill, showing her every corner of the gardens and outhouses, even the mansion itself, though Kate was fearful of discovery.

From the dense shrubberies, they watched an army of servants tend to the sweeping lawns and tidy flowerbeds. They saw uniformed maids and grooms go in and out of the house, the place bustling with activity.

Kate was puzzled, 'so many servants for one person?'

'Especially when that person doesn't live there most of the time!' retorted Pat, 'and how do you think all his staff get paid? By the sweat of our labours to provide him with rents, that's how!'

Another day, they again spied the small herd of roe deer grazing underneath a spreading chestnut tree, so tame that they hardly noticed their watchers. Kate was enthralled, having never seen the delicate creatures so close before, and Pat declined to tell her that the herd was there to provide sport in the form of hunting if ever their landlord graced his Irish home.

It was on that day that Pat looked into Kate's wide eyes, and gently brought is mouth down onto hers. Kate was startled at first, but then relaxed, as powerful feelings swept through her, leaving her dizzy and shaken. Pat lifted his head, and smiled into her eyes, making Kate quiver with emotion. She had never experience such feelings before, and she was moved to the depths of her being. Again, Pat explored Kate's mouth gently with his own, his tongue probing softly as she closed her eyes, giving herself up to her emotions.

When the weather finally turned too cold to walk out, they sat companionably in Kate's home, while the family chattered around them, warming themselves by the peat fire, kept going night and day for warmth and for cooking the potatoes. Strangely, they never sat in Pat's home, but Kate was too happy to question the reason.

Then in the spring, as the flowers started to bloom on the hillside, and birds began to herald the coming of the new season, Pat asked Kate to marry him. They were at their 'trysting place', the mighty oak that had witnessed much of their courtship. Kate was silent for a moment, remembering the fear she had experienced that dreadful day at the lough. But since then, Pat had caused her no fears and alarms. He was unfailingly gentle and kind with her, and she loved the exploring they had done together, and his extensive knowledge of the world around her. Even when she spoke to Conor, he did not betray any anger or temper. She looked up into his melting brown eyes, and brushed the tumbled lock of hair from his forehead.

'Yes Pat, I will marry you'.

Chapter 3

Kate sped home, bursting into the cottage that had been her home for sixteen long, happy years.

'Ma, Pa, Pat has asked me to marry him.' Seizing her father round the waist, she whirled him around, causing imminent danger to the crude but crowded contents of the low roofed building.

'Kate, Kate' scolded her mother, as she grabbed earthenware crocks, and clutched them to her ample breasts out of harm's way! 'Hush now, girl, and tell us about this nonsense you bring?'

'It's true, Ma, he's asked me and I said yes!"

'He has not asked me' grumbled Daniel, 'he should have come to me first'.

'Oh Pa', and Kate whirled him around again. Then she rushed out of the cottage, searching for her sister Mari, with whom she shared all her secrets. She found Mari near the lough, minding a trio of unruly boys, their brothers, who were bent on hurling clods of mud at each other. Mari, two years younger than Kate, was almost a carbon copy of her. But her eyes were not such an intense blue, and her hair was a paler version. But she was pretty enough.

'Oh Mari' whispered Kate, hugging her sister with affection. 'It's Pat. He has asked me to marry him, and I have said 'yes'!' The sisters seized hands and swung themselves around, nearly tipping their brothers into the lough in the process. Laughing, they sank to the ground while Mari bombarded Kate with questions.

The news spread like wildfire, and the young women of Clonarty were soon crowding round Kate, oohing and aahing as she retold the story of her proposal. Suddenly, Conor was there, frowning before her, demanding attention. He took her hand and led her away from the chattering knot of girls. He made no pretence of his anger as he stared into her upturned face, as if seeing her for the first time.

'You cannot be serious, my Kate. You know you were meant for me. What do you see in that miserable specimen?'

'You have no right to speak to me this way' retorted Kate. It is nothing to do with you who I marry. An' how dare you speak about Pat that way'

'Indeed it is' flung back Conor, 'you know full well that you were meant to marry me!'

'And who decided that? I don't remember you asking me, an' if you had, the answer would have been no! Pat is a good man, an' he loves me.'

'But so do I' breathed Conor softly, 'so do I'.

Kate spun on her heels and walked away, choked with emotion. She remembered the days when she had chased after Conor, hoping against hope for a kindly word or an admiring glance. But all she had ever received had been taunts and teasing.

'You are too late, Conor Murphy,' she muttered under her breath. 'Just too late; perhaps if you had told me sooner?'

The months sped by, and Daniel and Eileen became reconciled to the fact that their eldest, and tacitly accepted, favourite daughter, was to marry a man that they had never managed to become close to. They were a close knit family, which easily showed their love for each other. They could not understand Kate's adoration for such an apparently dour person, for they had never heard him speak of his thoughts and theories with such passion, when his face, normally in sullen repose, became alive. They had never witnessed the smile that lit his brown eyes, and then melted when they looked into Kate's.

But they accepted their daughter's choice; indeed there was little else they could do in the face of her determination, and they had no wish to alienate her. Then one day in mid-summer, Daniel escorted his wife and daughter the ten long miles to Dublin town. He had some coins squirreled away from selling eggs and cash crops, and he had promised his exuberant Kate that she would be married in clothes fit for the 'Queen of England'. Kate laughed, skipping away, so clearly full of happiness that their hearts too, filled to overflowing. The journey flew by, and soon they were close to the town, and searching for the Quaker shop. This emporium run by the 'Friends' would allow them to buy clothes that they could not otherwise afford, as these kindly folk collected the cast off garments of the gentry, and sold them for a few pence to help the beleaguered poor, for it was sure that no-one else would!

Kate was, for once, rendered speechless at the pile of clothes in front of her. A soft shift and a russet overdress in a dense, lustrous weave, which would enrich her rippling red gold hair, would suffice as wedding clothes. The kindly ladies added a pair of soft shoes, noting that Kate was not used to wearing shoes, and they didn't want to mar her day.

'Oh Pa' breathed Kate, 'can you…?

'Hush girl, I don't expect to fit you out more than once!' Daniel tried to look stern, but failed dismally. He also added a fustian skirt for his wife, only too aware that it was many years since he had bought her anything new, with so many hungry mouths to feed. But soon it would be Pat's business to feed and clothe his new, young wife, and if a father couldn't spoil his favourite daughter once in a while, where would he be?

The happy trio walked back to Clonarty, laughing and chattering, and planning the day. The villagers would all help with food, as they always did when one of their own got married.

Then one morning in the dying days of August, Kate emerged from her parents' cottage, and ran barefooted to the lough, hand in hand with her sister, Mari. She wanted to bathe before anyone else stirred, and indeed, she was much too restless to sleep for it was her wedding day. Mari helped her strip to her old shift, and immerse herself in the chill waters of the lough. Kate gasped as the water came up to her small breasts, but Mari laughed, and using the pan she had brought for the purpose, emptied the bowl over Kate's head. She rubbed a tiny piece of soap, another gift from the Quaker ladies, into the rippling tresses and then ladled clean water onto her sister's head. Finally, as Kate stepped onto the bank, wound her in a soft piece of cotton, twining her arm around her waist, held her close as they went back to their home. Mari was saddened by the thought that she and Kate would no longer lie together in the night and share their secrets. And Kate, too, was saddened by the thought that it would be the last time she would call it home!

There they found Eileen, but no-one else. All of her siblings, except Mari, had been dispatched to a neighbour. Tomos and Michael, Bernadette and Theresa, and the irrepressible Fergus, had all disappeared so that she could get ready. Mari rubbed her hair dry, and polished it, until the curls shone like burnished silk. She had already fashioned a chaplet of late summer flowers, and this she placed on her sister's head, standing back with her head cocked to one side to survey the effect. Eileen took Kate's wet shift and rubbed the girl's body until it glowed pink in the light of the peat fire. Then she slipped the soft, new shift over her head, and followed it by the russet dress. Finally she cinched the impossibly small waist with a plaited girdle, and she and Mari stepped back to survey the effect. Kate held her breath, looking anxiously at her mother and sister, until their faces softened into loving smiles. Eileen gathered her firstborn to her breast and whispered in her ear,

'You are beautiful, my Kate. Be happy with the man you have chosen.'

Mari, too, gave her a hug, and they ducked through the low door, blinking in the sudden sunlight.

Chapter 4

When Kate emerged into the sunshine of that late August morning, it seemed that the whole world had gathered to see her marry Patrick O'Hara. All the Clonarty families were there, including those who had migrated to other villages through their own marriages, but now returned to support her. Conor Murphy was there, flanked by his brothers, Liam and Dominic. The O'Connells, the O'Sullivans, the Donaghs with their numerous progeny, and many, many more, crowded the village centre, so all Kate could see was a blur of smiling faces. She could make out the face of Pat's father, Kevin, sour and wizened like an old apple, and looking much older than his forty years; even on this, his son's wedding day, he was grim and unsmiling. With him, and shuffling their feet nervously, were his other three sons, Pat's brothers, Seth, Calum and Michael, cowed and repressed in the presence of their father. As the crowd shifted and swayed, she spotted her mother chatting to old Bridget, the village midwife; Mari marshalling her siblings while Fergus was already planning mischief among the legs of the assembled villagers.

Then she felt a hand on her arm, and turned to see Daniel by her side, a broad grin creasing his face, as sunny and good natured as Kevin O'Hara was gloomy and dour. Daniel tucked her small hand into the crook of his elbow, and bent to whisper,

'Are you ready a cara?' Kate nodded.

The crowd parted as if by magic, and beyond them she could see Pat standing next to Father Muldoon. The old priest, his lined face crowned by white hair, tonsured naturally by age, looked towards Kate and gave her a beaming smile; he so loved to marry or baptize his parishioners. Daniel and Kate started towards the two men, as voices from the crowd whispered how beautiful was the bride, glowing in her russet dress, the colour of the autumn bracken. But it was not towards the priest that Kate looked, but at the man who stood by him, tall and handsome, his dark hair tamed by lough water, save for one curl that flopped onto his broad forehead in a suitably romantic fashion. His brown eyes smouldered with suppressed emotion as he caught sight of his lovely bride, moving towards him on her father's arm. He had also visited the Quaker store with his hard earned coins, and stood resplendent in black breeches, snowy white shirt and brogues on his feet. The shoes were slightly too small, and were cruelly pinching feet unused to shoes, but he would have walked on burning peat at that moment. Kate felt a familiar lurch behind her breastbone, and her very bones seemed unable to support her as she moved to his side. Pat held his hand out to her, and Daniel felt her spirit go from him to the young man, and his father's heart broke as he gave her up. Pat and Kate heard Father Muldoon's voice, as though through a mist, as he began the Nuptial Mass,

'In the name of the Father and of the Son and of the Holy Ghost.'

The sound of a fiddle wielded by expert hands filled the air, as couples swirled in the dust of the village centre. Young ones laughed and chattered as their elders circled in more stately fashion. They all loved a ceilidh, and hardly needed the excuse of a wedding to forget the harshness of their lives if only for a few short hours. Children screamed with high spirits, running between the legs of their elders. Food and drink had been generously donated by everyone present, regardless of possible shortages later; not a soul among them would have begrudged the two young people about to start a new life together. Men huddled in groups, sampling he poteen distilled somewhere high in the hills by Conor's father, a useful supplement to his family, for he was a lazy farmer!

Sometime in the afternoon, Kate, who had not missed a single dance, found herself whirled off her feet by Conor. He set her down and looked into her flushed face, with errant curls escaping from her chaplet of flowers and whispered softly,

'Why didn't you wait, me darling Kat, you know I wanted you?'

Kate gazed up into his eyes, blue as her own, set in his handsome, rugged face, though softer featured than Pat. She felt a momentary pang of regret as she imagined married life with this man, devoid of the turbulence of her courtship by Pat. But the moment was gone like a zephyr, for Conor might feel affection for her, but it was his pride rather than his emotions that were bruised.

'I'm sorry Conor, but you see, you forgot to tell me how you felt!'

Conor gave a shout of laughter, and swung her off her feet, earning him a scowl from Pat. But later, Kate saw him dance with Mari, holding her close and whispering in her ear, and knew she had been right. Whatever Conor might claim, his heart had not been touched by her defection.

It was towards evening, when the revelers were beginning to tire that they heard horses approaching, an event rare enough to bring the dancing to an abrupt halt. The fiddler carried on playing, unaware that his audience was distracted, until the tense atmosphere reached him, and he ceased with an eldritch screech. They saw a young man in his mid-twenties, dressed in expensive and fashionable clothes astride a glossy chestnut mare. His face above a high, starched collar would have been handsome in a florid, high coloured fashion, if it had not been set in a sullen scowl. But it was the presence of his companion, Agent O'Leary on his moth eaten cob that told them that the handsome young man was none other than their landlord, come to visit them from across the Irish Sea instead of keeping himself decently away from them like his forbears. The two men on horseback were accompanied by half a dozen men on foot, with brutish faces and armed with blackthorn shillelaghs. These were cutthroats from out of the district, hired as bodyguards to protect the precious person of the unwelcome visitor.

The presence of Lord Danforth in his estates in Ireland was not from choice, as his usual haunts were in the fashionable streets of London town.

But a foolish and illegal duel fought in the dawn mists of Hampstead Heath, over a lady of uncertain morals and equally uncertain age had left his opponent with a ball lodged in his chest and fighting for his life. Charles Danforth had perforce to flee the country while his erstwhile rival either recovered or gave up his fight for life. If the former, he planned to return as furtively as he left, but if the latter, he would be involved in a lengthy and costly battle to clear his name. He reasoned that he might as well look over his Irish estates and see if he could not wring some more income from them as he was a man of expensive tastes!

What he had seen so far had not lifted the mood of black depression that had descended as he had left London. All he had seen was ragged peasants in malodorous cottages surrounded by potato fields, barely wresting enough from the soil to pay their rents that had not risen for many a year, He had chosen this day to visit Clonarty, the last of his tenancies, but found himself in the midst of some sort of celebration. The villagers stood in sullen silence, waiting for their unwelcome visitor to take himself off and away to his mansion on the hill. They dare not show any outward sign of their true feelings, as awful retribution could follow. O'Leary spoke, his voice sharpened by nervousness as he had borne the brunt of his Lordship's temper for several days now,

'What's goin' on here, why aren't you about raisin' your crops instead of drinking 'n dancing in the middle of the day?'

Charles Danforth looked about him, his spirits lifting a little as he noticed that this group of villagers seemed better dressed and cleaner than those he encountered already. He guessed that the occasion was a wedding, and the bride, distinguished by a crude chaplet in her glorious red gold hair, was by far the prettiest he had seen, and he was a man susceptible to feminine beauty! He thought briefly and wistfully on the long forgotten 'droit de seigneur', but felt it expedient to suppress such thoughts if he wished to survive his impromptu exile. Inclined to be magnanimous on such a sunny and festive day, he fumbled in his purse that hung at is waist, and flung a handful of coins at the feet of the bride,

'A wedding gift for the loveliest bride I've ever seen, even in England!'

His words met with a stony silence, and Danforth felt a frisson of fear, as though a chill wind had swept through the village. O'Leary whispered nervously,

'They haven't much English, your honour'.

Danforth felt the black depression descend again,

'A pox on you and your stinking village, your hovel and your everlasting rain', he shouted, and set spurs to his horse. Villagers scrambled to avoid the hooves of the chestnut mare as the party moved up the hill towards the mansion, O'Leary scowling fiercely at these people who would cause him to receive a tongue lashing before the day was out.

Kate stared down at the coins at her feet, but made no move to pick them up. She, like all the others understood full well what had been said, though they preferred not to use the hated English. Suddenly she shook herself and tossed back her glorious hair,

'Will we let the dirty English spoil me wedding? Pat, you've yet to dance with your wife', and she lifted her arms to her scowling husband. The fiddler struck up a lively jig, and very soon everyone was dancing again, determined not to let the visitation ruin the day. The coins remained where they had been flung, for all that they could have spared them hardship in the future. No-one wanted to soil themselves with the English coins, and within a very short time, they were ground into the dirt by the dancing feet, and as they disappeared, the lighthearted mood returned. Kate danced with renewed energy in her softly slippered feet, though she laughed when she noticed that Pat had kicked off his smart brogues!

Chapter 5

The sun was sinking behind the hill when Pat took Kate's hand to lead her away from the ceilidh. Children were being gathered up, yawning and quarrelsome, their parents anxious to rest feet that had danced the afternoon away. Father Muldoon had long since gone to his cottage in nearby Clarne, accompanied by members of his flock. Pat led her to where her family waited, gathered together, dreading the impending separation. Eileen looked deep into her daughter's face, and then enfolded her to her ample bosom.

'Be happy, my Kate', she whispered.

'I will, Ma, I will'.

Then it was Daniel, with tears in his eyes as he held her close,

'A cara, my little one; don't forget yer old Pa!'

Kate felt her throat swell and she hugged this man, who had been the only one in her life for sixteen years.

'Pa, you know you will always be my very best man!'

'Hush now, and go to that husband of yours'.

Kate hugged them all, Mari, who had done so much for her this day; Tomos and Michael, blushing as their sister kissed their downy cheeks; Bernadette and Theresa, hand in hand as always, and finally Fergus. He fought as she swept him up and kissed him soundly on both cheeks before setting him down again, laughing at his furious expression.

She turned to find Pat, who was with his father and brothers. No hugs in this group, not even from his father. Pat shrugged; it was after all what he had always known. His brothers solemnly shook his hand, wishing they could hug their older brother; wishing they could tell him how much they would miss him, and wishing that they could come and live with him and his enchanting bride. But nothing was said.

And then it was time to make their way to their cottage on the edge of the village. A shebeen lovingly built by Pat and his brothers during the months since Kate had promised to marry him. A simple structure, like all the cottages, it was made of mud and straw, with a low doorway, and thatched untidily. Even if Pat had the means to make a better place for his bride, he would not, as that would bring O'Leary sniffing round and insisting he pay more rent, 'for didn't he have the wherewithal to pay more, with all this grandeur?' He had vowed as he worked, that he would make it snug inside, with wooden furniture, and a pen to house a pig when he could have one of the piglets due any day to his father's sow. But for now, there was a simple bracken bed, a three legged stool and little else.

As they strolled through the village, the couple was greeted on all sides by the villagers, wishing them a long and happy life, with more ribald suggestions coming from the young men. Conor was the only who held back, sadness in his eyes as he watched the pair climb a slight rise to their new abode. He had meant what he had said to Kate; for all that she had not believed him. He had loved her, and had been waiting for her to be old enough before declaring his feelings, only to find her snatched away by Patrick O'Hara. But it was too late, and Conor was nothing if not pragmatic. Mari was almost as beautiful as her sister after all and only had eyes for him! Perhaps he would woo her; some time!

Kate and Pat walked in silence, their thoughts turning to the night ahead. They knew what to expect; how could they not, living in such close proximity to their parents, and their nighttime activities. How could they not, when the boar, come visiting to serve the sows grunted and screamed his passion as he heaved and strained. They knew, but they did not speak of it. They were agonisingly shy of each other.

They ducked their heads to enter the shebeen, and Kate caught her breath. Someone had been in before them, and had lit a peat fire, its warm glow lighting the simple space. And thrown onto the bracken bed was a pair of woolen blankets, and a shawl, crocheted from soft lamb's wool.

'Ma?' breathed Kate, and then as she saw an earthenware bowl by the bed, filled with flowers picked from alongside the stream, 'Mari?'

Pat scowled, angry that she so easily assumed that the gifts were from her family, and that she had guessed right, as he had not thought of such gestures. Suddenly it was all too much, the cottage seeming to close in on him.

'Come' he said gruffly, and took Kate's hand.

Frowning in puzzlement, Kate did not resist, as he drew her out of the cottage and started upwards by the stream. The sun had gone, but a full moon was rising and lit their way as they took the well worn path. After a while they found themselves retracing their steps of that day long ago in April, when they had fallen in love, and later in June when that love was threatened. Gradually the familiarity of the scene and memories of past emotion helped them through their barrier of constraint. Finally they reached the top, and headed towards the walls of the estate, towards their 'trysting' oak, with its leaves just beginning to turn brown at the edges. They reached the shelter of the branches, and saw a glow in the sky as the big house was lit by a myriad candles, outshining the stars appearing above them in honour of its distinguished arrival. Pat shook his fist in the direction of the glow, remembering Danforth's appearance that afternoon and the arrogant way he had looked down at his tenants.

'One day', he muttered, 'One day. He and his kind will get their just deserts'.

Then he felt a small hand creep into his, and looked down into the face of his wife. She looked up at him, with love glowing in the blue eyes, darkened now in the moonlight.

'Not tonight Pat, he is not important.'

Pat took Kate's face between his hands and drank in the heart shaped face; the long lashed blue eyes, the high cheekbones, and the cascading red gold hair. He gently covered her mouth with his and kissed her, long and deeply, parting her lips gently with his tongue. He felt her tiny gasp, and her body trembling against his. Fire coursed through his body as his manhood awoke, and the need for her became compelling. He had held himself back all the months of their courtship, but now he allowed his instincts to break free. He brought his hand up to her breast, and caressed it through the soft fabric of her gown. Kneading and caressing, he felt her body seeming to melt into him.

'Kate, oh Kate, I've wanted you so long'.

Pat gently lowered his bride onto the soft turf, too impatient now to return to the cottage. He pulled the ruined chaplet out of her tumbling curls and buried his face into their soft shining mass, smelling the scent of the flowers and herbs that had rested there. He loosened the laces that held up her russet dress, and unclasped the girdle. Kate lay before him in her shift, her eyes darkened with unknown sensations.

'I love you Pat' she whispered as he kissed her again, exploring with his tongue deep in her mouth. He stood up to loosen his clothes, and shed the restricting breeches. Kate gazed at him with wonder dawning in her eyes, and held her arms out to him. Pat came down to her with a groan, releasing her breasts from the restriction of the shift and teasing her erect nipples. He lifted the shift and gently, so very gently, entered her. He felt her gasp, and cry out as he felt her resistance to his passage. And then the resistance was gone and she started to move with him. He held himself back as best he could but then it was over, as his passion spent itself inside her.

'Kate, Kate…. Oh Kate'.

Chapter 6

Kate giggled, in a state somewhere between sleeping and waking. An errant stalk from their bracken bed had found its way onto the gray blanket and was tickling her nose. At first it became part of a lovely dream, in which Pat was covering her face with light kisses. But the scratchy stalk intruded, rousing her to reluctant wakefulness. She opened her eyes drowsily and saw that a new day was just beginning as a ray of sunshine lit up the top corner of the low doorway. It was March, a full six months since her wedding day, and spring was beginning to shake off the megrims of winter. The sun was very welcome, with its first appearance for many a long dank, dreary week. The weather had been cold and bleak that winter and occasionally stormy, but there had been little snow.

Kate turned onto her back, lazily observing a spider, rimmed with gold in the shaft of sunlight. It was attempting to start a web across the doorway, and Kate marveled at its tenacity as it tried to swing itself across the gap to secure a silken line. Time and again it failed, and in unconscious empathy with a the long dead Scottish Robert the Bruce, Kate silently applauded as at last the line was firmly anchored, and the web finally begun.

Growing bored, Kate turned again onto her side, and contemplated Pat's features as he lay flat on his back, snoring gently. The strong, clean lines of his profile, and dark hair tousled in sleep, caused the same, strange sensation behind her breastbone as that far off day, high on Clonarty Hill. She sighed deeply as she looked back over the months since then. How wrong everyone had been about him; he had been a kind and thoughtful husband. And the passion that had flared on their wedding night had grown to such heights and Kate blushed to think of their nights together.

Their early months together had been taken up with harvesting the various crops. Having none of their own, the couple had helped their respective parents in return for a share of their bounty. At the time of their wedding, the grain harvest had been in, and most of the early potatoes had been lifted. But there was threshing to be done, and later the big 'lumpers' had been lifted, and it was these large potatoes that would supply the main sustenance during the year to come, carefully stored in a pit and covered with dried peat. The 'cash crops' had been dispatched to Dublin's market to raise the money needed for the annual rents and to allow for a few luxuries. The harvest had been good, and Charles Danforth had not raised their rents, so the village of Clonarty breathed a collective sigh of relief, and began to plan for the year to come.

Pat had then turned his attention to the fields his father had allocated to him. These had been fallow for a number of years, and needed some backbreaking work to get them ready for planting. He had turned them over roughly, ready for the winter frosts to break the sods to fine tilth. He had dragged a crude sled to the coast, five miles to the east, and hauled back load after load of seaweed, to spread on the fields as fertiliser. By the time winter winds swirled down the hill, to nip toes and noses, Pat and Kate had cut a stack of peats from the nearby bog, and stacked them outside their cottage.

Forced, then, to stay inside for days on end, Pat and Kate turned their crude shelter into a home. Using his sled, Pat had dragged some of the rocks that scattered the fields, and piled them outside the cottage. From them he fashioned a hearth and chimney to draw the smoke out of the cottage. At the far end, he constructed a pen to house the piglet promised from his father's sow that had farrowed around the end of November, and was even now growing apace on scraps thrown to it after their meals. The manure from the growing sow piglet was raked outside and allowed to pile up near the door, ready to spread onto the fields later in the year.

Finally, Pat turned his hand to woodworking, and fashioned bowls, spoons, stools, and innumerable other items for his wife, for he had inherited a skill as a woodcarver from his father. Kate's drowsy eyes wandered round the cottage, and a smile curved her rosy lips as she counted all the things Pat had made for her, many embellished with intricate carvings, making them into things of beauty.

But there was small cloud that marred the sunshine of those months together; so far she had not quickened with Pat's child. She yearned for a baby of her own; a miniature Pat that she could love and cherish, and raise in the home they had created together, but so far there had been no sign of conception. Anxious questioning of her mother merely brought a chuckle and a warm hug, for Eileen reminded her that she had waited four long years for Kate herself to make an appearance; though Eileen remarked ruefully, that she had made up for lost time since! And, continued Eileen, seeing Kate's crestfallen face, she was more than welcome to practice on her brothers and sisters, especially Fergus who was growing more of a handful with each passing day! Kate had laughingly rejected the offer, and had been comforted, though her body still ached for motherhood. Then a delicious thought popped into her head, for was there not only one way to make babies after all?

Armed with the bracken stalk that had awoken her, Kate leaned over Pat, and gently tickled his ear, but apart from a slight intake of breath, there seemed to be little effect. She leaned over once more, but suddenly found herself flat on her back with her arms pinned by her side, and Pat leaning over her scowling fiercely. Kate felt a small frisson of fear scurry up her spine, but then saw the twinkle lurking in the depths of his brown eyes,

'Ah, so you're awake at last, you lazy lummox', Kate simpered up at him, 'the sun's been up a long while and it's about time you were gone to your fields!'

By way if reply, Pat slid his hands under the blanket, and began to caress her sleek hips and thighs. Presently the hands slid up to her breasts and began to fondle her nipple, bringing it erect as Kate gave a gasp. Seeing that she was beginning to be aroused, he moved away from her slightly and whispered,

'So, I'll be off to the fields then?'

Kate's breathing was coming in ragged gasps, and she seized his arms in a vice like grip, then wound her arms around his neck and drew his mouth down to hers in a long, lingering kiss. The spider was an uninterested spectator as Pat slowly drew her shift over her head and studied his beautiful wife, watching her face as he entered her, saw her eyes open wide as he moved, gently at first and then with increasing ardour as she joined with him, until they climaxed together, and then lay still.

Warm and sated from their loving, Kate trailed her fingers across Pat's chest and twined them in the hair that curled vigorously round his navel. She remembered her earlier daydreaming, and putting her lips close to his ear, whispered,

'Wouldn't it be lovely if we had a babe, Pat? If we had a son he would look just like you!'

By way of reply, Pat heaved himself up abruptly, donned his shirt and breeches, and without a word, ducked under the low doorway and made his way to the earth privy he had dug behind the house. Bewildered, Kate called after him,

'Pat, Pat, what's the matter? Don't you want something to eat before you go?'

There was no reply, and she was left puzzled by Pat's abrupt change of mood. It had been so good between then until she had mentioned a wanting a baby. She considered that thought, but then shook her head determinedly,

'Can't be that. All men want a son of their own. Doubtless he had a pain in his belly!'

Shaking off doubts, she set about tidying the cottage, and feeding the young sow, who grunted happily at her. Later she would talk it over with Mam. She might be a married woman herself but she still thought of her mother as the fount of all wisdom and knowledge!

If Kate did not understand Pat's abrupt change of mood, neither did the man himself! He simply did not understand the sudden surge of anger that had swept over him at the mention of a baby. He had caught sight of Kate's startled expression, and knew that he had to get out of the cottage before he said something that would really hurt her. He had realised in a flash of intuition, that the very idea of sharing her with anyone else was repugnant, even a child of his own blood! After leaving the privy, Pat made his way up the hill to his fields, ready to work the anger out his system. The weather had obviously taken a turn for the better, and there was a hint of warmth in the air. It was time to complete the digging and start to create rows of trenches to receive the seed potatoes once all threat of frost had passed. He saw without really seeing that a number of his neighbours were heading in the same direction. They called out greetings as he passed by, but he did not acknowledge them, earning scowls of disapproval. Then they shrugged their shoulders and got on with their business, for they were more than used to the surly O'Hara's?

Pat reached his fields and gazed at them sightlessly for a while, but quickly realised that he could not concentrate on them that day. He turned and headed further up the hill, following the stream high above the fields, tracing his usual path to the Danforth estates. Once there, he leaned against the bole of 'their' oak tree, just beginning to show fat buds ready to burst forth with spring freshness. He tried to fathom out his emotions, and let his thoughts drift to the first person in his life that he had ever loved; and lost – his mother. He could remember her so clearly, though he had been only six years old when she died. She had had a gentle oval face, with a fall of straight brown hair, and brown eyes that had always had the slightly anxious expression that could be seen on the seals that swam off the beaches of the Irish Sea.

Briginne had grown up in the nearby village of Kilgarth, the eldest of a brood of seven children. Kevin O'Hara had been returning from market in Dublin one day, and had been caught in a sudden downpour of rain as he passed through the village. He had sought shelter in the nearest cottage, and with the customary Irish hospitality, had been welcomed inside to share the family meal. By the time he resumed his journey, he had requested the hand of Briginne from her parents, who were only too happy to accept, for they had too many mouths to feed, and Kevin looked to be a prosperous enough young man. Kevin had been on the look out for a quiet, biddable wife, as he had recently inherited his father's farm. Briginne had not been consulted, and had not voiced an opinion, though in truth she was nervous of her black browed suitor! Within three months she was married and pregnant with her first child.

Pat was a big baby, and a breech presentation. It had taken all the skill of the Clonarty midwife, Brigid's predecessor, to save the mother and child. But after many hours of agonizing labour, Briginne was finally delivered. She barely had the strength to suckle her child, but as her milk dried up, she found she was pregnant again!

This child miscarried at four months, with a loss of blood Briginne could not afford. Her slight, frail body was weakened further, and anxious neighbours spoke quietly to Father O'Flaherty when he visited his flock in Clonarty. The kindly old man sat down with Kevin, and over a pipe or two, spoke of restraint, and that a woman's body was a holy grail, and should be looked on with reverence rather than a breeding machine, especially when that body seemed to be so weak. Kevin turned on the priest, and told him brusquely to 'mind his own business' and 'keep his nose where it belonged, in his prayer book'. The affronted priest took himself off, and told the neighbours to keep a look out for Briginne, for he feared for her.

Two more boys were born in the space of two years, and by this time Briginne O'Hara looked like a woman of forty rather than the twenty three that she was. Pat adored his mother, and as he grew older, he tried to help her, and reduce her burden, without really understanding why he needed to. When Kevin was out in his fields, the cottage was a peaceful place, and Briginne would sing in a husky voice to her young sons, and play finger games with them. But when the doorway darkened with Kevin's return, fear returned with him, for he was ever ready with his belt to chastise them. The boys learned early in life that their best defense was silence.

When Pat was nearly six years old, his mother became pregnant again, and managed somehow to carry the baby to full term. Throughout the pregnancy she had ailed, but had forced to continue with her normal chores, and caring for her three sons. Neighbours who came to offer help were turned away with a snarl by Kevin. Up on the hillside of Clonarty, Pat shuddered as he remembered his mother screaming with the long, protracted labour. The midwife fought valiantly to ease the passage of the child, for it was another big baby, another son, and at last it was born. Exhausted by her struggles, Briginne lay as white as a ghost as she haemorrhaged; her life blood and spirit draining away together. When Kevin was told of his wife's death, he had merely shrugged and prepared to raise his sons alone. The only help he would accept in the days following his wife's demise was milk from a villager who had recently given birth and had plenty to spare for the motherless infant. But after that he managed alone. The boys were fed, housed and clothed, for Kevin was a successful farmer and made extra money from selling carved wooden household goods. But he never showed them affection by way of a gesture, a touch or a word. They were his sons and they would do as they were told.

The young Pat, already shy and withdrawn, became more introverted as the years passed, and he took the habit of escaping the cottage and wandering the hills around Clonarty, finding beauty and peace in the lush Irish countryside. He always completed his tasks before going, as he did not wish to court his father's ready temper. He became a good husbandman by observing his father, but appeared bitter and morose to those he met.

And it was so on that fateful day less than a year ago that he had looked, really looked at Kate O'Malley, as she sat with her father. Oh yes, he had noticed her growing up among the pack of Clonarty children, a leggy brat with tangled red hair and dirty face. And he had envied her, with her easy laughter as she raced around in endless games of tag. But that day, well, it had been like the sun coming out after along, dark winter, and Pat had fallen hopelessly, helplessly in love. No-one could have been more surprised than he, when he had found the courage to speak to her, and ask her to walk with him, and she had accepted! Even after the walk, when Pat had opened his heart to her, just a little, there had still been some constraint. He had feared that she would spread his inmost thoughts to all the others that she normally ran with; but she had not. Instead she had returned his love wholeheartedly.

But cruelly, as he his love deepened, Pat found in himself a fierce jealousy towards anyone who showed her affection; her mother, her father, even young Fergus whom she would swing high into the air and spin around. He thought he had managed to hide such base feelings when he had come across Conor Murphy sitting close and seemingly nuzzling her ear. A red mist had fallen over his eyes, and he could not remember anything until he had been dragged away forcibly. Pat knew at that moment that he was capable of killing another man, and he was shaken to the core of his being. Worse, he had seen the contempt in her eyes, and believed he had lost her forever. He thought that she would reject him, but the miracle had happened, and instead she had married him.

The months since their wedding had been the happiest of his whole life. He could even blank out memories of Briginne for days on end, while he worked for his bride at home or in the fields. He kept his jealousy under firm control, not reacting when Kate was her usual affectionate self to her family and friends. But suddenly she had caught him unawares with her talk of a baby; talk of another creature that would claw its way into her heart and take the love that was due to him. Being deprived of his mother so young, Pat could not remember Briginne' love expanding as her new sons came along, while Pat himself was her first born, her first love! Pat groaned aloud at the thought, but gradually he became calmer and more rational, and as sense returned, he acknowledged to himself that he could lose her if he did not show some understanding, for what woman did not want a baby of her own? And was it not lovemaking that caused conception, and that was the cornerstone of their marriage? Memories of nights, with Kate wrapped in his arms, and returning passion for passion. And yet, Pat reasoned cunningly, many couples never had children, and Kate was very young after all! Somewhat comforted, he prepared to return to the cottage and reassure her that all was well. Suddenly he saw her, coming up the hill towards the tree.

'Kate, Kate,' he shouted.

She looked up and started to run, straight into his arms.

'Where've you been? I've been looking all over for you. What are you doing up here?'

'I just felt like a walk. I had the gripes this morning when I got up.'

Reassured, Kate let herself be enfolded in his close embrace, resting her head in the hollow of his shoulder, and told herself she was making a fuss about nothing. Pat rocked her gently back and forth, but his eyes gazed into the distance, they were cold and bleak as the Irish Sea on a gloomy, winter's day!

Chapter 7

The potato haulms stood proud in their trenches, marching along in serried rows along the gentle slope of the hill Spring rains followed by warm sunshine had raised the crop to a respectable height already, and Kate, hoeing out the worst of the weeds, thought that they had the best crop in the whole of Clonarty. Pat was behind her, pulling earth up almost to the top of the haulms, for he believed that the longer the potato tops stayed below ground, the bigger his final crop would be. Kate was perfectly willing to believe this, as Pat certainly seemed to have a magic touch with all growing things.

But she had more reason to feel lighthearted this day, for in her heart she believed that she was with child. Lately, her breasts had felt very tender, and throbbed at the slightest touch. And once or twice lately, when she had risen from her bed, she had felt nauseous to the extent that she had had to rush out to the dugout privy behind the cottage. She felt sure that these were good signs, but she hugged the knowledge to herself as she worked along the row, humming quietly to herself. She wanted to be sure before she said anything to Pat, not willing to admit as yet, that she was reluctant to do so. The one person she needed to turn to for advice was her mother, and just then she saw Eileen making her way to the loughside with Kate's younger brothers and sisters. It was the ideal opportunity to have a cosy chat.

'Pat, I'm just away to see me Mam,' she called to Pat, setting down her hoe. She turned away with a cheery wave as she spoke, and so did not see the scowl that crossed Pat's face, or hear the muttered,

'Always running off to her mother; why can't she stay where she belongs, next to her husband?'

Kate found Eileen sprawled by the water's edge, keeping a lazy eye on her offspring, in the company of some of her neighbours. Kate gazed fondly at the older woman, and gave her a fulsome hug of welcome. She thought how much closer she felt to her mother since she had been married. Eileen was nearing forty years of age, and constant childbearing had robbed her figure of its shape and her skin of its suppleness. But her face was attractive in its gentleness, and her bosom comfortable enough for any small child to find succour there. Nearly all of her family was by the lough, except Mari, who was 'walking out' with Conor Murphy, and it was widely considered that another O'Malley wedding was in the air. Young Fergus had grown in height and mischief since Kate's wedding, and even now was busy running in to the water as fast as he could, throwing up sheets of spray and shrieking with laughter as he did so. He was not often allowed into the lough for his mother feared the deeper water. He had been found in there once by his father, and tanned to an inch of his hide, a rare event in the O'Malley household, so he had not repeated the experiment. But with so many adults about, his mother had taken pity on him and allowed him into the shallows.

Tomos and Michael, both teetering on the brink of adolescence, with voices ranging from descant to bass within the space of a sentence, were busy searching for frogs to hide in their shirts and then track down their sister Mari, busy with her swain, and drop them down the back of her dress!

Bernadette and Theresa, as close as twins, and still in the magical years of childhood, were closely examining the shoreline, wrapped in a fantasy in which the marks they observed were the footprints of the 'little people' whose stories they had grown up with, curled up on their father's lap in the long summer evenings.

'What a day,' puffed Kate, as she plopped down onto the grass next to Eileen, 'when was it ever as hot as this?'

Eileen smiled at her eldest daughter, always happy to see her.

'Look at that Fergus,' laughed Kate, 'where does he find his energy?'

'Where's your Pat?' asked Eileen, 'doesn't he know better than to be out in the heat of the day? It's not good for a man to be out in this hot sun!'

'He's alright, Mam. I just wanted to talk to you, ask you....'

Eileen glanced at her daughter's flushed face, and noted the glow of her skin, and the aura of vital health. She suspected what was on her daughters mind, but waited patiently for Kate to ask in her own time.

'How...how... would I know....how is it that... how would I know if I was with child?' Kate managed to blurt out at last. Eileen smiled at her confusion but said gently,

'When did you last see your flow?'

'Ah,' said Kate, 'of course!'

She thought this over a while before answering, as she was inclined to be careless on these matters, but finally,

'It was just before the potato planting.'

'Hmm, any other signs?'

Kate described her various symptoms, and Eileen pronounced firmly that she was indeed expecting a baby. And she clasped Kate to her bosom, shedding a few happy tears, which started Kate off. The two women discussed the likely time when Kate's baby was due. Eileen was not gifted with counting, but long experience of her own and others' pregnancies made her decide Christmas or early in the New Year. She then, in time honoured fashion of long time mothers, fell to recounting all the calamities that could befall a woman in childbirth, breech delivery, haemorrhages, milk fever.... Kate's eyes widened in horror, until. With a laugh, she called a halt to the fearful reminiscing,

'Whist, Mam or you'll be scaring me half to death!'

Eileen chuckled, but desisted, 'We could call old Fiddler Finigin next time he's by, and have a ceilidh in honour of the little one; what d'ye think, child?'

Kate was silent for a moment, mulling over the idea, when Pat's brooding face crossed her mind,

'No. Let's wait a while, I...I haven't told Pat yet, you see. There's plenty of time after all!'

In truth, Kate was not sure how Pat would take the news after the strange way he had acted when she had broached the subject before. They had not discussed the matter since that day he had stormed out of the cottage, and though she had managed to convince herself that all was well, now .... well now she was not so sure. Eileen sighed, troubled for her daughter, and for the look of sadness that had replaced the earlier joy. But she believed that married couples should work out their own destinies, and it was not for a mother, no matter how loving, to interfere.

'Ah well, child, you take your time and …..'

Whatever Eileen might have said was drowned by a succession of shrieks; high pitched girlish ones followed by the cracked laughter of young males, and finally a bloodcurdling scream that ended in a loud splash. Kate and Eileen jumped to their feet and looked aghast at the lough, where they could just see the top of Fergus' head disappearing under the water. Kate acted swiftly and wading into the water, grabbed a handful of hair and dragged the yelling child back to the bank.

Everyone talked at once; the girls claiming that Tomos and Michael had dropped frogs down their dresses, and the boys, far from denying the charge, argued that the girls were too silly for words, and what harm would a frog do after all? But the fact was that the girls' shrieks had distracted Fergus in the act of running into the lough, and causing him to misjudge his run, trip and tumble into deep water. Peace finally descended, and the boys were severely admonished and told to take their mischief elsewhere. This they were happy to do, for their chief victim, Mari, had not yet been tracked down. They had merely practiced on the girls by way of preparation for the real thing! The girls were finally placated and calmed by the promise of one of Pa's stories that evening, and Fergus was forcibly stripped of his clothes to dry in the sun, and within minutes he had renewed his game with unabated energy in spite of his dunking. The neighbours had all drawn close when the shrieking had begun, and were busy chattering among themselves, so there was no further opportunity for mother and daughter to speak of the burgeoning pregnancy.

Kate kept her news to herself for several days, not at all sure how to break it to Pat. She knew that she must speak soon, as he was sure to notice the changes in her body. Already her breasts strained at her bodice and though she could detect no swelling of her abdomen, it was only a matter of time. But she really did not comprehend her reluctance to speak, for did not every man yearn for a child of his own, especially if that child was a son? In truth they had had no secrets from each other before this, talking of every subject under the sun, but this….. Kate sighed deeply. And then she decided on a ploy as old as time itself; she would soften Pat with a good supper and drink, and then give him the news when he was relaxed and mellow.

Once she had decided her strategy, Kate felt her spirits lift, and she put her plans into action that very day, anxious now to tell Pat, and move on in harmony together. She walked to the nearby village of Kilgarth and accomplished some judicious bargaining, exchanging early potatoes for some cheese and bacon. Her own hens were laying well, and would provide some eggs for the feast.

Finally, she detoured on her way home to visit old man Murphy, Conor's father. She felt like a criminal as she sought him out in the hills behind Clonarty, where he kept moonshine still. It was not supposed to exist as brewing of the lethal stuff was highly illegal, but it was the best kept secret for many miles around. She found Murphy dozing, but at the sound of her soft footfall, one eye opened, and he gave her a quizzical look.

'What brings you here, lass,' he growled at her, 'does yer Pat know yer by?'

Kate stood nervously at the entrance to the hideout, its entrance disguised as a natural cave, and its still buried deep in the hillside, with only a tell tale wisp of smoke and steam emanating further up the hill hinting at the secret buried beneath it. She twisted her hands and explained her mission, the purchase of a small flask of poteen, for hadn't Pat been working so hard for many a day, and didn't she want to surprise him with her gift. Murphy merely grunted and handed over the flask in exchange for a packet of new potatoes. If he was surprised he did not show it, for he knew full well of the Daniel O'Malley's hatred for of the fiery brew, and his louring disapproval of those who made use of it. He also knew full well that Daniel's family had been raised to think the same. But he raised a questioning eyebrow when Kate stammered,

'Don't be telling Pat, will you? I do so want to surprise him.'

Murphy gave her a wink and a leer, and patted her hand in avuncular manner as he waved her away, before settling himself back to doze the afternoon away.

The next day dawned bright and clear, and Pat departed for his fields as usual. He noted the air of subdued excitement about his wife, but put it down to the news that had broken only yesterday that Conor and Mari had 'named the day' and another O'Malley wedding was in the planning. He was privately relieved that Conor was now spoken for, as he was convinced that Kate secretly hankered after her old flame, though in truth she had given him no cause. Whistling to himself, he set off with a loving kiss, leaving Kate to her preparations. By evening, all was ready. A veritable feast of bacon, cheese and eggs nestled on a platter, surrounded by a circle of early potatoes, cooked in their skins ad tossed in a little precious salt and buttermilk. The flask of poteen rested close by, dew gathering on the earthenware as it had been all day cooling in a bowl of water hidden in the shadows. Kate had washed herself and her hair carefully, bringing water from the lough back home, and emptying it into a wooden trough, fashioned by Pat himself, for he knew how Kate liked to cleanse herself regularly. She combed her hair until it gleamed in the glow of the peat fire and the fading sun peeking through the low doorway. She looked beautiful and she knew it, her pregnancy giving her skin a pearly sheen of youthful health and fecundity.

Pat ducked under the low doorway, drawing back in amazement as he saw the feast laid out, and his wife glowing with healthy vitally and utter beauty.

'What's this then? Have I missed a feast day?'

'No,' replied Kate, laughing.

'Maybe a wedding? Did Conor and Mari get married today?'

'No.'

'A wake?'

'No. I just wanted to celebrate – us,' answered Kate, 'Sit you down and I'll do your supper directly. You have worked so hard all these days, Pat, an' I just wanted to make a special evening – just you and I.'

When they had eaten and drunk their fill, Pat of the poteen, which had surprised him for he knew his wife did not approve of it, and Kate of some buttermilk, Pat leaned back on his stool and lit a clay pipe with some of his precious store of tobacco. He was filled with contentment; could a man ask for more than a beautiful, loving wife, a full belly and a smallholding that was flourishing, rewarding him for all his backbreaking work; he sighed with pleasure. He began to think fondly of their bracken bed in the corner, and of taking Kate to it, and, perhaps…? Kate leaned against his knee, her chin resting on it, Pat's hand gently stroking the gleaming red gold mass,

'Pat.'

'Mm'

'I've some wonderful news for you.'

'Mm'

'We're to have baby in the New Year.'

Pat's hand ceased its stroking, and his body stiffened. The cottage suddenly felt chilled, as though an icy wind had swept through it. Kate looked up at Pat's face in alarm, and saw the face of a stranger, cold and forbidding, with eyes like two black pits. He rose so abruptly that Kate fell sideways to the floor. Ignoring her, he headed for the door and disappeared into the evening. As he went, Kate's arm reached out in supplication, but he did not see it. In the distance, a rumble of thunder could be heard, effectively drowning her cry of anguish,

'Pat, Pat, tell me what's wrong for pity's sake!'

But there was no reply from the empty doorway. Kate's arm fell back, sweeping the crocks from the table, so lovingly prepared that day. She thought of going to her usual source of comfort, but reasoned that if Pat returned, it would only aggravate him that she had 'run to mammy' as he often accused her. No; she would have to deal with this herself. She dragged herself to the bed, and curled up like a foetus, around her own growing infant. She rocked herself to sleep, sobbing heartbrokenly. Towards dawn, she woke to find herself alone. Cold and stiff, she pulled up the blanket, and cradling her stomach, vowed,

'Don't worry, little one, I love you, and you will want for nothing as long as I live!'

She fell asleep again, comforted by her own inner strength, and did not wake again until the sun was high.

When he left the cottage, Pat took his usual path up the hill, blindly letting his feet take him where they would. He found himself by their 'trysting tree', the mighty oak that spread its branches over the wall of the Danforth estate. He shook his head to clear it. What was he doing there? In anger he smashed his fist against the bole of the tree, and the pain of his ruined hand finally jerked him back to reality. A vision of Kate rose in his head, and he groaned; Kate, his Kate, was going to have a child; a creature that would take her arms, her breast and her love. He swore soundly, and looked about him. He could see a few lights in the mansion, but mostly it was in darkness, its master long gone, back to the headier delights of London society. Further away were the lights of Agent O'Leary's cottage, where he lived with his slovenly woman and a brood of children. Further away still were the cruder huts of the thugs O'Leary hired to protect him as he went about Danforth business.

Another clap of thunder rent the air, and a few large spots of rain fell on Pat's unprotected head. He looked around for shelter, and scrambled over the wall, using the oak's branches to help him. As he approached the main house, he spotted an outbuilding with its door slightly ajar, and squeezing through, he found himself in a storehouse, with shelves stacked with jars of all shapes and sizes. Pat grinned mirthlessly as he recognised the distinctive size and shape of Murphy's brew. He reached down a jar, meaning to take a small pull; one that would not later be noticed. But the raw spirit soothed the pain in his heart, and later in his hand, and later still, the tempestuous thoughts that crowded his head. When the storm finally broke over the outhouse, it highlighted the sprawling body of an unconscious man, an empty jar of poteen lying on its side. The man murmured in his sleep,

'Kate, Kate.' And then he was silent.

Chapter 8

Kate could hear the wind raging outside the cottage as she woke from a sound sleep. She lay quietly for a few moments, not at all sure what had disturbed her. Then it came again, an ache low down in her back. She sighed; this had been the first night for many weeks that she had been able to get to sleep without the baby becoming boisterously active as soon as she lay down. She sighed again and turned over; trying to find a comfortable position for her swollen belly, for it was early January and close to the time when she believed her baby would be born. By her side, Pat lay flat on his snoring stertorously, his breath reeking of poteen, an all too familiar condition these days, or so it seemed to Kate.

As Kate tossed restlessly, she thought over how long it had been so. Pat had returned to the cottage the day after she had announced her pregnancy with a sore head and sorer temper. He had not told her where he had gone, and she resisted questioning him, fearful of rousing his temper. Since that day, he had not spoken of the coming baby at all; indeed, their free and easy relationship all but vanished. She thought he had lost all feelings for her, for on the rare occasions he chose to couple with her, it was done without tenderness, and usually when he came home the worse for drink. Twice he had turned her roughly to him as she lay dozing on the bracken bed, forced her knees apart, and without preamble had entered her. She had lain, mute and still as he grunted and heaved on her, until at last he climaxed; rolling away from her without a word. Kate had been left, sore and aching, a tear trickling down her face and wondering how such a crude act could be termed 'lovemaking'. But even that small attention had ceased as her body swelled, and he looked away from her when she removed her dress to bathe herself, seemingly finding her fecund body distasteful. More lately, he had spent more time away from home than in it, either in the fields, or gone some place where there seemed to be an endless of poteen.

Kate had been left alone so much that she began to spend more and more time with her family, playing with Fergus, or taking long walks with her sisters to the seashore, or up in the hills. Once she had seen Pat climbing the oak and disappearing over the wall in the grounds of the mansion and in spite of his cruel treatment of her, her heart had leapt to her throat as she thought of the danger he was putting himself in. If her parents wondered why she was with them so much, they didn't say, waiting for her to speak if she wished, steadfastly believing that she and Pat must work things out for themselves. But it had not escaped their notice that his fields were not tended as carefully as the previous year, and that Pat was often seen staggering back to the village late in the evening. Their hearts ached for their daughter, so they welcomed her when she appeared, but kept their counsel.

The weather had been mild and wet right up until Christmas, with sweeping mists that settled like a blanket on the valley, paying 'peek-a-boo' with the goats sent out to graze on the lush grass at the valley bottom. Christmas Day had brought an improvement, and the day had dawned bright and clear, with a crisp tang of frost just before dawn. But the sun had risen and the warmth had melted the frost, and chased away the lingering wraiths of mist. Father Muldoon had arrived, suitably mounted on a donkey, to celebrate the Christmas Mass. The air was so pleasant that all stood outside to sing their Christmas songs, their voices resounding around the hills above them. Later, families visited each other, bearing small gifts, especially where there were small children in the cottage. It should have been a happy time, sighed Kate to herself as she shifted her position yet again, the pain in her back become more persistent. But it had merely served to remind her of the happiness she had felt the year before, and she found it hard to join in with her family's festivities, try as she might. And none of them had breathed a word about Pat's absence, that day that should have been for her own small family!

But after that day, the weather had changed again, the wind veering round to the east, bringing icy blasts that crept into the smallest nook and cranny of their cottages, usually so snug with their endlessly burning peat fires. It nipped at fingers and toes, and froze the dew drop on Agent O'Leary's nose when he came to collect his year end rents. The villagers shivered in their scanty clothes, huddling together for warmth in their cottages, only venturing out if strictly necessary, for there was no work to be done in the fields. Even Pat stayed in his cottage, busying himself with carving more utensils, averting his gaze from Kate's swollen body and answering her timid questions in monosyllables. But that day he had taken advantage of a slight lessening of the wind and had disappeared for several hours, reappearing at sunset, lurching under the low door, and reeking of poteen.

The wind had picked up again that night, and seemed bent on destruction, as Kate listened to its keening round the cottage. The ache in her back grew steadily stronger, then for the first time, she felt a tightening sensation across her belly. Suddenly, she gave a chuckle; of course, her baby was anxious to be born! She lay quietly for a while, savouring the thought of the imminent arrival, reluctant to move lest she let an icy draught into the bed, but after a while, the pain grew more insistent, and she began to feel more than a little frightened.

'Pat, Pat' as she shook his shoulder, 'fetch me Mam, quick, the baby's coming!'

She shook him again, more fiercely, feeling him stir at last in response.

'Wha.. whas the matter?' came Pat's slurred voice.

'Quick Pat, the baby!'

The urgency in Kate's voice finally penetrated his drink fuddled brain, and he started up wildly, heedless of the cold blast of air that hit him. Throwing a piece of blanket around his shoulders, Pat stumbled to the door, and disappeared outside. He staggered the short distance to the O'Malley's cottage and ducked inside, stumbling over recumbent bodies, and managing to rouse the whole family.

'Who's there? What is it?' came the voice of Daniel from the dim light of the peat fire.

'It's Kate, the babe's coming. For God's sake help her,' shouted Pat.

Eileen got herself out of her bed, exclaiming at the cold, and seizing a piece of sacking, prepared to go out into the night.

'Don't worry, Pat. She's young and strong; she'll be fine presently. Rest you here until it's born.' And she was gone into the night.

Reaching Pat and Kate's cottage, Eileen stooped to enter, and saw Kate's face bleached white with fear in the glow of the fire.

'Gently, child, there's nothing to worry about, there's plenty of time yet.'

Eileen soothed the girl until she lay back again, and then was able to examine her and assess how far labour had progressed. Satisfying herself that there was indeed plenty of time, she busied herself about the place, stoking up the fire to keep out the worst of the east wind, and warm up a great iron pot of water. She had brought some herbs with her, long prepared in preparation of this day, as she intended to infuse some tea which would ease the worst of the labour pangs as they grew fiercer towards the end. She debated with herself whether to call for old Brigid, the midwife, but it seemed too cruel to drag her out on such an inclement night, when everything was progressing as it should. Kate lay much calmer now, soothed by her mother's presence.

Encouraged by Eileen, she tried to breathe through her contractions instead of fighting them. The night wore on, and the two women talked quietly or held hands during the contractions, which slowly increased in intensity, until the light began to grow outside and peek through the low door, and it was clear that the birth was not far off. Eileen drew Kate's knees up, and propped her back against a bracken bundle,

'Right now, me Kate, it's time to push this baby into the world; come on now, push, push!'

Kate's face went crimson with effort, as she responded to her mother's urging, and Eileen could just make out the crown of the baby's head. With more encouragement, the head was born, and Kate lay back panting.

'One more push, that's me girl, come on now.' And the baby slithered out into Eileen's eager hands. She wasted no time, with cold draughts sweeping round her as she tied off the cord, cut it, and wrapped the infant in a piece of soft material. She placed the baby, now crying lustily, into Kate's arms, saying,

'There you are, me darlin' girl, you have a handsome boy, so you have.' Kate lay back, sighing with contentment, all the hard work and pain forgotten the moment she gazed into her son's face, which was crumpled and red as he yelled his indignation at being thrust out into a cold world.

His head was streaked with birth blood, but she could see a fuzz of reddish hair, and she just knew that later he would open eyes as blue as her own.

'Sean, my little one,' breathed Kate, 'you are beautiful!'

Eileen busied herself, seeing to the afterbirth as it appeared, and gently washed Kate. Taking the baby from her, she laid him gently down beside his mother, and then helped Kate into a clean shift, and replaced the soiled bedding. After all the activity, she suddenly felt weary, but didn't want to leave her daughter alone. She looked down at the girl, hardly more than a child herself, gazing adoringly at her newborn son,

'Where's Pat, Mam? Is he waiting to see me? Will you shout for him to see his son?'

Kate's voice drifted away as she fell into a light doze, Sean cradled in her arms. Eileen went to the cottage entrance and peered out. She saw Daniel standing outside their cottage and looking anxiously up at her, so she waved him over. Of Pat, she saw no sign. Daniel hurried over to be given the wonderful news of his first grandchild, and a grandson at that! His seamed face broke into a delighted smile and he peeped in to see his daughter sleeping peacefully with the new born babe tucked up in her arms.

'Where is he?' demanded Eileen. Daniel shrugged,

'He stayed 'til daybreak, and then went off up there,' jerking his head towards the hill. 'I don't understand the man; you'd think he'd be over the moon with his first son; an' he don't even know it yet!'

Eileen nodded. What could she say? She understood Pat no better than her husband, and she felt infinity of sadness for Kate sleeping so peacefully.

After Pat had roused Eileen to attend to Kate, he had slumped by the O'Malley fire, his head whirling as he fought the effects of the poteen. The rest of the family had settled back to sleep, all except Daniel who fretted about his daughter and her coming ordeal, though he had perfect confidence in Eileen's skill as a midwife. Nevertheless, there were so many hazards for women in childbirth. He glanced over at Pat, sitting by the glow of the fire,

'Don't worry, lad, she'll come through all right!'

Pat looked up, then,

'But what happens after … I mean ….. will she still care ….. or will she just want the babe … I don't know, I could lose her..?'

His voice trailed off. Daniel stared in complete perplexity. What was the lad talking about? What did he mean by 'losing her to the babe? Daniel had never suffered such doubts; he had loved Eileen wholeheartedly, and had welcomed each of his children in turn. Luckily, Pat did not need a reply as he had closed his eyes and appeared to be dozing. As the sky lightened outside, the howling wind seemed to die away, and there was a perceptible rise in temperature. Pat roused himself and looked outside.

'I'll just go and see how she is,' he muttered, slipping out of the low door. He lurched the short distance to his home, and then stopped abruptly as he heard Kate cry out in pain as the climax of the birth approached. His face turned paper white, and he turned and stumbled away, up the hill; away from the village and the sounds of Kate's pain.

All through that day, visitors came and went to the O'Hara's cottage for the news of the new arrival soon got around. Kate had slept a while, and had woken refreshed to see the smiling face of her sister Mari, who was cuddling her brand new nephew. She had come to give Eileen a chance to return home and rest awhile, though she had promised to return soon. The two young women chatted in their old, easy way, exchanging news and gossip, and gazing admiringly at the crumpled face of the infant, snugly swaddled in a woolen blanket. Mari took the chance to talk about the wedding she and Conor were planning for the spring. Then their younger sisters, Bernadette and Theresa arrived, cooing and gurgling over the baby until they managed to wake him up, and the cottage was filled with his lusty cries. Eileen then reappeared and chased them all away, so that Kate could put Sean to her breast for the first time. She would never forget the moment when she felt the first tug of her son's mouth on her nipple and the sense of primeval joy that coursed through her body.

Later still, her brothers, Tomos and Michael appeared with a reluctant Fergus in tow. He looked at the new arrival, pronounced him to be very boring, and when would he be ready to get up and play with him, and why this, and why that until Eileen chased them away again. Kate lay, enjoying the bustle, and enjoying being in her mother's charge again, for all that she was a mother herself!

Neighbours called by, bearing small gifts; some warm material to swaddle the infant, milk and eggs for his mother, and most precious of all, their good wishes, and blessings. And all the while, Kate's eyes strayed to the door, and every visitor brought a look of hope that faded as they entered, for all she was pleased with all the attention. Eileen watched her with troubled eyes, for she knew what Kate yearned for, and cursed the man that was causing her such pain. Towards evening, there was a lull in the stream of visitors, and Kate whispered to her mother,

'Where is he, am, why doesn't he come?'

'Hush child, he'll be here soon.'

And as she spoke, they heard footsteps outside the door, and then Pat ducked into the cottage, his face paper white, and his eyes anxious. He didn't notice Eileen in the shadows, but came to Kate's bedside and gazed down at her. She returned his gaze a little fearfully, though she noted with relief that he seemed to be sober. Indeed, he had gone to his store after running from Kate's cries, but had not broached the supply. Instead he had passed the day huddled in the storeroom of the mansion, wrestling with his troubled thoughts and his terror at the thought of losing Kate in childbirth; her screams convincing him that she would surely die. At his son, he did not look. Kate held out her free hand, and he fell to his knees beside the bed, and he buried his head in her shoulder, hiding himself in her glorious red gold hair,

'I'm sorry …Kate ……I love you so, please forgive me.'

Kate stroked his head gently and sighed. With a wisdom beyond her years and experience, she knew that she had two children to care for, but only one would grow up!

Presently, the three on the bed fell asleep; baby, Sean, with the wise old look of the new born; Pat with his face temporarily wiped clean of its lines of anguish; and Kate the eternal mother. Eileen looked at the three of them and prepared to leave. Her work was done. She offered up a silent prayer that all would be well in the O'Hara household, but in spite of her indomitable Irish optimism, she had serious misgivings for the future.

Chapter 9

Young Sean O'Hara throve from the moment of his birth, nourished by his mother's abundant milk, kneading and gasping at her full breasts. She carried him everywhere with her, secure in the folds of her shawl, ready to suckle him whenever he so much as whimpered. She crooned lullabies to him when he was fretful, circling him in her warm maternalism. He soon shed the ancient, crumpled look of the new born, and had a smooth clear skin; the downy fuzz on his head that later grew into bright, coppery curls, and his eyes were the same startling blue as Kate's own. He was a contented baby. When he was not enfolded in Kate's shawl, he would lie in a basket fashioned from reeds collected by the loughside, and lovingly fashioned into a bassinet by Kate herself, sucking his thumb or playing with his toes and gurgling infant nonsense to himself. Later, as the weather grew warmer, Kate would put his basket outside the door of the cottage to catch the sunshine, and every passer-by felt obliged to stop and exchange burbled nonsense with him, to which he would chuckle fatly.

By the age of three months he could hold his head up sturdily, and by six months could sit for a while, before toppling sideways. By the next harvest he was crawling about the dirt outside the cottage, and giving Kate palpitations at the speed at which he would set off across the village, invariably making for the lough. Fortunately for Kate, Sean had self appointed guardian angels in the shape of his aunts, Bernadette and Theresa, who forgot about their 'little people' in order to mind their own, very special little person. By the time the year was out, he was pulling himself to his feet by grabbing a handful of his mother's skirt, and teetering on his chubby legs, before sitting down heavily.

To Sean, his mother meant sunshine and joy, and crooned lullabies, and a soft breast to lay his head on when he grew sleepy, or hurt himself. But his father meant a harsh voice and sombre face, a shutting out of the sun and the joy. With an instinct for survival, he fell silent when his father entered the cottage, and later, when he was mobile, he would find a darkened part of the cottage and remain there until Pat left again. As for Pat, the only way he could cope with his son was to ignore him as far as possible, and if he could not, when Kate was nursing him, he would leave the cottage altogether.

In the spring following Sean's birth, as the sun was beginning to warm the land ready for planting, Mari married her Conor. The couple had spent the winter planning their home and wedding, as Kate and Pat had done before them. Lent had come and gone when Kate, with Sean snug in his basket, went to the O'Malley cottage to prepare the young bride. Mari's hair was more gold than the red of Kate's own, and fell to her waist in a shimmering waterfall. She had chosen a dress from the Quaker shop in a soft blue, which brightened her pale blue eyes to the colour of summer skies, and gave her a dreamy look. Her younger sisters had picked a posy of spring flowers, and had woven them into a chaplet for her hair. Kate's eyes misted as she looked at her sister, memories of her own wedding day bringing a lump to her throat as she gave the bride a hug and a kiss.

Later, when the ceremony was over and the dancing began she found herself whirled around by Conor,

'It should have been you, y'know,' she heard him say in a lighthearted tone. Kate looked up into his handsome face and into his eyes, and saw that, though the tone was light, his expression was serious.

'Hush you,' she replied banteringly, 'an you an old married man!'

She knew it was the last time they would speak of it and felt heart sore for the carefree days of their courtship that never was. She thought about what life would have been like wedded to Conor. She knew he would have cherished her and any infants they might have had without the intensity of possession that marked her relationship with Pat. But, she sighed, there was no explaining the dictates of the heart, and in spite of everything, she knew her love of Pat would endure for all time. She squeezed Conor gently, and said,

'Take care of her ….my sister is very precious to me,' and moved on to dance with her father.

Later, the newlyweds departed for their new home, sent on their way with good wishes from them all, and ribald comments from the young men. Pat stood apart, watching the banter, perhaps remembering his own wedding day, mused Kate with a sigh. They strolled back to their cottage in companiable silence, Sean asleep in his crib, after all the fuss that had been made of him all day. Kate set the crib down, and took off her dress so that she could wash by the light of the peat fire. She became aware of Pat's gaze on her, and her heart beat faster; as he had not attempted to touch her since Sean's birth.

'Kate,' whispered Pat, 'you're so beautiful. The bride couldn't hold a candle to you!'

Kate held her breath, praying that his mood would last. Perhaps this night they would recapture the joy they had once shared? She turned towards him in the fading light, and held out her arms,

'I love you,' she whispered. Pat came into her arms and buried his face in her tumbling red gold hair. He breathed the perfume of the flowers she used to freshen it, and began to tremble. His mouth came down on hers, and he kissed her deeply, his tongue exploring hers, gently, so very gently. He murmured,

'Kate, my Kate.'

But then Sean stirred. His body reminded him that he hadn't been fed for several hours in the all the excitement. Kate turned an anguished glance towards the crib, willing him to settle again, if only for a little while. But the cries grew lustier and she could see his fists start to wave in temper as he demanded attention. She hesitated, torn between her maternal instincts and her longing for her husband. She turned back to him, trying to resurrect the closeness they had briefly shared, but one look at his face told her that the choice had been made for her. Without another word, he turned away with a scowl, and disappeared through the door. Kate knew she would not see him again that evening. With a sigh, she picked Sean out of his crib, and settled down with him at her breast, crooning a gentle lullaby.

It was much later, in the darkest part of the night that Kate heard him return. She had fed Sean, and settled him back to sleep, and had then lain on her own bed, curled up in a ball of misery. Pat had lurched to the bed, breathing heavily, and she knew, before the waves of poteen rolled over her, that he was very drunk. He fell across the bed, muttering'

'Kate, me darlin' girl.' She felt him fumble for her breasts under her shift, and then sliding his hand down to its hem, tried to pull it up,

'No Pat, not like this, wait 'til you're sober,' pleaded Kate, trying to push him off her.

'You're me wife, you'll not deny me!'

Pat succeeded in moving across her body, pinioning her arms above her head, as she fought him. He forced her knees apart with his own, and entered her roughly. Kate cried out in pain at the roughness of his entry after so long, but no more attempt to stop him. He soon climaxed and rolled away onto his back. Within moments he was snoring stertorously. Kate lay still, tears sliding down her cheeks, her body sore and abused.

'Pat, oh Pat. Where have you gone?'

Chapter 10

The summer sky was a cerulean blue, and a skylark poured out its liquid song. But Kate's heart was heavy as she gazed down into the basket where Sean lay peacefully asleep. She looked up and traced the contours of the land as it swept away from the village, past the ravaged peat bogs, and on towards the sea, hidden beyond a stretch of gently rising land. But the beautiful landscape could not ease the pain in her heart for it was desolate as she knew for certain that she was pregnant again. The surging joy she had felt when she had guessed she was pregnant with Sean was entirely absent this time. This child was not conceived as a result of mutual passion and shared, joyous lovemaking; this child was the product of one of Pat's drunken assaults on her body, usually carried out in the dead of night, and carried out in a furtive manner that Kate had the feeling that he was ashamed of the whole process. She could not feel pleasure in the presence of this embryo, lodged under her heart, and as if in acknowledgement of the fact, it seemed determined to make her suffer. For three months, she experienced almost constant nausea and an equally constant, nagging pain in her side. To compound her misery, she had to bear an increasing amount of the field work if she and Sean were to eat, as Pat's pride in his fields decreased as his drinking increased. He would alternate between spells of frenetic activity, and great lethargy, and for days on end, would disappear altogether.

Soon after Christmas, when Kate was in the sixth month of her pregnancy, Pat came home unexpectedly one evening. Kate was relieved to see that his mood was mellow, and that he appeared to be sober. She forbore to question him about his whereabouts, only too aware from bitter experience, that it was likely to worsen his temper, so she greeted him with a smile.

'Will you be wanting some supper, then Pat?' she asked as she was preparing food for herself and Sean.

'Aye, I'll take some food.' He sat down and ate in reasonably companiable silence, with Sean gazing at his father, round-eyed with anxiety. Pat did not even glance at his son, as he stood up to get his pipe.

Kate finished feeding the baby with potato mashed with buttermilk, and then set him on the floor. At almost a year old, the sturdy youngster pulled himself unsteadily to his feet with the aid of his mother's skirt, and swaying gently, set off on a lurching rush for the bed, where he tripped and plumped down onto his bottom. Kate laughed and clapped her hands at her son's achievement, and turned to Pat to share the moment, but the inwardly sighed as she saw Pat studiously ignoring the lad. She turned away to clear the supper crocks, revealing her swollen abdomen in profile to her husband's lowering eyes.

'Since when have you been with child again?' he shouted at her, 'whose brat have you got under your skirts?'

Kate's face drained of all its colour and she swayed as her head swam. She stared at him aghast,

'It…it's yours Pat,' she whispered, 'I've only ever lain with you.'

Pat stared at her in disbelief, having no memory of his drunken assaults in the night, the recollection lost in poteen fumes. He moved towards her, his fists raised. Sean screamed in fright as his father swung his arm, but at the last minute, he turned the punch and swung away in disgust. But as he did so, the flailing fist caught Kate a blow on her side, causing her to lose balance and she fell heavily to the beaten earth floor, catching her side against the table as she fell.

She lay where she had fallen, waves of nausea rising to her throat, and more frighteningly, she felt a sharp, stabbing pain in her groin. Suddenly, this baby that she had not welcomed now seemed to be infinitely precious to her, and she cried out in fear and pain,

'Help me Pat, this baby's not ready for the world yet!'

Pat was still standing over her as he had been since he had struck her accidentally. By the bed, Sean whimpered in terror at the sight of his father looming threateningly over his mother lying stretched out on the ground.

He let out an anguished wail. The sound finally awoke Pat out his trance, and he rushed out of the cottage to seek help from Eileen O'Malley.

'Quick, it's the baby,' he shouted at Eileen, discovering her on the way to Mari and Conor's cottage.

Eileen took one look at his face, and changed direction instantly, and bustled off to the O'Hara cottage, where she could hear Sean screaming and Kate whimpering in pain. She took one look at her daughter, and sent Pat to find Brigid, as her instincts told her that this birth was not going to be straightforward; it was too soon for one thing. She helped Kate up from the floor where she lay with her legs drawn up in agony.

'Mam, Mam, it hurts much worse than last time.'

Eileen nodded grimly, for she could tell that the contractions were coming far too violently for this early stage of labour. She heard a movement behind her, and turned to find Pat hovering at the door.

'I didn't mean …. '

Eileen simply nodded, the scooped up the wailing baby, and thrust him into Pat's arms.

'Here,' she said, 'take your son to Mari; this is no place for him.'

Brigid arrived as Pat hurried away, and examined Kate while Eileen stoked up the peat fire. Soon after, the baby was born, with Kate screaming with agony as the violence of the birth. Eileen took one look at the tiny crumpled face, and shook her head at Brigid. It did not need the weak, mewling cry of the infant girl, like that of a new born kitten, to tell them that the small scrap of humanity was not long for this world.

'Kate, a cara, you have a daughter. What do you want to call her?'

'Cora,' whispered Kate, not wondering why her mother needed to know so urgently. Eileen scooped up some water from a pitcher, and dabbing the baby's forehead, made the sign of the cross.

'I baptise you, Cora, in the name of the Father, and of the Son and of the Holy Ghost.'

She then wrapped the tiny girl in a soft piece of blanket, and laid her gently in Kate's arms, where her struggle for breath gradually grew weaker until they ceased altogether.

While Cora was fighting and losing her battle for life, Brigid was fighting for Kate's, for the young woman was hemorrhaging badly after the violence of the birth. The old midwife gently massaged Kate's abdomen until, with a sigh of relief, she caused the afterbirth to be delivered. Slowly, the flood of blood became a trickle. Kate lay as white as a sheet, looking as lifeless as the baby in her arms. Her mother gently removed the tiny bundle from her arms, and went to the door, where she found Pat hovering, terrified by Kate's screams, and riven with guilt. He believed that he had caused the death of the one person he cared about in the world!

'Here' said Eileen brusquely, for she was still anxious for her daughter's life, and sure that Pat was responsible for the crisis.

'Make yourself useful to your wife for once, and arrange to have this baby buried. Youse better pray that Kate won't be joining her!'

Pat blenched, but went off to do her bidding, more than ever convinced he was about to lose Kate.

Kate hovered between life and death for several days, and Eileen despaired for her spirit as much as her for her body as she seemed to have lost all will to live. She smiled briefly when Sean was brought to see her, but soon tired and turned away with a sigh. Sean could not understand why he had to stay with his grandparents, much as he loved them. Nor could he understand why his mother did not seem to care about him any more and he broke his heart. At night, he screamed out with nightmare visions of his father looming over his mother while she lay in the floor crying with pain.

Finally, Daniel came to see his daughter, against his wife's better judgment. His face softened as he gazed at his daughter, but then he hardened his expression.

'So you've had enough of us all then?' Kate's eyes fluttered and opened, her expression anguished,

'What d'you mean Pa? I love you all, you know that.'

'Well child, if you go on like this, you'll leave your son without a mother. As it is, he has nightmares every night over you. Is that what you want?'

'Oh Pa, I don't know what to do. I love Pat, but I can't reach him. I can't go on like this!'

'What's the matter with you, lying there whimpering about the things you haven't got, instead of counting your blessings like I always taught you? And you an O'Malley before you were ever an O'Hara!'

Kate smiled weakly, for she knew her father's stern words hid his anxiety and his love for her.

'I'll try, Pa, I promise. Ask Mam to bring Sean home; if he's having nightmares, he's best off with me'. Daniel patted her hand and left her then, satisfied with his efforts.

Kate turned the corner after that, and began to regain her strength. Sean slept with her at night and gradually the nightmares faded, until they only occurred intermittently, and then finally faded altogether. And by the spring, Kate felt her usual robust self.

One day, when the weather had turned warmer, and puffball clouds scudded across the sky, and the air was filled with birdsong, Kate left Sean with Mari, while she went to visit the tiny grave in the middle of Clonarty cemetery. She carried a posy of spring flowers, which she laid in front of a carved wooden cross. She noted with wonderment, the beautiful lettering and swirling patterns carved in the tiny cross. She wondered who had done this beautiful work, until she remembered, with a jolt, that Pat was the only one that she knew was skilled enough to do this, except his own father, and he would not! She sat and mused awhile at this revelation, and the cold band she had put around her heart thawed a little. Perhaps he does care; just a little? Then,

'I'm sorry, little one, that I didn't seem to love you. It wasn't true you know. If you had lived, I'd have cherished you just as I do Sean.' And she felt the tears come then, and her heart felt eased as she asked forgiveness from the tiny being that was her daughter.

Kate left the cemetery, her face resolutely turned to the future. Her father was right, and she would count her blessings and not grieve for what she did not have. She counted Sean, her enchanting son, now a sturdy fifteen month old toddler, and into all sorts of mischief once he had got over the fright of nearly losing his mother. He would run to her to be swung high in the air and then bury his face in her neck, mingling his coppery locks with her own red gold hair, and blowing fat, wet kisses at her. She counted her family. Her parents who had supported her all her life; her sister Mari, her friend and confidant for so many years; the boys, fighting their way to adulthood, but never too busy to give Sean rides on their broad backs; the girls, only now emerging from their childish dreams of fairies and leprechauns, who guarded their young nephew so carefully; Fergus, suddenly grown up as an uncle and very much on his dignity. She counted her friends in the village, the older ones who had watched her grow up, and her contemporaries who had roamed the hills and valleys with her in her growing years. And she counted Pat, the man she had chosen and still loved in her inmost heart. He may not have turned out the way she had hoped, nor did she understand his dislike of his son; but she knew with feminine instinct, that he loved her, indeed perhaps too much, wherein lay his problem. She sighed deeply. She would endure, and she would make a happy home for Sean, and any other babies she may have, and for Pat, if only he could be persuaded to share it!

Chapter 11

The O'Hara's settled to a rhythm of life that was the echo of their parents before them; the enduring succession of plantings and harvestings followed as night followed day!

Pat, frightened by nearly losing his precious Kat, shook himself out of his depressed and drunken state, and regained pride in his fields. If he could not quite recapture the ecstasies of their courtship, at least he treated his wife with due respect, and if his lovemaking was perfunctory, at least it was not a drunken assault.

A year after losing little Cora, Kate was safely delivered of a son, named Kevin after Pat's father. The pregnancy was trouble free, not even burdened with nausea, and Kate felt fit and well throughout. The birth, too, was quick and easy, like 'popping a peapod' said she, laughing. Kevin had his father's dark hair, and eyes that promised to darken to the same brown. Kate looked into her son's crumpled face and thought,

'You may have your father's and grandfather's looks, but I will not let you have their unhappy souls. You will grow up with laughter and joy, my little one, I promise you this.'

Sean was fascinated by his baby brother and hung over his basket for long periods, trying to copy Kate's crooning lullabies. He felt no animosity towards the newcomer for he knew that he had a special place in his mother's heart.

But in the two years following Kevin's birth, the weather and the harvests were poor, in spite of Pat and Kate's labours. Soon there were some deaths among the old and frail of Clonarty, and Kate was mortally afraid for her sons, and she went without herself so that they could be fed. Even so, she went through agonies as she watched their cheeks become hollow, and their bellies distend with hunger.

In spite of the lean times, they dared not use their cash crops to feed themselves. Rents had to be paid, and on time, hunger or no. If they were tempted, their neighbours, the O'Sullivans, soon demonstrated how foolish that would be.

It was approaching Michaelmas, when rents fell due, in the second year of poor harvests, and Kevin's second birthday. The O'Sullivans had a brood of six children, born at a rate of one a year to their fecund mother and feckless father. Jim O'Sullivan was a poor husbandman, and even in good years, his yield of crops was poor. He did not have the energy to spread seaweed and manure over his fields in the autumn, or to keep them weeded during the growing season. By the end of the first year, his family did not have enough to eat, though the village did what it could in the face of their own shortages. As the second year advanced, the youngest baby sickened and died as its mother's milk dried in her breast. The next child, a toddler of eighteen months, soon followed its young sibling to the graveyard on the hill. Jim felt despair as he saw his second harvest was likely to fail, and he knew that there would not be enough to carry the remains of his family through another year. So Jim took his precious store of shillings to Dublin where he purchased food for his starving family.

O'Leary came to the village soon after, and set up his trestle in the middle of the circle of shebeens. He was flanked by two burly thugs armed with blackthorn shillelaghs, for O'Leary was wary of villagers made desperate by hunger. He brought out his list of tenants, reminding the assembled souls that he held his position by virtue of his ability to read and write. One by one they shuffled forward to pay their rents when called by name.

'O'Sullivan.'

Jim stood before him, twisting his hat in tortured hands.

'Me little ones are starving; me wife couldn't feed the babe; I had to buy them some food, or they would all've starved. I'll pay by Christmas, I promise you.'

'Just how do you propose to do that? If you havena the rent now, where'll you find it by Christmas?'

'I'll get it; just give me time.'

O'Leary shrugged his shoulders and called the next tenant. Jim breathed a sigh of relief and moved away, thankful that he earned a reprieve.

Later that night, heavy footsteps could be heard tramping through the village. They all tumbled out, knuckling sleep from their eyes. A phalanx of large and thickset men was making its way to the O'Sullivan cottage.

'Out you,' shouted O'Leary, who had led the procession, 'Otherwise you'll be smoked out.'

Jim and his wife Maeve, appeared in the door, surrounded by their wide eyed little ones.

'You canna turn us out,' pleaded Jim, as Maeve flung herself at O'Leary's feet, 'Winter'll be here soon, an' we've nowhere to go.'

'You should've thought of that before you spent your rent,' snarled O'Leary, kicking Maeve away from him.

The Clonarty men surged forward, but were faced with a line of hired thugs, with shillelaghs and pitchforks. The movement faltered and died, and they watched helplessly as the O'Sullivans were bundled unceremoniously out of their home. Then the thatch was pulled down using the pitchforks, where it fell into the ever burning peat fire and burst into flames with a loud 'whoomph'.

Once satisfied that the family could not possibly use their shebeen, O'Leary and his bodyguards moved away, O'Leary cautiously hiding in the midst of his men as he avoided the glances of the Clonarty folk. A well aimed gob of spit hit him full in the face, but without breaking stride, he wiped the mess away.

Jim, Maeve and the children found refuge with their neighbours, but the following morning, they gathered the pitiful belongs that they had managed to save, and prepared to take to the road.

'Where'll you go, Jim?' asked Daniel, his seamed face creased with pity.

'I'll find work somewhere' replied Jim, 'Somewhere'.

Their future now lay in tramping the highways and byways looking for casual work. Jim had too much pride to beg from his neighbours, who had little enough of their own, but it was unlikely that they would all survive the coming winter. Clonarty never saw them again.

The O'Haras endured, and before Sean and Kevin grew too weak and unhealthy, food was once again coming in. Kate had begun two pregnancies during the lean time, but her weakened body had rejected the growing foetuses by the third month. But the following year, as the Sean and Kevin's cheeks returned to roundness, Kate quickened again, and this time she carried to full term. But she still wasn't in full health when she started her labour, and Eileen once again despaired of her and her infant's lives. But Kate did survive, and contrary to everyone's expectations, her baby girl clung to life, her cry as weak as a mewling kitten. But in time she began to thrive, much to everyone's astonishment. They called her Eileen after her grandmother, but very soon she was known by all as 'little Eily'.

While Kate was distracted with her sickly daughter, changes were underfoot all around her. Pat ducked into the shebeen one morning, turning his head away at the sight of Kate suckling the tiny infant,

'Me brothers are away to Dublin, so they are. I've just come from Pa's and they left yesterday morning.'

Kate looked up in mild curiosity,

'Who's gone; and why?' she asked.

'Seth and Calum. They've been muttering about getting work in Dublin to raise enough for a passage to America. Can't get away fast enough from working in the fields according to Pa. Young fools!'

Kate kept her counsel, only too aware that Pat wasn't interested in her opinion. But she couldn't find it in her heart to blame the boys, for that's all they were, for trying to escape from their dour and bad tempered parent. But she felt it unlikely that the boys would succeed in raising enough money, and was shocked to her core when the boys returned to the village to announce their imminent departure. After disappearing into the O'Hara shebeen, the boys emerged looking stony faced. Clearly, their meeting with their father had been singularly unpleasant. The pair made their way to Kate, where she sat outside nursing Eily, with Sean and Kevin playing nearby.

They both hugged her close, for they were fond of their pretty sister-in-law.

'We've come to say goodbye, Kate' muttered Seth. 'We leave for America in three days time. But we'll be back, won't we Calum' he added hastily, as he saw Kate's face and the welling tears.

'Oh aye,' affirmed Calum, 'With pockets full of American dollars.'

Calum gently touched the baby's cheek as he turned away, tears in his own eyes at the moment of parting. He hugged Kate again, and then his nephews, followed by his equally tearful brother.

'We're away to find Pat. Take care of yourself, Kate, an' these little ones.'

Kate watched them go towards the fields, where Pat toiled to feed his family. She knew Pat would not understand their burning need to escape, and she sighed deeply.

But she was soon to be shocked to her very core, by her own brothers.

Tomos and Michael had been mere lads when she had married, but while she was raising her own young family, they had been busy growing up, fighting their way through cracking voices and gangly limbs; finally emerging as a pair of handsome youths of sixteen and eighteen. They had been close as twins during their growing years, and loved nothing better than roaming the hills or frightening their sisters. But lately, Kate had noticed a certain restlessness, especially following Pat's brothers' defection. She often heard the sound of lively 'discussions' taking place in the O'Malley shebeen, followed by one or both brothers storming out and disappearing onto the hillside. Kat hoped and prayed that the stormy times would pass, and the boys would settle to taking over her father's fields as he grew too old to cultivate them properly.

But when Kate was busy preparing supper one day, with Sean and Kevin chattering happily together, and Eily dozing in her crib, Michael ducked through the low doorway and slumped onto a stool. Kate's cheerful greeting died as she saw his ravaged face.

'What ails you?' she whispered, aghast.

'It's Tomos…. He's gone. Oh Kate, what'll I tell Pa,' and more stridently, 'What'll I do without him?'

'Hush now,' said Kate, as the boy began to weep, great gulping sobs tearing at his throat. Sean and Kevin looked up, frightened by the sight of their young uncle crying. Kate was equally appalled, as he had never wept, even when sorely hurt from boyhood escapades.

'Tell me what happened; where has Tomos gone?'

Michael made an effort to calm himself, and was finally able to speak. He told of Tomos' increasing restlessness, and how he had started to criticize their way of life, rowing with their father about the futility of it all – scratching a living out of fields that they didn't even own!

. 'It was Seth and Calum that started it, with their talk of places to go – America, India and the like.'

Kate listened quietly to the halting words, never dreaming that so much had gone on without her knowing and not comprehending why Tomos should be so restless in the midst of such a loving family. Were they not all happy here, in their beautiful valley?

'It was about six weeks ago that he made up his mind to leave. He said it was now or never; if he didn't break away soon, he'd end up betrothed to some girl and soon enough be saddled with a family; begging yer pardon, Kate, but that's what he said!'

'Never mind,' urged Kate, 'Go on.'

'The thing is, he wanted me to go, and for a while I thought I would. But then, I couldn't see myself anywhere else, an' I couldn't make up my mind to go. An' I thought about Ma and Pa, an' how they would feel an' what they would say if we just went. But this morning, we were down by the shore, and Tomos stopped, looking out to sea. An' then he shook himself, and an' said, 'that's it, I'm going – now.' An' he started to walk away fast. I ran after him, but he just kept walking. He said that if I wouldn't come, then he'd just go alone, but he wouldn't wait any longer, an' then one day he would be back with a fortune, havin' seen the world, an' tell us all about it; if we hadn't died of boredom by then!'

The boy fell silent for a while, and Kate hugged him close, as she thought he had finished. Her gentle heart ached for him, as he had just lost his dearest friend. Then Michael pulled away and gazed into Kate's eyes, and she saw a soul in torment,

'How'll I tell Pa, Kate, for he's gone to Dublin to join the army?'

Kate sat back, appalled. Of all things, this would be the hardest for her father to bear. He hated the British and all that they stood for; hated the rapacious way that they had taken over Ireland and destroyed the pride of its ancient people; hated their absentee landlords; hated most of all, their army, billeted in large towns and cities such as Dublin, and enforced their rule without mercy.

'You see, Kate, he said that it didn't matter; that he'd use them to get rich, come back and buy Clonarty and all its lands and then laugh at them!'

'Oh how can he be so stupid,' cried Kate, 'it doesn't matter how rich he gets, he cannot buy an inch of Irish soil! Michael, you mustn't tell Pa about the army. It would kill him the same as if Tomos held a knife to his heart. It must rest here between us.' Kate looked anxiously into Michael's face, aware that it was a terrible burden she was asking him to carry. The boy nodded slowly,

'I promise,' he whispered.

The going of Tomos cast a blight over the O'Haras for many a month. Michael roamed the countryside alone; a lost soul with his brother. Daniel and Eileen could give him no comfort, ravaged as they were by the loss of their eldest son, with nothing to turn to for solace as they did not know where he had gone, or worse, why! Michael kept his promise to Kate, and had simply said that Tomos had walked off towards Dublin, and that was all he knew. As day followed day, the grieving parents slowly came to terms with their loss, and turned to their remaining children for comfort.

As for Kate, she hugged the secret to herself, not even sharing it with Pat, who was saddened enough by the loss of his own brothers.

But time passed, and the children grew, and it was with some surprise that Kate gazed at her reflection in the pellucid waters of the Lough, and wondered at the image she saw there. In her heart, she was the 17 year old girl who had wed her Pat on a sparkling autumn day. She had been aware of the passage of seasons; how could she not with three growing children! But she had not thought of the effect of those years on herself. So, she gazed at herself and saw a self-possessed young woman, not a lissome girl. Her hair was still red gold, and her skin still had a bloom to it, and while her figure was still slender, her stature now was upright and graceful. The youthful exuberance had gone to be replaced by a character that had been moulded by adversity, and the loss of her babies along with her dreams. She pondered a while, and thought,

'Why! I am nearly thirty. Where have the years gone?'

Turning around, she looked across the village to where he children sat in a semi-circle round her father. He was clearly telling the stories that he had once told her, and in her children, she saw the passage of years. Sean, her first born, and her pride and joy, was just entering adolescence, but still had the chubbiness of boyhood. But the rounded cheeks hid a good bone structure that gave a hint of the handsome man to come. His eyes were still the bright blue of his mother's, but his hair, once so like her own, had darkened to a burnished copper. His nose was a little snub, with a scattering of freckles across the bridge, but the shape promised to firm in the years to come.

Leaning against him, as usual, sat Kevin. At two years younger, he had the angular, awkward limbs of a boy, and a face that was usually streaked with dirt. His hair and eyes were dark like his father's, and could give him the same brooding look. But his nature was more open and warm, nurtured by a mother's love, which had countered his innate shyness, and he was a happy, if quiet, child. Three years younger, sat little Eily, almost a changeling in looks and character. Her eyes were grey, a changeable colour that varied with her mood or the weather. She had a fall of silky straight brown hair that reached her waist, never tangling no matter what she did. She was a silent, secretive child; not given to wild games with the other children, preferring to walk alone. Even at such a tender age, she had an almost mystical effect on small creatures and birds, bringing them home when injured, and nursing them back to health. Kate often gazed at her daughter with wonder, not knowing that she was in fact very like Pat's mother Briginne, who had died so many years before, for Pat never spoke of her.

'Yes,' whispered Kate to herself, 'That is where the years have flown! But it isn't over yet!'

She ran her hand down her body, but there was no overt sign of pregnancy, just her conviction that it was so. She was glad, for she enjoyed carrying and bearing babies when times were good. And, she reflected, it the very best time as her relationship with Pat had slowly improved over the years, and he now treated her with gentleness rather than as a body on which to slake his lust

'Indeed,' she said finally, 'The good God is surely smiling on us!'

And it did indeed seem so, as she carried the baby to full term, and after an easy labour, gave birth to her lastborn, Nuala.

Chapter 12

The sun blazed down from an inverted bowl of blue. Sean lay on his belly, high up on the hillside overlooking Clonarty. It was the month of June, and an early shower of rain had washed the air clean, leaving it sparkling, and with such clarity that Sean was sure that he could see forever if only he could summon up the energy to climb to the top of the hill. From his vantage point he could see the village spread out below him, with their untidy thatches and odiferous dung heaps romanticized and sanitized by distance. The shebeens looked much like the little wooden models that Grandpa O'Hara loved to whittle, and its people like so many ants, though unlike those energetic creatures, their movements were sluggish in the soporific heat of the sun.

Between Sean and the village were the cultivated fields, lining the lower slopes with a patchwork of varying shades of green. The predominant colour was the vivid green of the potato haulms, interspersed with wheat and barley, just beginning to turn to gold. Above him, Sean could see the serried ranks of young bracken marching up the hillside, green for now, but would later turn to russet with the onset of Autumn. The patch where Sean was sprawled was covered with short, springy turf, so thickly starred with summer flowers that it looked as if an unseasonal snow shower had passed over it. Above his head a sky lark kept flinging himself ever higher, pouring out its liquid, trilling notes to the whole world.

Near him sat Nuala, close on a year old, and an enchanting imp. She had sparkling blue eyes as vivid as Sean's own, and a pert little snub nose dusted with a scatter of golden freckles. Her hair was the same red-gold of her mother, and it curled over her head riotously. She sat engrossed in some mysterious game of her own that involved pulling up handfuls of daisies and letting them fall in a white shower, all the while chuckling richly to herself.

Sean watched her, absolutely enchanted with his youngest sibling. He had fallen in love with her the day she was born, and was her self-appointed guardian. He was fond of Kevin and Eily, and had never suffered a moment of jealousy when they had come along, but Nuala he adored. He lay watching her antics, musing on the effect that this very small person had had on his family, and in particular, his father.

Sean had never understood the brooding, surly man who had fathered him. He had compared his own family with others in the village, and saw the warm affection that they shared, notwithstanding the occasional raised fist or loud voices. But for him, there lingered a memory of his early years when he had cowered in fear whenever Pat entered the shebeen, and the violent rages he had witnessed. Those days had long passed, but over the years Sean had yearned for a gesture of love, some evidence that he was cared for. But that hope had long since died, and he had perforce to accept that his mother's presence meant sunshine and joy, while his father's brought a feeling of gloom, much like a dark cloud passing the face of the sun.

Sean recalled questioning their old priest, Father Muldoon, believing in his innocence that the cleric stood in place of Jesus and knew everything. He had met the peripatetic pastor making his way to Clonarty, during one of his interminable rounds of his scattered parish, and had fallen into step with him.

'Why,' he had begun, struggling to find the words to explain his incoherent thoughts.

'Why doesn't God make me Pa smile more often?' The words tumbled out in a rush, and he was not really sure if they were what he had meant to ask.

The kindly old priest, with his fuzz of white hair framing a round, cherubic face, looked down into the troubled face of the boy, and he sat down on a convenient tussock, patting the turf next to him for Sean to sit.

'Ye see, Sean,' he began, 'God gave us all two sides to our nature. There is the light side that is full of joy, and there is the dark one, which is full of sadness and misery. For all of us, there will be times when one side wins over the other, and if it is a bright day, nothing will make us sad, but if it is a dark day, nothing will make us happy. It is up to us to try and make our happy side show to the world as much as possible, but some folk find this difficult. Your father has troubled heart, and finds it difficult to let the light in, so you must try and help him find joy. It doesn't mean, ye know, that he doesn't love you. He provides you with a comfortable home and food on the table doesn't he?'

Sean pondered the words for a while,

'But me Mam is so beautiful, why doesn't he smile at her – I do – all the time!' The priest had to smile as he looked down at the earnest little face,

'Maybe he does, inside where you can't see it. Give it time, my child, and all will be made clear in the Good Lord's own time.'

Father Muldoon wasn't at all sure he had helped Sean, for in truth he did not understand Pat any more than Sean did. Who could not find joy in a lovely wife like Kate, and a son like this one? But he had a long way still to go, and with a sigh, he hoisted himself to his feet.

'Give me your shoulder my son, these old bones do not take kindly to a damp seat!'

The unlikely pair walked in companionable silence to the village, where Sean was soon diverted by a game of tag and soon forgot his earnest questions.

But all of this had been before, well Nuala! Sean remembered the day of her birth last June as clearly as if it was yesterday. The sun had shone then too, and he had been outside the cottage playing a game of stones with Kevin, too hot and lethargic to do anything more energetic. Kate had been cradling little Eily who had solemnly sucking her thumb, and soothed by a gentle lullaby, the pair of them drowsy with heat. Kate had grown great with this pregnancy, greater than she had ever been before, and she felt extremely lethargic. Then Sean looked up as she stopped singing abruptly, putting her hand to her back and taking several slow, deep breaths. When the spasm had passed, she had spoken quietly to him,

'Go and fetch me Mam, and take Kev and Eily for a walk. Quickly now, for this one is impatient to be born!'

Sean's eyes had widened with alarm, but he had run to his Grandma Eileen as he was bid, and taking Kevin and Eily's hands firmly in his own, had led them away from the cottage, and towards the lough. He had seen his father coming down the hill from the fields, and had waved vigorously. Pat had grabbed the boy's arm and shaken it more roughly than he had intended, is his concern,

'What ails you, boy, is it your Mam?'

'The baby's coming, Pa, and me Mam sent to fetch Grandma O'Malley and take Kevin and Eily out of the way,' Sean had responded breathlessly.

Then Pat had surprised them all by reaching out to his children and taking Kevin and Eily's hands himself.

'Come, we are not needed here. We'll get away and give yer Mam some peace.'

He had led the way up the hillside along by the stream until they had reached the very spot where Sean now sat. Sean had looked up into his father's face as they walked, and had been strangely moved by what he saw there. Surliness he was used to, but not the deep anguish he was witnessing.

'Why,' thought Sean, 'He's afraid of losing her!'

With a maturity beyond his years, Sean had reached out and touched his father's arm,

'Don't worry Pa, God won't let anything happen to Mam, we love her too much.'

Pat had smiled then at this simplistic notion of the workings of the Almighty, but that smile captivated Sean just as it had his mother so many years before. Pat was a man who kept his feelings deeply hidden, but when they did peep out, the effect was devastating!

They had all sat awhile on the hillside, and Pat had entertained his children with stirring tales of old Irish heroes, every bit as exciting as Grandpa O'Malley, whom they had considered to be the world's best storyteller. Eily had busied herself with collecting treasures, and had brought them to deposit in Pat's lap, each time gazing into his face as if expecting him suddenly to change back into his usual taciturn self. She had found a stone polished by the stream, a posy of summer flowers, and a leaf skeleton that had drifted there from the previous year's fall.

Pat had kept watch on his cottage from their vantage point, and as the shadows of evening had begun to creep across the hill, he had seen Eileen emerge from the low doorway of the shebeen, glance around, and then duck back inside,

'Come,' Pat had said quietly, 'It's time to return.'

They had made their way down the hill with gathering excitement until the young ones could contain themselves no more, and had broken into a run. They had tumbled into the cottage and had crowded round their mother, who lay back in bed with a new infant cradled in her arms.

'See,' she had smiled, 'You have a wee sister.'

Then the cottage had darkened as Pat entered. He had hung back till then, memories of previous births slowing his steps. The three older ones had moved back instinctively as he came to Kate's side. For the first time in all Kate's birthings, Pat had looked first at his new daughter, putting out a cautious finger to touch her fist, the tiny hand curling round it instinctively. Perhaps he had seen in the new born features a reincarnation of his Kate, or perhaps the magic of the child to come was already working, and the first time, Pat had felt his heart lurch with a surge of paternal pride. Kate found that she had been holding her breath, and had let it out with a long sigh. Pat had truly come home at long last.

Kate's milk had flowed in abundance, for that year had been one of plenty, and the infant Nuala had thrived. On warm and sunny days, Kate had put her outside in a wicker cradle, jealously guarded by her older brothers and sister, cousins, aunts and uncles, and indeed any of the numerous friends and neighbours, for she had enchanted them all. And if Kate had looked out to find the cradle missing, she did not fret, knowing that Nuala had been taken to another cottage to be clucked and cooed over. She had been a placid baby, content to lie gurgling and chuckling to herself and the world about her.

Sean had been her especial guardian, and when she had reached an age when she could hold her head up sturdily, he had hoisted her onto his back, tying her firmly before taking her for long walks. He had taken her to the coast, and shown her the crashing breakers flung there by a long distant storm. Burying his face in her neck, from which rose that particular warm odour that babies have, he had whispered to her of his dreams of travel to faraway lands, and she had seized his hair, pulling it hard and gurgling with delight. He had taken her to the walls of the Danforth estate and perched her on top of a low section and told her of the injustices meted out by a long line of Danforths, and how one day the Irish nation would rise up and throw off the hated British yoke. He had taken her to all the neighbouring villages and introduced her to friends and neighbours there, who also fell in love with the enchanting child.

The early magic that Nuala had wrought on her father had continued, and Pat had not only discovered the joy of his youngest child, he had discovered his older children as well. He had discovered little Eily, a slight, solemn child with her river of brown hair and dreamy grey eyes. She still brought him gifts, though she rarely had much to say. He had discovered his son Kevin, so like himself in looks, but with Kate's love surrounding him, he had escaped the introversion that had troubled Pat all his life. And he had discovered his eldest son, Sean, so like Kate in looks and temperament, and with a maturity beyond his years.

'My fault,' thought Pat guiltily, 'He's had to shoulder the burdens of my family for far too long.'

And he rediscovered his joy in Kate, wooing her anew with flowers from the hedgerows and small gifts purchased from itinerant tinkers, so that she glowed in the rebirth of his love.

And all the while Nuala had thrived, until a year later she sat on the hillside with her favourite brother, playing her infant game. Suddenly she tired of destroying showers of daisies, and with a swift wriggle, she flung herself onto Sean's back, crowing with delight. Sean managed to turn himself over and held her aloft, both arms outstretched.

'So you thought you would beat me, did you?' And Sean shook her in mock anger.

'Mm, mm, mm,' was the only reply he received, and laughing aloud, Sean got up, and hoisting the baby into his arms, he headed downhill towards the village.

'There Nuala, there's our valley where'll grow up, and one day, a handsome young man like me will come courting you!'

'Mm, mm, mm,' crowed Nuala, seizing handfuls of his hair.

Sean could not know, as he gazed at the peaceful scene below, that his village was to be overrun by events beyond anybody's control; events that would cause the death or migration of whole communities of people, and reinforce the hatred of the Irish for their English neighbours.

Chapter 13

It was March, in the year or Our Lord 1845, and the O'Hara family prepared to plant their new potato crop. The previous winter had been long and dreary, and Sean had counted off the days by watching his baby sister, Nuala grow and develop. As the previous harvest had been gathered in, she had taken her first, faltering steps, lurching straight towards the lough. As Christmas approached and the days contracted in a welter of gloom and fog, she had uttered her first clear word, 'angel' which the besotted family put down to an innate saintliness, until Sean observed that Grandpa O'Malley always greeted by throwing her in the air, crying 'hello my wee angel' as she descended. After that, the words came thick and fast, until she could lisp Mam and Pa, Sean, Kevy and Eily, and Gara and Gally for her two grandfathers, names that were promptly taken up by the rest of the family!

Grandma Eileen received the dubious title of 'Gump', which also stuck, much to her irritation and the amusement of her irreverent grandchildren!

Soon after Christmas, the weather had turned bitterly cold, and a rare snow shower had given Clonarty a picturesque charm as it coated the manure heaps and smoothed out the rough thatches. Nuala had been enthralled when she had caught sight of the new, white world outside the shebeen doorway. She had rushed outside clad only in diminutive shift, and had fallen with a flurry into a minor snow drift that had piled up around the door. Her expression of comical dismay had made the family erupt in laughter, even the taciturn Pat. She had recovered soon enough, and having been cuddled by Kate and dressed more warmly, she had ventured out again with Sean, and joined in the fun with the rest of the delighted Clonarty children, already busy throwing snowballs at each other.

The weather had grown colder and colder, until the lough itself had frozen over, apart from a central channel where the stream entered and exited. The children had tested it nervously for soundness, and a few hardy souls ventured a few feet from the edge, but before anyone had grown too rash and received an icy ducking, a sudden thaw had set in and the snow had vanished overnight. The adults had breathed a sigh of relief as they huddled over their peat fires, and had begun to look forward to spring!

But the winter had one last surprise, and the dying days of February were riven by gales that had roared across the Atlantic Ocean, cunningly working their way round the southern tip of Ireland, and then flinging themselves up the east coast to nip the toes of unwary travelers, and hang an impressive dew drop on the sharp nose of Agent O'Leary.

But March arrived, bringing in train the first hint of spring, as the winds died away and veered towards the south. Nature began to stir from its long winter sleep, and air filled with the clamour of birdsong, as males strutted busily in front of prospective mates.

After waiting a week to be sure that winter had well and truly departed, Pat declared it time to begin work in the potato fields. For the first time, he took the trouble to talk with his sons, particularly deferring to Sean as the oldest, and together they planned the work. Pat would start digging at the top of the field, completing the work that the winter frosts had started in breaking down the large clods of earth left after the autumn harvest. This would ensure that the manure and seaweed that they had spread at that time would be well and truly dug in, giving heart to their precious soil. Sean and Kevin would follow, rendering the earth to a fine crumb, which would receive the precious seed potatoes into their prepared trenches, dug with their trusty 'spuds'. Kate, with Eily, and the dubious help of Nuala, would shift any stones that had risen to the surface, and lay them by the side of the fields, for Pat still harbored thoughts of converting his shebeen to a sturdy stone cottage. Finally, they would all share in the planting.

The weather aided their efforts, and day after day, they rose to a fine mist that shrouded the village, whispering between the shebeens. But it quickly dispersed, sucked up by the gentle spring sunshine. Sudden showers of rain would send them scurrying for shelter, but these were short lived, and they were soon back at their labours. At this rate, said Pat, they would have nothing to do all summer but play in the sun and watch Nuala grow! Nuala was a delight to watch, as she insisted on 'helping', not only her own family, but everyone else as well. Stones removed from one field were solemnly buried in another; but best of all, Sean caught sight of her following in the wake of Kate who was carefully dropping the seed potatoes in their trenches and Nuala was equally carefully removing them and depositing them at the side of the field in lieu of stones. He threw back his head and roared with laughter, effectively stopping all work while everyone joined in the joke. In spite of Nuala's efforts, potato planting was completed in record time, to be followed by the grain crop and the vegetable patch. The village celebrated by holding a ceilidh in honour of the best planting season that anyone could remember for many a long year.

During the ceilidh, Sean took a little time out, and spent it looking around at his family and friends, thinking himself the luckiest person in the world to be surrounded by so much love and affection.

Daniel and Eileen O'Malley were especial favourites of his, ever since his earliest childhood when had had fled to them for comfort from his father's anger. Both were approaching their sixtieth birthday, but were hale and hearty for all that. Eileen was a round dumpling of a woman and her hair was completely grey, but her expression as always, was kindly, and her generous bosom was still a refuge to her numerous grandchildren. Daniel was as lean as his wife was plump, his arms stringed with muscle, and his face seamed with wrinkles. He could be found in the evening, puffing on a clay pipe, and regaling village children with stories of the long ago days of Ireland's turbulent past.

Of Daniel and Eileen's own children, only Fergus remained, and who could tell how long it would be before he 'flew the nest'. Mari was placidly settled with Conor and a gaggle of children of her own, who had arrived at two yearly intervals until there were six in all. Clonarty had waited for the next to arrive, but for some reason there were no more, and if Conor was relieved, he gave no sign of it. If Mari ever felt that she had been second best to his first love, she gave no sign either, and appeared truly content.

Michael had not been able to settle after his brother's defection, and had mooned about the place aimlessly for many months. His normally placid father became so exasperated that he had shouted at the lad to 'pull himself together and not behave like a lovelorn maiden!' Hurt and bewildered, Michael had disappeared off in the direction of Dublin, and was not seen for three days. Daniel was beside himself with worry, blaming himself, and being berated by Eileen for his short temper. But the youth had returned with joy written all over his broad, freckled face. He told them of how he had reached Dublin and had wandered about until he had found himself at the wharf where the fishing boats were moored, ready to leave for sea. Michael had been the interested witness of a row between a fisherman and his mate which had resulted in the mate stalking off in high dudgeon. The fisherman had spotted Michael loitering nearby and had shouted at him in turn,

'Instead of hanging about, why don't ye do something useful and help for the day. I'll pay you with some of me catch!'

Without giving it a second's thought, Michael had jumped on board, and spent the best day he could remember for a very long time. He brought his share of the catch home to his worried parents, and told them that he had promised to return and learn the fishing trade, as he had fallen in love with the sea. Clonarty had seen little of him since then, as Michael had made his home in Dublin. The fisherman had allowed him to lodge with him and his daughter, for he was a widower. In due course, he had married the daughter and inherited the fishing boat when his friend and mentor had died of a heart attack, having taught Michael all that he knew about the fishing trade.

The girls, Bernadette and Theresa had finally grown out of their daydreams of the 'little people', and turned their thoughts to boys instead. Like their older sisters before them, they had grown into beautiful young women and had been carried off to neighbouring Kilgarth by a pair of brothers, who had fallen in love with them simultaneously. Clonarty had enjoyed a lively double wedding, and the girls had settled happily in Kilgarth, as inseparable as ever.

And so there was only Fergus left at home, as irrepressible a scamp as he had been at the age of five, when Pat was courting his Kate. He had grown into a strikingly handsome young man, who had all the maids in the village swooning after him, and enraging the other village youths. Some while ago he had bought an old fiddle from a passing tinker who had found it in a ditch. He had lovingly restored it, and then badgered the fiddler from Kilgarth to teach him to play. The village had endured his eldritch screeching until time and teaching had improved his playing so much that he was in demand at ceilidhs and weddings far and wide. Indeed, he was busy playing at this one, his blue O'Malley eyes alight with laughter and mischief, and surrounded by his usual circle of adoring young women. Unfortunately for them, he would swear to each and every one that his 'aged' parents needed him and he could not possibly settle down with any one of them while this situation existed, but a 'wee kiss' would keep him interested for now! It is as well that neither Daniel nor Eileen heard these outrageous statements!

Sean's other grandfather, old Kevin O'Hara, had become more and more reclusive as the years passed. All of his sons had left home now, the youngest to follow his brothers to the emigration ship, leaving only Pat to tend the fields. Strangely for a man who seemed to dislike his own children he tolerated, indeed welcomed his grandchildren, particularly the youngest, Nuala. He rarely spoke to them, but if they came by he would sit and whittle small creatures, cottages and all manner of wonderful things out of pieces of wood. The children would watch, enthralled, as the object took shape before their eyes and would bear the prize away to be cherished until it broke apart from all the handling.

He rarely worked in the fields now, leaving Pat to do all that was necessary, as his food requirements were meagre compared to a growing family. But Pat had found himself with more land to cultivate than he could comfortably cope with, a fact that he took care to conceal from Agent O'Leary, for fear of losing it. Instead 'Gara' spent his time on a small plot behind his shebeen growing a few vegetables and many more flowers. The flowers were a source of wonder to his neighbours, for they only had time for the essentials of living, and grew what was needed to survive. And, too, they could not reconcile this morose old man with raising things of such beauty. He collected seeds from the long neglected flower beds of the Danforth gardens, uncaring whether Agent O'Leary saw them or not, as 'he couldn't tell a petunia from a potato if it jumped up and bit his dewdrop off!'

Of all his grandchildren, Nuala loved the garden the most, and for all her tender years, would treat the flowers with gentle care and tenderness, cupping the blooms in her chubby hands, and shedding tears when the inevitable happened, and the bloom faded and died. Clonarty shook its head in amazement at the sight of Old Kevin, dried up and sour as an old prune, sitting in the middle of his garden with Nuala paying wrapt attention to his lesson on the best time to plant the tall hollyhocks, or tiny primroses.

Sean's musings were brought abruptly to an end as he found himself being whirled into a jig by his cousin Siobhan, Mari's eldest girl.

'Why're you so quiet Sean, on such a lovely day?' Sean did not reply, but holding the younger girl firmly round the waist, he twirled her round so vigorously that they both fell to the ground, dizzy and laughing.

The weather continued to be glorious and the usually hard pressed potato farmers had little to do, but apply a hoe between the growing haulms, earthing them up to encourage more growth underground. Clonarty basked in warm sunshine that had begun in March and continued well into July, interspersed by vigorous showers.

The families all enjoyed such a rare season of continuous fine days, and throughout the spring and early summer the children would be out all day, racing up and down the hill, splashing in the lough, or running between the shebeens. Everyone looked forward to a bumper harvest, which would sustain them through the winter. And the precious cash crops should allow some spare cash to buy a few luxuries such as tea, tobacco and a few gewgaws of the women.

On several occasions, the O'Hara's, often accompanied by the Murphy's, would take a parcel of food and make their way to the coast. They used the occasion to collect seaweed that would be dried and spread on the fields in the autumn as fertilizer. But in truth, they simply enjoyed the day out, and looked forward to a stroll along the shore, dipping their feet in the turbulent Irish Sea. Once the job of collecting the seaweed had been done, and the bundles lashed firmly to sleds constructed by Pat and Conor to drag the stuff home, the day was given over to enjoyment. The youngsters would race around the sands playing tag, while the girls scoured the shore for shells that could be drilled and fashioned into necklaces or other ornaments. All of them enjoyed dashing into the sea, rolling in the tumbling surf. Nuala had to be continually watched as she had no fear of the waves. Time and again she dashed into the sea on her plump little legs, often disappearing from sight as a wave broke over her head, but would emerge spluttering and laughing.

When her siblings and cousins got tired of rescuing her, Sean hoisted the reluctant toddler onto his shoulders, and the whole gaggle of them explored the beach, picking up flotsam and jetsam thrown up from far distant ships.

The adults spent their time more lazily, enjoying the respite that this year was giving them. Sprawled on the sand, the men sucked at clay pipes and discussed the many injustices meted out to them by the hated English, and Agent O'Leary. Lord Danforth had been away so long, that the agent had become something of a tyrant, enjoying carte blanche to do what he would, as long as the revenues from the farmers continued to flow over the sea to London. Recently he had decided to increase the Danforth sheep herd, and had moved a Kilgarth family from their plots where they had farmed time out of mind. He had generously given them land near the peat diggings, where no crops would grow until extensive digging of drainage ditches had been carried out, and how would the family survive until then? Meanwhile Kate and Mari chatted of motherhood and their children, and reminiscing about when they were no older than their own children. Later, Pat pulled Kate to her feet, and they strolled along the base of the cliffs hand in hand.

These halcyon days would surely be looked back on with nostalgia, or so they thought during the long, lazy days. For how could they know that the seeds of their destruction had already been sown far away across the Atlantic Ocean?

The year before, a potato farmer in North America had noticed that his crop had been blighted by a strange disease. It had not spread too far, so he chose to ignore it, and began to harvest his crop. The bulk of it was transported to the east coast to be exported to Europe, as was his custom every year, and he made sure that the diseased tubers were well hidden by sound ones. The shipper loaded them with crops from other farms without noticing anything amiss, and set off to cross the Atlantic, heading for England. He made a fair crossing, and landed at Southampton to offload a parcel of tobacco for a merchant there. On entering his hold, the ship's captain encountered a stench, the like of which he had never experienced before. It was akin to a putrefying body, and the captain had no difficulty in identifying the source; the entire cargo of potatoes was rotten with disease. The captain promptly ordered the offensive load to be shoveled into sacks and unceremoniously dumped on the quay. Anxious to catch the outgoing tide, he ordered the mooring ropes cast off, and he sailed away bemoaning the loss of revenue, but glad to escape the stench of his rotten cargo.

The failure of the captain to organize the disposal of the diseased potatoes meant that the festering sacks lay on the quayside for a day and a night, until the local people noticed that the new stench managed to outsmell the normal ripe odours that were there and immediately dumped the cargo into the harbour. Unfortunately, by then the pores of the fungus that had caused the rot had been released into the wind, and would, in the fullness of time, waft on air currents far and wide; to the Isle of Wight, to the rest of England, to Northern Europe, and most devastating of all, to Ireland!

The O'Hara's, unaware of the disaster that awaited them, continued to enjoy the summer, but soon after mid-July, with the crop looking heavier than for many a year, the weather changed to days of cold and gloomy skies, unrelieved by a glimpse of sun. There was something strangely oppressive about the lowering sky, and they all shivered, as much with a primeval fear as with the chill. Waking up to yet another day of grey mist, Nuala summed up their feelings by asking plaintively,

'Mam, where's the sun gone? When's it coming back?'

Pat checked the fields every day, concerned about the ripening potatoes, though not really sure why it should be so. The haulms looked sturdy enough, and healthy, even if the brilliant greenness was muted by the dank, dismal days.

One morning, with harvest time not far away, little Eily woke early as she often did. She would slip out of the shebeen and wander up the hill, searching for the little creatures that were still scurrying about in the half light. A heavy mist swirled around her, reducing her field of vision to no more than a few yards, but she had no fear as she knew the hill as well as her own shebeen. She was aware of a strange odour in the air, but could not identify it in the cloying mist, and she was more than used to multifarious odours that hung around the shebeens! But this was somehow different, all pervading and evil. She wrinkled her nose in distaste and looked about her nervously, but she could still see nothing. She finally arrived at her favourite spot high up the hill by the stream and sat quietly, waiting for her visitors to come to her, voles, hedgehogs, rabbits and other favourites.

As she sat quietly the fog started to lift, and she raised her head, sniffing like a dog. As the air cleared, she was able to see the potato fields below her come into view. She studied them with disquiet; the fields so green just a day before seemed blackened, as though a fire had swept over them. And it was from the fields that the smell emanated. Eily jumped to her feet and ran down the hill screaming at the top of her voice,

'Mam, Pa, come quick. The potatoes have gone funny, Mam, Pa.….'

Chapter 14

Sean stood next to his father and gazed at the devastation before him. As far as the eye could see were fields of brown, oozing potato haulms. An evil, foetid stench arose from them; a rank odour that spoke of the charnel house, while here and there, shockingly, were islands of green where the rot had not yet struck, and elsewhere fields of barley and wheat mocked the eye with their healthy vigour.

'What is it?' whispered Kate, clutching at Pat's arm. She was holding Nuala on her hip, the little girl solemnly sucking her thumb, while gazing around her, round-eyed with wonder. All around the O'Hara's, other families gathered, roused by Eily's screams as she had raced down the hill.

Pat shook himself out of his trance and kneeling down, reached down into the sodden earth, scrabbling with his fingers to find the tubers. His hands re-emerged, dripping with slime that stank even worse than did the fields.

'God help us' he whispered, 'for we cannot.'

After a while, as the initial shock of discovery began to wear off, the groups of villagers began to shift and re-assemble; the men coming together to discuss the best course of action, as the women huddled together, clutching their infants to their breasts and talking anxiously in low voices. Sean hovered uncertainly by the men talking in low, urgent voices. He felt a tug at his sleeve, and turned impatiently to find his cousin, Dermot, Conor and Mari's eldest boy, looking at him with questioning eyes.

'D'you know what 'tis, what's done this?'

'How would I know,' hissed Sean, 'whisht – I'm trying to find out.' The boys fell silent and strained their ears to catch snatches of conversation.

'Did you ever see the like?' came from Liam Murphy.

'I mind back in '22 we had a terrible crop failure. 'Twas every bit as bad as this,' said old Fergus, husband of midwife Brigid. He was said to be the oldest man in the village, with toothless gums and wizened face, and who put on an air of wisdom due to his weight of years!

'We've never seen anything like this before,' asserted Daniel O'Malley, effectively silencing all arguments. 'Any crop failures have been down to bad weather and late frosts; nothing as bad as this!'

'Why don't they DO something,' thought Sean, 'instead of talk, talk, talk. We don't even know if all the 'taties are rotten or not, so why don't we just dig them all up?'

He did not yet have the experience to understand that the men were putting off the final discovery as long as possible, for beneath their fields lay their sole means of survival for themselves and their families. As long as the answer lay hidden, they need not face the terrible truth.

Finally a decision was reached; they would all split up and visit the neighbouring villages, and try and discover the extent of the problem. If it was just their valley, perhaps they could come to some arrangement with their neighbours. The Irish were nothing if not supreme optimists!

Sean saw his father break away from the group and head south towards the village of Colkenny, some two miles away. He fell into step and the two walked silently for a while. Their relationship was an easy one these days, so the silence was amicable enough, each busy with their own thoughts, but presently, Sean said,

'What will we do if it's all gone?'

'God knows, son. A poor harvest we can bear, but no harvest…? Maybe our landlord can help us!' And Pat laughed mirthlessly.

Father and son finished their journey in silence, and as they neared Colkenny, saw to their horror that these fields were in devastation as were their own. A knot of men was gathered in the middle of the huddle of cottages, as Pat and Sean approached, they were greeted with relief, for they were well known here.

'Did you see our crop? Whatever it is it came in the night without warning; yesterday they were green and healthy, and now…!'

The voice tailed off as the speaker saw the look on Pat's face,

'Your's too?' Pat nodded, too overcome to speak.

'If it's here and in Clonarty, then it must be all over these parts,' spoke another Colkenny man, 'what are we to do?'

'That's what everyone keeps saying,' though Sean, 'does no-one have the answer?'

After some more exchange of news, Pat and Sean retraced their steps back to Clonarty. By the time they arrived, the day was well advanced, and the women had returned to their homes to prepare some food, instinctively making the meal small in anticipation of what was to come.

By evening, all the men had returned with similar stories of stinking corruption. They gathered in the village centre to discuss the way forward, while their wives sat with their infants cradling in their arms, rocking them gently, as much to comfort themselves as persuade them to sleep. Older children sat in groups according to age, and were unnaturally quiet, their usual bickering suspended for once. The men were conscious that the fate of their village rested upon their shoulders, for they were very sure that no help would be offered by their landlord and his detested agent, O'Leary. They would be more than ready to see the lot of them thrown off their land to give it over to sheep grazing.

Though there was no designated leader, Daniel O'Malley was generally regarded as talking good sense, and he spoke now,

'It seems that the whole of this area of the Danforth estate, and beyond, has been hit by this plague, and further afield for all we know! No-one seems to know what 'tis for no-one's seen it before. Tomorrow, we must start harvesting, an' see just what we have. Though Pat here says he dug down, and only found a stinking mess, we cannot know if 'tis the same all over. An' someone must go to Dublin and see the people in charge 'n see if that know what 'tis about and what we should do. '

Daniel fell silent, and looked about him for other opinions. Finally, after a painful silence, came another voice, Conor Murphy,

'We must send word to Agent O'Leary – he could stop our rents for this year while we get through this trouble. Even Danforth, God rot him, won't expect to be paid if we've nothing to eat!'

'What,' exclaimed Pat, 'Like the O'Sullivans a while back? Agent O'Leary threw him out quick enough; I didn't see him given time to pay!'

There was a murmur of agreement. But Conor persisted, 'but it's everybody this time, it must be worth a try!'

'What'dya all say then?' said Daniel, quietly, looking around him. He saw some heads nodding agreement, while others shook their heads in denial. It was finally put to the vote with a show of hands; Conor would go and see Agent O'Leary while Daniel would go to Dublin to try and get some information from the Castle there. Presently, the assembly broke up with subdued villagers making their way back to their cottages, still trying to come to terms with the tragedy that had befallen them.

The O'Hara's settled the little ones, Nuala and Eily, in their bracken beds. Kate leaned against Pat, fearful of their uncertain future. Sean drew his knees up, folding his arms over them, while Kevin leaned on his shoulder, each boy busy with thoughts of their own. Finally Sean said,

'Well Pa, at least we'll be doin' somethin' now, instead of just talking 'bout it.'

Pat's face broke into a rueful smile, 'There talks youth! When you get older son, you'll know that sometimes it's better to talk than find out the truth, for the truth can be hard to bear!'

Effectively silenced, Sean went to his bed, but lay brooding a long while, troubled thoughts going round and round his head. Suppose they did not have any potatoes, suppose O'Leary did not give them relief from rents, suppose….? He finally drifted into a troubled sleep, to the sound of his parents' whispers. Sean's sleep was disturbed by nightmares, where he was holding out a bowl of sweet, new crop potatoes to Nuala, but as she reached for them, they turned to a brown, slimy mass that oozed between her fingers. She began to wail at him. The sound growing more and more insistent, until Sean woke to find it morning and Nuala was wailing pitifully; the events of the day before making her uncharacteristically fretful. It was time to begin harvesting.

For two weeks, the whole village laboured. The older men and boys dug until their backs ached and their hands were blistered. The women and younger children followed behind their menfolk with baskets and collected the tubers, tipping them at the ends of the rows. Some of the tubers were so rotten that the slime oozed through the baskets as they were being carried; and all the while there was the stench. They all awoke to it clogging their nostrils, overriding their habitual rich odours with its rancid sweetness. It filled their nostrils and throats as they dug and carried, so that from to time, they had break off from their labours to heave and retch. It followed them back to their cottages at night, suppressing their appetites for the little food they allowed themselves. It accompanied them to their beds and journeyed with them into sleep, inducing restlessness and nightmares, night after night.

When the harvest was complete, it was clear that more than half had been totally destroyed by the ravages of the disease, and it was fit only to be buried in a large pit, dug for the purpose away from the cultivated areas. Of the remainder, few potatoes were completely sound; most showing signs of rottenness, promising further decay. Their storage pits were opened, and the remains of the previous year's crop removed to make way for the pitiful and diseased new crop, for they believed that the safest place for it was out of the light.

During the harvest, Conor and Daniel left for their quests, but soon returned. Conor had gone, cap in hand, to plead their cause with Agent O'Leary, to plead with him to contact his master, Lord Danforth and ask for a stay of their rents. O'Leary bared his gums in a mirthless grin, and vowed that Lord Danforth had already proclaimed that rents must be paid on time, and any defaulting would result in immediate eviction. In vain did Conor plead eloquently on his village's behalf, citing their excellent record of payment hitherto. O'Leary's grin did not fade as he listened to the rhetoric, until finally getting bored, he turned away from the impassioned Conor. Finally, Conor lost his temper, which he had vowed not to do,

'How can you be so sure; he cannot even know yet?'

O'Leary merely shrugged, and edged behind two stalwart thugs in the guise of bodyguards. Conor clenched his fists and moved forward, but the sight of stout shillelaghs in the brutes' hands gave him pause, as he realised the futility of argument. He turned away, sick at heart at his failure to stir O'Leary's pity, and he returned to Clonarty to give the bad news that there would be no stay of rents, so their cash crops would have to used for rent rather than feed them. He told the villagers that he believed it was O'Leary had made the decision for himself without even informing his master. He was not totally accurate, as O'Leary did send a message, but it was true that the agent took malicious pleasure in pre-empting the reply.

Presently a missive arrived from England; the Danforth coffers were in urgent need of filling to settle gambling and other debts, and he taxed his agent with the task of collecting the rents with all due dispatch. Danforth had no intention in giving up any part of his luxurious life, so any defaults followed by evictions would allow an increase in the Danforth herd prize sheep and revenues that would flow from their wooly backs! It did not occur to Lord Charles, for he did not think of them at all, that he was effectively handing out a death sentence to his hapless tenants.

Daniel had gone to Dublin, going first to his son, Michael in his house overlooking the quay. The door was opened by his daughter-in-law, Colette, whose pretty face wore the same worried expression as everyone else he had met on his journey.

'Michael is from home,' answered Colette to Daniel's query, 'but he is due back tonight with the evening tide. Will you bide here for him?'

Daniel politely declined the offer of hospitality. He hardly knew the pretty lass in front of him, as Michael had left Clonarty immediately after his wedding to the fisherman's daughter, and had not since returned for a visit. Daniel absently patted a diminutive version of his own son, sitting in the parlour. Life should be easier for this family, thought Daniel, as they sold their fish to buy their potatoes. But where would they get their potatoes, and who would buy the salt fish, if the potato farmers could not? Daniel sighed at the uncertainty of all their futures and went on his way.

Leaving the small terraced house, Daniel made his way to the Castle. He was granted access by a high nosed servant who haughtily demanded to know his business. Having been informed, the servant bade Daniel wait in a small, draughty room and disappeared. After kicking his heels for over two hours, Daniel was on the verge of losing his patience and was about to search for someone to listen to him. But just in time, a black robed clerk entered, and again enquired haughtily of Daniel's business. Daniel tried to explain about the crisis that faced his village, but the clerk, in peremptory fashion, responded,

'Be off with you. We have more to worry about than your village; don't you know that there is widespread disease in the potato crop!'

In vain did Daniel try to explain that he too was there to report the disease in their area, and to seek advice on how to deal with it.

'All in good time, my good fellow,' insisted the clerk, 'the Government will inform you of their intentions in due course.'

Like Conor, Daniel perforce to return home with his mission unfulfilled, and no hope or help to offer his beleaguered friends and neighbours.

Towards the end of the harvesting, a stranger rode into the village from the direction of Kilgarth and Dublin. He was a portly little man, clad in a cutaway coat, breeches and a round, curly brimmed hat. His face was florid, evidence of a more than comfortable living, with a network of broken veins over his nose and cheeks; clearly a man who enjoyed his food, and even more, his drink! He was mounted on a sturdy brown cob, and was flanked by a couple of thugs who would not have disgraced O'Leary's bunch of ruffians. He rode to the edge of the potato fields where the devastated crops lay in mouldering heaps, and raised a handkerchief to his nose.

Sean watched the stranger, fascinated by his air of affluence, which along with his rotund figure, was in sharp contrast to the villagers who gathered round him. The little man, one Nathaniel Spratt of London, gazed around him, apparently looking for a person of authority to address. He caught the eye of Daniel, and decided that he was the most likely candidate,

'The, harrumph, government of Her Majesty, harrumph, have sent me to ascertain, harrumph, the extent of the blight that has afflicted the potato crop, harrumph, so that proper provision may be made, harrumph, for the indigenous population, harrumph.'

Delivering this speech appeared to sap the energy of Nathaniel Spratt as his cheeks empurpled with his efforts. The villagers were momentarily stunned by the high flown language which they found difficult to follow, though they did take its meaning well enough. Before Daniel could respond, Pat interjected, his ready temper rising at the sight of this pretentious little man interrupting their labours,

'And when you've, er, ascertained, what will you do for us, eh?'

'Gently Pat,' murmured Daniel in Irish, 'there's no need to antagonize the man 'til we find out what he's about.' Then to Nathaniel, in English, 'what's that you called this disease, blight; we've not heard that before.'

'Yes,' replied Nathaniel, it has afflicted crops in England, harrumph, and across Europe as far as is known, harrumph, but until a proper survey can be carried out, we will not know its full extent, harrumph.'

Clonarty village took a collective inward breath, shocked to hear that the wealthy neighbour across the Irish Sea were likewise afflicted. This was serious indeed. Nathaniel Spratt gazed again at the ruined fields and asked,

'How much of the crop has been spared?'

'Less than half,' answered Daniel, 'and what we have is already goin' mouldy.'

'Harrumph, that is about the same in all the places I have seen. I have been told that if you were to, harrumph, dry the tubers and then bury them with freshly burned lime and sand, harrumph. I have also been told, harrumph, that they are quite palatable if you grate them and soak them in water before cooking, yes indeed, harrumph. There is no need for anyone to go hungry, y'know.'

Sean looked at the distended belly straining the buttons of his waistcoat, and murmured to his brother,

'That one's never known what it is to be hungry, even for a day!'

With a final glance round, Spratt prepared to be on his way, beckoning to his escort to follow him.

'One moment,' said Pat, grasping the stirrup of Spratt's cob, 'what does Her Majesty's government plan to do once you've surveyed; you've not told us yet? Or will it wait 'til we all starve – that'll solve the 'problem!'

'There's no need to take that tone, my man, harrumph. There are many souls afflicted as badly as you and we are doing all we can, harrumph. Unhand my stirrup this instant!'

Pat looked up at the pretentious little man, with his florid, overheated face and rotund body. He muttered in Irish,

'Better be gone, otherwise it's not hunger that you'll be dyin' from.'

The hired thugs roughly elbowed Pat aside. They had no feelings towards their charge, but if he was not delivered back to Dublin unharmed, they would not get paid. The small procession headed off in the direction of Colkenny.

A mood of despair settled over the village, as deep as any of them had known. They had believed until then, that the problem was local, and perhaps they would be able to buy potatoes from further afield by using the remains of their cash crop money left after the rents to buy. But if the blight had cast its net as far as England and beyond, what hope could there be for them? For the first time, the spectre of famine stalked them.

In the O'Hara cottage that evening, Kate sat nursing a fretful Nuala, who was uncharacteristically grizzling. Pat sat close by with Sean, Kevin and Eily quietly sitting as close to their parents as they could for the comfort they sought. Pat stirred,

'It's obvious that our 'taties will only last a few weeks,' he observed, 'that fool with his talk of burnt lime. Where will I get the money to buy burnt lime! We've almost raised our rent with the barley crop, but without the early potatoes to sell, we will be short; the pig will have to go – we can't feed it anyway!'

'What then Pa?' asked Sean, 'It's a long time 'til next harvest.'

'I know, son, I know. What comes next is in God's hands, though he's been pretty backward at caring until now!'

'Whisht,' said Kate, in alarm, 'that's blasphemy. The good Lord sends these things to try us!' And she buried her face in Nuala's neck and started to croon a lullaby to the toddler. Pat laughed mirthlessly,

'Yes, he has indeed sent to try us. We'll have to try and get work, son, and see if we can buy enough to survive!'

Neither he, nor anyone of his family, thought that every able bodied Irishman, intent on feeding his family, would be doing the very same thing!

Chapter 15

Sean was having his nightmare again, the same one that had haunted his sleep every night for a week. Through a swirling mist he could see Nuala holding out her chubby hands to him and crying,

'Give me taties, Sean', the infant sobbed, 'give me taties.'

He reached forward, and in his hands was a bowl full of sweet, new potatoes, tossed in buttermilk.

'Here you are, Nuala, come and get them, they're all for you.'

Nuala dipped her hands into the bowl, but all she brought out was a handful of stinking slime that dripped through her fingers, reeking of corruption.

'Sean, Sean, you're nasty. I hate you. I hate you,' and the little girl's face puckered as she began to cry brokenheartedly.

''Tisn't my fault,' muttered Sean, tossing and turning in his bed, as the sound of Nuala's sobbing broke through the edges of his sleep and woke him up. And as had happened every morning that week, he had awoken to find that Nuala was really crying, and it had become part of his dream.

Nuala cried most of the time now, no longer the bubbling infant that she had been until the harvest. She cried because she was hungry, and she was hungry because she would not, could not accept the rotten potatoes that the rest of them forced down their throats. Kate did her best to make them palatable. She had tried soaking them as the little government agent had suggested, flavouring the resulting mess with cabbage water, wild nettles, wild garlic, herbs; any and everything had been tried to take away the appalling taste of corruption. Even apparently sound tubers tasted of decaying matter, and carried the same smell that had nauseated them during harvesting, and it took a supreme effort of will to force the stuff down, as the stomach revolted and heaved. The older O'Hara's knew that they must eat, as the remnants of the potato crop was rotting as it lay in the storage pit, and if not eaten soon, then it would be wasted altogether. They all understood this, except Nuala.

From the very first day, Kate had tried to force the little one to eat, but she had stubbornly refused, pushing the spoon away and turning her head. Her favourite Sean tried persuasion with their favourite rabbit game with the spoon,

'Look Nuala, it's a little rabbit, running across the hill,'

And he would wave the spoon as it imitated a rabbit running to its hole. Nuala would chuckle at his antics, clapping her hands with delight, momentarily distracted; but the moment the spoon neared her mouth her lips would tighten, and she would knock the precious mouthful to the floor. Pat tried coercion, pinching Nuala's lips while Kate inserted the spoon, but Nuala simply spat out the mess and screamed, throwing herself about to avoid a repetition.

But in the end, they all gave up, too distressed to attempt any more force feeding, and hoping that hunger would do what they could not. Kate had given her the last of the previous crop and boiled cabbage leaves, but there was little nourishment in cabbage for a growing toddler.

It was now November, and Nuala had been hungry for a long time, but still she would not eat. Even before Autumn set in, she had shed her 'bangles' of infant fat, but she had been a sturdy child with rounded limbs and round, rosy cheeks, glowing with good health. Now, her cheeks were sunken in, and she had purple shadows under her eyes. Her limbs were sticklike, while her belly was distended in shocking parody of the rotund agent for Her Majesty's Government, Nathaniel Spratt, who had not been seen again with advice to offer, neither good nor bad!

Sean got up from his bed, shivering in the early morning gloom. He could see a blanket of mist lay over the village, but even so, he felt too restless to lie abed. He picked up Nuala, speaking words of comfort, which quietened the grizzling toddler momentarily. Then wrapping Nuala and himself with a blanket, he set off for a walk, first telling Eily, who was awake early as usual, what he planned to do, to save his parents from worry.

Sean took the path towards the coast, moving instinctively, as he could see nothing through the swirling mist. He held Nuala close to his chest for warmth, crooning a gentle lullaby he had learnt at his mother's knee. He saw her eyelids begin to droop over eyes that seem to sink further by the day. Her red-gold curls, so like his own and once glossy and vigorous, had turned lank and lifeless, but were now beaded with moisture, giving them a spurious vitality. He carefully skirted the bog that provided them all with peat, and started down the long and gentle slope to the ocean's edge. As he approached the coast, he could hear the gentle shush-shush of the breakers, eternally expending themselves on the beach. By this time, the light had begun to improve as the mist started to lift with the approaching dawn.

He reached the top of the cliff, and stood quietly, nursing the slumbering infant, musing over the vagaries of Fate that could bring them all from prosperity to abject ruin with one savage swipe of her wand. Was there really an Almighty Being up there that would send these things to test them, as his mother averred, or was everything a matter of chance as his father insisted? And where had this disease come from? If the village elders were to be believed, there had been nothing like it before since time out of mind. Did it come from the air blown on the wind? And why were there no more visits from Dublin with offers to help? Sean's head ached with his questions, and for the first time he felt frustrated with his way of life, scratching a meagre living from soil that his family didn't even own, ignorant of the world around them. For the first time, he understood the restless longings of various uncles who had chosen to make their way in other lands. Then he sighed. He could not desert his family right now, and where could he go even so? Why, he thought to himself, it would break his mother's heart. He knew, without any sense of inflated importance, that as much as Kate loved Kevin, Eily and Nuala, he was her firstborn son, and as such was infinitely precious to her.

He looked out to sea which was a lighter shade against the looming sky, the line of surf glimmering ghostly white below him. The sky was slowly lightening, though the sun was well hidden, and he could see the sea more clearly now, moving restlessly, green and deep blue in turn as a slight swell moved the surface. As he stood there, silently watching, Nuala stirred and he hoisted her up so that he could see the glory that was unfolding before them. Right on the horizon, a golden ray appeared, beaming upwards, heralding the dawn. It was swiftly followed by a horizontal bar of liquid gold that shimmered on the surface of the sea, turning it opalescent. Bars of vivid reds, oranges and ambers appeared on the lowering clouds. A ball of flame ponderously rose from the depths of the ocean, until the very heavens were on fire. With a final heave, the sun climbed slowly upwards, beginning its short, autumnal journey through the sky before it committed suicide behind the dark clouds.

Both Sean and Nuala had held their breaths during the spectacle, but now Sean shook himself out of his reverie, both chilled by the long cliff top vigil. He turned for home, chatting to Nuala as much to take her mind off her hunger as to have a sounding board for the ideas that were surging around his head, ideas that would be lost if not expounded to someone there and then!

'You see, Nuala, there must be something – someone up there. A sight like that couldn't happen by chance – could it? We ought to go to Dublin, Pa 'n me, and try to find out what is being done – it's no use waiting for them to come to us – like that funny little man!'

'Funny man, funny man,' Nuala crooned, thumping his chest, 'funny man, funny man.'

'I'm sure the government'll've sorted something out by now – they've had long enough. I'll talk to Pa as soon as we get back. You'll have something to eat before you know it – you wait'n see!'

He gave the little girl a hug, which startled her, momentarily stopping her croon, but she soon started up again,

'Funny man, funny man....'

Sean and Nuala arrived back to their shebeen to find Pat and Kate waiting for them.

'Ah, there you are son; I've been waiting for you. Get yourself some food, we're goin' to Dublin, so we are!'

'I was goin' to suggest that meself, Pa, we may be able to find some food for Nuala that she will eat?'

'Yes, son, Hamish McFadden from Colkenny came by a while back. He's heard rumours that there's food to be doled out, that it landed in Cork a week or so back. It won't hurt to take a look. There may be work to be had, too.'

This last was said with little optimism, for their last attempt had met with total failure. There was no market for unskilled labour!

'Anyway, we must do something, for this little one is fadin' away in front of us.'

He touched Nula's cheek as she peered out from the blanket, and the little girl responded with a wan smile, reaching out for her father, who took her in his arms with a saddened look, then gave her to Kate to settle. Sean went inside to prepare for the journey, for the ten miles separating them from Dublin would mean that they would be gone all day.

Outside, Pat and Kate stood talking quietly, mulling over the possibility of finding either food or work. Privately, Pat held out little hope, and was undertaking the journey to please Kate as much as anything. He had no faith in the openhandedness of the British Government; after all, why should he? Then Fergus came across the village from the O'Malley home to speak to them.

'Mornin' Kate, Pat. I hear you're off to Dublin? Mind if I join you?'

'Yes. Why not – there's safety in numbers, tho' I hate to say it.'

Pat spoke bitterly, for the Irish were hospitable folk, but a spate of attacks on travelers recently spoke louder than any words of the feeling of desperation abroad!

'I'll be with you directly, then. Don't wait – if I'm not back when you're ready, I'll soon catch up.'

And Fergus retraced his steps to his shebeen. Soon after, Pat and Sean set out soon after, leaving Kate alone with Nuala, already grizzling, as Kevin and Eily had gone out to play already. Kate rocked the little girl, grieving over the slightness of her body. When her eyelids finally closed in exhaustion, Kate laid her on her bed, praying she would sleep for several hours, for sleeping babies did not feel hungry and cry! As she straightened up, the cottage darkened as someone entered. She turned, half expecting Pat or Sean returning for something they had forgotten; but she was startled to see Fergus.

'They've only just gone; hurry now, you'll catch them before they've left the village,' cried Kate.

'I - I know they've gone; I was watching from across the way. I wanted to see you before I left, to – er – say goodbye!'

Kate was puzzled. What did he mean? He was only going to Dublin, wasn't he? But then she looked at him more closely, noting the sizable bundle he carried, and his fiddle, which he carried in a bag over his shoulder. She was not surprised at the fiddle, for he rarely strayed far without it, but what was the bundle for?'

'You're leavin' 'em, aren't you? Just when they need you most, you're goin'?'

'Aw Kate. There's nothin' for me here. It'll mean one less mouth to feed. I'm tired of this life. One year, we've full bellies, and the next – this. Ireland's finished. All that talk of heroes; that was ages ago; we've no more hope of getting' back our land as the potatoes turning sound again!'

'At least wait until this is over,' Kate pleaded, 'If you go now, they'll have no-one.'

'They've got you and Mari. You'll mind them, I know you will. They'll not miss me.'

'That's nonsense an' you know it, you're their darlin' child. It'll break their hearts!'

'You said that when Tomos went, an' they survived. I tell you, he had the right of it, him and Seth and Calum and the rest. There's a huge world out there waiting to be explored, instead of scratching a living here.'

Kate looked at her 'baby brother', really looked at him for the first time. Instead of the handsome face, she saw flaws hitherto unnoticed. The bright blue O'Malley eyes had shiftiness about them, and were, even now, sliding away from her, unable to look her straight in the eye. His chin had a weakness about it, and his whole demeanour spoke of self-seeking. Yes, Fergus would survive.

'Well, why don't you go, or d'you want me to sob all over you? No doubt you've left Ma doin' that already?'

But when she looked at him again, he fidgeted, uncomfortable at last,

'So, you've not told 'em, have you? You want me to do your dirty work for you? Well go. I'll tell 'em what kind of man you really are. Why should they grieve over someone like you?'

Fergus turned to leave, but at the last, Kate could not bear to see him go forever with such hateful words for company. Before he reached the door, she ran to him for a swift hug, whispering in his ear,

'Goodbye Fergus. I hope you find what you are looking for.'

Fergus pulled her tight to him and then turned away quickly, going out into the bright, sunny morning.

Kate stood where she was for a long moment gazing sightlessly at her brother. Instead of a doorway, she saw a small boy with her own bright blue eyes and red-gold hair, full of mischief and racing around among revelers as she was wed to Pat. She saw the growing boy, always in trouble and always forgiven for the sweetness of his smile. She saw the boy/man, practicing his fiddle with an eldritch shriek until he finally mastered it. She saw the man grown, fluttering the hearts of the village maids and flirting with them all. She did not see, for she refused to see, the selfish man with the weak chin who had left for lands unknown.

Pat, Sean and Fergus, accompanied by sundry other Clonarty men arrived in Dublin soon after midday to find streets in turmoil of excitement. They made their way by the Liffey to the docks where they found a mass of people congregated, and surging to and from in an aimless fashion. Pat looked about him.

'We need to find out what this is about,' he muttered, and grabbing a passer-by by the arm, began to question him.

Sean stood by his father and observed the milling crowds. His gaze swept over ships being loaded and unloaded at the quay, and what he saw made his eyes widen in horror. There were ships being stuffed full of produce of Ireland; grain, butter and cheese, were all being carried up the gangplanks by dockers, apparently oblivious to the fact that their own countrymen were in desperate need of these very foodstuffs!

'Pa, Pa,' he said urgently, tugging his father's sleeve.

'Just a minute,' retorted pat angrily, 'can't you see I'm talking?'

'Sorry Pa.' Sean subsided and waited patiently for his father to finish, and all the while the ships were being loaded; one was even now edging out into the tide. So intent on the scene was he that it was some time before he noticed that Fergus was no longer with them. He turned quickly, and spotted the familiar red-gold hair, so like his own, disappearing into the crowd, and immediately lost from view. Sean shrugged. After all, Fergus was old enough to look after himself, but it was strange though, that he should take himself off like that!

'Well son.' Pat turned back to his son at last, having thanked the stranger. It seems that there's been some sort of meeting. There are to be proper plans drawn up for relief at last. There's to be food brought in for us, and work laid on and everything.'

'Thank god,' breather Sean, 'but look Pa. Look at those ships. Why is all that food bein' taken away?'

'I don't know son. Nothing the British Government does makes any sense; never has! Let's see if we can find out more. We need to get work too, if we're to feed Nuala.'

Pat and Sean, separated from the rest of the Clonarty men, made their way to the Castle and waited in the same dusty ante-room that Daniel had kicked his heels in some weeks before. While they waited, Sean told his father that he had lost sight of Fergus in the crowd.

'He'll doubtless make his own way back,' muttered Pat, none too happy with the wait.

Eventually, a high nosed official came in to send them on their way.

'You'll be informed in good time, along with everyone else. We will get a lot more done if we were not continually interrupted like this, you know.'

Sean felt his father stiffen, and feared his formidable temper, but Pat had himself rigidly under control.

'Me little one is dyin' for lack of proper food, and you tell me to mind me business!' Pat spoke quietly, but with such venom that the man stepped a pace or two backwards.

'There's no need to take that tone, my man; we're doing all we can. We're all badly off you know.'

Pat's gaze travelled up and down the official, taking in the sleek pomaded hair, the rounded limbs and the stout belly straining his handsome black coat.

'Hungry, are you?' he said pointedly.

'Well. We'll be informing all of you. Watch out for notices – they'll be posted all over Dublin.'

The man was clearly anxious to be gone, very nervous of his black browed inquisitor.

'We live ten miles away – an how're we supposed to read your notices?'

'I can't help you further – no decisions have been reached yet.' And with that parting shot, the man left the room hurriedly.

Father and son left the Castle and made their way back to the town centre. As they walked, they began to hear drums beating, and the steady thud of marching feet. They turned to see a body of soldiers moving at a brisk pace towards them; part of a regiment normally quartered in the Dublin Barracks. In spite of being raised to hate all things British, Sean could not help being stirred at the sight and sound of the military display. They were a brave sight, resplendent in scarlet coats crossed by white webbing straps, white breeches tucked into black boots, and crowned by tall shakoes. They were kept in step by the efforts of two drummer boys, of an age with Sean himself, but bearing themselves with great pride as they marched ahead of the phalanx. Sean turned to his father to comment, but then held his silence as he saw his father spit into the road after the passing of the soldiers. But curiosity got the better of them, and Pat remarked,

'I wonder where they're away to. Let's follow them and find out.'

They soon discovered their destination, a warehouse that was being besieged by a mob of angry men, armed with all manner of makeshift weapons. A pair of nervous looking clerks stood in front of the great doors, and was clearly relieved as the phalanx of soldiers came towards them, cleaving a way through the mob. Upon reaching the warehouse, the soldiers about faced, deployed in a line in front of the doors and leveled their guns menacingly.

'Now,' said one of the clerks, clearing his throat, 'if you will form a line, there is grain enough for all.'

'Only if you've money for it,' yelled a voice from the crowd.

'We can't afford to give it away, y'know. Very soon there'll be none left for anyone! Very soon there'll be Indian corn for all of you; no-one will starve.'

There was the sound of mirthless laughter in the crowd. Clearly, it had all been heard before. The mass of people shifted this way and that, the corporate body trying to make a decision. Close by Sean, voices could be heard,

'If we rush them, we'll be able to get through; there's only a handful of soldiers, and who's to say those guns are even loaded! Anyway, we're behind the front row – they'll get the shot and then we can get in and get a sack or two!'

Sean was aghast at the words he had overheard. He was pretty sure that these men were not after food for their families; they looked to be thorough going ruffians, and could only imagine they were selling the grain. Before he could even tell Pat what he had heard, the men vanished towards the back of the crowd, and within a short time, the crowd began to surge forward, no doubt egged on by the troublemakers. There was a rising growl and the front row moved forward menacingly on the thin line of soldiers. These stood firm, urged on by their officer, who gave orders in a quiet voice,

'Steady men; hold your fire until I give the order. Take aim…..'

The crowd held back for a moment, deterred by the menace of the guns leveled at their bellies, but the pushing from behind became insistent. There was a movement like a wave, and the whole crowd surged forward. There was a crackle of gunfire followed by screams as men were hit, but the surge carried forward until it reached the warehouse, pushing aside clerks and soldiers alike. There was a pause as the doors were pounded by insistent shoulders, then a backward move, then a forward rush; once, twice and the doors gave way. The crowd rushed in and began to tug at the piles of grain sacks without method or design. In the next moment, there was a shout,

'Watch out, it's goin'!'

And a pile of sacks started to slide, trapping some rioters underneath, their screams adding to the confusion.

Pat and Sean, at the very edge of the crowd, could only hear what was happening in the confusion, but once or twice, Sean thought he saw one of the insurgents, for he sported a bright red scarf around his neck. He was moving forward stealthily but purposefully, clearly intent on seizing a sack or two. Suddenly, Sean heard another sound behind him, one of the drummer boys was beating the Advance, and then,

'Charge!'

Another body of soldiers, reinforcements, came by at a steady run and charged into the crowd, laying about them with their rifle butts. There was panic as the rioters turned to face them, trapped in between the fallen grain sacks and the charging soldiers. Sean, intent on watching the melee, did not see a soldier coming up behind him, and was felled by a glancing blow from a rifle butt. As he fell, he thought he saw a man with a red scarf heading out of the great doors, bearing a sack of grain, before darkness descended.

When he came to his senses, he sat up shakily. Order appeared to have been restored, and a large crowd of bewildered Irishmen were surrounded by redcoats. One of the warehouse doors hung drunkenly on one hinge, and injured soldiers were being tended to by their comrades. Felled Irishmen were ignored. Most had suffered no more bruises during the skirmish, but one or two concussions had to be dealt with. Sean gazed groggily around him, and squinted to focus his eyes on the prisoners, finally identifying his father. It appeared that the group of Irish was being formed up ready to be marched away. Sean shouted in horror,

'Pa, no, don't let them take you!'

Pat looked towards his son and put his finger to his lips. Clearly he wanted Sean to be silent; there was no sense to them both being marched away.

'Go home an' tell your Mam,' he mouthed at the bewildered boy.

Sean, still too dazed to rise, watched his father being marched away. Why had it all gone wrong? They had come to Dublin to find food and work. First, their hopes had been raised by the news at the quayside, but now, no food, no work and Pat marched away by the hated English to heaven knew where! Sean put his head in his hands, and for the first time in many years, wept.

Chapter 16

Sean remained slumped on the ground as the warehouse and courtyard slowly emptied of people. Men injured by the fall of sacks were being roughly handled and dragged unceremoniously away after the body of marching men. One of them seemed to have broken his leg, which stuck out at an awkward angle, and he screamed aloud as he was dragged past Sean. The last of them, two soldiers with makeshift bandages round their heads, were placed on stretchers and carried away. He remained silent and unnoticed in the shadows, nursing an aching head and sick heart. Finally, one of the great doors was closed, but the second, damaged one was pushed as far as it would go. There was an eerie silence, as Sean slowly dragged himself to his feet, tottering slightly.

Inside the warehouse there was a jumbled mass of grain sacks, some split open, spilling their precious contents onto the dusty floor. Sean looked at the grain, and then at the door; there was no sound from without. He was by nature, totally honest, and in normal times would have walked away. But times were not normal, and the grain could mean the difference between life and death for an infant who could not eat the rotten mess of potatoes that was all she could have. He would take it, and think of the seizure of his father, who was only guilty of being in the wrong place at the wrong time and be comforted. He looked around again; nothing, nobody stirred. Taking off his scarf, he filled it as much as he could, tying the corners together firmly to contain the precious load. Used carefully, this bundle could keep little Nuala going until the promised government aid arrived.

He left the warehouse gingerly, squeezing through the gap left by the door with the damaged hinge. At any moment, he expected a strident voice demanding to know his business. He sidled out of the courtyard; still no-one in sight, and then he out in the streets, forcing himself to walk calmly and nonchalantly.

While he walked, Sean considered the problems that he yet faced. Firstly, the journey home; ten miles on his own with vagabonds on the loose who would find a sixteen year old boy easy prey. And he already felt weary to his bones! There was no sign of Fergus and the other Clonarty men to give him companionship, and the air was getting decidedly chilly; soon it would be dark. Then he remembered that his Uncle Michael had a fisherman's cottage down on the quay. His footsteps quickened with renewed hope as he made his way to the quay, where their disastrous day had begun in such hope! He had a moment of doubt, fearing his uncle might be away from home on a fishing trip, but as he approached, he saw him sitting outside his front door mending a net, his clay pipe stuck out of the side of his mouth, though unlit!

'Uncle Mick, Thank God yer here. I couldn't bear the thought of setting off home again without a rest, 'n in the dark, 'n something to eat, 'n on my own.'

His voice tailed off wearily as he realized that his uncle was looking at him strangely,

'What ails you boy? Sit yerrself down awhile and tell me where yer Pa's got to.' Michael shouted to his wife to fetch something for the boy, 'though it'll not be much,' he remarked, 'we're no better off than everyone else!'

'I know, Uncle Mick, I know.'

While he waited for Colette to bring him a drink, and perhaps a small bite to eat, Sean told Michael all that had happened that day, ending with the arrest of his father. Michael clucked over the bump on the side of the boy's head, but pronounced it not too serious. He was more worried about Pat!

'He could get locked away for a lengthy spell an' then where will Kate 'n the rest of you be?'

Michael sucked on his pipe awhile as he mulled over what to do.

'You say Fergus was with you this morning?'

'Yes, but we lost him by the Liffey, an' I haven't seen him since.'

'He came here acting very strange; asked questions 'bout ships leaving and then went off without so much as a goodbye!'

Finally, Michael reached a decision.

'I'll come to Clonarty with you, boy. Colette'll be alright here; we've good neighbours 'n she's used to me being away. I want to talk to yer Mam, and then we'll come back tomorrow 'n see if Pat appears in the courthouse. Anyways, it's a long walk home, especially carryin' a bundle like that!'

Sean started guiltily; he had not mentioned the grain for fear that his uncle would think the worst of him, but Michael merely shrugged.

'Times are hard, boy, an' it's not easy watching the little ones suffer.'

The two set out soon after and reached Clonarty when it was full dark. They had met no-one on the way, but had kept their eyes and ears open 'just in case' as Michael wryly observed. Sean was exhausted when he got in, and left it to his uncle to explain to a frantic Kate what had happened to Pat. She insisted that she would return with them the next morning,

'Mari'll mind the little ones when she hears what has happened.'

Her eyes widened when she saw Sean's bag of grain, and crushing a handful, made it into a porridge for Nuala. She offered some to her exhausted son, but he refused,

'I took it for her, Mam, I couldn't eat it. I'll do alright on our 'taties as long as they last.'

Sean managed to swallow some of the nauseating mixture that Kate had prepared earlier and took himself to bed. As he lay in a semi doze he could hear the low voices of his Mam and Michael discussing Fergus, the voices coming and going as he drifted into sleep,

'...how could he......time like this....break their hearts so he will.....who'll help next Spring?'

'Ah,' though Sean, drowsily, 'he's gone and left 'em!'

And the boy slept as it had been a long and exhausting day, both physically and emotionally. He slept on late in the morning, as Nuala had gone to bed with a full belly for the first time in weeks, and the infant slumbered soundly. He slept until roused by Kate's urgent shaking.

'Come on son, we must get back to Dublin to see your Pa!'

The trio set out in somber silence, after taking the little ones to Kate's sister, Mari. Kate was torn between worrying about Nuala and worrying about Pat. Mari had only been too willing to mind Nuala, so that worry at least was lifted from Kate's shoulders; she trusted her sister implicitly.

'Just feed her a little of that grain at a time; she's been too long without proper food 'n she'll likely throw up!'

Mari nodded; she was a placid soul, accepting life's ups and downs with a serene expression and a deep faith in God; a perfect foil for the volatile Conor. Kate often wondered if any deep thoughts went on behind that smooth brow, but she was loved her sister dearly and they were still the best of friends. The sisters had discussed Fergus before they left, and the heartache that the older O'Malleys would suffer.

'Leave it 'till I get back,' suggested Kate, 'if they ask, just say he's decided to bide awhile in Dublin 'n find work.'

Mari nodded, hugged her sister and brother, relieved her of Nuala and waved them off.

The journey seemed endless, but at long last the tallest of Dublin's buildings could be seen. Michael knew the city well, and led them straight to the courthouse. An officious court clerk was inclined to bar their entry, but Michael encouraged him to think again by the simple expedient of clenching his fists and moving forward determinedly. They sat down in the public gallery to find that the rioters were already in the dock, and the magistrate in the process of hearing the case.

Kate spotted Pat at the back of the crowd, and gave a small gasp. Sean followed his mother's gaze and saw that Pat sported a black eye, and his clothes were torn and ragged. Later they were to learn that Pat had been involved in a scrap in the gaol when meagre rations had been flung into the cell the night before. Far from holding back, Pat had relished the chance to work out his frustrations of the day in violent, physical action and threw himself into the fray; managing to grab a handful of food. He now waved surreptitiously but cheerfully enough to his wife.

The hearing had obviously been in progress for some time, and the magistrate had already heard the evidence of the warehouse clerks and officers in charge of the soldiers, and was now in the process of summing up the situation before dealing with individuals. Each of the prisoners was brought forward and asked if he had anything to say. Each in turn declined to offer any defense and was sentenced summarily to a short term of hard labour 'to learn their lesson the hard way,' as the magistrate caustically suggested. It was clear from the lightness of the sentences, that the court was inclined to be magnanimous in the light of the prevailing problems of the famine. It was also clear that the instigators of the riot had escaped, and that the prisoners who had been rounded up had not been guilty of injuring soldiers; a matter that would have been dealt harshly. Just then, Pat was brought forward and his name read out,

'Have you anything to say?' asked the magistrate in a bored voice. The morning was well advanced and he was looking forward to a substantial lunch with his colleagues in a nearby hostelry; not for him the problem of a restricted diet!

'Yes,' asserted Pat firmly.

'No, Pat, no!' Kate cried out.

'Well,' said the magistrate testily, ignoring the interruption from Kate. Pat gathered his thoughts; the hearing was conducted in English, and he did not have a perfect command of it, though he understood it well enough.

'I took no part in the riot; I was just lookin' on with me son.'

'What were you doing there if you were taking no part?'

'I was looking for some food for my youngest child who is starving,' replied Pat, flatly. 'him over there,' pointing at one of the warehouse clerks, 'said we could buy some.'

'You have some money then?'

Sean drew in his breath; his father would have been searched and they would know he did not.

'Well?'

'No I don't, but I thought to beg for some grain.' The words were forced through clenched teeth, for Pat was a proud man and did not care to admit that he had been willing to beg.

'Oh Pat,' whispered Kate under her breath.

'If you took no part in the riot, why were you taken?'

'I was standing with me son when the soldiers ran in, and as I turned to look, one of them raised his gun and hit him on the head. He went down, and I went to help in, but the soldier raised his gun to hit him again, tho' he was on the ground. I tried to get the gun from him but another soldier came up from behind and grabbed my arms. The first one hit me in the belly, 'n while I was fightin' for me breath pushed me into the yard with the others.'

Far from being sympathetic on hearing that Pat was merely trying to protect his son, the magistrate was outraged,

'You lifted a hand against a soldier of the Queen; sent here to keep law and order; you tried to get his gun?'

'Only to stop him hitting me son!'

'I cannot accept that. The man was doing his duty. You had no business being at the warehouse. At your own admission you had no money so could not buy the grain. You are clearly a troublemaker and I intend to make an example of you.'

The magistrate banged his gavel on the table,

'One year's hard labour.'

There was an audible groan from the assembled crowd, and an anguished cry from Kate. The military officers looked uncomfortable, and even the warehouse clerks looked shocked, in spite of their fright the day before.

'No,' shouted Pat, before court officials could move to drag him away, 'what right have you to pass judgment? I've done nothin' wrong 'cept watch me little one fade away for lack of proper food. You sit there, fat'n pompous an' say I can't do anythin' to save her; I can't do anythin' to save me son bein' hit as he lay on the ground…..'

Two burly officials managed to get hold of Pat's arms and dragged him to the floor. The magistrate was on his feet, purple with rage and nose pinched with fury.

'I'll teach you to hold this court in contempt; you are animals, you and your kind. Flog him before you throw him into the sty of a gaol where he belongs!'

And full of righteous indignation, the magistrate drew his robes around his rotund belly and swept out of the court, forgetting the handful of rioters still waiting to be dealt with. He was not destined to enjoy his lunch, however, his rage causing him to suffer a severe attack of dyspepsia; small revenge for the man he had condemned to a year of hard labour, often synonymous with a death sentence, the conditions in the gaol being as bad as they were. And what of the other sentences he had thoughtlessly meted out? Without their mainstay, what hope had his family of surviving the year, especially at such a time of privation?

There was a short period of silence after the magistrate had gone, and then confusion reigned as everyone tried to talk at once. In vain did court officials try to re-establish order and clear the courtroom. Kate had collapsed onto the hard wooden bench while Michael and Sean did their best to comfort her. Sean looked up and across the crowded courtroom to meet the eyes of one Captain James Willoughby. The two silently appraised each other, the sixteen year old Irish boy, distraught at the recent events and Captain of the hated British Army, totally unaware that their future lives were to be inextricably linked.

Sean saw a man resplendent in his scarlet uniform and gold lacings of Her Majesty's Foot Regiments, his shako punctiliously held under his right arm, his whole bearing the very epitome of military prowess. He was a man in his mid-twenties who stood an inch below six feet in his stockings, and with regular features. His upper lip was adorned with a magnificent set of moustaches, slightly more ginger than the brown of his hair, and green eyes. Those same eyes were now watching Sean and his mother with a quizzical look. Sean thought it strange that he felt no animosity towards this member of the hated English upper class; indeed he sensed a measure of sympathy from him. True, he had not been directly responsible for his father's predicament; that was down to his father's own volatile temper and the magistrate's petty vindictiveness. But he had been weaned on tales of how the filthy English had taken over his native land, and how not one of them could be trusted. But try as he might, he could not rid himself of the notion that this was a man who could be trusted; and indeed respected!

Captain Willoughby saw a youth, possibly fifteen or sixteen, with an intelligent brow and a shock of dark hair, the colour of a newly opened horse chestnut. The boy's features were strong and clear cut, though fined by hunger, but not yet gaunt from privation. The Captain supposed that the woman he was comforting was his mother, and from her reaction to the prisoner being dragged away, that he was his father. The other man who was comforting her also had a family look, brother, cousin mayhap? Like most of his fellow officers, Captain Willoughby had purchased his commission in the army, but unlike many of those same fellows, he was an intelligent man who took the time and trouble to ponder on the duties he was called upon to perform. The control of the food riots the day before, he had found particularly distasteful. He had been in command of the small squad of soldiers that had been dispatched to protect the grain warehouse the day before. On his arrival, he has disposed of his men in front of the mob, and had quickly assessed the situation. He could see that the front ranks were nervous of their guns and were more inclined to slink away than force a confrontation. It had come as a shock, therefore, when the crowd had begun to surge forward, but he had quickly realized that there had been agitators hidden in the crowd, but at that moment, he had caught the sound of approaching reinforcements, and it was he who had ordered his men to fire over the heads of the mob, and use their rifle butts to protect themselves until help arrived. He had encouraged his men to use the minimum of force in their dealing with the rioters; after all, who could blame a man for trying to feed his starving family? Others were not so understanding, however, and Willoughby could see the lump on the boy's head, bearing witness to his father's testimony. Willoughby sighed, for there was no easy answer to the problems they were facing.

The Irish could help themselves by diversifying their crops and lessening their dependence on potatoes, couldn't they? And did his own countrymen have the right to prevent the Irish from owning their land? And if they did, could they not do more to help them in their extremity now? He did not approve of rioting and theft, but he did have a strong measure of sympathy for these beleaguered people. Unlike most of his compatriots, he did not believe that all Irishmen were necessarily stupid and ignorant; barely raised above the level of the animals they lived with; witness the distress of the man who had been reduced to begging for food for his starving child!

Captain Willoughby watched as Sean and Michael helped the weeping Kate from the courtroom. They made their way to the gaol nearby and banged on the door.

'What d'yer want,' said the creature who answered their summons. He had a brutish fighter's face, with a low brow and mop of unkempt black hair. Even though the trio outside were used to multifarious odours, he had such a rank smell that they instinctively drew back apace!

'I...I'd like to see me husband,' asked Kate, softly, not wishing to antagonize the man, 'he was just brought in.

'The one who's to be flogged is it?' His lips drew back in a wolfish grin. 'Mebbe tomorrow. Orders.'

And the man shut the door in their faces. The only way to get help from such a creature would be to grease his palm, and they did not have the wherewithal to do that. They turned away, Kate weeping inconsolably now, almost fainting on Sean's arm.

Captain Willoughby, who had left the courtroom soon after the trio, came upon the scene, and rapidly assessed the situation as the gaoler banged the door.

'Can I be of service to you,' he asked Michael, with a slight bow.

Michael stiffened and muttered in Erse,

'Haven't you done enough? Come away, Kate, we'll try again tomorrow.'

But Sean looked into Willoughby's face and saw that he genuinely wanted to help.

'Me father's been taken in there, an' the gaoler won't let us in see him.'

Willoughby pounded on the door with a hand encased in a snowy white glove. While they waited, Sean eyed him surreptitiously, from his coiffured hair to his gleaming black boots, and felt again a strange affinity for the man.

'I told yer, come back tomor...' The gaoler had reappeared, but his angry tirade died as he caught sight of the Captain.

'Beggin' yer pardon, yer honour, I didn't see ye for these people cluttering up the doorway.'

'That's enough,' said Willoughby, wrinkling his nose distastefully at the rank odour. 'These good people want to see the prisoner....' 'O'Hara,' supplied Sean.

'Er yes, O'Hara. Be quick about it, I haven't all day!'

Fawning ingratiatingly, the gaoler took them to a small room inside the gaol.

'I'll just find out what's happened to the - er – prisoner,' and tugging his shock of hair, the oaf took himself off.

They waited in silence, Willoughby polishing the brim of his shako with his sleeve, Kate still weeping in hopeless fashion, Michael glowering at being beholden to one he considered to be his mortal enemy and Sean pondering on this strange turn of events. Presently, the brutish gaoler returned and called Willoughby out of the room. The others could only hear a muttered conversation, but the Captain soon returned to the room. He turned to Kate with a slight bow,

'I'm sorry ma'am; the flogging's already been carried out. Your husband is – er – recovering in a cell. I think you should see him tomorrow!'

'Please,' whispered Kate, her face ashen, 'Mayn't I see him now?'

'I don't advise it, ma'am, he will look a lot better in the morning.'

He turned to Michael,

'Do you live here, in Dublin?'

Michael forced himself to answer politely,

'I do, yes, but me sister from a village a distance away. She has little ones to mind.'

'I see. Can you stay in Dublin, tonight?' This was to Kate.

'I'll stay with me brother; but will they let us in tomorrow? We've no..'

'I know ma'am. Meet me here at ten o'clock. I'll see that you get in to see your husband.'

Willoughby was blithely unaware that the O'Hara's had no way of telling the time, but no matter, thought Kate, I'll be here at dawn!

They left the gaol, then, Michael thanking the Captain through stiff lips, but Sean and Kate adding theirs warmly.

'Tomorrow, then.' And touching his shako, now donned, Captain James Willoughby strode away.

It was a subdued trio that made its way from the prison to Michael's cottage by the quay. They were made welcome by Colette and given a scanty meal of salt herring, while Michael brought his wife up to date with their news. Their three children came and went all the while, though tending to stay out of the cottage as much as possible as it was cramped by the unexpected guests. The three boys all seemed to be diminutive versions of Michael himself, especially the oldest, named Mickey for his father. Later, they all crammed in somehow to sleep, though that was a precious commodity for Sean and his mother, worried about the morning. Sean could hear his mother in the darkness, weeping hopelessly, helplessly for hours on end.

Next morning found Sean and Kate outside the cottage soon after dawn, waiting for Michael; Kate red-eyed, but calmer now, and Sean filled with the optimism of youth. Michael appeared, knuckling sleep out of his eyes.

'You go on,' he said to Kate, 'yon soldier will mind out for you; you don't need me!'

'But Uncle Mick; he was only trying to help!'

'I know, boy. It's just that I can't abide English soldiers...' And Michael's voice tailed away.

'I know,' murmured Kate, 'Its Tomos, isn't it?'

'Don't be stupid, Kate,' snapped Michael, 'I haven't thought of him in years. It's the sight of those uniforms that puts me back up. I must get out in me boat today, anyway, or none of us'll be eatin'. Not that many are buying me catch these days!'

'Goodbye Michael an' thanks for all you've done. Come Sean, we don't want to miss the soldier!' And with a quick hug for Michael and a sleepy Colette, they set off, unsure what the day would bring.

Kate and Sean arrived at the gaol and settled down to wait for their helper. Neither of them doubted for one moment that he would keep his promise, no matter how long they had to wait, which was odd considering their long term distrust of all things English! Promptly at tem, the tall Captain could be seen making his way towards them, flanked by two privates. He seemed taller than ever with his shako, and made a stirring sight as she strode with measured step towards them, though only Sean was in the mood to appreciate it! Willoughby was carrying a cane today, and he touched his shako with it.

'Morning to you both. I'm Captain Willoughby, by the way. You must be Mrs. O'Hara and ...?

'Sean,' returned the boy, unsure of how to respond to such formal address, 'An' this's me Mam.'

The Captain touched his shako again, watched by the bemused privates. What was their Captain thinking of, treating these ragged, dirty Irish with such deference!

Willoughby rapped on the gaolhouse door with his cane, and it was opened promptly by the same lout of a gaoler, Carey, as the previous day. He silently surveyed the group, and led them to the same room as before.

'I'll just see if he's ready for you.' And the creature went out again. He returned shortly after and jerking his head towards the door, said

'This way.'

'Wait here,' said Willoughby to his men, and followed Kate and Sean as they trailed after the gaoler. He led the way through the building, past cells crowded with men, some hanging onto the bars, but most sitting on the floor sunk in apathy. The odd face was upturned with a vague glimmer of hope as they went by, but for the most part no-one took any notice of their passage. The stench was appalling, and Sean recognised the source of the gaoler's stink! Finally, they arrived at a cell with a single occupant. He lay face down on a crude bench, and the fresh blood sluggishly oozing from his back suggested that he had just been brought in and flung down onto the bench. The man groaned, and Kate started forward with a cry,

'Pat, oh Pat, what've they done to you?'

'He's bin flogged, that's what,' said the gaoler maliciously.

'Take yourself off,' snapped Willoughby, 'lock the door if you must. I'll call when we're ready to leave.'

'I can't do that. Me orders....'

'I think you can.' A coin quietly changed hands, and the oaf bowed himself out with cringing servility.

Willoughby returned to the bench where Kate was ineffectually dabbing at Pat's wounds, tears streaming down her face while a horror struck Sean stood mutely by.

'Excuse me, ma'am,' murmured Willoughby, 'let me see. I 'm more used to flogging and its effect, I've no doubt.'

Kate stood back and watched, as the Captain gently eased the shreds of shirt from Pat's back. What he saw made him compress his lips and stride to the door, shouting for the gaoler, Carey. He came at a run, for the Captain had been more than generous once and might yet be again!

'Water and clean linen strips, quickly now!'

'Yes, yer honour, at once yer honour.' And Carey scurried away, returning shortly with a bowl of water and some scraps of sheeting.

Willoughby gently bathed the weals criss-crossing Pat's back, and noted that none were deep, in spite of the groans he caused. He finally grunted with satisfaction.

'It's alright ma'am, whoever did this knew his job, and the cuts are shallow.'

Presently the Captain was finished, and he stood back to let Kate back to her husband's side, where she took his hand, murmuring to him. Pat had tried to remain silent during the treatment to his back, carried out by one he considered his enemy, and he couldn't begin to understand what was happening!

One moment he had been lying in a crowded cell where he had been unceremoniously flung the previous day, after the flogging; untended and apparently forgotten. The next moment, he had been carried into an empty cell and the door opened to admit wife, son and an English officer who had proceeded to attend to his wounds!

Sean had watched all the proceedings in silence, but when Willoughby stepped back, spoke quietly to him,

'Why're yer doin' this; we're nothing to you?'

'Let's just say, I believed your father, and I don't think he should have been condemned as he was.'

'But…but, why should you care?'

'Why do you question it? We all do things we can't explain sometimes.'

Sean nodded. He still didn't understand the Captain's motives, but realised that he wasn't going to get anything further by way of explanation. Just then his father broke into his reverie and spoke for the first time,

'Sean, Sean.'

'Yes Pa,' and Sean knelt down by his side to catch the words,

Take care of yer Mam, son. Make sure you plant in spring; yer Mam knows; you'll need to sell a thing or two, but get the money somehow.'

'I will Pa, you can rely on me.'

'I know, son, I know.'

'Come on now or I'll be losin' me job,' the rough voice of the gaoler intruded,

'You'll have to go.'

'Bye Pat,' sobbed Kate, 'I'll pray for you.'

'Bye Pa, don't worry, I'll take care of everything.'

The cell was unlocked and they were hustled out. Willoughby knew for certain that, as soon as their back was turned, Pat would be flung back from where he had been dragged.

'Wait for me outside,' he whispered to Sean and Kate,' I'll not be above a moment!'

Then the Captain, having waited for Sean and Kate to disappear from sight, seized Carey's shirtfront, wrinkling his nose with distaste at the smell. The gaoler was a short, stocky man and found himself almost lifted off his feet!

'Listen, you sniveling little worm, I'm stationed here for many months and I intend to visit this gaol regularly. If you treat that man decently, you'll be well rewarded, but if you don't; if I find his back is not healing, or he is left without food and water, I'll see to it that not only will you lose your job, but you will be treated in kind by my soldiers. Understand?' And he shook the apoplectic little man until his teeth rattled.

Carey, who was having trouble breathing, tried to nod, but the Captain's fist under his chin made that movement difficult, and he could only manage a strangled choke.

'Good.' He let go of Carey so abruptly that he fell in an untidy heap at the Captain's feet. The next moment, a handful a silver coins landed on the floor beside him,

'I'll not be announcing when I shall come,' and the Captain strode away, jamming his shako on his head as he went. Collecting the privates from the ante room, Willoughby made his way outside where Sean and Kate were waiting patiently.

'I cannot thank you enough,' said Kate in her gentle voice, 'he didn't do anything wrong; it's just our little Nuala…'

'I know ma'am. Don't fret yourself about it anymore. The time will pass, and he'll be home before you know it,' the Captain replied, equally gently, inwardly vowing that Pat would be home a lot sooner than they could imagine!

'I would like to accept this for your little one, Nuala,' and he held out a small purse. Kate's face blanched of any colour that remained,

'I cannot… you've done enough. We'll be alright, truly,' and she turned anguished eyes to Sean.

'Pardon me ma'am, I mean no offence, but all of this would have been in vain if your daughter has nothing to eat!'

'It was an appeal that Kate could not refuse, and seizing the Captain's hand, she tried to stammer her thanks, much to his embarrassment.

Willoughby gently extricated his hand, and pressing the purse into her palm, he tipped his shako with his cane once more and strode away, followed by his bemused privates.

Kate and Sean hugged each other and wept for all that had happened; for the worry about Pat, the sight of his wounds and the generosity of the English Captain. Then they set off to seek out some food to tempt a little one and perhaps a little luxury for themselves and the other young ones at home. Then they trudged home.

Chapter 17

Nuala began to lose the pinched look of long term hunger by Christmas, though her limbs still resembled sticks, and her hair hung limp and lifeless. But none of them looked particularly healthy, thought Sean, looking around with a sigh, as he cuddled his little sister; the monotonous diet of mashed, diseased potatoes gave them constant belly gripes, so they all had pasty looking skins and dark circles round their eyes. The family were all crammed into Conor and Mari's cottage, the largest of the family's, to celebrate Christmas, though celebrating was not exactly how Sean would describe the atmosphere.

Father Muldoon had visited Clonarty earlier that morning to say Mass for the villagers, and had led them in earnest prayer to the Good Lord, begging Him to end their trials, but if that was not His will, to give them the strength to strive to continue. The elderly priest's face had shone with a simple fervor as he intoned the words of the Mass, though like his congregation, his once robust frame showed the effect of privation. The older women in the flock found the service moving and hoped that it would sustain their spirits during the long, cold months ahead. But others, Sean among them, had great difficulty reconciling a loving God with such a trial, and he could not conceive of a divine purpose behind the blight that visited such suffering on little ones like Nuala.

After the Mass, families had dispersed to spend their day together. In the Murphy cottage were crammed Conor and Mari, with their brood of six and Conor's father Seamus; Eileen and Daniel O'Malley were there, but without their son Fergus and Kate sat with her four children and her father-in-law, Old Kevin but missing her Pat. The atmosphere was quiet and subdued, in contrast to the previous Christmas, when the table had groaned with food provided by them all; eggs and bread, butter and buttermilk and even a little tea for the women. Flasks of poteen had circulated, while tales of past heroes or horror stories made the children's eyes as round as saucers, while stories about the 'little people' brought a sparkle to them. But now, the assembled family spoke quietly among themselves about the events to date, and discussed their future. Even poteen was in short supply, its production forbidden as it used up precious foodstuffs. The little they had was all that was left in the store.

Sean was flanked by his brother Kevin who leaned against him in his usual way, and his cousin Dermot, the oldest Murphy, and across his lap lay a listless Nuala. Little Eily sat nearby with a trio of Murphy girls, four heads bent in earnest conversation. Sean looked about him, noting with a shock the changes wrought by months of poor diet. His grandpa, Old Daniel, wasn't much changed, his rangy features perhaps more lined; but Grandma Eileen had lost her buxom roundedness, her comfortable bosom now sagging to her waist. But the biggest shock to Sean was seeing his Mam; last summer she had been a handsome woman, the years sitting lightly on her and her glorious hair still glowing red and vital. Her carriage had been upright and proud and she had had the contented look of a fulfilled wife and mother, the early, difficult years with Pat firmly put behind her. Now her face was lined, with twin grooves running from nose to mouth, the glorious hair hung lank on her shoulders, and wings of white etched her temples. She looks old, thought Sean sadly, knowing that worry over Nuala and now Pat had caused the changes more than hunger.

'How's yer Pa?' Dermot's voice broke through his reverie.

'Fine, just fine, though dyin' to be home, especially today.' Dermot nodded in understanding.

Sean preferred not to discuss his father's situation with anyone, even his soul mate, Dermot, as it was a continuing puzzle to him and his Mam. Ever since Pat had been incarcerated in Dublin gaol, they had trudged the ten miles to see him once a week, through cold, mists or even driving rain. They had feared the effects of prison on Pat's spirit, and even more they had feared the many dangers he would encounter there, gaol fever, infection of his lacerated back or abuse from gaolers or fellow inmates. But instead they found Pat in a cell on his own, with permission to exercise for an hour a day in a small courtyard and an adequate supply of food. In spite of the sentence he had received, he had not been called upon to do hard labour, so that his back had healed and no longer pained him. His worst problem was not so much boredom or loneliness as he was, by nature a solitary individual, but separation from his family.

'I don't understand any of it,' Pat had said once, 'I keep waiting for that Carey to throw me out of here and into the labour gangs.' And another time he had remarked,

'I hear them return from the quarry sometimes, an' the noise they make, moanin' an' groanin' an' keeping me awake, an' I thank God I am not one of their number! A man got killed last week; he just raised his shovel to the head gaoler an' the guard shot him in the back!'

But over and over, Pat said, 'Why're they treating me like this? D'you know, Kate?'

His last was said with some suspicion, and Kate had had to soothe him; but in truth she did not know herself.

Sean kept his counsel. His father did not ask his opinion and he did not volunteer it, but he could only suppose that it was the doing of the English Captain, Willoughby. Sean not help remembering the courtesy shown to himself and his mother, and the sense of justice that had driven the man to act on their behalf. Nor could he forget the generosity towards them with the gift on money, to which Nuala owed her very life! Sean could not work out how his influence continued to keep Pat safe, but could only be glad of it. But the *why* continued to elude him. *Why* should a member of the British aristocracy care what happened to a poor Irish family? The only other member of that class he knew of was Lord Danforth, whose indifference to his tenants was legendry. The man was hated by all, as it was noted that he had been to see them in their time of trouble, nor had he sanctioned a reduction of rent. O'Leary had told them so, with great relish and reminded them that the penalty of default was the loss of their smallholdings.

If Sean had had the chance to discuss his dilemma with the Captain himself, he would not have been any nearer an answer, for the man could not have supplied it. The younger son of Lord Willoughby whose family estates covered many acres of Yorkshire countryside, he had been raised to follow a strict code of conduct, where justice and fair play were paramount.

He had an innate courtesy and was by nature a true gentleman. But for all that, he was known to be a strict taskmaster to the men under his command.

Taking his ease one evening with a glass of fine red wine in his hand, he listened to his fellow officers discussing their situation,

'They're little better than animals,' offered one very junior cornet,

Have you seen the hovels they live in?'

'Some of the women are quite handsome, though,' ventured another, 'have you visited Bridie's yet?'

'No thank you,' replied a third, 'I prefer the company at the Balls held at the Castle to a dose of clap! How long d'you think we'll be stationed here? I've my eye on the sweetest colleen you ever saw. But her father's an alderman, so I'll have to be careful in my courting!'

'Aiming to marry the girl?' asked the cornet.

'Gad no, but I've a mind to bed her!'

James listened in disgust. Did none of them think about what was going on around them, or about the reason that they were stationed here? Did they not know that the land was blighted by famine, even here in their cushioned luxury of their Dublin barracks? These same officers would consider he had run mad if they knew that he had not only bribed a brute of a gaoler to look after one of the Irish peasantry, but was still visiting the gaol to ensure that his orders were being carried out. Furthermore, he was importuning the Prison Governor to affect an early release for the man, which he had been promised. What was it about this group of people that had stirred his pity enough to cause him to act? He had noticed the boy's intelligent good looks, but he was no pederast, so that was not it. The woman had obviously been attractive in her youth, but worry and hunger had aged her fine features. Finally, the man himself could not be accused of an appealing nature, with his lowering scowl and bad tempered outburst. Perhaps it was simply that his sense of justice had been stirred, and it was also perhaps his way of repaying for all the injustices that these people had suffered under his own kind for many generations!

James shrugged. His was a tenacious nature, and he would see this thing through to the end now, which should not be too long, if the Prison Governor was to be believed. Rumour had it that the Regiment was due to be posted soon to India soon to stiffen 'Johnny Company' who was having its own trouble with their natives! He could shake the dust of Ireland from his boots and see some real action, instead of policing these distressing food riots!

Soon after Christmas the bag of grain that Sean had brought home was finished. Soon after this, the last of the small bag of coins had been spent, the price of food in Dublin markets having risen steadily since the harvest had failed. Then in February, he had gone to the potato pit and found the remaining tubers were rotten through and through. All he could see was rottenness and corruption. The optimism he had felt last November, in spite of Pat's imprisonment began to fade again. Unless the English came to their aid soon, not only Nuala but all of them would start to starve. By tacit agreement, neither Sean nor Kate told Pat of the crisis they were facing; there was nothing he could do after all, and he had enough to brood about locked away from his loved ones.

Once again, Nuala began to fret and then to wail with hunger, while she still resolutely refused the rotten mess of potatoes that the rest of them forced themselves to eat. The infant had not fully recovered her strength before the food ran out, so this time, she went downhill rapidly. Soon she no longer wailed, but lay in her cot, her eyes huge in her head, her wasted legs drawn up to her distended belly. With the insight of maternalism, Kate knew that her darling baby daughter was not long for this world. She kept this knowledge to herself, why upset the rest of them for they would know soon enough. She sat for long hours holding the infant close to her breast, crooning lullabies in her gentle voice. Sean would take the child from her on milder days, the winter had been largely kind in that respect, and carry her to the seaside, or up their hill or to their various relatives, hoping to raise a spark of interest, But day by day she faded.

Towards the end of March, when it was nearly time to consider planting, Sean discovered that the Government had finally started to give out food in Dublin. He had gone to Dublin alone to see Pat, as Kate was reluctant to leave Nuala. He found his father peevish at his wife's absence, brushing aside Sean's explanation, so much so that he cut short his visit, angry that his father seemed not to care about his youngest child! As was his wont, he went to visit his Uncle Michael to find out if there was any news. He was informed that, 'no, there was no public work to be had yet, but yes, there was food being handed out.' This was some stuff called 'Indian Corn' and had come from America, and everyone was saying how marvelous it was and how it was going to save them all!

'But I don't know,' observed Michael, scratching his head, 'it's bright yellow an' hard as bullets, an' no-one seems to know how to cook the stuff!' And as an afterthought, 'how's yer Pa?'

'He's fine,' replied Sean, distracted, 'It's Nuala we're fretted about. She's very weak; I must get some of this Indian stuff.'

He left the little house on the quay, and following his uncle's directions, found the warehouse, joining a lengthy queue waiting with stolid patience before the great doors. He shuddered at the memory of his last visit to a warehouse and was thankful of the subdued nature of today's crowd. This time there were no soldiers, just bored looking officials doling out small bags of the precious corn. Sean looked at it curiously; it was indeed bright yellow and looked hard as bullets!

'How d'you cook it?' he asked the man who handed him his ration. He merely shrugged,

'How d'you expect me to know, I don't eat the stuff. Next!'

Sean set off home alone. He had done this journey so often that he no longer felt nervous of being molested. Any travelers he met were usually too intent on their own affairs, and for sure, none of them had anything to steal! Occasionally, he and Kate had joined with other villagers making their way to Dublin, but they had gone so frequently, they could not rely on it. On this occasion, Sean could have welcomed some company. As he grew progressively weaker, the road seemed to grow longer and more arduous, and in spite of the advancing season it still fell dark long before he reached Clonarty. Fortunately the day was mild, as had most of the winter, which was about the only thing to be thankful for, mused Sean.

To help the time and distance to pass more quickly, Sean fell to predicting
the reaction of everyone to the new foodstuff. Suspicion certainly, as the Irish did not like anything new, and even worse, foreign! But hunger

would drive them to try it, if they could master the art of cooking it; surely boiling it like the potatoes would soften it?

Another step, another mile and he began thinking about Nuala and what the new food might mean to her. Would she accept it or turn her head away in disgust? He did not yet realize that Nuala was beyond hope and that no food in the world was going to save her.

Another step, another mile, and to his right, the sun was setting in a blaze of scarlet and orange.

'Perhaps we'll have a fine day tomorrow, an' then we can start thinking about buying some seed potatoes; none of last year's are fit to plant!' And he shivered as the air grew chill in the gathering darkness, as the sun finally slipped away behind the distant mountains.

Another step, another mile and he pulled up the collar of the jacket he was wearing, an old one of Pat's that hung on his slighter frame. It was of good sturdy wool, but it would have to be sold along with a lot of their household goods to find the money for seed. He tried to do some counting in his head having been taught the way of it by his Grandpa O'Malley, but his head soon ached with the effort.

'One wool jacket, two shillings perhaps? One fine bed frame, handcrafted by the finest carpenter for miles around, his father of course; ten shillings or more?' He shook his head. He would have to seek help from his more experienced Grandpa.

Another step, another mile. A silver moon was rising but it was the merest sliver, so did not give much light for him to find his way, so it was as well that he knew every step between Dublin and Clonarty! Unbidden, a sudden memory jumped into his head. He could see a group of children in a semi-circle round old Daniel as they huddled next to a peat fire. He saw himself in the group, face rounded by boyhood sitting with a diminutive Kevin, even then leaning against him, and little Eily cradled on his knee as now he cradled Nuala. Sundry other village children and cousins were with them, and they were wrangling among themselves as to why the moon kept changing its size, and finally they appealed to old Daniel, contentedly puffing his pipe, to settle the matter.

'Well it's like this. Once upon a time, the land was flat as an oat cake with no hills, no loughs; it just went all the way to the sea and then stopped! In fact, folks had to be very careful that they didn't fall off when they went walking!'

The children giggled and nudged one another.

'There was a princess called Naoimh who lived in a castle. She was beautiful as princesses always are, with golden hair that reached the ground. She spent much of the day combing her hair and singing with her beautiful voice right at the top of the castle where everyone could see her. And in those days when the land was flat, the sun shone every day and was never covered with clouds, and every night when the sun went to its rest, it bowed to the moon which rose up to take its place. The sun was all golden but the moon was silver, and the princess loved the moon even more than she did the sun. She was guarded by a giant, Hogan, for princesses always need to be guarded. This giant was an ugly old brute with a bald pate, just like Father Muldoon, a huge wart on his chin and a dew drop on the end of his nose ten times bigger than O'Leary's!' Daniel's audience hugged themselves with delight, but did not make a sound as they waited for the tale to continue.

'Well, the old giant fell in love with the princess, but she would have none of him, ugly old thing that he was. She sighed over a handsome young man who lived in Clonarty. His name was Diamid, and he returned her love, gazing at her as she combed her long hair in the moonlight. But the giant was jealous and he couldn't bear anyone to see her beauty, especially Diamid, so one night, he pulled the night sky down over the moon so that its silvery light could not be seen, and the next day, he did the same with the sun. But the sun's light was too strong and the sky was still light, but covered in a mist that men called clouds. The princess wept and pleaded with Hogan to give her back her silvery light, and Diamid stormed and raged as he could no longer see his princess properly. But there was nothing he could do; he could not reach to pull back the sky.

Diamid set off to find someone to help and he came upon another giant called Grogan, who lived not far away and groaned and sighed because he had no princess to look after. Diamid told him what Hogan had done, and Grogan lumbered to his feet, shaking the ground as he did so. The two set off, Diamid having to run very fast to keep up with Grogan whose head touched the clouds, making it rain wherever he passed. Very soon, they were back in Clonarty, and the villagers ran out of their homes to see the new giant. He called out in a loud voice, causing thunder to roll round the cloudy sky.

'Uncover the sun, you old goat'.

'Who's telling me what to do?' and Hogan appeared, his dew drop trembling with anger.

Hogan and Grogan ran at each other while villagers scattered and ran for their very lives. The giants swayed back and forth, both trying to throw the other down. All that day and into the dark night they wrestled, neither willing to give way. Then the princess called out in her sweetest voice,

'Is that you, Hogan dear?'

And the distracted giant let go for a moment, and Grogan got his leg behind Hogan's knee and threw him to the ground. Hogan landed with a crash that could be heard the length and breadth of Ireland, making a great hole in the ground and throwing up mounds of earth. Where he landed became the valley of Clonarty and the earth he threw up became our hills, and where Hogan's head rested became a lough. Grogan jumped up and down with glee, and made the ground all soft an' marshy an' it's where we dig our peat to this day!'

'But Grandpa,' whispered Eily in an anguished voice, what about the princess an' the moon an' ……'

'Hush child, all in good time! Well Grogan waited for Hogan to get up, but his pride was hurt, being thrown down in front of the princess 'n all, so he lay there sulking. So Grogan reached up and uncovered the moon. But Hogan leaped up and covered it again. They're still doin' it now, because, as you know, giants live forever.'

'But what happened to the princess?' came from Kevin,

'Like all good princesses, she married her young man an' lived happily ever after. But Hogan was so busy battling with Grogan over the moon, he never noticed!'

Sean smiled to himself in the near darkness, his musings having carried him to the very edge of the village. He quickly made his way to their cottage and ducked under the low doorway,

'Mam, look what they're givin' out in Dub….'

The words died away as he took in the scene before him. Kate sat rocking Nuala against her, tears running down her cheeks. Old Daniel and Eileen sat near her, each with an arm round Kevin and little Eily, who sat white faced and silent.

'No..o..o,' shouted Sean, 'look, I've brought food. Mam, see here.'

But Kate just turned her anguished face to him, and held out the baby. Sean gathered Nuala to his chest; she felt no heavier than a sparrow. Dark smudges ringed her eyes, and her lips were drawn back from her teeth in a grotesque parody of a grin. She was scarcely breathing, just a slight movement of her chest. Sean's shout had startled her momentarily, and she opened her eyes, gazing up at her adored older brother.

'Sean.' He had to put his face down to her lips to hear, the sound was so faint, and as he did so he felt her breathing stop. Aghast, he raised his head to look at her. Her arms fell away from her body and hung limply; her eyelids rolled upwards to show a rim of white. She did not stir at all.

'No..o..o,' cried Sean again, and pushed the frail body back to his mother.

'Hush Sean, the little one's at peace now in the arms of the Lord,' said his Grandma, trying to comfort him.

'What's she done that the Lord made her suffer so? She didn't do any harm to anybody.' And he bent his head, heartbroken.

Kate rocked back and forth, keening her distress, while the rest remained frozen in a tableau, the bag of Indian corn forgotten on the floor.

Father Muldoon stood on the hillside, surrounded by the entire village of Clonarty, come to give their support to the bereaved O'Hara's. Nuala was not only the first of their community to die, but she was a much loved infant, and there was not one of them, man or woman, who did not wipe away a tear. Sean stood close to his mother, trying to give her the strength to come through her ordeal, though in truth he did not have much strength for himself. His grandparents stood close by with Kevin and Eily, and even old Kevin was there, tears streaming down his leathery, sour features.

'Why,' thought Sean, 'he really did care for someone, after all.'

'This little one is already sitting at the feet of Jesus,' the old priest was saying, as distressed as they all were, 'it is not her for whom we now pray, but for her unhappy family who will miss her sorely.'

'Please stop,' muttered Sean under his breath, 'finish with these words. Leave us to grieve in private instead of out here.'

'Kate, Kate, what's happening up there?' The shout made them all turn round, to see Pat climbing the hill towards them.

'Pat.' And Kate was away, running down the hill to meet him. Sean watched his parents come together and stand close in earnest conversation. Kate was clearly telling him about Nuala as Sean saw his head rear back as though he had been struck, and then he bowed his head over Kate's hands. They stood awhile in silence, before making their way slowly back up the hill, neighbours reaching out gentle hands to a father who had come home to this!

'Come,' Sean heard Daniel say, 'let's go back down. Are you coming, Father, though we've not much to offer you.'

'Thank you,' said Father Muldoon, wearily, 'I'll be glad of a rest before I move on. There are many needing comfort these days.'

And they all went in sad procession down the hill, away from the cemetery, leaving behind a very small grave with a small posy of spring flowers on the freshly dug earth.

Later that evening, Pat told them how he had been released that morning, with no word of explanation, but merely an injunction to mind his manners and keep to the law in future. Kate tried to cook the hard yellow grains of corn, but after an hour they were still as hard as bullets. They tried to eat them as they were, but the grains caused gums softened by scurvy to bleed, and their stomachs revolted at the unaccustomed fare, regurgitating it violently.

That same evening, Captain James Willoughby was whirling around the ballroom of Dublin castle with a widow lady by the name of Mary Kavanagh. She was a lady of mature charms who was casting languishing glances from under her magnificent sweeping eyelashes, her bare shoulders rising milky white from the ruffled neckline of her ballgown, and a heady perfume wafted from the discreetly shaded valley between her voluptuous breasts.

Captain Willoughby was a contented man. Earlier that day he had overseen the delivery of an order for the release of the prisoner, Pat O'Hara, and unbeknownst to that man, had waited in an anteroom until he had gone on his way. A final payment to the obsequious gaoler Carey for 'services rendered' brought a smile to the brutish face, and Willoughby could put the family O'Hara out of his mind forever. If the sight of the laden supper table brought a qualm or two, he suppressed them, for had he not done more than most to put things right?

As he whirled the lady round in a waltz he made plans for a pleasant dalliance with Mary Kavanagh, the urgency to shake the dust of Ireland off his boots suddenly dead, drowned in the massed coiffure of glossy brown curls topped with two enormous feathers; or in the neat waist above an enormous crinoline. Mary Kavanagh could indeed make a man forget the misfortunes of her countrymen.

Later, in a secluded side room, when James essayed a foray on putting lips, traveling from there to the swelling globes above her dress, James could not understand why he saw an image of a youth with chestnut hair and an intelligent brow holding out a charming little sprite of two, or maybe three years. He heard the boy say,

'You forgot her, 'n now she's dead….your fault…..fault…'

And the image faded as he lifted his head from the widow's breast.

Chapter 18

In the days following Nuala's funeral, the O'Hara's drew in on themselves, trying to draw strength in each other. In time to come, Pat would again puzzle over his imprisonment and release, so different to his expectation, but for now, the shock of returning home to find his darling baby being placed in the ground was almost too much for him to bear. Sean watched his mother and father, faces lined and haggard in the light of the peat fire; sit close together as if proximity itself would cure their heartache. As for himself, grieving deeply for his baby sister, he too drew comfort from Kevin and little Eily, hoping that together they could defeat the shadows that threatened to overwhelm them. For two, maybe three days they stayed shut away from the world, but on the fourth day, the spell was broken by old Daniel, who ducked beneath the low doorway and surveyed the tableau within.

'Are ye goin' to hide away brooding for the rest of yer life? You've lost a little one, but there's the rest of yer family to care for!'

'Pa,' whispered Kate, 'that's cruel. Pat's only just returned and...'

'I know, I know. But the days are warmer 'n there's planting to be done. Come on, man, pull yerself together.'

'Get out.' Pat spoke for the first time between clamped teeth, 'can't you leave me in peace to mourn me daughter?' And his fists clenched threateningly. Suddenly he rose from where he had been crouched by the fire. On his face was the glowering look that Kate had come to know so well in the 'bad years', the look that said he was away to his secret place in the hills, and would doubtless return stinking of poteen, though God alone knew where he got it from! She did not try to stop him, reasoning that he needed to work through his torment in his own way, but Daniel was not so understanding.

'Where d'you think yer goin' man; you're needed here.'

For a moment, it looked as if he would raise his fist to the smaller man to strike him out of his way, but then he broke down, and turning back into the cottage, began to weep, great tearing sobs that wracked his very soul.

Daniel looked on, pity on his seamed old face.

'That's it,' he murmured quietly, and to Kate, 'he'll be all right now. We none of us will forget the little maid, but life goes on!'

'I know,' nodded Kate, but nothin' seems to matter anymore.'

'You too, Kate? And you an O'Malley! Look at young Sean here, an' yer other young ones, are they not worth yer care?'

'Aye. Yer right, as always. We'll be fine now.' And she hugged her father close.

Two days later, the seed merchant arrived in Clonarty with a cart piled high the seed potatoes, and sacks of wheat and barley seed. It also bulged with household goods as his customers were more inclined to pay in kind, this year more than most. Pat and other Clonarty men haggled to get the best price they could for their precious clothes, utensils and blankets. The wonderful bed frame that Pat had fashioned for Kate had to go, as did Sean's warm jacket; hand crafted stools and even the chair that Daniel sat in to recount his wonderful tales. This final item was for an extra purchase that Kate had urged Pat to make. They had already managed to buy enough seed to plant their potato trenches and the grain fields, but Kate had spied a goat tied behind the cart, doubtless from some other hapless smallholder, but she felt it could help them all return to health.

'Please Pat!'

And he could not resist. So the famous chair went with the merchant, his avaricious eyes gleaming as he saw it in his snug house in Dublin's Clare Street.

'I'll make another, an' a bed, an…'

'Hush,' said kate, 'It's putting roses back in these cheeks that's important now,' and she pinched Eily's gently. The goat could occupy the long since empty pigpen at night, and Eily could take her to crop on the hillside during the day. Its milk, for the udders swung heavy and full, would be shared by the entire village, and might even provide a little cheese to sell in exchange for goods they had just lost!

Sean sighed. Such plans should bring a little light into their eyes after the terrible months they had endured, but the memory of a chubby faced infant kept intruding. What a difference goat's milk would have made to her! Would this pain of loss ever pass? He saw his mother cross herself and murmur,

'Mary, Mother of Jesus, help us now out of our despair!'

'Aye,' muttered Sean irreverently, 'an' where was She when little Nuala lay dying for want of an animal like that?'

And so they planted. The days passed quickly enough in hard, physical labour, doubly hard now that they were all weakened by hunger. Ironically, the fittest of them all was Pat, who, in the normal way of things should have been the most deprived after three months in Dublin's stinking gaol. He would never know why he had been treated and fed so well, but he thanked God for it, and tried to spare his family as much as possible. His sons worked alongside of him, while Eily was sent to graze the goat. Kate did what she could, but preferred to spend more time with her mother, for in the older woman she found the comfort she sought. With Eileen, she could talk about Nuala, while with Pat she could not. He kept his pain deep and let it fester there, etching fresh lines on his face and deepening his scowl.

Sean worked with memories his constant companion. As he dropped the precious seed potatoes in the trenches, he could see a red haired sprite following her mother, carefully lifting out the precisely planted tubers and building cairns with them, until Sean's shout of laughter stopped all labour for a while. He could see the same mischievous sprite looking solemnly in her father's eyes, and explain to him how he should handle his spud, he could see….. he could see…… he rubbed his eyes; this way lay madness, but he could not rid himself of his visions no matter where he looked.

One day, he dragged himself up the hill to their favourite spot, where Nuala had loved to pick daisies and throw them into the air with fat chuckles of delight,

'Why?' He cried to the cloud sodden sky, 'if You're up there – why?'
And he lowered his head and wept.

Once the planting was over, the families of Clonarty came together
to discuss their survival until the autumn harvest; for they had no food
reserves to sustain them as in previous years. There would be many a
dreary month before their precious tubers could be lifted. Milk from the
goat had already allowed the children to regain strength and colour on
their faces, but that alone was insufficient for their needs.

'Maybe they'll start that work they're always on about,' ventured
Hogan, the O'Hara's nearest neighbour, and worried father of seven wraith
like children ranging from 17 years to four.

'Maybe pigs might sprout wings like an angel,' returned Conor, sourly,
'the day the English give us anything!'

'Hush Conor,' said Mari mildly, 'didn't they give out Indian Corn?'

'An' didn't bother to tell us how to cook it.' This from Kate, more
intolerant of the English since Pat's imprisonment, in spite of help from
the gallant Captain.

'There's always the hills; there's things growing there!'

'But that's not goin' to keep us going till harvest time.'

'We must go back to Dublin an' ask for work again.'

'Nay. Demand it! You'll get nothin' with asking, cap in hand.' Pat
spoke for the first time, his voice deep and angry as it always was now.

Sean listened a talk was thrown back and forth. He was sitting with
his arms wrapped round his knees, Kevin leaning against his shoulder and
Dermot close by, as always!

'Why do they do this every time?' he asked himself, 'There is nothing
to be gained by talking. Pa has the right of it; go and demand, but don't
just keep talking all the time!'

Then he remembered his father's words when all this had started;

'Sometimes it's better to talk than find out the truth!'

'But is that right? Surely it's better to *know* what you have to face than to pretend it may never happen. But at least it stopped me thinkin' 'bout Nuala for a while!'

Then he realized that the meeting was breaking up and that some sort of decision must have been reached. He nudged Dermot, knowing from past experience that he'd get a clearer answer from him than his brother Kevin, who was inclined to get totally confused!

'What's bin decided?'

'Weren't you listenin'? All the men are goin' to Dublin tomorrow; they're goin' to the castle as a depu…something…'

'Deputation is it?' asked Sean, proud of his knowledge of such words, gleaned from years of listening to Grandpa O'Malley.

'Yes. That's it, deputation.'

Sean got up and moved to his father's side. He had been raised not to interrupt his elders, so he waited impatiently for his chance to speak, hopping from one foot to the other.

'What is it son?' his grandfather asked in some amusement.

Can I come tomorrow, Pa?'

'I'm counting on it,' replied Pat, quietly.

Sean felt a surge of pride. He had thought that in his pain of loss, Pat had turned his back on his eldest son; but not so,

'I'm counting on you.' The words rang in his head, and he left the group to return to Kevin and Dermot.

'You comin' Sean?' Dermot enquired, 'we're away to trap rabbits in the copse.'

The rabbits in question had little to fear, for many had tried since the hunger began, with no success; but at least it would give them something to do instead of thinking of their stomachs. There was also the spice of danger attached, as the copse in question was deep inside the boundary wall of Danforth House.

'Perhaps rabbits choose to live there for a reason,' mused Sean with a laugh.

Next day, the men and youths were out bright and early, impatient to be gone. Some of the younger boys, like Kevin, were inclined to be sulky at being left behind, scowling in perfect imitation of his father! He was somewhat placated when his father told him 'to be a man and take care of your mother and sister.'

Kate took Sean to one side just before they left, and said quietly, 'Try an' stop him getting into trouble; I don't want to lose him again!'

'Don't worry, Mam, I'll keep a close watch.'

Kate smiled and hugged him close, though in truth she knew that no-one could stop her husband if he was determined on a confrontation.

The men and youths were waved off by their womenfolk, and by the too old and too young. The procession set off towards Dublin, gathering strength as it went, for groups from other villages of the Danforth estate had agreed to join them; men of Kilgarth and Colkenny, Ballymore and Clarne. Before they had gone but a few miles, more than a hundred pairs of feet marched in unified resolve; they must get work if their families were to survive.

Sean was gratified at the numbers who had turned out, for surely if there was trouble with the soldiers, his father would be less likely to take part. But unknown to Sean, his mother had already pleaded with Pat, first of all to stop him going, and failing that, to keep well clear of any fighting,

'For I couldn't bear it if you didn't come home again,' she said, gazing wistfully at him.

'Never fear, Kate a cara. I promise you I'll be home tonight.' And Pat had looked deep into her eyes. He did not notice the lines of care and sorrow, or the wings of startling white against the dimming red-gold of her hair; all he saw was the the fresh young face of his young wife when he had known that he loved her more than life itself.

Kate had been relieved by the promise, but nonetheless, had later spoken with Sean!

'It is a wonder,' thought Sean, 'how a journey is so much shorter when shared.'

How many times had he walked the weary miles to Dublin last winter, sometimes with Kate, sometimes alone, to see Pat? More times than he could count; more times than the whole of the rest of his life up to now!

Eventually they entered the outskirts of Dublin to find an undercurrent of excitement prevailing; men and women milling about in all directions. Pat managed to grab the arm of a man as he hurried past,

'What's happening here?'

The man was inclined to pull away without replying, a surly look on his face, but the sheer numbers of the Danforth group made him pause,

'They're goin' ter start road works; they're setting up trestles down by the Liffey.' And jerking his arm form Pat's grasp, he made off rapidly.

'D'yer hear that?' said Pat to Conor, with a laugh,

'We've come to demand work. They must've heard about us and got it ready!'

Others in earshot joined in the laughter, and with uplifted spirits, they walked briskly towards the Liffey quay. There, they indeed find activity, with trestle tables set up, and high nosed officials ensconced in state behind them. Nearby was gathered a group of earnest gentlemen of unmistakably English origins. They were smartly dressed in cutaway tail coats and tall hats, and carried rolls of paper under their arms. Later, they would discover that these were engineers, sent to Dublin with the instruction to set up public works in road building. These men had been told something of the crisis facing the Irish, and of the hunger they were suffering, but nothing had prepared them for the reality. They had seen emaciated men, women and children begging in the streets of Dublin; numberless small farmers from outlying districts pouring in stinking hordes into the city, clamouring for work that would enable them to sustain life for themselves and their families.

Sean noticed one of the engineers surveying the assembled masses with a look of sympathetic horror on his face.

'Why, he cares; just like that soldier. We think all Englishmen are unfeeling, but it's not true! But then, don't they think we're all ignorant bogtrotters? Mind, looking at some of us, perhaps they're right!'

He was startled when his father grabbed his arm,

'Stay close son, the Clonarty men are goin' to try and get taken on for the same job.'

'Yes Pa.'

And they shuffled forward in the crowd, getting close to a table apparently overseen the Englishman that Sean had been watching earlier,

'Pa,' said Sean, grabbing his father's sleeve, 'what would've happened if we hadn't come in today? Would anyone have come to tell us there was work, d'you think?'

Pay looked down at his son's earnest face, and forbore to answer; let the boy keep his illusions!

'Name?'

They had reached the front, and a fussy looking clerk with round, steel rimmed spectacles balanced on the end of his nose glared at them, as though they were to blame for him missing his lunch!

'Patrick O'Hara and me son, Sean.'

The clerk wrote on his list. Sean watched fascinated as the patterns appeared on the paper.

'That's what separates us. He can write 'n read, so he's a clerk, 'n I'm not.'

But he knew it was more than that. No Catholic could hold a position of authority, even a minor one like this fussy little man. So it wouldn't matter if he did learn to read and write, he would still end up a farmer like his Pa.

'Perhaps that's why the others left? Uncle Tom 'n Fergus.'

The clerk was speaking again,

'Bring your own shovel, you'll be building a road. Eightpence a day and sixpence for the boy,' jerking his head at Sean.

'Me son does the work of any man; he should get paid as a man,' said Pat, ominously calm.

'It's alright Pa,' whispered Sean urgently, for he could see the irritation in the clerk's prissy face. No doubt the smell of Irish peasantry was causing him severe stomach disorder!

'It's not alright, son. If we have to slave for these people to feed yer Mam and the young'uns, at least you should get paid properly!

The clerk could obviously understand the Irish that Pat was using as he swelled visibly with anger,

'Slave! Slave! I'll have you know that the Government is letting you work as an act of charity. If you don't want the work, take yourself back to the bog you came from and I'll give the work to those who do want it!'

Sean looked on with alarm. The very thing he had promised to prevent was happening. He noticed a group of soldiers lounging nearby, watching the scene with interest and it would take but a moment for them to get involved nif the clerk summoned them. Then intervention came from an unexpected quarter.

'He's right,' came a soft spoken English voice, 'the boy's full grown and should have a man's wage.'

The clerk blustered and seemed to be inclined to argue further, but a steely stare from the engineer, at odds with his mild appearance, put an end to discussion.

'Put your mark there,' the clerk snapped, pointing at the paper. Pat gripped the quill like a dagger, dipped it into the ink, and made a large cross where the clerk pointed, managing to spray ink on his lily white hand as he did so.

As Pat straightened up, he found the Englishman looking at him with an amused smile on his face; he had no more love for the prissy little clerk than Pat himself did!

'You'll be with my project,' he said, in his mild, cultured voice, 'I'm Joseph Harrington, by the way. How do you do?' And he held out his hand.

Pat and Sean stared, mesmerized by the courtly manner, and by the fact that it was directed at them, so they solemnly shook hands with the engineer.

'I'll expect you tomorrow, then, at noon. All workforces will meet here, and we will make our way to the site. After that, work will start in the early morning. One meal a day will be provided. Good day.'

And touching his hat brim, Joseph Harrington, Civil Engineer of London went back to his knot of compatriots. Pat and Sean stood rooted to the spot, mesmerized by the man.

'Come on man,' said Conor, breaking them out of their trance, 'we've all bin taken on. Let's get home to Mari and Kate 'n give them the good news.'

The journey home was like a triumphal procession, the men from Danforth estate forgetting that they had come to demand their rights, only to find them freely given!

So they arrived home, and Pat went to hold Kate in close embrace. There was hope once again. They would survive. They would eat until harvest time came round again.

Chapter 19

So they went to work, the men of Clonarty and the other Danforth villagers, shovels over their shoulders, feet stomping the road between their homes and Dublin. Sean thought that he could walk the way blindfolded; his feet knew every rut, every stone designed to catch the unwary, every hill, and every bend. And he would walk this way many times yet, he thought ruefully. The distance was too far to return home every night after a day of physical labour, but they would spend Sunday with their families, bringing food bought with their hard earned money.

The Clonarty contingent had all been assigned to the same project, and they all arrived at the meeting place by the Liffey in good time. Once again there was a scene of great confusion, as disappointed men wrangled to be taken on. As Pat had suspected, many villages had not been told in time, and frantic men surged into the city to plead for work. The trestle tables were still set up, but only as rallying points and not for more signings, and the atmosphere was rapidly becoming full of tension when a squad of soldiers at a brisk march and forced their way through the milling mobs. They took up station in front of the tables and smartly turned about face, a manouvre that he recognized with a shudder. To complete the feeling of déjà vu, he recognised the officer in tall shako and Captain's epaulettes; it was none other than their old acquaintance, James Willoughby. His feelings towards the Captain were equivocal, but he had to admire the man for his mastery of the situation. An engineer and clerk positioned themselves near a table and the clerk read out a list of names; the men thus identified moving as a group to a place indicated by the river. When the list was complete, they moved off as a body and were soon lost from sight. One by one, groups of men were called, and all the while, the soldiers remained fully alert, ready to suppress any outbreak of violence from unsigned workers. Sean was so intent on watching the process that he nearly missed his own name being called, and was only alerted by a nudge from his father.

'Wake up son, or you'll be sent home with the little ones!'

'Sorry Pa.' And shouldering his shovel, he moved off to the river.

Soon after they were marching out of Dublin, and after two to three miles, they were called to a halt. The engineer, Joseph Harrington, stood before them. Sean noticed that he had changed his clothes of the previous day, the smart cutaway coat and tall hat replaced by plain breeches and jacket, though he recognized that the material was finer than anything he had ever worn! Harrington was a mild mannered man of unpretentious appearance, but he held his audience in absolute silence, for was he not their saviour, the man who had brought them work, their guardian angel?

'We will be building a road from here, and in due course will complete it towards Dublin. Those of you who wish may set up cabins in the fields by here; the road will not progress very fast.'

There was a bark of laughter from the crowd at this, but it was quickly hushed. He went on,

'The rate is eightpence a day for a full day's work, with one meal of soup and bread to be taken in the evening. Anyone leaving before the end of the day will receive neither food nor pay. Is that understood?'

'Aye,' said Pat under his breath to Sean, 'beneath that soft looking face is a heart of stone, just like all the rest of 'em.'

'But Pa, if it hadn't been for him, I wouldn't be getting the same pay as you!'

'You think so? He knew a worker when he saw one. These people give nothin' without they want somethin' in return.' Sean kept silent. There was nothing to be gained from arguing with his father in this mood, a mood he was in most of the time these days. Instead, he found Dermot, and told him about the English Captain who had reappeared in Dublin.

'Just like a black penny,' said Dermot.

'No, not like that,' replied Sean thoughtfully, 'there's somethin' about him that I can't help liking, though I daren't tell Pa. He thinks all

Englishmen, especially soldiers, have two horns and a forked tail!' Dermot laughed and linking arms, the pair wandered off to find their fathers.

The would-be workers spent the afternoon in constructing themselves shelters that would last them as long as was necessary. These so called 'scalps' were no more than holes in the ground, two or three feet deep, roofed over with sticks and turfs gathered by the younger members of the party. In these they would be warm and dry when they were not working. Peat fires could be lit and the smoke allowed to escape as it could, a condition similar to their shebeens in Clonarty if the owner hadn't bothered to fashion a stone chimney.

'Where're we to find peat?' grumbled Conor, 'we've no time to dig and dry it if we're to start work at the crack of morn!'

But Harrington had thought of that too, and towards evening, a rumble of carts could be heard, coming up the rough track that they had just marched along. The carts were piled high with dried peat, ready to be lit. Also on the carts were several large cauldrons and sacks of provisions necessary for preparing the broth, and the greatest wonder of all, several round loaves of coarse bread. The men's' eyes widened at the sight, for most had not eaten properly for as long as they could remember. But even so, not one of them but thought of their families and wished they could be there to share in the bounty! Any fear that they would have to wait until they had done a full day's work to taste their first full meal was quickly dispelled, as the new arrivals quickly offloaded their peat stacks in the middle of the ring of scalps and dispatched willing volunteers to fetch supplies of water from a nearby stream to charge the cauldrons.

'Will you look at that,' said Sean to Dermot, their eyes nearly popping out of their heads at the sight.

'This workin' may not be so bad after all; what d'yer say Pa?' as Pat and Conor joined the boys.

'Well son, unless they're doin' all this to feed yon engineer and his mates, we'll eat properly for the first time in months!' observed Conor.

'You'd think they could've done this long before,' said Pat in a voice full of rage, 'a little earlier 'n we might still've got Nuala with us.'

The hatred in Pat's voice effectively silenced the rest, and they drifted apart, embarrassed by the raw emotion hovering in the air. Sean wandered away, deeply hurt by his father's words.

'Sure they could've done this before, but they didn't,' he muttered to himself, ''n now he's goin' to spoil it for the rest of us. We all loved Nuala, but the rest of us need to live, if only to remember her!'

His musings had brought him close to the engineer. Harrington had set up a pole, marked along its length, at which he appeared to be squinting closely. Sean watched in silence, and following the man's gaze beyond the stick, noticed another man further along the track with a similar device. Then Harrington straightened up and waved. The man far off moved his pole slightly, and the process was repeated. Finally, Harrington seemed to be satisfied with his efforts, as he began to write in a notebook he carried with him, laying the pole down as he did so. It was then that he became aware of the intense scrutiny he was being subjected to, and turning to Sean, smiled rather shyly,

'Well hello. It's Sean, isn't it?'

Sean's eyes widened in surprise at his name being remembered, and Harrington laughed at his amazement,

'I saw you yesterday at the signings, didn't I?' The words were said kindly enough, but Sean coloured as he remembered why he had been noticed. But Harrington seemed amused by his embarrassment,

'Don't worry lad, these petty clerks need to be put in their place, occasionally!'

Sean nodded, emboldened by the man's friendly manner,

'What are you doin' with those sticks?'

Harrington looked into the boy's face, noting the earnest expression, the broad intelligent forehead and wide enquiring eyes.

'D'you see the other pole along the track there?' Sean nodded. 'We're lining up the poles so that the road will end up level for as much of its length as we can make it. When we meet hills and valleys, we will try and make the slope as shallow as possible, otherwise yon poor old donkeys would have a hard time of it!' This last was said with a laugh, but Sean did not think that he was laughing at the Irish or their donkeys, but at the quaint thought. As with James Willoughby, Sean had the feeling that this was a man he could trust and respect.

'How d'you do that if there's a hill in the way?'

'We cut the road round the side and fill in the valley floors, which will be the job of you people. If we were Romans, doubtless we'd go straight up and over that,' and he pointed at a towering hill rising about a mile away from them, and directly in the line that the engineer had been surveying.

'An' where do Romans come from, England?' asked Sean politely.

Harrington suppressed a smile, for after all, what would this boy know of Romans?

'No. Romans conquered England many years ago, and to get about, made roads that were mainly very straight, regardless of hill and vale.' Sean's eyes widened again.

'Conquered England,' he asked incredulously. Harrington let out a shout of laughter this time at Sean's expression.

'Yes, even the English got conquered sometimes. But it was a very long time ago.'

He went on to describe how the road would be constructed; first of all to the correct width to take wheeled traffic, and then curved over its surface to allow rain water to run off, and the ditches dug alongside to drain away the rain water, 'of which there seems to be more than enough' said ruefully.

'We'll be good at that,' said Sean with a smile, 'we dig a lot of trenches at planting time.'

Harrington fell silent, working on figures in his notebook, drawing sketches and calculating angles, with Sean alongside, an interested spectator. He did not sense that Harrington was irritated by his presence, and he had an irresistible desire to learn more about the whole process. He felt anew, as he had done in Dublin, that this ability to read and write and figure was one of the things that set people like himself apart from those like Harrington. It prevented them from making progress in life and condemning them to a subsistence existence. Suddenly Harrington remarked,

'Why is your father so angry?'

Sean started and looked over to where his father was lounging on the grass near their scalp, empty clay pipe clamped between his teeth, and glowering at the engineer and himself. Sean could not bring himself to explain to this mild mannered Englishman that Pat hated all of his kind and all that they stood for.

'He's not so much angry as sad. We lost our little one at home, Nuala, and she was not yet three years old.'

'I'm sorry lad. What was it took her?'

'Hunger,' replied Sean simply, 'she couldn't eat the rotten potatoes, an' there wasn't much else.'

Harrington regarded him in silence. Such tales were distressingly common, and his pity was stirred. He had come to Ireland with romantic notions swirling in his head about how he was going to help the poor downtrodden peasantry with his wonderful schemes, and save them from hunger in their hour of need. The reality was so very different. Confusion, incompetence, an attitude of laissez faire among those in authority, all had prevented the swift execution of schemes such as this road. And people were already dying; little Nuala was not an isolated case.

Harrington was a kindly man with philanthropic tendencies, and he had organised his road works more carefully than most. He had taken it upon himself to approach the owner of the land hereabouts, fortunately resident at the time, and sought permission for the labourers to build their scalps, realizing that they would need warmth and shelter during inclement weather. It was he who had arranged the delivery of peat turfs and provisions for the first day's meal. None of these things would be financed by the Government but would come out of his own pocket. In time to come, his team of workers would compare their experience with others, and discover just how generous their supervisor was! But even now there was almost a festive atmosphere prevailing as dusk fell, with spirals of smoke rising from the peat fires, and the smell of cooking broth permeating the still air. In spite of his efforts to help these people, Harrington felt ashamed. Ashamed of his countrymen who had allowed the country to get into this state; ashamed of people of his own class, landowners who neglected their estates and were impervious to pleas to defer the rents in times of disaster; ashamed of those back home who knew what was happening here, and *simply did not care!* With such thoughts in his head, he had nothing to say to Sean in answer to the unconscious accusation behind the words, 'she couldn't eat the rotten potatoes and there wasn't much else!'

The work began early the following morning, and a routine was quickly established. Men were assigned to digging and moving earth in large barrows in a way that seemed to be haphazard, but nevertheless produced results with surprising rapidity and the road began to creep towards the large hill, curving southwards as it approached. There was a break in their efforts at noontide and if there was any bread left over from the night before, it was doled out. Strangely, there always seemed to be bread over! Then the afternoon session began and went on until the evening, when the soup ration was distributed. It was a nourishing and tasty concoction, which owed much of its substance and flavor to Harrington's purse rather than the Government's meagre ration allowance.

The man himself returned to Dublin to sleep, but would often spend the hours of dusk at the site, puffing on a clay pipe and chatting to the workforce, as well as his fellow engineer, another Londoner by the name of Saul Maynard. Pat still kept himself apart, but most of the Clonarty men grew slowly to respect and then to like this quietly spoken Englishman. They discovered the two engineers had their own criticisms of their Government.

'Yes,' observed Maynard, puffing vigorously on his pipe, from which more smoke rose in the still air than did from the peat fires! 'Robert Peel has no love for the Irish. Why, when he was Secretary of State here, he encouraged the most severe repressions. Your own Dan O'Connell called him 'Orange Peel' for his favouritism of Orangemen. There's no reason to expect any better of him now that he's Prime Minister!'

'But,' objected Harrington, 'that was thirty years ago and he is said to be a man who knows his duty. After all, it was he who has worked to repeal the Corn Laws, and it was he who brought in the Indian corn.'

'Did he ever try the stuff himself?' asked Conor, 'when it first came it was as hard as iron, and no-one seemed to know what to do with it!'

'What would you suggest, then?' replied Harrington. Conor shrugged,

'How would I know, living in a village miles away from Dublin, what can be done!'

'What about all the food leaving Dublin on all those ships? I've seen them with me own eyes!' came from Pat. Tired of sitting alone, he had decided to join the discussion. 'Why, I stood by the Liffey one day an' watched six ships leaving, loaded down with Irish grain while one came in with your Indian corn.'

'I must admit,' returned Harrington gently, mindful of the man's tragedy and trying to calm the anger in his voice, 'I cannot explain it and it certainly cannot enamour you people towards our Government!'

'Huh,' said Pat shortly, 'use yer long words, but yer famous Peel and his ilk have taken away our freedom, an' now that we're starving, dole out their charity in small handfuls. Perhaps they think they'd be better off if we all starved to death?'

Harrington looked up at Pat standing over him with a glowering expression.

'I can understand your bitterness, but the British are trying to do something, maybe not as well as you would like, but they are trying. And most of the ordinary people don't even know how bad it is here!'

Pat turned and stalked back to his scalp. Harrington clearly would not accept the premise that the British had no business in the country, and left alone, the Irish would not have got into this situation.

Sean sighed. Why was it that the first time that Pat had joined them there were harsh words rather than a reasoned discussion? He was not being fair either. Lately he had heard of Irish landlords, albeit Protestants, who were every bit as bad, if not worse, than the English ones. And some English ones were treating their tenants really well, not only suspending their rents but providing food as well! They were not all like Danforth! All of these facts Sean had heard during the discussions round the peat fire during the evening.

'Strange,' he thought, 'Some good comes out of everything. I never heard about the world outside Clonarty and Dublin at all until now.

The working week ended mid-afternoon on Saturday and the men received their meal early and were paid for the week. They duly noted that they had been paid for a full 6 days and not just five and a half, though they were again unaware that their supervisor had been responsible for the extra! The Clonarty men went off in a group, taking the road to Dublin to buy food for their families. They found their earnings allowed some small luxuries; a twist of tea, a handful of tobacco for long empty clay pipes. They found that the much despised Indian corn was still the cheapest of all the food stuffs available at a penny a pound. They always walked with a spring in their steps, for in spite of the hard, physical work, they were at last providing for their loved ones. They were, after all, more than used to digging trenches!

The arrival of the men in their villages was always an occasion for rejoicing, those left behind running out of the shebeens when the first sighting was made. Women and children and the older generation, milled around their menfolk, hugging them all, and chattering at the parcels they carried.

On Sunday, following Mass if Father Muldoon happened by, was followed by an inspection of the fields tended by their womenfolk and older sons. Pat acknowledged that Kate and Kevin were doing a good job without him and Sean. Though old Daniel confided to Pat that it was largely Kevin's efforts that had produced these results, while Kate still spent much of the day gazing forlornly into space.

'But she's just getting' over Nuala. It is worse with you'n Sean away so much!'

'What'm I supposed to do?' asked Pat morosely, 'we've got to earn until harvest.'

'Don't take on. I meant no blame. But I'll be happier when you two come home to stay though!'

Pat looked anxiously at the growing haulms. They seemed healthy enough, but the weather was not as good as it might be; day after day was overcast and dank. But he consoled himself,

'But we had fair weather last year an' look what happened, so perhaps it's not so bad.'

Pat also took the opportunity to check on the old folk and how they were dealing with the situation. Old Daniel and Eileen seemed to be coping well, having each other for mutual support, and Kate to mind them. But he was worried about his own father, old Kevin. Since Nuala's death, he had grown ever more reclusive, scarcely venturing from his cabin. Pat would stay and talk awhile, but for two fundamentally morose men, this was an effort, and Pat would soon leave, leaving some of the precious food. His father did not seem to eat much, seeming to be thinner and more desiccated every time Pat returned.

And so the season advanced.

'We won't have to do this much longer, son, with the 'taties nearly ready. Though I wish we could have at least a few days of sun!'

Sean did not answer. His feelings about the end of road building were equivocal. Part of him would be pleased to resume their lives, independent of the whims of others. They could rebuild and replace all that they had lost this last year, except of course, the most precious of them, Nuala! But another part of him was enjoying the present way of life. He enjoyed the company and the talks around the peat fire in the evenings. He enjoyed the more varied diet, without realizing that they were particularly fortunate in this respect! He enjoyed most of all the company of Joseph Harrington who had taught him so much of the world outside. The man was never too busy to explain what he was doing with his surveying poles, and would sketch diagrams in the sand to illustrate his point. In truth, Harrington enjoyed the encounters every bit as much as Sean, finding in the boy a shadow of the lad he once was, listening to his own father, himself a civil engineer of note.

The road had, by this time, reached the hill it was to skirt around. The labourers were even now in the process of building up the side of the hill as it fell away, and cutting into its flank to make a level platform. Harrington, busy with his plans, heard disquieting rumours during his visits to Dublin, where he was expected to report to the Castle at regular intervals. It was whispered that the Public Works were due to close very soon in anticipation of the harvest.

'But why not wait until it is time for the harvest?' he asked a supercilious official. But the man simply shrugged and did not vouchsafe a reply. But even more disquieting were the vague rumours emanating from further south, that the new crop of potatoes were beginning to show signs of blight. But no-one could say where this was happening. Harrington looked closely at the potato fields as he drove to the road works, and the haulms looked green and healthy enough. 'Scaremongering,' he muttered to himself.

'I wish it would stop raining, though,' he thought, not for the first time that summer.

He had another reason to be anxious about the continuous rain, as the road was biting deep into the hillside which until banked properly, would be unstable, and that would be difficult as long as it rained! He had left Maynard in charge for the day while he reported back to the Dublin officials. But now he hurried back, overcome by a presentiment of disaster.

'You are getting as fanciful as these people,' he admonished himself firmly.

Harrington came round the curve of the hill and stopped his donkey cart, taking in the scene before him. In spite of the rain falling steadily from the lowering clouds, the men were hard at work; after all, no work, no pay! He could see a rope stretched up the hillside above the road, and a man pulling himself up with his shovel on his shoulder. At the foot of the rope, two or three others were shoveling soil into barrows, cutting into the hillside, and leaving a vertical face. Further away, there was a large group of men busy on the furthest reach of the road, starting to level it off. He spotted Maynard standing some way off and surveying the scene, and quickly drove forward to join him.

'Why have you got that rope up the hill? It's a small matter precarious in this rain; that man up there could cause a slide!'

'That's why I'm doing it,' explained Maynard, 'there's an overhang up there,' pointing, 'and I want it cut away before it tumbles on its own.'

Harrington shook his head, still unhappy, but not sure why.

'I think we should leave this section 'til it dries a bit, and come back to it.'

'I don't agree. We'll end up with bits of road unfinished all over the place.'

'At least move those men from the cliff foot; if that lot comes down….'

At that moment there was a cry, and the two men stood aghast as a tragedy unfolded before their shocked eyes. The man pulling himself up the rope had nearly reached the overhang as Pat, working at the cliff base, had begun to walk along the road to talk to Sean. Sean himself was some way off and had raised his hand to wave to Pat when a shower of loose soil pattered down the slope above him. Sean's wave turned into a violent gesticulation and the boy screamed out,

'Pa..a..a' as the overhang began to break away, carrying the man with it. Gathering speed, a whole section of the hill fell down, down towards Pat, who could only stand and stare, rooted to the spot, unable to move as the deadly rumble drowned Sean's cry.

'Pa..a…a' came through the last decaying clatter of a few delayed pebbles, then the silence, except for the sound of running feet.

Sean reached the pile of earth and begun to dig frantically with his bare hands, until a gentle but firm tug on his shoulders stopped him.

'Let the men near, they'll be quicker with their spuds.' Sean backed off then, and watched with dazed eyes as Conor and the rest took turns to shovel the wet, cloying soil away.

The man who had gone up the slope, a neighbour from nearby Clarne, lay groaning nearby, and he was picked up gently, causing an anguished scream. The reason was soon apparent; his leg stuck out at an unnatural angle, and the shockingly white head of his shin bone showed through the torn flesh.

'God preserve him,' said his rescuers, crossing themselves.

Sean was oblivious to the scream and the activity, his whole attention focused on the diggers, who seemed to be taking an eternity to reach their goal. Once, twice, he leaned forward as though to hurl himself on the dwindling pile, but a gentle but firm pressure held him back. It was Harrington himself who restrained the boy, his face as white as a sheet, as intent on the digging as Sean himself. Suddenly, a hand appeared, and then a shoulder, and soon after, Pat's head. The men soon revealed the torso, and with a concerted effort, pulled him clear of the cloying earth. He lay quite still. Maynard knelt by Pat's side, and put his cheek close to Pat's lips. Looking up at Harrington, he shook his head. Conor shoved him aside and knelt down to put his ear to Pat's chest, but it was a token gesture as he had seen the full weight of the slide fall exactly where Pat had been standing, but he felt the need to satisfy the straining Sean that everything had been done that could be done.

'Oh God, no,' muttered Harrington. But Sean did not hear him, did not see the Clonarty men exchange glances as he flung himself on Pat's chest,

'Pa, oh Pa, don't leave us,' he wept piteously. The teeming rain washed the muck off Pat's face and mingled with Sean's tears as his neighbours and friends gently but firmly pulled him to his feet and led him away from the scene. Conor turned back for a moment, and saw that the teeming rain had washed away more than the muck. As the cleansing process went on, the lines wrought by the years appeared to wash away too. Gone were the scored furrows of bitterness across the forehead and mouth; gone were the marks of sorrow and anger; gone was the rage. The handsomeness of the man could plainly be seen, and for the first time, Conor saw and understood what Kate had fallen for so many years before.

While Sean had mourned over Pat, Harrington had been briskly taking charge of the situation. Though shaken by witnessing a man die before his eyes, he knew that swift action was called for. Later he would deal with the pain of knowing that it was *his* road works, *his* guidance, and *his* men that had suffered. Leaving Conor and the other Clonarty men with Sean, he called the rest of the men, and Maynard together.

'Right all of you. You will be paid until the end of the week and need not report back until Monday. It is possible that the work will close anyway with the harvest so close. Draw your wages and food from Maynard, then you may use my cart to transport the injured man, Callaghan isn't it, and also O'Hara to their villages. I will come and see the families within a day or two.'

'Aye, do that,' came an anonymous voice from the crowd, 'I'm sure you will be able to explain why their menfolk can no longer provide for them.'

Harrington's face blenched whiter than ever, but he did not reply. The accusation was unfair, and he knew it; his workings had the lowest accident rate than any other, a fact borne out by his visits to the Castle. But that knowledge did not comfort him at this moment in time! He knew that he should have taken charge and moved the men immediately on his return rather than argue with Maynard. Now he turned to his deputy, noting that he seemed singularly unconcerned at the events, and brusquely gave instructions about the wages, food and cart. Then Maynard simply shrugged and moved away.

Harrington returned to the tableau on the hill. Conor was holding Sean in close embrace, as the boy's shoulders heaved in distress. Conor felt a deep affection for Sean, partly for the affection he had had for Kate, and for the boy himself with his red gold hair and blue eyes, so like his mother's, and his cheerful personality. Dermot hovered close by, uncertain what to do or say, dumbstruck by the speed with which tragedy had struck. As Harrington approached, he heard the muffled voice of Sean from Conor's chest,

'What'll I tell her? What'll she do, Uncle Conor?'

'Hush boy. 'I'll be with you an' I'll tell her.'

Harrington stood awkwardly for a moment, unable to break in, but then coughed gently to attract attention.

Conor raised his eyes questioningly.

'I've made arrangements for your friend to be taken to his home. You and Sean, and his father, will be paid for the week. I'm so sorry, Sean.'

Sean did not raise his head, unable to look at the man. At that moment he held him to blame for his father's death, but he could not bring himself to say the words.

Within an hour, the site was cleared. The men from other villages had carefully placed the injured man, Callaghan and Pat on the donkey cart, and then they quietly moved off, murmuring words of sympathy for the small family group standing mutely by. Callaghan had fallen unconscious with the pain of his shattered leg, 'which is as well' muttered Hogan, making him as comfortable as he could with makeshift splints. Then carrying parcels of food, and with their wages tucked out of sight, they set out for home, a sombre procession, with Conor and Dermot flanking a dazed Sean.

Harrington and Maynard watched them go as the rain continued to pour, until they were lost from sight. Then collecting as much of the surveying equipment as they could carry, set off for Dublin. They walked in silence, Harrington only too aware of the consequences of the day's events; Maynard apparently unperturbed.

The procession reached Clarne, and Callaghan was carried carefully into his cottage to be treated by the local midwife. He would be most unlikely ever to walk again, but more likely be carried off by gangrene within a few weeks!

The Clonarty group walked slowly through the centre of their village, past the meeting place, past the dancing place, past the celebration place, and stopped by Kate's door. This homecoming had not brought happy faces to greet them as they had not been expected. The men walked quietly away leaving Conor, Dermot and Sean by the cart bearing Pat's body. The donkey stood patiently with its sad burden. Kate came to the door and stepped outside and gazed at the tableau. Then she saw the cart and its burden and raised anguished eyes from the cart to Conor, who nodded slowly. Kate shook her head as if to give a lie to the scene before her,

'No..o..o.' the wail tore at their hearts, and Sean began to weep, his tears mingling with the rain running down his face.

'Not this as well!'

Conor looked at Kate in surprise, and followed her gaze as she turned towards their fields. As far as Conor could see, marching in serried ranks up the hillside, circling the village, was a brown and stinking ruin. And all over, there was the smell of destruction and decay.

Chapter 20

Sean stood at the edge of their fields, the desolation of the landscape echoing the desolation in his heart. The rain fell obliquely, driven by a soughing, westerly wind that susurrated dully through the weeping haulms and sullen barley stalks. He curled his bare feet into the clinging mud, feeling it ooze between his toes. Useless to even hope that there were any healthy potatoes beneath the sodden earth; unlike the previous year, there were no islands of green amid the sea of brown slime.

He was alone with his despair, the rest of the villagers sensibly staying in their cottages and out of the rain. But Sean had felt too restless for the confines of their shebeen, and had wandered out to investigate the true extent of this latest disaster. He was not bothered by being wet as this had been his daily lot during the latter stages of the road building, and he had spent day after day in sodden clothes. At night, they all discarded their clothes and set them round the peat fire as they slept in their scalps.

He turned his face up to the weeping heavens, feeling the rain run down his face with his tears,

'Why?' he shouted up at the infinity of grayness, 'haven't we enough to bear?' It seemed that he could hear his father's voice in the sighing wind,

'I'm relying on you, son. Take care of yer Mam and the young'uns. You're the man now.'

'How Pa? How can I take care of them with no harvest? I don't know what to do. Help me Pa, help me!' And he felt his youth slip away from him as his frail, adolescent shoulders bent at the weight of the burden.

'Take care of them, care of them….' The sound faded as the breeze died away, leaving only the sound of the driving rain.

Sean turned towards the village, and for a brief, terrible moment beheld an awful sight. Before his eyes lay destruction and ruin, with a few charred shells where there had once been sturdy cob cottages. He rubbed his eyes and shook his head, as the rain eased somewhat, and saw a scene as it should be, with cottages intact, with smoke rising from peat fires within. Was it a fancy born of despair, a sleepless night, or a terrible glimpse of the future?

Yesterday they had laid Pat's body at Kate's feet, and she had slowly sunk to her knees by him; this man who had stolen her heart so many years before, and to whom she had remained constant in spite of his moody and mercurial nature. Then Conor had gently raised and enfolded her in his embrace as Eileen and old Daniel arrived. Eileen had taken in the scene at a glance and directed them to carry Pat's body into the cottage. Leaving Kate in Conor's embrace, she had set about laying him out, cleaning the remaining mud and grit from his face and generally tidying his clothes; he had no others to change him into. Finally she placed two tallow candles by his head. She could hear the murmur of voices outside, as Conor recounted the events that had led to Pat's death, but inside it was quiet and peaceful, with just a low

bubbling sound from the ever burning peat. While she worked, Eileen talked softly to the inanimate Pat,

'Now what've you done? You know this will break her heart? An' how is she to manage for food with the harvest ruined again? But yer a handsome devil, I'll give you that. No wonder my Kate took a fancy to you.' She sighed and laid his hands upon his breast,

'There, lad, it's all I can do; not even a clean shirt for yer burying.' She looked up then, aware of a soft sound, and found that her namesake, Little Eily, had crept in, and was sitting by her father, gazing into his face. She was such a silent, secretive child, that no-one ever knew what she was thinking, but Eileen saw the anguished look on her face, though her eyes were dry. The older woman's generous heart was touched by the child's grief,

'Aye, you truly loved him, didn't you?' and she stroked the child's shining brown head abstractedly, thinking ahead of the uncertain future for them all, with Pat gone. How would Kate cope with this little one and young Kevin?

'Thank God for Sean,' she muttered to herself, 'there's an old head on young shoulders.' Leaving Eily in silent vigil by her father, she went outside in time to hear Conor say,'

''Tis all the fault of that English man; he should never have started digging just there when it was so wet!'

'But it wasn't Harrington,' protested Sean, 'he wasn't there, it was that Maynard.' Earlier, in the throes of shock, he too had blamed Harrington, but time and his innate sense of justice had made him recall things as they really were.

'Mebbe,' replied Conor, 'but he was responsible for the works, 'n he should be paying you for losing yer man, Kate.'

'He said he would come'n see us,' insisted Sean.

'How can you say such things,' cried Kate, 'how much money'd bring back my Pat?' And she turned and went into the cottage.

'Leave her be,' said Eileen to Conor, 'you mean well, but it's not the time to be talking so.'

'I'll be away to Dublin Castle tomorrow,' said Conor grimly, 'Kate may not want to know now, but she'll need all the help she can get in months to come with that,' jerking his head in the direction of the foetid fields.

'I'll try'n get a message to Father Muldoon, ter say his prayers over Pat's burying,' said Daniel for the first time, 'and I'd better tell old Kevin. He's going ter take it hard; Pat was the only left of his sons left in Clonarty, tho' tis hard to tell what the man's thinking. You look exhausted, lad,' he turned to Sean, 'go in ter yer Mam. She's going to need all of you more than ever now.'

Sean nodded, and followed by Kevin he ducked under the low doorway and disappeared.

During the long night, after he had settled his younger siblings, and after a meagre supper of their precious food, Sean sat with his mother in vigil. They did not speak. From time to time, Kate would take Pat's hand, or stroke his face, murmuring all the while in her low, sweet voice. She would brush the thick, dark hair away from his forehead and softly kiss his brow. Sean looked on, unable to ease his mother's torment while his own heart broke. More than once, he put his arm round Kate's frail shoulders, and just for a moment she rested her head on his shoulder. But then she would gently detach herself, and return to Pat.

Neighbours had called earlier, each one bearing a small gift from their own meagre resources, leaving Sean touched by their generosity. One had even found some more of the precious tallow, and more lamps burned bravely, adding their light to the gentle glow of the peat fire.

At last the long night ended, the awakening day evidenced by a lightening of the doorway. Just before dawn, the younger ones had awoken, and joined Sean and Kate, forming a circle of shared grief. Finally Daniel arrived, and shocked by the scene, he fetched Eileen, who coaxed the three dazed youngsters out of the morbid scene and took them back to her cottage. Daniel sat down by Kate,

'Well, my Kate, Father Muldoon'll be here soon.'

'You're not taking him,' said Kate fiercely, 'I canna live without him.'

'Hush now, you know you can't be keeping him in here. His body may be lying here, but his souls with God up in Heaven.'

'Do I know that? Pat always said that there's nothin' up there but emptiness. What've I done to be punished like this? I love him 'n no-one's goin' to take him away!'

'You don't know what yer saying,' said Daniel, shocked, 'It's at a time like this you should be turning to the Good Lord, not away from Him!'

'I ask you again, Pa, what's He done for me; he's taken my baby, taken away our harvest, taken away our clothes, our belongings, 'n now he's taken away my Pat, an' you ask me to turn to Him!' Kate's voice rose steadily, becoming harsh and strident. Daniel shrank before the onslaught, unable to find adequate answers to the tirade.

'Yer bitter now, Kate. Give it some time, 'n you'll see things differently.'

'Aye, when we're all dead! Look at me, Pa,' and she held out her arm, slender as a wand, 'Look at you. We none of us'll be alive next year unless your God does something!'

But the outburst had broken Kate from her hypnotic state, and without further argument she allowed Daniel to lead her out of the cottage. Conor arrived with the men who had helped escort them home the day before, and placed him on a makeshift litter. Outside, with the morning already saturated with a heavy mist, a procession formed, led by Father Muldoon intoning prayers for the dead.

Immediately behind the litter came Kate, flanked by her sons, and followed by Eileen holding Little Eily's hand, followed in turn by old Daniel and Pat's father, Kevin. The latter had not said a word on hearing the news about the last of sons, nor had he visited his cottage to pay his respects. Now he walked with a face carved out of granite, furrowed by lines of age and bad temper. The rest of Clonarty brought up the rear, and the sad procession made its way up the hillside to the cemetery, singing hymns and responding the Priest's prayers.

They laid Pat to rest next to the tiny grave of his beloved daughter, while Kate, Sean and Kevin stood impassive and dry eyed. Little Eily had vanished, seemingly to avoid witnessing her father being laid in the ground, but at the moment when the first sods were about to cover his face, she ran as light as thistledown to the head of the grave. In her hands was a posy of flowers gathered from the fields nearby. She knelt and placed the bouquet on Pat's, and whispered quietly,

'Bye Pa.'

Then Daniel and Eileen took the O'Hara's back to their cottage to escape from the increasingly heavy rain, while Conor hitched up the donkey to the cart in preparation for his trip to Dublin,

'Before I get locked up for thievin'!' he said. He planned to return the cart and then go to Dublin Castle to find out if anything was being done about Pat's death. If not, he intended to report the matter himself, for 'why should a breadwinner lose his life through the carelessness of a Public Engineer?' Daniel agreed, but advised him to approach the officials with deference and caution or he would get no help at all! It was after seeing disappear through the mist and rain that Sean had taken himself off to the fields to gaze at the ruin of their harvest.

'We'll never get through another year,' he muttered to himself. He had only to look at himself to see the difference between now and this time last year! Then he had been glowing with health from the previous good

harvest and the long, sun-filled days of summer. This year, they were all stick thin, in spite of the improved rations from their wages. Last year, there had been some sound tubers to salvage and keep them going until past the middle of winter, while this year there were none; the evidence stretched away before him in the totally brown fields, and he had no need to dig beneath the oozing earth for corroboration. Last year, the barley fields had been healthy, and had ensured them of money for their rent. This year, after weeks of driving rain, their heads drooped, sodden and forlorn, threatening to be totally inadequate for their purpose. Last year they had been ignorant of the blight, had not even heard the word. This year, they suffered under the weight of knowledge; they knew that this was total disaster!

Conor reached Dublin and delivered the donkey and cart to the depot where the Engineers had their base. Then he made his way to the Castle, where he was put to wait in the usual anteroom. And as usual, he was left to kick his heels for a lengthy period until an official deigned to spare him a moment.

'What's your business? Be quick, there is much to do.'

Conor retailed the events of the tragedy at the road works, while the clerk listened impassively, then,

'I have read the report the report submitted by Mr. Harrington. It is clear that the accident was caused by the weather conditions prevailing at the time. Good day!'

'That's it?' asked Conor, 'a man has lost his life because a hillside fell on him, an' you blame weather conditions? He was killed by diggin' bein' done where it shouldn't, an' I want justice for his widow an' children.'

The clerk eyed him coldly'

'If we paid for every accident you people suffered through your own stupidity, the Government would be destitute. Good day.'

He turned to leave the room, and Conor shouted in desperation,

'Where's Harrington; I demand to see him. He'll tell you that it was no accident! Pat just happened to be there when the slide started.'

The clerk turned back, his face suffused by anger,

'*Mister* Harrington,' he began with heavy emphasis, 'has been called away to London. Be off with you before I call the guard, and be thankful that I am a patient man.' And he strode from the room before Conor could gather his scattered thoughts.

'Called to London,' he muttered in a daze, and then more strongly, 'he's run away 'cause he knows he's to blame!'

In fact Conor could not have more wrong. On his return to the Castle after the accident, Harrington had made his report, laying the blame on himself and Maynard, and had recommended that adequate compensation be paid to the man's dependents. He had also intended to add to the payment himself, and planned to go to the village in a day or two to make this payment directly, once the first shock of loss had died down. But his plans were thwarted by cruel fate, for as he returned to his lodgings, he found an urgent message from London informing him that his father had suffered a stroke and was close to death.

An anguished Harrington was torn between fulfilling his self-imposed obligation to the O'Hara's and fulfilling his filial duty to a much loved parent. After much cogitation, he decided on a compromise. He visited Maynard at his lodging and explained the situation to him,

'The thing is Saul, I'm not entirely sure that the Castle will pay out compensation; they are not known for their generosity, and I suspect that they will try and wriggle out of their obligation. Can I rely on you to see that the family is taken care of?'

'Of course,' replied Maynard, blandly, 'but it wasn't our fault, y'know. We were trying to make the road safe; the man should not have walked there just then!'

Harrington looked at him in shock, but the mounting urgency to reach his father overcame his doubt, and thrusting a purse into his hand, said to Maynard,

'Be that as it may, the family will be in grave difficult without their man, so I'd be obliged if you would take this to the village in a day or two. The Castle can doubtless give you directions.'

'Very well,' replied Maynard, 'safe journey. Er, will you be returning? I hear that the works are being closed as the harvest is due in!'

'I don't know. It will depend on my father's state of health. If the works are closing, I'll not be needed. Goodbye Maynard.'

And Harrington left. He hurried to the castle, lodged his report in charge of the Public Works, and informed him of the reason behind his hurried departure.

'But be sure to get in touch with me if you need any more information. I will be glad to oblige. It wasn't the man's fault and he should be compensated. My assistant is still in Dublin and can also supply information.'

Harrington left Dublin of the next available sailing, noting wryly that it was a cargo vessel stuffed full of foodstuffs. His mind was still troubled at leaving the situation unresolved, but worry about his father gradually came to the fore as he left the coast of Ireland far behind him.

He arrived home to find his father recovering from the stroke that had left him paralysed down the left side of his body. Young Joseph, as he was known in London to distinguish him from his father, also Joseph, found himself caught up with dealing with his father's affairs. He gradually took over all of his outstanding contracts, and it was many weeks before he thought of Ireland again, or the O'Hara's. He never returned to Ireland, but watched in horror from his cosy existence the continuing tragedy of that unhappy country. But his presence at the Dublin road works was to have a surprising legacy, though Harrington would never discover it!

Back in Ireland, Maynard cheerfully pocketed the purse that Harrington had left. He not only lacked imagination, but was completely amoral, and could not see any harm in his actions. It simply did not occur to him that the O'Hara's would be in desperate straits without the money he had pocketed. Neither did he pursue enquiries concerning Government compensation. When it was confirmed that the Public Works had indeed closed, he took ship to England, and like Harrington, never returned.

Conor returned to Clonarty an embittered man. But when he told Kate that there would be no money, she simply shrugged,

'I didn't expect any,' apathetically.

Sean, when told that Harrington had run away from his obligations and was directly responsible for the lack of payments, he vouchsafed no reply. But he thought about the matter deeply. He was intensely disappointed as he had grown to almost hero-worship the man, and had felt a reciprocation of his regard. Of Conor's accusations he had no doubts, but he did think that there had to be a good reason for the apparent defection. He just couldn't bring himself to believe that he and his family had been abandoned out of hand. But he kept these thoughts to himself; clearly they were not shared by Conor and the rest of the team!

Chapter 21

As Sean stood and gazed over the ruined fields of Clonarty in August of the year 1846, he felt he had reached rock bottom. He simply could not see a way forward; long term hunger, exhaustion, the loss of Nuala and now his father, his mother's withdrawal from them all and finally the lost harvest all conspired to beat him down, until he felt he was at the bottom of a pit with steep sides, and from which there was no escape. Bowing his head in acceptance of defeat, he made his way back to the shebeen and throwing off his sodden clothes, sank into a sleep that lasted twenty four hours.

For the first few hours he lay totally comatose, and the sounds of activity in the cottage went unheard. But then the dreams began, and he tossed and turned in anguish.

In his dreams he could see a mound of sodden earth which began to heave and tremble as he approached. Then two heads started to rise from it, one dark and one small and red haired. He started forward with arms outstretched and a glad cry; they were not dead after all! Then the heads turned and he could see that they were, in reality skulls with empty eye sockets and twin rows of gleaming teeth. Skeletal bodies followed the heads, reaching out there bony arms towards him. He could feel Kevin, Eily and Kate trying to push by him trying to reach the bony embrace. Kate whispered with a beatific expression,

'Pat, I'm coming, I'm coming.'

No matter how he tried, Sean could not stop them, and first Kate, and then Kevin holding Eily by the hand, reached the mound and scrambled to the top. They all stood, hand in hand with the skeletal Pat and Nuala, and slowly sank from sight waving to Sean as they went. Sean cried out in his sleep, his arms reaching out in an imploring gesture.

Little Eily, who had been sitting by him when since his restlessness had begun, took his hand and bowed her head over it. From the young girl's body emanated a feeling of peace of restfulness, flowing down her arm and through her fingertips into Sean's, until his unquiet spirit was calmed and he slept peacefully once more. Three times in the night and day that he slept, she quietened him, until towards the evening of the day after Pat's funeral, Sean finally awoke naturally.

He yawned and stretched and then raising himself up on his elbow, he looked round the cottage. Eily lay close by him, dozing lightly, her peaked little face and shadowed eyes telling of her own suffering that she bore with a fortitude, rare in one so young. Kate sat across the fire from him, her arms wrapped around her knees, rocking backwards and forwards. She had been there when he fell asleep, and Sean suspected all the time he had been asleep. Of Kevin, there was no sign. Sean pondered on the recent events, but of his dreams he had no memory, just a lingering sense of disquiet, and a feeling of gratitude towards his little sister.

With a lift of spirits given by his long sleep, Sean felt more hopeful about the future. True, nothing had changed, but his natural resilience and optimism had returned and he began making plans for the future. The fields would have to be cleared of their rotten, blighted burden, and then manured with seaweed ready for planting next spring. How he would achieve this with just his younger brother, and a bereft Kate, he did not dwell on. Nor did he dwell on the problems of raising money to pay for new seed. They would harvest the barley when the rain finally ceased, and the rent would be raised before the Michaelmas collection. Whatever else, they must raise the rent money, for without that they would have nothing; no cottage, no fields, no future, of that he had no doubt. Then he would return to Dublin and find out if there were Public Works still to be had. He did not yet know of Conor's abortive visit to the city, or he might not have been so sanguine in his planning!

This ability to come to terms with extreme adversity and make positive decisions about the future was a facet of Sean's character that had only surfaced since the start of the troubles. Ever an optimist, he now tempered that side of his nature with a more reasoned approach. Intelligent and deductive, resilient and resourceful were the properties that would enable him to survive the difficult times ahead, whereas so many of his countrymen would just give up and perish!

Having mulled over the situation and reached his decisions, Sean resolutely rose from his bracken bed, and went out in search of Conor, but his uncle had already left for Dublin.

But even the elements seemed to conspire against them all in the days following Pat's funeral, with thunder and lightning rolling around the western hills, bringing torrential rain in their train, and effectively dampening any hope of harvesting. The stream that normally sang and gurgled down the hill above the village rushed headlong in full spate and filled the Lough to overflowing. The excess water ran off into the marshes until the land to the east was one vast, shimmering sheet of water, making travel to the coast impossible, as was the cutting of peats to dry ahead of winter.

While work in the fields was impossible, Sean decided to travel to Dublin to find out for himself if all Public Works had indeed shut down. He had spoken with an angry and embittered Conor, who had reported that there was no money to be had and all works were closed, but he still thought to find out for himself. He hoped that knowledge of a second ruined harvest might have caused the authorities to reverse their decision. But he was to be sadly disappointed on his arrival in Dublin. The English Government, convinced that Ireland's troubles would be over with the harvest, had not only shut down all Public Works, but also the importation of foodstuffs, including the much maligned, but cheap, Indian corn. Until the ponderous machinery could be set in motion once more, they would be totally bereft of any help, and totally without sustenance. Sean spent the last of his wages on some depressed looking cabbages, and returned home with a heavy heart.

Back in Clonarty, with the weather slightly improved, Sean set Kevin, Eily and himself, together with their O'Malley grandparents to scouring the hills for anything at all edible. They scavenged nettles and other wayside weeds, nuts and fruit from bushes and brambles. They even probed the forbidden acres of the Danforth estate for orchard fruits off heavily laden trees, all the while keeping a sharp lookout for O'Leary and his thugs. These were a constant threat, as they were known to patrol the perimeters, and no-one would be safe from their blackthorn shillelaghs! But they had managed to avoid any encounters to date.

'It's not as if they pick 'em themselves,' grumbled old Daniel, after they had been forced to scramble to safety before they had been spotted by a roving bully boy!

The results of their scavenging did sustain them while they waited for the barley harvest as the weather gradually improved. And if the unaccustomed nettle soup tended to run through them like a purge, at least the new diet improved their skin and hair, and eased gums swollen by scurvy. Watching his family busy at their foraging, even managing some laughter as they did so, Sean felt that they had taken a step or two out of the black pit, toiling laboriously up its steep, slippery sides. But he must beware though, he told himself firmly; it would not take much to push them down again. And, he sighed to himself, Kate was not there with them as she remained in the shebeen, only rousing herself to prepare food from their days' gleanings. At night, she slept curled like a foetus by the fire, staring wide-eyed and sleepless at the glowing embers. Nothing Sean or his grandparents said reached through the wall that she had built round herself since the day she had watched Pat being buried, and day by day she grew more ethereal as she took very little of the food they brought home. Even little Eily could not reach her, though she would sit by her mother for hour after hour, softly singing.

The crisis came about two weeks after Pat's burial, when they had all returned from a scavenging trip to find the cottage empty. Sean's mind immediately turned to the swollen Lough, knowing of his mother's distressed state of mind. He rushed outside, followed by his siblings. It was a blustery day, with wavelets whispering across the surface of the Lough, now much bigger than they were used to. The tall willow tree that had always stood by its bank, under which Kate had sat watching her brother Fergus that fateful summer's day so long ago, now stood enisled, forlorn and sodden. But of Kate there was no sign. Then Sean felt a tug on his sleeve from Eily,

'She's up there,' said the little girl, pointing.

'Where Eily? I can't see anyone or anything; how d'you know?'

'She's up there,' the little girl insisted, shrugging.

Sean had much respect for the fey quality of his little sister, and taking her hand, they started up the hill, unknowingly following the path their parents had taken during their courtship. They followed the stream upwards, swollen and turgid with debris plucked from its bank as it roared by, twigs, leaves and even a tiny vole, flushed from its nest while it slept and drowned before it could struggle free. They left the stream at its source and found themselves by the Danforth boundary wall.

'In there?' questioned Sean. Eily nodded mutely. Ahead lay a break in the wall, through which they scrambled, and they found Kate at last, under the spreading branches of a large oak tree. Kate was leaning on the bole of the tree, her arms outstretched as though to embrace its thickness.

'Mam,' cried Sean, but she did not respond, as with eyes tight shut, she sobbed,

'Pat, Oh Pat, where are you?'

Suddenly, something snapped inside Sean. He took hold of his mother's shoulders and pulled her roughly from the tree, then forced her to turn and face him. Though her eyes were open, they were blank and staring. Sean began to shake her, gently at first, then with increasing violence, snapping her head back.

'Pa's dead. He's not comin' back, d'you hear? But we're here, an' we need you, me 'n Kevin 'n Eily. We love you!'

His voice rose to a shout, and then tailed away, as he stopped shaking his mother for there was no answering spark. But then, looking into his mother's eyes, he saw just a glimmer of life, a suggestion of warmth, of feeling. Slowly, Kate's head lowered, and then rose again, her eyes swimming with tears.

'Sean, Sean, is it you? It's just that I miss him so.'

'I know, Mam, I know.' And he held his arms out to her, this woman who had held him to her bosom, who had been the joy of his childhood and who now needed him. She stepped into the arms of her son, smaller now that the son she had borne. A noise behind them reminded them on the others, and they broke apart to take in Kevin and Eily. They were a family again; their mother had returned to them, and they took another step out of the pit.

At long last, Sean was able to start the harvest, and it was every bit as bad as he had feared. The ground was still sodden, but being on the side of the hill, was at least draining fast, and he could not wait any longer. Around him, others were hard at work; he could see Hogan several fields away, and the Flanagan's further up the hillside, but of Conor and the Murphy's, there was no sign.

'Strange,' mused Sean, 'they've the largest fields. Why haven't they started digging?'

He found that he soon tired, his body unable to sustain the effort required to dig. He tried to help himself by keeping some sort of rhythm, intoning softly to himself,

'WHEN we get enough to eat,' stabbing with his spud,

'THEN I'll learn to read,

THEN I'll get on,

THEN we'll never, ever starve again!'

He had no idea how he would ever accomplish this feat, though there were rudimentary schools to be found in the locality. But he did find that he had managed to clear almost a row of rotten, stinking tubers, piling them along the row to be collected later. Already their familiar stench filled the air bringing the remembered feeling of nausea.

'Sean, Sean.' He started at the sound of his name, and looked up to see Dermot waving frantically from down below. He waved back,

'Ho Dermot. Why'nt you and yer Pa clearing yer fields?'

'Pa sent me to fetch you 'n Aunt Kate. He wants to see you.'

'Can't it wait awhile? I've just started!'

'He said it was important.'

Sean shrugged and stuck his spud into the ground. In truth, he would be glad of the rest. Suddenly his fields looked very big, too much for him on his own! He started down the hill to where Dermot waited and the boys set off for the Murphy shebeen. Sean glanced at Dermot, but his cousin turned his face away. A chill band of dread closed round his heart.

'What's the matter, Dermot? Has anythin' happened to….?'

'No…no….. I don't know. Pa just said to fetch you.'

Sean frowned. The boys had grown up together, and were as close as brothers. They had never had secrets between them before! His steps quickened and they soon arrived at the Murphys' shebeen. On entering, Sean was surprised to find it full of people. There was Daniel and Eileen sitting close together the other side of the cottage; there were all the Murphy children complete now with Dermot's return, from his sister Siobhan down to the toddler, Brigid, solemnly sucking her thumb, and gazing at the assembled company with wide eyes. Near the door sat Kate, with Eily and Kevin close by. Conor was standing near the great, stone chimney, sucking on an empty clay pipe and looking ill at ease. By his knees sat his wife, Mari on a small, three legged stool. She always reminded Sean of the pictures of the Madonna that Father Muldoon carried with him, to hand out to deserving youngsters. Her placid face was framed by her smooth reddish hair, once so much less vivid than Kate's, but now almost glowing in comparison with her elder sister's dull whiteness. Only one year younger than her sister, Mari looked untouched by the troubles, as though they had failed to reach behind her smooth façade.

'Why,' thought Sean, 'she looks ten years younger than Mam. But then, she hasn't had the same sorrows to bear.' But he was startled out of his reverie by his Uncle Conor, who began to speak.

'Now that you're all here, there's something that Mari 'n me want ter say to you.' And he shifted awkwardly, 'you'll mind that when Pa was alive he was well known for his poteen, God bless him?'

They all nodded. No-one could deny that old Seamus Murphy was famous far and wide for the quality of his poteen, brewed in a still cunningly hidden in the surrounding fields.

'Ever since I can remember,' continued Conor, 'Pa'd sell his poteen for coin, or if paid in kind would sell it on in Dublin for coin. Over the years he made quite a hoard.' Again there were nods from the audience, not sure where this was going. Murphy was known to be astute, and his hoard of silver shillings had helped build their holdings into the largest and most productive in the district.

'Mind, he sometimes had to use it when times were bad, but he always promised us, me 'n Liam 'n Dominic, that he'd share it between us when the time came. Well, when Liam 'n Dom decided to go to America a year or so back, he paid their passage and gave them a bit more besides, but he promised that whatever was left would be mine when he went.'

Conor had all their attention now,

'Then of course, he was taken all of a sudden, an' there was no time to sort things out.' Indeed, it had been a seven day scandal when Seamus, who was supposed to be trading in Dublin, was taken by a heart attack in the cottage of the widow MacAfee in Kilgarth!

'Well we searched, Mari 'n me. Pa'd never said where he kept his hoard, so we couldn't find it; not then.'

''Could you not?' came Kate's soft voice from the corner.

'Of course not,' protested Mari vehemently, 'if we'd had the shillings d'you think we'd have let little Nuala be taken?'

'No, of course *you* would not,' Kate answered her sister, but her eyes were on Conor, who flushed and shuffled awkwardly.

'Well, with all this rain, 'n not bein' able to get outside, we were stuck in here, an' we had a real search; we hadn't had time before. An' we found it mortared in here,' and Conor indicated a spot in the stonework of the chimney.

Sean was shocked at first at his mother's words, and by her tone, but when he looked around, he noted that the family had all of their furnishings, table and chairs, beds and blankets, so clearly they had had money to buy seed last year. He chided himself, for what man would not take care of his own, but to let Nuala….. He could not finish the thought. Conor went on,

'Clonarty is finished. Mari 'n me, we've a mind to try for an emigration ship to America. After our passages, us 'n the littl'uns, there won't be much left over.' Sean saw Mari's eyes slide sideways, 'but if you could raise some, Sean, with yours and my barley crop, we could all go.'

There was a stunned silence for a moment, and then from Daniel,

'I can't blame you, Conor, for seeking a better life. But those ships! Such stories you hear; floating coffins, so they are, how many of you will arrive in America, eh?'

'An' how many of us'll live through this next year?' retorted Conor, angrily, 'our minds are made up.'

'Whisht, son. I said I understand. But Eileen'n me, it's too late for us. We're too old for journeying.' Conor shrugged, and turned to Kate. She spoke so softly that even Sean standing next to her had to strain to make out the words,

'I'll not leave here. I can't go.'

In spite of her soft tone, Conor responded angrily,

'Yer out of yer mind, woman. Pat's dead. D'yer think he would want you ter stay? Think of these,' his sweeping hand arm indicating Sean and his siblings. The others were surprised at his anger, but Kate thought she understood. Was there still a spark after all these years, or a fond memory from long ago?

'I'm sorry, Conor. I cannot leave, whether you understand or not. These young ones must decide for themselves, but I can't leave me Mam and Pa, nor can I leave Pat.' Sean, Kevin and Eily immediately moved closer to her side, their decision made.

'Yer wrong,' said Conor quietly, perhaps not even surprised. 'If we've no need to wait for the harvest, we'll be goin' soon, er, tomorrow! Sean, get whatever yer can from the fields, an' all of you use anythin' we leave behind.'

Sean nodded, speechless. The full import of Conor's words had just reached him. Not only would he lose his cousin and lifelong friend, Dermot, but also a much treasured aunt in Mari. And worst of all, the support and advice from an Uncle who had been a second father to him. The months ahead looked bleak indeed, and he was hard put to hold back the tears.

But worst of all was the sense of betrayal. Clearly, Conor had anticipated the outcome of the discussions, and the family was already packed and ready to go. Their departure had been carefully organised, and like as not, they already had their passages booked.

The Murphy's left early next morning, taking only what they could carry in bundles on their backs. Little Brigid was tied firmly to Siobhan's back with a shawl, and the remaining children straggled along behind their parents. Kate hugged them all, and then held Mari closely, their girlhood memories holding them transfixed momentarily. Then she embraced Conor,

'Take care,' he whispered into her hair, you've got a good lad in that Sean, an' he'll be minding you.'

Kate nodded; they had said all that there was to say; the past was finished. Dermot and Sean said their own farewells, each knowing that it would be forever. Then the procession wound its way out of the village, other friends and neighbours reaching out hands as they went. Soon they were lost to sight in the early morning mist. Sean held a small purse that Conor had pressed into his hand out of Kate's sight,

'I wish it were more, but you'll use it carefully; don't tell yer mother.' And he had gone. Sean felt the sides of the pit closing him in again; was there no way out?

A week after the Murphy's departure, Hogan came to their shebeen with his diminutive wife, Bridie. Sean was fond of his neighbours and his parents had been good friends over the years, and he had not forgotten the man's kindness when Pat had been killed. Hogan, as he was ever addressed, being another Patrick, spoke first,

'Mornin' Kate, Sean. We've, er, come to say goodbye!'

Kate looked at them, wide eyed in shock,

'Oh no! Not you too! Where will you go? What about your little ones?'

'There's nothin' for us here. We'll not raise the rents, and already the babe is sickenin'. We're goin' ter try for Wales; there's money to be had in the iron towns.'

'But how'll you get there?' put in Sean. Hogan shrugged.

'We'll go south and try for a crossin' to Anglesey.' Sean nodded. He too had heard there was money to be earned in the 'Iron Empires' of South Wales, either in the mines or the blast furnaces. Such was the power of rumour to a hungry people that they had heard of money to be had, but not of the hardships endured by the workers, especially the immigrant Irish, fleeing the effects of famine. Sean felt his heart stir with envy for a moment, but they had made their decision for good or bad; Kate would not leave so neither would they.

The Hogan's were followed by others, until there was a mere handful of cottages occupied, and the village took on a forlorn, neglected air. Sean was reminded of his vision, yet these cottages were, as yet, intact! Ironically, the remaining shebeens were all re-furnished from the items left behind by the likes of the Murphys, so they all had tables and chairs and bedding at least. But the sense of community that had sustained them through the previous year was slowly vanishing, replaced by a sense of 'every family for itself.'

Day followed weary day, as Sean struggled to finish the harvest, with Kevin a willing if meagre helper. The barley crop was pitifully small, even supplemented by Murphy's grain, and when he took it to sell in Dublin, he had not the adult cunning to drive a good bargain. The only way to pay the rents would be to use the purse that Conor had pressed on him, and so it could not be used to purchase food. Already they were feeling the effects of their inadequate diet of gleanings from hedgerows and the hillsides. Their limbs were ever more sticklike, and their skins more transparent.

While in Dublin, Sean kept asking about the re-opening of the Public Works, for he realized that it was the only way to survive the winter, when even their foraging would have to cease. He discovered a building that housed the 'Board of Works' in total chaos, with furniture piled outside on the streets, and much coming and going on the part of official looking personages. When accosted, these officials merely looked harassed and could not, or would not offer any information concerning any imminent projects. One individual, either more kindly or less busy than the rest, noted the boy's pinched cheeks and desperate air, and took time to talk to him. He explained to Sean that the Government had changed the rules concerning the funding of these works, and were now requiring local landowners to pay for any work that benefitted them directly.

'It's all very complicated,' the man sighed, 'and not easy to persuade owners to pay for relief of their own countrymen.'

Sean nodded, unsurprised at this further evidence of the rich landowners' inhumanity!

'The situation is further complicated by the absence of many of the owners, which delays things considerably,' the helpful official went on, 'why, we are at this moment waiting on a reply from a landlord south of here, a Lord .... er....Danforth, or some such. We want to drain some land near the coast, which could supply work to the local villages. We've communicated, but so far, we've heard nothing.'

'Aye, an' not likely to,' said Sean bitterly, 'he's our landlord, an' we've never had any help from him, not last year nor this. I've never even seen him, though Mam said he visited at the time she was wed to Pa.'

'Be patient if you can,' the official said kindly, 'we're doing our best.'

'Sean nodded, a lump in his throat preventing further speech. The man meant well, but that would not put food in his or his family' mouths. Not for the first time he felt despair threaten to engulf him, and he just wished that he could lay his burden on the shoulders of someone older and sturdier than himself.

The official watched him go, noting the dragging steps, and the bowing of the slight shoulders, the limbs thin to the point of emaciation. Yet it was not an unusual sight. Daily, in Dublin, bodies of the poor were discovered in hidden corners and alleyways, and the populace all wore the same pinched, starved look. If it was up to him, he thought, he would open all the food depots where harvested food was stored prior to export. It did seem somewhat immoral to be depriving the native population of the harvest that they themselves had gathered, and shipping it off to the more affluent mainland! Already there had been riots outside the depots, and outside the Board of Works by desperate, hungry men. They were ruthlessly suppressed by soldiers hastily summoned. He understood, but what could he do? Get on with his job, he supposed, and try and get some sort of Public Works going as soon as possible. But would there be enough able bodied men to carry out such works? By the look of the youth who had gone on his way, time was running out.

Back in Clonarty, Sean counted his shillings slowly and carefully for the fourth time that morning, It was now Michaelmas, and O'Leary was due with his coterie of thugs, to collect the rents. Sean wondered what the agent would make of the village, with many of its inhabitants gone away and few rents to collect. But they couldn't be thrown out, could they? Not with the rent money forthcoming. Nevertheless, he had an icy pit of dread in his stomach, or perhaps O'Leary had always had this effect on him!

Just past noon, the clop, clop of horse's hooves could be heard approaching from the direction of Kilgarth, and a moment later, O'Leary rode into the village, mounted, as always, on his sturdy cob. The years had not dealt kindly with the agent. His face was empurpled with broken veins, caused by better living than any of the tenants could possibly imagine, and his nose was enlarged by a triangle of warts, its tip constantly festooned with a dew drop that resisted the briskest of westerly winds. His body was shaped like a barrel, underpinned by a pair of skinny legs, so he was seen to his best advantage mounted on his cob. Trailing behind the agent was his usual retinue of bully boys, ever watchful for trouble from the downtrodden tenants. Apparently they had not already heard that the majority of the able bodied men in this village had already departed!

With practiced ease, a trestle table was set up in the village centre, and O'Leary settled himself pompously in the travelling chair behind it, accompanied by heavy wheezing. He spread out a piece of paper on the table in front of him and began to read out the names of the tenants. As each name was called, eliciting no response, the agent looked up, as though in surprise, but Sean soon realized that it was all an act, and the agent knew exactly who remained. After four or five names had been called, and not responded to, he paused, shaking his head,

'I don't think Lord Danforth goin' ter like this. If he don't get his rents, he might as well turn the whole lot over to sheep! No profit in empty fields!' He shook his head ponderously, almost dislodging the dew drop!

Sean felt a chill run down his spine. O'Leary was just playing with them, pretending he hadn't known about the absentees. He looked at the others, and knew that they shared his thoughts.

'O'Hara… Kevin.' Sean jumped at the name, but it was his grandfather being called. Kevin shuffled forward and put a handful of coins down. Sean's eyes widened,

'Where'd he get it?' he asked himself, 'he hasn't worked his fields for years!' Then he shrugged. It wasn't his business; old Kevin was a total recluse these days and neither asked for or offered help of his son's family.

'Still,' thought Sean, 'if he has money, it would help us; we could share, after all we are his only kin now, the only ones he has left!'

'O'Hara…Patrick.' Sean swallowed and stepped forward.

'Pa…Patrick is dead. I've got the rent, though.' And he put his shillings down on the table.

'Just a minute, boy,' O'Leary squinted up at him. This tenancy is in the name of Patrick O'Hara. I don't even know you.'

'But..but..I'm his son, an' I've brought the harvest in, an'…' then Sean realized that the agent was playing with him, as a cat with a mouse. There was nothing, nobody that O'Leary did not know about.

'Well I don't know,' O'Leary shook his head again, 'Lord Danforth is very anxious to get his sheep running here. So what shall I do, boy? Shall I plead your case, even at the risk of losing me job?'

'Please sir,' said Sean, feeling sickened at the need to humiliate himself to this brutal man, but what was pride at a time like this? 'O'Leary sighed heavily and picked up the money, counting it carefully before dropping it into a draw string bag,

'Well I'll just take this until a reply comes back. Mayhap I won't have ter worry with winter coming on, an' maybe Lord Danforth'll get his sheep after all….eh…eh?' And the man gave a belly laugh at his own humour. Sean stepped back from the table, disgusted and frightened by the agents' words. Would they still be here come springtime?

The list continued with few responses, until,

'O'Malley…Daniel.'

Daniel stepped forward,

'I don't have it. There was not enough barley that wasn't ruined. I'll have to owe ye 'til the next harvest.'

'An' how'll you raise it, old man? You've no money for rent, so you've no money for seed…eh?'

''Please,' begged Daniel, 'we've not much time left to us, let us live in our own home.'

'You know the rules; no rent, no cottage an' no land. Be out by tomorrow or we'll put you out.' O'Leary grinned wolfishly at him,

'One less ter worry about!'

'Don't worry, Pa,' whispered Kate, putting her arms round her father and noting pityingly that he seemed to have shrunk in the last few moments,

'You 'n Mam can move in with us; it'll be warmer come the winter if we're all together.'

Daniel nodded and moved to where Eileen stood patiently waiting. They entwined their arms together and walked away, heads erect, back to their doomed cottage.

The list was soon completed with the few remaining villagers paying their rents. Those that couldn't, with the exception of the O'Malley's, had already left. Soon after, O'Leary and his ménage packed up, and the agent mounted his cob, with much wheezing, and threatening to return the next day to carry out the eviction. They did not doubt his words. The departure was watched with hate filled eyes, for the villagers knew that they were helpless. Only Lord Danforth could waive their rents, and he either did not know, or if he did, did not care about their plight.

Kate tried to persuade her parents to move in that evening, offering to help with moving their meagre belongings. But they gently resisted,

'Let us have one last night in our cottage. It's been our home since we wed, an' you were all raised in it!' How could Kate resist such a plea? But mysteriously, her mother brought a small shrine that had stood in the corner since before Kate was born. It was a simple carved wooden statue of the Virgin and Child mounted on a base with a place for a candle, though that had not been lit for a very long time. Daniel had bought it from a passing tinker for his young bride. Eileen passed it to Kate,

'Take care of this, an' I'll bring the rest in the morning.' And Eileen held Kate close to her for a moment.

That night, Sean awoke and noticed a glow illuminating the doorway of the shebeen. He lay for a moment, puzzled at the light, but then sat up in alarm. Fire! And it was coming from across the green, the direction of the O'Malley cottage. He shook his mother and Kevin awake, and rushed out to investigate. When he reached the site of the blaze, he found O'Flynn, the nearest neighbour, already there, and gazing at it in bemused fashion.

'Grandpa, Grandma,' screamed Sean, and then felt his mother at his shoulder. She tried to approach the flaming thatch, but the heat drove her back. Sean held Kate close to him to prevent her trying again, for it was clear that the old folk could not be saved. Kevin and Eily were suddenly there, their faces as white as sheets. By then, also, everyone else in Clonarty had arrived, and they stood in silent vigil to a much loved old couple who most of them had known all their lives. And not one of them but believed that the old couple had chosen their own way of leaving their home of so many years. Kate and her family had tears streaming down her face, as she spoke to her parents.

'Pa, Mam, why did you do it? I'd've taken care of you.' But she knew, as they all did, that this was no accident. At least her parents were at peace now.

By the morning the fire had mostly gone out, and O'Leary and his thugs arrived to find a smouldering ruin. O'Leary looked disappointed at being deprived of an eviction,

'Not much left ter bury,' he noted cruelly, as he kicked his cob into motion. The silent villagers stared at him with cold, implacable stares, making the agent's back prickle as he left the village.

Sean had already realized that the agent's word were accurate, and decided that his grandparents had the best burial place that they could hope for. He sent Eily up the hill for flowers to weave a wreath which could be placed when the ashes had cooled. He would ask Father Muldoon to say some prayers when next he came, but in truth, the old priest had not been seen for some weeks now.

As he stood by the ashes of his beloved grandparents, and the cottage that was his second home, Sean felt the sides of the pit closing in once again!

Chapter 22

Sean stood on the cliff top overlooking the Irish Sea, and gazed with apathetic interest at the scene below him. Lined up along the water's edge and just above the high tide mark, were five or six curraghs. He wondered idly who they might belong to as it was not a stretch of beach frequented by inshore fisherman. Some way offshore, riding at anchor, was a two masted sailing ship of the kind that regularly sailed out of Dublin laden with foodstuffs bound for their wealthy neighbour across the sullen grey sea. Again, this was a most unusual sight, though Sean supposed that it had put in for repairs, as there was a small boat loaded with sailors making its way to the stern by hauling on lines hanging over the sides. On the beach were a handful of men, presumably there to collect seaweed like himself, though they were currently engaged in gazing out to sea at the two master rather than going about their business.

Sean could understand their lethargy, as he was finding it increasingly difficult to raise any enthusiasm for necessary chores these days. The death of his grandparents two weeks before had hit him hard, for if that indomitable pair had given up the fight for life, what was the point in his continuing the struggle?

Strangely, by contrast, Kate seemed to have regained her own inner strength, and had taken back from Sean the task of keeping up the family's spirits. It was she who now organised the daily forage for edible wild plants, they these were rapidly diminishing with the onset of winter; and the setting of rabbit snares, though these were of doubtful use, as they rarely, if ever, caught anything. During the lengthening evenings, she would sit by their peat fire, often inviting their few remaining neighbours to join them. She would brew tea from a mixture of herbs and sundry other greenstuffs and they would exchange reminiscences. Or she would sing an Irish ballad in a voice that was low and full, with Eily joining in with her childish descant that was slightly off key, giving it a minor quality that had a charm of its own.

It was Kate who had bullied Sean into finishing the harvest, such as it was, and then sending him off to the coast to collect seaweed for manure, promising to send Kevin on later when he had finished foraging with her,

'You never know,' she had said brightly in encouragement, 'I might be able to make seaweed soup!'

So Sean had made his way to the coast with dragging step, and was now glaring morosely at the turgid grey Irish Sea rollers committing suicide on the beach. The wind was westerly, so the sea was more sullen than angry, which exactly matched his mood. Even so, there was a nip to the air presaging the winter just round the corner, and he stirred himself to move down to the beach.

'If it isn't Sean O'Hara? Where's yer Pa, lad, I've not seen him for a year or two?'

Sean turned in surprise. The man standing next to him was Calum McCabe from Colkenny. He had been a crony of his father's for many years, during Pat's heavy drinking era, and perhaps for that reason, Sean couldn't like the man. Nonetheless, he answered politely enough,

Didn't you know? Pa was killed a while back working on a road out of Dublin.'

'What's that you say? Pat dead? No, I hadn't heard. I've bin over the water in Liverpool, trying ter find work. How did it happen?'

Sean related the events leading up to Pat's death, though the telling of it brought a lump to his throat. McCabe nodded once or twice, and then,

'An' I've no doubt you've had little help from those fat arsed officials in Dublin neither, eh lad?'

'No; I didn't expect it, though Uncle Conor tried. But they said it was Pa's own fault!'

'D'yer see that ship there, lad?' said McCabe, changing the subject abruptly. Sean nodded.

'It's crammed with food; the holds are bursting with it. There's wheat 'n oats 'n barley, eggs 'n cheese. What d'yer think of that?'

'It's always bin so; it's how we pay our rents, so it is.'

'Why do we have ter pay rents? So some fat English pig can keep a string of horses an' mistresses in luxury over there.' And he jerked his head seaward towards the invisible English coast.

'Why do they have the land, eh? Because some protestant oaf years ago decided to take it after some battle or other, that's why!'

'I know,' said Sean, quietly. He might privately agree with the man's sentiments, but he could not see what could be done about it right now, and all the talk of food was a torment to his aching belly. McCabe did not look as if he had gone without for very long, so his time in England had apparently not been unrewarding. Again, McCabe abruptly changed the subject,

'Are you a man now Sean, now that yer Pa's gone? Are you the man of yer family?'

'What d'you mean? I do my best, but it's not easy.'

'I know, I'm sure you do. Well, that ship there has put in for repairs, as you can see. You see, it had a bit of an accident with its rudder while loading in the Liffey, and they didn't realise until after they left.'

'How d'you know?' asked Sean, suspicion clouding his mind.

'Well now, accidents can be helped to happen! Yer see those curraghs along there?' Sean nodded again, 'they're waiting for it to get a wee bit dark, and then me 'n me mates'll take them visiting yon ship, and then the Captain will give us a little of all that food mayhap!' After all, it belongs to Ireland, doesn't it?' Sean looked at him, eyes huge in his wasted face,

'You mean – steal it?'

'What d'yer mean, steal? I'm tellin' you it belongs to us. What they're doin' is stealing. They don't need it over there. You don't see them walking around with legs like sticks and little'uns with huge bellies on them, let me tell you.' Sean winced at this reminder of Nuala. Perhaps it was that that which decided him in the end, for when McCabe said,

'Are you comin' in with us?' he mutely acquiesced.

'Well, we've to wait an hour or two. Them along there are keeping an eye on it, just in case they finish the repair quicker'n we thought!'

Just then, Sean heard his name being shouted from the top of the hill, and turning, saw his brother, Kevin, running down the hill towards him.

'It's me brother,' said Sean, 'don't tell him of the plan. We're supposed to be collectin' seaweed, but then I'll send him home while I stay on.'

McCabe nodded and moved away towards his cronies along the beach. Kevin was curious about Sean's companion, but accepted Sean's explanation that he was an old friend of their Pa and had to be told about his death. The boys worked steadily to gather a good sized bundle of seaweed. The rest of the men had vanished from the beach, and Sean supposed that they had hidden themselves in one of the many caves that were scattered along the cliff, to await coming of darkness. He told his brother that he should return home with the collected bundle, while he would continue to load the sledge and follow on. Kevin was inclined to argue, but the habit of obedience to his elder brother was strong in him, and he stood patiently while Sean lashed the seaweed firmly to his back, and told him to go.

'Don't be long,' urged Kevin, 'it'll be getting dark soon.'

Sean nodded,

'Tell Mam I'll be home in good time, an' not to worry,' and he walked with Kevin to the top of the hill, and waved him off cheerily.

He ran back down to find McCabe watching out for him.

'Alright? We'll be leavin' soon, just as soon as the sun gets low enough, they won't see us very well, especially in these curraghs, bein' so low in the water. You'll be home to yer Mam in no time, with a decent supper for her 'n the rest of you.'

Presently, Sean and McCabe went down to the edge of the beach, where the rest of the men joined them. With six curraghs lined up, there would be two in each; not a pleasant prospect in a sea that looked distinctly choppy when viewed close to! Sean had learned to swim after a fashion during family outings to the sea, but he had never strayed out of his depth before, and the ship suddenly looked a long way away! He offered up a silent prayer that he would not disgrace himself, but would prove himself the man he claimed to be! He was assigned to one of the group, a surly looking individual, who did not look happy at being given a boy as his partner. In spite of his miserable expression, the man, 'call me Mickey' was surprisingly sympathetic when he saw how nervous Sean was, and said encouragingly,

'Sturdy little craft, so they are. Just sit still, an' ye'll not even get yer feet wet!'

It was growing perceptibly darker, and though the sun was hidden behind a bank of grey clouds, it was plainly close to sunset. The ship could still be seen, silhouetted against the lighter sky, and it was also clear that the small, dark curraghs would not easily be seen against the darker land mass.

'Ready lads,' came from McCabe, who was clearly the leader of the team. Sean sensed rather than saw the nods, and added his own. He could not have answered just then, for his throat had closed with fear, and his palms were damp with sweat, while his belly heaved, empty though it was. McCabe went on quietly,

'When we get there, use the lines to haul yerselves up the side. We'll have the curraghs all the way round, an' all go up tergether. Don't forget ter tie them on, though, or we'll all have ter swim for it! If you see anyone on deck, he must be silenced before he can make a sound.'

Sean suddenly realised how desperate this venture was. Not only was he involved with robbing a Government ship, but there might be men hurt! But then a vision of Nuala rose up before his eyes, and his grandparents going to their cottage with heads held high, and he strengthened his resolve.

The curraghs set off across the choppy sea. There had been a bad moment when trying to launch them on the surf, slight though it was, and they were all soaked by the chill water before it was achieved. Sean was told to sit in the middle and not move a muscle, whilst Mickey knelt at the front and propelled them along using a single oar. It looked cumbersome and unwieldy, but they moved along surprisingly briskly, and before very long the vessel was on top of them. There was absolute silence among the attackers as they moved with precision, three curraghs moving to either side. The lines still hung from the ship, and each curraghs was secured with a slip knot, ready for a rapid getaway. Mickey showed Sean how to release it when the time came, in case he could not do it himself. Sean nodded mutely, his heart pounding and his throat drier than ever; he shivered violently; not entirely due to his earlier soaking. Mickey gripped his shoulder firmly to steady him, and brought his mouth close to Sean's ear,

Ye'll be alright, lad, stay close ter me. You don't look as if you'll be able to climb that rope so I'll go first an' pull you up,' Sean nodded again, and with a final pat on the back, Mickey grabbed the rope and swarmed up it, agile as a monkey, and disappeared over the side. Sean tied the rope round his waist and the next moment felt it tighten. Bracing his feet against the side of the ship, he went quickly up its side, and joined his companion. So far, there had not been a sound from the raiders, but there were sounds emanating from below the deck, men laughing, a clink of dice, coarse swearing by two voices, seemingly involved in an argument. Mickey took Sean's arm and the pair moved to the bows of the ship where the others were gathering. Suddenly there was a muffled shout, then a thump and the sound of a body falling. As Sean and Mickey arrived, the found their comrades gathered round a body lying crumpled on the deck.

'Keep a sharp look out,' hissed McCabe, 'this'un won't be the only sailor wanderin' about, tho' it does seem they're mostly below deck right now. The hold's just here. You three,' touching them, 'keep watch while we get the cover off, an' no noise!'

One man produced a crowbar and got it under the hatch cover. There was a creaking noise as it began to lift. They all held their breath as they looked around, but no-one appeared to investigate.

'Must all be at their supper,' thought Sean. The hatch lifted further and McCabe moved forward to peer in, and then he reared back with an oath. Below him, instead of a dark hold bulging with grain sacks or rounds of cheeses, he saw rows of bunks on which lounged men in uniform proclaiming them to be of Her Majesty's Army. The scene was illuminated by the light of two lanterns, and the men could be seen to be engaged in various activities as they sprawled on their bunks; reading newssheets, rolling dice or drinking. As the hatch cover had lifted they had all looked up startled, looking like so many moons as their faces swam in the smoky light. For a moment all movement was suspended, soldiers and raiders immobilised by shock, but then, with a shout, first one and then another soldier slid off their bunk, making for the steps leading up from the hold.

'Quick lads,' shouted McCabe, all need for silence gone, 'over the side or we're done for!'

Sean joined the rush for the side of the ship, disoriented by the rapid turn of events. A figure appeared in front of him. He put his head down and charged forward, meeting the oncoming man in the midriff with the top of his head. 'Oof' Sean heard as he reeled slightly from the impact, and dodging ran past.

'Where was the curragh? Should I jump in the sea an' find it,' raced through his mind, as he tried to dodge another figure who was suddenly before him, but this time the figure gabbed his arm,

'Steady, it's only me,' came a familiar voice, 'Here take this.' And Mickey thrust the end of a rope in his hand, 'hold it 'n don't let go. Up yer go now.' And Mickey heaved him up the side of the ship and pushed him over. Sean hit the water, the cold making him gasp out loud, but he kept the rope in a tight grip. Then he heard Mickey's voice again,

'C'mon lad or we'll not get away.' An arm reached down to him, and he was helped over the side of the curragh, that rocked alarmingly. But the next moment, he was inboard, and the craft was already moving across the water, back towards the shore, barely visible. Behind was noise and confusion; men shouting, feet pounding on the deck, much shouting and swearing and giving of orders. They were moving steadily towards the sliver of white surf when they heard,

'Take aim. Fire!' Muskets cracked behind them, and Sean instinctively ducked. He felt the wind of a musket ball by his left cheek, and in the next moment, a startled oath from Mickey.

'Are you alright?' asked Sean anxiously.

'Yeh, I'm fine. Don't worry, we'll soon be there.'

Other noises could be heard coming from the ship, and then a loud splash.

'Mother of God,' swore Mickey, 'they've launched a boat, 'we'll not get out of this so easy.'

In the next moment, they shot over the surf and landed. Sean jumped out and pulled the curragh up the beach, and then prepared to run. But then he noticed that Mickey was moving very slowly. The boy peered at him through the gloom,

'Mickey, what is it? Did you get hit? Here, let me help you.'

'It's me leg; they got me in the thigh. Aargh!'

A groan was forced from him as he got out of the curragh, leaning heavily on Sean. Looking back out to sea, Sean could make out the ship's boat being rowed briskly towards them, muskets silhouetted against the evening sky. It would not be too long before the beach would be swarming with soldiers! Around them, curraghs were beaching and their occupants running away as fast as they could. It was clearly 'every man for himself' and equally clearly, Mickey would not be running anywhere. Sean wracked his brains for a way of escape, then,

'I know,' he said urgently, 'there's a cave not too far away. If we can get to it, we'll be hidden an' they'll never find us.' He dragged the groaning Mickey as fast as he could towards the cliff, fear giving him the strength he did not possess. He prayed that the soldiers would not see them as they entered the crack in the cliff that he knew from past games of hide and seek with his siblings and cousins so many years before! He did not look back, but was aware that the soldiers had landed and the soldiers were splashing through the shallows, shouting to each other,

'Fan out and catch those Irish bastards.'

Sean's breath came in agonised gasps, but he was close to his goal. He heard a shout behind him,

'Halt or I'll fire.' Staggering on, he found the crack more by instinct than sight, for it was too dark to see. Pulling Mickey in behind him, he laid him down, and turned back to the entrance to ensure that the undergrowth that normally covered it was in place. The he rejoined his companion. The two sat silent, as the hunt went on around them,

'Where'd those bastards go? They didn't run by me.'

'They've vanished like one of their 'little people'!'

'Leave'm, there's plenty more to chase.'

'Yes, but I swear one of'm was hurt.'

The sound of the hunt faded, then returned, then faded once more towards the sea. Sean chanced a look through the undergrowth, and reported that he could see them down by the beached ship's boat.

'We'd best stay here a while, they're still there.'

Mickey nodded. They were both shivering with cold and shock, but there was nothing to be done until the boat moved off. While they waited, they speculated on what had gone wrong with the raid.

'Those stupid idiots in Dublin,' said Mickey, bitterly, 'they were supposed to damage one of the cargo ships, not a transport. Or it could be that someone thought it worth his while to warn the Castle of our plans!'

He fell into a troubled doze, and Sean took the opportunity to look at his leg using the faint moonlight that filtered through the undergrowth hiding their cave. He could see an entry hole at the back of the thigh, but there was no sign of the musket ball's exit. It must still be lodged in the fleshy part of the leg, and would need more expert help that he could offer. He kept a close eye on the beach, as well as the risen half moon allowed, as it played hide and seek behind the ragged clouds. Mickey continued to doze, though clearly in pain as evidenced from occasional muffled groans. The soldiers clearly thought that some of the raiders were still in the location, and were prepared to outwait them. He had never felt so cold in his life before. Hungry, he may have been, but the cottage had an ever burning peat fire and could not ever remember such a creeping numbness that was now consuming him. Through the long night they lay, huddled close for warmth, but the boat did not move.

Finally, dawn broke, the sky lightening imperceptibly by degrees. More carefully now, Sean peered through the curtain of undergrowth to see soldiers scanning the cliffs and beach around them. One of them had a telescope, and was making full use of the sharp contrasts given by the sun rising from behind him.

Suddenly there was a shout, and the man with the telescope pointed, setting a group of soldiers running across the beach directly towards their cave. Sean started back, his face ashen.

'They've seen us,' he whispered to Mickey, but he was mercifully still asleep. He heard the pounding of boots coming closer, but then they passed by, coming to a halt some twenty yards beyond. With extreme caution, Sean peered through the 'curtain' again to see two soldiers reach down, and drag a body from where it had lain on the sand. Sean could not tell if the man was dead or unconscious. The soldiers dragged their victim back to the boat, loaded him on board, had another sweep of the beach and cliffs with the telescope, and then pushed off from the surf, heading back to their ship. Sean released the breath he didn't know he had been holding. Whoever the unfortunate was who had lain wounded on the beach all night, he had saved Mickey and himself, and Sean offered up a silent prayer of thanks for the man, and another prayer that his punishment would not be too harsh, if he was, indeed, alive!

He crawled out of his haven into the grayness of dawn, and looked about him. The beach looked totally deserted, and he pondered on the next problem; how to get Mickey back to the safety of his village, and find the skilled help that he needed. Casting about him, he spotted his sledge lying where he had abandoned it the night before; if only he confined himself to gathering seaweed; but no use to agonise on that when positive action was needed! He fetched the sledge and rearranged the seaweed to make a reasonably comfortable couch. Fortunately, his father had made it long and narrow to accommodate the long, kelp fronds, so Mickey would be able to lay full stretch without his injured leg dragging on the ground. The thought of dragging the sledge with its burden across the beach and up the cliff path was too much to bear, so he refused to dwell on it; one thing at a time. Ducking back into the cave, Sean found Mickey awake, but dazed with pain and fever,

'That you, Sean? What's happened? Have the soldiers gone?'

'Yes, they went a while back taking someone from the beach; I don't know who, but they'd there all night! Its morning now an' there's no sign of anyone else. If you can get outside, I've a sledge that can help get you home. Are you from Colkenny like McCabe?'

Mickey nodded, then

'How're you goin' ter help me lad? I'm a mite big fer you an' you don't look as if you've bin fed for a while!'

Sean didn't answer, but leaning down, got Mickey's arm round his shoulder and started to heave him up. Mickey tried to help, but as his injured leg moved, he groaned out loud and fell back.

'You go lad. I can't get up. You go and get someone to come back fer me; McCabe must be back in Colkenny by now!'

Privately, Sean did not trust McCabe, and did not want to leave Mickey here alone. It was just possible that the ship might return for a more thorough search.

'If I could just get you to the entrance, the sledge is just outside; it'll be easier then.'

By dint of Sean heaving and Mickey shuffling, they somehow managed to get to the entrance and the sand bar outside it onto the beach outside. A further combined effort brought forth a string of oaths, but got Mickey laid full length onto the sledge, close to fainting with the pain. Sean stepped into the straining rope and began to heave but the sledge did not move. Looking down, Sean saw that the runners had dug themselves into the sand with the heavier burden. He stepped out of the harness and collected more seaweed to throw down in front of the runners. He tried heaving again, and this time, the sledge started to move. Slowly, steadily, inch by inch, they moved from the depression that they had sunk, and then onto the firm sand where they made better progress, though Sean needed frequent rests. He was heading for the path that left the beach less steeply than the rest, though as he approached it and looked up, it still looked impossible to climb! But then he heard a shout,

'Sean, Sean. Wait there, I'm coming down!'

Never had Sean been so pleased to see his brother. Perhaps with two of them, they just might succeed!

Kevin bounded the cliff, scattering sand all over them when he arrived, and talking all the while,

'Where've you bin? Mam's bin frantic. Why didn't you come home? Who's that an' what's happened to the ship an' him?'

Sean couldn't help but laugh at the breathless tirade, so unlike his solemn brother.

'Hold on. One question at a time. And how'd you know about the ship?

'That Calum McCabe came by last night, just as Mam was getting' really worried, you know, the man you were talkin' to yesterday? An' he told Mam she should be proud of you, an' that you were strikin' a blow for Ireland, 'n you'd be home soon, 'n not to worry. But you didn't come home, so she worried all night an' wanted to go out an' search, but I said no, as you might've come back a different way!' Sean nodded,

'You did the right thing, Kev. There were soldiers on the beach all night. I'll tell the whole story when we get home. This man's hurt and we're both frozen!'

The boys both looked at Mickey, who smiled bravely, but he was clearly in great pain, and there was a pinched, bluish look around his mouth. With Kevin pushing and Sean heaving, the boys began the ascent. Every few yards they were forced to rest, their breath coming in shuddering gasps, while they leaned against the sledge to stop it sliding backwards. They were close to the top when they spied a group of men coming from the direction of Clonarty. Sean's heart leapt in fear until he recognised his compatriots from yesterday, and not soldiers.

'Ho there, Sean. Who've you got there, lad?' It was McCabe running towards them. 'I've just bin by yer home to see if you were back safe an' found yer Mam frantic instead. She's on her way now. Hey Mickey, what happened to you?'

McCabe knelt by the injured man and examined his leg gently. Watching him, Sean felt that he might have misjudged the man. After all, he had taken the trouble to visit his Mam last night and this morning. McCabe turned to Sean and asked,

'Have yer seen anyone else, Sean? Three of yer didn't get back last night. Sean told him of the man he had seen dragged off the beach, and of him and Mickey hiding in a cave.

'C'mon, let's get you back home, lad, you look exhausted.'

McCabe took up the straining rope and set off up the cliff path at a brisk pace. Sean couldn't but compare how easily the man managed the load, while he and Kevin had struggled so hard. Once again, he noted the general air of well being all the raiders exuded, even Mickey, injured though he was! As he hauled, McCabe spoke of the happenings the night before,

'Those bastards were waitin' fer us, so someone informed, an' no doubt got well paid for his trouble. If we hadn't gone so soon after sunset, they'd have bin waitin' on the deck 'n not down below. T'was the only thing that saved us!'

'Mickey said so last night,' said Sean, 'd'you know who?'

'Aye.' The reply came softly, and with infinite menace, and Sean felt a frisson of fear, and could even feel sorry for the informer, whoever he was!

'There's Mam,' cut in Kevin, and he set off at a run. Sean followed a bit more slowly, conscious of his dignity as a man! But Kate was having none of it, and reaching him, she flung her arms around him.

'Sean, Sean. I've been so worried!'

'I'm alright, Mam, really. There was no need to be worried. I'm full grown an' can take care of meself y'know!'

'I know son, I know,' replied Kate, tremulously wiping away a tear.

'If you 'n the lads want to return home, Kate O'Hara,' interjected McCabe, 'I'll take care of Mickey here. Thanks for the help, Sean. Yer Mam should be proud of you. Kept his head in a crisis, so he did.'

Sean knelt down by Mickey, whose eyes were glazed with pain,

'Bye Mickey. I hope yer leg gets better. Thanks fer lookin' after me. I'd never have got out if not fer you.'

'Sure you would. You've a cool head on those young shoulders. You just need a bit of flesh on those bones of yours.'

'Yea, don't we all.' He squeezed Mickey's hand again, and the sledge moved off. McCabe turned back to shout,

'I'll return your sledge soon. Bye!'

The O'Hara's wended their way home, skirting the boggy area which was still partly flooded. Kate spoke quietly to Sean,

'That's a man to be avoided, Sean. He always meant trouble to yer Pa all those years ago.

'I know, Mam. But what he said was true. Why should all the food we produce be taken out of the country when we need it so badly? If I hadn't had to pay the rents, we'd be eatin' now, wouldn't we?'

'But that one. He's not fightin' because of hunger. Did ye not see the flesh on him? He's fightin' because he likes fightin' and thievin'!'

Sean was too tired to argue, and in fact privately agreed with his mother. Presently, Clonarty came in to view, and there was Eily running towards them as fast as her weakened legs would allow, her river of brown hair streaming out behind. She flung herself at Sean, wrapping her arms round him in silent rapture.

'Hey, little one, did you think I had gone forever?'

Together, they all entered the cottage without the bounty Sean had longed to bring, but to the warmth and security of their peat fire.

Chapter 23

In the days and weeks following the raid on the supposed cargo ship, Sean underwent a series of moods. During the first few days he felt extremely anxious, convinced that soldiers would come marching into Clonarty and drag him off to prison, as they had done with Pat. He skulked in the cottage, jumping at shadows and every passing footstep until Kate chased him out to 'do something useful' and to 'pull himself together'! Kate was of a mind that her son had carried the mantle of responsibility for too long, for one so young, and she knew that she had been partly to blame. To add to his woes, Sean had suffered from a low fever after spending the night in the cold, damp cave.

On the third day, McCabe had come by with their sledge, and reported sadly that Mickey had not survived the removal of the musket ball by the Colkenny midwife. This information was imparted quietly to Kate, as McCabe correctly summed up the atmosphere in the O'Hara shebeen.

'I've a mind that he's better off this way, as the leg had already started to go bad, an' he was full of fever after the night in the cave. Don't tell the lad; they shook down well together, so they did.'

Kate nodded in agreement, and asked politely,

'What d'yer plan now?'

McCabe answered somewhat bitterly,

'Never fear, Kate O'Hara. I'm not after yer boy again. Soldiers have bin seen snooping about, an' I've a mind ter get back ter Liverpool before they get too nosy.'

Kate waved him off with a sigh of relief, and went inside to give Sean an edited version of the conversation; simply that McCabe had returned the sledge and was leaving Ireland soon.

Sean seemed to turn a corner after the news, and his spirits lifted, though he still suffered nightmares about the raid, waking in a sweat of fear as he saw soldiers approaching him with fixed bayonets. But even these died away in time.

But the sense of futility and helplessness lingered. He brooded on the food ships leaving Ireland and on their own hunger, and he sunk into such a state of lethargy that Kate was in despair. She suggested that they all go foraging at the beach, but

'What's the purpose of it?' asked Sean, bitterly, 'we're all goin' ter die in the end!'

Kate tried again,

'Shouldn't you try for the 'Works' again in Dublin?'

'Why? They aren't goin' ter start again, and if they do, d'yer want me to be killed like Pa?'

Then the weather worsened. To a country used to soft, damp weather, or at worst, a few days of frost in January, this was literally a bitter blow! An icy wind from the north east blew across Russia and flung itself on the suffering populace of Ireland. Snow fell in early November and frost was continuous, night after night of it, and still the icy gale blew, hurling hail and snow down chimneys, through doors, and into every nook and cranny of the cottages where their miserable occupants huddled together. Sean now had the perfect excuse to do nothing. He could not dig fields, spread seaweed manure, go foraging or collect more seaweed, or seek out Public Works. He and his family stayed in for days on end, and Sean spent his time gazing at the ceiling, sunk in a morass of misery.

In the end, it was not Kate's pleading, or Eily's increasingly pinched look, as she never complained or Kevin's scowl of anger at his adored elder brother, that brought Sean out his lethargy, but his Grandfather O'Hara. That crusty old curmudgeon had withdrawn to his shebeen after paying his rents in Michaelmas, and had hardly been seen since. Even before that he had been almost totally reclusive, having lost the one person who could coax him out of his 'grumps', Nuala. Kate had done her best after Pat had died, and had gone to visit and share the little that she had. But her efforts had been constantly repulsed, and she had finally left him to his own devices, simply watching for the curl of smoke drifting from the roof. It was a few days after the onset of the arctic gales that she noticed that smoke no longer emerged from the O'Hara shebeen, but couldn't say when it might have stopped.

'Sean, will you run across to yer Grandpa and see if he's alright; there's no smoke an' he may be too weak to keep his fire goin'. Tell him to come here and warm up.'

'What's the point,' grumbled Sean, in his usual way these days, 'he'll just tell me to mind me business as usual.' Then Kate lost her temper,

'The point is, I'm askin' you to. He may be bad tempered, but he's yer Grandfather, and you owe him some respect. So go now!' Her voice had risen to a shout and a startled Sean found himself making for the door without further argument, throwing a piece of sacking over his shoulders to offer some protection from the biting wind. Even so, it caught him by surprise, and he made his way as quickly as possible old Kevin's cottage on the edge of the village. It was difficult to even see properly as the wind blew up snow flurries and flung them into his eyes, making progress very difficult.

'My God,' thought Sean, 'even the weather's against us. Have you no pity?' he shouted at the unrelenting grey sky! Then he was outside the door, where he hesitated, seized by a frisson of fear. A squeaking noise could be heard from within. He cautiously opened the door and peered inside, his eyes slowly adjusting themselves to the gloom. He made out the form of his Grandfather lying on his back by the fireplace, but as his eyes grew accustomed to the gloom, he realised that around the body were several large rats that had clearly been about their business for some time. The fingers of both hands and almost an entire foot had been eaten away, and worst of all, his eyes had gone, leaving gaping sockets. The rats did not even pause from their business as Sean stood transfixed by horror, merely tugging at the body and giving it a spurious vitality. Sean stood rooted to the spot unable to move, until a rat ran over his foot' He backed out of the door with a scream, and collapsed in the snow, vomiting up what little he had inside him. Kate, who had been watching anxiously from their cottage, quickly ran over to her distressed son,

'Mam, Mam, don't go in there. Grandpa's....!' shouted Sean frantically, 'Rats! Oh Mam!' Kate helped him up and led him back to the cottage, where she hugged him closely, rocking backwards and forwards, as Kevin and Eily looked on, puzzled. Eventually, Sean calmed himself, and told his mother quietly what he had witnessed. Getting up, he took a bundle of reeds that had been stored to repair their thatch, and thrust it into the fire. When it was alight, he strode out again, and crossed quickly to the 'house of horror' where he thrust the firebrand deep into the thatch. It smouldered briefly, and then, as the wind fanned the flames, they spread across the roof which collapsed with a roar. Sean stood back, nodding to himself. Whatever else, he and his family was not going to end up being eaten by rats, perhaps even before they were fully dead. He felt rather than saw his mother stand beside him.

He patted her hand, 'Mam, I'm goin' ter Dublin tomorrow. It's time I started work again.' And bowing his head, he whispered 'Sorry Mam.' Kate sighed in relief.

That evening, a mood of quiet optimism prevailed, now that Sean was back to his usual self. Kate spent the evening fashioning a coat and foot bindings for Sean out of some old canvas sacks, gleaned from the Murphy house. She used several pieces, laying them in different directions to make the coat as windproof as possible. Sean sat with Kevin, amicably wrangling, while Eily, as usual, sat quietly gazing into the fire.

'Why can't I come with you, Sean,' argued Kevin, 'you 'n Pa always used to leave me behind, though I'm near as big as you? Now he's gone, I should work as well.'

'And who will take care of Mam and Eily, if we're both gone?'

Sean's hand affectionately stroked the girl's head,

'The fields have got to be properly prepared. Once the weather clears, you've to start the diggin' an' manuring ready for planting. This cold wind can't last forever.'

'What's the point,' returned Kevin, aping his brother of not so long before, 'we've got no seed!'

'We'll worry about that come spring; we'll think of something! Perhaps this littl'un will talk to her fairy friends for us!'

Eily smiled at him and hugged her knees in delight at the attention.

The next morning found Sean on the road before sunrise, for the days were shortening, and he wanted to reach Dublin by mid-morning and he knew he couldn't travel fast in his weakened state. The sacking coat did a poor job of keeping out the wind, and the cold from the road soon struck his feet through the wrapping, and he shivered in the raw, morning air.

He kissed Kate and Eily, and slapped his brother on the back, telling him to good care of them, and he stepped out as briskly as he could. To help take his mind off bodily discomforts, he mused to himself as he trod the familiar road, his natural optimism reasserting itself.

'If I can get work today to keep us goin' through the winter, and Kevin gets our fields ready, we should be able to raise seed money from Uncle Conor's things even if it's only a small crop this year. Then when we're back on our feet we'll....'

His thoughts were interrupted as he was passing through Kilgarth, and he was taken aback to discover the real impact of the Irish disaster; the silence! He was used to villages like this being alive with sound; children screaming and laughing as they played; adults gossiping in small groups; women, arms folded across their bosoms shredding the character of a mutual enemy, or errant husbands; babies crying, always babies crying; and best of all, the greetings received from everyone,

'Is that you, Sean? Grand day, so it is. Give Dublin my good wishes. God bless you son.'

But now, the few remaining occupied cottages were silent with their occupants huddled around their fires. The rest were derelict or burnt out, just as in Clonarty. The few faces he saw were pinched with cold, with jaws clamped by starvation, the children's' bellies hugely distended above stick-thin legs. As he left the village, he flung his head back and shouted at the leaden sky,

'What've you done? You've taken away our voices! Don't you care?' And for a while he could hardly see his way forward through his coursing tears. It was the same in every village, every hamlet he passed, and it was with considerable relief that he saw Dublin appear through the murk ahead. He dragged his way wearily to the Board of Works, and found a milling crowd of desperate men, all seeking work. He joined the seething mass, which was being funneled into the building and then diverted into several rooms. At least it was warm in the midst of so much humanity, and in a surprisingly short time, he found himself in front of a desk behind which was a weary looking official.

'Name?'

'O'Hara.'

D'you have a ticket for employment?'

'No, er, no… I didn't know I needed one. Last summer…'

'This is not last summer. Now you need a ticket. Clear the room, Sergeant, I'm overdue for my break, but I'll just finish with this one.'

Sean sighed with relief, for he thought he was going to be cleared out with the rest. The Sergeant, who had been lounging in the corner with three privates, organised his men, and with muskets held horizontally across their chests, soon had the room cleared.

'Now, O'Hara, I'll issue you with a ticket that entitles you to work. Don't lose it as you'll not get another.'

'No sir, I won't to be sure. Er, where is the work?'

'There's a road going out of Dublin; it starts just out of the town to the North-West. They're starting in two days time. Report early. Eight pence a day an' one meal.'

All the while the clerk had been writing out Sean's ticket, and had not noticed the boy's face blench.

'M..m..must it be there… isn't there anywhere else… I don't care where or what I do…. it's just…'

'What's the matter, boy? All the rest are filled. If you don't want the work, there's plenty who do. Just take a look outside!'

'No… that is yes….of course I want work. But….but…me Pa was killed there,' he finally blurted out.

The clerk raised his head and looked properly at the youth in front of him for the first time, noting the extreme pallor and sunken cheeks, just now overlaid with an air of desperation. He was not a hard man at heart, but he had trained himself not to look too closely at those he had to deal with, otherwise he would never sleep easily at night in his snug little house, and swallow the meals served by his ample bosomed wife. But this one reached through the barrier of indifference he had erected.

'I can only offer you this work, but if you want to try another room, they have different works. But if you'll take my advice, you'll be better off with this, as all of them are likely full.'

'Thank you,' said Sean, in a low weary voice, 'it's just that I wasn't expecting to be sent back there!'

'I understand,' said the clerk kindly, 'good luck.'

When Sean left the room with his ticket, the clerk signaled for the soldiers to leave as well, and locking the door behind them all, effectively shutting out the babble outside, he went over to the window and looked out over Dublin. From his window he could see the Liffey and the harbour teeming with ships, and the streets outside teeming with men. It had been this way for some time now; gangs of desperate men, some with families, making their way to the harbour, desperate to board ships, desperate to find a better life. But the clerk knew only too well how futile most of these hopes were, for he was a literate man and read the news sheets every day.

Those that took ships to Liverpool found, that contrary to their expectations, the mainland of England had little to offer. They too, were in the grip of hunger, with the failure of their own potato crop and the Repeal of the Corn Laws that had made the price of grain tumble. So the poor of England had little pity to spare for the very poor of Ireland.

Those that took ship to America stood no more than an even chance of arriving there; their transport ships were not called 'Coffin Ships' for nothing. Typhus and starvation wreaked havoc among the human cargo before they were even halfway across the Atlantic. And if they did reach the other side, their troubles were not over as they were herded together in colonies on Staten and other islands. If they had escaped typhus on their ships, they would, like as not, succumb there!

And those that made for the Iron Towns of South Wales fared no better. Flooding into the valleys, they also flooded the labour market, undercutting wages and so making life difficult for themselves and the indigenous Welsh. Burrowing like rabbits underground to fetch out the coal or iron ore, or manning the blast furnaces, their labour and their lives came cheap to the Iron Masters such as the infamous Crashaw Bailey!

The clerk sighed heavily,

'Oh Ireland, what have you come to? This business of Protestant and Catholic; it's all so unnecessary!' And then shaking off this unaccustomed introspection, he unlocked his door and made his way to a nearby tavern where he soon forgot the O'Hara boy and the troubles besetting Ireland in a few jars of good Irish ale!

Outside once more, Sean wandered disconsolately through the heaving crowds. He was pushed this way and that until he found himself by the harbour, and by the row of cottages that had housed his Uncle Michael and his brood of miniature fishermen. He wondered, not for the first time, what had happened to his Uncle, but it didn't really touch him as he was too deeply upset at the thought of going back to 'those road works.' In his mind he could picture the scene as vividly as if it happened the day before; his father standing at the foot of the hill, smiling for the first time in weeks and raising his arm in greeting. And then the fall; the other man descending, windmilling in a shower of debris as Pat disappeared from view, to die with his mouth full of Irish dirt. Sean shuddered briefly, and looking again at the fisherman's cottage, noticed that a wisp of smoke curled lazily from its chimney. Before hope had time to rise, it was vanquished. The door opened and a stranger emerged who stared briefly at Sean before walking briskly away.

Sean wandered back into the City streets. He knew that he should set off home soon, but he could not rouse himself from his torpor. His dragging feet took him to a more prosperous area of Dublin, down Henrietta Street, where a row of elegant Georgian houses bore mute testimony to a world far removed from his own. He stopped outside one of the houses, set back behind wrought iron railings with a short flight of stone steps leading up to a handsome door framed by fluted columns. Over the door was a delicate fanlight, and either side of it were tall, sash corded windows that spilled light into the street, even though it was the middle of the day. He gazed in wonder at the scene within, grasping the railings to lean forward, heedless of the cold on his bare hands. A group of people within swirled and eddied, dressed in the height of fashion and clearly strangers to hunger and privation.

By some quirk of fate, Sean was standing outside the house of the widowed, Mary Kavanagh, mistress of his one time acquaintance, Captain James Willoughby. The lady was entertaining the Captain and a group of fellow officers with a light luncheon and witty repartee, totally oblivious to the desperate situation outside their snug walls.

Sean gazed with fascination at the elegant company within, particularly at the voluptuous Mary; at the smooth white skin and shining brown hair swept up into an elaborate coiffure; at the sweeping blue velvet dress that came to a smooth vee at the front of the impossibly tiny waist and then belled out over a crinoline so full that the skirts swayed as she moved round the room, tending to her guests. Mary Kavanagh was a contented woman as she had held the dashing Captain Willoughby in thrall for many months now, and she had yet noticed any slackening of his ardour. She was also a wealthy woman who had married a rich old man, who had decently died quite soon afterwards, leaving her this house and the wherewithal to live a life of luxury. She could afford to indulge her appetites, provided she kept within the bounds of discretion. If she thought at all about her starving countrymen, it was with annoyance should they happen to impede the progress of her smart conveyance through the streets of Dublin.

Sean was leaning further forward to get a better view into the room, when the section of railing he had been clutching gave way, pitching him into the void beyond. He had, in fact, been leaning on a gate that opened onto steps leading to the servants' basement, and someone had failed to fasten properly. He tumbled down the flight of stairs to fetch up with a grunt at the kitchen door, winded and dazed. Through his daze, he heard a door open and a shrill voice cry,

'Ooh, it's a vagabond. What shall we do?' Another voice, softer and gentler, answered,

'You silly wench. It's no vagabond. It's naught but a boy, and it looks like he's fallen down the stairs. Who left that gate open? He might have killed himself!' The voice faded momentarily, and then returned, ordering another person to 'pick 'im up and be careful of broken bones.' Sean felt himself raised from the cold flagstones, and carried into the warmth and light of the basement kitchen. The person carrying him spoke for the first time, a deep masculine voice close to his ear,

'Whew Mrs. M! This one stinks, and just look at his rags!'

'Stop complaining. Can't you see he's nothing but skin and bone? How's he able to keep himself washed? Just set him down near the range and leave him to me.'

'I hope you know what you're doing. If Mr. Baines catches you taking in waifs and strays, you'll be for it!'

Then Sean felt himself being lowered into a chair next to the source of heat, where he stayed still, gathering his wits for a few moments. The source of the friendly voice had apparently moved away, and he decided that it was safer to keep his eyes closed. But curiosity overcame his fear and opening his eyes carefully, he began to take stock of his surroundings. He was seated in front of a long, black metal contraption from which radiated wonderful warmth. On top of the contraption was a row of pots and pans, from which emanated a delicious odour which made his beleaguered belly groan. The room was large, though low ceilinged, and was whitewashed. From its walls hung various cooking implements and bunches of dried herbs for as far as he could see, and set in the middle of the floor was a long, scrubbed wooden table. Suddenly the kindly voice was back, making him start,

'So, you've come round? Are you hurt bad anywhere?' Sean felt his limbs picked up and moved about one by one. Then the voice said,

'I don't think there's any damage, except perhaps your head?'

Sean nodded then groaned as his head agreed with the question. The owner of the voice had come into view now, and Sean gazed at his saviour. He saw a round kindly face adorned by white hair, topped by an even whiter cap. She was clothed in a long black dress covered by a fiercely starched white apron. Sean spoke for the first time,

'Where am I? Is this your house?'

'Bless you, no,' said his saviour with a laugh, 'the house belongs to Mrs. Kavanagh, and is in Henrietta Street. I'm the cook, Mrs. Markham, and that there,' jerking her head at another female similarly clad, 'is Kelly, the maid. Over there is Sykes, who carried you in.' Sean cautiously turned his head to see Sykes scowling at him from the other side of the table. Just then, a bell clanged somewhere over his head, making him wince, and Sykes got up and left the room, grumbling under his breath.

Mrs. Markham bustled about the stove, her starched apron crackling about her,

'By the look of you, you've not had a good meal for many a day. I'll pour you some soup, shall I?' Sean nodded mutely. He couldn't trust himself to speak as saliva rushed into his mouth for the first time in months. Mrs. Markham went over to one of the larger pots and ladelled some soup into a bowl and set it down on the table to cool. All the while she chatted to Sean in a monologue that didn't require him to answer,

'Her up there, she don't know what's going on in the world out there. I don't suppose you're the only one who looks like that. I've heard tell of whole villages wiped out. But do she stop with her fancy lunches, and her fancy dinner parties, 'soirees' she calls'em. You'd think she'd be ashamed serving all that food with so many starving, wouldn't you? But no. And that fancy Captain of hers. He could say something. If she gave away half of what she serves up, they wouldn't go hungry!'

Sean watched her, fascinated, while she worked and talked. She was rolling out a huge round of pastry, and her plump fingers deftly turned the pastry this way and that, finally throwing it over biggest pie dish he had ever seen! Then she stopped to test the soup bowl, and satisfied with the temperature, handed it to Sean with the advice 'you take it slowly. You've been hungry for a while, and I don't want to see good soup wasted!' Sean nodded and took a cautious sip causing his stomach to heave in protest, but then settle; another sip, and the same result. Slowly, sip by sip, he drank the soup, feeling strength return with every mouthful. With the bowl empty, he felt full and contented, though under it all, he remembered his family and wished they could have shared the bounty. The cook was a kindly person, and a discerning one, and she caught the look on Sean's face,

'You've got family, lad, haven't you? What's your name; I can't keep calling you lad? Tell me about yourself.'

Shy at first, Sean gave her his name, and then, encouraged by her kindly face, began to tell of Clonarty and his family, of his father's imprisonment and of losing Nuala. As memory took hold, he lost his shyness and the story flooded out like a spring tide. By the end, his rescuer's face was wet with tears and her heart ached with pity. But she knew full well that this was not an isolated story. In her own small way she carried out a crusade for the poor. Unbeknownst to her employer, the waste food from the tables upstairs found its way to a nearby street where families living nearby carried it off within minutes. Mary Kavanagh did not know that she sustained the lives of several impoverished families!

When Sean was finally finished and lapsed into silence, she silently hugged him to her ample bosom, and then poured him another bowl of soup to sustain him on his journey,

'For you must go soon of you are to get home tonight!' She busied herself making up a bundle for him to take home, so that his family would, after all, share in the treat. Some soup was ladelled into a wide-necked jar with a lid, and the jar placed carefully inside an old but serviceable canvas sack. The soup was followed by a round loaf of white bread, a cabbage, and most precious of all, a large ham bone, with which his mother could make a sustaining broth. Sean's eyes were as round as the loaf, but still he said,

'Can you spare these; won't it cause trouble?'

Mrs. Markham laughed at that,

'God love you. What would her ladyship up there be doing with a bone?' Sean had to smile at the vision of that elegant lady earnestly standing over a cooking pot.

'That's better; you've a lovely smile, Sean. Now I think you should go; you've a long walk by your own account.'

Sean nodded, his spirits sunk again, and it was all he could do to tear himself away from the warm range and the warmer kindliness, but if he didn't leave now, he wouldn't leave at all. Mrs. Markham, seeing his hesitation and understanding it, encouraged him,

'If you're not gone before Mr. Baines comes down; he's the butler y'know, and an ogre if ever I saw one; he'll see that I'm put out without a character.'

Sean got up hastily. The last thing he wanted was to cause trouble to his benefactress. He was not to know that Mr. Baines was even softer hearted that Mrs. Markham, and carried the basket of scraps every day for that kindly lady to feed her poor!

He left the warm kitchen with strict instructions to visit any time he was in Dublin, and then set off for home. It was full dark by the time he arrived, cold and weary. He had had no trouble finding his way as there was a gleaming full moon in a cloudless sky, presaging another frosty night. The nourishing soup sustained him on his way, as did the vision of Kate's face as he presented her with the food. It was gestures like this that restored his faith in human nature and gave him hope, once again, for the future!

He reached Clonarty and saw his home silhouetted against the enormous moon, as the canvas screen was flung back,

'Is that you, Sean?' cried Kate. He was home at last!

Chapter 24

Eily woke up in the middle of the night, her belly distended by cramping pains brought on by the unaccustomed food brought home by Sean. The family had so enjoyed the broth boiled up by Kate using the ham bone and cabbage and served with a small wedge of bread. While they had eaten, Sean had told them of the road work he had signed up to, but not that it was the same one as before; he had made up his mind to deal with that himself. He also told them of the kitchen he had literally tumbled into, and the kindness he had received. For the first time in many months, they went to bed replete.

Eily stretched, trying to ease the cramps, willing them to go away. She was a fastidious child, and would not soil her bed, but it was so cold outside where a privy had been dug at the back of the cottage; and it was so warm in here, cuddled up to Sean's back. She had developed the trick of inducing a state of dreaminess when physical discomfort, or sadness threatened to overcome her, and she would transport herself to the hillside where it was perpetual summer, and she would sit surrounded by birds and small creatures.

But another cramp shook the frail little girl, and sighing, she slid from her position between Sean and Kevin swiftly and silently. Not even pausing to throw a shawl around her shoulders, she scurried to the back of the cottage just in time to relieve herself in the privy. Sighing again, this time in relief, she straightened up, but was then struck by the beauty of the night scene. The full moon looked huge, as it lay low down on the horizon. It cast a silvery glow over all it touched, causing the frost encrusted landscape to glisten as though scattered with tiny jewels. Gentle plumes of smoke meandered upwards from a few of the cottages, or lay on their thatches, giving them the appearance of being wreathed in bridal veils. The little girl was so entranced that she sank to the ground to savour the scene for a little longer. She did not feel the cold as the beauty of the scene induced a state of euphoria. The moon dropped lower and lower, until it was no more than a silver rim on the horizon, and then it was gone, plunging the world into darkness. Eily let out a pent up breath in a long sigh, and thought vaguely of returning to her bed, but a delicious lethargy had stolen over her, as she gazed in rapture as the stars appeared to fill the sky with myriads of twinkling lights. She hugged her knees and gave herself up to the cold night air as it stole the little warmth that she had left. Her last thought was that her mother had told her that every star was the soul of someone who had died, and was up there waiting for their loved ones to join them.

'Pa, Nuala,' whispered Eily as she slipped away.

It was Sean who found her next morning, sitting upright on the bank behind the house and her arms wrapped tight around her knees, a beatific smile on her face. He had wakened early and felt the little girl's absence; the cold patch on his back suggesting that she had been gone for a while. Now he looked at the diminutive figure of his sister, not wanting to touch her for that would tell him what he feared was true, that she was dead. He felt numb, as though his heart could not take any more of this pain. Finally, shaking himself out of his torpor, he bent and tried to lift her. It was difficult, for even though she had the substance of a bird, the cold night had set her limbs and he could not easily get his arms around her. He hurried to the front of the cottage, and whispered urgently to Kevin to come and help, but at the same time trying not to disturb Kate; but it was no use,

'What is it, Sean? What's the matter?'

'It's Eily Mam. She must've gone to the privy in the night, an' she didn't take her shawl!'

Kevin came out, shivering in the raw morning air, and between them, the boys managed to lift Eily and bring her into the cottage, setting her down by the fire in a vague hope of warming her back to life. She sat upright still, and the glow of the fire gave her cheeks a spurious lustre of health. Kate gazed at her child, and then sat and cradled the icy body. Slowly the limbs relaxed until she could be laid down on their bracken bed. Kate smoothed the long hair from her forehead, and spoke wonderingly,

'She looks so peaceful. I wonder what she saw out there. Ah little one, you are at rest now in the arms of the Virgin Mother,' and Kate crossed herself. Sean watched his mother, and could not understand her acceptance of yet another tragedy.

'Why did the Virgin Mother choose now, Mam? Just when I've got a job and can provide. Why now?'

Kate could only stroke his arm sadly, for she had no answer, just her own endless grief.

Later that day, Sean and Kevin carried their sister to the cemetery and laid her down. No use to wait for Father Muldoon, who hadn't been seen for months; and no use to try and dig a grave, the ground frozen as hard as iron. They laid her on a bracken bed, 'just like home' and built a cairn from the stones that littered the landscape. Kate said some prayers over the cairn, recommending the soul of 'this innocent child' to the Holy Mother up above.

Later that day, Sean prepared to leave for work, for he dared not be late on the first day. There was no question of Kevin joining them, as they both knew that Kate could not be left alone, and the boy would have enough to do preparing the fields. Sean held his mother close, and they wept together for a while. Breaking away, he slapped his brother on the back, bade him to be a man, and set his face for Dublin.

The task work was so much harder this time around. Without the companionship of his father and their village friends, Sean suffered from intense loneliness. The rest of the work force were mainly full grown men, who had little time for a strange youth in their midst, and a feeling of 'every man for himself' prevailed. To make matters worse, the weather continued to be unremittingly bad, with icy winds, snow and frost. To an

Irish native used to staying snug in his cottage during the worst of winter, the hardship of being outside all day was almost unendurable, particularly as they were constantly hungry.

But surprisingly, the moment he had dreaded most, the moment when he would revisit the scene of his father's death, passed easily and painlessly. He had arrived at the road in the early morning light to discover that the rock fall had been cleared, and the actual site of the disaster unrecognizable. He had sighed with relief, and hefting his spud, reported to the Engineer. He had nursed a secret hope that he might meet Joseph Harrington again, but instead he met a dour Yorkshireman, Peter Grimes, who spoke English with such a heavy accent that Sean and the rest were hard put to understand their instructions.

The workers took over the scalps dug the previous year, as the ground was too hard to dig new ones nearer the site of the work, even though it meant an extra trudge at the start and end of the working day. The new Engineer had no intention of laying out his own resources as Harrington had done, and he provided the barest minimum for his work force, for which he had clearly scant respect. The turfs they used for their fires were those left over the previous summer, and the one meal a day that was supplied was a poor quality soup and coarse bread. For the first time, Sean really appreciated what Harrington had done for them all, and was further convinced that it was not his fault that there had been no help given them after his father's death.

The work force was not just made up of males from the surrounding villages, but also women who had lost their husbands, children even as young as five, and older folk who could barely lift their spuds. This group was paid a pittance of four or five pence a day, the full amount only given to those who brought their own implement and could do a full day's labour. Sean's heart ached for little ones staggering along with a basket of stones, and he spent some time from his own labours trying to help them, until he found his own wages docked!

So Sean spent his days enduring the freezing conditions while hardening his heart against the pitiful sights around him. At night he curled up by a meagre peat fire along with three other adolescents like himself, trying to provide for their depleted families. For the most part they slept, too exhausted to do anything else, but occasionally, when the icy wind howling round their scalp kept them awake, they would exchange bitter thoughts about the iniquities of the British Government, and made earnest plans about what they would do when they were back to normal times again.

'We must rise up as one,' said one serious youth, about the same age as Sean, 'O'Connell tried to change things in their parliament, an' got nowhere, so we must fight!'

'How can we fight?' replied Sean, bitterly, 'have you seen the state of us? How many will be left when this is all over?'

'We must get strong again,' admitted the other, 'and when they are not expecting it, then strike!'

Sean turned away from him. The lad was a dreamer, for it would be many years before they would be capable of action. Even now the villages were emptying with their residents joining the growing streams feeding the cemeteries, the emigration ships or the Welsh Iron Towns. At the end of the week they were paid in coin, but there were weeks when the money chest did not appear in time, so they were forced to go home empty handed, with promises of double the next week, though how they could feed their families on promises was never explained. Or they were permitted to buy food from the agent who had failed to supply the coin, 'not his fault, you understand, it is a matter of supply!' But through his generosity, bags of oats could be purchased, or bread, or a handful of tea, with only the smallest charge to cover the cost of the loan, 'to cover expenses, you understand?' But somehow the following week's wages seemed to be smaller than ever.

Then Sean would trudge home through the silent, decaying villages, and note, week by dismal week, the slowly dwindling numbers of occupied cottages. He would drag himself the weary miles to be greeted by Kate and Kevin who had spent their in trying to work the frozen fields in readiness for the spring planting.

There were lighter moments in the midst of gloom; one grey Sunday, when the O'Hara's were sitting round their fire engaged in desultory conversation, the doorway darkened and they looked up in surprise to see Father Muldoon!

'God bless all here,' said the old priest cheerily enough. He was welcomed almost ecstatically and invited to sit awhile and share their oatcakes. Sean noticed with a pang that the robust priest with rosy cheeks had long since vanished, and Father Muldoon was as thin and gaunt as the rest of them.

'Where've you been Father?' questioned Kate, 'we've been looking out for you for many a long week.'

'I know, but it's a long story. You'll remember my old donkey, Maira?' They all nodded, 'she was as stubborn as only a donkey can be, and she chose to depart this life just as I was coming down the hill by Clarne. And if that wasn't bad enough, she chose to roll on me!' The priest's scraggy jowls quivered indignantly, making Sean chuckle as he remembered that the old priest was always fond of a joke against himself.

'Well there I was, and would be still, if a 'Good Samaritan' hadn't happened by and picked me out from under that old donkey. He carried me to his cottage, and I've been there for a number of weeks mending my broken leg. Just as I was mended, I was called to a meeting of priests in Dublin to see what was being done in the district.'

'An' what is being done, Father,' said Sean politely, for in truth he had seen little evidence of anything happening.

'There's little the church can do, my son, for we've no money to help succour the poor. The only good thing is that the Castle has admitted our existence.'

'For that we must be thankful?' asked Sean angrily, as Kate clutched his arm to try and calm him down.

'Easy now, my son, everything comes in time. Its patience you need.'

'An' while we're bein' patient, how many more will die?'

The old priest had no answer for him and Sean flung out of the cottage in disgust, not wishing to hurt the old man. He was clearly still weakened by his fall, and Sean wasn't taken in by his apparent anger at the donkey, for the old priest had been inordinately fond of the stubborn beast, which had carried him for many a mile over the years.

Inside the cottage, Kate quietly brought Father Muldoon up to date with village affairs. She listed all those who had left, pausing briefly at the Murphy's and Hogan's, for those she missed the most sorely.

'And your good parents?' asked the priest, 'did they go with Conor? Though I'm surprised as I felt sure they would not have left you here?'

'No Father. They're still here, in their cottage.' And Kate recounted the events leading to the O'Malley's deaths, though she fiercely insisted that it had been an accident,

'Pa was so distressed at losing his home that he was careless with the fire,' she maintained, 'and Father, we've lost little Eily; she died one night out there. We don't know how or why; we just found her the next morning.'

Kate's voice broke, and Kevin moved close to comfort her.

'Come daughter, we'll pray for all their souls.'

Father Muldoon led Kate and Kevin in prayers while Sean stayed stubbornly away. Later, the priest toured the village, stopping by the ruins of the O'Malley cottage to say prayers for the dead, and then he made his way to the cemetery, now noticeably fuller than his last visit. The old priest sighed. It was the same wherever he went. The only village relatively intact was the largest of the Danforth group, Clarne, where he maintained his small, thatched church and priest's house. He was a simple man with a deep faith in the Almighty, but that faith was being sorely tested as he gazed at tiny graves in the many cemeteries he visited. He could understand Sean's bitterness, and his heart reached out to the youth, but he could not reach him with his words and he could only hope that time would heal his wounds.

Soon after Father Muldoon's visit, another visitor called by, though this time Sean was away at his road working. A man appeared at Kate's door,

'Would you be Kate O'Hara of Clonarty?'

'I am,' replied Kate, 'an' who are you?'

'I've come from Nantyglo in Wales on me way to Dublin. I've a message from Patrick Hogan who says he was a neighbour of yours?'

Kate's eyes widened with joy,

You've seen Hogan an' his family? How are they? Come in, come in, an' tell us everything.'

The man came in, pulling off a cap, and seating himself by the fire, brought them up to date with the Hogan's doings,

'Though you'll understand I've been a while on the road. Patrick said to tell you that he's doin' well, an' his missus, but they've just lost the littlest one!' Kate crossed herself.

'The work is hard, for they're all underground. He's diggin' for the iron ore an' his missus is hauling wagons an' one of his lad's on ventilation.' The words could not begin to describe the reality of Hogan and his family's existence. For many hours every day, Hogan hewed for iron ore, stripped to the waist and laid full stretch; while his diminutive wife hauled wagons like a beast of burden and their six year old son sat for hour after hour in darkness waiting for the shout to open the ventilation doors in the mine shafts. But the stranger continued,

'They've food in their bellies an' hope for the future, an' he says that if you've a mind to join them, he'll find you work.'

Kate thanked the man politely, but after he had gone on his way to Dublin to take ship to Liverpool, thought long and hard about his words. She told Sean of the visit, and for the first time, voiced doubts about the wisdom of staying,

'We should've gone with Conor, shouldn't we?' Sean hugged his mother,

'You did what you thought was right, Mam. If everyone left, what would become of Ireland?'

'It wasn't that, Sean. I thought I could hold on to him by staying here, but I couldn't; I can't even remember his face clearly!' She wept then, and Sean comforted her.

'Too late now,' he thought to himself. If we take to the roads now, we will surely perish.'

And all the while, O'Leary's threat hung over them. He would ride through the village, inspecting the growing dereliction, aware that his master in England was none too pleased with the declining rent returns. He took every opportunity to bait Kate, or Sean, if he was there, with the threat that the lease was in Pat's name and that a letter was even now on its way to turn them out. Sean endured the threats as well as he could, fighting to hold on to his temper,

We've paid. Why should he throw us out?'

'Because he'd rather turn all that into grazing for sheep,' said O'Leary waving at the fields, 'he can't be bothered with your piddling little plots!'

Had Sean been gifted with foresight, he would have been gratified by the fate that awaited O'Leary. The agent had indeed predicted accurately that Lord Danforth was extremely displeased with the lack of rents, but the long awaited letter carried the notice that O'Leary was held to blame, and that a new agent was on his way. The agent was summarily dismissed and told to take himself off from Danforth lands, and to take nothing with him that was the property of the estate. O'Leary hastily threw his belongings together, along with a cache of silver coins, stolen from rents over the years, and prepared to go, mounted on the sturdy cob that had carried him for so many miles. But he was too late. An officer of the law, backed by the very thugs who had protected him, awaited him as he opened his door. The cob was confiscated as Danforth property, and a search soon revealed the cache of silver which was also removed from the protesting agent. He was forced to walk away with his meagre possessions, to an uncertain future, and was seen no more.

Towards the spring, Sean began to hope again. The terrible weather at last began to ease its grip, and they still alive, albeit weakened even further by privation. But Sean's meagre wages kept them going, as did a soup kitchen opened in Dublin, run by Quaker ladies, and discovered by Sean. These good people were famous for their philanthropy, and had taken it upon themselves to offer succour to the starving populace. Sean had enjoyed their largesse, and was also able to take a pot home for his mother and brother. He did try to persuade Kate to go to Dublin every day to be fed while he was working, but she would not hear of it,

'What will happen if we go to Dublin an' leave the cottage empty? O'Leary is just waiting for the opportunity to pull it down and claim it was abandoned.' None of them knew as yet, that their erstwhile enemy had long departed!

Sean did not try to persuade her any more, but observed,

'Kevin has done a good job on the fields. Soon I must see if there is seed to be had; I've heard it said at the Works that there are loans to be had. As soon as the weather warms, we'll get in a crop of early 'taters and we'll be eating them in no time!'

Sean's mind conjured up a vision of a kish full of steaming tubers, their skins bursting open in the heat, and waiting to be tossed from hand to hand as they were peeled. He nearly groaned aloud at the memory. Kate laughed at her son's enthusiasm and made no attempt to cast doubts on his hopes. It was good to have hopes once again, so it was.

Sean was at work one day in March, when Clonarty received another visitor. The man had come up from the south, and like so many travelers before him, was making for Dublin. He enquired politely at the villagers of the distance he had to travel, and was told he would not manage it by the end of the day. With typical Irish hospitality he was offered a bed by O'Flynn in return for the man's news, though little in the way of food! All the remaining families gathered in O'Flynn's to hear the news, and they heard that things were every bit as bad where he had come from, and that he had a mind to emigrate,

'Though I'll have to work my way, mind, for I've no money!'

What the man did not tell them was that he was also fleeing from typhus that had entered his village ten days earlier. His whole family had died of it, but he believed he had escaped the deadly disease by taking to the road as soon as he could. But it was already too late and the disease was racing through his bloodstream, and the lice that had feasted off his blood were already transferring themselves to the bodies of his hosts, huddled together as they were. Every one of them would be bitten in time and would succumb to the disease, among them, Kate and her son Kevin.

That night, the O'Flynn's were woken by the sound of their guest groaning on his bracken bed. They crept to his side, and their horror filled eyes saw reddish blotches that sprawled across his chest and abdomen, and crawled up his arm from the wrist; the dreaded typhus rash. The man was delirious and feverish, his tossing body exuding a stench that made the O'Flynn's gag as they ran from their hovel. They spent the night huddled in a derelict cottage, waiting for the morning and praying for deliverance.

In the morning, Danny O'Flynn cautiously approached his own doorway, and peering in, saw the man lying sprawled in his own ordure and quite dead. He sighed. They had endured so much, survived for so long. Would they now fall victim to this most terrible of diseases? Turning away with dragging steps, he told his neighbours, who were all peering out of their doors at him. They all silently gathered to watch Danny O'Flynn set fire to his own cottage. Kate and Kevin looked at each other wordlessly. There was nothing to do but wait.

Towards the end of that week, Sean was looking forward to going home. The air had a touch of warmth that heralded the return of spring, and he longed to get the fields planted. He talked with the other youths in his scalp, and they all agreed to visit the Castle as they passed through Dublin on their way home, and find out if the promised seed potatoes had arrived, and if they could arrange a loan to buy them. The mood was one of buoyant optimism, brought on by the sun that peeped through ragged clouds,

'D'you think these'll be blighted too?' said one less hopeful than the rest. Sean answered thoughtfully,

'I don't think so. I've a mind that the cold winter we've endured will've cleared the ground. Anyway, it's the only thing we know, the only thing to do!' The other boys nodded their agreement before they all faded off to sleep.

Sitting by their peat fire a few days after the stranger had left, Kate and Kevin began to suffer from headaches that came and went. At their worst, they felt as if a band of iron was being tightened round their foreheads. Kate knew that they were in the early stages of the disease that had killed their visitor. Old Daniel had described epidemics of it that had swept across Ireland in years gone by, and had told of whole villages being wiped out. Kate bowed her head in prayer, not wanting to frighten Kevin, who had no idea what was the matter just that his head hurt! She knew that few people survived the illness, especially when weakened by hunger. Her heart turned towards her other son, who did not know what was happening and would find out the hardest of ways. She bowed her head in grief, and prayed that Sean, at least, might survive.

The agent arrived with the weekly wages. As usual, Sean had to turn away from the pittance being doled out to those who laboured without tools, or could only work a few hours a day. He had schooled himself to harden his heart by conjuring up images of his mother and brother waiting for the little that he could bring!

The boys collected their wages, and hefted their spuds onto their shoulders before setting off to Dublin in a cheery state of mind.

'It's passing strange,' though Sean, 'that a bit of warm sunshine an' we all start to hope again!' Already he had mentally planted his early 'taters and healthy green haulms were breaking through the soil. They arrived at Dublin and presented themselves at the Castle.

'Yes,' said a supercilious clerk, 'there is a committee even now sitting down and discussing the feasibility of supplying potato and other seed.'

The boys, somewhat overawed by the high-flown language said that they would return when the committee had finished sitting, and would they please not take too long! The clerk shut the door in their faces.

They then wandered cheerfully onto the streets of Dublin to find a market for their purchases; some oats to bake into cakes; some salt herring, buttermilk and a little tea. Sean was delighted that he had enough to buy the tiny quantity of tea, for he knew how much his mother loved it.

The visit to the Castle had delayed them, and it was now too late to start their journeys home. They crossed the Liffey and penetrated the slum district where they found an abandoned hovel, where they curled up like puppies, and fell into an exhausted sleep.

Kate awoke in the night. In spite of the glow from the peat fire, she could not see for a mist before her eyes, and wondered vaguely how it had got into the cottage. In the darkness, she heard Kevin groan and reached out blindly for him. He was burning hot, or was it herself? Then she knew. Both the fever and the mist were the result of the typhus. She felt quite calm now, knowing that the end could not be far off.

'Mam.' Kevin's voice came faintly out of the swirling fog, and again, 'Mam.' She could sense the fear in it for he sounded like a small child again.

'Hush my Kevin, it will pass. Here.' And she gathered him to her vanished bosom and rocked him as she had as a baby, ignoring the pain in her head.

For herself, she did not fear death as she had longed to be reunited with Pat, and she had only fought for survival for her children. But now, Eily had gone, and Kevin was slipping away. That only left Sean, her eldest, and she could now admit, most loved. She prayed that he would find the strength to go on when he discovered their deaths in the stinking hovel, for he was due very soon.

'Do not grieve, my son,' she whispered into the darkness, 'you have your life ahead of you, leave this place and make a new life for yourself!'

She shut her eyes against the pain, and tried to transfer her thoughts to her distant son, but soon the effort was too much to bear, and she lay silent, cradling Kevin, hoping to last as long as this son needed her. Towards dawn, Kevin began to cry,

'Mam, Mam, take it away!' She kissed him, unable to do more, and as the sun rose she felt him slip away. Sighing, she gave herself up to the waiting shadows, and with a final prayer to the Good Lord to keep her son Sean safe, she followed Kevin.

In Dublin, Sean tossed and turned in the throes of a nightmare, and he whimpered aloud in his sleep. It was the same one as he had had before, when Pat had died and he had seen his and Nuala's skeletons rising from a mound of earth, and beckoning to him and his family. This time, though, they were not skeletons but were fully restored to health. But then he could see Eily holding hands with Grandpa Daniel and Grandma Eileen, all smiling and waving. Daniel even had his clay pipe clamped between his teeth and puffing contentedly. They all looked so happy that Sean felt isolated and alone. Then all of them started waving vigorously at someone behind Sean. He turned and saw his mother and Kevin wave back, and start to walk towards the mound with happy smiles. As they reached the mound and started to climb, Sean shouted,

'No, no! Don't go. Don't leave me!'

But his words went unheeded, and they scrambled up the steep sides, where Kate ran into Pat's arms. Then they all formed a circle and began to sink back into the mound, all the while smiling and nodding. At the last moment, they all turned and waved at Sean before vanishing below the surface.

Sean gave a despairing wail as the sun was breaking through the door of the hovel.

The other boys, roused by Sean's cry, sat up complaining loudly and knuckling sleep from their eyes. With one accord, they decided to make an early start to spend some time with their families before making their way back to the road works. As they reached the edge of Dublin, ready to go their own way, they all said a cheery 'see you tomorrow.'

Sean felt the sense of unease that had clung to him since he had awoken slip away in the watery sunshine. But soon the sun faded, and a chill wind sprung up, raising a frisson of fear down his spine.

He hurried through past the villages along the way, averting his eyes from their pitiful inhabitants for there was nothing he could do to help them; while everywhere the silence shouted!

It was before noon when he saw Clonarty and immediately knew that something was wrong. There was no smoke rising from any cottage, none at all!

He began to run. Reaching his cottage he stepped inside, only to reel back, gagging at the stench within.

He sank to his knees and threw back his head, gazing at the indifferent sky. He rocked back and forth, keening his agony to the indifferent sod cottage, a wild ululation of grief and despair.

Chapter 25

The man stood looking down at the body huddled at his feet. The boy's breathing was barely perceptible, and it seemed that in a very short time, it would be stilled forever. So much was obvious to the man, but he was gripped by a terrible inertia that prevented him from taking any action to prevent the inevitable. His mind was numbed by the many tragic sights he had so recently witnessed and it seemed futile to make a move to save this one soul from perishing when so many had already succumbed.

The man had reached Clonarty from the south, unknowingly following the footsteps of the typhus carrier. Strangely though, he was neither a peasant farmer, nor even Irish. It was a man whose fate seemed destined to cross with that of Sean's, though he was far from recognising the boy in the gaunt huddled wretch at his feet. Captain James Willoughby of Her Majesty's Army currently stationed at Dublin's Barracks; his presence in Clonarty at that precise moment in time was wholly coincidental, but it was the nature of the man that he had decided to find out for himself the true state of affairs in the country, away from the cushioned luxury to be found in Dublin. But the timing of the tour was a direct consequence of his tempestuous relationship with the widow, Mary Kavanagh.

James Sebastian Willoughby had been born some five and twenty years before, the younger son of Lord Charles Willoughby of Bensham Manor in Yorkshire. His father had also been a soldier, for he too had been a younger son, and had not expected to succeed to the family estates. At the age of eighteen, his own father had purchased a commission for him in one of King George's finest foot regiments. He had joined the Regiment in the company of his boyhood companion, Gerald Deluce, whose family estates marched alongside his own. The young men, resplendent in their dashing uniforms, quickly became absorbed into army life, and by their early twenties had both attained their captaincies. They were dispatched to the Iberian Peninsula where England and her allies were fighting a series of desperate battles against the seasoned veterans of Napoleon's armies. The pair distinguished themselves time and again by their acts of extreme bravery, or maybe it was foolhardiness, as they vied against one another? Many an olive skinned Spanish lady was dashingly courted by the two handsome young officers, who seemed more interested in winning his rival's lady than winning one of his own!

The friends and rivals both survived the Peninsula Campaign and were sent home for a well earned rest. There, they counteracted their boredom by rivaling each other during hunt meets, or at the Balls arranged by their doting families. When Napoleon shook off his silken chains and escaped incarceration from Elba, they were overjoyed, and hurried to London to rejoin their Regiment, and to embark to Belgium. There, they took part in the great clash between Wellington and Napoleon near the small village of Waterloo, their platoons being caught up in the thickest of the fighting. Charles was seen to save his friend from the sweeping sabre of a French dragoon, but Gerald, not to be outdone, saved Charles from an exploding cannonball by flinging himself on top of him. Both survived the epic battle with nothing more than a few minor cuts that would leave them with some interesting scars to beguile the ladies with in due course!

A week later, Charles received the shocking news that his older brother and heir had been killed during a hunt when his horse had flung him over a high fence and broken his neck. With tears in his eyes, Charles arranged the sale of his commission, and took the packet boat home to don the mantle of responsibility. Before leaving Belgium he embraced his friend with deep emotion, prophesying a great future for his boyhood companion and rival; 'doubtless you'll be a general before you know it!' They swore eternal constancy, but both knew in their hearts that their closeness would wither away as their paths diverged; Charles' to estate duties and the 'carrying on of the line', and Gerald's to serve King and Country in a martial role.

Charles arrived home to comfort his bereaved parents, and he took over his brother's duties without a backward glance. He gave to his new way of life the same dedication that he had given to soldiering, and eventually found fulfillment thereby. Within five years he had courted and won the hand of Lettice Ashton, whose family were also close neighbours, and very soon was the father of two sons, the first named Gerald in honour of his dearest friend, and the second, James Sebastian. Within ten years, By then, his parents had died and he was the Lord of Bensham Manor, with a steadily increasing family, though no more sons were born to him.

Young James spent a happy childhood on the rolling dales of his father's estates. He was raised on stirring tales of soldiers and battles, and was his father's willing helper in the setting up of battle scenes with legions of tiny, painted lead soldiers. Time and again the two would re-enact the battles of his father's military career, his favourite being the last and most renowned, the Battle of Waterloo. His older brother, Gerald, was not at all interested. He was a serious boy who took after his mother and would be ideally suited to take over the estates in due course, 'if he wasn't so damned dull,' sighed his father to himself.

James had always known that he was destined to be a soldier, a fact with which he was in full accord. And equally naturally he would enter his father's old regiment, where Charles' former soul mate was now Colonel, having not yet fulfilled the prophecy of reaching generalship!.

Charles and Gerald met one evening in the Officer's Mess to talk over old times and discuss James' commission. Charles' eyes misted over as he looked round the familiar setting and the dress uniforms of the Junior Officers. He struggled to contain his nostalgic emotion as Gerald described the events during the years since their parting, 'damned boring, if you ask me. No decent battles to speak of once Old Boney had gone!'

Charles spoke of his family in general and his younger son in particular, urging Gerald to keep an avuncular eye on him. Gerald himself had never married, but promised stoutly to be a second father to the young man, 'though I'll not show favour, you understand?' Charles did understand perfectly, and two old comrades drank a toast to James' future and to the new generation of officers coming along.

Next day, James presented himself to his new Colonel. Resplendent in his new uniform, scarlet jacket adorned by the correct amount of gold lace as befitted a junior officer, snowy white breeches and gleaming, knee high black boots, he definitely thought he cut quite a dash! His black shako, also adorned with gold braid, boasted a handsome tassel that swung bravely as he marched, but was now tucked firmly under one arm as he entered the Colonel's office.

'Well, my boy,' said Colonel Deluce gruffly, 'so you think you'll make a soldier?'

'Yessir,' smartly from James.

'As good as your father, eh?'

'Better sir!'

Gerald gave a snort that might have been derision or laughter, and turned to Charles, who was watching somewhat misty eyed.

'He'll do; he'll do!'

Father and son made their farewells, the older Willoughby almost overtaken by emotion, while his son swallowed a lump in his throat at the thought of losing the hand that had guided him since his birth, sixteen years before. After much slapping of backs and injunctions to 'take care', they parted.

James fell happily into army life, enjoying everything from early morning parades; to mock 'set piece battles'; to learning to shoot at the ranges; to the Regimental Balls; to the Mess Nights when the junior officers took part in wild games which often resulted in bloody noses and black eyes! Within a few years he had attained his Captaincy and had earned a reputation as a good officer, who treated the men beneath him firmly, but fairly. Watching his protégée from a distance, Gerald was well pleased. True to his word, he had shown the young man no special favour, but had watched his progress with immense satisfaction, a fact he imparted privately to Charles in his sporadic letters. He also admitted that he had had to do nothing to ease James' passage through the early years of his military career, for he was a 'natural'.

While stationed in London, James also developed a liking for the pursuit of the fair sex. He had been raised to respect truth, justice and ladies of his own class, so he did not include delicately nurtured damsels in his chases. Instead, he developed an unerring instinct for discovering the courtesans in his set, and had soon notched up a string of conquests among these females.

The only cloud on Captain James Willoughby's bright horizon was the lack of any 'real soldiering'. To date, the Regiment had not left London let alone the shores of England, nor had he experienced any battles. He was uncomfortably aware that at the same age, his father had been a war veteran, with medals and commendations for bravery to his credit.

'But it's not my fault,' he told his friend and drinking companion, Edward Colby, during a particular heavy bout of drinking in the mess, 'if only there was a decent war somewhere!' Edward owlishly agreed, though at that moment he would have agreed to anything!

'I 'shpect we'll be posted soon; rumours, don't y'know.'

A week later, Colonel Deluce presided over dinner in the Officers Mess. He gazed sternly at the officers ranged either side of the long table, looking very smart in their dress uniforms. He watched the port circulate, and when it had completed its third circuit, banged on the table for silence. He got it,

'I have just received orders for our posting. The Regiment is to be posted...' The assembled company held its collective breath; would it be India as had been strongly rumoured, or Europe, Africa, Australia?

'......to Ireland. To be precise, to Dublin. They have famine over there, and there is a need to keep public order.'

The Colonel got up amidst a stunned silence, walked slowly to the door, and turned,

'We have two weeks before embarkation.' He shut the door firmly behind him.

James sat silent, completely taken aback by the news, while a hubbub rose around him,

'It can't be true; the old man jests!'

'Tomorrow he'll tell where we are really going.'

'Ireland! They live like animals!'

'They live with their animals.'

Round and round the noise reverberated, until James thought his head would burst after freely imbibing of the port. Dreams of glorious battle faded to ashes as the reality of the posting sunk in. Quietly he got up from the table, and staggering slightly, left the room. Reaching his quarters, he vented his anger on his hapless servant, snarling at the man to fetch him a bottle of the best brandy. His groom foolishly expostulated, gently suggesting that the Captain mayhap had had enough already. He received a kick in his rear for his pains. When the groom returned, having taken longer than was necessary for the errand, he found the Captain stretched out on his bed, snoring stertorously, and fully clothed down to his gleaming boots. The groom spoke softly to the recumbent form as he deftly removed his boots, and the beautifully cut scarlet jacket,

'So you've 'eard the news 'ave you? It's not like you to fly off the 'andle like that. Never mind. Mebbe it won't be for long.'

The groom took himself off to his bed, leaving James to sleep off his woes, though he would doubtless wake with a head like thunder on the morrow!

Before he embarked, James took some long promised leave, arranging to rejoin the Regiment in Liverpool immediately prior to embarkation. He was still low in spirits about this cruel twist of fate, but he had become reconciled to it during the bustle of preparations for departure. He braved the Colonel's den to take his leave and also to find out more information about the posting, and was told that it would likely be of short duration, with a reward in the end; India!

Charles Willoughby was sympathetic to his son's disappointment, but reminded him gently about that all important word, duty, and that a soldiers lot what not always the desired one.

Father and son spent a contented week together, finding pleasure in each other's company that had deepened with the passage of time. Charles spoke of his eldest son,

'He's gradually taking over the running of the estates, with my blessing d'you see. Your mother and I have a mind to do a bit of travelling.' James thought about his rather timid mother and wondered about the 'spot of travelling,' but he understood his father's restlessness. He had given up the challenge of a soldier's life to do his duty by the estates and now he felt he could relinquish the reins.

'He's doing a damn fine job of it don't y'know, but if only he wasn't such a dull dog! Have you met the gel he's courting? Spirited little squab of a thing; just right for him!'

James smiled at the description and hoped that Gerald would not get to hear of his father's opinion of his lady love, for the old soldier's voice had a carrying quality!

All too soon the leave was over. James took affectionate leave of his family, his parents, brother and three sisters. He hugged his diminutive mother, who told him sternly to 'ensure his servant aired his smalls properly,' as she had heard that Ireland was a 'dreadful damp place.' Gerald slapped him on his back and warned him against the Irish peasants, as he had heard 'went about armed with cudgels and were prone to fighting over the slightest thing!'

He was introduced to Gerald's intended, the 'little squab of a thing' according to his father. She turned out to be a trim young lady of even shorter stature than his mother. She shook his hand firmly with her own tiny one, and told him firmly to 'try and help the poor starving people.' James was startled, as he had not yet given a thought to the reasons he was going to Ireland, but only the anger he had felt at the decision. Before he could ponder on this, his father was hugging him warmly and telling him 'to be sure to come again before he was sent half way round the world.'

James reached Liverpool with time to spare, and was soon involved in the chaos of embarkation. Upon arriving at Dublin's harbour, there was the further chaos of disembarkation and settling into their barracks. For a day or two the barracks were full to bursting as the departing Regiment sorted themselves out prior to their departure. In the interim, the various ranks exchanged news, the 'old timers' regaling the newcomers with horror stories of Ireland in general and Dublin in particular. James refused to listen, preferring to form his own opinion in the fullness of time.

Once they had the barracks to themselves, the Colonel gave his officers a stern briefing, with the order to pass his instructions to every last man. He warned his officers that their duty was to keep order with the minimum of force and the maximum of tolerance. He reminded him that there was famine in the countryside and the people were severely distressed. When going out and about, they were warned to always travel with a companion or in a group, and to treat the citizens of Dublin with respect, 'just remember, it is their country!'

It was the very next day that James' squad was sent out to oversee the dispensing of grain at a warehouse, and where he would meet Pat and Sean O'Hara for the first time. James commanded the first of the soldiers to arrive at the warehouse and who had to face the mob that was gaining in strength and in anger. He had quickly assessed the situation, and noted that the majority were only intent on buying food and were peaceable enough, but the temper of the crowd was being whipped up by agitators in the rear. Mindful of the Colonel's words, he gave the command to prepare their guns but to aim high. However, as the mob rushed forward, panic set in amongst his line of inexperienced privates and several of them aimed at the advancing crowd.

In the melee that ensued, James was involved wherever the fighting was thickest and did not see the reinforcements arriving. Nor did he witness the incident that felled Sean and led to Pat's arrest. But when he saw the O'Hara's in the courtroom the next day, he instinctively felt that Pat was telling the truth, borne out by the swelling on the side of Sean's head. He took the trouble to study the people round him and found his preconceived notions of the Irish to be completely false.

'Why, they're just like us,' he thought, his pictures of a bovine race of limited intellect melting away as he studied Sean's intelligent brow. That he would become involved with the family was not an intentional act, rather an impulsive gesture, born out of his innate sense of justice. Later, he again acted impulsively when he agreed to meet Sean and Kate outside the gaol, but had no regrets when he saw the nature of the brutish gaoler, Carey. James realised that he would have to see this business through, as he understood that Pat would likely die on gaol if he did not oversee his imprisonment. But in truth, he was heartily glad when Pat was released, and he could get on with his life!

But during those months, James became increasingly restless with the nature of the duties he and his fellow officers were required to perform. Maintaining law and order wherever they were summoned was not exactly their idea of soldiering and inevitably they sought other distractions. True to his own code of ethics, James did not pursue the inexperienced maidens he met at the regular balls and soirees they were expected to attend, and he was too fastidious to use the high class brothels frequented by his fellows. But by the time Christmas came and went, he was frustrated in more ways than one! It was at such a vulnerable time that he met Mary Kavanagh at a New Year's Eve ball in Dublin Castle, and fell head over heels in love for the first time in his life.

Mary was the widow of Jerome Kavanagh, a hitherto confirmed bachelor of fifty, who had been captivated by a ravishing seventeen year old girl. He was a wealthy merchant, and had been pursued by many an avaricious mother intent on securing a good marriage for their numerous daughters. But he finally met his match when he laid eyes on the youngest daughter of an impoverished gentleman. Mary had not an ounce of sentimentality in her exquisite frame, and she viewed the aging Jerome as a means of escape from the genteel poverty she had endured during her upbringing. Jerome punctiliously requested her hand from her father, who invited Mary to say if she wished to accept,

'Of course, Papa, why wouldn't I?'

Her anxious mother questioned her youngest daughter as to her feelings for her suitor, so much older than herself. Mary had ingenuously replied,

'Why Mama, I shall adore him, of course!'

They had married on Mary's eighteenth birthday, the lavish wedding and reception paid for by the adoring groom. He took his new wife on a tour of France, where he shyly disposed of her virginity, with many apologies. By the age of twenty one, Mary was in full possession of the Kavanagh fortune, including its properties, chief of which was the elegant Georgian house in Henrietta Street. The malicious among Dublin's society were unsure whether it was the physical or financial demands of his young bride that had caused the apoplexy that carried off the bemused bridegroom, but he lived long enough to make a will leaving everything to his young widow.

Mary surveyed her way of life with great satisfaction and decided that the widowed state exactly suited her, and she no intention of shackling herself to anyone else, even after the customary year of mourning was over. After all, another husband would have the right to dispose of her fortune any way he wished, and that did not suit her at all! However, she discovered in herself a taste for the baser passions, barely awakened by the fumbling Jerome, and she determined to have discreet affairs conducted under her own terms. By the time she met James at the Dublin ball, she was five and twenty, and at the height of her splendid looks. She was currently without a suitor, as her last affair was with a major who had recently departed from Ireland with his regiment. But his attraction had already begun to pall, and Mary had not been sorry to see him go, but it had been a while since she had welcomed a man to her bed and she was ripe for a new affair.

Mary had arrived before James, and was standing near the entrance to the ballroom, chatting in desultory fashion to a wispy female of indeterminate age, who had the unenviable task of acting as chaperone to Mary, to lend an air of respectability to her establishment. Her first sight of James was the top of his head as he bowed punctiliously over the hand of the hostess, and as he straightened up, Mary's eyes widened with interest. She studied him covertly from behind her fan as he exchanged words with the Governor and host for the evening, noting the breadth of his shoulders that strained the seams of his splendid scarlet jacket. His legs, encased in skin tight overalls, were shapely and well muscled, and he carried himself proudly. Finally, he turned from his host and approached the ballroom, and Mary was able to study his features, dominated by a pair of green eyes fringed by long dark lashes. His moustache, slightly more ginger than his hair, enhanced rather than dominated a handsome face with firm lines and a cleft chin. Mary was satisfied; she had selected her next victim!

James entered the ballroom, resigned to another tedious evening dancing attendance on the polite society of Dublin, and fending off the efforts of mothers with marriageable daughters to engage his interest. He felt that there was something rather obscene about the entertainment that invariably included a lavish supper when so many were starving and dying in the countryside, and in the city itself. He kept his thoughts to himself in deference to his hosts, but he could not imagine he would enjoy the evening in the slightest. The only bright spot as far as he was concerned was, on that very day, he had achieved the release of the man, O'Hara, who should even now have arrived home to his wife and son. James could not know that Pat's infant daughter had died of starvation, and that Pat would arrive home in time for her funeral!

As he entered the ballroom, he was met by a vision of loveliness that took his breath away. It was just the panacea that his depressed spirits needed right then when he saw a young lady of medium height, dressed in a sweeping ballgown of peach coloured silk that belled out from of tiny waist over a crinoline of noble proportions. The low cut bodice was embellished with peach rosebuds, artfully revealing a glimpse of a voluptuously swelling bosom. White shoulders rising from the gown met an elegant, swan like neck that in turn supported a face of classic features, oval in shape, with a firm rounded chin and crowned by glossy brown curls, somewhat darker than James' own, arranged in an elaborate coiffure. James' eyes travelling upwards met a pair of large grey eyes that were surveying him with some amusement. He turned away in some confusion, determined to discover the identity of the lady. Presently, he came across a fellow officer who admitted that he knew the lady, could introduce him, and that she was a widow of some few years, a Mrs. Kavanagh. James' delight was complete. This was no shrinking maiden who he would be unable to pursue without the noblest of intentions, but someone he could court, and perhaps…..? But first he must be introduced.

At that moment, the orchestra was tuning up in preparation for the first dance and James crossed the ballroom floor and presented himself to Mary and her companion with a smart click of his heels,

'Mrs. Kavanagh. I believe this is my dance.'

'Why, er, Captain,' replied Mary, correctly relating the lavish gold epaulettes to his rank, 'I don't think…'

'Can it be you have forgotten,' returned James with mock wistfulness, 'let me show you.' And plucking her dance card deftly from her wrist, he studied it carefully, and then with a few strokes of the attached pencil, he declared triumphantly,

'There you see!'

Mary looked at the card, eyes widening in amusement at the temerity of the man, 'Captain James Willoughby' had been firmly penciled in for the dance about to start and for two others, including the coveted supper dance.

'Well, Captain Willoughby, it seems you are correct.' And Mary allowed herself to be swept into the dance, turning away with a choke of laughter at the face of her ousted dance partner just now approaching, his face red with rage. James appeared not to notice the spluttering civilian, but gathered his partner firmly into his arms, and steered her onto the dance floor.

'Well Captain. Are you as decisive in battle as you are on the dance floor,' asked Mary, archly.

'Of course! It is the only way to carry off battle honours.'

'Am I then a battle honour?'

'You are a prize any sane person would want to win,' returned James, lightly enough but with a trace of seriousness. Mary experienced a frisson of anticipation as she swept round the ballroom.

At the end of the dance, James returned Mary to her companion, promising to return and claim her for the supper dance. This he did with determination when the time came, causing a youthful lieutenant to beat a hasty retreat in the face of superior fire power. Mary was delighted with the attention and James could not remember when he had last enjoyed an evening as much. The problems of the O'Hara's and the starving populace were well and truly forgotten in the excitement of the chase.

After the third dance that James had so shamelessly stolen, he steered Mary into a small anteroom, ostensibly to recover from the exertions of the dance. Mary was a little alarmed at the speed at which matters were progressing, as she fully intended to thoroughly enslave her Captain, and an early capitulation would jeopardize her plan. In the privacy of the anteroom she allowed James to kiss her thoroughly, feeling her own passion rising to match his, but she kept her head and when James' lips started to wander to her neck, then on to her silky shoulders and finally to the swelling mounds of her bosom, she rapped him smartly with her fan,

'Captain Willoughby, you forget yourself!'

James looked up startled, to meet her steely glare.

'I beg pardon, ma'am; your beauty caused me to be quite overcome.'

'I wish to return to the ballroom this instant, if you please.'

Contritely, James escorted Mary back to her companion, and with a formal bow and click of his heels, he excused himself, and sought the quiet of the refreshment room to calm himself down. There he found Edward Colby gazing gloomily into a glass. He choked as James clapped him on the back and told him to 'lose that long face before he curdled the cream on the desserts'! Edward was not amused and bemoaned the lack of excitement.

'What d'you mean; I've had a wonderful evening.' Edward surveyed his friend with jaundiced eyes: James usually shared his views.

'What you need,' said James earnestly, 'is to meet some of the local society; there are some interesting people out there!'

'Ah!' replied Edward, realisation dawning, 'you've found yourself a wench.'

'That's no way to talk about the most wonderful lady you could ever meet!'

'Humph,' retorted Edward, succinctly.

After the ball, James continued his pursuit of Mary Kavanagh with great determination, making sure he was invited to all the social events to ensure that he would meet her. Mary allowed him to think that he was determining the pace of the courtship, and even invited him to one of her soirees, but if James thought he was going to find his way into her bed after it was over, he was sadly mistaken. At the end of the evening he found himself, politely but firmly, escorted to the door by the Kavanagh butler, Baines. This went on for three weeks as James' ardour mounted to fever pitch, and Mary herself was finding it harder to resist his advances. Too soon and the Captain's ardour would cool as rapidly as it had flamed; too late, and he would find himself another, more willing partner. Finally one evening, after an excellent supper and some musical entertainment, Mary sat down beside her admirer and murmured low,

'Return one hour after midnight.' She moved away so quickly that James thought he had imagined the invitation, but his senses flamed with anticipation.

Promptly at one hour past midnight, he knocked quietly on the door. It was immediately opened by Mary herself, clad in a loose peignoir, her glorious hair freed from restraint and tumbling about her shoulders. She placed a finger on his lips, and taking his hand, led him up the stairs to her bedchamber. There, the two came together with a passion that surprised them both, reaching their climax together.

Afterwards, James lay nuzzling Mary's ear gently, as she lay in voluptuous contentment,

'You are a wonderful woman, Mary love,' he whispered in her ear.

'I must agree, sir,' replied the lady, archly, 'and am I a battle honour?'

'Ah Mary, a man would charge a row of cannon to carry you off!'

Later, they made love again at a more leisurely pace, bare limbs entwined among the tangled silk sheets. Towards dawn, James quietly let himself out of the door before the servants started moving about, and made his way back to the barracks. He had completely forgotten the injunction against roaming the streets of Dublin alone, either by day or night, but arrived safely enough, carried along a wave of euphoria.

The affair flourished to the satisfaction of both parties, and to the amusement of James' fellow officers and the Kavanagh servants, who were always aware of their mistress's affairs in spite of her efforts at discretion! Mary had judged her capitulation to a nicety as James was completely enthralled by her; deeply in love as never before. Without neglecting his duties, James danced attendance on his lady love at every free moment. Many a morning parade was attended in a state of near stupor, having been kept awake the night proving his manhood again and again to an increasingly insatiable Mary. Edward Colby became seriously concerned for his friend, and warned him to take care lest a report of his behavior reached the Colonel,

'Y'know you're not supposed to roam the streets of Dublin at night alone; it's just not safe. There are desperate men abroad who'd think nothing of relieving you of your purse and your life!'

'Don't be an old woman, Edward! I always go armed.'

'But what about the parades? Only the other morning you were actually swaying on your horse and the Old man's got eyes like a hawk; he doesn't miss a thing!'

James laughed and slapped his friend on the back,

'You're just jealous. Find yourself a woman like Mary, and lighten up that long face of yours. You remind me of an old nag of me father's as it was being led away to be put down!'

It was inevitable that the Colonel would become aware and would take action. He had always kept a discreet eye on his friend's son, but until recently had had no cause for concern. The affair did not surprise or concern him, as James was as lusty as the next man, and the Colonel was just thankful that the lady was a widow who was 'old enough to know what she was doing'. However, the Colonel would not tolerate James bringing the Regiment into disrepute, which was something that could well happen if the reports and rumours were to be believed.

So it was that James found himself sitting next to the Colonel in the mess on a night that he was obliged to stay in the Barracks. The Colonel was in the habit of joining the junior offices in the mess, as he was an approachable and sympathetic commanding officer, so James was not alarmed at the attention. But then he noticed that the others had quietly dispersed, leaving him alone with a unusually stern faced Colonel Deluce. James began to feel uncomfortable.

'Well, my boy. How d'you like Dublin now, eh? I know you youngsters were keen to prove yourselves on a battlefield somewhere, just like your father and myself at your age!'

'Yes sir, but it isn't so bad, after all.'

'Keen to move on then?' asked the Colonel slyly.

'Is that likely, sir?' questioned James, somewhat anxiously.

'It's possible. This was only meant to be a temporary posting y'know. I thought you youngsters couldn't wait to leave?'

'Of course,' said James, somewhat desperate. How much did the Colonel know? 'We shall be ready to do our duty.'

Surprisingly, the Colonel chuckled,

'Don't get too enmeshed with the lovely widow.' And then more seriously, 'it is an order that no-one, officer or private, is to leave the barracks alone. This will be rigorously enforced; a Corporal was found floating in the Liffey yesterday, and I've no wish to be responsible for informing your father of your demise in like fashion.' James eyes widened in shock; he had not heard about that! The Colonel continued,

'Just between you and me, my boy, your father and I cut something of a dash among the ladies in the Peninsular Campaign, but I don't believe that we were in the danger that you would be in this place! I do understand young blood, but be very careful as these are desperate times. Take a friend with you, and above all else, remember the reputation of the Regiment; I will not have that brought into disrepute!'

The Colonel rose and patted James' shoulder before leaving him to ponder his words. The younger man could only be thankful for a sympathetic Commanding Officer, and realised just how careless he had been of his safety, and just how badly an unpleasant incident could have reflected on the Regiment.

James discussed the situation at the next soiree he attended at Mary's, taking Edward along to meet with the other guests. Mary was inclined to be petulant as she was used to having James at her beck and call, and she condemned the Colonel as 'an old fussbudget'. But James was not now in the first throes of infatuation, and was taken aback at the attack on the Colonel who commanded his highest respect, and he told his paramour so in no uncertain terms! Mary shrugged her elegant shoulders and punished James by refusing to see him for a full two weeks, only relenting when her own needs became too strong to resist. Grudgingly she agreed to the presence of Edward Colby when she wanted James to stay the night, having been assured of his discretion.

During the progress of their affair, James had kept up to date with Irish affairs, and knew that the farmers were keeping themselves by attending Public Works, though he had no idea what these works consisted of. He was intermittently troubled at the callousness with which Mary treated her distressed countrymen, regarding them as little better than animals. When the second harvest failed, her only reaction was to remark,

'Perhaps this will get rid of some of them; always swarming about Dublin and getting in the way!'

James found himself increasingly at odds with Mary, and found it hard to hide his distaste for her remarks, and they began to quarrel frequently. But still their mutual attraction kept the affair smouldering on. But strangely, it was an unwitting Sean O'Hara who finally precipitated the end of their relationship.

On the day that Sean had tumbled down the stairs into the kitchen of the house in Henrietta Street, James and Mary were upstairs having yet another row about Mary's attitude towards the starving populace. James had previously suggested that she keep a less lavish table and to donate some of the food to the poor. In retaliation, Mary had ordered an even more sumptuous spread than usual for her next luncheon. The scene that Sean had witnessed through the elegant window, as Mary moved among her guests in her blue velvet gown had seemed tranquil enough, but James was hiding a simmering anger, while Mary was hiding her satisfaction at 'scoring a hit' over him!

When all the guests had gone, except the compliant Edward dozing in the drawing room, Mary and James retired upstairs, where for a while their resolved their differences with their mutual passion; that had least had not changed since their first coupling. Later, Mary got out of bed, and wrapping a peignoir around her, she crossed to the window overlooking Henrietta Street. She saw the figure of a youth leaving the gate from the kitchen basement, and noted that he appeared to be carrying a bundle. She had long suspected that her housekeeper had been giving away food from her kitchen, but had been unable to prove it, and this seemed the ideal opportunity to confront her servant. She swept out of the bedroom in high dudgeon, leaving a startled James to scramble into his clothes. Mary reached the kitchen in time to hear Mrs. Markham remark to Baines,

'That little bit of food'll put heart into that boy and his family for a while. Poor lamb. Did you see his wrist; no thicker than a chicken leg bone!'

'And just what did you give that beggar from my larder?' demanded Mary in peremptory tone from the kitchen door. Mrs. Markham looked up startled,

'Why, just a bit of stale bread, ma'am,' she answered, calmly enough. But Mary was not to be placated,

'How dare you give away my possessions? You have no right!'

Mrs. Markham was foolish enough to remonstrate,

'But ma'am, there's folk dyin' all over for lack of a bit of food. You've more than enough!'

'How dare you,' hissed Mary, 'you are dismissed. Do not expect a character. Be out of here tonight!' Mrs. Markham stood aghast. Where would she get another post without a reference in these hard times? Next to her, she felt Baines stiffen,

'Then I'll have to go too.'

'Then get out, both of you. Ingrates, the pair of you!'

Mary spun round and collided with James, who had listened to the exchange with growing horror,

'Then I will be off as well. I have closed my eyes to your heartless nature for too long.' He spoke to the stricken servants,

'If you present yourselves at the Barracks tomorrow, I'll see to it that you're given work.' Mary almost screamed with fury and swung a stinging blow towards James' face. He caught her wrist just before the blow landed and held it tightly as Mary's bosom heaved with temper. Looking into eyes that glittered with hatred, James wondered how he had ever found her attractive. When she had calmed a little, he released her abruptly, and then returning to the drawing room, he roused the slumbering Edward. He told his friend that they were leaving and would not be returning. Edward asked no questions, realizing instinctively that the affair was over,

'Thank God,' he murmured to himself.

With his tumultuous affair well and truly over, James began to look about him properly once more. Though he had been called out many times on law enforcement duties, to food queues, work queues and the like, he had not been fully aware how desperate the population had grown, so wrapped up was he with his lady love.

The failure of the second harvest had caused a rush for the emigration ships, and the Public Works had restarted. But more recently, alarming rumours of a typhus epidemic had begun to spread in the Barracks. James felt ashamed at his indifference, his magnanimous gesture to the O'Hara's seemed an eon ago. He wrote to his father in Yorkshire and arranged for some funds to be transferred to Dublin which he planned to use to finance some of the Quaker soup kitchens that were being opened across the city. He had already persuaded the Officer's Mess to take on Baines and Mrs. Markham in their kitchens, so that they would be sure to get a reference should they chose to move on. In these small ways, he sought to quieten his troubled conscience, though with only partial success.

Towards spring, Colonel Deluce gave his Regiment the news that it had waited for, for so long. Again, he chose a Mess Night, but did not bother to wait for the port to circulate more than once, and rapping on his glass, he spoke quietly,

'Gentlemen, we are off to India!'

The cheers swelled around the smiling Colonel, but he was observing James and was troubled by the expression on the younger man's face; it did not appear that he was pleased at the news. But surely the affair with the widow was over, pondered the Colonel, he had heard that it was so, but perhaps the rumours were wrong? He determined to investigate the matter, but reassured himself that within a short time they would be leaving Irish shores and that would certainly put an end to the affair once and for all!

Colonel Deluce could not have been more wrong. James was not thinking of Mary Kavanagh at all, except that he now resented her for preventing him doing his duty properly! He mentally castigated himself for not doing more for the Irish people, as he had urged Mary to do. Perhaps his guilt was in reaction to his infatuation with such a heartless woman, as he now described his erstwhile paramour, and he just could not bring himself to join in the euphoria than prevailed in the Officer's Mess, especially now that the Colonel had quietly slipped away. Listening to the excited chatter swirling around him, an idea began to slowly form itself in his mind. Before he left Ireland he would go and see for himself the extent of the problems the rural population was facing, especially as he had some long overdue leave.

James laid his plans carefully. Though he was entitled to leave, the order had gone out that no member of the Regiment was to leave Dublin for their own safety and James had no wish to incur the Colonel's wrath. Sympathetic and understanding he may be, but he would brook no disobedience. He took his closest friends aside and swore them to secrecy as he knew that someone needed to know where he was going. Edward Colby and Robert Harding were both horrified, and tried their hardest to dissuade James from his foolhardy venture. It was only when they realised that he was bound and determined on his course of action, and would carry it out with or without them, that they agreed to help him. The three friends gave out that they planned a few days in a local hostelry and would be incommunicado for a while.

The trio set off together in civilian clothes and made for their favourite hostelry. As they travelled, the friends made a last ditch attempt to dissuade James,

'What can you do?' asked Robert, 'you can't feed them all!'

'I can see for myself,' replied James, 'we've been told so many stories; how can we know if they're true.'

'What happens if we are recalled to barracks while you're gone?' asked Edward. James shrugged,

'You'll think of something. I just have to go!'

The friends parted company as they approached the road south out of Dublin. James was dressed in rough clothes, borrowed from a grateful Baines who fully understood the Captain's quest, but urged him to be careful. He carried a small budget containing enough food to sustain him for three or four days and an even smaller quantity of money. He hugged his companions and bade them to stay away from the Barracks for as long as possible.

James soon encountered one of the Public Works, where a ragged gang of workers was lengthening a stretch of road. The gang comprised men, women and even children trying to carry stones in baskets. James' heart wrenched in pity, as none of the gang seemed to have an ounce of flesh on them. Most coughed incessantly, in spite of the milder temperature and their limbs were covered with running sores. They looked at James' passing with lack lustre eyes; their native Irish curiosity long since dimmed by privation.

From the end of the road, James took a large sweep through the hills west and south of Dublin. Everywhere he encountered the same scenes of devastation; villages either completely deserted or housing a few pitiful families. Children with sticklike limbs and distended bellies peered out of hovels, voices stilled by long term hunger. No-one seemed to be working the fields in readiness for the spring planting, but perhaps, he thought, they had nothing to plant?

Within two days of leaving Robert and Edward, James had the answer he sought, and knew that the situation was a hundred times worse that he and his friends had supposed. While he had danced attendance on the heartless Mary, with her lavish suppers and flamboyant lifestyle, these people had been suffering unimaginable torment. No wonder they grew desperate in the food queues he had been called upon to oversee. James found he could not eat the little food he had brought, but nor could he give it out, for what good would so little do in the midst of so much want?

As he journeyed, first further south, and then swinging back to the northeast to return to Dublin, an idea was forming in his mind as to what he could do to really help some of these people. It would need the help of Mrs. Markham and Baines as he would be gone before the plans could come to fruition.

He slept his last night in the bracken, waking shivering with the dawn, but welcoming the discomfort as a balm to his troubled soul. He set off early, determined to reach Dublin by nightfall and set his friends' minds at rest, for he had no desire to see them punished. He slaked his thirst in a nearby pool, and looked once again with distaste at the food he had brought. He would leave it with someone on his journey back, he decided.

He stepped out resolutely enough and covered the miles steadily, approaching a village an hour or two after noon, unaware that it was Clonarty, the village from whence had come the O'Hara's. It looked totally derelict, as had so many villages, but a frisson of fear ran down his spine as he drew near; then he noticed the smell. Though a soldier of a few years, his lack of campaigning experience had not prepared him for the stench of a typhus victim, but his instincts told him that something was very wrong. Holding a kerchief to his mouth and nose, he walked slowly through the village, looking out for any sign of life. Then he saw what looked like a bundle of rags on the ground outside a cottage, but closer inspection showed it to be the body of a youth who seemed to be actually breathing!

Shaking off his initial inertia that had gripped him on first discovering Sean's inert form, James approached the cottage and peered inside. As his eyes grew accustomed to the gloom, he could make out the shapes of two bodies, that of a woman and adolescent boy, and unlike the older boy outside, clearly dead. He could see the slinking shapes of rats moving in the hovel and the stench was appalling making him beat a hasty retreat to the slightly less malodorous air outside. He quickly inspected the rest of the intact cottages, only to find that every single one housed only corpses. Strangely, one cottage only housed one victim, while its neighbour was crowded. Now, at last, there was something he could actively do. One person he could and would help, but the rest needed to be cremated as soon as possible, along with the rats that he understood to carry the typhus plague. Moving quickly and decisively, he formed a bundle of reeds from a thatch and ignited it. He thrust the flaming torch into each thatch in turn, finishing with the one adjacent to the youth. Once all the thatches were well and truly alight, he turned his attentions to the sole survivor. Burying his fear that this one might also be diseased, he lifted him away from the flames engulfing his home, noting the lightness of the frame, and carried him to the edge of the lough. The youth stirred and opened his eyes. Looking past James' shoulder, he saw flames engulfing all the cottages and his eyes widened in horror.

'Mam, Kevin, no.o.o!' he called out in Irish. James did not understand the words but understood their meaning, and his heart stirred in pity.

'Quietly, lad. There's nothing you can do for them.' Sean looked at him in puzzlement, unable to cope with the English.

'D'you understand me, lad?' queried James. 'But your face is familiar; aren't you the lad I met in the courtroom, Sean isn't it?' Sean just continued to stare at him in puzzled fashion, and James surmised he was probably in shock and forbore to question him further. Taking off his jacket, he wrapped it round the light form, noting that the lad's skin was icy cold,

'Small wonder,' he muttered, 'I was cold enough in that warm jacket and this one has only sacks!' He scooped some water from the lough in a cup he had for the purpose, and taking bread and cheese from his budget, he softened the bread with water, and cut the cheese into slivers. He had already noted the boy's gums swollen and spongy with scurvy. All the while, he spoke softly to the boy to reassure him.

'Come on, lad, eat something. Put some strength into you. I'm taking you to Dublin when you are ready, and you'll need all you have for the journey.'

After his outburst, Sean had lapsed into a stupor. His mind could not comprehend the presence of the Captain, or cope with the fact that the Captain was actually feeding him with his own hands. He closed his eyes, convinced that he had, in fact, died and that this was all a dream. James looked at boy's face, fine drawn by hunger but showing a strong bone structure, and the intelligent brow he had noted before, and he felt unaccountably moved. He could not quite understand why he felt so deeply for this lad as he had never been attracted to boys; his tastes ran entirely to the female of the species. Perhaps he felt that he epitomised all that was wrong with this society. Here was a boy, apparently intelligent and resourceful, reduced to this pitiful condition due to being born a Catholic, whereas someone like Mary Kavanagh and her ilk in Dublin could live so much more comfortably because they were Protestants.

The cottages were well and truly ablaze by now, and James decided that it was time to move on. The early spring sunshine was weakening, and there could not be many hours of daylight left. Besides, he wanted to get the lad away from the scene as rapidly as possible. He gently pulled Sean to his feet, and supporting him as best he could, began the long journey towards Dublin. Stumbling and tripping, Sean was only half aware of the journey. After an hour or two, James realised that they were not going to reach Dublin that evening, and the air was already getting decidedly chilly. The pair came across a collection of cottages that looked relatively intact, and furthermore, had no telltale smell about them. Gently lowering Sean to the ground, James inspected the hovels, and choosing the least unsavoury, helped Sean into it. Then he spotted a stack of turfs piled outside the door, and with this unfamiliar fuel, attempted to make a fire in the empty hearth. At first he got more smoke than fire, but after a while a respectable red glow could be seen, giving out a pleasant heat.

Further exploration unearthed a cooking pot, so James was able to heat some water, which he used to brew some tea with a handful of leaves he had brought with him. He held Sean's head while the boy swallowed some of the brew, and then fed him some more bread and cheese, even taking a little of it himself. Afterwards, James leaned back with a sigh and lit his pipe, pondering over the events of the day.

'Why are you helping me?' came Sean's voice, startlingly out of the gloom.

Chapter 25

The man stood looking down at the body huddled at his feet. The boy's breathing was barely perceptible, and it seemed that in a very short time, it would be stilled forever. So much was obvious to the man, but he was gripped by a terrible inertia that prevented him from taking any action to prevent the inevitable. His mind was numbed by the many tragic sights he had so recently witnessed and it seemed strange indeed to make a move to save this one soul from perishing when so many had already succumbed.

The man had reached Clonarty from the south, unwittingly following the footsteps of the typhus carrier. Strangely though, he was neither a peasant farmer, nor even Irish. It was a man whose fate seemed destined to cross with that of Sean's, though he was far from recognising the boy in the gaunt huddled wretch at his feet. Captain James Willoughby of Her Majesty's Army currently stationed at Dublin's Barracks; his presence in Clonarty at that precise moment in time was wholly coincidental, but it was the nature of the man that he had decided to find out for himself the true state of affairs in the country, away from the cushioned luxury to be found in Dublin. But the timing of the tour was a direct consequence of his tempestuous relationship with the widow, Mary Kavanagh.

James Sebastian Willoughby had been born some five and twenty years before, the younger son of Lord Charles Willoughby of Bensham Manor in Yorkshire. His father had also been a soldier, for he too had been a younger son, and had not expected to succeed to the family estates. At the age of eighteen, his own father had purchased a commission for him in one of King George's finest foot regiments. He had joined the Regiment in the company of his boyhood companion, Gerald Deluce, whose family estates marched alongside his own. The young men, resplendent in their dashing uniforms, quickly became absorbed into army life, and by their early twenties had both attained their captaincies. They were dispatched to the Iberian Peninsula where England and her allies were fighting a series of desperate battles against the seasoned veterans of Napoleon's armies. The pair distinguished themselves time and again by their acts of extreme bravery, or maybe it was foolhardiness, as they vied against one another? Many an olive skinned Spanish lady was dashingly courted by the two handsome young officers, who seemed more interested in winning his rival's lady than winning one of his own!

The friends and rivals both survived the Peninsula Campaign and were sent home for a well earned rest. There, they counteracted their boredom by rivaling each other during hunt meets, or at the Balls arranged by their doting families. When Napoleon shook off his silken chains and escaped incarceration from Elba, they were overjoyed, and hurried to London to rejoin their Regiment, and to embark to Belgium. There, they took part in the great clash between Wellington and Napoleon near the small village of Waterloo, their platoons being caught up in the thickest of the fighting. Charles was seen to save his friend from the sweeping sabre of a French dragoon, but Gerald, not to be outdone, saved Charles from an exploding cannonball by flinging himself on top of him. Both survived the epic battle with nothing more than a few minor cuts that would leave them with some interesting scars to beguile the ladies with in due course!

A week later, Charles received the shocking news that his older brother and heir had been killed during a hunt when his horse had flung him over a high fence and broken his neck. With tears in his eyes, Charles arranged the sale of his commission, and took the packet boat home to don the mantle of responsibility. Before leaving Belgium he embraced his friend with deep emotion, prophesying a great future for his boyhood companion and rival; 'doubtless you'll be a general before you know it!' They swore eternal constancy, but both knew in their hearts that their closeness would wither away as their paths diverged; Charles' to estate duties and the 'carrying on of the line', and Gerald's to serve King and Country in a martial role.

Charles arrived home to comfort his bereaved parents, and he took over his brother's duties without a backward glance. He gave to his new way of life the same dedication that he had given to soldiering, and eventually found fulfillment thereby. Within five years he had courted and won the hand of Lettice Ashton, whose family were also close neighbours, and very soon was the father of two sons, the first named Gerald in honour of his dearest friend, and the second, James Sebastian. Within ten years, his parents had died and he was the Lord of Bensham Manor, with a steadily increasing family, though no more sons were born to him.

Young James spent a happy childhood on the rolling dales of his father's estates. He was raised on stirring tales of soldiers and battles, and was his father's willing helper in the setting up of battle scenes with legions of tiny, painted lead soldiers. Time and again the two would re-enact the battles of his father's military career, his favourite being the last and most renowned, the Battle of Waterloo. His older brother, Gerald, was not at all interested. He was a serious boy who took after his mother and would be ideally suited to take over the estates in due course, 'if he wasn't so damned dull,' sighed his father to himself.

James had always known that he was destined to be a soldier, a fact with which he was in full accord. And equally naturally he would enter his father's old regiment, where Charles' former soul mate was now Colonel, having not yet fulfilled the prophecy of reaching generalship!.

Charles and Gerald met one evening in the Officer's Mess to talk over old times and discuss James' commission. Charles' eyes misted over as he looked round the familiar setting and the dress uniforms of the Junior Officers. He struggled to contain his emotion as Gerald described the events during the years since their parting, 'damned boring, if you ask me. No decent battles to speak of once Old Boney had gone!'

Charles spoke of his family in general and his younger son in particular, urging Gerald to keep an avuncular eye on him. Gerald himself had never married, but promised stoutly to be a second father to the young man, 'though I'll not show favour, you understand?' Charles did understand perfectly, and two old comrades drank a toast to James' future and to the new generation of officers coming along.

Next day, James presented himself to his new Colonel. Resplendent in his new uniform, scarlet jacket adorned by the correct amount of gold lace as befitted a junior officer, snowy white breeches and gleaming, knee high black boots, he definitely thought he cut quite a dash! His black shako, also adorned with gold braid, boasted a handsome tassel that swung bravely as he marched, but was now tucked firmly under one arm as he entered the Colonel's office.

'Well, my boy,' said Colonel Deluce gruffly, 'so you think you'll make a soldier?'

'Yessir,' smartly from James.

'As good as your father, eh?'

'Better sir!'

Gerald gave a snort that might have been derision or laughter, and turned to Charles, who was watching somewhat misty eyed.

'Hell do; he'll do!'

Father and son made their farewells, the older Willoughby almost overtaken by emotion, while his son swallowed a lump in his throat at the thought of losing the hand that had guided him since his birth, sixteen years before. After much slapping of backs and injunctions to 'take care', they parted.

James fell happily into army life, enjoying everything from early morning parades; to mock 'set piece battles'; to learning to shoot at the ranges; to the Regimental Balls; to the Mess Nights when the junior officers took part in wild games which often resulted in bloody noses and black eyes! Within a few years he had attained his Captaincy and had earned a reputation as a good officer, who treated the men beneath him firmly, but fairly. Watching his protégée from a distance, Gerald was well pleased. True to his word, he had shown the young man no special favour, but had watched his progress with immense satisfaction, a fact he imparted privately to Charles in his sporadic letters. He also admitted that he had had to do nothing to ease James' passage through the early years of his military career, for he was a 'natural'.

While stationed in London, James also developed a liking for the pursuit of the fair sex. He had been raised to respect truth, justice and ladies of his own class, so he did not include delicately nurtured damsels in his chases. Instead, he developed an unerring instinct for discovering the courtesans in his set, and had soon notched up a string of conquests among these females.

The only cloud on Captain James Willoughby's bright horizon was the lack of any 'real soldiering'. To date, he had not left London let alone the shores of England, nor had he experienced any battles. He was uncomfortably aware that at the same age, his father had been a war veteran, with medals and commendations for bravery to his credit.

'But it's not my fault,' he told his friend and drinking companion, Edward Colby, during a particular heavy bout of drinking in the mess, 'if only there was a decent war somewhere!' Edward owlishly agreed, though at that moment he would have agreed to anything!

'I 'shpect we'll be posted soon; rumours, don't y'know.'

A week later, Colonel Deluce presided over dinner in the Officers Mess. He gazed sternly at the officers ranged either side of the long table, looking very smart in their dress uniforms. He watched the port circulate, and when it had completed its third circuit, banged on the table for silence. He got it,

'I have just received orders for our posting. The Regiment is to be posted...' The assembled company held its collective breath; would it be India as had been strongly rumoured, or Europe, Africa, Australia?

'......to Ireland. To be precise, to Dublin. They have famine over there, and there is a need to keep public order.'

The Colonel got up amidst a stunned silence, walked slowly to the door, and turned,

'We have two weeks before embarkation.' He shut the door firmly behind him.

James sat silent, completely taken aback by the news, while a hubbub rose around him,

'It can't be true; the old man jests!'

'Tomorrow he'll tell where we are really going.'

'Ireland! They live like animals!'

'They live with their animals.'

Round and round the noise reverberated, until James thought his head would burst after freely imbibing of the port. Dreams of glorious battle faded to ashes as the reality of the posting sunk in. Quietly he got up from the table, and staggering slightly, left the room. Reaching his quarters, he vented his anger on his hapless servant, snarling at the man to fetch him a bottle of the best brandy. His groom foolishly expostulated, gently suggesting that the Captain mayhap had had enough already. He received a kick in his rear for his pains. When the groom returned, having taken longer than was necessary for the errand, he found the Captain stretched out on his bed, snoring stertorously, and fully clothed down to his gleaming boots. The groom spoke softly to the recumbent form as he deftly removed his boots, and the beautifully cut scarlet jacket,

'So you've 'eard the news 'ave you? It's not like you to fly off the 'andle like that. Never mind. Mebbe it won't be for long.'

The groom took himself off to his bed, leaving James to sleep off his woes, though he would doubtless wake with a head like thunder on the morrow!

Before he embarked, James took some long promised leave, arranging to rejoin the Regiment at Liverpool immediately prior to embarkation. He was still low in spirits about this cruel twist of fate, but he had become reconciled to it during the bustle of preparations for departure. He braved the Colonel's den to take his leave and also to find out more information about the posting, and was told that it would likely be of short duration, with a reward in the end; India!

Charles Willoughby was sympathetic to his son's disappointment, but reminded him gently about that all important word, duty, and that a soldiers lot what not always the desired one.

Father and son spent a contented week together, finding pleasure in each other's company that had deepened with the passage of time. Charles spoke of his eldest son,

'He's gradually taking over the running of the estates, with my blessing d'you see. Your mother and I have a mind to do a bit of travelling.' James thought about his rather timid mother and wondered about the 'spot of travelling,' but he understood his father's restlessness. He had given up the challenge of a soldier's life to do his duty by the estates and now he felt he could relinquish the reins.

'He's doing a damn fine job of it don't y'know, but if only he wasn't such a dull dog! Have you met the gel he's courting? Spirited little squab of a thing; just right for him!'

James smiled at the description and hoped that Gerald would not get to hear of his father's opinion of his lady love, for the old soldier's voice had a carrying quality!

All too soon the leave was over. James took affectionate leave of his family, his parents, brother and three sisters. He hugged his diminutive mother, who told him sternly to 'ensure his servant aired his smalls properly,' as she had heard that Ireland was a 'dreadful damp place.' Gerald slapped him on his back and warned him against the Irish peasants, as he had heard 'went about armed with cudgels and were prone to fighting over the slightest thing!'

He was introduced to Gerald's intended, the 'little squab of a thing' according to his father. She turned out to be a trim young lady of even shorter stature than his mother. She shook his hand firmly with her own tiny one, and told him firmly to 'try and help the poor starving people.' James was startled, as he had not yet given a thought to the reasons he was going to Ireland, but only the anger he had felt at the decision. Before he could ponder on this, his father was hugging him warmly and telling him 'to be sure to come again before he was sent half way round the world.'

James reached Liverpool with time to spare, and was soon involved in the chaos of embarkation. Upon arriving at Dublin's harbour, there was the further chaos of disembarkation and settling into their barracks. For a day or two the barracks were full to bursting as the departing Regiment sorted themselves out prior to their departure. In the interim, the various ranks exchanged news, the 'old timers' regaling the newcomers with horror stories of Ireland in general and Dublin in particular. James refused to listen, preferring to form his own opinion in the fullness of time.

Once they had the barracks to themselves, the Colonel gave his officers a stern briefing, with the order to pass his instructions to every last man. He warned his officers that their duty was to keep order with the minimum of force and the maximum of tolerance. He reminded him that there was famine in the countryside and the people were severely distressed. When going out and about, they were warned to always travel with a companion or in a group, and to treat the citizens of Dublin with respect, 'just remember, it is their country!'

It was the very next day that James' squad was sent out to oversee the dispensing of grain at a warehouse, and where he would meet Pat and Sean O'Hara for the first time. James commanded the first of the soldiers to arrive at the warehouse and who had to face the mob that was gaining in strength and in anger. He had quickly assessed the situation, and noted that the majority were only intent on buying food and were peaceable enough, but the temper of the crowd was being whipped up by agitators in the rear. Mindful of the Colonel's words, he gave the command to prepare their guns but to aim high. However, as the mob rushed forward, panic set in amongst his line of inexperienced privates and several of them aimed at the advancing crowd.

In the melee that ensued, James was involved wherever the fighting was thickest and did not see the reinforcements arriving. Nor did he witness the incident that felled Sean and led to Pat's arrest. But when he saw the O'Hara's in the courtroom the next day, he instinctively felt that Pat was telling the truth, borne out by the swelling on the side of Sean's head. He took the trouble to study the people round him and found his preconceived notions of the Irish to be completely false.

'Why, they're just like us,' he thought, his pictures of a bovine race of limited intellect melting away as he studied Sean's intelligent brow. That he would become involved with the family was not an intentional act, rather an impulsive gesture, born out of his innate sense of justice. Later, he again acted impulsively when he agreed to meet Sean and Kate outside the gaol, but had no regrets when he saw the nature of the brutish gaoler, Carey. James realised that he would have to see this business through, as he understood that Pat would likely die on gaol if he did not oversee his imprisonment. But in truth, he was heartily glad when Pat was released, and he could get on with his life!

But during those months, James became increasingly restless with the nature of the duties he and his fellow officers were required to perform. Maintaining law and order wherever they were summoned was not exactly their idea of soldiering and inevitably they sought other distractions. True to his own code of ethics, James did not pursue the inexperienced maidens he met at the regular balls and soirees they were expected to attend, and he was too fastidious to use the high class brothels frequented by his fellows. But by the time Christmas came and went, he was frustrated in more ways than one! It was at such a vulnerable time that he met Mary Kavanagh at a New Year's Eve ball in Dublin Castle, and fell head over heels in love for the first time in his life.

Mary was the widow of Jerome Kavanagh, a hitherto confirmed bachelor of fifty, who had been captivated by a ravishing seventeen year old girl. He was a wealthy merchant, and had been pursued by many an avaricious mother intent on securing a good marriage for their numerous daughters. But he finally met his match when he laid eyes on the youngest daughter of an impoverished gentleman. Mary had not an ounce of sentimentality in her exquisite frame, and she viewed the aging Jerome as a means of escape from the genteel poverty she had endured during her upbringing. Jerome punctiliously requested her hand from her father, who invited Mary to say if she wished to accept,

'Of course, Papa, why wouldn't I?'

Her anxious mother questioned her youngest daughter as to her feelings for her suitor, so much older than herself. Mary had ingenuously replied,

'Why Mama, I shall adore him, of course!'

They had married on Mary's eighteenth birthday, the lavish wedding and reception paid for by the adoring groom. He took his new wife on a tour of France, where he shyly disposed of her virginity, with many apologies. By the age of twenty one, Mary was in full possession of the Kavanagh fortune, including its properties, chief of which was the elegant Georgian house in Henrietta Street. The malicious among Dublin's society were unsure whether it was the physical or financial demands of his young bride that had caused the apoplexy that carried off the bemused bridegroom, but he lived long enough to make a will leaving everything to his young widow.

Mary surveyed her way of life with great satisfaction and decided that the widowed state exactly suited her, and she no intention of shackling herself to anyone else, even after the customary year of mourning was over. After all, another husband would have the right to dispose of her fortune any way he wished, and that did not suit her at all! However, she discovered in herself a taste for the baser passions, barely awakened by the fumbling Jerome, and she determined to have discreet affairs conducted under her own terms. By the time she met James at the Dublin ball, she was five and twenty, and at the height of her splendid looks. She was currently without a suitor, as her last affair was with a major who had recently departed from Ireland with his regiment. But his attraction had already begun to pall, and Mary had not been sorry to see him go, but it had been a while since she had welcomed a man to her bed and she was ripe for a new affair.

Mary had arrived before James, and was standing near the entrance to the ballroom, chatting in desultory fashion to a wispy female of indeterminate age, who had the unenviable task of acting as chaperone to Mary, to lend an air of respectability to her establishment. Her first sight of James was the top of his head as he bowed punctiliously over the hand of the hostess, and as he straightened up, Mary's eyes widened with interest. She studied him covertly from behind her fan as he exchanged words with the Governor and host for the evening, noting the breadth of his shoulders that strained the seams of his splendid scarlet jacket. His legs, encased in skin tight overalls, were shapely and well muscled, and he carried himself proudly. Finally, he turned from his host and approached the ballroom, and Mary was able to study his features, dominated by a pair of green eyes fringed by long dark lashes. His moustache, slightly more ginger than his hair, enhanced rather than dominated a handsome face with firm lines and a cleft chin. Mary was satisfied; she had selected her next victim!

James entered the ballroom, resigned to another tedious evening dancing attendance on the polite society of Dublin, and fending off the efforts of mothers with marriageable daughters to engage his interest. He felt that there was something rather obscene about the entertainment that invariably included a lavish supper when so many were starving and dying in the countryside, and in the city itself. He kept his thoughts to himself in deference to his hosts, but he could not imagine he would enjoy the evening in the slightest. The only bright spot as far as he was concerned was, on that very day, he had achieved the release of the man, O'Hara, who should even now have arrived home to his wife and son. James could not know that Pat's infant daughter had died of starvation, and that Pat would arrive home in time for her funeral!

As he entered the ballroom, he was met by a vision of loveliness that took his breath away. It was just the panacea that his depressed spirits needed right then when he saw a young lady of medium height, dressed in a sweeping ballgown of peach coloured silk that belled out from of tiny waist over a crinoline of noble proportions. The low cut bodice was embellished with peach rosebuds, artfully revealing a glimpse of a voluptuously swelling bosom. White shoulders rising from the gown met an elegant, swan like neck that in turn supported a face of classic features, oval in shape, with a firm rounded chin and crowned by glossy brown curls, somewhat darker than James' own, arranged in an elaborate coiffure. James' eyes travelling upwards met a pair of large grey eyes that were surveying him with some amusement. He turned away in some confusion, determined to discover the identity of the lady. Presently, he came across a fellow officer who admitted that he knew the lady, could introduce him, and that she was a widow of some few years, a Mrs. Kavanagh. James' delight was complete. This was no shrinking maiden who he would be unable to pursue without the noblest of intentions, but someone he could court, and perhaps.....? But first he must be introduced.

At that moment, the orchestra was tuning up in preparation for the first dance and James crossed the ballroom floor and presented himself to Mary and her companion with a smart click of his heels,

'Mrs. Kavanagh. I believe this is my dance.'

'Why, er, Captain,' replied Mary, correctly relating the lavish gold epaulettes to his rank, 'I don't think...'

'Can it be you have forgotten,' returned James with mock wistfulness, 'let me show you.' And plucking her dance card deftly from her wrist, he studied it carefully, and then with a few strokes of the attached pencil, he declared triumphantly,

'There you see!'

Mary looked at the card, eyes widening in amusement at the temerity of the man, 'Captain James Willoughby' had been firmly penciled in for the dance about to start and for two others, including the coveted supper dance.

'Well, Captain Willoughby, it seems you are correct.' And Mary allowed herself to be swept into the dance, turning away with a choke of laughter at the face of her ousted dance partner just now approaching, his face red with rage. James appeared not to notice the spluttering civilian, but gathered his partner firmly into his arms, and steered her onto the dance floor.

'Well Captain. Are you as decisive in battle as you are on the dance floor,' asked Mary, archly.

'Of course! It is the only way to carry off battle honours.'

'Am I then a battle honour?'

'You are a prize any sane person would want to win,' returned James, lightly enough but with a trace of seriousness. Mary experienced a frisson of anticipation as she swept round the ballroom.

At the end of the dance, James returned Mary to her companion, promising to return and claim her for the supper dance. This he did with determination when the time came, causing a youthful lieutenant to beat a hasty retreat in the face of superior fire power. Mary was delighted with the attention and James could not remember when he had last enjoyed an evening as much. The problems of the O'Hara's and the starving populace were well and truly forgotten in the excitement of the chase.

After the third dance that James had so shamelessly stolen, he steered Mary into a small anteroom, ostensibly to recover from the exertions of the dance. Mary was a little alarmed at the speed at which matters were progressing, as she fully intended to thoroughly enslave her Captain, and an early capitulation would jeopardize her plan. In the privacy of the anteroom she allowed James to kiss her thoroughly, feeling her own passion rising to match his, but she kept her head and when James' lips started to wander to her neck, then on to her silky shoulders and finally to the swelling mounds of her bosom, she rapped him smartly with her fan,

'Captain Willoughby, you forget yourself!'

James looked up startled, to meet her steely glare.

'I beg pardon, ma'am; your beauty caused me to be quite overcome.'

'I wish to return to the ballroom this instant, if you please.'

Contritely, James escorted Mary back to her companion, and with a formal bow and click of his heels, he excused himself, and sought the quiet of the refreshment room to calm himself down. There he found Edward Colby gazing gloomily into a glass. He choked as James clapped him on the back and told him to 'lose that long face before he curdled the cream on the desserts'! Edward was not amused and bemoaned the lack of excitement.

'What d'you mean; I've had a wonderful evening.' Edward surveyed his friend with jaundiced eyes: James usually shared his views.

'What you need,' said James earnestly, 'is to meet some of the local society; there are some interesting people out there!'

'Ah!' replied Edward, realisation dawning, 'you've found yourself a wench.'

'That's no way to talk about the most wonderful lady you could ever meet!'

'Humph,' retorted Edward, succinctly.

After the ball, James continued his pursuit of Mary Kavanagh with great determination, making sure he was invited to all the social events to ensure that he would meet her. Mary allowed him to think that he was determining the pace of the courtship, and even invited him to one of her soirees, but if James thought he was going to find his way into her bed after it was over, he was sadly mistaken. At the end of the evening he found himself, politely but firmly, escorted to the door by the Kavanagh butler, Baines. This went on for three weeks as James' ardour mounted to fever pitch, and Mary herself was finding it harder to resist his advances. Too soon and the Captain's ardour would cool as rapidly as it had flamed; too late, and he would find himself another, more willing partner. Finally one evening, after an excellent supper and some musical entertainment, Mary sat down beside her swain and murmured low,

'Return one hour after midnight.' She moved away so quickly that James thought he had imagined the invitation, but his senses flamed with anticipation.

Promptly at one hour past midnight, he knocked quietly on the door. It was immediately opened by Mary herself, clad in a loose peignoir, her glorious hair freed from restraint and tumbling about her shoulders. She placed a finger on his lips, and taking his hand, led him up the stairs to her bedchamber. There, the two came together with a passion that surprised them both, reaching their climax together.

Afterwards, James lay nuzzling Mary's ear gently, as she lay in voluptuous contentment,

'You are a wonderful woman, Mary love,' he whispered in her ear.

'I must agree, sir,' replied the lady, archly, 'and am I a battle honour?'

'Ah Mary, a man would charge a row of cannon to carry you off!'

Later, they made love again at a more leisurely pace, bare limbs entwined among the tangled silk sheets. Towards dawn, James quietly let himself out of the door before the servants started moving about, and made his way back to the barracks. He had completely forgotten the injunction against roaming the streets of Dublin alone, either by day or night, but arrived safely enough, carried along a wave of euphoria.

The affair flourished to the satisfaction of both parties, and to the amusement of James' fellow officers and the Kavanagh servants, who were always aware of their mistress's affairs in spite of her efforts at discretion! Mary had judged her capitulation to a nicety as James was completely enthralled by her; deeply in love as never before. Without neglecting his duties, James danced attendance on his lady love at every free moment. Many a morning parade was attended in a state of near stupor, having been kept awake the night proving his manhood again and again to an increasingly insatiable Mary. Edward Colby became seriously concerned for his friend, and warned him to take care lest a report of his behavior reached the Colonel,

'Y'know you're not supposed to roam the streets of Dublin at night alone; it's just not safe. There are desperate men abroad who'd think nothing of relieving you of your purse and your life!'

'Don't be an old woman, Edward! I always go armed.'

'But what about the parades? Only the other morning you were actually swaying on your horse and the Old man's got eyes like a hawk; he doesn't miss a thing!'

James laughed and slapped his friend on the back,

'You're just jealous. Find yourself a woman like Mary, and lighten up that long face of yours. You remind me of an old nag of me father's as it was being led away to be put down!'

It was inevitable that the Colonel would become aware and would take action. He had always kept a discreet eye on his friend's son, but until recently had had no cause for concern. The affair did not surprise or concern him, as James was as lusty as the next man, and the Colonel was just thankful that the lady was a widow who was 'old enough to know what she was doing'. However, the Colonel would not tolerate James bringing the Regiment into disrepute, which was something that could well happen if the reports and rumours were to be believed.

So it was that James found himself sitting next to the Colonel in the mess on a night that he was obliged to stay in the Barracks. The Colonel was in the habit of joining the junior offices in the mess, as he was an approachable and sympathetic commanding officer, so James was not alarmed at the attention. But then he noticed that the others had quietly dispersed, leaving him alone with a unusually stern faced Colonel Deluce. James began to feel uncomfortable.

'Well, my boy. How d'you like Dublin now, eh? I know you youngsters were keen to prove yourselves on a battlefield somewhere, just like your father and myself at your age!'

'Yes sir, but it isn't so bad, after all.'

'Keen to move on then?' asked the Colonel slyly.

'Is that likely, sir?' questioned James, somewhat anxiously.

'It's possible. This was only meant to be a temporary posting y'know. I thought you youngsters couldn't wait to leave?'

'Of course,' said James, somewhat desperate. How much did the Colonel know? 'We shall be ready to do our duty.'

Surprisingly, the Colonel chuckled,

'Don't get too enmeshed with the lovely widow.' And then more seriously, 'it is an order that no-one, officer or private, is to leave the barracks alone. This will be rigorously enforced; a Corporal was found floating in the Liffey yesterday, and I've no wish to be responsible for informing your father of your demise in like fashion.' James eyes widened in shock; he had not heard about that! The Colonel continued,

'Just between you and me, my boy, your father and I cut something of a dash among the ladies in the Peninsular Campaign, but I don't believe that we were in the danger that you would be in this place! I do understand young blood, but be very careful as these are desperate times. Take a friend with you, and above all else, remember the reputation of the Regiment; I will not have that brought into disrepute!'

The Colonel rose and patted James' shoulder before leaving him to ponder his words. The younger man could only be thankful for a sympathetic Commanding Officer, and realised just how careless he had been of his safety, and just how badly an unpleasant incident could have reflected on the Regiment.

James discussed the situation at the next soiree he attended at Mary's, taking Edward along to meet with the other guests. Mary was inclined to be petulant as she was used to having James at her beck and call, and she condemned the Colonel as 'an old fussbudget. But James was not now in the first throes of infatuation, and was taken aback at the attack on the Colonel who commanded his highest respect, and he told his paramour so in no uncertain terms! Mary shrugged her elegant shoulders and punished James by refusing to see him for a full two weeks, only relenting when her own needs became too strong to resist. Grudgingly she agreed to the presence of Edward Colby when she wanted James to stay the night, having been assured of his discretion.

During the progress of their affair, James had kept up to date with Irish affairs, and knew that the farmers were keeping themselves by attending Public Works, though he had no idea what these works consisted of. He was intermittently troubled at the callousness with which Mary treated her distressed countrymen, regarding them as little better than animals. When the second harvest failed, her only reaction was to remark,

'Perhaps this will get rid of some of them; always swarming about Dublin and getting in the way!'

James found himself increasingly at odds with Mary, and found it hard to hide his distaste for her remarks, and they began to quarrel frequently. But still their mutual attraction kept the affair smouldering on. But strangely, it was an unwitting Sean O'Hara who finally precipitated the end of their relationship.

On the day that Sean had tumbled down the stairs into the kitchen of the house in Henrietta Street, James and Mary were upstairs having yet another row about Mary's attitude towards the starving populace. James had previously suggested that she keep a less lavish table and to donate some of the food to the poor. In retaliation, Mary had ordered an even more sumptuous spread than usual for her next luncheon. The scene that Sean had witnessed through the elegant window, as Mary moved among her guests in her blue velvet gown had seemed tranquil enough, but James was hiding a simmering anger, while Mary was hiding her satisfaction at 'scoring a hit' over him!

When all the guests had gone, except the compliant Edward dozing in the drawing room, Mary and James retired upstairs, where for a while their resolved their differences with their mutual passion; that had least had not changed since their first coupling. Later, Mary got out of bed, and wrapping a peignoir around her, she crossed to the window overlooking Henrietta Street. She saw the figure of a youth leaving the gate from the kitchen basement, and noted that he appeared to be carrying a bundle. She had long suspected that her housekeeper had been giving away food from her kitchen, but had been unable to prove it, and this seemed the ideal opportunity to confront her servant. She swept out of the bedroom in high dudgeon, leaving a startled James to scramble into his clothes. Mary reached the kitchen in time to hear Mrs. Markham remark to Baines,

'That little bit of food'll put heart into that boy and his family for a while. Poor lamb. Did you see his wrist; no thicker than a chicken leg!'

'And just what did you give that beggar from my larder?' demanded Mary in peremptory tone from the kitchen door. Mrs. Markham looked up startled,

'Why, just a bit of stale bread, ma'am,' she answered, calmly enough. But Mary was not to be placated,

'How dare you give away my possessions? You have no right!'

Mrs. Markham was foolish enough to remonstrate,

'But ma'am, there's folk dyin' all over for lack of a bit of food. You've more than enough!'

'How dare you,' hissed Mary, 'you are dismissed. Do not expect a character. Be out of here tonight!' Mrs. Markham stood aghast. Where would she get another post without a reference in these hard times? Next to her, she felt Baines stiffen,

'Then I'll have to go too.'

'Then get out, both of you. Ingrates, the pair of you!'

Mary spun round and collided with James, who had listened to the exchange with growing horror,

'Then I will be off as well. I have closed my eyes to your heartless nature for too long.' He spoke to the stricken servants,

'If you present yourselves at the Barracks tomorrow, I'll see to it that you're given work.' Mary almost screamed with fury and swung a stinging blow towards James' face. He caught her wrist just before the blow landed and held it tightly as Mary's bosom heaved with temper. Looking into eyes that glittered with hatred, James wondered how he had ever found her attractive. When she had calmed a little, he released her abruptly, and then returning to the drawing room, he roused the slumbering Edward. He told his friend that they were leaving and would not be returning. Edward asked no questions, realizing instinctively that the affair was over,

'Thank God,' he murmured to himself.

With his tumultuous affair well and truly over, James began to look about him properly once more. Though he had been called out many times on law enforcement duties, to food queues, work queues and the like, he had not been fully aware how desperate the population had grown, so wrapped up was he with his lady love.

The failure of the second harvest had caused a rush for the emigration ships, and the Public Works had restarted. But more recently, alarming rumours of a typhus epidemic had begun to spread in the Barracks. James felt ashamed at his indifference, his magnanimous gesture to the O'Hara's seemed an eon ago. He wrote to his father in Yorkshire and arranged for some funds to be transferred to Dublin which he planned to use to finance some of the Quaker soup kitchens that were being opened across the city. He had already persuaded the Officer's Mess to take on Baines and Mrs. Markham in their kitchens, so that they would be sure to get a reference should they chose to move on. In these small ways, he sought to quieten his troubled conscience, though with only partial success.

Towards spring, Colonel Deluce gave his Regiment the news that it had waited for, for so long. Again, he chose a Mess Night, but did not bother to wait for the port to circulate more than once, and rapping on his glass, he spoke quietly,

'Gentlemen, we are off to India!'

The cheers swelled around the smiling Colonel, but he was observing James and was troubled by the expression on the younger man's face; it did not appear that he was pleased at the news. But surely the affair with the widow was over, pondered the Colonel, he had heard that it was so, but perhaps the rumours were wrong? He determined to investigate the matter, but reassured himself that within a short time they would be leaving Irish shores and that would certainly put an end to the affair once and for all!

Colonel Deluce could not have been more wrong. James was not thinking of Mary Kavanagh at all, except that he now resented her for preventing him doing his duty properly! He mentally castigated himself for not doing more for the Irish people, as he had urged Mary to do. Perhaps his guilt was in reaction to his infatuation with such a heartless woman, as he now described his erstwhile paramour, and he just could not bring himself to join in the euphoria than prevailed in the Officer's Mess, especially now that the Colonel had quietly slipped away. Listening to the excited chatter swirling around him, an idea began to slowly form itself in his mind. Before he left Ireland he would go and see for himself the extent of the problems the rural population was facing, especially as he had some long overdue leave.

James laid his plans carefully. Though he was entitled to leave, the order had gone out that no member of the Regiment was to leave Dublin for their own safety and James had no wish to incur the Colonel's wrath. Sympathetic and understanding he may be, but he would brook no disobedience. He took his closest friends aside and swore them to secrecy as he knew that someone needed to know where he was going. Edward Colby and Robert Harding were both horrified, and tried their hardest to dissuade James from his foolhardy venture. It was only when they realised that he was bound and determined on his course of action, and would carry it out with or without them, that they agreed to help him. The three friends gave out that they planned a few days in a local hostelry and would be incommunicado for a while.

The trio set off together in civilian clothes and made for their favourite hostelry. As they travelled, the friends made a last ditch attempt to dissuade James,

'What can you do?' asked Robert, 'you can't feed them all!'

'I can see for myself,' replied James, 'we've been told so many stories; how can we know if they're true.'

'What happens if we are recalled to barracks while you're gone?' asked Edward. James shrugged,

'You'll think of something. I just have to go!'

The friends parted company as they approached the road south out of Dublin. James was dressed in rough clothes, borrowed from a grateful Baines who fully understood the Captain's quest, but urged him to be careful. He carried a small budget containing enough food to sustain him for three or four days and an even smaller quantity of money. He hugged his companions and bade them to stay away from the Barracks for as long as possible.

James soon encountered one of the Public Works, where a ragged gang of workers was lengthening a stretch of road. The gang comprised men, women and even children trying to carry stones in baskets. James' heart wrenched in pity, as none of the gang seemed to have an ounce of flesh on them. Most coughed incessantly, in spite of the milder temperature, and their limbs were covered with running sores. They looked at James' passing with lack lustre eyes; their native Irish curiosity long since dimmed by privation.

From the end of the road, James took a large sweep through the hills west and south of Dublin. Everywhere he encountered the same scenes of devastation; villages either completely deserted or housing a few pitiful families. Children with sticklike limbs and distended bellies peered out of hovels, voices stilled by long term hunger. No-one seemed to be working the fields in readiness for the spring planting, but perhaps, he thought, they had nothing to plant?

Within two days of leaving Robert and Edward, James had the answer he sought, and knew that the situation was a hundred times worse that he and his friends had supposed. While he had danced attendance on the heartless Mary, with her lavish suppers and flamboyant lifestyle, these people had been suffering unimaginable torment. No wonder they grew desperate in the food queues he had been called upon to oversee. James found he could not eat the little food he had brought, but nor could he give it out, for what good would so little do in the midst of so much want?

AS he journeyed, first further south, and then swinging back to the northeast to return to Dublin, an idea was formulating in his mind as to what he could do to really help some of these people. It would need the help of Mrs. Markham and Baines as he would be gone before the plans could come to fruition.

He slept his last night in the bracken, waking shivering with the dawn, but welcoming the discomfort as a balm to his troubled soul. He set off early, determined to reach Dublin by nightfall and set his friends' minds at rest, for he had no desire to see them punished. He slaked his thirst in a nearby pool, and looked once again with distaste at the food he had brought. He would leave it with someone on his journey back, he decided.

He stepped out resolutely enough and covered the miles steadily, approaching a village an hour or two after noon, unaware that it was Clonarty, the village from whence had come the O'Hara's. It looked totally derelict, as had so many villages, but a frisson of fear ran down his spine as he drew near; then he noticed the smell. Though a soldier of a few years, his lack of campaigning experience had not prepared him for the stench of a typhus victim, but his instincts told him that something was very wrong. Holding a kerchief to his mouth and nose, he walked slowly through the village, looking out for any sign of life. Then he saw what looked like a bundle of rags on the ground outside a cottage, but closer inspection showed it to be the body of a youth who seemed to be actually breathing!

Shaking off his initial inertia that had gripped him on first discovering Sean's inert form, James approached the cottage and peered inside. As his eyes grew accustomed to the gloom, he could make out the shapes of two bodies, that of a woman and adolescent boy, and unlike the older boy outside, clearly dead. He could see the slinking shapes of rats moving in the hovel and the stench was appalling making him beat a hasty retreat to the slightly less malodorous air outside. He quickly inspected the rest of the intact cottages, only to find that every single one housed only corpses. Strangely, one cottage only housed one victim, while its neighbour was crowded. Now, at last, there was something he could actively do. One person he could and would help, but the rest needed to be cremated as soon as possible, along with the rats that he understood to carry the typhus plague. Moving quickly and decisively, he formed a bundle of reeds from a thatch and ignited it. He thrust the flaming torch into each thatch in turn, finishing with the one adjacent to the youth. Once all the thatches were well and truly alight, he turned his attentions to the sole survivor. Burying his fear that this one might also be diseased, he lifted him away from the flames engulfing his home, noting the lightness of the frame, and carried him to the edge of the lough. The youth stirred and opened his eyes. Looking past James' shoulder, he saw flames engulfing all the cottages and his eyes widened in horror.

'Mam, Kevin, no.o.o!' he called out in Irish. James did not understand the words but understood their meaning, and his heart stirred in pity.

'Quietly, lad. There's nothing you can do for them.' Sean looked at him in puzzlement, unable to cope with the English.

'D'you understand me, lad?' queried James. 'But your face is familiar; aren't you the lad I met in the courtroom, Sean isn't it?' Sean just continued to stare at him in puzzled fashion, and James surmised he was probably in shock and forbore to question him further. Taking off his jacket, he wrapped it round the light form, noting that the lad's skin was icy cold,

'Small wonder,' he muttered, 'I was cold enough in that warm jacket and this one is only in sacks!' He scooped some water from the lough in a cup he had for the purpose, and taking bread and cheese from his budget, he softened the bread with water, and cut the cheese into slivers. He had already noted the boy's gums swollen and spongy with scurvy. All the while, he spoke softly to the boy to reassure him.

'Come on, lad, eat something. Put some strength into you. I'm taking you to Dublin when you are ready, and you'll need all you have for the journey.'

After his outburst, Sean had lapsed into a stupor. His mind could not comprehend the presence of the Captain, or cope with the fact that the Captain was actually feeding him with his own hands. He closed his eyes, convinced that he had, in fact, died and that this was all a dream. James looked at boy's face, fine drawn by hunger but showing a strong bone structure, and the intelligent brow he had noted before, and he felt unaccountably moved. He could not quite understand why he felt so deeply for this lad, as he had never been attracted to boys, his tastes being entirely normal. Perhaps he felt that he epitomised all that was wrong with this society. Here was a boy, apparently intelligent and resourceful, reduced to this pitiful condition due to being born a Catholic, whereas someone like Mary Kavanagh and her ilk in Dublin could live so much more comfortably because they were Protestants.

The cottages were well and truly ablaze by now, and James decided that it was time to move on. The early spring sunshine was weakening, and there could not be many hours of daylight left. Besides, he wanted to get the lad away from the scene as rapidly as possible. He gently pulled Sean to his feet, and supporting him as best he could, began the long journey towards Dublin. Stumbling and tripping, Sean was only half aware of the journey. After an hour or two, James realised that they were not going to reach Dublin that evening, and the air was already getting decidedly chilly. The pair came across a collection of cottages that looked relatively intact, and furthermore, had no telltale smell about them. Gently lowering Sean to the ground, James inspected the hovels, and choosing the least unsavoury, helped Sean into it. Then he spotted a stack of turfs piled outside the door, and with this unfamiliar fuel, attempted to make a fire in the empty hearth. At first he got more smoke than fire, but after a while a respectable red glow could be seen, giving out a pleasant heat.

Further exploration unearthed a cooking pot, so James was able to heat some water, which he used to brew some tea with a handful of leaves he had brought with him. He held Sean's head while the boy swallowed some of the brew, and then fed him some more bread and cheese, even taking a little of it himself. Afterwards, James leaned back with a sigh and lit his pipe, pondering over the events of the day.

'Why are you helping me?' came Sean's voice, startlingly out of the gloom.

Chapter 26

James looked at the boy over the peat fire glow, noting the newly alert look in his eyes. Apparently he had got over the worst of his shock. He also noted that the lad had spoken in English.

'Are you feeling more the thing,' he enquired gently. Sean's brow creased with the effort of remembering,

'I know you. You're the soldier who helped us when Pa was taken?'

'Yes, that is so. We seemed destined to meet.'

'Why are you helping me?' asked Sean again, 'An' why are you here at all?'

'It's a long story, but suffice to say that I wished to see for myself just how bad things were for your people.' Sean struggled to follow the polished speech of the older man, and pondered on his words. He could not truly comprehend why this English Captain was wandering through the countryside to find out about their troubles. Why should he care? The Captain's voice came again,

'Where is your father now?' And very gently, 'I assume that was your mother in the cottage where I found you?' Sean nodded, his throat swelling with emotion when he remembered his discovery in the cottage.

'Take your time lad. D'you want to tell me about it?' For a while Sean could not reply as he struggled for control, but finally he took a deep breath and nodded. He felt at ease with this man, and he desperately wanted, needed to talk to somebody. The story came out, haltingly at first, as he sought for the right words in a language he could understand, but which did not come easily to him in speech. James did not interrupt throughout the telling, in spite of the many silences. He recognised that the troubled youth needed to exorcise his demons.

Sean told him of the events during the past year; of his father's arrival home to find his youngest and dearest daughter dead from starvation; of the sale of all their possessions to find money for seed and the subsequent planting in hope of a change in fortune; of the search for work while they waited for the crop to mature. When he came to the road building, James could sense that the youngster had enjoyed those weeks, in spite of the hard work, as he waxed enthusiastic about an engineer who had taken the trouble to explain what he was doing to his inquisitive audience, and about all that he had learned during those weeks. But the tale turned to horror again and he told of the landslide and the loss of his father, followed swiftly by the total destruction of the harvest from the return of the blight.

James marveled at the resilience of these people who could recover from such a deep tragedy. But there was more to come; the departure of his Uncle Conor and his family, and various other friends and neighbours leaving the O'Hara's to struggle on almost alone,

'Mam wouldn't leave Pa and Nuala, you see.' Sean fell silent for a while, his head bowed. James thought he had finished his telling, but it was not so, he was simply gathering his strength for the rest. Then there had been the rent money to find, and the constant threat of eviction from the agent in spite of their payment; and then the loss of the elder O'Malley's and of Grandpa Kevin O'Hara. 'Did the lad's troubles never end?' thought James to himself. So Sean had gone to Dublin to seek task work again, which he had found harder this time, but he had also found friendship in a house there. It was that meeting, related Sean that had given him the heart to carry on, though the loss of his sister, Eily, had nearly destroyed him again.

James looked up in surprise when Sean recounted the events in the house in Henrietta Street that had so heartened Sean. Could it have been the same event that had opened his eyes to the shortcomings of his mistress, and the final rift between them? If so, he had cause to thank him; and reflect that they indeed seem fated to meet!

The story was finally drawing to its terrible conclusion, and Sean's voice was beginning to slur with weariness,

'I thought if we could plant some seed we might just keep going. I was sure that the cold weather would've killed the blight. I was on me way home to tell Mam and Kevin that seed potatoes might be given out, when…when' He could not go on, but James knew the rest anyway. Sean put his head in his hands and wept at last. James let him be; it was what he needed most of all.

Presently Sean slept, and James leaned back against a pile of bracken, and lit a cheroot. He needed time to think about his future. He knew he would face disciplinary action when he returned, having failed to meet his friends on the appointed day. He should have been back to meet them this very night, and the threesome would have reported back for duty with no-one the wiser. Sean's weakness had prevented him from carrying out his plan, but for the life of him, he could not feel any regret. Leaving aside his own behaviour during the recent months, did any of the Regiment really know what had been going on in Ireland while they had carried on their business behind the barracks walls, or marched out to keep the peace from time to time? Did they really understand the meaning of the word 'starvation'? James confessed to himself that he had not until he had made his journey away from the confines of the city. He could not be sorry that he had his eyes opened.

A plan he had begun to form in his mind prompted by Robert's remark, 'you can't feed them all,' returned to him, and of course, his friend was right. But he could, and would help a few, particularly children. It was clear from his travels that, while many children had died, there were many others who were orphaned. These he could help by sending them to his father's estate. He had no doubt that his father would support the enterprise, and when the youngsters were grown and trained in forms of husbandry other than simply potato farming, they could return to Ireland or seek some other way of life. His imminent departure from Irish shores would prevent him carrying out the project himself, but he knew he had readymade deputies in Mr. Baines and Mrs. Markham, who could take responsibility and administer the funds that would be necessary for the passages. He, unlike his erstwhile mistress, had long known that the pair was feeding the destitute of Dublin, but had maintained a discreet silence. So he knew that their hearts were in the right place, and he felt instinctively that they could be trusted.

Had James been gifted with foresight, he would have been gratified to find his faith vindicated. The ex-servants of Henrietta Street gathered up a dozen orphans from the slums of Dublin, and using the funds entrusted to them, transported them to Yorkshire and the security of Bensham Manor. There, James' brother had built a dormitory to house the children, and there they flourished. They were educated as were the estate children, and taught the necessary skills they would need for their future, while Mr. Baines and Mrs. Markham acted as their surrogate parents.

James also considered Sean's future. From the boy's own account he had no family left; he was totally alone. As a man with close family ties of his own, James could empathise with the lad's utter grief. If he could be persuaded, there was no reason why he should not join the Regiment as a drummer boy; he seemed to be old enough, and the Regiment had recently lost one of theirs in a tavern brawl. However, James knew that many Irish were antagonistic towards the British Army and the lad may resist the idea. But there again, James argued with himself, he had little to be grateful to Ireland either, having met with hostility from some of his own countrymen. But the lad would have to decide for himself. The immediate problem was to get him to the barracks and feed him back to full strength; James was determined on that. With this decision made, he drifted off to sleep, more at peace with himself than he had been for many a month!

Early next morning the unlikely pair set off for Dublin, having shared a meagre breakfast of very stale bread and scraps of cheese that was all that remained in James' budget. Though Sean had been used to tramping the miles between Dublin and Clonarty, the events of the previous day seemed to have drained him of his strength, and James had to half carry him for most of the way. The boy tried to remonstrate feebly protesting that it 'was not right' for an English Officer to be carrying such as himself, but James just ignored him and simply strode out as briskly as he could.

In spite of frequent rests, they arrived at the outskirts of Dublin by mid-morning, and shortly afterwards found themselves at the barrack gates. The sentries on duty, seeing the disheveled pair, were inclined to refuse them entry. But after a blistering delivery of cultured English, the sentries drew themselves to attention and looked extremely uncomfortable, but James then took pity on them and commended them for their vigilance before passing through. He led the way to a block housing his own A Company, for he knew there would be a vacant cot, caused by the recent loss of their drummer boy. Sean was too tired to take in his surroundings, but meekly followed the Captain who seemed determined to take control of his life. Presently they found themselves in a long, low room that seemed to be crowded with half dressed soldiers occupied with various activities; polishing buckles and boots, playing cards, lounging on cots. At one end of the room appeared to be a large cooking pot, surrounded, surprisingly, by a gaggle of women who bickered together in shrill voices.

James stopped by the cot nearest the door and deposited Sean on it. The boy felt enormously weary and closed his eyes, too weary even to listen to the conversation going on over his head, even though it concerned him directly. James had summoned a Corporal to the cot, and Sean heard words in vague snatches as he drifted in and out of consciousness,

'Sleep for hours.....feed him when he wakes.....to me for further orders...' The voices faded away and Sean slept deeply and dreamlessly.

James left his protégée there and made his way to his own quarters. He needed to see his friends as quickly as possible, but first he needed to change into his uniform before he was spotted by a senior officer. He found his groom unpacking the portmanteau he had taken to the hostelry where he had supposedly spent his leave, so he could only guess that his friends had returned and had brought his baggage with them. His servant, Briggs, was clearly relieved to see him, but was inclined to grumble in usual garrulous fashion,

'Looking all over they've bin, yer friends. Said to get this unpacked for you. Major Williams sent for you an hour or so back.' He continued to grumble until James latched on to the one piece of important information,

'What did Major Williams want?'

'Don't know, Sir, just wished to be informed when you returned. Shall I send a message?'

'No. I'll do it myself. God, this jacket needs pressing!'

'Sorry Sir, the bag only arrived an hour ago, an' I've not had time....'

'It's alright Briggs, I'm not blaming you. There's no time now; it will have to do.'

Fastening the gold frogs across his chest, and tugging his jacket down, James set off for the Mess. He needed to see Robert and Edward to find out what they had said already, before facing his superiors. He found his friends moodily quaffing claret. They looked extremely relieved to see him and prophesised all sorts of disasters. Edward told him,

'The order went out two days after you left. All leave cancelled; we're due to ship out in under a week. There is some sort of trouble brewing in India and they need reinforcements for Johnny Company,' rather irreverently referring to the soldiers of the Honourable East India Company, 'we delayed as long as we could, hoping you'd be back when you said you would, but we got another message demanding our presence immediately, as the Old Man wanted to address us at dinner. Sorry James, we had to report back!'

'Can't be helped. It is my responsibility. I would've been back but I came across a boy who needed help. I just couldn't leave him or he would have died.' He was about to recount the finding of Sean, when an Officer in the uniform of a Major, with a round face and bristling moustache, strode over to their table.

'Captain Willoughby. What are you doing here drinking when I expressly gave an order for you to report to me on your return?' Standing smartly to attention, James faced the irate Major,

'Sorry Sir. I didn't realise the urgency of the message.' Major Williams spluttered,

'Didn't realise. Didn't realise. You appear to be as stupid as you are insubordinate!'

As the Major had the reputation of having the intelligence of the pig that his features so closely resembled, James was hard put to keep a straight face. He simply stood impassive while the Major railed against him, his friends and finally James again. When the tirade finally petered out, he delivered the coup de grace,

'Report to Colonel Deluce immediately. I have recommended that you be suspended!'

James stood there aghast, his dreams and plans in ruins at his feet. Suspension from the Regiment would mean that he would not embark with the Regiment to India, the posting he had set his heart on. How could he have been so stupid as not to imagine such a punishment? Major Williams then made his departure, muttering about 'young whippersnappers! Think they can do as they please!' James did not wait to discuss the situation with his friends, but hurried back to his quarters to collect his shako, and then made his way to the Colonel's office. There he was made to cool his heels by an aide who told him brusquely that the Colonel would see him at his convenience, and that he had much more important business to attend to than a disobedient Captain. The enforced wait did nothing to calm his agitated nerves, so by the time the Colonel was ready to talk to him, he saw himself returning to Yorkshire in heavy disgrace, never to go campaigning and to the utter disappointment of his father.

Even as he considered this worst case scenario, James just could not regret his decision to tour the countryside, 'they should all go and see,' he muttered to himself.

'Captain Willoughby.' The voice of the aide startled him out of his abstraction, 'the Colonel will see you now.'

A moment later, James stood rigidly to attention in front of the Colonel's desk; shako clamped under one arm, looking every inch a soldier; surely a sight to stir an avuncular eye! But Colonel Deluce was looking far from avuncular, his blue eyes as cold as ice as he gazed steadily at the young officer before him. The silence lengthened into minutes and James began to feel acutely uncomfortable, as a cold sweat broke out under his stiff collar. Finally, the Colonel spoke,

'How d'you expect to command obedience from your men when you do not know the meaning of the word?' The accusation was made quietly, but with deadly effect, as James did have an answer to it. He swallowed hard, finding his throat constricted and dry.

'I had occasion to reprimand you once before about going off on your own, and yet you saw fit to repeat the performance. Do you have an explanation, eh?'

'I..I'm sorry Sir. It is just that I had heard so much about the state of the Irish people that I thought to see for myself before we left.' James thought that honesty had to be only policy, and could only hope that the Colonel would understand if only a little.

'Do you consider your curiosity gives you the right to take yourself off for days on end, in direct opposition to orders? You could have been killed out there, and no-one the wiser.'

James kept silent. There was no answer to the charges; they were absolutely just, and he had known it even as he had left.

'I have been considering what action to take. Major Williams has recommended suspension, and I am bound to say, I deem it to be a fair punishment.'

The room spun round as James heard the dreaded words,

'No,' he thought, 'anything but that; I'll do whatever you say, but please don't suspend me now!' If the anguish on his face moved the Colonel, it was not apparent.

'Unfortunately, I cannot spare you at present. Captain Craig has been taken ill and has requested sick leave. However, I feel that this matter is so serious, that you will carry out extra duties for a period of three months, and after that I will review the situation, and may well extend the period. In the meantime you are confined to barracks, and may not set foot outside until we leave for embarkation. Is that clear?' This last was delivered with such force, that James jumped, but came back instantly with a click of his heels and,

'Yes sir!'

Colonel Deluce continued to regard him steadily so that James wondered if there was more to come. The punishment was fair, and so much more preferable than suspension, though he was not looking forward to extra duties and confinement to the barracks, but the alternative did not bear thinking about. Once again he began to feel extremely uncomfortable under the Colonel's steady gaze, and sweat broke out anew under his collar. Finally, Deluce put him out of his misery, and observed in a mild voice,

'What would I have told your father if you had not returned?'

By now James felt completely demoralised, all trace of bravado long departed, he stammered,

'I'm desperately sorry Sir. I just didn't think….'

'I know. Youth never does. Do you want to tell me what you learned in your travels?'

'Well, I found that things were much, much worse than we have been told. There are whole villages out there full of corpses. It is frightful, Sir.'

'I know,' came the surprising reply, 'I too have taken a look. But unlike you, my boy, I took an escort! Had you not also heard that there is typhus in the district? You could have brought it into the barracks with you; either yourself, or that ragged urchin you returned with.'

This time, James' jaw dropped open in astonishment; did nothing escape the Colonel? And the possibility that he could have introduced a killer disease to his men simply had not occurred to him. This was the worst punishment of all. He would spend the next few days in an agony of suspense as he waited to see if Sean or himself succumbed, and subsequently others.

Watching him closely, the Colonel nodded, apparently satisfied,

'You see, James. We must all accept the consequences of our actions. You have seen too many people since your return to consider isolation now. I suggest you spend the next few days in prayer!'

James left the office with his mind in turmoil. He made his way back to his quarters to put at least some distance between himself and his fellows, though he realised that it was a futile gesture. But later, he remembered that the Colonel had not questioned him further about the 'urchin' or what he intended to do with him, so presumably he entrusted James to behave responsibly towards him. On the subject of typhus, he just didn't know what to do. He did not wish to spread panic among his men by spiriting Sean out in precipitous fashion, and as the Colonel suggested, could only pray that they were both clear of the disease. For himself, a good wash down must help; he felt particularly filthy from his travels anyway. He did not know how the disease was spread, except that somehow rats were involved. He had to hope that he had not gone near enough to any of the bodies he had seen to pick it up. He had to hope; it was all he could do!

Sean opened his eyes slowly to behold an unfamiliar sight, a raftered ceiling. He lay quietly, marshalling his thoughts and trying to remember where he was. He was aware that he was lying on a bed, and the various

sounds around him brought memories flooding back, Of course, he was in an army barracks where he been transported to in extraordinary fashion by Captain Willoughby. The sound of a cough close by brought his eyes to the foot of his cot, and he beheld a figure that looked for all the world like one of the leprechauns of his Grandpa O'Malley's tales. The leprechaun was perched cross-legged on the end of his cot, and looked about his own age. He had a round face with a pointed chin, a shock of brown hair that stood up in an untidy crest. A pair of large ears stood out either side of his head, and his forehead was corrugated with concentration as he gazed at Sean with a pair of brown eyes.

Seeing that Sean was truly awake, the leprechaun's face split into a broad grin that showed gaps in his prominent front teeth. The gap-toothed smile was so infectious that Sean found himself smiling in return, at which the leprechaun broke into rapid speech,

'You've opened yer eyes at last. The Corp'ral said to fetch him as soon as you woke up.' No leprechaun this, speaking as he had in English, but then he jumped off the bed and hurried away, to return even before Sean had time to wonder where he had gone, followed by the Corporal who had witnessed his arrival. The man looked down at Sean with such hostility that he felt extremely uncomfortable. He was not to know that Corporal Dunster thought the world of his Captain, and held Sean directly to blame for the Captain's predicament; that news had spread rapidly through A Company's dormitory some time before! However, the boy's extreme pallor and weakened frame were obvious, even to the Corporal's jaundiced eyes, and he spoke reasonably enough, echoing the leprechaun's words,

'So, you're awake at last. The Captain left orders of you to be fed, and then to go and see him.' With a curt nod, the Corporal turned away. The leprechaun gave Sean a wry grin and hurried after him, returning within a short time with a steaming bowl. The appetizing smell from the bowl made Sean's stomach lurch and he hauled himself up to a sitting position to take it. It was a stew of dubious quality, but to someone who had not eaten properly for a very long time, it was manna from heaven! He ate slowly, every spoonful making his stomach heave, but he managed to keep it down. But very soon he felt sated and handed the half filled bowl back. The leprechaun kept up a non-stop flow of chatter as he watched Sean eat, undeterred by Sean's silence. He spoke English, but of a sort that Sean had never heard before; almost as incomprehensible as the Yorkshire Engineer, Peter Harvey.

'Cor, you don't look as if you've eaten for many a day. I'm Christopher Barnet but everyone calls me Kit. Christopher for the church where I was found as a nipper, and Barnet for the part of London where the church was. Cor, 'ad enough already? Want some bread? Where was I, oh yes. I was an orphan, brought up in a children's 'ome. Couldn't wait to get away so's I took the Queen's shillin'. 'Ad to lie 'bout me age, but they didn't worry too much about that. You finished? Better go an' see the Captin.'

Sean felt overwhelmed by the flood of words, as he dutifully tried to rise. But his head swam, and his legs could scarcely support him, so he sat down again abruptly.

'You alright?' came anxiously from Kit, 'it's prob'ly 'cos you slept so long yesterday and the night an' most of today!'

Sean finally managed to stay upright, and he slowly followed Kit towards the door. The chatter continued unabated as they entered a long corridor and made their way outside.

''Ere, mind yer step. Take me arm 'til yer sure of yer feet. D'you want the latrines, they're down 'ere? No. Well just 'oller when yer do. This 'ere's the parade ground, an' over there's where the stables where the officers keep their 'orses.'

Sean looked about him in wide eyed wonder. The parade ground looked vast, and he could imagine it filled with soldiers marching in time to drums beating and bugles playing, as he had seen them do in the streets of Dublin more than once. In spite of himself, he had found it a stirring sight; a pity the Irish didn't have their own army; he would have joined it in an instant!

The pair entered a building at the far side of the parade ground, but by this time the chatter was going unheard as Sean concentrated on staying upright and keeping up with his guide. His head ached more and more, and in spite of the long sleep, he still felt weary to his bones. But all at once he was jerked out of his reverie when Kit remarked,

'An' 'ere's the schoolroom.' Sean looked at the room, much like all the others they had passed except for a few tables scattered about and some slate lying where they had been left. He spoke for the first time since he had awoken; startling Kit so much that he was silenced for a moment,

'You mean,' asked Sean, breathlessly, 'you can go to school?'

The flow started again,

'So you can speak English? I wasn't sure. The Captin didn't say. Yes, some of the men go to learn their letters. You git extra pay for that. Not for me though, I've got better things to do wiv me time!'

Sean found this beyond his comprehension. How could anyone pass up the chance to learn to read and write, especially if you got extra pay for it! However, there was no time for more as they had reached a door, apparently their destination as Kit tentatively knocked. For the first time he looked apprehensive and he explained to Sean,

'I don't like comin' 'ere where all the officers are. It's like when yer in trouble an' they send for you. Never mind. I'd better wait or Captin Willoughby won't be pleased. 'Es alright is the Captin, 'e's as fair as they come. Not like some, let me tell you.'

The door finally opened and an officer looked at them enquiringly, especially at the ragged Sean. Kit explained his errand and they were ushered into a large room where several officers were working at desks. Kit began to look acutely uncomfortable. Sean was too fascinated by everything he saw to be frightened, but his continuing physical weakness was of concern and he earnestly prayed that he wouldn't disgrace himself by passing out! Finally, Sean was summoned into another, smaller office, while Kit was curtly told to remain where he was. Sean found Captain Willoughby seated behind a large imposing desk, and dressed in his uniform as Sean had first seen him; an imposing figure to the nervous youth. But the smile of welcome he received was friendly enough. James had given much thought as to where he should talk to Sean. He would have preferred an informal chat in his quarters, as he was aware that the grandeur of the surroundings was unsettling to the youth, but he also knew that gossip abounded in the closed society of the barracks, and rumours about his relationship with his 'stray' would very soon circulate! If Sean was to make any sort of success of army life he did not any unpleasantness at its start! But of course, he did not yet know if he would be interested.

'Well Sean. How are you feeling now? I hear you have slept the clock round! Sit yourself down on that stool before you fall down!'

'Yes sir. I feel a bit strange, but it'll pass. I want to thank you. You saved my life. I don't think I would have left Clonarty if you hadn't come by.'

There's no need for thanks, lad. It would have been a waste of a life and I've a feeling you've places to go yet! Have you given any thought to what you'll do now?'

'N...No. I can't go back to Clonarty. There's nothing left for me there. I'll have to find work in Dublin, but there's so many doin' that!'

'Have you thought about joining the army? You won't be the first Irishman to do that, in spite of the rules!'

Sean's eyes opened wide as he considered this novel idea. Ever since his Uncle Tomos had ran off to join the army so many years before, and caused such anguish in the family, he had thought of it as a heinous crime. In spite of the efforts to keep the truth from Daniel O'Malley, he had discovered it and his wrath had been monumental! A very young Sean could remember it to this day, and shuddered at the memory. He realised that James was speaking again,

'I know you haven't much time to thank the British for, but from what you have told me not long since, you haven't had much to thank Ireland for either. But I can't give you long to decide, Sean. We leave Dublin for India in three or four days time, and there is much work to do. If you feel you cannot do this, then I've something else to offer you,' and he told Sean of his plan for the orphaned Irish children and the involvement of the servants, Mr. Baines and Mrs. Markham. Sean's eyes widened again at hearing the names, and he burst in with,

'Why, Mrs. Markham is the lady who took me into the house, you remember, I told you about her?' James nodded. He had suspected that it was so. He promised that Sean could meet her, whatever he decided, but he gently pressed for a decision.

'Think carefully about this Sean. I've not been to India myself, but I have been told that there is money to be made whether you are a private soldier or an officer. In time you could return and mayhap buy some land for yourself.'

'No. That I could never do. We're not allowed you see!' James was momentarily silenced by the bitter tone, indeed he had forgotten that Catholic Irish could not own an inch of their own soil! The Sean surprised him by asking,

'I saw a schoolroom on the way here. Kit, er, Christopher Barnet told me that the men can learn to read and write?'

'That's right. The Government wants to improve the education of the soldiers, so they are invited to join the classes, and they even get a bit of extra pay. But even that doesn't seem to encourage many to come. Why do you ask?'

'I've long wanted to learn. I'm sure it's somethin' that stops us getting on, you see?' James didn't quite see, but it was clear that Sean was more than a little interested in this aspect of a soldier's life.

'Well?' pressed James when Sean had fallen silent for a few moments, 'I must ask you to decide quickly; there is much to do.'

Sean's face cleared of its anguished expression, as he had sought to choose between abandoning his beloved country and joining the army with the lure of learning and of leaving his nightmares behind. He straightened his back, and looking James straight in his eyes,

Yes. I will. You are right. There is nothing for me in Ireland. I will learn to read and write and one day I *will* come back!'

'Well done lad. I'm sure you won't regret it. I'll get you taken back to A Block with Drummer Barnet, and you can sign up tomorrow. The uniform of our last drummer boy will have to fit as there's no time to get another.'

James got up, but paused as Sean asked one last question,

'Is it true that the Irish like me change their names when they join?'

'I don't know lad. I'm sure if you ask around your quarters you'll find one of your own kind who can tell you.'

James shouted for an aide to fetch Kit from where he had been waiting, hopping from one foot to the other in nervousness. James gave his orders,

'Take Sean to the kitchens; there's someone there he wants to meet! Then take him back to A Block and give him the uniform of that drummer boy; what was his name?'

'Benson, Sir,' mumbled Kit, desperate to get away from his exalted surroundings.

'Of course; Benson. Then tomorrow morning, after parade, take him to the Recruiting Office. I will see you both there.'

'Yes sir. Is that all Sir? Can we go Sir?' James smiled at Kit's eagerness and waved them away. The boys made their way to the kitchens, where Sean found the motherly figure of Mrs. Markham, who was inclined to be tearful at the sight of him. Enfolded in a soft bosom, poignantly reminding his of his Grandma O'Malley before the blight, Sean managed to give an account of all that had happened and how he managed to be here in her kitchen. Kit listened to the tale unfold with a look of profound sadness creasing his brow, while Mrs. Markham clucked as each new disaster was revealed. Then she introduced Mr. Baines, reassuring an alarmed Sean that he wasn't the ogre she had made him out to be! Then she fed the boys some of the delectable food that she was preparing for the officers' dinner, and sent them off with strict instructions to come back and see them before the whole garrison departed.

Kit led the way back to their dormitory block, concerned by the increasing pallor of Sean's face. He suggested to Sean that he rest while he would search out the belongings of the late Drummer Benson. Sean did so gratefully, falling asleep within minutes, in spite of the activity around him.

When he awoke, it was evening. And the low room was lit by rush lights and lanterns, that cast surreal shadows to the eyes of the dazed youth. He spotted Kit across the room and waited patiently to catch his new friend's eye, while pondering on the twists of fate that had picked him up from the depths of despair at losing the last of his family, to this place with its promise a future. He was absolutely certain that had it not been for Captain Willoughby, he would have perished as he lay on the cold ground; and a tiny resistant core of him wondered if that wouldn't have been preferable. As it was, he was in an English barracks, surrounded by people who had been taught were his enemies throughout his formative years. But, he argued with himself, it was an English soldier who had helped Pa and been courteous to Mam. It was the same English soldier who had taken the trouble to rescue him and bring him to Dublin and safety, and who was now taking an interest in his future. Well, he had made his decision, good or bad, and leastways he would get to learn to read and write! He was full of confidence in his ability to learn, he had only lacked the opportunity before!

At that moment, Kit came over and took him to the communal cooking pot. He explained to Sean that all of their rations were thrown in together and brewed up by the women gathered around it; the wives or followers of some of the soldiers. When the Regiment left Dublin, Kit confided, they'll have to draw lots as to who will go with them, married or not.

'You'll see,' chuckled Kit, 'there'll be a screeching and wailing then!'

Sean was doled out a share according to his lowly rank, and after supper, Kit showed him the uniform of the drummer boy, Benson as he related what had happened to the unfortunate youth,

Got mixed up in somethin' as he shouldn't. Tried to pick the pocket in a tavern, and the next minute there was chairs and tables flying, and Tim – that was his name – got a knife in his ribs. Never mind, he wasn't wearing his uniform, so's there's no rips!'

Sean blinked at Kit's callousness but soon forgot the hapless Tim as he tried on the outfit. It was far too large for his emaciated frame, but Kit told him kindly that he would soon fill it out. There were white trousers that tucked into black boots,

'Got ter keep'em tidy, or you're for it.'

There was a scarlet jacket, with crossed straps of webbing that glowed with snowy whiteness,

'Pipe clay!' said Kit, succinctly, 'Got ter keep'em white or you're for it.'

Finally, to crown it all, there was a shiny black shako, that settled itself right down over Sean's ears, causing Kit to shriek with laughter,

There's a good reason for 'aving big ears,' he chuckled, dancing up and down with glee. And then,

''Ere,' and he stuffed some rag under the brim to keep it in place. Sean found he was holding his breath, and let it out in a sigh. He was more moved than he cared to admit, but at least it set the seal on his decision to join up; he had never owned such a splendid set of clothes in his life before.

Later that evening, the boys sat among the soldiers as they sucked on clay pipes and they exchanged conversation. Very soon, the low ceilinged room filled with evil smelling smoke, but it did not worry Sean in the least having been raised in a sod cottage which was constantly filled with smoke from the ever burning peat fire. The talk was all about India, of which many had heard stories, but none had visited. They spoke of dark skinned men who were fabulously wealthy, and lissome women who could not wait to throw themselves into the arms of the handsome English soldiers!

After a while, Sean felt his eyelids starting to close; would he ever have enough sleep? He sidled away to his cot, to sleep soundly until the next morning.

He was awoken to the sounds of much activity, and a very loud shout from somewhere near the foot of his bed,

'Get yerselves up, you lazy scum. Get on parade before you feel the kiss o' the lash!' The voice moved away, and Sean cautiously opened an eye. He saw Kit hastily donning his uniform, but when he saw Sean awake, he gave an enormous grin and said,

'Time for parade. Want to come'n see? If you sign on, you'll be out there tomorrow!'

Sean did as he was bid, donning his filthy rags with a sigh of distaste. Even the casual clothes of the soldiers put them to shame. Kit saw the grimace and interpreting it correctly, pointed out a trunk stowed under the bed,

'Look in there. Poor old Tim won't want them anymore!'

Sean opened the trunk, and his eyes widened with delight; there were breeches in serviceable cloth, a shirt and some good shoes. These last were far too large, so Sean regretfully put them back. When he was dressed, with his old rags stuffed under the bed, he hurried out after the scurrying soldiers, only to collide violently with Corporal Dunster who snarled at him to 'mind where he was going.' Sean could not understand the man's animosity, but decided philosophically that there was nothing he could do about it, and he would try and avoid the man whenever possible.

When he reached the parade ground, The Regiment was already lined up ready for inspection. Sean was dazzled by the gleaming ranks of men, and the extra dash cut by the officers in their ornate uniforms. He watched from a discreet vantage point as Colonel Deluce appeared, and escorted by his top ranking officers, inspected the serried ranks. It was a stirring sight, and Sean thoroughly enjoyed the spectacle, thrusting to the back of his mind that he would have to learn all the actions that were necessary. He spotted Kit standing alongside the Troop Sergeant, a drum slung on his left hip, supported by an extra crosswise strap. Sean stared at the drum, for it had just occurred to him that this was something else he have to do!

'Ah well,' he sighed, 'somethin' else to learn.'

Later that morning, Kit took him to the Recruiting Sergeant, where he was met by Captain Willoughby, looking suitably serious,

'Still of like mind Sean?' Sean nodded.

The Sergeant gave him a bible to hold, and told him to repeat the words of the oath after him. Sean swallowed. During the morning, he had wrestled with the problem of a name. Part of him wanted to keep the one he had; he was proud of it, after all. But another part of him wanted a clean break with Ireland and all the heartbreak he would ever associate with the place,

'I, Joseph Harrington......' James looked startled. What a strange choice; he had assumed that Sean would simply take the dead drummer boy's identity. But he did remember the engineer that Sean had so admired, so perhaps there was sense in it after all; though that acquaintance had ended with his father's death!

When the oath was done, Sean was instructed to make his mark to indicate that he had signed on, and then he symbolically received a shilling; the 'Queen's Shilling', that bound him for a period of many years to the service of the Queen of England.

Three days later, Sean and Kit leaned over the side of the ship that was to carry them, first to England and then on to India, and would sever Sean; no Joe from Ireland for an indefinite period. The three days had passed in a blur of activity, as the Regiment prepared for departure. Sean...Joe.... (when would he get used to his new name?) found that his stamina had improved with regular eating, and the slow recession of shock at the loss of Kate and Kevin. There had been so much to do and learn, that there had been no time left for mourning. With Kit's guidance, he had played a few tentative raps on his drum, but soon realised he had a lot to learn. Then there were all the commands to respond to on parade, and the discovery that he had two left feet when it came to marching, though the oversized boots did not help.

Corporal Dunster had not made things easier for him either, as he seemed determined to pick on every mistake that inevitably a new recruit would make. Kit tried to help as much as he could, but he could not explain the man's hostility any more than Sean...Joe could. But it was the only sour note in three days of wonder and magic, as everything was new and exciting.

But then it was time for parting. He had sneaked into the kitchens to bid a fond farewell to Mrs. Markham, who had warned to be careful of 'those heathen, dark skinned people and to return to with his pockets bulging with jewels!'

At last it was time to board. He was determined not to look back, but the compulsion was just too strong, and so here he was, hanging over the rail with Kit, as the sailors ran about preparing for departure; running up and down rigging, sure footed as cats. The ship began to edge away from the quay, and Sean felt his eyes fill with tears, which he angrily brushed away. Kit was hopping from one foot to another, as he did when he was excited or nervous. Soon they were out in Dublin Bay. He could see the city rising out of the early morning mist, and mountains beyond the city looked blue and purple, let by a rim of sum showing from the east; enough to lighten the city but not to show the squalor. The heartbreaking beauty of it all caught at Sean's throat; he had never seen Dublin or Ireland quite like that before. How could he bear to leave it?

'I will return; I will; I will,' he vowed with clenched fists. Overhead, seagulls screamed mockingly, the sound beating about his ears,

'Sean O'Hara's dead; Joe Harrington lives; Sean O'Hara's dead; Joe Harrington lives,' the birds mocked.

...... and Monsoons

The Ballad Of East And West

Oh, East is East, and West is West,
and never the twain shall meet,
Till Earth and Sky stand presently at God's great Judgment Seat;
But there is neither East nor West,
Border, nor Breed, nor Birth,
When two strong men stand face to face,
tho' they come from the ends of the earth!

Rudyard Kipling (1865–1936)

Chapter 1

'Joe; hey Joe.' The voice demanded attention and the born again Joseph Harrington blinked his eyes to focus them. It was Kit shouting to him to 'come an' see this', we're 'ere, we really are.' Joe crossed the gently heaving deck of Her Majesty's transport ship, Gloriana, to join his friend at the ship's rail, where he was gazing earnestly into the distance, his forehead corrugated with concentration. Joe followed his gaze and saw, low down on the horizon, a purple line between the bright blue of the sky and the darker blue of the sea. As he watched, the purple haze took on a form and solidity until Joe could see that it was, indeed, land. The boys took hold of each other's arms and jumped up shouting,

'Land…land…..India at last!'

Other soldiers lounging on the deck and sailors going about their duties, smiled indulgently at the boys for they were lively and popular youngsters, and furthermore they reflected everyone's feeling of excitement after so many tedious weeks at sea; India at last.

The weeks since their departure from Ireland had been filled to capacity with new experiences for Joe. The early days had found him coming to terms with his new name and learning to respond to it. The adoption of the new name had not been as easy as he had thought, and many an order from an irate NCO had gone unheeded, and he had despaired of ever answering to it automatically. Sometimes, he wished he had never embarked on such a course, and had kept his own name, as others clearly seemed to have done.

But in the quiet moments in the middle of the night, when he found it difficult to sleep, the answer came clearly enough.

As Sean O'Hara, he could not have joined the British Army even to save his life. It would have been a betrayal of his father, grandfathers and generations of O'Hara's and O'Malley's before them. He had been weaned on tales of British injustice, and the intolerable burden of having their country trampled on by foreigners, a humiliation difficult to bear. To add insult to injury, they had been forced to pay rent for their land, otherwise face eviction, by agents such as O'Leary and his thugs; so they paid, but grudgingly. Better to have perished outside the sod cottage close to his mother and brother than to perpetrate such an act of betrayal.

But as the Englishman, Joseph Harrington, he could take what the British Army had to offer, learn from it, use it, and some day return to resurrect the lost Sean O'Hara and plant him back in his Irish soil to grow anew. So he rationalized his action, and found that he could live with it. Indeed, there many Irish soldiers in A company who were not so particular and simply dropped the O or the Mac to become Connell or Kelly!

So Joseph Harrington determined to learn as much as he could from these people he found himself among, and his appetite for learning was insatiable. Even the indefatigable and irrepressible Kit found himself exhausted by the barrage of questions and was forced to protest,

'Leave it out, Joe; you've fair worn me out! Go ask someone else.'

So he did. Any and everyone found themselves the subject of interrogation, but he was a likeable enough youngster, and on the whole it was taken in good spirits. Joe soon discovered who best to avoid, like the surly Corporal Dunster, but the rest would recount their favourite anecdotes while puffing solemnly on their clay pipes.

The first hurdle for Joe was to improve his grasp of the English language, but luckily he was a natural learner with youth on his side. But another problem was, which version of it should he copy? It seemed that there were as many ways of speaking English as there were men speaking it. There was Kit who came from the slums of the East End of London that Joe had found almost incomprehensible at first. Then there men from all over England, from the slow speech of the West Countrymen contrasting with those from the north like the Engineer, Peter Harvey. And the Irish soldiers all spoke English with a lilt that unmistakably proclaimed their origins, and these, Joe was determined not to copy. And finally there were the officers, and Joe soon realised that it was their speech as much as anything that set them apart from the rank and file, but even with them there were differences; some spoke with a slow drawl while others favoured a clipped mode of speech.

Joe listened to them all, and came to the conclusion that if he was to succeed as an Englishman, he would have to adopt the speech of the officers. But to survive, he must adopt the speech of those around him. So he set himself the task of learning English twice over. Among the soldiers he developed an accent that was an amalgamation that borrowed elements from all he listened to, except the Irish. Then in private, he practiced the speech of any officers he came across. He would often be seen muttering to himself at quiet a moment, which was put down to his Irish background, as they were known to be 'odd people'!

For the rest, Kit was his mentor for all procedures necessary to survive as a drummer boy in the British Army. His uniform had to be taken care of and donned in correct fashion, otherwise, as Kit had predicted, he was 'for it!' Then there were the drum beat patterns to master, advance, retreat and many more; his head reeled with them all. Then there was the Army hierarchy to learn, and he was warned that it was almost a hanging offence to address a Major as Captain, or a Sergeant as Corporal! But he soon discovered for himself that drummer boys were at the very bottom of the heap and were expected to run errands for absolutely everyone else, including the female followers, who would complain to their protectors if the boys refused to do their bidding.

He also learned that A Company, in which he had been placed, was one of four companies, and together they made up a Regiment of close on seven hundred men. Above the drummer boys were the privates, the 'the scum of the earth' as Wellington had once described them, the dregs of society. Many of them were ex-felons, and many more were Irish. Then came the Corporals and Sergeants who had gained their position by promotion and used it to make life hell for those beneath them. Finally came the commissioned officers, but about these, Kit was a bit vague, as he was not at all sure how they had come to reach their exalted positions, but clearly they were of a class above the men they commanded. Joe was intrigued to note that many junior officers looked as young as himself, and certainly younger than the men they commanded. The mystery was finally solved by an old soldier, Private Kershaw, who had taken a liking to the new recruit, and did his best to protect him from the worst of the bullies.

He explained that these officers were all from the monied and aristocratic classes who had all bought their commissions. So their rank had little to do with their abilities at soldiering, and was more to do with their families. Kershaw went on to explain that it was a tradition that younger sons were dispatched to the army to earn themselves a bit of glory, as they could not hope to inherit the family estates. Of Colonel Deluce, neither Kit nor Private Kershaw could tell Joe much, as they seemed to put him on a level with God. They only saw him on morning parade, and were not anxious to be summoned to his presence as it meant that they were to be disciplined!

Joe's education continued against a background of the removal of the Regiment from Ireland and their transport to India, via a brief sojourn in England. After Joe had taken his emotional farewell to Ireland and his Sean O'Hara persona, the transport ship had covered the short crossing to Liverpool, where it had made a brief landing. As they approached the port, Joe asked Kit if it was London, a question that was greeted with great mirth by Kit,

'You're so funny Joe. This ain't but a small place compared to London,' he said with the natural pride of a cockney for his birthplace!

A few of the officers disembarked with the intention of spending some long awaited leave with their families before the longer mission to India began, and many of them hailed from estates in the North of England. Their numbers did not include Captain Willoughby, still in heavy disgrace and confined to ship in lieu of barracks. Colonel Deluce relented enough to allow him to dispatch a letter to his parents asking if they could join him in London before final embarkation. James did not chafe at the restrictions to his liberty, knowing the punishment to be fair. He had been badly frightened by the thought of bringing typhus into the barracks, and while his fears had been unfounded, he still suffered pangs of conscience over it.

Only in the matter of Sean, now Joe, could he feel vindicated, and also in his plan to adopt some orphans. He now kept a distance from Joe for in such a close community, tongues would soon wag, but from a distance saw the friendship that had sprung up between him and Kit. He knew that the more experienced drummer boy would steer Joe in the right direction, and help him over the difficult period of adjustment to Army life in the rabble in which they were placed.

Within two days, the ship set sail again for London, where the Regiment would transfer to larger ships for the longer voyage. Joe was able to see the coastline of England as they beat their way south. The weather was fair as it was well into April, and there was freshness about the countryside that brought a yearning for his native land, and an itch to be digging the earth ready for plating potatoes. He ruthlessly suppressed such longings and turned his back on the land.

There were a few anxious hours as the transport rounded the southeastern tip of England where a lighthouse gave warning of dangerous rocks, but then they began to make their way up the channel at a spanking pace, driven forward by a brisk westerly wind. On past Plymouth, the Isle of Wight and then the deadly Goodwin Sands the ship sailed serenely, while sailors gave dire warning of ships being caught fast and sucked down to their doom in the shifting sand banks. Escaping such a fate they sailed on past the white cliffs of Dover and into the Thames Estuary, and finally berthed in the Port of London.

The entire Regiment disembarked and marched in good order to a nearby barracks, in spite of feeling a little shaky on their legs after their time at sea. Once settled, most of the officers and men were given three weeks leave to visit their families or visit the local taverns! The few who remained on duty were those who had nowhere particular to go, and of course, Captain Willoughby. The Colonel also stayed in the barracks, as the Army and the Regiment were his life, and he had long since lost touch with his family from the estate that marched alongside Bensham Manor.

Kit asked Joe if he would like to spend his leave with him, as he planned to go visiting 'Ma Baker'.

'But I thought you were an orphan?' asked Joe, perplexed.

'Well I am. But Ma Baker was the cook at the foundling 'ome, an' the only one who had any time fer me. Then she left 'n married an old soldier who was goin' ter take over a 'ostelry in Clerkenwell. It was after she left that I ran away, but I know she'll be pleased to see me!' he said with true Cockney optimism.

'Yes, but she doesn't know me.'

'Any friend of mine'll be welcome,' replied Kit, loftily, and would brook no further argument.

Joe went with him but with a lot of apprehension. Only the thought of spending the next three weeks in the almost deserted barrack amongst the few soldiers left, most of whom he didn't know had made him agree to the venture. He need not have worried. Ma Baker was a buxom woman who put him in mind of his Grandma and Mrs. Markham, and as the boys walked into the Spotted Cow she gave a shriek of delight, abandoning a customer as she bustled over to them. She enfolded Kit in a fulsome embrace. Kit almost disappearing into her apron front, from whence Joe could hear muffled sounds,

''Ere, put me down, I want you to meet someone.'

He was finally released from a tearful Ma and Joe was introduced as 'me bestest friend and another orphan'. And so Joe was also enfolded to her ample bosom. Called to order by her irate customer, she told the boys to go through to the back where they would find her husband stowing some barrels.

'See, told you, didn't I?' Joe had to admit that the welcome was every bit as genuine as Kit had predicted and he felt easier in his mind about tagging along with Kit. The boys soon ran Barney to ground in the bowels of the inn's cellars where he was sorting out barrels of ale. Joe took an instant liking to the man, and was intrigued to see him hopping about with one leg replaced by a wooden stump. The handicap in no way seemed to bother him as he deftly managed the heavy barrels with an ease that would have shamed many an able bodied man! It was some days before Joe plucked up the courage to ask what had happened to his leg, and was told that it had been lost at the Battle of Waterloo some thirty years before. Though he knew nothing of this apparently famous battle he listened avidly to the tale, though horrified at the aftermath,

'It was like this Joe. We was defending this bit of a hill when we saw the French Dragoons lining up to charge. It was a fearsome sight, let me tell you; big 'orses they were, 'n big men too. They looked fifteen foot tall. An' they had sabres; deadly they were; take yer 'ead off if yer weren't careful. Well, we 'eard the order shouted; I s'pose it were 'charge' in Frenchie, then they came at us. We stood firm tho', Joe. Steady we were; then the order came to 'take aim'. We waited an' waited, an' still they came; you could almost count the 'airs on the 'orses manes; towering over us they were. At last we got the order to 'fire'; our muskets sang then let me tell you. My shot hit an 'orse right in front of me 'n down it went. Trouble is, it landed on me an' rolled about a bit I was knocked out then by a hoof, an' knew no more of the battle. When I woke up it was all over, an' they were searching fer wounded; nearly passed me by, they did, lyin' under the 'orse, but I managed to croak out loud enough to be 'eard. They took me to the 'ospital tents an' that's when me trouble started. This leg,' tapping the wooden one, 'was all smashed up, so they decided to cut it off. So they did, without as much as a by your leave! A tot of rum was all they gave me, an' then sawed it orf!' Barney fell silent for a moment, lost in the memory at the agony of amputation. Joe was equally silent, appalled at the very thought of it, and uncomfortably aware that such a fate might him one day!

'Well, I near died soon after. Shock, they called it. But I didn't. Then the wound went bad an' I near died again. But I didn't. Then they put me on a cart and took me to Ostend then 'ome. All that lurchin' about, I near died again, but….'

'But you didn't,' chorused the boys as Kit had arrived half way through the telling. Barney was taken aback, and was inclined to be peevish, but the boys begged him to finish the tale,

'Yes, well. Then they chucked my art the army. Unfit fer dooty, they said. Me! Gave me leg for Queen and country an' that's all the thanks I get!'

'And then what happened,' breathed the boys, as Barney lapsed into a disgruntled silence,

'I came 'ere, didn't I? Me brother owned this place. 'E took me in, God bless 'im. 'Ad this leg made an' he 'elped me learn the trade, then 'e went an' snuffed it! Left me the inn an' everythin'. Well I met me Agnes; that's yer Ma Baker, Kit, an' we got 'itched, but no thanks to 'eh Majesty's army let me tell you!'

'No,' thought Joe, 'I wonder if they treat all their wounded like that?'

The boys thoroughly enjoyed their three weeks leave, roaming the streets of London all day. Though well used to the noise and crowds of Dublin, Joe was amazed at the size and bustle of London. Kit showed him the church of St. Christopher where he had been abandoned as a baby; St. Paul's Cathedral where they enjoyed whispering messages to each other in the gallery; and finally Buckingham Palace. They were fortunate enough to see the Queen ride out in her carriage, accompanied by her husband and Consort, Prince Albert. Joe looked at the dumpy figure of the woman who held such power in her diminutive hands and could not help but exclaim,

'But… she looks so ordinary!'

Kit also took Joe to slum areas where he could see that the contrast between rich and poor was every bit as wide as his own country. Rows upon rows of tenements were filled with emaciated men, women and children. Many of the women held a baby to their withered breasts, while with their other hand they drank deeply from a bottle whose contents Kit described as 'Mothers' Ruin'. Joe supposed that it was something like poteen when he saw the effect that it had on these poor women.

In other, smart streets, he saw ragged waifs ready to sweep a road clean for a lady or gentleman to cross without soiling their elegant crinolines or pantaloons,

'D'you think there are rich and poor in India too?' he asked Kit.

'Dunno, but I 'spect so. They seems to be wherever you go, eh Joe.' He solemnly agreed.

In the evening, they returned to the inn and to Ma Baker's wonderful food. She had taken one look at Joe's emaciated form and decided that he needed 'feeding up' before he left. She set about the job with much gusto so that Joe would rise from the table feeling bloated, sure that his stomach must be visibly swollen. By the end of the three weeks he felt much better than he had since the first harvest failed. The prominent bones of his face began to soften and his limbs took on a rounded appearance; less like the sticks they had resembled for so long. But best of all, he no longer suffered from fits of weakness that had dogged him since his collapse. He was now able to spend his days running the streets with Kit and sit up half the night listening to Barney recount anecdotes of his army days, so many years before,

'Seeing you boys in uniform brings it all back,' he said nostalgically, 'you'd think it was yesterday 'stead of thirty years back!'

But then it was time to return to barracks. The boys took a fond farewell of Barney and Agnes, who would always be Ma Baker to them. They could not know how many years would elapse before they saw each other again, and tears were shed on all sides. Ma enfolded them in her expansive embrace and besought them to take care. Barney shook them by the hand and admonished them to be good soldiers and not fail their country,

'In spite of what it's done to him!' thought Joe angrily to himself.

James Willoughby had spent the leave in much quieter fashion in the barracks as duty officer for the entire three weeks. Colonel Deluce had come close to relenting on more than one occasion, but on reflection had decided that James needed to learn the hard way what obedience really meant! Moreover, he knew that the letters sent to Bensham Manor from Liverpool had had the hoped for results, and James' parents had arrived two days after the Regiment and were comfortably installed in a hotel for the rest of the leave period.

Charles Willoughby met his old friend and erstwhile comrade in arms for a private meal. The two men partook of a generous dinner, talking in desultory fashion of the politics of the day until the servants had removed the remains of the last course and had left them with a full bottle of port and some fine cigars.

'Well,' said Charles, drawing on his cigar and emitting a cloud of fragrant smoke, 'what is this escapade that James indulged in, and please don't spare me the details?'

'Don't get agitated, my old friend. It is a matter of discipline above all else. That boy of yours has some fine qualities; no doubt of his parentage, what!' But he is wont to think that he knows better than those more experienced than himself, and acts impulsively.'

Gerald went on to relate how James had decided to roam the Irish countryside, in spite of strict orders forbidding it, 'alone, damn me' with gangs of desperate men and raging typhus abroad.

'My blood ran cold, let me tell you, when I heard that he had gone. He also involved two others in the plot, though they didn't go with him; I might have been less worried if they had!'

'I see,' returned Charles thoughtfully, 'he was ever one for seeing for himself. I doubt if you'll ever cure him of that. We can only hope that the punishment at least makes him stop and think next time! I'll have a word with the boy while I'm here.'

The two men spent the rest of their evening reminiscing about their escapades in the Peninsular Wars, and their last great battle together, Waterloo. Charles sighed lustily,

'You're a lucky devil, Gerald. If my brother hadn't died…..'

'Yes, but you wouldn't have a fine son to follow in your footsteps. And I have to admit that it's been deuced dull soldiering since Boney was tucked away!'

Charles then spent another evening dining, this time with his son in his Officer's Mess. He noted the planes of James' face had a new maturity to them since he had sailed for Ireland. Over the customary port and cigars, Charles listed to James' own version of the events leading to his confinement,

'It knew it was wrong, Sir, but we had been there all those weeks and we still did not know the full truth of the matter. There were those that said that the Irish had brought it all on themselves, and that they were a shiftless lot. If only they had been prepared to work harder, then they would have been able to feed their families without coming cap in hand expecting the Government to do it. Well it wasn't a bit like that. Those villages, emaciated children, burnt out cottages; it was ghastly, absolutely ghastly! When I came across that lad, Sean, his whole family and the village had been wiped out. Yet when I met him the year before, he was obviously an intelligent lad, capable of hard work and more than willing to do it. I can't say that I regret my actions, though I must confess that I didn't pay enough attention to the threat of typhus at the time.'

'Don't let the Colonel hear you say that, he thinks you've learned your lesson! Well James, are you looking forward to India?'

'I can't tell you! We should be able to do some real soldiering at last. I hear that some of those hill men are ferocious opponents.' Charles smiled at his son's exuberance,

'It's thought in some quarters that it isn't quite the thing to serve time in India, y'know. I could arrange a transfer for you.' James looked utterly appalled,

You can't mean it Sir; I've waited so long for this chance!'

'I'd a mind to mention it, but wanted to hear what you had to say. Fact is, my boy, your mother and I might see something of you out there! Your mother's sister, Esme, married a planter, and they're settled out there. Owns a parcel of land somewhere near Lucknow; calls himself a 'Zemindar'. Well, they've been inviting us for an extended stay for many a year, but I have always been too busy with the estate. But now that your brother is due to marry that little dab of a thing…'

James smiled at the memory of a tiny hand and a firm handshake, '… during the summer. Pity you won't be at the wedding, but it couldn't be arranged in time. He'll take over the estate; almost runs it now, don't you know, …'

James waited for the added,

'….if only he wasn't such a damned dull dog,' and smiled when it duly came.

'Well, your mother and I will set off when they're established; I've no mind to kick my heels around the place and get underfoot. Between you and me, James, I'll be glad to get rid of it all. I envy you your life of soldiering!'

'Yes, but you'd seen some action by the time you were my age; and you were at Waterloo!' returned James, wistfully. His father chuckled,

'It seems we're never satisfied, eh?'

Father and son then fell to discussing the arrangements for the transfer of Irish orphans to the estate, which was apparently well in hand,

'They should be arriving soon after you leave, James. Gerald is willing to see to it all, though I've a mind that it's that fiancée of his that's the prime mover.' Remembering the young lady's parting shot to him so many months before, James was inclined to agree. He was also silently acknowledged that it was probably her words that had inspired his expedition to the countryside!

Next day, James was able to entertain his mother to tea, while his father took a nostalgic tour of the barracks, escorted by Gerald Deluce. James was shocked to see his mother's face looked wan and drawn, and she had clearly lost a lot of weight. He waited until she had finished pecking at her food for a while, and then asked quietly,

'Are you quite the thing, Mama? You don't look as robust as I remember?'

Lettice's eyes flew up to meet her son's, and she coloured,

'I'd forgotten how long it has been since you left for Ireland,' she replied inconsequently, 'your father's not noticed as he sees me every day. You are not to say anything to him; he just lives for the day when we set off for India ourselves.'

'But you are not well enough!' protested James,

'A sea voyage is just what I need, you'll see. Anyway, I'd rather travel than sit at home waiting…'

'What's wrong, Mama? D'you know?'

'I've seen a physician. There is a lump here,' and she pressed her hand to her left breast, 'there's nothing to be done. I hope I will see my sister, it has been so long since we said goodbye. But I'm in God's hands. You won't tell your father, promise me James?'

He looked at her in anguish, but taking his face between her hands, she gazed fondly into his eyes,

'I've been lucky, you know. Your father has been a good husband; better than many I could mention. And you and Gerald and the girls have been my especial joy. Now you are all able to take care of yourselves; the girls are married and Gerald about to be and you are off with the Regiment. None of you need me anymore, except Charles. So you see…?' And James did. They finished their tea together, and James knew that they would not speak of it again.

The leave period passed, and the soldiers began to return to barracks to prepare for the long voyage. The great barrack rooms buzzed with noise as the female followers squabbled over their cooking pots and laundry sinks. Soon they would have to draw lots, for very few of these women would be able to go with their protectors. Many arguments broke out, as long term 'wives' claimed that they had a prior claim over the newer arrivals. It would not matter though, for when the time came, the ballot was strictly controlled by an officer, and there would be no appeal.

At last the day of departure dawned and they were all roused soon after sunrise, and lined up in the parade ground ready for inspection.

In spite of himself Joe was stirred by the sight of the massed ranks of men, resplendent in their scarlet jackets with gold frogging, pristine white breeches and high, black boots. The jackets were crossed with pipe-clayed webbing to match the equally white belts, and the uniforms were crowned by shakoes of glossy black, with a cockade set at a jaunty angle, held firm by a strap passing under their chins. Wonderful to behold, but how would it be in battle, thought Joe irreverently. The Colonel appeared to take the inspection, passing up and down the serried ranks, his uniform outshining them all in its quantities of gold braid and plumed shako.

With inspection over, the ranks of soldiers led off, their rhythm beaten out by the drummer boys preceding each squad. Joe marched alongside Kit in his inherited uniform, the overlarge boots more comfortable stuffed with rags, and the jacket noticeably better filled by Ma Baker's cooking! His drum was silent, though, as he had not yet mastered the technique, something he would have to do during the long voyage.

Through the streets of London they marched, heading for the docks, with ragged urchins running alongside and shouting insults and obscenities at them. Here and there, a woman not selected by ballot trailed a hapless soldier, weeping and wailing for him not to abandon her as she was surely with child. As they approached the docks, they could see well wishers waiting to see them off, especially families of the officers.

James had taken a private farewell of his parents the night before, and had begged them not to come to see him off. He had hugged his mother closely, and looked into her face long and hard, for he knew like as not, he would not see her again, and it tore him apart. Then he embraced his father warmly. Quietly, his father spoke,

'Don't worry my boy. I'll take good care of her. This is the best way!' And James knew that it was no secret after all, and felt easier in his mind. With many instructions to 'take care' and promises to see each other in India, they parted. But now, the Willoughby's were at the docks, placed so that James would not notice them, but they would be able to catch a last glimpse of their handsome son.

Joe and Kit had no-one to see them off and were eager to board the ship. As soon as possible they did so, and were directed to stow their belongings below. Surveying the gloomy hold where all the soldiers would be crammed during the voyage, the boys pledged to spend as little time below as possible. Finding a dark corner to deposit their meagre possessions and their drum kits, they ran back up on deck. All was bustle and confusion and noise, with sailors swearing at soldiers for getting under their feet, and officers trying to chivvy the men below. The boys watched the sailors in fascination,

'Cor, Joe. See that?' as two barefoot seamen raced up the rigging and inched their way along a boom many feet above their heads,

'D'you think they'd let us do that?' asked Joe. Kit shook his head dubiously, not at all taken with the idea.

Within a remarkably short space of time, the ship was ready to sail. Soldiers kept bobbing their heads up on deck 'to take a last look' and sent below again by harassed officers. Shouts of 'cast off forrard' and 'cast off aft' followed in quick succession, and the ship inched away from the quayside. The boys had managed to escape the eagle eye of their Sergeant, and wedged themselves by the rail where they could get a good view of the quay. The crowd gathered close to the dockside to wave them away, handkerchiefs fluttering white in the morning sun, abandoned wives still pleading as the width of water between dock and ship widened. At the last moment, James spotted his parents waving, and had to stare very hard to prevent tears forming. Kit was strangely silent, his natural ebullience quelled by the thought of the years that would pass before he saw England again. Joe too was silent. He felt no sadness for this was not his land; he had already made his farewells; but plans for the future raced through his head, and the long weeks of the voyage would give him all the time he needed to learn!

The ship made its way out of the Thames Estuary and began the haul along the English Channel, heading westward and tacking against a brisk southwesterly wind. As the Channel widened, they lost sight of land and inched nearer the French coast, bound for the Bay of Biscay where they would have the chance to try out their sea legs, and then on down the Iberian Peninsula, finally heading for the southernmost tip of Africa.

The soldiers crammed into the large holds which rapidly became foetid with human ordure. Most were inured to living in close proximity with unwashed humanity, but preferred to spend as much time as possible in deck, away from the gloomy interior. On a ship as crowded with men as this one, there was little opportunity for free movement, and the sailors resented the soldiers, a feeling born of an age old rivalry between the two services.

In order to preserve the peace as much as possible, the naval and army officers established a routine for their men. Every morning the soldiers were ordered up on deck for drill and inspection, but in small numbers due to the restricted space. They were made to exercise in various fashions by the officer of the day, or they had bouts of boxing or wrestling, all of which fulfilled the purpose of using up as much of their energy as possible in the forlorn hope of preventing outbreaks of violence below.

After breaking their fast, the men would turn to other activities, or simply pass the time in gambling, which was strictly forbidden, or merely whiling away the hours on their bunks.

Joe found the days filled with continuous excitement. Every morning he spent time with Kit, learning the various drum beats, discovering in himself a natural sense of rhythm. When the voyage was well underway, and to Joe's delight, he was able to attend classes held in a small enclosed area of the deck, where at last he was able to learn to read and write. These classes were his especial joy, and again he discovered a natural aptitude to learning. The other soldiers in the group, while happy to receive the small addition to their pay, had little interest or aptitude, but at least they did not hold Joe back as they simply spent the time dozing! Kit declined to join Joe in class insisting that he wasn't in the least bit interest, an attitude Joe found difficult to understand.

The tutor was Sergeant Adam Swales, a gentle man who seemed totally out of place in the world of rough and brutal soldiery. Certainly he was no adept at keeping disciple and only held his rank in deference to his education and ability to teach. He had been born to a West Country parson and the daughter of a minor landowner, who had promptly disowned her after the wedding. They were much in love, a state that would endure throughout their married life, and they raised a large brood of children with boundless affection but little else. The parson educated them all, boys and girls alike, to a high standard, and then sent them out into the world to earn for themselves the living that he could not provide. Adam Swales, the third of six sons, discovered in himself the strong desire to pass on his education to those less fortunate than himself, and was delighted when he secured a post at a village school not twenty miles from his home town of Dorchester. The school had been set up by a local squire who demanded that all his tenants' children should attend every day except at harvest time.

Adam arrived to find a small wood and stone building that housed the schoolroom, a living room, and very little else. Sighing for the loss of the shabby but cosy home he had left, he tried with the aid of a local village girl, to make it into a home for himself. After a few months, Adam was forced to admit that teaching those unwilling to learn was a frustrating task, and if it had not been for one or two brighter sparks among his brood, he would have admitted defeat and gone elsewhere.

Sadly for Adam, his peaceful existence was not fated to last. The squire's daughter, an exquisite blond of some seventeen years, arrived home in disgrace from her first season in London. She had taken society by storm with her violet eyes and trim figure, and could have had her pick of a dozen eligible bachelors, including more than one with a title, much to her mother's delight! But the minx discovered in herself a penchant for young and handsome army officers, particularly of the cavalry regiments, with their dashing mess uniforms. She fell in love with a Captain with dark brown eyes and an elegant moustache, and the affair blossomed to the point of elopement. Just in time, her frightened maid disclosed the dreadful truth to a thoroughly alarmed aunt and chaperone, who packed her off back to her father to cool her ardour in the somnolence of the Dorset countryside.

After brooding on the injustices of the world of her elders, the young lady, Penelope, took to riding round the countryside on her glossy chestnut; a dashing figure in a riding habit styled on the uniform of her favourite cavalry regiment. Her sharp eyes soon noticed Adam as he strolled along the lanes of the estate. His looks were romantic enough for the most discerning of maidens, with melting brown eyes and Byronic black curls tumbling over his forehead. Penelope reined in the chestnut, and spoke to him,

'Who are you? You weren't here when I left for London,' she enquired in her low, sweet voice. Adam looked up and was lost in a sea of violet eyes and riotous blond curls. Stammering, he tried to explain that he had not long become the village teacher. Within a week of the first meeting, the would-be lovers were keeping trysts in quiet corners of the estate. The squire happened upon them one day as they strolled among a beech copse. He had spotted Penelope's chestnut nearby and surprised them exchanging a gentle kiss. A roar of fury brought the pair to their senses, but Penelope recovered first. Affecting a touching sob, she related how Adam had lured her to the spot had forced the kiss upon her. The enraged squire raised his riding crop and brought it down across Adam's face, raising a weal that would take months to fade, and bade him to be gone from the estate forthwith, or face a flogging. The squire was later to question his decision, having had the opportunity to observe his daughter's behaviour over some weeks, but at the time, there was no reasoning with him.

A sadder and wiser Adam packed his meagre belongings and left the estate, his life in tatters, his love soured in his breast. By dint of trudging and begging lifts from passing carts, he headed towards London, convinced that he would find new employment there. As he drew closer to the city, he came upon a group of soldiers bent on recruitment. They called to him to join them, to fight for Queen and county; so he enlisted.

His advancement was rapid and entirely due to a sharp eyed captain who had spotted him reading a volume of Shakespeare in the barracks, oblivious to the hubbub around him. Aware of the treasure he had in an educated soldier, the Captain promptly promoted him to Sergeant, and put him in charge of teaching the common soldiery.

Adam fared no better with his adult students, their bovine expressions no more rewarding than those of his youthful charges. That is, until he met Joe on board Her Majesty's transport ship, Gloriana. As soon as he saw the alert expression in the lad's big blue eyes, and the frown of concentration on the intelligent forehead, Adam's spirits rose. Within a short space of time, Joe could recite the alphabet, and outline the letters on the slate. The elementary readers were soon devoured and Adam had to search among the crates in the hold to find books to stimulate the budding intellect. Eventually the lessons passed on to other subjects; History, carefully avoiding the subjugation of Ireland, as Adam had soon learned of Joe's background; Geography, tracing their route on the globe Adam had brought with him; and as many others as Adam felt would interest his youthful student. Joe discovered a world that he had never known existed outside the narrow confines of Clonarty, and a relationship started to develop between the tutor and student that was to last a lifetime.

When not involved in lessons of any sort, Kit and Joe roamed the ship. Though the official dictum was to stay below decks and out of the way of the busy sailors, the boys found ways of avoiding discovery from the Corporals and Sergeants. The sailors turned a blind eye to their escapades, and taught them to scamper up the rigging and out along the booms. They showed them how to handle the great billowing sails, and scramble out on the bowsprit until they could perch on the figurehead of the 'Queen in Splendour'.

Apart from a brief spell of stormy weather that taxed the sea legs of all those unused to ships, the weather was set fair for the voyage. One sparkling summer day as the ship was nearing its first stop at Cape Town, Joe was perched up in a crows nest high above the deck of the ship. The crows nest swung back and forth with the movement of the waves far below, and the scurrying figures of the sailors on deck looked like so many ants. Suddenly Joe spotted three porpoises swimming alongside the ship, leaping as they went, their snouts in a permanent smile. Around the porpoises and the ship, the wave tops glittered in the sun, lighting the sea with liquid gold. Beyond the end of the sea, the infinity of blue that was the sky made his eyes ache with the wonder of it all.

Joe felt a thought slip into his mind that so surprised him, he had to hold his breath while he took it in, and examine it carefully. He was happy!

The tragedy that had happened to his family and friends, and so to him, would always be there in a graveyard in a corner of his mind. But since the day that Captain Willoughby had found him close to death outside his cottage, his life had spiraled onwards and upwards. He had lost his father but had gained many mentors, Captain Willoughby, Private Kershaw and now Sergeant Swales. He had lost his mother, but had met the likes of Mrs. Markham and Ma Baker. He had lost his best friend and cousin, Dermot, but had found Kit. He had learned so many things that his head sometimes reeled with it all, but the most magical of all, he could read! His immediate horizons had grown from the limits of Clonarty and Dublin and he felt that one day they would encompass the world.

A tiny corner of his mind nagged at the disloyalty of his joy, but he felt with growing conviction that he would not have been content to pass his days as a simple potato farmer. What he could have done about it he could not imagine, and now there was no need after all.

As Joe looked down from his eyrie, he caught sight of Captain Willoughby strolling about the upper deck with Captain Tucker, the ship's commander. James had enjoyed the voyage so far, sharing a cabin with Edward Colby and Robert Harding. His punishment still technically continued, and he was duty officer more often than his fellow officers; but being 'confined to barracks' was hardly onerous aboard ship. Best of all, Colonel Deluce was aboard one of the other transports, and though James liked and respected his Commanding Officer, he had felt his disgrace keenly and he was glad that there would be time for memories to fade.

Every night, the officers dined with the ship's captain and his officers, and the talk ranged freely among myriad topics as the port decanter circulated. None of their daytime duties was particularly onerous, merely seeing to their men's inspection and exercise, and being ready to step in when needed to settle disputes in the men's quarters. Yes, James was content. Though he nursed a secret sadness at the thought of his mother's illness, his martial heart was stirred with excitement at the thought of India and the fighting to be done there.

The voyage was not wholly without unpleasantness. As they had made their way towards Cape Town at the southern end of Africa, the water became more and more malodorous, and the fresh meats and vegetables had long since turned bad. They were heartily glad to see the approach of their first port of call, to restock their food and water stores. The soldiers were fascinated by the table shaped mountain rising above the port, and their glimpse of dark skinned people. Joe and Kit hung over the rail, gazing at the small boats that darted towards them containing a motley collection of different coloured skins. Kit nudged Joe,

''Ere Joe, d'you think it washes off, or are they always like that?' Joe was able to answer as he had seen pictures of these dark skinned men in one of his readers,

'No, it doesn't wash off; it's there all the time; probably due to all this sunshine!'

Their stay was all too short, and having revictualled, they set sail again on the last leg of the voyage, heading for Bombay on the west coast of India. Their fair winds continued to push them along until halfway between the two great continents, they were becalmed. For four days they stayed motionless, the great sails hanging loosely in the stifling air. For once, the soldiers were allowed more time on deck away from the foetid, steaming holds. As many as could find space to do so, slept on deck, cursed by the sailors who thought it their sole right.

The breathless air and ancient hostility between the two groups of men were bound to cause an eruption, and sure enough on the third day of their becalming, it happened. A small group of sailors and soldiers were dicing in a patch of shade, strictly against orders. Pennies were being gambled on the fall of the dice, and one sailor was doing very well at the expense of the others. He was a rat faced man, with a greasy queue of hair hanging down his back and a powerful, rank smell. As he rolled the dice and reached for the pot of money when yet again the dice fell in his favour, a burly private shot out his hand and caught the sailor's sleeve. Two dice rattled from it to lie on the deck like two accusing eyes. The first to react was the sailor. He jumped to his feet and backed to the rail, a knife appearing as swiftly from his sleeve as the dice had done. The soldier moved cautiously, aware of the danger he was in. The other dicers backed off, willing to let the protagonists sort out their differences. But some of them edged closer, forming a semi-circle, avidly waiting for some action to relieve their boredom.

Suddenly the private moved, surprisingly quickly for a man of his size. Feinting to the right and away from the knife hand, he swerved back and then threw himself forward, reaching for the vicious weapon. As fast as he moved, the sailor was faster. Sidestepping, he allowed the private to rush under his arm and collide with the rail. Swiftly the knife lifted and plunged into the soldier's side. A blood gushed from the wound the sailor reached down and seizing the man's legs, tipped him over the side. With a gasp, the onlookers rushed to the rail to see a large triangular fin cutting its way towards the wounded man. Within minutes it was over with a swirl of bloodstained sea. If the soldier had not been dead when he hit the water, his end would have been swift indeed.

'Seize that man,' came a shouted command from Captain Tucker, who had witnessed the incident from the poop deck, but had been powerless to stop it, so swiftly had it occurred.

The sailor was flung below in the rope locker, and the next day was hauled out to receive his punishment, twenty lashes from 'the cat', a multi-headed whip with metal claws. The entire ship's crew and as many soldiers as could crowd the deck were present; the Captain wished to make it clear that he would brook no breaches of discipline on his ship. The sailor was tied by his wrists to the corners of a large wooden frame, and as the 'cat' whistled through the air for the first time, raising a bloody weal across his back, there was a collective sigh from the watchers and a scream from the victim.

Joe and Kit stood silent in the crowd. They had witnessed the fight the day before, and had been horrorstruck at the speed at which a man's life had ended. Joe was no stranger to death, but never before caused by a deliberate act of violence. Now they watched the punishment with equal distaste, though recognising that justice had to be done.

'But,' thought Joe, 'does it have to go on for so long?' as the man's back was reduced to a bloody pulp and his anguished screams faded as merciful unconsciousness took over.

As the flogging came to an end, Joe felt a zephyr touch his cheek. Unsure of the sensation, he looked upwards, and the sight of the mainsail flapping gently, and then more vigorously, caused him to yell excitedly,

'Wind! Look everyone; wind!'

They reached Bombay a week later.

Chapter 2

The coastline of India drew closer and closer until the watchers crowding the rails could make out more detail. Two points reached out as if to greet them; to enfold them in their embrace. Although it was mid-morning, the air was stiflingly hot from the sun beating down from the vivid blue sky, and soldiers and sailors alike, though dressed simply in shirts and breeches were drenched in sweat. But none thought to seek the shade; they were much too eager to drink in the view.

Kit and Joe had climbed the rigging to get a better view and were perched like monkeys on top of the mainsail,

'Can you just smell that Kit?' The odour of India seemed to creep across the oily sea until it seemed to envelop the ship. It had almost a tactile quality, compounded of multitudinous facets. There was human ordure certainly, but they were used to that; the same stench wafting through the cracks in the decking from the holds below. There was animal ordure too, and rotting fruit and vegetables. But overlying it all was a new smell, spicy and exotic, that told them that they had arrived at the fabled shores of a fabled land.

Behind them, in line astern, were their sister transports, Britannia and Victoriana; majestic enough names for majestic looking ships. It was passing strange, thought Joe, that throughout the long weeks at sea they had hardly caught a glimpse of them, and yet, within hours of them sighting land, they were there once more. The three masters had all sails set to catch the slight breeze that propelled them to the waiting arms of Bombay, and Joe was stirred by the sight of these handsome vessels.

Soon the origins of the some of the smells became obvious as refuse, both animal and human, began to float by them. Here and there were dotted the floating corpses of animals; dogs, cows, and surely more than one human! The sailors began to scamper up the rigging, preparing to furl up the great sails, and they chased the boys from their vantage point.

They slid past a fort, a relic of Portuguese possession, which was surrounded by a collection of tumbledown sheds, godowns that were packed with the goods that India traded with the rest of the world. On the other side of the bay rose a hill clothed in lush vegetation. Under the barest of sail, Gloriana came to her berth and touched as gently as a sigh. Activity among the sailors reached fever pitch as they made fast, their faces bright red with exertion. But then their job was done, and the sailors could rest until the soldiers departed.

"C'mon,' Kit nudged Joe as the order came to leave the ship, 'best go down or old Dunny will be chasing us!' irreverently speaking of their Corporal Dunster. The boys hurried below where the heat hit them like a hammer blow. Pouring with sweat, they hastily and regretfully donned their uniforms, and gathered their immediate belongs; the rest were in the hold and would be delivered to them all later. Then they made their way off the ship that had been their home for so many weeks.

'Why does the land seem to move?' whispered Joe, as they lurched across to where A Company was assembling. After so long on a heaving deck, solid land felt very strange indeed. The heat seemed to be rising with every minute and the men's faces above their tight collars were turning an alarming shade of puce. Chivvied by their Sergeants and Corporals, the men formed up.

Around them there appeared to be bedlam, with brown-skinned people in multi-coloured garments surging round them. Joe's eyes swiveled back and forth as he tried to take in every detail,

'Look,' he nudged Kit, as a gorgeously dressed Indian with jewels flashing about his person was carried by.

'Wake up there!' bawled Corporal Dunster, and the boys came to attention. The officers had disembarked and had been met by the guides who were to lead them to a cantonment just outside the city. With drummer boys beating time, and led off by A Company, the Regiment left the docks in remarkably short time, Colonel Deluce sensibly realizing that there would be men fainting in the torrid heat.

Joe marched alongside Kit, proudly beating the rhythm learned during their time at sea. His head felt as if it was bursting as it seemed to expand inside his now tight fitting shako; as they marched through streets lined with people, much as London had been when they left it. But here the people were brown and mostly semi-naked. They squatted on their haunches at the side of the streets sunk in apathy, reaching out a hand to beg from time to time. Many sported hideous mutilations or held out babies with emaciated limbs and swollen bellies. But the soldiers marched by oblivious, their eyes firmly looking straight ahead, eager to get to their destination and out of the appallingly hot sun. Joe averted his eyes from the babies as the memories were just too poignant to bear!

'Company..y..y halt!' and the ranks came to a crisp stop in the parade ground of the cantonment. Around the perimeter lounged a number of men watching their arrival with curiosity. When all four companies had lined up, Colonel Deluce stepped forward to address them,

'Well men, we have arrived in India at last. We will stay here in Bombay for some little while; as yet I do not know for how long. You will be allocated quarters, but these are currently being occupied by the Regiment we are here to replace, so there will be crowding for a day or two. You will kindly conduct yourselves in the manner that I expect from men of this proud Regiment, and if I hear of any trouble perpetrated by any one of you, the offender will be severely punished. That is all!'

'Now there's a nice welcome,' hissed Kit out of the side of his mouth, earning himself a rap over his knuckles from Sergeant Shaw. The men were directed to the various barrack rooms, only too thankful to escape from the merciless sun. Inside was a little cooler thanks to high ceilings with heavy strips of cloth wafting back and forth over their heads, giving an illusion of a breeze. It soon became clear that there was a shortage of beds for them all, as the soldiers of the resident Regiment were determinedly lying on theirs to protect them from the newcomers! The boys found a bench running along an end wall, and thankfully stripped off their red woolen uniform jackets. The shakoes soon followed, leaving a band of red around their foreheads.

The boys sprawled gratefully on the bench for a moment, overcome by heat and weariness, but before long the resilience of youth allowed them to sit up and take notice of their surroundings, Then they noticed a soldier stretched out on a nearby cot, apparently clad only in a strip of cloth round his waist and between his legs, and sucking on an empty pipe. His face and hands were burnt to a deep brown, though his body and limbs were much paler; he had clearly been in India for some time, so the pair drifted over to him intent on asking a few questions.

The object of their curiosity was quietly daydreaming on his cot, oblivious to the sounds of activity all around him; a trick he had learned from Indian holy men who were capable of self-inducing a trance. But presently he became aware of being the subject of intense scrutiny, and opening his eyes found two faces peering closely at his own. One face looked just like one of the monkeys indigenous to India, even to the corrugated brow; but the other was more intelligent, with keen blue eyes that stared into his own,

'Whaddya want?' he said, none too pleased at being disturbed in the midday heat.

'We've just arrived,' said Joe, breathlessly, 'an' we were wondering if it's always this hot?' The man chuckled,

"Ot? This ain't 'ot. It'll get a lot worse before it gets better!' Then he relented at the horrorstruck expression on their faces,

'It'll rain soon, 'n then it'll cool down a bit.'

'What, today?' The man chuckled again. And then realizing that he wasn't going to be left in peace, and in truth taken with the pair of inquisitive youngsters, he propped himself up on his elbow and began to explain,

'This country's not like back 'ome. It doesn't rain all the year round; especially where you come from!' pointing his pipe at Joe, who frowned in vexation for he had worked so hard to rid himself of his Irish cadences. But no matter, the soldier was speaking again,

'No. It gets 'otter 'n 'otter for several weeks, and then the 'eavens open, and it rains for weeks on end. Rain like you never saw, it fair falls down! Then it gets cooler around November time, an' it's a bit like summer at 'ome. Then it gets 'otter again. The punkahs help a bit,' pointing his pipe at the wafting cloth above their heads, 'but nothin' really works 'til it rains.

The officers do alright though. They go off to the 'ills where it's cooler, 'n take their womenfolk with 'em.'

'What's that you're wearing?' asked Joe, intrigued by the strip of cloth. The man chuckled again,

'My, but you two are full of questions! It's called a dhoti, an' you'll see a lot of natives wearing 'em because they're cool. You should get one for yourselves if you're to stay 'ere. The officers don't like it, but if you're off dooty, they can't say much. Now leave me be, there's good lads. It's too 'ot to talk,' and closing his eyes, he made it clear that he wouldn't answer any more questions. The boys settled themselves on their bench, and in spite of the heat, fell into a doze.

'Stuck here until October at the earliest! But my dispatch clearly spoke of an urgent situation!' Colonel Deluce glared at the man opposite him, Colonel Manfred of the outgoing Regiment, who chuckled wryly at the outrage on his visitor's face.

'I'm afraid your notion of urgent and that of those residing in Calcutta are clearly not the same. I applied for my Regiment to be relieved nigh on two years ago, and was finally informed that the replacement would arrive by the end of the year. You caused a furore when you sent word that you had left Dublin and would be arriving in June or July. Dispatches buzzed back and forth like angry hornets! Their lordships finally decided it was best if we met up in Bombay and exchanged command formally here. It's alright for them sitting in comfort of the Residency in Calcutta; they didn't have to travel across the country through the worst of the hot weather. We did all of our travelling at night, let me tell you.'

'But,' queried Deluce, still puzzled, 'what about the emergency that needed urgent reinforcements?'

Manfred laughed out loud at that, making the diminutive punkahs wallah in the corner wake with a start from a doze and begin to fan them with a burst of energy,

'Emergency! Just some minor skirmish with some hillmen. If we'd had to wait for reinforcements we'd have been wiped out long ago! Y'know,

I think that our Commissioners in Calcutta have lost touch with reality. Never mind, you're here now, and I'll be glad to see good old England again. You must give me all your news before you leave; ours is always several months behind hand.'

'But you still haven't explained why we must stay here until October. Surely if you've left your headquarters, they must be empty?'

Manfred chuckled again; Deluce was getting more than a little tired of that chuckle,

'You don't know this country yet! The rains are due any time now, and the roads will be impassable for a good three months. No; best wait until October; that's the best time to travel.'

Colonel Deluce was not a happy man. He had acted with great expedition, removing his Regiment from Dublin and then commissioning transports to carry them half way round the world; all because he had been led to believe that there was a crisis happening in India. And now they would have to kick their heels in this place for two to three months, if Manfred was to be believed. He knew only too well what mischief that bored and restless soldiers could get up to. Surely the so-called rains couldn't be that bad!

A soft footed servant entered bearing some iced sherbet, and the two colonels sipped it gratefully. Manfred said sympathetically,

'Look. Leave it for now and get some rest until the sun goes down. It won't seem so bad then. I've had a room prepared at my bungalow; you'll be taking it over once I'm gone. I've also arranged for a mess dinner for us all. Give us a chance to exchange news; what!'

Gerald smiled wanly and thanked him. Following the servant, he was escorted to a bungalow set apart from the barracks and surrounded by a well tended garden. He was shown into a comfortable room, aired by the now familiar punkahs, but even so it was stiflingly hot. He threw off his uniform jacket and stretched himself on the bed with relief; and surprisingly fell into a light doze.

Later that evening, the officers of the two Regiments met in their Mess, and were seated in grand style at great mahogany tables. James Willoughby, positioned halfway down one of them, gazed about him appreciatively. The gold faced scarlet of their own regimentals contrasted with the deep blue trimmed with silver of the other Regiment, the colours glowing in the light of myriad of candles in handsome silver candelabra spaced at intervals down the long tables. The candlelight reflected off polished silver cutlery and chafing dishes and winked off elegant china tableware and crystal glasses. A magnificent silver epergne dominated the top table, where the colonels and their aide-de-camps were seated, already engrossed in earnest conversation.

'It could almost be a Mess back home,' mused James, 'if it wasn't for the servants and this damned heat!'

The servants in question wore matching livery of emerald green tunics tied with enormously wide white sashes that ended in gold fringes, above loose white trousers. They sported neatly bound turbans of the same emerald green, bearing an upright scarlet feather, and they were a magnificent spectacle. There seemed to be a great many of them as they padded in and out wearing soft slippers and carrying large silver dishes. The food was unfamiliar, consisting of several types of curry. James sampled them appreciatively; always willing to try new tastes.

The heat affected them all, and it soon became clear who were the newcomers, as they sat red-faced above their tight collars. The experienced India men, though obviously hot as evidenced by beads of sweat on their foreheads, seemed to cope so much better. They even seemed to have less constricting collars; or did it just appear so? There was a buzz of conversation round the table, and James dragged himself from his musings and joined in politely. Away to his left he could hear Lieutenant Carless' whining tone; why did he dislike that man so much? He was busy protesting about the inconvenience of being stuck in this 'God forsaken hole' for all the world as if he was a veteran of the country. James sighed; the man was intolerable.

'I hear the women of this country are well worth pursuing. And they know a trick or two! What d'you think,' persisted Carless,

'You'd best be careful who you pursue,' returned his neighbour, bearing a Captain's insignia, 'some of them are very high-born, and their families protect them closely; with knives if necessary!' The Captain's mouth was curled with disdain as he answered Carless who clearly had the same effect on him as he did on James! The conversation continued to ebb and flow,

'What news from London?'

'Is the Irish famine over?'

'Is it true it rains for months on end?'

Are the Rajahs as wealthy as they say?'

'Have you ridden an elephant?'

'Have you hunted tiger?'

And over the buzz, the strident whine of Carless kept intruding like an angry hornet,

'There's always one in every Regiment,' drawled a quiet voice on James' left. The speaker was eyeing James with an amused twinkle in his deep brown eyes, 'it's the heat that makes it seem worse than usual!'

As the owner of the brown eyes was deeply tanned and arrayed in the Royal Blue of their hosts, he clearly spoke for experience. He also sported the insignia of a Major, and James replied with due deference,

'I'm sorry. I didn't realise my thoughts were so obvious.'

'Don't worry. Men like that,' nodding towards Carless, 'aren't worth raising a sweat over.'

'You've been in India long?'

'I came over with the Regiment ten years ago. A fascinating country, tho' it doesn't suit everyone. I've a mind to end my days here, and I've only come to Bombay to arrange the sale of my commission. Then I've my eye on an estate in the mofussil near Lucknow.' James raised an enquiring eyebrow,

'Mofussil?'

'Yes. It's the wild country away from the so called civilizing influence of the British!'

'You don't think much of the civilizing influence then?'

'There have been civilizations here when the British were running about in woad! However, that's beside the point. It's a fascinating country, as I said, and I've no ties to draw me back to England. Though I'm bound to say that this hot weather could make a man change his mind!' And he drew his finger round his collar,

'Why on earth we persist in wearing these uncomfortable uniforms I cannot imagine. You'd think our long experience here would have taught us better. But we must keep up the standards, eh?' Then catching the look on James' face, he added hurriedly,

'Don't take any notice of an old cynic like me; you make your own judgments.'

'No. Please go on. I'd like to hear more about the country. I feel woefully ignorant. None of us expected it to be this hot, or to find we cannot travel due to the rain! Not something we are used to back home.'

'No indeed. Well....'

And James Willoughby listened enthralled as his companion regaled him with descriptions of the life he could expect when he finally reached their destination halfway across the country in the province of Oudh.

At the top table, Colonels Manfred and Deluce were once more discussing the problem of staying in Bombay.

'It's no good thinking of leaving now,; insisted Manfred, 'the distances are vast, and you'd hardly get underway before you were bogged down. Take my advice and keep the men busy here. Get a 'munshi' to teach 'em a bit of local language and that sort of thing. Let 'em find out what India's about. Bombay's not such a bad place y'know. And let 'em get the diseases out of their systems before you move off!'

Deluce felt that he had no choice but to bow to the greater experience of the other man. Truly he felt very ignorant about it all, and wished that he had studied the country more than he had, rather than rushing to get here.

The evening wore on with course after course of highly spiced foods. Wines flowed freely, and then came the port as they nibbled sickly sweetmeats.

James had spent almost the entire evening listening to the brown eyed Major, and had taken a definite liking for the man. Their voices were inclined to become somewhat slurred as the evening progressed, but the intense heat was forgotten as the conversation flowed,

'See those fellows there?' said the Major, pointing to the servants busily engaged in clearing debris from the tables, 'you think they all look alike, eh? Well they're not. Some of 'em are Hindus. Now they will serve us with food, but they'd rather die that eat with us. Caste, y'see.' James didn't, but he was too interested to interrupt.

'And they won't touch a cow. Sacred y'see. And the others; they're Moslems, and they won't touch a pig! Unclean y'see. Leave them alone and they'd be at each other's throats inside a week!'

'Where'd you say you were going to have your estate?' asked James'

'A few days out of Lucknow. Not that far from your cantonment, where you'll be stationed. Perhaps you'd care to spend some leave there?

Not many Europeans though; you'd get to see a bit of real India! The only ones within a day's journey are a planter and his wife. Damn, what are they called? Ah; Ferguson. They've been there years. Nice couple and they respect the country. They were telling me last time I was there that they were expecting a visit from England in a few month's time. Yes; that was it; the Willoughby's.'

James looked at him with startled surprise,

'Good God! You're talking about me father and mother! They are the Willoughby's. Me too, of course. James Willoughby at your service.'

His companion gave a crack of laughter and the two men owlishly shook hands.

'Major, or soon to be ex-Major, John Carlton, at your service indeed. Well, well,' chuckling, 'so I'll be sure to see something of you!'

Three days later, the Bluecoats left Bombay. The transport ships had revictualled in record time, anxious to be away before the monsoon rains arrived, and they awaited their human cargo in the calm waters of Back Bay.

The entire content of the cantonment rose at five thirty in the morning, the departing Regiment to form up; their replacements to cheer them off. In truth, they were glad to see the back of each other, as the short time they had spent together crammed together in accommodation designed for half the number and in the torrid heat had stretched tempers to their limit. Frequent fights had broken out over trivialities, and Sergeants and Corporals had spent much of their time separating the warring factions. So now the Redcoats leaned over the verandah rails of their barracks, and silently watched the Bluecoats form up in their Companies. Orders were bawled out, sounding with startling clarity in the crisp morning air. It was a beautiful morning, the moments before the sun gained any power, and the air was pleasantly mild rather than unbearably hot.

Colonels Manfred and Deluce solemnly shook hands.

'Bon voyage,' said Deluce politely, trying hard to show that he was not glad to see the back of his opposite number, as he had spent much of their time together showing up Deluce's ignorance.

'Thanks old man. I wish you joy of India! Don't forget; try and get the diseases out of their system; yours too!'

Manfred clapped Deluce on his back, much to his annoyance, before turning to his officers,

'Let's be on our way before this damned sun gets up!'

Kit and Joe leaned over the rail and waved at their new friend and mentor, who was looking more soldierly now that he had exchanged his dhoti for his uniform. They were sorry to see him go as they gleaned a lot of valuable information about India from him. They noticed that he had kept out of the way of the troublemakers, and had told the boys that he had learned the art of detachment by association with a Hindu holy man,

'You just sort of empty yer mind. Just let yerself go and see yerself out of yer body.' And he had shut his eyes and gone totally limp, his breathing becoming slower and shallower until the watching boys thought it would stop altogether. Before they could get too anxious though, he slowly returned to normal, and looked at the boys' bemused expressions,

'It's a great trick when the heat, or this mob,' indicating the crowded room, 'get too much. You just sort of; go away!'

And now he was going away in reality. And Joe especially felt bereft.

Once they were in sole possession of the cantonment, parade was called, and the men returned to the rooms to dress. The large barrack dormitories looked strangely deserted, and they fought for ownership of the cots, or charpoys, ranged down the walls. Joe took over the deserted charpoy of his departed friend and felt strangely comforted by it.

Later, after the Companies had paraded and been inspected, they raised their standard alongside the Union Jack. At last they felt that they had truly arrived.

Ten days later, India dealt her first blow. Dysentery broke out.

Chapter 3

The men had joked of this most humiliating of maladies during the long voyage from England. 'The gripes', 'the runs', Indian belly'; the variety of descriptions matched the variety of names. But nothing had prepared them for the reality of it when the first soldier was struck down. It really isn't so funny, thought Joe, as he watched Kit curled into a foetal ball, clutching his distended belly and groaning. Around him, the majority of men in A Company were in a similar state, and groans filled the large dormitory. Joe fanned his friend anxiously, knowing that soon he would stagger to his feet, and with a helping arm round his shoulder, would lurch to the privies already sticking from the exertions of others.

'Why have I been spared,' pondered Joe, 'as so few others have been?'

The sickness knew no class distinction. It had visited the men in all four great barrack rooms. It had visited corporals and sergeants in their neat rows of single room dwellings. It had visited the officers in their spacious bungalows, surrounded by English style gardens on the outskirts of the cantonment. It had even visited Colonel Deluce himself, and he groaned and sweated and heaved in involuntary accord with his men, from his second-in-command to the lowliest drummer boy. Joe had wandered unhindered through the cantonment early that morning and heard the groans emanating from all sides, and thought to himself that the dreaded dysentery was indeed a leveler of men! He could only suppose that his own immunity was due to the privations he had suffered; perhaps in some way it had hardened his belly against the disease. But whatever the reason, he was heartily grateful for it, as he and the handful that had been spared did their best for their friends.

The Indian servants also did what they could, offering advice from their long experiences of such diseases. Joe looked up from fanning Kit to see a lanky fellow, clad only in a dhoti and a strip of white cloth flung over his shoulder. Long, straight black hair, redolent with coconut oil, hung down either side of a cadaverous face, and brown eyes gazed at the groaning Kit with concern,

'Try and make him drink, sahib,' he said with a sing-song voice, 'it is the only thing to do, I am telling you.'

So Joe fetched a dipper of water from a chatty and held it to his friend's lips, only to have it flung away as Kit suffered further convulsions. But he persevered and managed to drip some of the precious water into Kit's mouth.

No, it really wasn't funny at all, for as the disease began to lose its grip, the first fatality occurred. He was an old soldier, a 'lifer' who had suffered chronic and debilitating seas sickness throughout the voyage, so perhaps it wasn't surprising. But nevertheless, he was the first to die in India; a sobering thought. And as the Regiment, at least those who were fit enough, gathered together to bury their comrade, news came of another death; Major Williams. The very same Major Williams who had delighted in James Willoughby's disgrace, had suffered an apoplexy during a particularly violent bout of cramps, and his overstrained heart had given up its struggle. He had been found by an Indian sweeper who had gone to his bungalow to attend to the privy, lying in his own ordure. He had not been a popular officer, with his porcine features and unpleasant mien, but the manner of his passing shocked them all. They had been in India less than two weeks and already two of their number were dead.

But the disease followed its course and loosened its grip on its victims, who slowly recovered, only to be afflicted by boils and prickly heat. Searingly hot days followed one another without relief, and tempers flared all too easily. Colonel Deluce knew that his men needed something to help them endure until the monsoon rains arrived to cool them all down; so he paid them.

The men's pay had followed them near half way round the world, though they had not known of it. Deep in the hold of Deluce's ship had been three brass bound chests full of the 'Queen's shillings'. He had deliberately withheld payment while on the high seas, knowing that that it would have caused endless trouble in the confined spaces of a transport ship, as men fought to guard their precious hoard. And since they had arrived, there had no time.

So one morning soon after the funeral of Major Williams, the men were paraded at the crack of dawn; the only time of day when it was bearable to don their uniforms, and were ordered to line up in front of the Company Paymasters. Deluce had also had the foresight to engage Indian traders, bunnias, to bring Indian currency to exchange. Joe and Kit received their allocations, with Joe's slightly enhanced by his 'classroom bonus', though he felt somewhat guilty at being paid for something he enjoyed, but his friend had no such qualms as he was blessed by the rare quality of being totally without envy. The pair decided to exchange their coins for rupees and annas; though it meant little to Joe as it meant exchanging one set of unfamiliar coins for another! Kit showed him how to fashion a money belt and advised him to keep it always around his waist whether in the barracks or outside,

'You just can't trust nobody,' he said with worldly wisdom. Joe thought sadly of his simple home, where the door had never been closed to anybody, whether empty or not,

'Maybe we didn't have much,' he told himself, 'but what we had we shared!'

That evening, along with a party of soldiers given leave to explore Bombay, the youngsters left the barracks in high spirits, even Kit, still a little shaky from his bout of dysentery. They were ordered to 'stick together' and to return by ten o'clock at the latest!

The air was so stifling that it seemed to have almost a liquid quality, and soon they were all sweating profusely, even though the worst of the day's heat had passed. However, nothing could dampen their high spirits after being cooped up on the ship and then the overcrowded cantonment for so long. They found the local inhabitants largely occupied in cooking their evening meal, and smoke from the cooking fires fuelled by animal dung rose on all sides, adding to the furnace like heat bouncing off the closely packed dwellings. Gasping with the effort of breathing, the group made its way slowly through the streets, noting with interest, that in common with cities the world over, there was a striking difference between rich and poor.

They saw handsome houses, built in extravagant fashion, and pierced with by delicate trellises worked in stone, topped by ornate minarets and towers. They saw streets of hovels, where naked potbellied children played among human and animal ordure. Everywhere, they saw the lower part of every building stained blood red, the result of the universal habit of chewing betel nut and directing streams of blood red saliva at the nearest wall.

Everywhere, too, there were traders, with their wares spread out in front of them laid out on strips of cloth, so that they could be rolled up in a moment. There were glass bangles and other gaudy ornaments on offer; there were unfamiliar foodstuffs that the boys tentatively tried, and mostly liked; and best of all there were handsome slippers with curled up toes, decorated with beadwork and gold braid. Kit was very taken with the slippers, and paused at several traders trying to choose between them.

As they made slow progress along the crowded streets, they were accosted on all sides by potbellied children with outstretched hands and beseeching brown eyes. Joe was prevented from pressing some small coins into the nearest hand by Kit's pragmatic advice,

'If you do, you'll never be rid of them!' Joe recognised the sense in that, though it hurt him to resist those huge, begging eyes in the emaciated faces.

Then Joe suddenly found himself separated from Kit, who had stopped to haggle over a pair of particularly outrageous slippers and the rest of the group who had sauntered faster than the boys. He wandered slowly in the direction of Back Bay, recognising some of the landmarks in the fading light, from their arrival there. Several tall masted ships rode at anchor out in the bay, lights beginning to twinkle from their mast heads, though their own transports were long gone. The scene was one of languorous bustle, as this was a principle trading port, where once the East India Company had once carried out much of its business. Though now 'Johnny Company' was now involved with the administration of the sub-Continent, Bombay was still a thriving trading centre.

Joe was intrigued to see two Englishmen in close conversation lounging near the waterfront. Dressed in lightweight alpaca suits, they were the first civilians he had seen since their arrival. He was rather envious of their lightweight clothing, so much more sensible than the woolen uniforms they had to wear on parade! However, the average Indian was even more sensibly dressed, in fact, hardly wearing anything at all! Many wore the dhoti that he was familiar with, or baggy thin cotton trousers and tunics. There were few women to be seen, presumably busy with their cooking, but those he saw were either swathed in brightly coloured garments he had been told were called saris, or entirely enveloped in sombre 'bourkas'. He silently thanked his erstwhile mentor from the barracks for his vast knowledge of India, willingly passed on to Joe and Kit.

Joe leaned against a convenient wall and let the scene shift in front of him. The stifling quality of the air made everyone appear to move in slow motion as though they were swimming, though the heaviness was gradually lifting as darkness approached, particularly near the waterfront. He presumed that Kit would soon find him and for the present, he was content to watch the new world of India go by. Looking away from the waterfront, he saw a small procession approach. The leader of the group was splendidly dressed in a bright blue brocade tunic, tied around the waist with a sash of gold through which was thrust a tulwar, a broad curved bladed sword. Baggy white trousers were tucked into gleaming black boots, and the outfit was finished by a scarlet turban tied impeccably and topped with a white feather fastened with a blood red ruby set in gold. The man was mounted on a gleaming chestnut horse, whose proud carriage declared a long pedigree, and from its height, the rider looked about with haughty mien.

Joe looked at the animal with admiration with an Irishman's innate appreciation of horseflesh. He supposed from his dress and small group of attendants, also smartly dressed and wearing tulwars that the man was of some importance, and certainly wealth! The procession had reached a point alongside the two white men, still deeply engrossed in conversation, when a small child dashed out in front of the chestnut. With consummate ease the rider brought the animal to a halt, throwing it back on its haunches. The chestnut sidled on its hind legs trying to restore its balance, so that its hindquarters swung perilously close to the Englishmen as the child ran off, oblivious to its recent danger. Again the rider corrected the horse's movement and persuaded it to edge away from the two men who had looked up in alarm. While Joe admired the horsemanship of the resplendently dressed Indian, one of the Englishmen looked up at him and snarled,

'Can't you watch what you're doing, you damned coolie!' and he turned back towards his companion.

'Joe's mouth dropped open. 'Coolie' was an epithet he had already learned was used for the lowliest of servants and could not be appropriate for this man, who even now was glaring at the speaker. Pure hate filled his brown eyes, and a deep colour suffused his face as his blood rose at the deadly insult. At that moment, the Indian noticed Joe for the first time, and the outraged expression on his face. Perhaps he saw in the boy's face the unspoken empathy that he felt; and he began to calm down, while the hand that had dropped to his tulwar relaxed and fell away. For a moment, Joe and the Indian looked at each other, committing each other's faces to memory. Joe saw a handsome face, near as young as his own, with light brown skin and deep brown eyes. The Indian saw a white boy with chestnut hair, close in colour to his horse, and skin reddened by the sun, and a pair of bright blue eyes. The moment passed, and the procession moved off, leaving Joe with a strange prescience that he would encounter that particular Indian again. Just then he heard a familiar voice,

''Ere Joe. Look at these,' and there was Kit holding up the most outrageous slippers that Joe had ever seen; the curly toes as least six inches long, and encrusted with glass beads and gold braid. Kit was deeply offended when Joe threw back his head and burst out laughing. The two Englishmen looked up in mild curiosity.

Ex-Major John Carlton presented himself at Colonel Deluce's office. He was no longer in the uniform of the departed Regiment, but was now attired in a spanking new alpaca suit in light grey, and he felt comfortably warm, as it was still early in the morning. He noted with approval that the newcomers had soon caught the habit of beginning their day as early as possible, as it was just after six, and the place was already bustling with activity.

Gerald Deluce came in from morning inspection, and greeted his visitor cheerfully. He was at last feeling better after his debilitating bout of dysentery, and he had noticed that his Regiment was also looking close to normal again. He invited Carlton into his inner sanctum, and bade him sit down before asking him to state his business. Carlton smiled at the clipped speech of the Colonel; it epitomised the British military that he was very glad to have left behind!

'Good of you to see me without an appointment, Colonel. I presume you know that I have bought myself out of Regiment and plan to return to the District of Oudh?' the Colonel nodded, 'like yourselves, I will find it difficult to travel until the rains are over, and I've a mind to sort out some business affairs before I leave. It won't occupy me for long, and there's not much in the way of Society as they're all away in the hills.' The Colonel listened politely, waiting for Carlton to come to the point, though he had an inkling of what was in the wind!

'Well, I thought I could be useful to you as an advisor as I know the country, and can help with travel arrangements and all that. It is generally the done thing to consult one of the 'Company' men, but I think you'll find me more understanding of the army's needs!'

Deluce's face broke into a smile. He much preferred the erstwhile Major to his departed Colonel, feeling instinctively that Carlton sympathized with his ignorance rather than laughed at it,

'Delighted, old man. I'll put you on the payroll forthwith. If you could give me a few hours a day, I'd be more than grateful.'

The two men shook hands in agreement, and Carlton took himself off to find James Willoughby and tell him the good news. The two men had met several times since their first mess dinner together and the friendship had rapidly deepened. He discovered James eating a light breakfast in his bungalow, amusedly watching the rivalry between his servant, Briggs and Indian servant he had inherited along with the bungalow. Briggs was stiff with disapproval as he believed that he should be doing everything for his master, but was fighting a losing battle against the inscrutable Indian who knew his way round so much better than the perspiring Sergeant.

James greeted John Carlton cheerfully, calling for more cha. The two men discussed John's new appointment as adviser to the Regiment,

I think the first thing to be done is to hire a 'munshi' as Colonel Manfred suggested; it's about the only decent notion the man ever had!' James smiled at the irreverence with which John spoke of his ex-Colonel; clearly he had had no respect for the man. But then, John seemed to have little respect for the 'establishment' at all!

'Why did you remain a soldier for so long, if you felt so strongly about it all?' enquired James, with real interest. John shrugged,

'My family was impoverished even before they bought my commission which I thought would be the best way for me to make my way in the world. The men of my line seem to be tainted with the gamblers disease, and my father was no exception. He ran through what little money he had been left by his father, and then put a period to his life! My mother followed soon after, worn out with despair.' John was silent for a moment, and James could hear under the blunt words that he had loved his mother deeply. John continued,

'After that, it was matter of paying off the debts and making the best of things in the Regiment; not easy on army pay!' James tacitly agreed. Apart from buying their commissions, it was usual for families to pay their sons an allowance to cover the expense of living and entertaining in the Mess. James' own father did so for him, and he could not imagine how he would have coped without that support. Any officer who could not 'stand his round' tended to be despised by their fellow officers, particularly the likes of Carless. No wonder John Carlton had little time for the established order of things. John went on,

'Well things improved once we got to India. I arrived a Lieutenant and bought out as a Major, as you know. We were involved in several skirmishes over the years, and those Indian princes tend to go into battle decked out in all their finery, jewels and the like. I was able to put away a tidy sum against the day when I wanted to buy out, so here I am! As I told you before, I've no ties in England; I was an only child, and I've no wish to see the place again. You'll see, James, this is a fascinating country, but you've got to look with your eyes wide open. Don't stay stuck in your cantonments like some of the soldiers who come here. They only learn enough of the language to call for their whiskey and their clean laundry! I'll find a munshi and you must make use of him!'

James was a little taken aback at his friend's vehemence, in contrast to the casual way that he usually spoke, but he realised that much of John's sarcastic manner was a defense against the blows that life had dealt him. Small wonder he was bitter. He tentatively asked,

'Are you a gambler too?' John's lips curled sardonically,

'No. I seemed to have to have escaped that particular disease. I only invest in sureties, like my land in Oudh. I can't wait to get back and start. It's a wild area, ready for taming. You'll see James, the changes I will bring about; just give me a few years. That is, if the British don't spoil things in India with their high handed dealing with the natives. You'd think they would learn after the years that they have been in this country. But no, they go walking all over the hereditary rulers of the place with their shiny black boots. There'll be trouble, real trouble if they're not careful. Not like the petty skirmishes we have dealt with up to now!'

'What d'you mean?' asked James, and John went on to explain the principles of annexation, and some of the other peremptory ways the British had of dealing with Indians. It all left James with much food for thought when John finally left. By then the heat of the day was beginning to make itself felt, so he lay on his bed, fanned by the ever present punkahs wallah, finally falling into a dream filled doze where a troop of Indian Princes covered in dazzling jewels charged at him, shouting,

'You shall not have them; they are ours!' But James did not know if they meant their jewels or their land!

A few days later, the rains began. Kit and Joe were exploring the back streets of Bombay yet again, and poring over a selection of carved wooden elephants accompanied by a constant chatter from the vendor. They did not particularly want an elephant, but that in no way diminished the enthusiasm of the trader squatting behind his wares. Just then they heard a rumble of thunder, but as that had occurred several times over the past few days, they took little notice of it. A fat drop of rain fell on the trader's head, and he had rolled up his goods and moved to the shelter of a nearby awning before Kit and Joe had time to straighten up from their crouching position. The heavens opened then, and in a moment they were both drenched. They ran for the same awning sheltering as the trader, and looked out in amazement at the deluge. In the middle of the street was a group of small children, totally naked, jumping up and down in a frenzy of excitement, throwing their arms about and screaming with laughter. Kit and Joe looked at each other, and at their wet clothes, and then with a yell, rushed out to join the children who looked at them with mild alarm!

The deluge continued for some ten minutes, and then stopped as quickly as it had begun. Very soon the streets were steaming as the sun came out, and the atmosphere rapidly became as torrid as it was before. One of the small children ran towards a hovel nearby, and then stopped as a large snake reared up in front of him. It was a cobra that had been sleeping peacefully out of sight of the house dwellers, but the torrential rain had flushed it out of its snug hollow. The cobra's hood flared out either side of its head, and the upper body swayed in mesmeric fashion as the creature fixed the terrified child with its beady eyes. Joe nudged Kit, but like everyone else looking on, was momentarily rooted to the spot. Then the spell broke as a small, grey-brown mongoose ran out from between two hovels, and rushing at the cobra, seized it behind the head. A wild struggle ensued, with the snake's body thrashing about in wild paroxysms. The struggle finally ended with the mongoose triumphant, and it disappeared from whence it came, dragging the cobra's body between its legs.

The onlookers all discovered that they had been holding their collective breaths, and exhaled with noisy gasps. The child ran into the waiting arms of its mother.

The rains did not immediately alleviate the torrid heat. Every day there were downpours followed by brilliant sunshine causing steam to rise. Everything that Kit and Joe owned seemed to be permanently damp, from the bedding on their charpoys to their curly toed slippers. Shirts left on the floor overnight turned green with mildew and fat, hairy spiders scuttled from them as they shook them out in the morning. Monsoon toads squatted obscenely in puddles chorusing incessantly in shrieking unison. Almost they wished for the pre-monsoon days, forgetting how they had longed the drenching rains. The servants constantly reassured them,

'It will be better soon, sahib, I am telling you!'

'But you said that before the rain,' grumbled Kit, sulkily. But the little punkah wallah merely smiled through his gap teeth, and nodded inanely to himself.

Men who had so recently recovered from dysentery found themselves plagued by prickly heat which made them scratch themselves raw; or agues that rattled their teeth as they lay helpless on their charpoys. Fat beetles and scorpions joined the hairy spiders in the bedding and clothes until everyone in A Company heartily cursed India and wished that they had never left Ireland!

Meanwhile, John Carlton was true to his word and had found a munshi in Bombay. He was a Hindu, simply dressed in a lungi and muslin shirt, and carrying a staff. He was as bald as an egg, and had serene brown eyes that looked placidly on the world through round, wire rimmed spectacles. He was introduced simply as Gupta by Carlton when he brought him to Colonel Deluce to make arrangements for lessons in Urdu to commence.

Colonel Deluce was very pleased to see the munshi as he was only too aware of the depths to which morale had sunk. Trying to learn the local language would not suit everyone, but at least it would be a diversion!

As it was unthinkable for officers and men to share the lessons, it was arranged that the officers would have an hour or two immediately after inspection when the day was at its coolest and most pleasant. Later in the day the rest of the men would have their turn, in spite of the rising heat. A room was set aside, and the classes began.

At first the room was packed for both the officer's session and later general session. But the novelty soon wore off and the majority of the Regiment soon returned to the itchy boredom of their quarters.

Every day Gupta would arrive, lay his staff down carefully and seat himself cross legged on a table in front of his audience. His serene brown eyes would look round the class, quietly noting who was present, and then he would start intoning words in Urdu while pointing to objects that related to them. His audience, with varying degrees of success, would sound the words after him, trying to capture the same intonation, trying to ignore the drumming of the rain outside.

Among the officers, James sat with his friends Edward Colby and Robert Harding. These two having been bullied somewhat into attending, were inclined to treat the lessons with a certain degree of levity. James found that his pleas to take them seriously fell on deaf ears, so he was not at all sorry when their appearances began to taper off, and finally come to a complete halt. For himself, he found the lessons challenging, and as the monsoon dragged on, started to make real progress.

Among the men, enthusiasm rapidly diminished until there was a core of a dozen who attended regularly. Joe went every day, but had not been able to interest Kit at all,

'What do I want with that heathen nonsense?' he muttered, 'the Queen's English is good enough for me!'

Alongside Joe sat Sergeant Adam Swales, which he found strange at first as his erstwhile teacher was now a student! But their collective enthusiasm soon overcame any barriers and before long, the pair were in competition to increase their vocabulary.

As the weeks passed the weather grew perceptibly cooler and the rains slowly petered out. Men who had so recently cursed the country and its climate, found it altogether pleasant; more like England in the spring or early summer. Agues and prickly heat vanished and a new optimism burgeoned. Carlton had worked indefatigably during the rains, advising on transports for their provisions, mounts for the officers, servants to cater to their every need. They would need grass cutters to supply fodder for the horses; drivers for their carts and doolies; coolies to carry out all manner of menial tasks. When Deluce saw the list his eyes nearly started out of his head,

'There must be four, no five times as many servants as men! Are you sure we need all these, Carlton?'

'Believe me Colonel,' replied Carlton with a smile, 'these numbers are modest compared to most Regiments on the move, and nothing compared to an Indian Prince's entourage!'

Halfway through October they were ready to go. They had been in India some three months; lost two men to disease, and suffered unpleasant and debilitating illnesses. But they had experienced a new and exotic country and they all, from the Colonel to the lowliest drummer boy, were tended by servants; and even the weather was becoming more like 'home' every day! There were setting off on a journey across a country that was vaster than in any in their previous experience. They marched out of the Bombay Cantonment with a spring in their step, the drummer boys leading off their respective Companies. Joe's heart beat in time with the rhythm he was sounding, behind the scarlet cloth of his jacket. His webbing straps gleamed white as they crossed his chest, and his boots were polished to a shine in the sparkling morning sun. His shako fitted more securely now, and no longer tended to descend to his ears. They marched through the outskirts of Bombay with little picanninies running alongside. Joe felt anxiety at leaving the safety of the city; the future beckoned.

Chapter 4

Halcyon days they were. The trek from Bombay across the vastness of India took on the feeling of one long picnic, and he looked back on the journey, Joe could only remember the *fun* of it all. Doubtless there were unpleasant moments, or days when the weather was damp and miserable, or nights when the winter began to bite and frost nipped at their noses, but none of these seemed to impinge on his memory.

Every morning they awoke to a babble of sound that always seemed to accompany Indians whenever they were together in large numbers. Smoke from cooking fires would be rising in the still morning air, as servants brewed cha or prepared chota hazri for their new masters. Presently, a contingent would set off in advance of the main body in order to find a suitable stopping place for tiffin and rest around midday, and a camp site prepared of the end of the day's march. Cries of,

'Chuldi, chuldi,' would ring out, and the advance guard would be gone.

Then the main procession would form up, with A Company always in the vanguard. Colonel Deluce would lead off mounted on a showy chestnut stallion, splendidly accoutered and purchased from his predecessor. With him rode his senior officers, the Majors of the four Companies, with James Willoughby acting as Brevet Major in replacement of the unfortunately deceased but unlamented Major Williams. Deluce had confided his decision to James before leaving Bombay, with the earnest hope that he would be able to arrange the purchase of the commission when he had settled in their new headquarters.

Then would follow the Captains and Lieutenants, always excitable and given to galloping off from the column in pursuit of game, real or imagined. After them came the men, marching in 'easy order' and covering the ground more efficiently than their casual gait suggested.

Bringing up the rear were the doolies, bullock carts and other strangely assorted wheeled vehicles that bore the burden of the enormous amount of baggage that the Regiment had managed to accumulate already. This included the Regimental accoutrements that had come to India with them, buried in the holds of their transport ships along with the pay chests. In addition, each and every soldier, from the Colonel down to the newest drummer boy had made innumerable purchases in Bombay, where every saleable item seemed to cost just a few rupees. They had all had clothes made for them by native derzees from cool cottons, alpaca or muslin.

Milling among the baggage carts were the camp followers; the women who had won the right to follow their soldier husbands on the voyage and who spent their days in trying to hitch rides from the doolie drivers. These earthy ladies had found themselves with more free time than they were used to, as servants were so inexpensive, that even the lowliest private could afford a bearer or two. As a result, the women simply got bored during the overnight stops, and spent their time arguing shrilly among themselves over some imagined slight, and adding to the general cacophony, compounded of animal lowing, servants shouting and the dolorous notes of the bells hung around the bullocks' necks.

In addition to these females, there were a handful of Officers' wives. These adventurous creatures had followed the military transports in more comfortable of passenger vessels, and had docked in Bombay some weeks after their husbands. They had expected to find their menfolk long departed having made arrangements for their safe passage across the country, but instead had found them trapped in their cantonment awaiting the cessation of the rains. Many tearful reunions ensued, and the ladies, a few of which had their children with them, were able to accompany their husbands across the vast hinterland of the Indian subcontinent. They travelled in a miscellany of transports, from crude dak-gharies, that resembled large boxes on wheels, to elegant carriages hired in Bombay, with their occupants shading their delicate complexions from the noon-day sun with frilly parasols. The occasional dashing maiden, preferring to ride, was clad in well cut riding habit styled on one of the army uniforms and run up for them by the obliging derzees in Bombay.

Colonel Deluce occasionally viewed the spectacle from some vantage point with absolute amazement, as the procession moved steadily below him, stretching for a mile from to end. But somehow it managed to cover the ground at a steady twenty or so miles per day. Grass cutters kept the mounts well supplied, and they were able to buy fresh provisions to supplement their rations at villages along the way. The mounted Junior Officers were more than willing to supply the cooking pots with game such as pigeons, partridges, deer and such like. With progress so good, Deluce ordered a rest day every Sunday, and occasionally a longer break of two or three days when he felt it was necessary. He had been advised to do so by Carlton, who assured him that they were not expected in Oudh until the spring, and the breaks for good for morale.

He had also explained that that the cantonment was manned by a skeleton staff from the Mariaon Cantonment near Lucknow, supporting the resident Indian Regiment of sepoys, so there was no need for a headlong dash across the five hundred or so miles that separated them. Deluce had had the fact verified by cables winging back and forth from Calcutta, so was content with the steady but not overtaxing pace.

Every evening, the advance guard would find them all a pleasant spot to set up camp, and on their arrival the army of servants would erect tents, and within a remarkably short space of time a miniature city would rise amid the wilderness. The privates made do with very crude affairs, sharing five or six to a tent, but the officers had their own luxurious canvas quarters. The main mess tent was a wonder to behold, more of a marquee, and housed trestle tables set with travelling china and cutlery sparkling under lantern light. The officers and their lady guests were comfortably seated on campaign chairs that had to be dismantled every morning before being loaded onto a baggage wagon. The meal was invariably excellent, washed down with copious draughts of port or brandy,

'It must be hoped,' observed James wryly to his friend Edward, 'that we arrive at our destination before supplies run out!'

The Regiment swept away from the swamps of Bombay and headed towards the northern tip of the hills know as the 'Western Ghats', crossing land cleft by rocky ravines and thence onto drier sierras. From there they swung north, to pass through the plateau lands between the Aravalli and Vindhya hills on to the jungles of the Madya Pradesh. From there they would slowly make their way to the great Gangetic plain that straddled the province of Oudh, and their final destination of the cantonment of Kotepore, some distance north of the larger cantonment of Mariaon at Lucknow. The route had been suggested by John Carlton, who was accompanying them, mounted on a large grey stallion, and escorted by a coterie of servants,

'For all the world like a minor Maharajah,' laughed James. Deluce blessed his decision to take the ex-Major onto his payroll, as his advice was invariably sound. He was also a fount of knowledge when it came to dealing with the apparently limitless variety of religions and castes among the Indian contingent, so that they would not offend the Hindus with their sacred cows or the Moslems with their abhorrence of pigs!

James was thoroughly enjoying the journey. In addition to the promised promotion, which effectively laid to rest the ghost of his disgrace in Dublin; he had fallen in love.

The object of his adoration was a Miss Lucy Mainwaring, eldest daughter of Major Hilary Mainwaring of C Company. The last time James had met the young lady had been some four years previous, when she had visited the barracks with her father, when she was a pert young miss of fourteen years. Golden hair had tumbled in disarray down her back, and freckles had dusted a rather snub nose. She was also painfully shy, and had responded to his polite overtures with agonised brown eyes and total silence! So he had shrugged and forgotten about her, until she had entered the mess in Bombay on the arm of her father, accompanied by her Mama and a maiden aunt, no doubt travelling in the hope of relinquishing her spinster status. But James had had no eyes for anyone but Lucy.

Lucy! Grown four years in age and a lifetime in beauty. The snub nose had become retroussé, and the dusting of golden freckles enhanced a creamy skin. Her hair was still golden but was now swept up in an ordered array of curls and twists that crowned a perfectly shaped head balanced on a slender neck. The brown eyes were enormous and no longer agonised. With the passing years she had developed a poise that would have put royalty to shame, and James was instantly besotted. When introduced by Major Mainwaring, it was his turn to be tongue-tied, causing the young lady to arch an elegant eyebrow and to laugh gently at his stammers,

'Why, we know each other from long ago do we not, er, Captain Willoughby?'

'Yes indeed. And it's Major, or will be.......that is,' tailed off James in confusion. But Lucy merely smiled sweetly and passed on to the next introduction, one elegant hand with its long tapering fingers lightly resting on her father's sleeve.

Lucy Mainwaring was not as indifferent to James as she had made out! She too remembered their last meeting in London, when she had stood before him, totally overawed. Recently raised to his Captaincy, James had been resplendent in his spanking new dress uniform, with scarlet jacket almost covered by quantities of gold braiding, and sporting a handsome new dress sword. He had seemed so tall to the shy fourteen year old, and her heart had throbbed painfully behind budding adolescent breasts. Too shy to speak, and in spite of his friendly tone, she had watched helplessly as he turned away to exchange pleasantries with her mother, and then turn on his heel and march briskly away, tassels a-swing on his gleaming knee high boots. At that precise moment, Lucy vowed that one day, the dashing Captain Willoughby would be hers.

The rest of the visit passed in something of a daze for Lucy and she ignored her younger siblings as they raced around the barrack square, or peered in show cases full of ancient and yellowed documents or strange antique uniforms. She could not wait to return home and lock herself in her bedchamber. At long last, her Mama had seen enough of the barracks, and escorted by her husband, shepherded her brood back to their elegant London home. She had noticed Lucy's abstraction, but had put it down to adolescent megrims and had forbore to question the girl. Pleading a headache, Lucy took herself off to her room and sat down in front of her mirror. Studying her face in great detail, she decided that there was potential in it, especially if she made an effort to tame her wild curls. She had to hope that her nose would gain a more sophisticated shape as she grew older and that her freckles would respond to frequent applications of a special lotion she had seen advertised in their local emporium. Seizing her brush, she set to work to bring some order to her tangled golden mane, while she gave herself to dreaming.

From that day forth, a bemused Elspeth Mainwaring, Lucy's Mama, did not recognise her eldest daughter. From a hoyden who liked to tumble with her younger brothers and sisters in mock fights, or play hide-and-seek in their large garden, careless of her appearance and ignoring all pleas to keep herself tidy, she changed overnight into a demure young miss. Elspeth was suspicious of the change, and was inclined to think that it would be of temporary duration, but as the weeks wore on, she had to admit that this biddable and tidy daughter had come to stay.

Lucy's governess was also bemused by the change. Hitherto, her young charge had shown little interest in her lessons, ever eager to escape with her siblings. But now, she listened avidly to her mentor and attended to her lessons with an enthusiasm the governess, like Elspeth, did not believe would last! But Lucy firmly believed that James would only be interested in a female who could hold her own in intelligent conversation, and opinion that she had gleaned from the pages of romantic novelettes smuggled in to her by the newest parlourmaid, Daisy. She practiced assiduously on the piano, mastered the art of painting delicate water colours, and spent hours a day walking carefully round her bedchamber with a heavy book balanced on her head to improve her deportment. She lavished pots of special lightening cream on her the hated freckles, but sadly, of all her efforts, it was this that seemed to bring about no change, and eventually she gave up the struggle, and decided that they did not look so bad after all. She finally managed to tame her hair with the help of Daisy, who showed her how to pile the mass of it in sophisticated array, but as neither Daisy, nor her mistress had any experience, the result could not be deemed elegant!

Nevertheless, Lucy felt that at the advanced age of fifteen, she was now ready to meet James again, and began to drop heavy hints to her father that she would 'so much like to revisit the barracks where her dear Papa spent so much of his time.' But before her plan reached fruition, disaster struck!

Major Mainwaring came home one day with a heavy frown on his face, and kissing his wife abstractedly, had taken her arm and ushered her into the drawing room. He left the door slightly ajar, and Lucy could not but help taking advantage. The voices came and went from within, and once, her mother gave a startled scream, quickly soothed by the Major's soft tomes.

What Lucy heard appalled her utterly. The Regiment was going to Ireland for an indefinite period, and worse, could not take their families with them, (it was at this point that Elspeth had screamed as she was used to following her soldier husband wherever he was posted).

'There, there, my dear,' came Mainwaring's low tone, 'it will only be until autumn when the harvest's in. You'll see, I'll be home before you know it!'

'But Hilary, why can't we come with you. We have always done so?'

'I have explained, my dear,' replied Hilary patiently, as he was inordinately fond of his family, 'there could be trouble out with the local populace. There's famine d'you see, and it might be difficult to ensure your safety as we should. Why don't you get your sister to stay? You are always saying you should. You could take a house by the sea or stay here if you prefer. There, there,' he repeated hastily as his wife's eyes filled tears.

Lucy fled to her room as Hilary ineffectually patted his wife's shoulder while ringing for her chambermaid. He was a good but unimaginative husband and he felt helpless in the face of feminine misery and beat a hasty, if ignominious retreat as soon as the maid appeared. Upstairs, Lucy was sprawled across her bed, sobbing into the pretty satin coverlet,

'T'isnt fair,' she told the bed between sobs, 'he'll go away and find someone else, and I'll never see him again!' The fact that James could have met 'someone else' at any time simply had not occurred to her; she was totally convinced that as long as he was close by, he was simply waiting for her to grow up before falling for her devastating charms!

In spite of Elspeth's pleas and Lucy's tears, the Regiment set sail for Ireland. They left London to the doleful wails of their womenfolk, promising to be back as soon as the harvest was in and the Irish could eat again. None of them could have foreseen the failure of a second harvest and that it would be well over a year and a half before they saw their menfolk again.

Lucy's nature was naturally optimistic, so she pulled herself out of her misery once the Regiment had gone by convincing herself that James would be far too busy to notice the Irish women, and anyway, they would all be too ugly for him! It is as well that she did not know of the Castle Balls held in Dublin, or the striking widow Mary Kavanagh!

But her efforts had been rewarded, and now, close to her sixteenth birthday, she was a beautiful and poised young lady, trembling on the brink of womanhood. The elegant house in Chelsea, where her mother having decided to stay in London rather than go to the seaside, was besieged by a succession of ardent young admirers. At a ball held in honour of her sixteenth birthday, Lucy danced till dawn, her dance card filled from start to finish. She merely dallied with the callow youths, using them to practice feminine wiles, her heart firmly fixed on the absent James, who had taken on an almost godlike aura since she had last seen him.

As the months passed, Elspeth and her daughter drew closer together as Lucy grew up, and the older woman shared snippets of her husband's letters. They cried together when a letter informed them of the terrible news that they had to stay for 'an unknown number of months due to the failure of the second harvest'. Elspeth sighed wistfully,

'One feels sorry for them, of course, but with a little effort......!' Lucy could not reply for her throat was too swollen for speech. Surely he must find someone and then her constancy would be wasted,

'Soon I'll be too old,' said a voice inside her sixteen year old head!

It was just after Lucy's seventeenth birthday that another bombshell fell on them. It was spring, and Elspeth and Lucy were taking advantage of an exceptionally mild day, and were sitting in the garden. There was a riot of daffodils around them, while the almond trees seemed frosted by their delicate blossoms. On the lawn tumbled Harry and George, at twelve and ten still capable of enjoying a good scrap. Elspeth absentmindedly reminded the boys to 'mind their nankeen breeches' as she perused yet another letter from her husband, before sharing it with her daughter laughing at her brothers' antics,

'Let me see,' began Elspeth, 'ah yes, he is in good health, though the Irish people are falling prey to all sorts of ills that arise from starvation. Poor souls,' sighed Elspeth, unaware that her husband kept the worst of the news from her for fear of upsetting her and did not deem it necessary to mention the typhus that was raging in their district.

'He speaks here of Captain Willoughby, Lucy. D'you remember him, my love?' blithely unaware of her daughter's red cheeks, 'apparently he took leave and disappeared off into the countryside against the express orders of the Colonel. Well! Did you ever hear of such a thing? He will have got an ear wigging from the Colonel, I'll be bound. Ah yes; so he did. And listen, Lucy, they are to return, and…….. oh my goodness!'

'Mama, what is it? Pray don't keep me in suspense!' but Elspeth was busy scanning the letter rapidly,

'A moment, darling. Mm, they are to go to India…..but….yes, he says I am to go too.'

Lucy sat by her mother. She felt lightheaded and chilled, as though a cold wind had sprung up, though the spring sunshine shone as warmly as ever. She scarcely heard her mother's chatter,

'India! We have never been there. I have heard so much about it. Of course the little ones will have to stay with their Aunt and Uncle. I've been told that the climate is very bad for children. What d'you think Lucy? D'you think Emily is too young at fourteen? Yes; I am sure you're right,' though Lucy had not replied. She turned to her mother with a dazed expression,

'You mean I am to come too? Oh Mama!' And Elspeth found herself enveloped in a close embrace.

'Yes of course you are to come. You are as near full grown as makes no difference, and how can I bear to lose all my children! Never marry a soldier, my love, for you will find your heart broken one way or the other. I have been separated from your dear father for all these months and now I am to be separated from my little ones.' And she sighed histrionically and dabbed at her moist eyes.

'But wait. Let me just read this. He says he will be home very soon; probably hot on the heels of this letter, but they are summoned to India as a matter of urgency, and won't be in London above three weeks! Goodness. How can I be ready so soon?' But her audience had deserted her as Lucy had risen and wandered off to pursue her own thoughts. She passed her sister Emily, idly swinging beneath a stout oak tree while her brothers chased each other around with loud whoops. They called to her as she walked slowly by,

'Lucy, Lucy. Come and play, do. We'll hide and you can find us. Lucy….please!'

But Lucy hardly noticed them. So, she thought, he would be home soon, but then would go again, to India. But she was to go too. She wrapped her arms around herself in excitement. He could not fail to notice her if they were to travel together. India. She had read so much about that exotic far off land in her novelettes, unaware that those closely printed pages could not claim to contain accurate information! Romantic figures with melting dark brown eyes and gorgeous costumes floated across her mind. Towering minarets and elegant pavilions jostled with elephants surmounted by magnificent howdahs. Sloe eyed maidens at the world over diaphanous veils. India!

Two weeks later, Hilary Mainwaring strode through the front door of his Chelsea home, to be greeted ecstatically by his wife and joy by his children; three of whom were blissfully unaware that they were to lose their Papa again very soon! Dinner that evening was regaled by stories of the Regiment's time in Ireland, and in turn he was badgered by his young sons,

'Did you see any leprechauns, Papa?'

'Did you fall into any bogs?' Hilary fended them all off with a smile, loath to tell them exactly what went on in that benighted country; the starvation, the hopelessness, the despair, the sickness. Lucy listened avidly for a mention of her beloved, but in vain. Eventually, when she could bear it no longer, she was forced to enquire, putting on an air of nonchalance,

'Papa, what about Captain Willoughby? You wrote that he was in disgrace….?'

'Oh yes, I did write about it, did I not? He spent some time with Colonel Deluce, though no-one knows what passed between them. Major Williams, Willoughby's Senior Officer, recommended suspension, though I thought that a trifle harsh, though disobeying orders is a serious business. The countryside was rife with troublemakers and there was disease abroad. He even brought a boy back with him; I was told that he stank abominably!'

'But Papa,' urged Lucy, beside herself with impatience, 'what happened to Jam…. er….. Captain Willoughby?'

'He's been confined to barracks ever since. The Colonel could have sought his resignation, but another Captain was forced to request sick leave, so Willoughby was needed. Why d'you ask?'

'Oh no reason. I was just interested and I did wonder what it took to be in disgrace!' And with a tinkling laugh which sounded false to her own ears, she changed the subject. Fortunately Harry took up questioning his father, giving Lucy a chance to ponder on the information. So James was confined to barracks, so out of harm's way of the ladies in London; Lucy smiled in satisfaction.

Next morning, Lucy was summoned to the library where her parents had been closeted for over an hour in earnest conversation. She knocked and entered,

'Ah there you are. Come in child,' called her father, 'though I shouldn't call you that any more. You have grown up charmingly while I have been away. And your Mama tells me you have become as much as a companion as a daughter!'

'Thank you Papa.'

'Now my dear. Your Mama tells me that you know of the Regiment's transfer to India?'

'Yes Papa.'

'She also tells me that she would like you to accompany her when the time comes?'

'Oh yes, Papa.'

'I thought it best that you should listen to the arrangements, for your Mama is going to need your help and support during the coming weeks.'

'But Papa, are we not to travel with you; with the Regiment?'

'Not this time, m'dear. We are called to India as a matter of urgency and there is no time to arrange matters here before I must go. We could be away for some years!'

For the first time since entering the room, Lucy noticed that her mother was sitting with her head bowed and weeping quietly into a lacy kerchief,

'Mama, what is it?' she said, dropping to her knees beside her mother's chair. Her mother waved the kerchief vaguely, so Hilary provided the answer,

'Yes; well. It is not wise to take young children to such a treacherous climate…'

'I know,' interrupted Lucy, 'Mama said that when the letter came.'

'Yes, but she didn't know how long we would be gone. The boys and Emily will live with my brother until they are of an age to join us. I wrote to him before I left Ireland, and I received his reply this very morning. He and Aunt Elizabeth are willing to take them, and he should be here in a day or so to help sort out our affairs.'

Lucy was aghast. When she had first been told she could go to India, she had assumed it would be for a year or two, and that she and Mama would travel with the Regiment. She was very fond of her younger siblings and the thought of not seeing them until there were grown was too awful to contemplate. No wonder her Mama wept into her kerchief. But the alternative was worse; as much as she would miss the little ones, she would miss her parents more; and of course, there was James!

Hilary's brother, Humphrey, arrived two days later, post haste from his estates in Essex. The brothers were not close, but they knew their duty towards each other, and Humphrey did not hesitate to offer to take his young nephews home with him and raise them with his own hopeful brood. The boys, George and Harry would go to Eton, of course, at the proper time, and Emily would share his own daughter, Susannah's governess.

The brothers set about terminating the lease on the Chelsea house, which had been taken fully furnished as suited such a peripatetic family. But they had lived there for the longest period, and had grown attached to the place. Emily in particular declared that she could not *bear* to leave it, and did not *want* to live with her poisonous cousin, Susannah, and that the baby screamed *all the time*, and ………. until her mother threatened to box her ears, and only refrained by the thought that she would soon leave her behind! And it was not surprising that she taken to throwing tantrums at the upheaval to her young life!

All too soon it was time for Hilary to leave, and the entire family gathered at the quayside to wave him off. There were soldiers milling about everywhere, and Lucy strained her eyes in the hope of spotting James, but without success. Indeed, time had dimmed the memory of his face to such an extent that she was not at all sure that she would recognise him from a distance. However, she had learned patience over the years, and having waited so long, what were a few more weeks?

After the Regiment's departure, the house arrangements were soon completed, but there were still some weeks before the schooner that they had booked passages for Elspeth and Lucy, would set sail. Humphrey suggested that they would do better to wait out their time in Essex, and the offer was gratefully accepted. She was emotionally exhausted by the loss of her husband so soon after his return from Dublin, and the thought of the looming separation from her younger children. Normally a sensible, stout hearted person, she was now given to sudden bouts of tears, which the harassed Humphrey found difficult to cope with. Within a week of the Regiment's departure, the whole party set out for Essex. The weather improved again and their spirits rose as they drove by trees laden with blossom, and spring flowers a-riot everywhere.

They were greeted by Humphrey's placid wife, Elizabeth, who took over the task of soothing her fractious sister-in-law. The boys instantly disappeared off with their cousins, Jake, Tobias and Timothy in the direction of the gardens. Emily quickly became reconciled to her 'poisonous cousin', Susannah with a promise of a visit to the stables, to visit her new pony. Even better was a promise from her Uncle that she should have one of her own to help her over the loss of her parents and older sister!

Lucy seemed strangely bereft. Her mother was closeted with her Aunt and her brothers and sister had disappeared. She wandered out to the garden where she indulged in her favourite daydream, in which she walked up to James clad in an elegant ballgown, with rosebuds twined in her hair, and he held out his hand to her in complete adoration.

The weeks passed pleasantly enough and at last it was time for Elspeth and Lucy to return to London to board the 'Lady Grace' which was to carry them to their exotic destination. At the last minute, Elspeth's sister, Enid, who had also been staying with them, announced her intention of travelling to India with them. Until the very last minute, the redoubtable maiden lady had declared that nothing would drag her to 'those heathen lands'. But when she realised that her sister's departure would mean that she would have to return to lonely spinsterhood in her small property in Brighton, she suddenly discovered in herself a taste for travelling!

The parting with Emily, George and Harry was every bit as bad as Elspeth and Lucy had feared. Emily grew hysterical, causing Elspeth to blench with distress, and threaten to overset their plans. Fortunately, the promised pony arrived that very morning, and Susannah was able to coax her wailing cousin away to the stables. The boys were then hugged to their mother's bosom until they voiced a muffled protest from her lace fichu,

'Don't worry,' said Harry soothingly, 'I'll look after George,' and could not understand why his mother burst into a fresh bout of weeping. Lucy hugged the boys, and felt that her heart was breaking. Her throat closed up and she found it impossible to speak.

Humphrey, who was to escort them, finally managed to shepherd his charges into their carriage, and they set off, followed by another piled high with luggage. They stayed overnight in a comfortable hotel and early next morning boarded the Lady Grace, riding at anchor, and looking not nearly large enough to carry them nigh on half way round the world. The other passengers were also families of members of the Regiment, and also a sprinkling of young men recruited by the East India Company, and going out to join their employer.

Lucy found herself the only young, unmarried and passably good looking female on the voyage and her spirits rose accordingly. Within days of their departure, waved off by a mightily relieved Humphrey, every young man aboard the Lady Grace, whether passenger or crew had fallen madly in love with her. They vied for the privilege of standing at the rail with her gazing at the sparkling waves; they fought for the privilege of escorting her to the Captain's table for dinner every evening; they squabbled with each other to indulge her every whim. The purser even went so far as to passionately declare his love as they drifted down the Iberian Peninsula and begged her hand in marriage on bended knee. A more flighty young female might have had her head completely turned by all the attention, but Lucy merely flirted with them all without favour, and saved her heart for the one she was longing to see.

The voyage passed in leisurely fashion. Elspeth and Enid found other mature ladies to spend their time with in comfortable gossip, most of them old acquaintances. They were secure in the knowledge that Lucy would not come to any harm with so many admirers to guard her. Lucy herself spent much time gazing at the surrounding ocean, reflecting that her beloved had passed this way. He too must have seen the flying fish skimming the surface of the water, and the dolphins with their perpetual grin. He too must have marveled at the grandeur of Table mountain, when the arrived at last at Cape Town. It was as well that her numerable admirers did not know what she thinking or their hearts would have been broken!

There was a brief, uncomfortable interlude as they approached India, when a storm assailed them, but it soon passed, and the very next morning a blue haze in the distance proclaimed the presence of land.

For them, India put on a welcoming face. The monsoon storm had washed away the offal and ordure from the blue waters of Back Bay, and all they could smell was the exoticness of India. For them, the air was balmy and warm, not overpoweringly torrid.

But best of all, their menfolk, who they thought would have long gone across the vastness of the sub-continent, were there to meet them! Elspeth greeted her husband ecstatically, the pleasure of the reunion finally easing the pain of leaving her other children at home. Lucy was also enfolded in an affectionate hug, and Enid greeted with surprise before they were shepherded to a waiting carriage, to be wafted through the streets of Bombay and on to the cantonment. The ladies gazed around them with lively interest and bombarded Hilary with questions, which he did his best to answer.

He had them driven straight to their bungalow to rest, for, he explained, they were to be feted that very evening at a grand dinner. The ladies were instantly in a flutter, all thoughts of rest completely gone.

'But Hilary,' wailed Elspeth, 'how can we dine out? All our dresses are packed on board ship!' Hilary merely smiled and gesticulated. Outside, a line of coolies were carrying their trunks towards the bungalow,

'Unpack what you need, m'dear, these ayahs will help you.' Clapping his hands, he summoned two Indian women to the room, clad in simple white saris. They entered, and pressing their palms together, bowed to the three ladies. Lucy was fascinated. The ayahs' hair was glossy and redolent of coconut oil, and each had a smudge of red on their foreheads. Escorted to their bedchambers, the ladies found their trunks awaiting them, with more servants busily unpacking them. Crinoline cages were taken out and coaxed back into shape. Evening gowns were unpacked and shaken out from tissue wrappings, and then carried off for pressing. There was feverish activity for over an hour when finally the exhausted ladies rested on their beds, worn out by the excitement of their arrival and the unexpected greeting.

Lucy lay somnolent, experiencing a gentle rocking motion as though she was still on the ship. Wondering drowsily how long it would be before she lost the sensation, she fell asleep.

Later, she dressed in her best evening gown. It was peach satin, and finished round the scooped neckline by silk rosebuds, and there was a matching spray of rosebuds in her hair. Her ayah helped her dress her golden hair high on top of her head in elegant array, exclaiming all the while at the colour in heavily accented English. Lucy's heart beat fast, and a delicate flush stained her cheeks. She did not wish to question her father, but she hoped against hope that *he* would be there. He must be; she would die if he wasn't. At last she was ready, and made her way to the drawing room to await the others, her satin skirts shushing, draped wide over the crinoline frame. Her father rose to greet her, his face showing his love and pride,

'You look lovely, my dear. I'm so proud of you.'

'Dear Papa,' she murmured, giving him a quick hug. Then Elspeth and Enid swept in, resplendent in mauve and puce respectively. The houseboy entered and announced the arrival of Major Conroy of B Company. He had been pressed into service by Hilary to escort Enid to the Officers' Mess, but he had no intention of trusting his wife or daughter to anyone else! Tucking one elegantly gloved hand into each crooked elbow, Major Hilary Mainwaring proudly led the way with a beautiful lady on each arm. To him, they were as lovely as each other, his eyes seeing his wife as no older than the golden haired girl on his other arm. Followed by Major Conroy and Enid, they walked along the tree lined street from the bungalow and across the parade ground, deserted in the half light of evening. Then they mounted the steps leading up to the Mess, where the ladies were relieved of their wraps by two magnificently dressed and be-turbaned Indian servants guarding the door. Then they made their way along a short corridor and into the anteroom. The room was already full of soldiers in full dress uniforms, and quantities of gold braid dazzled the eye under candlelit chandeliers. Hilary began the introductions,

'You know Colonel Deluce, Elspeth. Colonel, my daughter Lucy and Elspeth's sister, Enid.'

The Colonel bowed over the ladies' hands and they moved on. Suddenly there was an eddying movement, and in the gap thus created, Lucy saw - *him*! The blood drained from her face and she felt faint. Taking a firm hold of herself, she drew herself erect, and by gentle but subtle pressure on her father's arm, managed to manouvre him in the right direction. He stood stock still, as though he had been waiting for her, every bit as handsome as she remembered. She studied him covertly as her father moved slowly in his direction, smiling and bowing to acquaintances as they progressed. Nigh on six feet tall, with broad shoulders and well muscled legs in the tight fitting breeches; his brown hair waved across a broad, intelligent forehead, and his green eyes gazed at her across the narrowing distance. He had grown his sideburns longer than she remembered, and they now joined the ends of the sweeping gingery moustache, which framed a sensitive mouth; the chin was clean shaven and deeply cleft.

In turn he studied Lucy as she approached, utterly captivated. Recognition had not been immediate, and it was only the fact that she was with Major Mainwaring that made him realise who she was. But he would have been hard put to relate this ravishing beauty to the golden haired, tongue tied urchin of four years before! Moving with grace, her slender figure enhanced by the wide skirted fashion of the time, she was a vision of loveliness. White shoulders rose from the peach satin of her gown, as creamy smooth as the silk of the rosebuds that framed the high bosom. Brown eyes, striking with the bright blond hair, seemed to be locked with his as nearer and nearer she came. Her perfume, as evocative of a rose garden on a hot summer's day, wafted towards him. Then she stood before him, poised and cool. Her father began the introduction, but she interrupted with a soft, slightly husky voice,

'Why, we know each other from long ago, do we not, er, Captain Willoughby?' And he found himself stammering some sort of reply for all the world like a callow, lovelorn youth as she moved away, the crinoline swaying gently.

Lucy took a deep breath as the moment passed. She had met him again at last, and had seen the admiration leap into his eyes exactly as she had hoped and dreamed. And she felt she had acquitted herself well; not humiliating herself by falling into a faint or blushing a fiery red. She moved like an automaton alongside her father, her mother long since having left his side to renew old acquaintances. She bowed to this scarlet jacket and that, until called to attention with the announcement that dinner was served. There was instant skirmishing by Junior Officers closest to her, striving to claim the privilege of escorting her to the dinner table, and Hilary found himself almost elbowed aside in the rush. Lucy smiled charmingly at them all, and chose the nearest, an ecstatic Edward Colby. Major Mainwaring relinquished his hold on his daughter, and went off in search of his wife, only to find her leading the procession on the arm of Colonel Deluce. Even Enid was bespoken by the attentive Major Conroy, and the one man who had arrived with three females in tow, suddenly found himself without a one! Sighing philosophically, he followed the rest of the unattached officers into the dining room.

With so few ladies among so many men, they were scattered along the length of the magnificently laid table. The Colonel had shamelessly used his position to have two ladies seated either side of him, including Elspeth, but the rest of the Officers had to make do as best they could. Lucy found herself between Lieutenant Colby and another Lieutenant who introduced himself is Simon Carless. He was a young man of interesting looks, somewhat akin to a Greek god, but who obviously thought highly of himself. He managed to convey to Lucy that she was highly privileged to have him by her side, and he proceeded to tell her of his various attributes in an upper class drawl that managed to achieve an irritating nasal whine. She noted that James was some distance away, and that the heavy frown on his face suggested that he was unhappy with that situation. She soon discovered that the frown deepened when she turned to converse with Carless, though only slightly when she spoke to Colby. A spirit of mischief moved within her and she turned back to Carless more and more, thereby reinforcing that young man's inflated opinion of himself.

Dinner was served by the Indian servants in their emerald green tunics, and comprised several courses of highly spiced Indian dishes. The ladies, new to such dishes, found themselves perspiring gently, in spite of the indefatigable efforts of the punkah wallahs, and were glad to sample dishes of yoghurt sweetened with honey.

When the meal was ended, the ladies rose and led by Elspeth, returned to the anteroom to partake of some cha, leaving the men to their port and cigars.

For once, the men did not linger over their drinks, the novelty of having lady guests among them again was too new, and very soon there was a crowd in the withdrawing room. Within minutes, Lucy was surrounded by an admiring audience so that James, striding in with the Colonel, could not even see her. Scowling heavily, he sat down with the Colonel on a leather covered chesterfield,

'Why the black looks, James?' enquired the Deluce innocently, though he had already surmised the situation perfectly.

'Nothing Sir. It's just that all these families arriving put me in mind of my own.'

'Have you heard from your parents recently?'

'Yes indeed. The Lady Grace not only brought these good people, but also a packet of mail. My father wrote a long letter after Gerald's wedding, and also says that he and Mama would be leaving soon. In fact, they should be on the high seas even now. They intend to disembark at Calcutta, as being the nearest port to my Uncle and Aunt's estate. By the way, Sir, did I tell you that Carlton's estate marches close to theirs?'

The Colonel shook his head.

'It is amazing, is it not? We travel all this way to this enormous country, and then will have to traverse it, and now I find that I am to be almost a neighbour of their hosts!'

'Tell me James. How did the wedding go off?'

'Very well by all accounts. Gerald and his wife Jane, appear to have had half the county as guests, and were joined together in fine style. His bride looked charming and Mama cried all through the ceremony. Papa says that he is glad it is all over and is looking forward to the sea voyage.'

'Yes he would,' said the Colonel quietly, 'for your mother's sake!'

'You know then?' asked James in surprise.

'We have been friends a long time, James; there are few secrets between us.'

James was silent for a moment, and then changed the subject,

'I intend to write to the estate as Papa as written the direction to address it. I want to tell him about the Major's post you have offered me and I am sure that there will be no difficulty.'

'I'm sure you're right. Your father is very proud of you, you know.'

James read into the gently spoken words the tacit admonition not to blot his copybook again. He truly hoped that such a situation would never again arise when he might be called upon to compromise his beliefs.

'Ah,' exclaimed Deluce, 'it looks as if some of the ladies are leaving us. They must be exhausted by their hectic day, and the unaccustomed climate!'

James looked up in alarm. He had waited hopefully for the crowd around Lucy Mainwaring to thin, and in any case was too polite to interrupt his conversation with the Colonel. But now she appeared to be leaving!

The two men rose as Hilary Mainwaring approached with his ladies. Elspeth and Enid had both admitted to being extremely fatigued, and had begged to be taken back to the bungalow. Lucy had had no choice but to accompany them, in spite of the appeals of her courtiers! With the advantage of youth, she was not in the least tired, but swallowing her chagrin as best she could, Lucy wished them all goodnight, and prepared to take her leave of the Colonel, only to find James standing next to him. She swept an elegant curtsey to both men to cover her confusion, and wished them both goodnight.

Later, lying beneath the soft draperies of a mosquito net, a novel experience for her, Lucy pondered on the evening. The effect she had had on James was all that she had wished for, but why, oh why had she behaved as she had done? She could have been polite to her dinner companions without acting the coquette. James would now think her a shallow minded hussy, and would pay her no more attention.

James tossed and turned on his cot in his bungalow, his thoughts filled with a golden haired beauty with gamin features, and striking brown eyes. Far from wishing to ignore her, he was busy planning on making a better impression on her, after his stammering greeting. He groaned aloud as he thought of the languishing glances she had bestowed on Carless of all people!

But the best laid plans are known to go awry, and so it seemed to Lucy. The day following the welcome dinner found all three ladies groaning on their beds from a surfeit of the unaccustomed spicy food. As Lucy curled up in agony, she had the added misery of believing that *he* would think she did not want to see him! For James' part, he had to go with John Carlton to visit a Bombay bunnia to arrange provisions for the impending departure of the Regiment. All day, a succession of visitors presented themselves at the Mainwaring bungalow bringing messages of cheer for the invalids; but not James. Lucy was in despair!

James returned from his trip to find that the Mainwaring ladies would not be gracing the Mess for dinner that evening, and illogically convinced himself that Lucy was ignoring him!

By the time the ladies had recovered enough to socialize once more, the situation had cooled to an alarming degree, so when at last they met, were perfectly polite to each other, but no more.

A week later, the Regiment left Bombay. Elspeth and Enid chose to travel in a well sprung carriage, procured for them by Hilary, who was unaware that he had been grossly overcharged by a smiling and bowing bunnia. Lucy preferred to ride, and for her, he found a spirited chestnut mare, with a white blaze on her forehead. She had a gentle mouth and sweet disposition, so Lucy dubbed her Doucette. The entire set of youthful subalterns instantly declared their wish to change places with the mare as Lucy showered endearments on the animal, and fed her tidbits from her palm.

She had had a derzee run up two riding habits, styled on the uniform of a French cavalry regiment she had once seen. One was midnight blue, faced with silver braid, and the other was bottle green, faced with gold. To complete both ensembles she had a matching hat, one side swept up and held in place by an enormous feather. She thought that she looked very dashing in both habits, an opinion shared by her coterie who rode by her side every day.

James found himself increasingly frustrated in his attempts to get close to Lucy without occasioning comment. In his brighter moments, he was convinced that she had shown an interest when they first met, but in his darker moments, decided that she had dismissed him as a stammering fool; and worse, one that was too old for her! To make matters worse, she seemed to favour the one officer that he just could not abide, Simon Carless. Every evening, when the officers and ladies met in a large mess tent for dinner, Carless managed to seat himself next to Lucy, so it did not take much to make the suffering James imagine that she favoured his suit. At such times, he would excuse himself immediately after the meal and take himself off with the excuse that he had to check the picquets.

Lucy was in despair. She disliked Carless wholeheartedly, but her encouragement on that first, fateful evening was enough to convince the arrogant young officer that she found him totally irresistible. While she enjoyed the admiration of most of the junior officers, she was convinced that James had dismissed her as a shallow hearted miss, too young for him to bother with. And yet, in their calmer moments, both would remember their first meeting when their eyes met across a crowded room!

The situation might have continued indefinitely if fate had not stepped in once more. Hilary Mainwaring was about to escort his bevy of ladies to the mess tent one evening, when Lucy discovered that she had forgotten her fan. For once, there was not a junior officer waiting to take her arm, so Hilary told her to fetch her fan and wait upon his return. Scorning such niceties when the mess tent was a mere thirty feet away, Lucy stepped out of her tent, busily arranging her full skirts, and bumped into James, also bound for the mess tent. He begged her pardon most profusely and offered to make amends by escorting her. Conscious that the collision was entirely her fault, Lucy was stricken with shyness, and simply nodded. Misreading her silence as a wish to be escorted by anyone rather than him, James said stiffly,

'If you prefer, I will find you another escort?'

Lucy in turn thought that he preferred to be elsewhere, and stammered,

'No, no. That is if you have duties to attend to….. I would liefer it was you who…..'

James stopped then and tried to look into her face, downcast from his. She looked up then, and he saw that her eyes were swimming with tears.

'What is it? Have I offended you in some way?'

'No. Oh no. Please may we go on and I will be better presently.'

That evening, James managed to sit next to Lucy at dinner, bringing a heavy scowl to Carless' face, which pleased James immensely, and another to Colby's, which did not! For the first time, James and Lucy seemed to be at ease with each other, and James was able to see that the young lady he was attracted to had hidden depths. It was during dessert that Lucy asked him what had been on her mind since her father had mentioned the incident in his letter, so many weeks ago,

'Major Willoughby?'

'Please call me James.'

'What did you do to earn a reprimand from the Colonel? Father spoke of an unauthorized excursion?'

James looked at her steadily and she returned the look with a quizzical expression. Satisfied that it was not just idle gossip that prompted the question, James marshaled his thoughts to provide a serious answer,

'We had been in Ireland for a long time, Lucy, and had seen the situation grow from bad to worse. Food queues, riots, men fighting for a place in the Public Works, soup kitchens and the like. We saw the worst that desperate men could do to each other, but in all that time we never left the city of Dublin. Reports would come in of villages starving and populations dying or drifting off to the emigration ships. We would talk about it in the Mess and say how terrible it was for them, but we really had no idea of the reality of it, and deep down we were just a little smug about ourselves. There was a prevailing feeling that if only they would try a bit harder, and not be so dependent on their potato crop they would be able to feed themselves.'

Remembering her mother's reaction to her father's letter, Lucy nodded mutely in understanding. James continued,'

When we were told of our impending transfer to India, I felt that I had some unfinished business to do; I wanted to see for myself. I had some leave due, so I left the barrack, ostensibly to spend a few days on a hostelry with some friends. Lucy, I cannot begin to describe what I saw; it was far, far worse than anything I had heard. I saw a field in the distance, not far out of Dublin, and I thought that it was covered in crows. As I got nearer, I realised that it was people, mostly women, picking over the ground in the hope of finding something edible. The villages that I had heard about were indeed deserted; I have never seen anything so desolate; no smoke from chimneys; no children's' voices; just an eerie silence and an icy wind that blew through empty doorways. I took some food with me for the journey, but when I tried to eat it, I felt nauseous. On my way back, I saw yet another deserted village. Just a collection of cottages, shebeens they call them, but it must have been a pretty enough place in the summer. There was a small lake, and a hill rising the other side of it. There was an odour that spoke of recent death, and I was about to hurry through, but in front of one of the cottages, there appeared to be a bundle of rags. I thought I saw the bundle move, but put it down to the wind that whistled round the place. What made me stop and take a second look, I will never know, but I did, and saw that it was a boy, and he was alive, though only just! Well, I thought, if I do nothing else for that poor benighted country, I would try and save this one boy. Doing what was needed took longer than I anticipated as he was desperately weak, but I couldn't just leave him there; there was no-one else to leave him with! So I was late and my exploit discovered.'

'And the boy; what happened to him?'

'That is what made it all worthwhile, Lucy. He not only survived, but is here with the Regiment in India, as a drummer. For those that claim that the Irish are all ignorant peasants should take a closer look at that boy! He has learned to speak English properly, so you would be hard put to guess his origins, and has learned the rudiments of reading and writing during the voyage. He is quite extraordinary and I'm sure he will go far!'

'I'd like to meet this drummer of yours; perhaps you could point him out to me sometime?'

'Lucy.' Elspeth's voice interrupted their low conversation. Lucy made a moue of annoyance, but her mother insisted,

'The ladies are leaving.'

'I'll be out very soon,' assured James, as Lucy hurried after her mother, who did not go further than a neighbouring tent to partake of their last dish of tea, while the men smoked their cigars and circulated the port. It was truly amazing, mused Lucy, how they took their 'civilized habits with them wherever they went!

That evening brought an ease between James and Lucy, and the discussion they had shared encouraged an intimacy they had both wished for, but had been unable to initiate. Lucy came to realise that the man she had admired for so long, albeit from afar, was not the demi-god of her imagination, but a warm, humane person who had been prepared to defy his superiors to defend what he believed in. For his part, James discovered that Lucy was a sensitive soul, who seemed to understand instantly the motives behind his escapade.

Though it cannot be said that the relationship blossomed without any setbacks, at least the foundations had been laid. There were occasions when her coterie of admirers made it difficult to get near her, and the imp of mischief within her made her encourage them, even the hated Carless, even though she knew it would enrage him! At such times, he simply took himself off to inspect the picquets, or go on hunting forays with Edward, thereby ignoring her for a day or two. But these were but minor setbacks, and as time went on, they made steady and inexorable progress towards complete commitment to each other.

Joe was happy on the journey as each new day brought new discoveries, new experiences and new friendships. From the moment he had left Ireland, his life had seemed to have blossom, much like the rose he had once seen in Grandpa O'Hara's garden. The plant had been stolen from the grounds of Danforth Manor one winter, and his Grandpa had planted it lovingly in his own small plot. He had manured it with seaweed, and carefully clipped it as spring advanced. Sean had watched as the early leaves began to open, and the plant made vigorous growth. At last, a flower bud had appeared which swelled and swelled, until it was ready to burst forth. It had slowly unfurled day by day, a deep red colour, layer upon layer of velvety petals gradually curling outwards. Now Joe felt that his life was like that rose bud, slowly opening his life to new layers of experience.

The early days had been marred by physical weakness and grief, but these had gradually faded until he was whole in mind and body. He would never forget his family and his home, but now he could remember them without the gnawing heartache.

For him, the change had begun on the ship carrying them to India when he had begun to learn to read. He had sat in the small cabin of the troop transport, and unraveled the mysteries of the strange shapes that made up the letters of the alphabet. Then came the discovery that they could be put together to make words that he used in speech; wonder upon wonder! Under Adam Swales tutelage, he had pored over the elementary readers, tracing the words with his forefinger and mouthing them as he went along, totally oblivious to the noisy, disinterested class around him.

Then had come India and the myriad new scenes that ravished the eye. In spite of the appalling heat and stifling air, ha had loved it from the moment he had stepped ashore. Let the others grumble about the gripes and the prickly heat; for him there was just too much to see and do. Anyway, he had been prepared from the start to dress like a native in his off duty time, and soon found the torrid heat easier to endure in muslin shirts and pyjamas.

The classes in Urdu were a further delight, and he loved to watch the Munshi, as he sat cross legged before them, clad only in a dhoti. First he would look at the motley collection of soldiers in front of him, noting those who came regularly, like Joe and Adam, and nodding at them would begin the lesson. Swaying gently from side to side, he would intone words in Urdu, followed by a translation in English, and would encourage his audience to copy him. Most of them ignored the invitation and talked among themselves, and it was left to those who really wanted to learn to take up the challenge. Joe found that he had a natural talent at copying the Munshi's intonation exactly, much like he had developed his own version of English. By the time the monsoons ended and they were ready to leave Bombay, he had acquired a respectable vocabulary. He liked to practice his newly learned words on any hapless bearer who came within his vicinity, and they would smile indulgently at his efforts, and if need be, correct him politely. Not long before their departure, he made a new friend among the army of servants, one who was always willing to listen to his efforts.

Gopi was the son of one of the bearers and was a year or so younger than Joe and Kit. He had lost his mother some years before and his father was training him to become a bearer like himself and wise in the ways of the English. Gopi's English was still rudimentary, and Joe decided that they could be of help to each other. Kit snorted with amusement as the pair tried out various words on each other, and took himself off to find some more congenial occupation. Within a very short time, Joe and Gopi were firm friends, and from each other, learned much about their respective cultures and religions.

If there was a cloud on Joe's horizon, it was his relationship with Kit. The boys had been fast friends since Joe had opened his eyes in the Dublin barracks, and Kit had steered him cheerfully through the hazards of his early days with the Regiment. On board ship, he had protected Joe from those men who found his chestnut hair and blue eyes attractive, especially when they were deprived of female company for weeks on end. And since arriving in Bombay they had roamed together, savouring the new delights of this exotic land. But Joe had the feeling that Kit wasn't interested in it for its own sake; the wonder at what made this country what it was; the people; their religions; their thoughts; their very difference to the English or Irish! He was convinced that Kit would spend his time in India as a casual spectator rather than become part of it. He was saddened by that but knew that there was nothing to be done about it; it was simply Kit's nature, but inevitably he felt a gradual drifting apart.

One evening, Joe and Gopi sat beneath a peepul tree contentedly puffing on bidis. The raw tobacco smoke stung Joe's eyes, as he was a newcomer to the habit, but he found pleasure in the shared experience. He tried to copy the relaxed way that Gopi sat, squatting easily with bony knees projecting upwards. He had seen Gopi stay in that position for an hour or more at a time, but he found ten minutes in that position caused excruciating cramps in his thighs. No matter, he was determined to persevere. Meanwhile, he shifted his position with a sigh and looked about him.

The camp was bustling with soldiers preparing for the night. Picquets were being changed on the perimeter, and muted commands drifted towards them. Innumerable cooking fires sent columns of fragrant smoke vertically upwards in the still air. The night was chill as winter was approaching, but Joe had bought himself a quilted garment in one of the larger villages they had passed through, and he felt warm enough. He admired Gopi's stoicism as he was, as usual, clad only in a dhoti and light shirt. To one side of them were the officer's tents, far grander affairs than their own, and between them strolled ladies, always surrounded by escorts, particularly the young Miss Mainwaring and Joe could see her golden hair lit by the fires, forming an aureole round her head. Joe had notice Major Willoughby's attentions to that young lady, as he noticed everything about the Major, and hoped he would be successful in his courtship. Joe felt something akin to hero worship for his saviour, and would willingly have kidnapped the object of his attention if asked to do so!

Above the boys' heads were a myriad of stars, sparkling in the frosty air, and Joe wondered idly if they were the same stars that had shone down on him in Ireland. He had never taken much notice of them before, except to admire their beauty. Gopi interrupted his reverie with the observation that he would have to find his father, before his father found him and cuffed him about the head as he was used to doing.

'Don't go yet, Gopi,' urged Joe, and then 'what do you want from life?'

'Why, to be a bearer, like my father, Sahib. What else is there?'

'But what if you had enough rupees to buy your own land and farm it, what then? You wouldn't have to serve others!'

'But Sahib. It is my dharma. What would I do with many rupees?' chuckling, 'I would be a rich bearer!' Joe looked at his friend, his mouth stretched in a grin,

'Dharma? What is that?' Gopi thought carefully, searching for unfamiliar words,

'It is what I am; what I was born to be. Why would I want more? It is my dharma to be a bearer. I am content.'

Gopi rose and left Joe to his thoughts. 'Dharma', he mused. It was a strange word and a stranger concept. Never to want more than you are born with, never desire to change, to move onwards and upwards. Perhaps that was Kit's nature too as he did not appear to want to learn new things, to find out more about life. Joe had already learned much about the caste system among the Indians he had met, and found that their class system was as rigid as the British one! He had also learned of their adulation of strange things, including cows. These creatures were encountered everywhere, gazing at them with soulful brown eyes, fringed by absurdly long lashes. Only the day before they had marched towards a village, and squarely across their path ruminated one of these beasts, dewlaps swinging and its large hump silhouetted against the sky. The animal was emaciated, for though the villagers revered them, they couldn't afford to feed them in hard times, and they grazed where they could. The column had parted and flowed round the cow like water flowing round an immovable object. As Joe had marched by, he looked at the cow and could have sworn that it winked at him. A bubble of laughter had risen inside him, earning a reprimand from Corporal Dunster, but he couldn't help it; the might of Queen Victoria's army diverted by a cow! He had tried to share the joke with Kit later that evening, but was rewarded by a puzzled frown.

'Dharma.' What was his dharma? Once he would have been content to live the life of a subsistence farmer, but now he had the unshakeable conviction that he had a long path to travel in his life. He had discovered in himself abilities that he didn't even know he had! Pride in his ancient Celtic ancestry rose within him; the spirit of princes that strode the fertile lands of Ireland and bowed their heads to no man; until it had all gone wrong and they were overrun by their more powerful neighbour.

'Dharma.' He came from a race that his fellow soldiers despised, and yet he had already proved himself more capable than they in learning the secrets of reading and writing, and the mastering of another language. All the common soldiers thought about was where their next meal was coming from, or chasing the camp women and tumbling them in the long grass beyond the camp perimeter.

Joe finished his bidi, and groaning from his stiffened limbs, made his way to the tent he shared with Kit and six other private soldiers. Muffled curses followed him as he stumbled over supine bodies, but they were light hearted, for Joe was a popular youngster among the soldiers of A Company, largely due to his unfailing cheerfulness and willingness to carry out errands without complaint.

The next night found Joe sitting under another tree; this time his companion was Sergeant Adam Swales. The scene was remarkably similar to the previous evening, for the land they were travelling through was flat and monotonous, punctuated by groves of trees, such as the one they were sitting under. Somewhere in the night, jackals barked and monkeys chattered as they settled down for sleep high in the safety of the trees. Tonight, Joe puffed on a cheroot, courtesy of Adam, and he puffed on the unexpected gift. He and Adam had become good friends in spite of their differences in age and rank. Born of genteel parents but raised in dire poverty, Adam was entirely devoid of class consciousness, and he had taken a liking to Joe on board their transport, and had recognised in the boy the same thirst for knowledge that he had always had himself. He also admired the dogged determination with which Joe tackled all new tasks, whether it was learning to speak 'correct' English, learning to read and write, or mastering a new language.

'Have you heard of 'dharma'?' asked Joe, sure that Adam would know the answer, as he seemed to know everything else!

'I've heard the word, as I have heard of 'karma', but I am not too clear on their meaning. Dharma seems to be ones role in life, and as far as I understand it, is as unchangeable as the seasons. Karma seems to be one's fate. These people believe that everyone is born more than once; reincarnation they call it. If they follow their dharma in one incarnation, then better fortune should follow in the next. It is hard to understand when our Christian beliefs tell us that we only have one life and we must use it to prepare for an eternity with God.'

''Do you believe in God, Sergeant Swales?' Adam was one of the few people that Joe could ask such a question, and it was a question that had taxed him for a very long time.

Adam puffed on his cheroot before answering, as he sensed in the question the need for reassurance,

'Look up there, Joe. What do you see?' Joe looked puzzled, but dutifully replied,

'Stars.'

'Yes, but just look at the numbers of them, Joe. If we sat here for a year and a day, we couldn't count them all. Look at the world around you; how did it all get here? There is so much that is beautiful that I cannot believe it is all accidental.'

'Yes; but isn't there also ugliness, and hunger and disease?'

'I know Joe. We cannot understand all of it. I do not know the rhyme or reason why we must suffer on occasion. But man has a will. He can do much for himself if he uses it. Yes, I do believe in God, and I also believe in a force for good and a force for evil. A man must choose his path, and when things go beyond his control, it is also a measure of a man how he copes with it.'

Joe sat quietly as he considered Adam's philosophy. There was a lot in what his mentor said, but still,

'What about when babies and little ones starve; what then? What sort of God gives them such suffering that they can do nothing about?' He sighed, as he did not have his answer yet. Adam watched the troubled face. Joe's features had matured over the previous months since he joined the Regiment, and now it was rapidly becoming a man's face, with a light growth of reddish hair on his chin, and the planes of his cheekbones and jaw line were much more defined. No, Joe was not satisfied and Adam could only hope that his unquiet soul would find peace one day. Perhaps it would happen in this country with its concept of Dharma and Karma. Many of his own kind would consider his thought heretical, but Adam was a free thinker in every sense of the word, and was always prepared to listen to other points of view, while holding firm to his own beliefs.

'Have you remembered that it is Christmas Day tomorrow, Joe?'

Joe looked stunned. He had indeed forgotten. Christmas. It had used to be his favourite day of the year. The whole of Clonarty would gather to hear Mass from Father Muldoon; old enmities would be set aside; old quarrels forgotten, as voices were raised in paens of praise for the new born Christ Child. In this strange land and unseasonably mild weather he had forgotten!

'Wait here, Joe, I've a gift for you.' Adam rose and stubbed out his cheroot and went down the slope to the tent he shared with other sergeants. Joe sat musing while he waited. A gift! What manner of gift would his mentor have for him and what could he give in return? Before he got too agitated at the thought, Adam returned with a heavy book. He chuckled,

'You would not thank me for this if you had to carry your own baggage. Thank God for doolies, eh Joe?'

Joe opened the heavy book carefully; it was a Bible bound in leather and tooled in gold lettering. Joe was too overcome to speak, as it was clearly a valuable book, and equally, well used!

'But Sergeant, I can't take this; it is your own; I've seen you use it many times!'

'There is no value in a gift easily given, Joe. This book has travelled far and brought me comfort more than once. I believe it might do the same for you if you will open your heart to the words you read. It is not an easy book, mind, and you will learn more about reading than all of my lessons could teach you!'

And again he chuckled. Joe sat with his legs drawn up to his chest, cradling the book to his heart. He whispered,

'I will treasure it always.'

Later, Joe gave Kit a gift. It was a statue of the Hindu God, Ganesh, the elephant headed son of Shiva and Parvati. He had bought it during one of their forays in Bombay, and had been told that by a particularly astute bunnia that it was the God of learning, and he had paid many times its worth at that thought! But he gave it to Kit with Adam's words whispering in his ears, 'there is no value in a gift easily given'. Kit returned the gesture with a pair of slippers with outrageously curled toes!

Next day, the entire Regiment attended service, conducted by their chaplain. Protestant and covert Catholic alike stood bareheaded under an Indian sky and sang songs to their God, alien to this land of Moslems and Hindus, Buddhists and Jains. Their servants stood watching, unaccustomedly silent as they pondered on a strange religion that seemed to worship a new born baby!

Lucy Mainwaring stood between her parents and prayed that her relationship with Major Willoughby would soon reach fruition and Lieutenant Carless would cease his unwelcome attentions, which were bidding fair to ruin everything!

Major Willoughby stood next to his Colonel, and remembered his parents on this special day, praying that his mother had not worsened too much since he had last seen her, and that the sea voyage might indeed have helped her condition. He also prayed that he would see both parents again soon after they reached their destination. Of Lucy, he tried not to think. Lately, she seemed to strongly favour Carless' suit, and he was rapidly convincing himself that he had been mistaken in her character.

Joe stood next to Kit and remembered past Christmases when he had prayed with his family for a good year to come and a fair harvest. The Protestant service did not offend him at all, as there was enough that was familiar to bring tears to his eyes.

Adam Swales stood nearby and dreamily pondered on the strange events that had brought them to this place. He too remembered his large and boisterous family, his indigent parents and the love that had enveloped them all. Of his lost love, Penelope, he did not think at all.

After the service, Colonel Deluce announced a week's respite from the journey and an extra drink ration all round. He was roundly cheered as the Regiment prepared to enjoy Christmas fare, and seven glorious days free of travel.

Chapter 5

'Please ask the Burra Sahib if I may attend him.' A splendidly dressed figure stood before Captain Forsyth, Colonel Deluce's aide, and delivered his words with a punctiliousness that spoke of careful rehearsal. Captain Forsyth blinked at the gorgeous apparition before him, and replied with equal correctitude,

'If you care to wait a moment, I will see if he is available,' and nodding at the visitor, went into the inner tent which served as an Officers' Mess, and where Colonel Deluce was enjoying tiffin with his staff officers.

Deluce listened to the message with a frown of annoyance; he had grown used to enjoying his tiffin in peace and quiet, and it was the last day of their holiday. The next day, the first of the New Year, would see them on the move again at dawn. However, at his aide's insistence that the visitor looked to be of some importance if his regalia was anything to go by, he swallowed his annoyance and followed his aide outside.

Blinking in the bright, midday sunshine, he took in the splendidly clad Hindu before him, who even now made solemn namaste. He was clothed in a tunic of brilliant scarlet satin, so brilliant that in the bright sunlight, it almost hurt the eye. A gold turban was meticulously wound around his head, and decorated with a white egret's feather held in place with an enormous ruby. The tunic was sashed with gold cloth above snowy white pyjama trousers tucked into glossy black boots. Behind the Hindu, a mettlesome black horse was held in check by a syce, an impressive moustachioed figure with a fearsome looking tulwar tucked in his belt.

'Burra Sahib?' said the Hindu, questioningly. The Colonel was amused; he was not accustomed to having his credentials questioned, but as he was out of uniform, he replied with equanimity,

'Yes. I am the Burra Sahib, Colonel Deluce. What can I do for you?'

'My master is the Raja of Kotepore. He has been travelling, and is now returning to Kotepore. He has learnt that your Regiment is also travelling to Kotepore and requests the pleasure of your company for dinner this evening.'

This speech was delivered in a sing-song voice, again in the manner of one who had carefully learned his lines, and his face was creased with concentration and anxiety. The Colonel spoke slowly and carefully,

'Tell your master that I shall be delighted to join him for dinner this evening.'

The heavy frown on the face of the Hindu reinforced the suspicion that he was committing the answer to memory, and then,'

'You may bring your officers and the esteemed Carlton Sahib. Eight o'clock. A guide will come and show you the way.' Making Namaste again, the resplendently dressed visitor mounted his horse and rode away before a bemused Deluce had had a chance to respond to the last instruction. He was still amused by the whole thing, but also intrigued. What manner of coincidence brought the Raja of the very District he was travelling to, to this place, at this time, given the vastness of the country? The answer would be sought this evening; clearly it would have been pointless to question the messenger.

Shrugging to himself, the Colonel returned to his officers and gave them the news that their presence was demanded at a Hindu dinner party that very evening. The reaction to the unexpected invitation was muted, as they had all looked forward to a New Year's Eve celebration with their lady guests; but there was nothing to be done; the Colonels tone brooked no argument!

John Carlton was there, and Deluce sat himself down beside the former Major and passed on the information that he was required to attend as well, indeed, had been demanded by name! Carlton smiled,

'The Raja and I are old acquaintances. I wish I had known who your visitor was; I could have helped with the language.'

'What is the Raja doing here?' enquired Deluce.

'He had arranged a marriage for his eldest daughter with one of the Rajput princes and the wedding trip had been planned for some time. It was sheer coincidence that the transfer of the Regiment was due to happen at the same time. Colonel Manfred knew of it, but clearly forbore to mention it. Indeed, in the all the years we were stationed at Kotepore, he had the feeling that we were not fully accepted, and that the Raja was not to be trusted.'

'Why was that?' asked Deluce.

'It's difficult to put your finger on a reason. We were regularly invited to the palace and royally entertained. But sometimes we had the feeling that they were watching us with distinctly hostile expressions, as if they would rather use their tulwars on us rather that feed us! Oh! By the way, they are strict Hindus and as such, will not eat with us as we are considered to be casteless. Nothing to be done about it, I'm afraid!'

Deluce nodded. He was aware of the caste system of the Hindus, though he found it incomprehensible!

'But that still doesn't explain his presence here?' persisted Deluce, 'if they left at the same time as us, surely they would have reached Oudh by now?'

'Indeed, that is so. But the Raja's son has reached an age when his father considered he should something of the rest of India, and at the same time, visit various members of their family who have married and moved to other provinces scattered across the continent.' In fact, their party left Oudh ahead of us, but arrived in Bombay around the same time. Then they had to wait for the same reason as us; the weather! I met with him during our stay there.'

Carlton and Deluce looked up as a commotion near the entrance heralded the arrival of a group of junior officers, squabbling amicably among themselves. James Willoughby brought up the rear, wiping the sweat from his forehead with a colourful silk scarf.

'And I say that Harding won the day,' expostulated a red faced Colby, 'what d'you say, James?'

Thus addressed, James cheerfully acknowledged Harding's victory, and so managed to start the wrangling all over again.

'Oh I say James, how can you say so? It was young Davey won the dash!'

'Yes, but the outright winner was Harding! I'll wager a month's pay!'

The argument raged back and forth, until James caught the Colonel's eye, and crossed the room to join him and Carlton.

'What's all that about?' demanded Carlton.

'We've been on the maidan indulging in some horse races. It seemed a good way to spend the last day here. The ladies came to cheer us on, but as you can hear, there seems to be some dissension over who actually won! We are all looking forward to the party tonight to see in the New Year! It seems incredible that last New Year we were in Ireland with no thought of release.'

'I've got some news for all of you, James,' said the Colonel quietly, 'the Raja of Kotepore is travelling the same road as ourselves and has camped nearby. He has asked for our company for Dinner tonight.'

'But the party tonight! We have planned for it, and all the arrangements are made!'

'Yes I know, and I am sorry. It is only the senior officers, though, so the ladies will have to be entertained by the junior officers; it will keep them on their toes!'

James was dumbstruck. He had looked forward to this evening as a means to make his peace with Lucy, and all being well, ask her to marry him. She had been at the maidan cheering on the contestants, and though she had been impartial with her favours, once or twice James had caught her looking at him in a way that encouraged him to press his suit. But now he would be forced to leave her to the less than tender mercies of Carless, who would doubtless make the most of the opportunity. None of the this mental turmoil showed on his face as he addressed the Colonel,

'Are the ladies not invited with us, Colonel?' He was answered by Carlton, fully aware of James' anxiety,

'I'm afraid not, James. It is not the Hindu custom to take their women into company, and they will expect us to behave in similar manner.'

'James,' interrupted Deluce, 'I rely on you to organise the escort. A dozen men will do with a couple of drummers. Make sure they smarten themselves up; we want to make a good impression!'

'Yes sir!' and James left to arrange the detail, his mind seething with angry thoughts. Why tonight of all nights? The fates seemed to be against him with a vengeance. He strode through the camp, his features set in a scowl, ignoring friendly greetings that followed his tempestuous passage. He stopped short at the sight of Lucy, ravishing on white muslin and twirling a wholly frivolous, frilled parasol. She was deep in conversation with Simon Carless, and as James watched, she threw her head back and laughed at something Carless had said. James spun on his heels and marched away, his thoughts as black as his tasseled boots! So that was it; doubtless she preferred the younger man, with his blond, Grecian good looks. If only she had the sense to see through the man, and recognise how shallow and self-seeking he was; but so be it!

It was a pity that James had not waited for a moment longer, for, as he had turned away, Lucy too had flounced away in the opposite direction, leaving an enraged Carless glowering after her. The laughter had been in response to a crassly delivered proposal of marriage, which she had rebuffed in the most damaging way possible; by mirth! Carless had seen fit to inform her how lucky she was that someone as high born and fastidious as himself should take an interest in her. It was at this point that Lucy, at first amused, and then irritated had turned away and disappeared into the tent she shared with her parents.

Unfortunately, as she had turned, she had caught sight of James' retreating back, and the stiff set of his shoulders told its own tale. He had seen Carless talking with her and had misconstrued the situation. Drat the man! Drat all men! She would have nothing more to do with any of them. With that firm resolution, she began to look forward to the evening, when she would take great delight in ignoring both of them. But her plans were doomed to come to naught, as her father entered the tent soon afterwards, greeted his wife and daughter abstractedly, and imparted the news that they would be without his company that evening, as all the senior officers were required to 'dance attendance on some heather potentate'!

'Hush dear,' admonished his wife, casting an anxious glance at the ayah, busily laying out their gowns for the evening.

'Humph,' growled Hilary Mainwaring, not at all pleased with the rearrangement of his evening, 'I'd liefer be with you tonight, m'dears. We've been apart for the last two New Years, have we not?'

'It can't be helped,' said Maud wistfully, 'Lucy, Enid and I will have to make the best of it. How many officers are going with you?'

'Why, Major Conroy, Grant, Willoughby; and oh, that fellow Carlton. Seems he is an old friend of the Raja.'

Lucy listened in silence, trying not to cry. So much for her plans to show both James and Simon that she really didn't care for either of them!

James strode across the camp and found the soldiers of A Company enjoying their midday break.

'Where's Sergeant Brittan?' he snapped at Kit who happened to be lounging against a tree trunk and whistling discordantly through his gap teeth. He jumped to attention,

'Yessir. I'll get him sir.'

Kit ran off in search of the Sergeant, accurately assessing the Major's mood. Any delay would likely bring his wrath down on all their heads.

'Funny,' thought Kit, 'it's not like Major Willoughby to be in a paddy!'

Luckily he spotted Sergeant Brittan quickly, and passed on the information that he was wanted instantly, if not sooner!

James tersely gave out the orders for the evening, emphasizing the need to be smartly turned out, or 'heads would roll'. Oh, and two drummers were expected.

'Phew,' muttered Kit, 'it's not like the Major to be h'aeriated!' Joe agreed, and busied himself with preparations for the evening. He had no wish to feel the lash of the Major's tongue if he were not smartly turned out. He eased on the jacket to check if it needed attention. It was getting increasingly tight across the shoulders, and his wrists stuck out of the sleeves a good inch or two. He was growing apace and would soon have to beg a new jacket from the Quartermaster if he was not to appear too ridiculous. It really was amazing how he had shot up upwards and outwards since joining the Regiment. It seemed only yesterday that the jacket hung on his emaciated frame, and the shako had descended over his ears.

That evening, the detail formed up outside the officers' tent, and awaited the appearance of the guide. He duly arrived; the same moustachioed syce from the morning, with the same fearsome tulwar stuck in his sash. He waited impassively while the Colonel and his Majors mounted up, along with Carlton, and the party set off to skirt the lake. The Raja's camp lay the other side of the lake from their own, and was screened by a grove of trees, so it was little wonder that they had not noticed their arrival. As they approached, the soldiers unconsciously stepped out briskly, marching in perfect time to the drummers' rat-tat-tat. They came to a halt with perfect precision outside a tent that was so large, it appeared to be a portable palace! Hung with rich silks and topped with miniature minarets, it could have been transported from 'Arabian Nights!'

At the entrance, bowing obsequiously was the same round faced emissary who had carried the invitation to them that very morning. This evening, he was gorgeous in vivid blue and silver, 'doubtless to match the hangings of the palace' though the Colonel inconsequentially as they dismounted.

Then the Raja stepped out, surrounded by his entourage and greeted his guests. The escort stepped back a pace and snapped to attention as the officers approached their hosts. Joe peered under the peak of his shako, drinking in the sights around him. He was dazzled by the colour and splendour of the Indians, and privately thought that they made the dress uniforms of the officers look positively dowdy. At that moment, a youth stepped forward to be introduced. Joe frowned, searching his memory; he was sure he had seen the youth before! But surely the last time he had seen him he had been mounted on a thoroughbred stallion that he had controlled with consummate ease, and had been called 'coolie' for his pains! It was the youth from Bombay. Small wonder he had been enraged at the epithet; the son of a Raja; and he, a lowly drummer boy, had had the temerity to sympathise with him!

When the introductions were done, the boy stepped back and looked along the line of soldiers drawn to attention. His eyes seemed to meet Joe's across the intervening yards, but if he recognised him under the shako, he gave no sign, and turning on his heel, he followed the party into the tent.

The Raja bade his guests make themselves comfortable on piles of cushions heaped about the tent on exotic rugs. The Colonel groaned inwardly; his aging bones would not take kindly to crouching on cushions, but he would have to bear it as best he could. He was seated next to the Raja with Carlton on the far side of his host. His officers were ranged round in a semicircle, interspersed with members of the Raja's court. A lavish meal was served by soft-footed khitmagars, but as Carlton had predicted, their hosts did not eat with them.

The conversation ebbed and flowed around them. Deluce was mindful of Carlton's warning about the Raja, and was on his guard, but as the meal progressed and much excellent wine consumed, he relaxed. The questions seemed to be innocuous enough; how was the journey; what did he think of India; was it as pleasant as England? The Raja was a handsome man of middle years, with dark brown eyes devoid of expression. He was softly spoken with a voice as silky smooth as black velvet; and then,

'Tell me Colonel, what do you think about the policy of annexation?'

Deluce heard a warning cough from Carlton, as he strove to clear the wine mists from his head. He knew about the policy having discussed it with Carlton, and also knew that it was a bone of contention with many Indians. He understood that it was to do with the British forbidding the Indian custom of adoption when there was no heir in direct line, and then annexing the districts involved, thus bringing them under British rule. While there had been great resentment at such treatment in many areas, so far protests had been fragmented, with the Indians too busy squabbling among themselves to take concerted action.

Deluce replied carefully, anxious not to offend his host, but equally he did not wish to deny a policy that was being meted out by his superiors in Calcutta!

'Your Highness, I have been in India for such a short time and would hesitate to express an opinion after such a brief acquaintance.'

The Raja stared at him impassively from slitted eyes; the only sign of annoyance being a slight flaring of his nostrils. Then he turned to Carlton and addressed his next remark to him while Deluce breathed a sigh of relief, vowing to drink no more wine that evening! It certainly behoved him to keep a clear head around this man! Carlton was right; underneath the hospitality there simmered a deep resentment against the British.

James found himself seated next to Prince Saeed, son of their host. The youth spoke impeccable and unaccented English, which prompted James to enquire where he had learned it.

'I was at school in England until a year ago, at Eton. You may know of it?'

'Yes indeed,' responded James, 'I was there myself, many years ago. Did you enjoy your time there?'

The Prince's eyes darkened and James got the impression that he had memories of the place that he preferred not to share.

'My father considered it necessary for me to have a British education so that I might understand the ways of the British in our country. The other boys were not used to brown skins.'

The reply was said in a flat, passionless manner, but it made the skin crawl at the back of his neck; he knew only too well how cruel young boys could be to anyone they considered to be different. Strange to hold his skin colour against him, though; it was hardly darker than James' own. Just then, he was distracted by his other neighbour, and when he turned back, the Prince had gone. James was disappointed as he had found the boy very interesting to talk to, and he hoped that his questions about his school days had not upset him unduly. He had appeared to treat the matter with stoicism beyond his years, but there was no telling what thoughts went on behind those heavy lidded eyes; so very like his father's.

The Prince strode out of the tent, shadowed by his bodyguard, who never let him out of his sight. Saeed was used to his presence that he generally ignored his existence, except to be aware at all times, that the man was in his father's pay and doubtless reported back regularly.

He searched for and found, the soldiers of the escort seated on a grassy mound nearby, waiting for the call to return to camp. Food litter scattered about told him that they had been fed, and now they were peaceably smoking bidis and playing cards. The Prince strode over to them, searching for a face he thought he had recognised. Joe looked up, startled as Saeed stopped in front of him where he was sitting chatting to Kit. He jumped to his feet and spontaneously greeted the Prince with a respectful namaste. The Prince looked surprised, but returned to greeting equably enough.

'You were in Bombay?'

'Yes, Your Highness. And you were on a beautiful stallion!'

'I am not 'Your Highness', and you may call me Prince. Do you want to see him?' This last was snapped out abruptly, as though he was surprised that he had said it!

'I would indeed, Prince.'

The Prince turned on his heel and strode away to the horse lines, where syces guarded the valuable horseflesh of the Raja's entourage. Saeed stopped by a chestnut stallion, with gleaming coat and proudly carried head. He fondled the horse's soft nose, whispering endearments in Urdu. He then stood back for Joe to take a closer look. Joe sensed the horse's nervousness; seemingly jittery around strangers. Approaching slowly, Joe made no attempt to touch him, but as he drew close, he leaned forward till his face was close to the stallion's and blew gently into his nostrils. The animal shied back and then leaned forward, snuffling at Joe's face. Saeed looked startled, and then laughed,

'You are the first Englishman to have gentled Shiva!'

'Perhaps it is because I am an Irishman, Prince,' answered Joe without thinking.

'Ah,' said the Prince enigmatically, 'let us talk a while.'

Joe fell into step just behind the Prince as he wandered to the edge of the lake, but at an impatient wave of a hand, he came alongside instead. He wondered what such an exalted young man should want from him, but waited quietly to find out. They reached the water's edge and seated themselves under a feathery neem tree. The bodyguard sat close by until an angry gesture from the Prince drove him further away. Night had fallen long ago, and now a bright moon lit the surface of the water with a silver sheen. A zephyr breeze touched them icily, but the Prince seemed not to notice the cold.

'That day in Bombay,' he began abruptly, 'you stopped me from being foolish. That ignorant man nearly had his head cut off by my syce's tulwar. It would have caused no end of trouble!'

Joe didn't know how to reply, so remained silent. The Prince continued,

'It seemed that you knew exactly how I felt and was willing me to stay my hand.' Saeed turned and looked Joe straight in the eye; he returned the look steadily,

'I don't know if what you say is true, but I just felt that he had no right to speak like that when he was a visitor in your country.'

The Prince laughed mirthlessly,

'Visitor? I thought the British owned the country!' he muttered with a bitter tone, 'but of course you are Irish. You must feel the same?'

'But how do you know about the Irish?'

The Prince smiled at his surprise,

'I know much about your history as I was at school in England for a few years. You would be surprised how much I know about the British habit of conquering every land they visit, and then plundering them for their riches!'

Joe felt uneasy. He could not disagree with all the Prince had said, but he was, after all, in the uniform of the hated conqueror. As if he divined his thoughts, the Prince said quietly,

'I felt that I could talk to you as I could not to any of the boys I met in school. Somehow I knew you would understand, even if you are dressed like that! Why did you join their army?'

'I was starving. My family was all dead or gone away. One of their officers found me, and took me back to the barracks. In the end it seemed to be the only thing to do.'

The Prince nodded. He understood the quirks of fate only too well.

From somewhere in the darkness a jackal barked and a night bird screeched. They could see the Regiment's camp fires twinkling across the lake. The night chill crept on them, but still they talked, low voiced, until they heard shouting from the royal tent warning them that the escort would soon be required to form up. They got to their feet and turned to go. Then the Prince looked Joe deep into his eyes, and taking both of his hands between his palms, he pressed them together. Joe felt a frisson down his spine; somehow he felt that their destinies, their karmas, were linked; he was sure of it.

Lucy Mainwaring found that her headache was getting worse as the evening progressed. It had started as a small pain behind her eyes when she had discovered that her father and all the senior officers would not be attending the New Year's Eve party after all, but would be entertained royally (she believed) by an exotic Indian Raja. For the first time since they had left England she felt homesick for their Chelsea house where she could have locked herself in her bedroom and have a good weep; or pour out her troubles to her obliging maid, Daisy. As it was, there was little privacy in their tent, and a bout of weeping would simply have brought about anxious questions from her Mama and Aunt, and that she simply could not bear.

So she dressed like an automaton, letting her ayah dress her hair how she liked, and paying no heed to the usual spate of extravagant compliments on its colour. When the time came, she accompanied her mother and aunt to the Mess tent where the junior officers awaited them, eager to do their duty in the absence of their seniors. The servants had excelled themselves, and the tent sparkled with their best silverware, unpacked for the occasion. The cooks had been sweating over their cooking fires all afternoon, and the feast could not have been surpassed had they been in permanent quarters rather than their peripatetic camp site.

Lucy's plans to ignore Carless' presence were quite unnecessary as he chose to treat her with rigid politeness when the ladies had first arrived, and then moved away so quickly as to earn a rebuke from Elspeth Mainwaring for his rudeness. The small pain behind Lucy's eyes began to spread, and soon her whole forehead throbbed under the elaborate coiffure. Edward Colby, delighted to have the field clear of both Carless and Willoughby for once, fought off all other admirers and claimed her arm to lead her into dinner. A small group of Regimental musicians were playing a selection of romantic pieces; the setting was perfect if only she had been in the mood for dalliance. Edward was a sensitive young man and simply grateful to have Lucy's company for the evening, made no demands for her attention. Equally grateful for his consideration, she made an effort to converse, and presently managed to forget her troubles; if only the intrusive headache would go away, she could have got through the evening reasonably well.

At last, the dinner was over, and the ladies left the men to their port as they retired to repair the ravages to their toilette, or partake of a dish of tea. There was no room in the Mess tent to dance, but for hardy souls who wished to brave the chill night air, there was an area of beaten earth outside the tent to twirl in a waltz or two. The evening dragged on interminably. Lucy vowed that as soon as the New Year had been toasted in, she would plead a perfectly genuine headache and take herself to her camp cot, and cry herself to sleep under the covers, in spite of the threat of unwelcome questions the following morning. Edward still persevered in trying to cheer her up, aided by the usual coterie of Captains and Lieutenants, but to no avail. Simon Carless shot her venomous glances whenever she happened to look in his direction, but in her present mood she was simply grateful not to have to deal with his unwelcome attentions!

Just as midnight was approaching the sound of drums a-beating could be heard, overlaid by the thud of horses' hooves. Lucy's heart beat faster, and for the first time that evening, the headache retreated a little. If only James would meet her halfway, she would explain about that afternoon and mayhap put things right between them.

The first to enter the Mess tent was Hilary Mainwaring, closely followed by Gerald Deluce. One by one, other Majors filed in, with John Carlton bringing up the rear. Edward, gazing at Lucy's profile as watched the procession enter the tent, thought that he had never seen anyone look so forlorn, and gave her hand a reassuring squeeze. She did not notice it at all!

'He isn't coming,' said a voice in her head, 'he doesn't care for me, after all.'

And then he was there, bowing to the ladies who stood near the tent flap, greeting Robert Harding, and fending off eager questions about their evening. He came closer, speaking to Edward and taking her hand, murmuring commonplaces, while she yearned to shout at him,

'He means nothing; I was telling him so but you turned away!'

The headache returned with full force, stabbing at her forehead until she nearly cried with the pain of it. James saw the unhappy look, but before he could enquire as to its cause, the Master of Ceremonies called them all to raise their glasses; it was midnight. They all stood and toasted the passing of the old year and the starting of the new. James looked into Lucy's eyes,

'It is a New Year, Lucy; let us make a new start?' Lucy's eyes filled with tears, her headache forgotten,

'Oh yes; please; may we?'

Across the room, Simon Carless looked at the pair with loathing. All tender feelings for Lucy had gone, swept away by her careless laughter that afternoon. How dare she snigger at his proposal when he, Simon Carless, scion of a noble family, albeit a minor one, had seen fit to honour her with it? And who was Mainwaring? Naught but the son of a baron after all. Well, he decided, Miss Mainwaring was not going to escape lightly if she chose to rebuff his advances. A plan began to form in his mind, his latent sadism rising to the surface as he contemplated his revenge. He would take Lucy Mainwaring; take her against her will, the thought of which merely added to his excitement; a piquancy; and he felt himself stir at the thought. For the first time that evening he smiled; but it was an evil, devilish smile, so that Captain Forsyth sitting close by involuntarily shivered, and moved away.

Back in their tent, Joe and Kit also toasted in the New Year with ale. Joe thought,

'This time last year I had a mother and brother, and we were all starving. Now I have no-one, but I do have a new life. I vow that I will not look back in sadness anymore; I will make something of myself in this land.'

'Ere Joe; I was just wishing you Happy New Year, but you was miles away!'

'Er, Happy New Year to you too, Kit.'

On the first day of January, 1848, the Regiment moved on again. It was not quite at dawn as the Colonel had hoped; too many sore heads were being nursed, not least his own, but by mid-morning they were on their way. Lucy rode with James and they chatted in companionable fashion. It was too soon to talk of their difficulties, but they knew that they would, that they could, in time; there was no hurry after all. Carless rode some way behind, brooding on his injured pride and plotting his revenge.

His chance came two days later. A party of riders took a gallop away from the marching column to find relief from the dust that was being raised. In the party were James and Lucy, Robert Harding, Edward Colby and Major Grant's wife, Abigail. She came with them to give propriety to an unattached girl's presence among so many men, but as she was but four years older than Lucy, she did not cast a damper on their spirits. They rode easily for a while, but then with a shout, found a long stretch of open ground and set their horses at a gallop. The thoroughbreds responded with a twitch of their tails, ecstatic at being allowed to stretch their aristocratic legs as they tore after one another. Doucette galloped with the rest, but Lucy felt her stride falter, and then the mare came to an abrupt halt, nearly tumbling Lucy from the saddle. She slid to the ground and looked at the mare standing with lowered head in obvious pain. The other riders soon realised that something was amiss, particularly James who had immediately noticed that Lucy was no longer matching him stride for stride. They all rode back and crowded round, exclaiming at the mare's dejection. James dismounted, and gently lifted Doucette's right foreleg,

'Look's as if she has picked up a stone.'

James worked at the hoof with his pocket knife and managed to prise out the offending stone, but then had to inform an anxious Lucy that the tender part of the hoof had been cut, and it was out of the question for Lucy to ride any further. The party all turned back towards the column, Lucy up behind James on his black stallion, which was well able to cope with the double burden, particularly at the leisurely pace they moved at, to allow Doucette to limp along led by Edward. For the rest of the day, Lucy was forced to share the carriage with her mother and aunt, a situation she thoroughly disliked as she loved the freedom of horseback, but the constant attention of James did much to lighten her spirits.

Carless discovered the mare's indisposition, as news travelled through the camp like wildfire. He decided to carry out his revenge that very evening, and laid his plans very carefully.

That evening, Lucy retired to her tent early, tired out by the day's events. Before she could disrobe with the aid of her ayah, a soldier presented himself at the tent, bearing a written message. It was unsigned, but Lucy supposed that it had come from James. It simply told her that Doucette was in pain and in need of her attention. If she cared to accompany the soldier who carried the note she could see for herself what needed to be done. Without considering the possible consequences of going out alone with a soldier to the horse lines, Lucy snatched up a warm shawl and told her ayah to wait on her return. The ayah looked at the retreating back impassively, hoping that the memsahib would not be long for she was tired and wished to go to her own charpoy strung at the end of Lucy's cot.

Out on the horse lines, Joe was on piquet duty. Though he was untrained with muskets as yet, he and Kit were expected to take their turn at guard duty, but they were always paired with a more mature soldier. Joe's partner on these occasions was a big shambling private called McKay. He was a man of limited intelligence, and with his shambling gait, had earned the nickname of 'Bear', but Joe got on well with him, and McKay relied on the younger man's keener vision and hearing to keep lookout for him. More than once, Bear had fallen asleep, knowing that Joe would rouse him if need be, but so far their nights on duty had been peaceful enough.

Joe loved being among horses. His father had never owned one, but in his youth, Joe had often ridden the Danforth ponies as they kicked up their hooves in boredom in the Danforth paddocks. He particularly like Doucette, for her nature was as sweet as her name, and he fondled the mare's silky nose as he fed her tit bits. He did not think that the injured hoof was very bad, and felt sure that it would heal quickly enough. As he murmured soft words to the mare, he heard footsteps approaching and in the light of a half-moon, he saw that it was Lieutenant Carless. He did not like this officer very much, having fallen foul of his acerbic tongue more than once, so he kept very quiet, fearful of being reprimanded for having the temerity to touch the horse of an officer's daughter. Then, to his dismay, he heard other footsteps approaching, and he peered round the horse to see two more visitors. Moonlight shone on a golden head, and he recognised Lucy Mainwaring. But what could she be doing meeting Carless late at night? Joe frowned; he, along with the rest of A Company, believed that all was well between the lady and captain Willoughby, so this situation was very strange indeed.

Lucy slowed as she neared the horse lines and looked around nervously. Suddenly she wished she had not come. It was very quiet here, away from camp noises and a chill wind sprang up, and she clutched her shawl close around her shoulders. There was no sign of James; where could he be? Then she heard a voice she had grown to hate,

'That'll do, private.'

'Yes sir.' And her escort saluted and marched away, leaving her alone with a man who she believed must cordially dislike her.

'It's kind of you to meet me here, Lucy,' said Carless with a sneering tone.

'I did not give you leave to use my name,' replied Lucy, trying to strike a haughty note.

'A female who meets a man alone at night has no cause to expect manners,' taunted Carless.

Lucy felt the clutch of fear; what did the man intend? Surely he did not lure her here to simply exchange insults? Carless could see well enough by the light of the moon, and accurately read her thoughts,

'Yes, my dear. You are quite right. I intend to enjoy myself with you, and you may tell who you please; your reputation won't be worth that!' and he snapped his fingers at her.

'You are being ridiculous,' said Lucy, with more bravado that she felt, 'I've only to say how you lured me here.'

'Lured you? But I have the very note I sent which clearly says that I asked you to meet me here. Who is going to believe you; afterwards?'

Lucy was silent. Carless was right. It did not matter in the least that she was innocent, and duped by this evil man. She had come out alone to meet a man, and that alone would condemn her in all eyes. As for James; he would not believe that she cared for him after all, as she had obviously chosen to meet with Carless.

Suddenly she was angry. How dare the toad treat her like this? To think that she had once liked him!

Carless watched her, a wolfish smile on his face. He accurately read every thought that was passing through her mind. He waited as her fury mounted, and then, almost contemptuously, he reached forward and seizing her shoulders, pulled her roughly to him and kissed her brutally on the lips. Lucy gasped and fought furiously. She dared not shout; she did not want to be discovered in this situation. She struggled, but Carless was stronger than he looked, and sexual arousal made him even stronger. Slowly but surely he dragged her away from the horse lines and away from the camp. He intended to enjoy the ravishment and he did not want a stray piquet hearing what was going on.

Joe heard it all from behind Doucette. The mare stamped nervously at the raised voice, but he quietened her with a gentle hand on her nose. His mind raced as he tried to think of a way to help Miss Mainwaring, realizing only too well the consequences of shouting for help. He had been among the English long enough to know the meaning of reputation and how easily it was lost. Bear must still be sound asleep as he had not appeared in spite of the noise. It was up to him to do something, and quickly, as the desperate sound of Lucy's struggles came to him through the chill night air. He went to where Bear was supine on the ground, heavily asleep. He eased the musket from under his arm, but still he did not stir. He shouldered the musket, and then strode off in the wake of the retreating noises, hearing Miss Mainwaring's anguished pleas and Lieutenant Carless' savage laugh, and he gritted his teeth. How could a man treat any woman so? He had an innate gallantry towards all females, and just couldn't understand Carless' actions.

When they had gone some distance from the camp, Carless neatly tripped Lucy so that she fell to the ground, and before she could move he was upon her, tearing at her clothes. The voluminous skirts and crinoline were but a minor impediment, and he rapidly set about disposing of them. Then a loud voice came from the direction of the camp,

'Halt; who goes there?' followed by the sound of a gun being primed, and then the voice came again, 'Halt or I fire!'

Carless swore bitterly, but got to his feet. Some idiot piquet was likely to take a shot at him if he didn't declare himself. But what was he doing so far out of camp? Cursing to himself, he moved away from Lucy, huddled on the ground, and trying to repair the ravages to her clothing,

'What d'you want?' he snarled.

'Sorry sir,' replied Joe, as innocently as he could, 'I thought I heard a noise. I was afraid for the horses; I thought there might be a horse thief, or a wild animal.'

Carless was silent for a moment. Joe had deliberately mentioned the horses in the hope that carless might surmise that he had been overheard. But he would not question him, of that he was sure; Carless could not risk admitting what he was about!

'Get back to the horses. There is nothing here,' Carless ordered.

'Yes sir.' Joe snapped to attention and retreated slowly. He did not think that Carless would attempt a further assault on Lucy knowing that he was in earshot, but nevertheless, he moved slowly.

Lucy stood up cautiously. She felt bruised and defiled, and wished she could crawl into some hole and stay there. She had heard the exchange, and like Carless, knew that they had been overheard. She wondered who her saviour was, but felt instinctively that her reputation would not come to any harm from the welcome intruder. But first she must get back to the safety of her tent. Carless stood before her with a look of pure hate,

'If you breathe a word of this, I will tell the world that you enticed me here; understand?' Lucy nodded bone weary.

'I just want to forget this, and you, as quickly as possible!'

Carless strode away into the night, leaving her alone. Lucy sank back to the ground and indulged in a fit of weeping. Then she heard footsteps and thought for one terrible moment that Carless was returning, but it was her rescuer,

'Ma'am, are you alright? May I escort you to your tent?' Lucy nodded, and rose from the ground. She tidied herself as best she could, and wrapping the shawl tightly round herself, began to walk with faltering steps. The youth, for she could see that he was very young, tentatively put a hand under her elbow to prevent her from falling as they made their slowly towards the lights of the camp. He spoke quietly as they went in surprisingly cultured tones,

'There was no need to come and look at your mare, the hoof is mending well, and she is not distressed.'

Lucy simply nodded, too tired to speak. She knew instinctively that the boy was going to be discreet, and if questions were asked, would state that she had gone to the horse liens to check on Doucette. Amazingly they reached her tent without meeting anyone she knew. Before she went inside, Lucy looked at her knight errant properly for the first time. She saw a handsome boy with copper red hair and striking blue eyes. He was but an inch or two taller than herself, for she was tall for a woman, but he was clearly going to make a well proportioned man.

'What is your name?'

'Drummer Joseph Harrington, Miss Mainwaring.'

So that was it. James' Irish lad who had far to go! James was right; he was extraordinary, with a sensitivity and intelligence beyond his years.

'Thank you, Drummer Joseph Harrington, for looking after Doucette,' and then 'and me,' sotto voce.

Lucy went inside her tent then, and was glad to see that her mother and aunt were still at the Mess tent. She felt that she had been away for a very long time, but clearly it was not so. Breathing a sigh of relief, she divested herself of her clothes without calling for her ayah, not wishing to see anyone in her disheveled state. Gratefully, she got into her bed and shut her eyes, but sleep eluded her for many hours.

The following morning, Lucy felt battered and bruised in mind and body. She rode in the carriage with her mother who exclaimed at her lowered spirits, but could not get anything out of her daughter save that she still had a dreadful headache, and a comment that 'perhaps I am a little homesick!' Elspeth put it down to another tiff with her suitor, though James was all attentiveness again.

'Girls,' sighed Elspeth to Enid, 'the sooner she was safely married, the happier she, Elspeth would be.' And she decided to speak to Hilary that very evening and warn him to treat James' suit with encouragement, should the Major speak out.

James was concerned when he found Lucy distrait for a day or two, but did not believe he was to blame. To his relief, she recovered her spirits as the mare's hoof healed, and she was able to ride again. Strangely, Carless now seemed to be keeping his distance, though he occasionally caught a venomous glance from him, and wondered at the cause.

The journey continued. They were traversing the great Gangetic Plain, and encountered innumerable villages, where the farmers were preparing for the spring planting. The villages were all curiously similar; simply a collection of untidy huts, flanked by water tanks where the precious monsoon rains were stored to water the crops through the hot season. Joe found that he could talk to the farmers with his halting Urdu and asked them questions about their crops. He could not but empathise with these simple folk, whose lives were dependent on the vagaries of the weather. Plenty of rain meant they could eat through the dry weather; poor rains and they would starve.

Most of the towns and villages were Hindu, but occasionally they passed through a Muslim area and heard the sound of the muezzin from a high tower, calling the faithful to prayer.

During their travel, James found the opportunity to question John Carlton about the Raja of Kotepore and his son. He had been fascinated with them while they were being entertained, and he was intrigued to know how John knew so much about them.

'We first met many years ago,' John began, 'I had not long been in India; just a raw young lieutenant! We had settled in Kotepore, but I was keen to see more of India,'

James nodded; he could relate to the idea!

'I found it fascinating from the start. On my first leave, I headed north towards the mofussil. I traveled light; just a couple of syces and camping gear. One day, we came on a low hill, and camped overnight. There were other people in the vicinity and we had met many hunting parties, but the country was at peace so I did not feel that I was in any danger. I got up at dawn to witness a spectacular sight. In the clear light of dawn, I could see the Himalayas far off. They were all colours; purples, blues, greens, and all capped with white. They seemed to float on a sea of green as the mofussil marched for endless miles right up to the foothills; but the mountains looked close enough to touch. The sun started to rise just then and turned the scene to pure gold for a moment, but as it climbed higher, the mountains vanished. I don't think I have seen anything so beautiful before or since. If you had been there James, you would have understood!'

'But what has this to do with the Raja?' asked James, impatiently.

'Patience my friend, I am just setting the scene. As I stood gazing, I was moved to exclaim, 'Why, that's magnificent!' A voice came from behind me saying 'yes, that is India at its best!' I turned to find an Indian behind me. He was one of the hunting party and though he was well dressed, there was nothing to proclaim him as high born. We fell to talking, and I professed a growing love for the country, and in turn he questioned me about England, and in particular, about the public schools. I was surprised to say the least! He invited me back to his camp to eat, and for the first time, I encountered 'caste', for though he sat with me while I ate, he didn't actually touch the food, which made me feel very awkward, surrounded by dishes, and a number of people watching me feed myself!' James laughed, having felt the same during their meal.

'The Indian introduced himself as Ajit Khan, but it was not until later that I discovered that he was heir to the Raja of Kotepore; his father was alive then. He spoke of his young family, and especially of his son, and said that he planned to send the boy to England to study. I asked him why he wanted to do that, and he replied, rather bitterly, that as the British were a fact of life, he thought that his son should learn all about them! It was the first time, James, that I questioned the rightness of our presence in the country. I'd grown up with the belief that the British had a right to go anywhere they chose, and that Indian was the 'Jewel in Victoria's Crown', and so on; but there was this man quietly putting the opposite side of the case. I stopped to think about how I would feel if an alien army ensconced itself in my country!' Carlton paused for a moment to light a cigar, and then continued,

'To cut a long story short, we parted company then, but when I returned from leave I discovered who Ajit Khan really was, chiefly because he invited me to the palace regularly. Colonel Manfred didn't like it, but there was nothing he could do without offended the Raja, and he had been told to keep on friendly terms with the Indians by the Commissioner in Calcutta!'

'It seems that the Raja did indeed send his son to England,' said James, 'the Prince told me that he had been to Eton.'

'Yes, but that did not happen until Ajit became Raja, as his father would not allow it. Also, there was a problem that needed to be solved with much consultation with saddhus, their holy men. You see, the Hindu believes that he will lose caste if he traverses the 'Black Waters' or 'Kala Pani', in other words, take a sea voyage! Of course, Ajit did not want that for his son, but he was determined that he should go; so what was to be done? It was agreed that he would not lose caste if he traveled overland until he reached the English Channel, which was deemed to be too small to be a threat. But all this took years to decide, so the boy was twelve years old by the time he left. It took a lot of courage from him and his father, for there was no certainty that he would survive the journey, even with a sizable escort. But somehow he did; all the way through Afghanistan and Persia where bandits and cutthroats abounded!'

'I don't think young Saeed enjoyed his stay,' said James reflectively, 'when I asked him about it the other night, he preferred not to say, and then slipped away quietly.'

'I'm not surprised,' observed John,' he was very young and had never been away from Kotepore let alone India. The Raja asked me to write to the school and make the arrangements, and the school insisted that he attend without his servants. That is demanded of all the boys, but it meant that he would be all alone in a strange country without one of his own countrymen to hand! No wonder he didn't care to talk about it.'

'And what does the Raja think about the British now?' asked James.'

'The same as he has always done. He hates their presence in his land. If he was powerful enough he would turn us out tomorrow. His son now knows the enemy better than any Indian Prince has done before. Me, he tolerates as he knows that I love the country, and have sympathy with his feelings, but I have no illusions; if I stood in the way of his getting rid of unwelcome guests, he would have me killed without a second's thought. As he cannot achieve it on his own, he has made a 'Talukda' instead!'

'What the deuce is that?'

'He has given me land to use as I will, and I must raise taxes from the people who live there. It's a common enough arrangement, but not usually with Europeans. They usually take what they want!'

'What about my Uncle and Aunt, then?' queried James, 'they have had an indigo plantation there for some years.'

'Yes I know. They have simply leased the land and pay for the privilege. The previous Raja, Ajit's father, was nothing if not pragmatic, and that land was not yielding much before the Ferguson's arrived. But they have no rights to the land and the Raja Ajit could turn them out tomorrow if it suited him!'

James pondered on all the information, and wondered at the strange relationship between his friend and the Raja. He was, as yet unaware, that his protégée had formed a similar relationship with the Raja's son!

The journey which had once seemed endless was nearly over. The Regiment, with its coterie of bearers, syces, dhobis, grass cutters, ayahs and other miscellaneous servants, was within sight of Lucknow. They had travelled up the slopes of the Western Ghats, penetrated lush jungle and swept through the corridor between the Aravelli and Vindhya Hills. They had gone cautiously through the primitive, feudal country of the Rajput princes before they had finally spilled onto the vast Gangetic Plain. Their position was ever proclaimed by a cacophony of noise and their passage marked by a vast dust cloud.

They crossed the River Jumna north of Allahabad, and the Ganges south of Cawnpore, and then swung northwards to approach Lucknow. Their arrival had been expected, and as they entered the city they were greeted by a contingent from the Regiment stationed in Mariaon Cantonment. These men fell in ahead of Colonel Deluce and his officers, and escorted them through the streets of Lucknow.

Though their final destination was a day's journey northwards, Lucknow would be the nearest large city to them, and where they would expect to spend their short leaves. Accordingly, they looked around with great interest. Like Bombay, Lucknow was a mixture of the exotic and the squalid. Minaretted palaces reared up above narrow streets, and walls everywhere were stained with betel juice, and close inspection of the splendid palaces revealed peeling stucco and an air of dilapidation.

By contrast, the Residency was neat and orderly and its buildings well maintained. They were not halting there, however, but made their way to the cantonment where they would rest overnight.

As they entered the cantonment, many of them experienced a feeling of déjà vu; they could have been entering an English country town. Spacious streets were lined with neat bungalows surrounded by gardens ablaze with flowers; zinnias, cockscombs and violets jostled with sweet peas and phlox. An exotic touch was added by quisqualis tumbling down walls, and competing with bougainvillea for climbing space; but everywhere was the glorious sight of roses. In multi-coloured and perfumed array, they filled the gardens and brought a homesick lump to many a soldier's throat. Joe was reminded forcibly of his grandfather's garden in Clonarty, and had to gaze sternly ahead to prevent a tear trickling down his cheek.

In the main barrack square, the resident Colonel greeted Deluce and his officers, and made arrangements for accommodation to be found for them all overnight. The ladies were carried off by resident wives to be clucked over, and their fashions examined by the ladies starved of fashion news from their homeland. The soldiers were crammed into the barrack blocks, as they had been in Bombay, but with cooler weather, the situation was far more tolerable.

Deluce found himself closeted with Colonel Smythe within an hour of their arrival, to be briefed about their duties in Kotepore. Smythe had despatches for Deluce to peruse at his leisure, but wished to personally warn Deluce personally of the situation he would expect to find there.

'How much did Colonel Manfred tell you of Kotepore?' enquired Smythe.

'Very little, I'm afraid,' admitted Deluce, 'he seemed anxious to get away from Bombay. He did say that the emergency that brought us to India was over.' Smythe frowned,

'The immediate emergency was over, but there is always a problem. Bandits roam the mofussil and are protected by the local populace in spite of our efforts to win them over to our side. We are tolerated in Oudh; no more than that. The Maharaja is aging and at present has no heir, and there could be trouble in due course when he dies. The Raja of Kotepore has a certain reputation for disliking our presence here. You've met him I understand?'

'Yes indeed. We dined with him one evening en route. I could see that he could be difficult!'

'I've a feeling,' went on Smythe, 'that the trouble in Oudh could be sooner rather than later. I hope I'm wrong, but it is as well to be prepared. As it is, Oudh supplies most of the sepoys in the Indian Regiments; it could be a recipe for disaster!'

The Colonels discussed Oudh and its problems for a while longer, and the Smythe invited his opposite number to stay in his bungalow overnight, muttering that his 'ladywife' would by only too pleased to welcome him.

That evening, the officers met in the Mess to be entertained by their hosts, reminding them of their arrival in Bombay so many months before. But this time, they felt themselves to be veterans of India. The pleasant cool weather added to a more relaxed atmosphere, as did the presence of the ladies, both visiting and resident.

The Mainwaring's had been whisked away to the bungalow of Mrs. Frenshaw, the wife of the most senior Major, and had been subjected to a barrage of questions from the lady and her daughters, aged sixteen and seventeen, about England, the current fashion, court gossip, in fact any and everything!

'I had a son,' said Mrs. Frenshaw in tragic tones, 'but he succumbed to typhoid fever within a year of our arrival.'

Lucy had already spotted a small portrait enshrined on a side table, but had forborne to ask questions!

The bungalow was crammed full of furniture in the Victorian manner, and plush covered tables fought for floor space with horsehair sofas and velvet covered chaise longue. Mrs. Frenshaw had a loud penetrating voice, and having gleaned all the information she could about England and its fashions, she began to complain of the difficulties of finding good servants in 'this God forsaken country'. As her diatribe was delivered in the hearing of bearers carrying tea trays and dishes of sticky sweetmeats, the Mainwaring's felt acutely embarrassed, but their formidable hostess went on, quite oblivious to the strained atmosphere. Lucy cast a quick glance at an Indian servant standing near her impassively, and she thought she could detect a look of anger deep in his brown eyes.

Thankfully, once tea was over, Mrs. Frenshaw recommended that they rest and refresh themselves ahead of the party later that evening. They were shown into two rooms, pretty with chintz covered chairs and muslin draped beds. Enid had been carried off by another memsahib, and Hilary was about his Regimental duties, so mother and daughter were alone, an extremely rare treat over the past weeks!

'What a welcome sight,' exclaimed Elspeth, 'a real bed after all this time! Really, I am getting too old for all this gallivanting after your father!'

'Mama! You know you wouldn't be left behind for the world! I hope our trunks arrive soon so we pick out our dresses for tonight. Lucknow looks big enough to have dressmakers, so we can have a few more made up. It will be fun showing the residents here a thing or two about fashion!'

'It's unkind to crow,' scolded her mother, 'in a while we will be in the same situation. Rest now my dear. You will want to look your best for your Major Willoughby tonight!'

'Mama! He is not *my* Major Willoughby!'

'Is he not? Well never mind; I am tired even if you're not. Elspeth kissed her daughter and left her in the care of an ayah who helped her disrobe and slip under the muslin drapes.

Lucy smiled to herself as she recalled her mother's remark. Little escaped her mother's eagle eyes, but she did seem pleased at the situation, and if she was, so would be her father! She was only thankful that she had been away from the tent that fateful night when Lucy had been brought back by the young drummer and had not witnessed her disheveled state She shuddered in the warmth of her bed as she relived those terrible moments when she had been convinced that Carless would was going to have his evil way with her. The following days had been nerve wracking as she had tried to behave as normally as she could in order to avoid comment. She had succeeded, in the main, and she had gradually put the event behind her, but memories would return in unguarded moments, and her slight frame would shudder violently until she got herself under control again.

Worst of all, Carless seemed to watch her from under his hooded eyelids as though he was still plotting her downfall. Since that day, Lucy had been careful that she was never alone near him, but the feeling of insecurity persisted. She drifted off to sleep with a vision of Carless' head gradually turning into an evil faun with pointed ears and horns growing out of his blond curls.

James arrived later at the Frenshaw bungalow in time to escort Lucy and her parents to the Mess. They all looked forward to the evening and the chance to meet new people and exchange news. James had heard that a parcel of letters had arrived for the Regiment and awaited them in Kotepore, and he confided to Lucy that he hoped to find a letter from his father.

The next morning, the Regiment set off once more, but only a short day's travel faced them before they would arrive at their destination. They marched up the main road through the neat rows of bungalows, all eager to catch sight of the place that would be home for an indefinite number of years.

The cantonment at Kotepore was built on the gentle slope of a hill, with parade ground and Mess set on flat ground at its foot. The bungalows climbed the hill on terraces, and gardens surrounded them, with well tended lawns. The town of Kotepore could be seen on the adjacent hill, crowned by the Raja's palace. Between the two hills was an extensive maidan, and the officers saw immediately its potential for races, or the increasingly popular game of polo.

There were rows of cottages for sergeants and corporals, and even a few modest ones for married privates. The main barrack blocks were set under groves of trees, and they did not look so large and prison like in such a setting. Kit summed up the general feeling of them all,

'Cor Joe; I could like it 'ere!'

Chapter 6

'Oh Major Willoughby!'

James looked with carefully suppressed irritation at the simpering, facile female in front of him. He had come to the Mainwaring bungalow in the hope of finding Lucy at home, but had had the extreme misfortune to encounter Miss Enid Fairweather, all alone. The lady was some two years younger than her sister, Elspeth Mainwaring and an established spinster, and she had a similar effect on the majority of her acquaintances.

When the Fairweather sisters had first been launched upon the ton of Regency society some twenty years before, they had been used to going about together, a measure of expediency on their parents' part, rather than a particular wish of theirs. Superficially similar, the sisters had a n abundance of blond hair and brown eyes; unusual enough colouring to catch the eye of the jaundiced Regency bucks. But on closer inspection, Elspeth's hair was seen to be a true, bright golden, whereas Enid's inclined to mouse, in spite of frequent application of lemon rinses. And Elspeth's brown eyes had faded to an indeterminate mud colour in Enid's rather sallow face.

'It isn't fair,' would bewail the hapless Enid in the privacy of her bedroom; but out in company she would try to compensate for her indifferent looks with an artificially bright and gushing manner.

The sisters were much invited out to functions, as hosts soon realised that if they wanted the attractive Elspeth, then they needs must invite

Enid! This situation continued almost to the end of the season, when a dashing Captain Mainwaring had espied the enchanting Elspeth, and had fallen head over heels in love with her. And wonder upon wonder, Elspeth, who could have had her pick of a dozen aristocrats' sons, lost her heart to the dashing Captain, newly returned from active service.

The pair swept all objections before them and were married in early autumn, and Elspeth ecstatically prepared herself to follow the drum. Her attendant at the wedding was her younger sister, Enid, fluttering in pink organdie, and praying for a gallant to sweep her off her feet. But it was not to be.

The following London season was singularly lacking in invitations for Enid, as the departure of Elspeth from the London scene meant that hosts were no longer obliged to invite her. Eventually, Enid retired to her parents' home in the country, and prepared for a long and lonely spinsterhood. With the demise of her parents within a year of each other, she found herself in possession of a generous patrimony, and she set up home in Brighton with a succession of companions. Brighton was much favoured by the Regency society as the Prince Regent was often in residence, and the constant presence of Regiments stationed in the locality gave Enid hope of dalliance more than once. But any possible suitors soon retreated in disorderly haste before the gushing manner which became more pronounced as time wore on.

Elspeth, living in a succession of army quarters, produced a parcel of offspring at regular intervals, and Enid finally found her niche in life, as a doting maiden aunt. Fortunately for her nieces and nephews, their travels did not bring them too often within their aunt's orbit until their extended stay in the Chelsea house, but by then they had learned to escape whenever they sensed her approach. Furthermore, her brother, Humphrey, also had a growing family, so Enid learned to divide her time between the two establishments and not to outstay her welcome.

Now Enid Fairweather gazed up at the embarrassed James, fluttering her eyelashes and fanning herself delicately with a silk fan stretched on ivory sticks,

'Oh Major,' she breathed, 'I'm sure you've come looking for Lucy, but she's just this minute gone out with my sister; I'm surprised that you didn't see them!'

'Actually, Miss Fairweather, it's Major Mainwaring I particularly wanted to see.' This remark caused Enid to flutter her eyelashes all the more, and she cooed archly,

'Why yes; the Major, of course! I mustn't ask what you wish to speak to him about?'

'If you'd care to ring, I'd be most grateful.'

'Yes, of course, how silly of me,' and Enid seized a small hand bell and rang it with a flourish of the wrist.

'Memsahib?' The soft footed house-boy spoke behind Enid, who had been gazing in adoration at the acutely uncomfortable James, and caused her to jump.

'Oh why must you creep up on one? See if Major Mainwaring is available to see Major Willoughby. At once d'you hear!' This last instruction was somewhat superfluous, as the servant, after looking enigmatically at the flustered memsahib, had disappeared as quietly as he had entered.

'I just can't get used to how they creep about, indeed I can't!' In truth, Enid just couldn't get used to the Indian servants at all. It was their differentness as much as their brown skins that bothered her, and she would often lie awake at night beneath her muslin drapes, convinced she would be murdered as she slept!

James just had time to form the prayer that Hilary would not be long, when the prayer was answered and Hilary Mainwaring strode into the room. He had been at Headquarters and had arrived home just in time to intercept the servant sent to look for him.

'Well James, this is a surprise. What can I do for you?'

'I'd like a word with you; in private!'

'Ah. Regimental business, eh?' he responded with a conspiratorial twinkle, which put James at his ease.

The men repaired to the study, where Hilary rang for a chota peg to put his guest even more at ease. Enid, left behind, lost no time in collecting her parasol against the steadily increasing midday sun, and setting off to find her sister and niece, agog with the news that James Willoughby had asked to see their husband and father, alone!

'Well James?' repeated Hilary, stretching out his long legs in a comfortable rattan chair.

'The fact is, Sir; I'd like to, er, that is,'

Hilary waited patiently. He was not a man overburdened with imagination, and did not immediately jump to the same conclusion as his sister-in-law. James began to colour up from collar, the flush rising to his cheeks, but at last managed to blurt out,

'I love your daughter dearly, and I'd like to ask her hand in marriage; if she'll have me!'

Ah,' replied Hilary, 'so that's it. Elspeth has been hinting for some time, y'know! How can I say no? Me wife made up her mind a long time ago,' and he chuckled at the look on James' face,

'You can't keep something like this quiet in a place like this. Well, my boy, I'd be pleased to have you for a son! Lucy favours her mother y'know. Looks just like Elspeth did when I first met her, and I tell you this, she doesn't look a day older!'

James was saved from the necessity of replying to this by the sounds of the arrival of the ladies. Elspeth knocked gently on the study door and entered, followed by a blushing Lucy and a simpering Enid.

'Hilary,' cried Elspeth, 'Enid tells me that you have a visitor; ah, Major Willoughby!'

'This young man wants to marry Lucy, what! Well puss?' and he gently pinched Lucy's scarlet cheek, 'what d'you say?'

'If it pleases you, Papa, I'd like to marry James; er, I mean Major Willoughby.' Her father chuckled and pinched her cheek again,

'It'd better be James if you're to be wed!'

Elspeth embraced her daughter, and then James. Enid did the same with much twittering, which momentarily stopped the conversation. Then Hilary called for sherry to toast the happy couple as conversation started up again, and plans were made. It would be the first Regimental wedding since they had all arrived in India, and they wished to make the most of it. After a while, Lucy caught James' eye, and reading the message in them, quietly left the room followed by her suitor. They went into the garden, where summer flowers and beautiful roses filled the air with their heady perfume.

James opened his arms, and Lucy came into them naturally. A tall girl, yet her man was taller, and she rested her head on his epaulettes and softly sighed,

'Happy, my dear?' asked James.

'Oh yes; especially as Mama and Papa seem to be pleased too.'

'It would seem,' observed James, dryly, 'that they have merely been waiting for me to declare myself!' Then he put a gentle hand under the girl's chin, and bending his head, kissed her softly on the mouth. He was momentarily surprised by a sudden shrinking away, but then it passed as quickly as it came, and he reminded himself that she was not used to a man's embrace. He could not know that the caress had brought with it a startling memory of Carless' sordid attack, and that Lucy had then to steel herself to continue the kiss, so that James would not suspect anything was amiss. Would she never forget?

The husky voice sang slightly off key. The song was a sad one; a haunting refrain that reminded Joe of the beautiful Irish ballads that his mother used to sing to them when they were small, and times were still good. Seeking the source of the sound, he listened,

Oh dear me, the mill is running fast,
And we poor shifters canna get nae rest,
Shifting bobbins coarse and fine.
They fairly make you work for your ten'n nine.
Oh dear me, I wish the day were done,
Running up and doon Pass is nae fun.
Shiftin', piecin', spinning warp, weft and twine
Tae feed an' clothe ma bairnies offa ten'n nine.
Oh dear me, the world is ill divided,
Them that works the hardest are the least provided.
But I maun bide contented, dark days or fine,
There's no much pleasure living, offa ten'n nine. **1**

Behind A Company barrack block he found a young lass up to her elbows in lye soap and attacking a mound of washing as she sang. She was an unkempt creature with a tangle of brown curls. Slightly built, with a barely formed figure, he guessed her to be some three or four years younger than himself. Catching his movement out of the corner of her eye, she looked up startled, breaking off her song with a tremulous quaver,

Whatcha staring at? Haven't you seen someone doin' laundry before?'

'Sorry. I didn't mean to startle you. I heard you singing and was curious; what was the song about?'

'Isn't it plain?' asked the girl, loftily.

'Well no. I haven't seen you before! Did you come here with the Regiment?'

At that, the girl threw back her head and laughed aloud, showing even white teeth in her peaked face. Now that he could see her clearly, he observed that she had elfin features, with grey eyes, though one eye was nearly closed by a swelling, blue-black bruise.

'Yes. I came with the Regiment! You mayn't've seen me, but I've seen you. You're Drummer Harrington, aren't you?' Joe nodded. 'The song's about the Jute spinning trade; those factories where folk slave from dawn to dusk for pennies. That's what's the song's about! I learned it from a Scotch lass.'

'So, you know me, but what's your name?'

'Nancy; Nancy Carter.'

'And how is it that I haven't see you before?'

'We was on diff'rent ships. An' then I was ill in Bombay, 'n me father kept me outta sight, 'n then I rode in a doolie 'cos I still wasn't well.'

Joe was puzzled about the situation. He knew the officers could bring their families, and a few of the non-commissioned officers, but rarely the privates; they were confined to drawing lots for bringing their so-called wives; but never their children. Seeing that he was full of questions, Nancy sighed, and wiping her hands on her soiled apron, she seated herself on a handy tree stump, and proceeded to tell him her story.

Her father, Will Carter, had worked in a cotton mill in Manchester, and in time was made foreman. He was a popular man, liked by the workers for his reasonableness, and by the owners for the efficient way he ran his shift. He worked hard, and the rewards bought his family a comfortable, if small, terraced house, coal in their grate and food on the table for his wife, Mary and their children; Nancy, the oldest, then twin boys. Will adored his wife, and counted himself a fortunate man. He was also moderate in his drinking, unlike many of his co-workers, indulging only in one or two pints on pay night. He enjoyed a single pipeful of tobacco last thing at night, before retiring to the tiny bedroom that he shared only with his wife, having a second bedroom for the children.

But then disaster struck the family. There trouble at the mill with unionists trying to gain ground. Will resisted them, fearful of agitation leading to the loss of his comfortable existence; but the unionists plotted behind his back and called the mill workers out on strike. For four bitter weeks, the strikers held out against hunger and coercion, but the sight of their family's hunger finally drove them back to work where Will waited, having reported for work every day. But his workforce were bitter at his 'blacklegging' and they conducted a hate campaign against the Carters. Night after night, stones were hurled at their windows, and they had to be stuffed with card and rags. Then rags soaked in pitch were lit, and lobbed through one of the recently broken windows, regardless of the possible consequences. Mary stood it as long as she could, but fearful for the safety of their young children, finally begged Will to move elsewhere.

Will finally gave in to his wife's pleading, and went to see the mill owners to get a reference for work at another mill away from Manchester. But for the sake of expediency, the owners refused to supply one as they were heartily sick of getting no work out of his shift for too long, and they were anxious to get rid of someone now deemed a 'troublemaker'. Will pleaded with them, reminding them that it was loyalty to them that had led to this, but they were adamant.

The family were soon faced with destitution, as Will could only get casual, poorly paid work. They moved out of their cosy terraced home, and into a one roomed hovel, and then to a dank, foetid cellar, whose walls ran with water, even in summer. One of the twin boys sickened with a fever and died, swiftly followed by his brother. Mary, broken hearted by the loss of her babies, and losing the will to live, soon followed her little ones to the grave. Will was a broken man. In a short space of time he had lost his home, his adored wife and his sons. He began to squander the little money he had on drink, leaving ten year old Nancy to earn what she could in a nearby mill as a child labourer. It's where I met the Scotch lass who sang that song!

Then one day, Will Carter announced his intention of leaving Manchester forever and making his way to 'the Smoke', where, he had been told, a man could become rich without even trying. Dragging Nancy in his wake, he trudged the miles to London, sleeping rough and earning casual money along the way to keep them from starving. The pair finally reached their destination, and Will found work in a hostelry, where he spent his earnings in ale, save for a few pennies he flung at his daughter to buy food. He never really knew how he came to enlist, but one day he awoke from a drunken stupor to find himself in the Regiment's London Barracks, with an aching head and the 'Queen's shilling in his pocket. He had become Private William Carter.

Nancy, left at the hostelry, thought that her father had wandered off again, or had been injured, or murdered in a street brawl. She made the best of the situation by running errands for the landlord's wife, a large bosomed, and large hearted woman, who took pity on the waif. Time passed by and just as Nancy felt settled at the inn, and was beginning everything had turned out for the best, the landlord came to her room one night and stifling her screams with a pillow, he forced himself on her. When he had done, he informed her that she would earn her keep more efficiently by servicing his best customers.

Nancy packed her meagre belongings as soon as the landlord had left, and ignoring the searing pain inside her, she robbed the till of its few shillings, and slipped out into the night. Morning found her making her way painfully near the barracks where the Regiment were quartered, newly returned from Ireland. It seemed, at last, that kindly fate was smiling on her, for the man on sentry duty was her father, hardly recognizable in his uniform.

He was as shocked to see her as she was to see him, and he was further shocked when he heard the reason why she had fled the shelter of the hostelry. He wanted to go and punish the man who had despoiled his daughter there and then, but Nancy pleaded with him to 'leave it be', as it could not change what had happened, just cause her father to be punished for abandoning his duty post. Will told her to return when he had finished his duty time, and he gave her a coin to get some food. He later smuggled her into his barrack block, telling Nancy that she must claim to be his woman, young though she was. It was the only way to keep her safe from other, equally lascivious men as the landlord.

And so they had departed for India. Will had made his daughter hide away in a rope locker, and shut away for most of the voyage, she had been miserable and sickly. Reaching Bombay, she had easily succumbed to the dysentery that had raged there, and very nearly died from it. She had still not recovered when they left for Bombay, and had traveled in a doolie. During the journey, with the frequent rest stops, she had gradually grown stronger, and was able to walk increasing distances during the day.

'An' that's how we got 'ere.'

Throughout her tale, Nancy had sat still, with her hands clasped in her lap. Her voice had a huskiness that was pleasant to the ear, but she had spoken in a monotone, except when describing the loss of her baby brothers, her mother, and later, the violent rape by the landlord. Then her hands had writhed together in her lap, and her voice took on a touch of hysteria, which she struggled to get under control. Joe looked at her profile, with her unbruised eye turned towards him, and could only marvel at her composure. She was surely too young to have suffered so much; though he could say much the same! And like him, her spirit seemed to have survived intact.

Yet the story was clearly not complete. Why was Nancy dealing with piles of laundry when everyone used dhobi-wallahs, and why was her eye blackened? These questions had yet to be answered. Again, she sensed his curiosity, and turning towards him, she looked long and hard at his face. Obviously what she saw satisfied her, and sighing once more, continued her tale in a voice so low, Joe had to strain to hear.

'I liked this place as soon as I saw it. I thought it was beautiful after Manchester, 'n London, 'n then the ship.' She gestured at the vista, and Joe looked at it with her. From where they sat they could see most of the cantonment, climbing the hill away from them, with gardens making splashes of colour between the neat bungalows. Looking in the opposite direction, the ground fell away gently until it reached a meandering stream that eventually ran into the sacred Ganges a mile or so beyond them. From their vantage point, they could see the ghats where the Hindus took their dead for ritual burning. Beyond the river could be discerned the rooftops of Kotepore, the skyline pierced with towers and minarets. Between themselves and Kotepore were dotted groves of trees; feathery neems, tall peepuls with their pointed leaves, and the strange banyans, with their habit of sending down tendrils to root in the fertile soil. It was indeed a lovely sight. Nancy sighed again,

'Me Da started drinking again. He'd stopped when he found me in London, and realised what his drinking had caused happen to me. But when we got 'ere, he found something over there that's even worse,' and she jerked her head in the direction of Kotepore, 'Opium! He said it helped him forget better'n drink. But it used up his money again, to buy it. That's why I have to earn a bit of money doing this!' She waved her hand at the laundry piled around her. Silence again; a sad, strained silence, and then finally a deep sigh. Joe waited patiently.

'When he was full of opium one day, 'im 'n 'is mate, 'e told 'im that I wasn't 'is wife, but 'is daughter. His mate suspected somehow, as 'e didn't use me at all. So 'is mate asked if 'e could?'

Joe was appalled,

'Did he make you?' he asked as gently as he could. She shook her head vehemently,

'No; no; I vowed that I would never be used against me will again. But 'he beat me with 'is belt.' Nancy spread her hands in a helpless shrug,

'It's only the opium; 'e wouldn't otherwise; 'is mate knows that and bides 'is time. But when they've 'ad a pipe or two, then 'e asks. So I have to 'ide.'

Joe looked at the gamin little face and thin limbs. But the look on Nancy's face resisted pity; she had too much dignity for that. He had asked for her story, and had got it in full measure!

'Is there anything I can do, Nancy?'

'What can you do? 'E 'as the right.' That silenced Joe, as it was true. Whether she was regarded as Carter's woman or child, he had every right in law to abuse her as much as he wished. And hadn't he suffered from an indifferent, if not violent father in his early years? The pair sat quietly until,

'Nancy'' A raucous bellow brought them out of their reverie,

'Aren't you finished with my shirts yet, girl?'

A soldier rounded the corner of the barrack block and strode menacingly towards them. He was a big man with a deep chest and powerful arms.

Thick black hair sprouted from his chest where his shirt was open to the waist, and his chin was unshaven, even though it was late in the day. Bleary, bloodshot eyes peered suspiciously from under thick black eyebrows. Joe had seen him before, though he did not know his name, just his unappealing reputation, and he was father to this slight elf of a girl?

''Ere. Whatcha doin' with me Nancy?' Carter lumbered up to the pair who rose nervously to their feet.

'Nothing. We were just talking,' said Joe, cautiously, as he saw Carter's fists bunch. He felt Nancy give him a slight shove,

'I've nearly finished; see! I'd just sat down for a moment.'

Just then, they heard the sound of horses, hard driven, coming from the north; from the direction of the mofussil. As they watched, the horses came into view, ridden by a soldier and a syce. The uniform was unfamiliar, but it seemed that the soldier carried a despatch bag. Carter's curiosity was roused, and as the riders passed out of sight behind the barrack block, he ambled away, forgetting his daughter and her unfinished laundry, much to her, and Joe's relief.

'You'd best go; 'e might come back,' suggested Nancy. Joe nodded.

'You'll not say anythin'?' she went on anxiously, ''ell only take it outa me.'

.No, I'll not say anything. But Nancy, if you need a friend, or help, or anything at all, you'll come to me; promise?'

Nancy nodded, then pushed him gently,

'Go now.'

Colonel Deluce frowned over the despatches. He had sent the exhausted messenger to find refreshment, but had told him to return as quickly as possible. There was a report from an outstation, a day's journey north of Kotepore and deep in the mofussil. The station served many of the scattered estates that supplied indigo and other commodities to the East India Trading Company, and was manned by a small group of their own soldiers. However, in times of crisis, they looked for aid to the cantonment in Kotepore. This was such a time, apparently. The bandits that Colonel

Manfred had spoken about, and that he had dealt with, had seemingly risen again, and had attacked the Ferguson's estate, and burned a number of indigo trees, frightening away the Indian workers. Fortunately, it seemed from the report, no-one was injured, but much damage had been done. The bandits had then sallied off to Carlton's estate, but that wily ex-soldier had hired himself a band of armed sepoys in Kotepore before taking his leave of them all. These had driven off these 'badmashes' without loss of life on either side. But, the despatches made clear that the bandits could, and probably would return, and the Colonel was requested to send help as soon as possible to round up the troublemakers once and for all.

Deuce digested the content of the messages, and then lit a cheroot before leaning back in his chair to think the situation over. Was it just coincidence that the Raja of Kotepore had very recently arrived back in his palace? Could it be that the Raja was flexing his muscles a little, and gently probing the nature of his adversary? Whether this was so, or not, it was a nuisance so soon after their arrival; why it was less than a week ago when they had marched in, and now at least some of them would have to march out again! Then he caught himself up with a chuckle,

'My God!' he muttered, 'I must be getting old! This is what we came for after all! Anyway, this is a job for a younger man; there will be a forced march if we are to respond quickly.'

Without waiting on the return of the messenger, he came to a decision,

'Captain Forsythe!' he yelled to his aide, who nearly jumped out of his skin; he had never heard the 'old man' shout like that before!

'Sir?'

'Send for Major Willoughby.'

Dawn the next morning saw one hundred men, two drummer boys, and the officers of A Company marching briskly out of the cantonment, led by the messenger and syce who had arrived yesterday. They set off northwards towards the mofussil, with Drummers Harrington and Barnet leading the foot soldiers with a stirring rat-tat, through a wispy blanket of morning mist, reminding the Irish among them poignantly of home! They were led by mounted officers, Major Willoughby, Captains Colby and Harding, Lieutenants Carless, Frogmore, Rose and Wilson. The rest of the cantonment turned out wave them off, many an onlooker envious of the marchers. But one onlooker dabbed at a tear with a lacy kerchief, as

Lucy Mainwaring tried hard to keep a smile on her face as she waved her soldier off in time honoured fashion.

They found the outstation a-buzz with excitement when they arrived as shadows fell in that evening. There were but a handful of sepoys and a small company of soldiers, in a modest collection of bungalows that were unprotected by even a bamboo palisade. Captain Clarke explained to James within minutes of their arrival that 'they were not used to trouble in their neck of the woods'. James looked round the station, noting the meagre attempts at defence in the form of a few sandbags.

'Set your tents up close to the bungalows,' James ordered his Captains, 'and set the sepoys and privates to start cutting staves. We should be able to throw up some sort of barrier tonight.' Then James motioned to Captain Clarke to precede him into the largest bungalow, where the telegraph was set up, and the administration of the station took place. The Captain looked ill at ease, as though he was being held to blame for the situation, and was, therefore, inclined to be truculent. James realised that he would be of more help if he co-operated, so made an effort to put him at his ease,

Well Captain; I see you have made a good start on the defenses. Tell me. When did you first hear about the attacks on the estates?'

'Two days ago, Major. These remote estates all have telegraphs so they can contact each other, and us, if necessary. It was the evening of; let me see; ah Thursday, that Mr. Ferguson signaled to say that he had seen smoke in the fields, and discovered that they had been deliberately fired.'

'Did he see anyone?'

'Not then. Later that evening, he saw a small group of bandits approaching the bungalow. He was worried about Mrs. Ferguson, but they veered off to the sheds where they fired some stored indigo, and then rode off. Mr. Ferguson didn't want to leave his wife, so stayed in the bungalow with his armed servants.'

'What happened next?'

'It was not until morning that he ventured out to see the damage and then we tried to telegraph the cantonment, but the lines were obviously down, probably courtesy of the bandits. So then we sent off the messages. By then a message had come through from Mr. Carlton to say that he had also been attacked, He has not had time to have his bungalow built, and was camped in the middle of the estate. But he had taken the precaution of installing a telegraph line ahead of his arrival, and came with a group of sepoys. Between them, they had beaten off the attackers. I must tell you Major, that I am very pleased to see you; there was no saying how serious this could become.' James nodded, and then mused,

'It seems passing strange that the bandits cut the lines to the cantonment, but not between the estates and you? It does seem that they wanted you to know, but not us; at least not too quickly. And they could have intercepted the messenger and his escort, and dispatched easily enough.'

Clarke looked puzzled; clearly he had not considered this fact of the affair,

'Perhaps they didn't know that I had sent a messenger?'

'Tell me Captain. You had trouble during Colonel Manfred's time, did you not?'

'Yes. We thought we had caught the ringleaders, for it has been quiet ever since, so I was very surprised at this upsurge after so long. The Ferguson's have always been popular; good to their workers; pay their rent on time, But,'

'Go on,' urged James,

'There have been rumours; no-one knows who starts them, but they say that the Ferguson's are planning to take over the land and not pay rent at all! It isn't true, because I talked to them about it. They are as puzzled as I am as to the origin of this.'

'How did the rumours start?'

'Who knows? You hear them whispered in the villages, in the market; everywhere! And when you ask where this person or that heard the story, they say it was their brother-in-law in the next village; and so it goes on.'

'I believe that this has been carefully planned,' said James, thoughtfully, 'why cut the line between here and the cantonment, but not between here and the estates? Why spare the Ferguson's when they were vulnerable? Why ensure that a detachment was sent from the cantonment but only after a delay?'

Clarke remained silent. He had no answers to these questions, and correctly surmised that James was simply airing his thoughts. Finally, James reached a decision,

'We'll camp here tonight, and in the morning, if you'll supply me with a guide, I'll go and take a look myself. You may not know this, Captain, but the Ferguson's are my Aunt and Uncle!'

And with that parting shot, James strode out, leaving a startled Captain, and went outside to see how things were progressing.

Joe sat near a small fire drowsily smoking a bidi and chatting in desultory fashion with Kit. Around them, the sounds of the camp settling down for the night eddied and swirled. From the horse lines came the gentle munching of the beast overlaid with the muted jungle of their harness. Kit had been recounting a long, involved anecdote of his early months with the Regiment, but his voice tailed away and Joe was amused to see him slide gently to the ground. It had been a long, exhausting march, and except for the picquets they would all soon make for their tents and their bedrolls. Sounds of laughter could be heard emanating from the bungalow, where the officers were doubtless sitting over their port, but the camp was gradually fading into somnolence.

By a nearby fire, two station servants were squatting, also drawing on bidis. A third man joined them, dressed in a shabby tunic and pyjamas, an untidily wound turban in the style of the Pathans. Joe looked at the newcomer, and noted drowsily that he didn't recognise him and felt sure that he hadn't seen him about earlier; but no matter, he thought, there must be many such. The trio began a low voiced conversation, and as the evening breeze died, the words came to Joe with startling clarity through the still, night air. He listened to the rapid Urdu and tried to make out as many words as he could; a habit he had grown into since they had said goodbye to Gupta, back in Bombay. Presently, he began to pay closer attention as the import of the conversation became more intelligible. He heard the word 'angrezi' spoken several times, then there came 'attack', 'dawn' and 'surprise'. The words were disconnected by many he couldn't interpret, but somehow, the way that the words were spoken as much as the words themselves, seriously disquieted him. He frowned and considered what he should do. No use waking Kit, who would shrug and say that it was none of his business; and anyway, if he could hear Indians, then they could probably hear him!

He rose as casually as he could and yawned, noting that the trio by the next fire gave him no more than a cursory glance and continued with their low voiced plotting, unaware that Joe had some knowledge of their language. He sauntered to the main bungalow and asked the sepoy on duty at the door to take a message to Major Willoughby.

Inside the bungalow, Captain Clarke was nervously entertaining his guests to an excellent dinner. The room was not designed for such a number and was gradually becoming more heated, in spite of the valiant efforts of a diminutive punkah-wallah. James and the Captain had been discussing the plans for the morrow, and James had been careful not to take too much wine, aware that he needed a clear head come the morning. He noted that Carless had no such inhibitions and the whining voice was taking on the strident note that it usually did as he became inebriated. James' lip curled with disdain; nevertheless, Carless had better be up to his duties tomorrow; he was not going to tolerate any mistakes on this first expedition he had been trusted with.

The port circulated, and Carless began to declaim to anyone who would listen on the foolishness of living so far from civilization, and expecting others to pull their chestnuts out of the fire. James was aware that this was a reference to the Ferguson's who were known to be related to him, but before he could respond, and much to his relief, Carless quickly rose to his feet, and made for the door, doubtless to lose the wine and port he had imbibed of so freely! He reached the door just as a sepoy was entering, and shoved the man aside and staggered onto the verandah, where he discovered an anxious Joe waiting on the sepoy's return. Carless recognised him, even through the haze of alcohol, and he snarled at the boy,

'So it's you, you little prig. Whad'ya want?'

Joe felt extremely uncomfortable,

'I've asked for a word with the Major, Sir.'

'Listen, you little turd,' hissed Carless, 'just take yourself off back to the stone that you crawled out from. Or has the Major sent for you? Fancies you, does he?'

Joe went white and prayed earnestly that the Major would soon appear. He couldn't disobey a direct order, but he would be in trouble if he disappeared having asked to see him. To his enormous relief, James emerged onto the verandah, and ignoring Carless, who looked at him venomously, said,

'What is it Harrington, that's so urgent that it cannot wait until morning?' He then noticed the look on the boy's face and went on,

'You'd better come in here,' and he ushered Joe into a small anteroom, where he said less formally,

'Well Joe?' Joe began to tell him of the whispered conversation by the dying camp fire, and the third man he thought had only just arrived. Even to his own ears it sounded lame, but what would the Major make of it?

'Are you sure, Joe?'

'Well; er; no Sir. That's the trouble. I couldn't understand everything, but it was the way they said it, as though they were angry about something and up to no good. If you, er, see what I mean?' he finished lamely.

The Major did. It wasn't like the lad to fuss over nothing, and he had the greatest respect for the youngster's linguistic skills. Also, it would go some way to answering his own questions. Why did the bandits cut the line to the cantonment, and why were the two attacks pushed through with more vigour? And why attack only English estates? Apparently, bandits were not usually so discriminating! It would be good tactics to draw the enemy to them, let them wear themselves out with a forced march and then catch them napping. All the while the Major mused, Joe stood quietly feeling extremely uncomfortable, but at least he hadn't been dismissed out of hand, but what was he thinking? James reached a decision,

'Thank you for coming to see me Joe. It won't hurt to take precautions. Go back to your tent now, but not a word to anyone yet.'

'Yessir,' said Joe and left the bungalow with a sigh of relief, passing by Carless who was too busy throwing up to notice him; much to his relief. He found Kit still curled up by the fire, so let him be; no use turning in if the Major was going to call them all out again. He saw that the three Indians had gone.

James returned to the dining room and banged on the table with a heavy bottomed glass. He had everyone's attention instantly, for they had all, except Carless, followed his example and gone lightly with the wine.

'I've just received a message saying that we may expect an attack at dawn tomorrow!' He looked round at the startled faces with a grim smile.

No-one asked where the message had come from; they simply accepted that it was so.

'We must double the picquets immediately, and those not on watch must rest fully accoutered. We will all rouse an hour before dawn, and make our dispositions. I did not yet know the numbers who may perpetrate this attack, so ensure that the perimeter is totally covered. That is all gentlemen. Go to it!'

James waited until all his men had left, and then turned to Captain Clarke,

'I received this information from one of my men, who heard what sounded like a plot being hatched.' James forbore to mention the age of the informant and the paucity of the information. He went on,

'Tell me; do you consider all your sepoys and servants reliable?'

'Normally I would say so, and many have been with the outstation for a long time. But last week, one of my most trusted men was called back to his village with the news that his son was ill. Two days later, two volunteers arrived, and as we were short handed, we took them on. But I couldn't vouch for them.'

'Hm. I suggest we look discreetly for the two in question, and quietly lock them up for the night. No need to make a fuss. Do you have a lock-up?'

'Er; yes. There's a store hut with a padlock. But what if we are wrong about them; and this situation?'

'Then we'll owe them an apology. But for now I want them under lock and key, with a guard on the door.'

'Very well Major,' said Clarke reluctantly, and left the room to arrange the arrest. Ten minutes later, James scrutinized the pair, and noted that they wouldn't meet his eyes when he questioned them about where they had come from, and why they came along when they did. They simply said that they had heard about the station needing help through their brother, or uncle or some such. James gave up and ordered them incarcerated for the night. He then made the rounds of the station and took a good look at the defenses, and their weaknesses, ready for action the following morning. There was a buzz of rumour, but he fended off questions with soothing platitudes of 'best to be alert, but it's probably nothing, but they would have plenty of time to rest when the job was done!' Finally, he found Joe, fallen across the gently snoring Kit, unable to stay awake any longer. The two youngsters sprawled by the fire stirred James as he gazed at them. He hoped devoutly that no harm would come to these boys.

James spent a fitful night, and several times he rose and made a round of the picquets. Each time he found them alert, stirred up by the rumours of imminent attack. But 'all peaceful' came the report each time he passed them by. He finally fell into a fitful sleep after telling Briggs to ensure he was awoken two hours before dawn. After a refreshing cup of cha, he sluiced himself with cold water to clear his head. His eyes felt gravelly and his forehead throbbed, and he wondered, not for the first time, if he was doing the right thing.

Colby and Harding emerged at that moment, and together the made a circuit of the station, noting areas that needed improvements to their defence. The night was very dark as the moon had set some hours before, but the fitful light of a myriad stars helped them see enough, aided by a few cresset on the bungalow walls. James did not want to give a warning to any possible bandits lurking nearby that they were wide awake and alert in the station.

An hour before the dawn, all the soldiers were aroused and told to 'stand to', the orders passed down from officers to the Sergeants and Corporals in subdued whispers. The horses were led closer to the building and tethered securely against possible alarm. By now rumours were rife, and anxious men knuckled sleep from their eyes as they stared at the barely discernible undergrowth.

Joe was acutely aware that all this activity was due to his action the night before, and he felt distinctly uncomfortable, One part of him prayed that he was right, and all this preparation was not for nothing, but the other part was terrified! Would dawn never arrive?

Then in the east could be seen a faint glow as the rising sun threw out its first tentative streamers of gold. Slowly but perceptibly, the sky lightened, and James made a last circuit of the station, and made sure that the men were lined up two deep at the most vulnerable spots, ready for a double volley from their rifles. Coming back from to his own position, he found Joe and Kit huddled together, drums at the ready in case they were needed for the advance, or, heaven forbid, the retreat!

'In there you two,' said James firmly, gesturing towards a small store near the lock up.

'But Sir,' came two agonised whispers in concert.

'Go!'

'Yessir!' And two chastened youths slunk into the hut, only cheered up by the number of windows from which they could watch the action!

Just then there was heard the cry of a hoopoe; or was it? The tension mounted. Then suddenly a band of Indians rushed out from the undergrowth to the south of the station. They ran waving tulwars, and apart for the sound of their passage through the bushes, were unnervingly quiet.

'Fire!' A volley of rifle fire crashed out from the front rank of soldiers, who then immediately dropped to their knees to allow the second rank behind them to take aim.

'Fire!' A second volley rang out, and the precipitous rush of the attackers turned to panic driven flight. The bandits rushed back into the undergrowth faster than they had come, leaving some of their number either writhing on the ground, or completely still. Now that they knew that their attack was not a surprise after all, would they slink away or try again?

The sky was lightening all the while and the defenders could make out vague shapes moving about beyond rifle range. James took another turn round the perimeter, and could see that the bandits were moving to surround them. At least they had some idea of the number sent against them; it was clearly going to be more than a brief skirmish. Checking that all reloading had been done, James encouraged them all to stand fast, and returned to his position where he found Clarke peering anxiously round him. It was the first time that James had seen him that morning and suspected the Captain had not believed that an attack was imminent, and had slept through the preparations. They could all have been slaughtered as they slept if James himself hadn't decided to follow his instincts, and a youth's sharp ears!

Shouting 'din, din' as they came, the bandits attacked from all sides.

'Fire.' And again 'fire'; the volleys rang out. Then there was no time to reload and fierce hand to hand fighting ensued. The attackers fell back momentarily, and then came on again, but the breathing space allowed enough time to reload, and two more volleys rang out. At such close range it was hard to miss, and slowly the defenders gained the upper hand.

James found himself in a hand to hand encounter with a tall Indian with a fanatical gleam in his eye. He wielded his tulwar with such ferocity that James was forced to give way, moving back inch by inch until he felt the verandah step behind him. Desperately he feinted, seemingly dropping to his knees, and as the tulwar whirled towards his head, he brought his sword up to pierce the shoulder of his adversary. The tulwar fell to the ground and the Indian sank to his knees. Attackers close by saw him drop and with a despairing cry, began to run back towards the surrounding forest. Within a short space of time, the station was empty of active fighters.

In the nearby hut, two youthful faces peered out. Joe saw Willoughby's fight, and in agony had watched his retreat and with triumph when he saw the Indian fall. Soon it was clear that the tide of battle was definitely going their way,

'C'mon Kit. Let's go out and see the finish.'

Joe headed for the door followed by Kit. As he reached the door, it was pushed open roughly from the outside. Four bandits rushed in, with a desperate gleam in their eyes and looking for revenge on the hated angrezi who were beating them. Their rush shoved Joe behind the door, still clutching the handle, so they only saw Kit standing before them, open mouthed in horror. Four tulwars rose and fell. The first nearly cleaved Kit's head from his shoulders, the others cutting deep into the already dying body. As the butchery went on, Joe's eyes turned upwards in their sockets and he slid to the ground, pulling the door back even further as he went down.

The bandits finished their grisly work, and rushed out again, their blood lust slaked, and anxious to reach the cover of the jungle. But they hadn't gone far before they were spotted by a group of soldiers. Two were shot outright and one was wounded in the leg, bringing him crashing to the ground. The fourth made it to the trees, but made the mistake of turning to brandish his tulwar and shout defiance. He was shot in the shoulder.

Joe did not hear the soldiers come in, or the inward drawn breaths as Kit's body was discovered, or the urgent,

'Where's Joe?' from Private Kershaw. Nor did he hear the sounds of searching, or the shout,

'Here he is!'

'Is he hurt?' This from Corporal Dunster, and Joe would have been surprised to hear the anxiety in his voice. The first thing that penetrated his consciousness was being lifted from the floor. As he opened his eyes, Corporal Dunster's face swam into view.

'What….what happened?'

'It's alright Harrington. It's all over now.' Painfully, memory slowly returned,

'Kit; he was; where's Kit?'

'I'm sorry, Joe. It's all over for him, too. They got him, I'm afraid.'

Joe shut his eyes tight. Not Kit? Not his friend? He was just standing there and he could do nothing to help. Memory rushed back with full force and he saw the raised tulwars, and Kit's head nearly severed. Bile rose in his throat. Dunster interpreted the expression on Joe's face and got him to his feet,

'Outside lad. It's the best place. And shielding Joe from the grisly bundle on the floor, got him outside just in time before he threw up. Major Willoughby strode over, aware that something was wrong. He had been overseeing the rounding up of any prisoners, mostly wounded men trying to crawl away,

'What is it Corporal? What's happened here?'

'The devils didn't just run away, Sir. They vented their spleen in there,' with a jerk of his head towards the hut, 'They've done for young Barnet, and just missed this one, fainted behind the door. Not surprising when you saw what those savages did!' James looked at Joe, who was now shivering violently with shock,

'Briggs!' to his batman,

'Sir?'

'Take this lad, and give him a hot drink.'

'Sir.'

'The rest of you finish rounding up as many prisoners as you can. Captain Colby,'

'Sir.'

'Mount a guard on the prisoners. There is no room big enough to contain them all, so we'll have to guard them in the open until we can interrogate them.'

'Yes Major.'

It was, amazingly, only an hour since the action had begun, but so fierce had been the fighting, that they were all drained. When the essential work had been done, and guards detailed to watch the prisoners, and picquets to check that the bandits did not return, James ordered them to stand down, and for chota hazri to be issued all round. When he had broken his own fast, he arranged with Clarke to have an interpreter ready to help with the interrogations.

'We'll leave the fancy devil until last, the one that nearly saw me off! He seemed to be some sort of leader, as they gave up as soon as he fell. While the worst of the wounded are attended to, I'll start with the more lightly wounded. God above! What is that noise?' James strode to the door and looked out. There was a roar; a great cheering coming from the edge of the forest. What he saw made his eyes open wide, and then his face suffused with anger. Two bodies dangled from a tree. James strode out followed by a white faced Clarke.

'What is the meaning of this?'

The group round the tree fell silent and shuffled awkwardly. Corporal Dunster turned to face his seething Commanding Officer. There was no trace of guilt in his face as he replied,

'It's the two bastards that did for Kit, Sir, and nearly for Joe if they'd seen him. Two unarmed boys, they didn't stand a chance.'

'How dare you take matters into your own hands. Sergeant Britten; arrest this man!'

'Yes Sir.' Reluctantly from Britten, and he gestured for two privates to step forward and take Dunster's arms.

James returned slowly to the bungalow, his anger slowly subsiding. He could understand the strong feelings of the men, as the two drummer boys had been firm favourites with them all, even the dour Dunster apparently; who would have known that he would feel so strongly about them! But that was by the way. He had had no business meting out summary justice!

The rest of the morning was spent interrogating the prisoners, but by the end of it, James felt that he was no nearer the truth. He called a meeting of the officers over tiffin.

'The only thing I have been able to ascertain is that these are simply poor farmers who have been led astray with promises of large sums of money if they would help attack the station. None of them seemed to know who would pay them, or what was the purpose of the attack? By all accounts, they were all approached some two or three weeks ago, even before we arrived at Kotepore, so this was no spontaneous uprising. It was carefully planned to unsettle us before we had even settled in at the cantonment, and then be forced to do a rapid march to get here.' James finished with his summary, and waited for contributions from his officers.

'What about the big fellow you dispatched, Major; have you questioned him yet?'

'No, Captain Colby. I was saving him until last, but I have a feeling that we won't get much out of him. He is very different from the rest!'

'Surely there must be some way of making him open his mouth?' sneered Carless. He had been at the fight that morning, white faced, but nevertheless there. He looked, if anything, even more whey faced now, thought James. He fought down the rising feeling of irritation,

'I don't think we need to resort to brutality.'

'It's no more than they did,' retorted Carless, 'you should have seen their faces when those two were strung up. They thought they were all going to get it!'

James turned away in disgust,

'What do you think, Captain Harding?'

Robert looked thoughtful,

'There is another way. These fellows are terrified losing 'caste'. I don't know all the ins and outs of it, but we could find out!' James nodded slowly,

'Captain Clarke, can you help here? We are still new to all this!'

'I believe that this man is Hindu, though we could check. They have various taboos, of course. The main one is the eating of beef, but also being forced to eat with someone of much lower caste, such as an 'untouchable' for example, would be pretty abhorrent.'

James pondered a moment; that could do it. 'Do you have any such?'

'The wallahs who see to the night soil would do, but you might have difficulty persuading one of them as the caste system is so engrained and everyone knows their place; but a large enough bribe should do the trick!'

The meeting was disbanded, and James began the difficult task of interviewing the big Hindu' He was brought into the bungalow with his shoulder wound roughly dressed, and clearly in some pain; but he stood proudly before James; not in the least bit cowed. He was dressed in a handsome tunic from which the buttons seem to have been torn off. James also noted that the jewel from his turban was also missing, and James frowned in annoyance. However, that was not the matter in hand.

'What is your name?' he began. He received a haughty glare.

'Very well. As I don't know your name, I will address you as 'coolie'' That got a ferocious glare,

'Chiranji Das,' came sullenly.

'Well, Chiranji Das; why did you attack the station, creeping up on us like thieves in the night?'

'Is it not you who are the thieves? We did not ask the angrezi-log to come here. This is not your land!'

'What did you hope to achieve? Even if your plan had succeeded, mare angrezi soldiers would come.'

'Then we would have driven them away too.'

'Who sent you to do this?'

'I am my own master. No-one sent me.'

'I don't believe you. Who sent you?' Silence.

'Very well. If you choose not to tell me, I will treat you like a common prisoner. James turned to the guards by the door,

'Take this man away, and put him with the sweepers and he can eat with them.' Chiranji's eyes darkened as he took in the threat, but he said nothing as he turned away. James said clearly to his departing back,

'And see that he eats, even if you have to force the food down his throat.' Then he waved the escort away, and watched from the window as he was taken to where a trio of sweepers was sitting with bowls of rice and dal in their hands. Chiranji began to struggle as he neared the group, but the escort forced him to sit by leaning on his injured shoulder, which effectively silenced any opposition. A bowl was placed in his hands, but he flung it away. The sergeant in charge of the escort gestured, and the Hindu's hands were seized and his head forced back. Even from his distance away, James saw tears start in the man's eyes, but he made no sound. He knew that the prisoner would say nothing, and sickened, he shouted,

'Sergeant, enough! Take him back with the other prisoners,' and he turned away defeated. He may have cleared up the immediate problem, but he was no near solving the cause of it!

They stayed there three more days. The most first and most pressing problem was the repair of the telegraph wire that joined them to Kotepore. The break was quickly discovered and repaired, and James was able to signal an anxious Colonel Deluce that the situation was under control, and that the ringleaders had been captured.

Then the dead and wounded on both sides had to be counted, and arrangements made to dispose of the dead. James was amazed to find that the British had lost only two privates and the hapless Kit, though there were numerous tulwar slashes to be dressed, which could yet cause problems. The bandits had lost ten of their number, including the two summarily hanged by Dunster, but they too had many casualties from gunshot and sword wounds.

The hardest decision of all was what to do with the many prisoners they had taken; some fifty sat in the station compound, gloomily smoking bidis, and looking thoroughly dejected. He decided, after discussions with Captain Clarke and his own officers that the majority had been telling the truth, and had indeed been led astray by promises of money to supplement their meagre income. Furthermore, it would enhance their reputation if they showed mercy to them. So leaving the obvious ringleaders, Chiranji Das and the two suspected of collusion, in the lock up, he had the rest released on a surety that they would not be tempted ever again. They were touchingly grateful, and showed an inclination to want to kiss his feet, so he bade them to 'be off,' and they left in small groups, carrying their dead with them to arrange for ritual burning in the Hindu manner.

Early the next morning, the soldiers buried their own dead. With no chaplain available, it fell to James to provide the prayers. Clarke unearthed a Bible, and James read from it the twenty third psalm, having always felt the words to be suitable and stirring for such an occasion. He glanced at

Joe during the short committal ceremony, but the lad seemed to be bearing up well; he stood white faced, but enduring.

Through Joe's head ran a prayer he had heard from his mother many years before,

'Out of the depths I have cried to thee O Lord,
Lord hear my voice,
*And let thine ears be attentive the voice of my supplication,'***2**

He couldn't remember any more, but the emotive words ran round and round in his mind like a chant. But he added to himself,

'Must I lose everyone I care for?'

That afternoon, after instructing Clarke to be on his guard, James rode off to the Ferguson estate with a small, heavily armed escort. It lay only an hour's ride away, and very soon he was clattering up a gravel drive, and reining in before an elegant, verandah'ed bungalow. An elderly couple came out to greet them and James had no difficulty in identifying his aunt, in spite of the many years that had passed since he had last seen them; and of course, a striking resemblance to his mother! The pair greeted him warmly and took him into the bungalow for refreshment and an exchange of news.

James was able to reassure them that the emergency was over for now, but admitted to being puzzled at the cause of it all. He told them of the prisoner Chiranji Das, and his refusal to tell them who was behind it. His Uncle conjectured,

'It's probably Rajah Ajit; he has no love for the British. We got on well with his father, the previous Raja, but we don't know quite what to make of this one!'

James recalled what John Carlton had to say on the subject, but kept it to himself, not wishing to cause further alarm,

'Maybe he was just seeing how we would deal with the situation; he cannot have believed that the bandits would win?'

They tossed the subject around between them, until his Aunt Esme interjected with,

James dear, there is a packet of letters for you from your Mama and Papa. We were planning to forward them to you when all of this blew up. They are presently in Calcutta, and your Papa says that Lettice needs to rest awhile before making the long journey here. We suggested that they take it in easy stages by boat. Is your Mama very poorly?'

'Yes, Aunt Esme. I'm afraid she is.'

'Oh dear; I was so looking forward to their visit. We were so close as girls,' and she sighed. James sought to lighten the moment,

'I've some news for them when they arrive; I'm engaged to be married!'

That piece of news brought a warm hug from his Aunt and a brisk handshake from his Uncle Richard, and the conversation grew more lighthearted with questions about his wedding plans, and a promise to travel to Kotepore for the occasion. They parted with vows to see each other again soon, and,

'Bring your young lady to see us, if you can!'

The troop went on their way, intending to return to the outstation via the Carlton estate. There they found John in his shirt sleeves helping to lay out the plan of his bungalow. In the meantime he was living in a tent that matched the Raja's for grandeur. He greeted James warmly, and ordering refreshment for him and the escorts, took him into the shell of the new bungalow to get a first hand account of the skirmish, having learned about it by telegraph that morning. When James had finished his account, he nodded somberly,

'You did the right thing in letting most of them go. They'll report back that you are a just Sahib, if a little soft! But I don't like it, James, I really don't. I've a feeling in my bones that the British are riding headlong towards disaster due to their high handed attitude in trying to take over everywhere.'

'You've said so before, John, but still you have chosen to settle here?'

'Ah! I'm a pragmatist; and this suits me very well. Apart from anything else, I'm away from so called civilization, and that suits me down to the ground. Once I've had this place built, I'll protect myself. Those amateur brigands who tried to storm this place didn't get very far! But enough of this James, have you proposed to the lovely Lucy yet?' James was startled at the question, but readily assured his friend that he had, indeed, done so.

'Don't look so surprised, James; it was pretty obvious to anyone with eyes in his head! Don't forget to invite me to the wedding. But I think you'd best be on your way now if you want to get back before dark. I don't think they'll be any more trouble just now, but you never know! By the way, what did you say that the leader was called?'

'Chiranji Bas. Why, d'you know him?'

'Mm. No, I've not heard the name, but I'll make enquiries.'

Early the following morning the troop left the outstation, seen off by a much relieved Captain Clarke. He could get back to his normal peaceful existence of administering his small area for the east India Company. Though this august body had given up their trading rights some years before, and were now concerned with administering crown affairs, Clarke found it useful to have his fingers in the movement of goods; a very lucrative addition to his modest Company salary!

A day's hard travelling brought them to Kotepore Cantonment, and a warm welcome from those left behind. The three prisoners marched sullenly, loosely tethered together, but the soldiers strode out jubilantly. They had proved their mettle in the fighting; for many it had been their first real engagement. Tactfully, Joe had not been asked to beat the rhythm alone, and he marched is a state of numb misery. Along the way, he kept recalling Kit's voice; and the way he would cock his head on one side when he was about to say something funny; or the way his forehead would corrugate and his ears stand out when he was puzzled. And when Joe would try and engage him in serious conversation, he would say,

'Cor Joe; 'ow'd you think of that? Your 'ead'll explode!' And on the subject of girls,

'It's all very well, Joe, but they're just not like us!' Oh, but he was going to miss his friend sorely.

Chapter 7

A volley of rifle shots rang out and echoed over the elegant bungalows and airy barracks of Kotepore Cantonment on a sunny day in April 1848, as Major James Willoughby emerged into the sunshine with his bride on his arm. He looked down at the radiant girl at his side and whispered,

'Happy my dear?'

'Oh yes,' returned Lucy, having recovered from her start at the deafening salvo.

'Oh yes,' she repeated to herself quietly, 'how can I not be when I'm Mrs. Lucy Willoughby?'

The salvo had been delivered by the men of A Company, lined up under the watchful gaze of Colour-Sergeant Cuthbertson, and it was immediately followed by a lusty cheer, for the Major was a popular officer. The newlyweds passed out of the chapel door and trod through an arch formed by the crossed swords of fellow officers in full dress uniform; the gold braiding on the scarlet jackets almost dazzled the eyes in the bright mid-morning sun, competing with the flashing blades. At the end of the arch awaited Colonel Deluce, ready to shake James heartily by the hand, and claim an avuncular kiss from the bride.

The pair had been followed by the few guests who had managed to cram into the tiny building. Elspeth Mainwaring emerged, gently dabbing at her eyes with a wisp of lace kerchief. Hilary Mainwaring held her arm having given away his favourite daughter with a small measure of reluctance, but aware that he respected and admired her new husband. Enid Fairweather cried more copiously than the mother of the bride, all over the scarlet jacket front of the long suffering Major Conroy, tacitly recognised as her permanent escort.

Charles Willoughby emerged more slowly, carefully supporting his wife, Lettice. The senior Willoughby's had travelled up the river in time for the wedding, and James had gone to nearby Cawnpore to greet them. He was hard put to stifle a cry of anguish at the sight of his mother, who appeared almost ethereal, so little flesh did she have on her bones. And her eyes were sunk into their sockets. But those same eyes lit up when she saw James and she sighed when she kissed her handsome son. She smiled wanly at his shocked features, and pressed his hand,

'I'm really quite well, my dear. The sea voyage did me so much good! Now tell me about this bride of yours?' James did so, holding a hand that was as delicate as fine porcelain, with skin stretched over the fine bones like one of Lucy's silk fans.

Esme Ferguson emerged on the arm of her husband, Richard, alternately joyful at the wedding of her favourite nephew and seriously worried about her sister. With them came John Carlton, taking time off from building his new bungalow to stand as James' best man. While he was pleased for his friend, and liked and respected Lucy, he had mixed feelings about the slowly increasing influx of British memsahibs. Most of them came with all that was worst of Victoriana, and had the firm opinion that what the 'heathen' needed was to be educated and converted to the British way of life. Few took the trouble to read the history of the peoples of India, or understand that their culture was centuries ahead of their own!

The wedding party made its way to the Officers' Mess, where they disappeared inside to enjoy a sherry reception and the wedding breakfast. On the way, James stopped with Lucy still on his arm, to thank A Company for their salute. He was cheered even more heartily than ever when he informed them that food and drink would be served in their Barrack block courtesy of himself!

'Just raise your first glass to my beautiful wife,' he admonished, turning away with their cheers ringing in his ears and a smile on his face.

The wedding breakfast was a lighthearted affair, with many toasts being drunk to the happy couple and many boring speeches endured beneath the swishing punkahs. The best speech was delivered by John Carlton, who surprised them all with his skill as raconteur as he regaled them with anecdotes about his early days in India, when the Kotepore Cantonment was still a collection of huts, and the Officers' Mess a large tent!

Later, when the ladies had retired to repair their toilettes, and the men were circulating the port and enjoying fine cigars, Simon Carless came to take his leave of the party, insisting that he had a duty to attend to. James knew that it wasn't so, but he was glad to the man go.

'I wish you joy of your, er, bride.'

Innocent enough words, indeed friendly, but the way that they were spoken caused James to look up sharply and frown. What did the man mean? But Carless had gone, and James was distracted by yet another toast to a happy future for the couple.

Lucy changed into a travelling outfit, in preparation for their departure for a destination as yet unknown to her. All that James would tell her was that they had a great distance to travel, taking some days, so she carried a small travel case and had had the rest of her trousseau packed into a large trunk already loaded onto a doolie. In fact, their honeymoon was a gift from their groomsman, John Carlton. He had made all the arrangements, and had sworn James to secrecy. Their journey would take them through the mofussil and beyond the terai, to the very foothills of the mighty Himalayas, where a pavilion set in a small valley awaited them.

The pavilion was the property of a Muslim friend of John's, one Jamal Shah, who had reason to be grateful to him; John glossed over the reason for that, but assured James that it was a delightful spot and he was welcome to stay as long as he wished. An escort had been arranged against possible bandits, 'yes, real bandits lurk in the mofussil,' he had said with a smile. When James tried to thank him, he simply shrugged,

'It's the best way for you and your charming lady to get to know the country; go out and see it, and its people as they really are! This isn't England, in spite of many people who come here think it should be, 'if only they would make the effort!'

After enduring tearful partings from her family, Lucy was glad when it was time to leave. Likewise James endured much backslapping and unsought advice on how to conduct himself on his wedding night and was more than happy to escape.

The cavalcade set out, Lucy up on Doucette, curvetting as she caught the stir of excitement. James was mounted on his black stallion whose coat had been curried to a high gloss by his syce. The escort led off, and James and Lucy waved their farewells. Lacy kerchiefs were applied again and again to feminine eyes, and Enid went pink with pleasure as Lucy threw her small posy and she managed to catch it,

'Oh I say,' she breathed at the perspiring Major Conroy.

With only a few hours of daylight left, the party made for a dak-bungalow on the edge of the mofussil. Carlton had planned the entire journey so that they would have somewhere to stay every night, though he had warned James that the standard of hygiene and comfort were liable to be highly variable. The first one, on the 'edge of civilization' was reasonably clean and comfortable. The party carried their own food and linen in the doolie, and on their arrival, the servants set about converting the crude bungalow to the standard that they had just left.

The newlyweds dined simply that evening after the splendour of the wedding breakfast, and they chatted in desultory fashion. Lucy felt highly nervous about the night ahead, though her mother had tried to prepare her in her own embarrassed fashion. She had grown accustomed to James' embraces and his kisses, and the spectre of Carless had gradually faded, until that very day! He had managed somehow to catch her alone for a brief moment at the reception, and had given her a wolfish leer,

'Enjoy yourself tonight; if you can! Or do you intend to lead your lap-dog Major on as you did me?' And he turned away leaving Lucy's stomach churning as the memory of that hateful night came rushing back.

So now she sat across the table from the man she loved, trying to control a frisson of fear that would persist, try as she might to suppress it.

'Will you go ahead to our room, Lucy?'

She started. James was looking at her with a gentle look on his face, seeming to sense her fear, though he could not know the whole of it. Perhaps he would put it down to maidenly nerves? At least she was not as ignorant as many Victorian misses, for her mother belonged to the school of thought that there was nothing wrong in the physical manifestation of love between man and wife, and had been determined that her daughter should know what to expect, even though she did it with pink stained cheeks!

Lucy rose and went to their room. The bed had been made up with fresh sheets and smelled of sandalwood. An oil lamp cast a soft glow on the bed with its muslin drapes, and there were fresh flowers on a side table. Lucy abstractedly pulled a rose bud from the bowl, crushing the velvety petals in her hands. Her ayah looked at her impassively,

'Does the memsahib wish to undress?'

'Yes; no; er yes, Meeta.'

Meeta helped her out of her riding habit, and unlaced her corsets. Then she helped Lucy into her nightdress. It was made of fine lawn, finished at the scooped neckline with delicate lace. It gathered under the bust and then fell in soft folds to the floor. Meeta released her hair and brushed it until it shone like burnished gold in the light of the oil lamp. Lucy sat quietly, looking at her reflection in the mirror; wide, frightened eyes stared back at her.

'I love him; I love him,' she intoned in her head like a litany. Then suddenly Meeta was gone and James stood behind her, dressed in nightshirt and dressing gown and holding her hair brush,

'Beautiful; so beautiful,' he murmured, picking up a golden curl and brushing it across his cheek, inhaling its fragrance.

Lucy rose and turned to him, her eyes glazed. James kissed her softly and then again more urgently. He felt her slight recoil like a douche of cold water,

'What is it my love?'

'Oh James. I'm; I'm just a little frightened, that's all!'

'Never be frightened of me; ever. Lucy?'

'Yes? What is it?'

'Do you know what is meant to happen between us?'

'Yes; that is, I think so. Mama did try to explain, but, er.'

James cursed under his breath. Oh this Victorian reticence; and in spite of himself, Carless' poisonous words intruded momentarily. Sighing, he said gently,

'Come to bed, my dear. We'll leave it for now; let it happen when you are ready.'

'Oh James, if we could! I am so sorry.'

'Don't be sorry; we have all the time in the world!'

Fine words, thought James grimly, and he hoped he could honour them after so many months of abstinence!

They settled themselves in the bed. It was not particularly comfortable, but James hoped that the ministrations of the servants would have got rid of any unwelcome residents! He lay on his back with Lucy' head on his shoulder. He could feel her body against his, the small breasts soft against his chest, and her golden hair spread over the covers like a golden fan. Slowly, her breathing deepened as she faded into sleep, and he repeated sadly to himself,

'You have all the time in the world!'

Lucy's last thought before drifting into sleep was that she had married the most wonderful man in the world, and that she must learn to overcome her squeamishness as soon as possible if she was not to lose him!

Sometime before dawn, James awoke with his arm numbed from the weight of Lucy's head. Her hair still lay across him, and as he gently eased his arm from beneath her, it slithered across him like shot silk. Her nightdress had become disturbed sometime in the night and James could feel her long legs stretched down the length of his thigh. He propped himself up on his arm and looked at his young bride. The pearly light of pre-dawn showed the oval face with its retroussé nose and gently pouting mouth. The brown eyes were hidden behind thick lashes, surprisingly dark for a blond haired girl.

He gently touched the soft cheek with the back of his hand and she stirred and nestled to his hand with a tiny sigh. Holding his breath, James touched her throat where a pulse beat steadily; did the pulse quicken slightly, or did he just imagine it? His hand slid to the top of her nightdress and he teased the bow holding the neckline tight, until it slid apart, revealing the pearly white skin of her breast. He caressed one rounded breast with feathery strokes, and then the other. The nightdress fell open, and he gazed on his wife's form in all its perfection. James raised his eyes back to her face where he found her eyes wide open and gazing into his. She said nothing, but he could see that the fear had gone, replaced with a small anxiety and a tremulous eagerness. She lifted her arms and pulled his down to hers, and they kissed, gently, and then with rising passion. After that it was easy. The nightdress and his shirt came off, and James caressed her until he thought that she was ready for him. Then lifting her hips slightly, he entered her; gently at first as he felt a resistance, and when he felt the resistance give way with a small cry of pain, he entered her fully. They travelled together on parallel seas of pleasure until at last it was over. James kissed Lucy's damp forehead and whispered gentle words of love as she lay with tears in her eyes,

'Why was I so afraid?' she whispered tremulously, 'it was so beautiful!'

Next morning they continued their journey. Each day was a fresh experience. Some dak-bungalows were flea infested hovels while others were havens of comfort; but no matter, James and Lucy were oblivious to their surroundings. The servants exchanged amused glances as the pair gazed at each other with languishing glances, hardly able to wait for the nights when they could murmur sweet love words as they lay together, and share their mutual passion.

They came across settlements deep in the mofussil, surrounded by fields of gram, millet and sugar cane. They passed indigo plantations and marshes where water fowl rose in their hundreds, alarmed by their passing, causing James to sigh momentarily for his gun. Then one morning when they looked out of their chamber window, they saw the Himalayas for the first time. At first they could not make out what they were seeing, but as the sun rose in the clear air, they could see the distant peaks, floating on a sea of green and while. The tops of the peaks vanished eerily into the pale blue sky, so that it was hard to see where mountains ended and sky began.

Soon after that, the dense foliage of the terai began to thin and they began to climb steadily. The weather, which had already turned hotter in Kotepore, cooled perceptibly, and there was blossom on many of the trees.

At last, they reached their valley. There was no warning; one moment they were travelling single file up a gentle hill and then when they rounded a corner, a scene of heartbreaking beauty unfolded before them. In the middle of the valley, surrounded by blossom covered trees, stood a pavilion, fretted and minaretted like the palaces of Kotepore. Beyond the pavilion was a small lake, fed by a waterfall that tumbled down a hillside at the far side of the valley. Lucy found that she was holding her breath, and let it out in a long sigh,

'James. It's enchanting!' James merely smiled and mentally thanked his friend, John Carlton who had given them the gift of paradise.

The procession curved its way down the hillside into the valley, led by James and Lucy. As they approached the pavilion, an Indian stepped out to greet them. They could see past the neatly turbaned head that the entrance of the pavilion opened into a courtyard where a fountain could be seen gently plashing into an ornamental pond.

James dismounted and helping Lucy down from Doucette, went forward to meet their host.

'Salaam, Major Willoughby, Mrs. Willoughby,' said their host, bowing low, and he introduced himself as Jamal Shah. James knew from John that he was a Muslim, and was surprised to see a woman emerge from the pavilion behind Jamal, albeit shrouded from top to toe in a black bourka. She too salaamed, and wished them welcome from behind her face veil. She spoke in a slightly husky voice, and reached out her hand to Lucy,

'Come Mrs. Willoughby, I will show you your room while my husband looks after Major Willoughby.'

She led the way into the pavilion, passing through the entrance and out into the sunshine of the courtyard. Lucy exclaimed at the beauty of the small formal garden surrounding the fountain, where the beds were a mass of colour. Her hostess chatted as she led the way,

'Ah Mrs. Willoughby, you are a lover of flowers, I see. I too love to see them in profusion! My name is Shaheda and I am first wife of my husband. Ah, here we are,' and she led the way into a delightful bedchamber, hung with beautiful silks and redolent of various perfumes, of which the strongest was sandalwood. Lucy managed to speak at last,

'It is good of you to entertain us in your home when you don't even know us!' Shaheda laughed, a pleasant tinkling sound,

'We will not be staying with you. This time of your new marriage is a time to be alone. No, the servants will see to your comforts.'

'But,' protested Lucy, 'you are giving up your beautiful home for us?' Shaheda laughed again,

'This is not our home! It is one of our hunting pavilions. We wished to oblige John Carlton, but now that we have met you and your husband, we shall be pleased to oblige you!'

Lucy noticed that Shaheda did not use the epithet Sahib or Memsahib, but spoke in a more familiar fashion, so perhaps she had know John Carlton for some time,

'Why did you wish to oblige John Carlton?' she queried, 'he would not tell us.'

'Ah. Our dear friend John is too modest. You see, it is very simple; he saved my husband's life! They were both on a tiger shoot with Raja Ajit Khan when they became separated from the main party. The beaters had gone out and they could hear them some way off, so they rested under a tree waiting for the hunt to come closer. Then Jamal got up and as he did so the tiger appeared from the undergrowth no more than a few yards away. He was gathering himself to spring when Carlton got up, stepped in front of the tiger and shot him between the eyes. My husband was very definite; if the gun had misfired or his aim less than perfect, John would have died, So you see, we have cause to be grateful.'

'Yes indeed,' murmured Lucy, then,

'You speak very good English, and seem to know Mr. Carlton very well?'

'We are very old friends, for the incident I spoke of happened many years ago. He made it his business to learn about this country very quickly, and learned its language, and we have learned from him in return. We have learned that Englishmen do not keep their wives out of sight of men, which is why my husband allowed me to come out and greet you both today.'

As she had been speaking, Shaheda had divested herself of the enveloping bourka, and now stood before Lucy dressed in a beautiful outfit of emerald silk. A long tunic reached almost to her knees over matching leggings, the tunic edged with gold and small emeralds sewn into the fabric. Lucy exclaimed at it, and at Shaheda's hair that fell past her waist in a glossy plaited rope entwined with seed pearls. Shaheda looked at her wide-eyed guest, eyeing her up and down, and then,

'Chup!; she exclaimed, and clapped her hands. An ayah entered noiselessly. The two spoke together in rapid Urdu, glancing at Lucy from time to time, and waving their hands in the air, so she knew that she was being discussed. Then the ayah went out, to be replaced by her own Meeta. She also spoke to Shaheda, and lifted her eyebrows in surprise. Shaheda laughed and clapped her hands softly in delight. Turning to Lucy, she said,

'I am sure you would like to get out of your traveling clothes and refresh yourself?'

'Yes indeed. I feel very hot and dusty.'

Meeta bustled about, helping Lucy to shed her riding habit and corsets. More ayahs came in carrying a hip bath and jugs of water. Shaheda showed no inclination to leave, so Lucy tried to swallow her embarrassment as she was stripped of her petticoats, pantaloons and bodice. Finally she stood naked and thankfully stepped into bath from which rose exotic aromas. She leaned back and allowed Meeta to wash her all over, sighing luxuriously as the scented steam tickled her nostrils. Shaheda looked on amusedly,

'It must be many days since you did that? I miss my bath if only for one day!' Lucy looked at her is surprise,

'You bath every day?'

'Why of course!'

At last Lucy stood up and was dried. She then had perfumed oil rubbed into her skin, and when she turned to put on a robe, she found that the first ayah had returned and was holding garments draped over her arm in a most beautiful shade of peacock blue, lavishly embroidered with gold thread. Lucy's eyes opened wide as she realised that the garments were meant for her, and that she was meant to wear very little underneath!

She was dressed in the beautiful garments, and then her hair was loosened from its pins, and brushed until it flowed in a golden river to her waist. Shaheda and Meeta spent much time admiring its colour, so very rare in India they informed her. Meeta then parted the hair in the middle, and put a smudge of red in the parting and another on her forehead. Finally, she polished the hair with a strip of silk cloth until it gleamed in the fretted sunshine streaming through the windows.

Lucy stood in front of Shaheda, who looked her up and down critically, before turning her to look at her reflection in a lavishly framed full length mirror. Lucy gasped, as Shaheda observed,

'Perfect. You are tall and slim, just like a hill woman; the style suits you. How you English ladies bear all those petticoats and crinolines I'll never know; especially in the hot weather!'

'I don't know either. I've been here such a short time, and James tells me that the hot weather has to be experienced to be believed.'

'Take my advice, Lucy, and dress like the Indians do, in saris or like these; you will be far more comfortable. Ah! Just the thing!' Two ayahs carrying trays entered the room carrying trays with sweetmeats and dishes of cha.

The two women sat and relaxed among the brilliantly covered cushions of the chamber, chatting amicably over their refreshments. From time to time, Lucy wondered vaguely where James was and what he was doing; but for the most part, she was perfectly content to sit with Begum Shaheda Shah discussing India; it was a completely novel experience for her. She amazed at her hostess' knowledge of the outside world as she had been led to believe that Muslim ladies were kept in complete seclusion. When she tactfully asked Shaheda if this was so, she said with a chuckle,

'There is no better place for gossip than a zenana!'

Finally, as shadows lengthened, Shaheda rose gracefully to her feet with a sigh, embraced Lucy warmly, and took her leave,

'I wish you a happy marriage, my dear. John Carlton has told me much about your James Willoughby. We will see you again before you return to Kotepore. Farewell for now.'

Lucy looked out of the window and saw Shaheda emerge, once more shrouded in her bourka, where she entered a covered palanquin, which was carried by four stout coolies. Her husband mounted a magnificent stallion, and escorted by a band of armed servants, the party set off up the valley from whence she and James had entered earlier that afternoon.

Lucy stood at the window long after her new friend had disappeared from view, and was so deep in thought that she did not hear someone enter the bedchamber. A discreet cough behind her brought her out of her reverie,

'Could you tell me where Mrs. Willoughby is?' Lucy spun round to face James standing at the doorway. When he recognised who was standing before him, tall and slender in peacock blue silk tunic and leggings, his mouth dropped open,

'Lucy! I didn't; my God; you look, er, magnificent! What do you think of this place?'

'Oh James, it is truly wonderful. We will never be able to thank Carlton enough for his wedding gift. I almost wish we could stay here forever!'

'Mm.' James took her into his arms and looked at the lovely oval face, the shape enhanced by the fall of hair from a central parting. Eyes, slightly almond shaped and deep brown in the gathering dusk, gazed back at him with love and trust. He felt something stir deep within him; a feeling that transcended mere desire; and he knew that he loved this girl beyond anything. He kissed her softly where her hair parted, and murmured,

'Come, my little Indian, they have prepared dinner for us.'

Two weeks they spent in the idyll. Together the explored the valley, climbing up by the waterfall, and walking for miles for miles along the ridge at the top. Lucy discovered that Shaheda had left instructions with the ayahs, and every day, riding or walking garments were laid out for her, all in Indian style. She had never felt so free and unencumbered in her life before; even as a child she had been imprisoned in innumerable petticoats!

James was delighted that she was no weak and vapourish miss who fainted at the thought of physical activity, and in tunic and breeches, she walked and rode with him like any male companion. The only experience she refused to share with him was when he stripped to the waist and flung himself into the lake at the foot of the waterfall. When he encouraged her to join him, she shook her head laughingly and declared that she had never learned to swim! Besides, she told him firmly, that water looked devilish cold! James would not admit it, but she was right, for the stream was born high in the mountains. He swam around noisily for a while. And then emerged, slightly numb to drip all over Lucy, sitting on the bank and dabbling her toes. She looked up at him admiringly, noting the muscles rippling across his chest, and had the unladylike urge to drag his dripping head down to her own and have him make love to her there and then! She chided herself sternly for her lack of modesty and hid her urgency in laughter. James flung himself down by her and lay with his head in her lap, soaking the beautiful silk robes!

Somehow they found themselves discussing the Regiment, though they had vowed not to on their honeymoon. James had never believed in hiding soldierly affairs from soldiers' wives; if Lucy was to be part of his life, he wanted to share everything with her.

'And what happened to the ringleader?' she asked, referring to the battle at the outstation,

'Chiranji Bas? He and four others were tried in Kotepore and sentenced to hard labour. I can't say I was happy with the result; he was a proud man, and will be a bitter enemy when, or if, he ever gets released. But it was an East India Company outstation, and they tried and sentenced him, and I must suppose that they know what they are doing?'

'But what would you have done; let him go?'

'Ah, there's the rub! He had to be punished. But I would have liked to have got to the bottom of it first. The rest we let go with a warning.'

'And Corporal Dunster? I heard that he was charged with insubordination. What did he do?' So James recounted the events of Kit's murder and subsequent hanging; sparing Lucy the worst of the details. Finally he said,

'Dunster was stripped of his rank and confined to barracks for three months; it's no more than he deserved; he cannot take the law into his own hands, no matter impassioned he may feel!'

Lucy was quiet for a while, pondering over everything she had heard, and then teased softly,

I remember hearing of an officer who took the law into his own hands; wasn't it in, let me see. Ireland or….!' She got no further, for James had leapt to his feet, and picking her up in his strong arms, held her over the lake,

'Well, little minx, who are you talking about, eh?' Lucy gave a token squeal in protest and struggled, but her heart wasn't in it for she was enjoying the sensation of being in James' arms. He buried his face in the mass of her hair and set her on her feet to kiss her. It was some time before the conversation resumed,

'And what about young Harrington? You said that he was sorely distressed by his friend's death?'

'Aye, poor lad. You'd think he had suffered enough in his young life without witnessing the brutal act that robbed him of his closest friend. But I think he will recover in time; he has strength of character that would shame many an older man!'

'Yes I know.' James raised an enquiring eyebrow,

'You've met him then?'

'Yes, he did me a, er, service some while ago.' Lucy hoped that James would not notice the hesitation. She had vowed to bury the incident with Carless deep in her past, for she felt that James could be capable of murder if he ever discovered the truth. But he did not appear to have noticed anything amiss,

'He's quite extraordinary; I know I've said so before; but did you know that he now reads better than all the other soldiers, with the exception of Sergeant Swales, and he was a schoolteacher! I suspect he reads better than many officers, I'm ashamed to say!'

'Before we left Kotepore, I noticed him talking to a girl; who is she?'

'I am not sure. She is supposed to be the wife of Private Carter of B Company, while others say that she is his daughter. I've yet to get to the bottom of it! But she and Joe do seem to have become very friendly, and it will help him get over Barnet's death.'

The pair sat quietly for a while, drowsing in the warmth of the afternoon sun. Though not as hot as Kotepore, where the heat had begun to rise even as they had left, it was as warm as an English summer's day, and induced sleepiness. Nearby, a small grey squirrel, encouraged by their stillness, scampered close by looking for food, doubtless to feed a growing family in a snug nest in a tree close by. The little creature had three dark smudges on its back, 'said to be put there by the Lord Krishna himself,' observed James drowsily.

The nights were their especial delight. Lucy was fast losing her shyness of James, and more than once, silently thanked her mother for raising her to think of the act of love as something to be welcomed rather than a sordid necessity! The first evening at the pavilion had set the pattern. They had returned to their bedchamber after dinner to find that lamps had been lit that cast a gentle glow over the lustrous hangings. Incense burned in a pierced and fretted brass bowl, and the fragrant smoke drifted round the room, discouraging the ubiquitous stinging insects, and dispelling the need for muslin drapes. James had helped Lucy shed the tunic and leggings, and she had stood before him, shyly hiding her herself behind her curtain of hair. They found their bodies well attuned, and their passion increased day by day. James could not remember any woman in his life so willing to match his ardour, even the experienced Mary Kavanagh of Dublin, who used the act of love as a weapon to use against him! He thanked his lucky stars more than once that this wonderful girl had come into his life. He never knew that her love had burgeoned over four years before!

All too soon, their time in Paradise Valley, as they had dubbed it, came to an end. Jamal Shah and his Begum Shaheda, returned, this time to bid them farewell. Again, Shaheda took Lucy into the bedchamber for a cosy feminine chat, and questioned Lucy closely about their relationship. When Lucy shyly remonstrated at the intimate questions, Shaheda gently chided her,

'Why do you not want to answer? Are not man and woman the same the world over?' Lucy had to agree, and gradually overcame her reticence. But some of Shaheda's advice still managed to bring a blush to her cheeks, though, which made the lady chuckle and pinch her cheek. Emboldened by their confidences, Lucy asked what it was like to share her husband with other women,

'It is nothing, child,' said Shaheda indulgently, 'I only share his body. I am his first and favourite wife, and the running of the household is in my hands. He would not dream of bringing anyone else here with him!'

Then it was time to go. Lucy and James led the way out of the valley, followed by their small coterie of servants, escorts and the doolie piled high with luggage. Lucy had with her all the clothes she had been wearing since her arrival, Shaheda pressing her to keep them, with the advice that she should wear them whenever she could, especially in the hot weather. Lucy promised that she would, though what the other memsahibs and her parents would make of them she could not imagine! They turned to wave at Jamal and Shaheda, the latter, of course, shrouded in her bourka, and they both made deep salaams just as the party passed out of sight. Lucy and James were deeply saddened; convinced that they would never be as happy again as they had been in this magical place. They had promised to return some day, and had begged the Shah's to visit them in Kotepore. Shaheda had smiled enigmatically, and told her that they had a house in Kotepore, and would doubtless see them there, but it would be difficult to visit them at the cantonment; they did not elaborate the statement with a reason.

The journey back was more tedious than the outward one, tinged as it was with regret. They planned to travel via Carlton's plantation to thank him for his wedding gift, and then to the Ferguson's to see James' parents.

They found John stripped to his waist, and helping to mix red clay with straw for bricks, He greeted them enthusiastically and without embarrassment. He led the way into his tent, and plunged his arms in a bowl of water, which turned red with sticky clay. He dried himself on a towel provided by a hovering bearer and pulled on a muslin shirt.

'No need to ask if you've enjoyed yourselves,' he observed, smiling indulgently at the quick blush that stained Lucy's cheeks, overlaying the light tan she had acquired, 'ah, there you are my dear.' A girl entered the tent, clad in a white sari, and John put his arm round her, drawing her close to his side,

'This is my wife, Dharshi.' Dharshi looked at them shyly out of enormous kohl ringed brown eyes. She made namaste to them, but otherwise said nothing.

'We can't thank you enough for your wedding gift,' said James. Jamal and his wife made us so welcome. By the way, you sly dog, they told us what you had done for Jamal.' John shrugged,

'My gun was loaded; what else could I have done? Anyway, they have been good friends to me, and I have learned much about this wonderful country and its people from them.'

'They think the world of you too,' put in Lucy.

Soon after, they left John and his plantation, anxious to reach the Ferguson's before nightfall. Neither of them mentioned the presence of Dharshi, though both had their own thoughts about her. James pondered to himself,

'Of course; why didn't I realise sooner that John would take an Indian woman to wife?' Lucy thought,

'What a lovely lady; she's just right for him. Would I have accepted it so calmly before my honeymoon? Probably not. I've changed so much these past weeks and I am so glad that I have.'

Just as the light was fading they reached the Ferguson's bungalow. Syces ran out to take their horses. And a house boy emerged to take them inside. The expression on his face was very grave, but before they could say anything, he spoke,

'The Sahib and Memsahib are with Memsahib Willoughby; she is very ill.'

They followed the houseboy inside, James full of fear for his mother. They were shown into an airy bedroom where his mother lay on a bed, looking more ethereal than ever. Fragile white skin stretched over the bones of her face, and skeletal hands lay outside the covers. Kneeling by the bed was Charles Willoughby; his head was bowed and his hands clasped in prayer. He did not notice the entrance of his son and his bride. Richard and Esme Ferguson stood close together, and looked round startled as James and Lucy approached the bed,

'Oh my dears. What a sad way to end your honeymoon!' said Esme quietly. James looked at her in anguish,

'Is she…?'

'Yes, I fear so.'

James knelt by his father, who turned to him and nodded briefly before fixing his gaze on his dying wife once more. James was shocked at the ravaged features of his father,

'Why, he looks old,' he thought.

Presently, Lettice Willoughby opened her eyes and saw her son kneeling next to her husband. She reached out her hand to him, and he took it gently, fearful of the fragility of it. She smiled,

'My son,' she whispered, 'how is your lovely Lucy?'

'She's here, Mama.'

'Are you happy son?'

'Yes Mama.'

'Ah, Charles.'

'Yes my love?'

'I love you.' Her eyes closed again, and they all heard her final breath, like a sigh; and Lettice Willoughby slipped gently from life.

No-one moved for several minutes, and it was Lucy who broke the silence with an agonised cry,

'Oh James, Papa Willoughby; I'm so sorry!'

Richard Ferguson took her arm gently and led her from the room, leaving Lettice with her husband, son and sister.

Later, when they sat in the withdrawing room after pretending to eat dinner, they discussed what should be done. Charles was not with them, preferring to keep vigil by his wife's body. James looked haggard, which wrenched at Lucy's heart; he had been so happy such a short time before. He announced that he would telegraph Kotepore that evening, as he would need an extension to his leave, and also he knew that Gerald Deluce would want to be told as Charles' closest friend.

Next day, they were all startled when a group of soldiers marched up the drive, flanking Colonel Deluce on horseback and the Regimental Chaplain. He had indeed been shocked by the news and had travelled at speed to support his friend. He also realised that there was a need for a minister to conduct the funeral service and had acted accordingly. Watching the long time friends embrace, James was further shocked when he realised that the Colonel too looked old. When had that happened, and why hadn't he noticed until now?

The funeral took place that evening; the rising heat making speed essential. Lettice Willoughby, nee Ashton, archetypal English rose was laid to rest in India, in the depths of the mofussil of the Province of Oudh. The grave was dug at the edge of the garden, where Esme vowed she would lay a flower bed round it, for 'Lettice loved her roses so.' Charles stood with his friend and erstwhile fellow soldier, Gerald who had made his life bearable when he had had to leave the army, before he met the wife that he now laid to rest. Choking on emotion, he murmured in Gerald's ear,

'For God's sake make them dig it deep enough for me!'

Lucy held on tightly to James' arm, not knowing how else to comfort him. The Chaplain ended the service by reading the 23rd Psalm, the emotive words bringing comfort to them all,

'The Lord is my Shepherd, I shall not want.'

Later that evening the women left the men to their after dinner port and brandy, tactfully realizing that they needed some time together.

'What will you do, Papa?' asked James, gently.

Charles raised his ravaged eyes to meet his son's,

'Richard here has kindly offered me a home for as long as I wish to stay. I've nothing to return to England for in the near future; young Gerald has the estate well in hand; runs it a damned sight better than I ever did, with that little dab of a wife of his. You don't know, James, but we had a letter, when was it? Must be three or four days ago; the first to have reached us here. They are expecting their first child; Lettice heard the news just before….just before….. she…. The end!'

James was overcome with pity. It seemed that his father had been torn apart by his bereavement. Perhaps it was best that he stayed awhile where his wife was laid to rest. He had a suspicion, though, that he would never leave! His brother's name sake, indeed the man that he had been named after, interrupted the lengthening silence,

'It's a good notion, my dear chap. I've a mind to retire in a year or two. Perhaps we could travel together, see more of the world. What d'say?' James looked at his Colonel with surprise,

'Retire? But…'

'Yes young man. It may surprise you, but I am not as young as I used to be! Oh, not straight away, but when the Regiment is settled, then it will the right time to make way for a younger man.'

James did not know what to say. He knew that the Colonel had been a young man at the time of Waterloo, as had his father, but he had never stopped to consider how many years had passed since then. Silently he prayed that he wouldn't retire too soon. He chided himself for being selfish, but if the Colonel would wait but a year or two he could gain experience as a Major, and could then apply for the Colonelcy! But now was not the time to air these thoughts, and he sensibly kept silent, as the men rose to join the ladies before the sad party retired to bed.

Two days later, the Kotepore contingent set off leaving Charles to grieve for his wife, but promising to visit his son and new daughter as soon as he felt able to do so. Later that evening, James and Lucy entered the bungalow that was to be their first home. Smiling for the first time since they had arrived at the Ferguson's Plantation, he swept his bride off her feet and carried her into the pretty drawing room.

'Welcome home Mrs. Willoughby,' he breathed into her ear. Lucy hoped that he would want to make love again that night, as he had not since mother had died. She vowed silently that she would soon make him come to terms with the loss of his arms with the comforting touch of her arms.

Chapter 8

A heat haze shimmered over the Kotepore cantonment, for it was approaching midday and the month of May was advancing. A man stood under a large peepul tree, gazing at the scene below. The bungalows of the cantonment were laid out in neat rows on terraces climbing the gentle slope towards the observer, with driveways running between them in a criss cross pattern. At the foot of the terraces the barrack blocks were almost dazzling in a fresh coat of lime wash, and above the long, low building housing the Officers' Mess, the Union Jack hung limply. Beyond the quarters of the British soldiers were barrack blocks for the sepoys, Indian soldiers recruited mainly in the region of Oudh, whose steadily increasing numbers had resulted in the erection of several new blocks in raw, red clay bricks.

In the rising heat, the few people that moved about appeared to do so in slow motion. They were mainly gardeners watering gravel paths or parched flower beds, or ayahs keeping a close eye on their juvenile charges and making sure that they kept on their sun bonnets. Soon it would be time for tiffin, and then activity would almost cease as sensible folk kept under cover during the hottest part of the day. Already, split bamboo chiks had been rolled down to cover windows, and awnings lowered to cover verandahs where the sahibs might wish to enjoy a post tiffin chota-peg.

The man sighed contentedly. It was cool under the peepul tree as the long pointed leave dripped moisture to the ground, making a screen of fine droplets. The resulting cool dampness made such trees popular with animal life other than human, and it behoved the wary to check for the presence of sleeping snakes and such like. Under this particular tree there was a bench, obviously of recent construction as the fine teak still had a bright freshness about it. A plaque proclaimed it to be 'in loving memory of Philomena Lynch', and the young man studied the simple message with a touch of sympathetic sadness before he seated himself, stretching his long legs out before him with another contented sigh.

The young man was tall, standing six feet two in his stockinged feet. He had broad shoulders above a slim waist and hips, and long shapely legs. The face was handsome, with strong lines to the cheek bones and a firm chin, slightly cleft by a shallow dimple. His hair was the colour of a polished horse chestnut, and his eyes under bushy dark eyebrows were a vivid blue. He had particular reason to be full of contentment, for that very day he had been promoted.

'Sergeant Joseph Harrington,' he said to himself, and then again, louder, 'Sergeant Joseph Harrington. Well Sergeant, you have come a long way since you arrived here!'

Settling himself comfortably on the bench, he allowed his mind to drift back over the five years since the Regiment had marched into the cantonment, drums a-beating and eager anticipation written on every face.

After the skirmish at the outstation, Joe had missed Kit dreadfully, never realizing how much he had grown used to the monkey face and his quixotic humour. He closed his eyes and conjured up the impish features and recalled the way his forehead would corrugate and the ridiculous ears would stand out more than ever when Kit was deep in painful thought. He could almost hear the bright, Cockney voice,

''Ere Joe, will you look at this!'

The vacuum had been slowly filled by his growing friendship with Nancy Carter. He father, Will Carter, had finally admitted that he had smuggled his daughter into India aboard his transport ship in complete disregard of regulations. He had pleaded that there was no-one else to mind her, but was severely reprimanded by Major Conroy and locked up in solitary confinement. While incarcerated, he suffered from a complete withdrawal from opium, and men remembered the screaming delirium that could be heard clear across the parade ground. The experience frightened him so much that he vowed never to use the drug again; a vow he managed to keep to several weeks until the urge overtook him again and he drifted back into dependency.

Joe had kept a close eye on Nancy during her father's imprisonment, fearful that the so-called friend might take advantage of the situation. Nancy pooh-poohed his fears, showing him a wicked little knife that she kept strapped to her calf at all times. Joe was aghast,

'But would you be able to use it, Nancy?'

'Course I would. What d'you take me for?'

Fortunately, Major Conroy solved the problem unwittingly. He recounted the saga of Private Carter over a Mess dinner one night, and the newly returned Lucy Willoughby questioned him closely about the fate of the daughter. Major Conroy looked uncomfortable and admitted that he did not know what had happened to her; that he had only been concerned with the disciplinary aspect of the case. Lucy looked scornful, and told him in no uncertain terms that all the dependents of B Company soldiers were also his responsibility; causing Major Conroy to look even more uncomfortable and mop his brow at the unexpected attack. The very next day, Lucy made her own enquiries and was told that Nancy occupied a corner of B barrack block. She sent for the girl and was impressed by what she saw. Untidy and dirty as she was, Lucy saw under the grime an alert and intelligent youngster. Without hesitation, she offered Nancy a position as maid, although with a surfeit of Indian servants on hand, she did not really need one. Nancy accepted with alacrity, though she had informed her would-be employer that her father needed to agree.

'He will!' asserted Lucy, grimly.

She told James of her action, and he went to see the sober and suffering Private Carter, recently released from gaol. The man was inclined to bluster and speak of his 'only comfort having lost me wife.' Fighting to keep the contempt out of his voice, James appealed to his venality and they struck a bargain for the person of one Nancy Carter, lady's maid. Unwittingly, James thus sealed the fate of the man, for with money in his pocket, he became re-addicted to opium and died within a year.

Nancy soon settled to her new job and showed a natural talent for her duties. She was devoid of servility, which Lucy found refreshing, though she always treated her employer with respect. Through her maid's friendship with Joe, Lucy found that she could keep abreast of barrack room gossip, and was usually better informed about the soldiers of A Company than their Major or their junior officers! With the permission of the Willoughby's, Joe was able to visit Nancy in the early evening, the pair sitting on the back verandah and exchanging news of that day's happenings.

Apart from Nancy, Joe had also found that he had grown closer to Adam Swales. He had been touched by the gift of the Bible that first Christmas, and had continued to make progress with his reading. Many of the stories had been familiar and invoked memories of his childhood in Clonarty when Grandpa O'Malley or Father Muldoon would recount Bible stories to a circle of wrapt youngsters. When Joe had finally mastered the difficult Biblical language, Adam had introduced him to Shakespeare and also some contemporary authors. Since their arrival at Kotepore, Adam's parents had sent him a case of books along with news of home. Joe had found immense delight in sitting with Adam on the porch of his small Sergeant's bungalow in the evening, puffing on cheroots and dissecting the latest literary offering.

Two years after their arrival in Kotepore, Adam had confounded them all by meeting, and then marrying a young woman he met in Agra. He and Joe had gone to that most famous of shrines, and dutifully gazed in awe at the fabulous tomb that Shah Jehan had had built for his beloved wife, Mumtaz. Stepping back to get a longer view, Adam had trodden on the delicate toe of Louise Plested. She was an Anglo-Indian, the only daughter of the union between an East India Company clerk and an Indian lady of the Brahmin class. Both sets of parents disowned the couple, but that did not deter them. They had lived in connubial bliss for three years, long enough to produce baby Louise. Then Barry Plested had succumbed to cholera one hot summer, and his heart broken wife had flung herself into the sacred waters of the Ganges to be seen no more. The baby had been raised by her mother's family as a strict Hindu, but one look at the handsome and romantic Adam Swales, and history repeated itself. Louise's family cast her off when Adam wished to marry her out of hand, and his Commanding Officer reprimanded him on their return to Kotepore for marrying without permission.

Adam and Louise calmly faced out the storms, and settled down to married bliss in Adam's small Sergeant's bungalow on the lower slopes of the cantonment.

Happily, Louise's arrival made no difference to Joe's welcome at the bungalow, and he found Louise very easy to talk to, and from her, learned much about the Hindu way of life, and in particular about the mysteries of the caste system. The lady herself had a serene beauty, and could not have been more different from the dashing, but shallow Penelope who had precipitated Adam's wanderings, with her blond hair and violet eyes. Louise had inherited an oval face, with a golden skin and brown eyes from her mother, and a serene temperament and enormous tolerance from her father. She had a willowy figure, which she swathed in saris of rainbow colours. Joe adored her, more than he felt he should, but Louise recognised the youthful crush for what it was and handled her young admirer with a gentle tact until his adoration turned to a deep and abiding friendship.

Since their marriage, the Swales had had a son, who sadly died within a week of his birth. The couple had coped with their tragedy with quiet stoicism, but Joe knew that they longed for another infant to heal the hurt, but so far they had not been blessed.

The Swales' son was but one of many funerals that had taken place in Kotepore, which served the highlight the fact that India exacted a price from Europeans who chose to live there. Every year, the ladies were escorted to hill stations by their husbands, taking bungalows in Simla and Musoorie, for the long, hot season and the following monsoons. They would return refreshed and pink cheeked, unlike those obliged to stay behind to man the cantonment. Every year, cholera or typhoid fever would sweep the community, invariably carrying off a handful of victims.

Then there were snakes to contend with, and more than one unwary soul had been bitten, sometimes with fatal consequences. Many of the bungalows had a resident mongoose, whose presence was welcomed when the residents discovered that these little creatures did sterling work at keeping snakes at bay.

Lucy Willoughby was one of a handful of wives who refused to desert her husband in the hot weather, preferring to stay and share his discomfort. Only when James was granted leave would she travel north with him, the two of them exploring the lower slopes of the Himalayas, or the lovely lakes of Kashmir. They too had had a child, a baby girl, but like Adam's son, she had scarcely survived two weeks before a tiny coffin made the short journey to the Regimental cemetery. 'Why is it so difficult for a British baby to survive here?' pondered Joe.

Deaths among soldiers had wrought many changes among them. Within one year of their arrival, Joe had been made up to full private, his place as a drummer boy being taken by a lad from nearby Lucknow, the son of an East India Company employee. His corporal was Dunster, newly reinstated after his demotion. Their relationship was much improved since the tragedy of Kit's death, and the two became good friends, but a year later, Dunster succumbed to cholera. It was then that Joe was promoted to Corporal. In spite of his youth, there was no grumbling among the men; they seemed to hold his ability to read and write in considerable awe!

Two sallies into Afghanistan had further depleted their number, while allowing others to cover themselves in glory. The latter included Major Willoughby who had led an audacious charge against a group of Afghans ensconced in their stronghold, and they had won the day. That had taken place only the previous winter, and they had all suffered grievously from the inhospitable mountains south of Kabul.

It was on their return that there had been a further reshuffle of officers, both commissioned and non-commissioned. There was also news that a contingent of soldiers had been dispatched from their London barracks to replace the losses sustained.

There was tacit recognition that James Willoughby was heir apparent to the Colonelcy, and it was only the need for him to gain maturity and experience that Colonel Deluce had not yet carried out his threat to retire.

Major Mainwaring had retired and returned to England with his wife, Elspeth, leaving behind Enid who had succeeded in capturing Major Conroy, whose defenses had finally crumbled before a determined assault. Major Grant of C Company and his wife Abigail also chose to retire, and travel awhile in India before returning to England. The two vacant Majorities were filled by James' old friends, Edward Colby and Robert Harding. The only Junior Officer overlooked was Lieutenant Simon Carless. After the Willoughby wedding, he had started to drink heavily, his mess bills becoming notorious among his fellow officers. He tried, and failed to spread poison about James and Lucy. He tried and failed to spread poison about Joe, suggesting improper relationships with Adam, or Willoughby or anyone his evil mind landed on. He was constantly reprimanded for being drunk on duty, and an exasperated Deluce was only too aware that he could not get rid of him, simply refuse his promotion, which only increased his bitterness.

So it was that very morning that Colonel Deluce had sent for Corporal Joseph Harrington. He had entered the Colonel's office with trepidation, having never rid himself of the notion that he was due to be reprimanded! Major Willoughby lounged against a wall behind the Colonel, his casual stance helping Joe relax.

'Well Corporal Harrington,' began the Colonel, 'I hear from Major Willoughby that you have been carrying out your duties thoroughly.'

'Than you Sir,' replied Joe, standing rigidly to attention, his shako tucked under his right arm.

'There is a vacancy for Sergeant. The Major here feels that you are the right man for the job. I have to say that I feel you are somewhat young for the responsibility, but the Major assures me that you are capable of it.'

'Thank you Sir.'

'Well, Sergeant Harrington, don't let him down. He seems to have a lot of faith in you!'

'No Sir; thank you Sir. Thank you Major Willoughby.' Joe was almost incoherent with excitement. Both the Colonel and Major looked at him indulgently.

'That will be all, Harrington', said James, shaking him by the hand.

'Sir!' Shako rammed back on his head, Joe saluted, spun smartly on his heel and marched from the room, his mind in turmoil. No, he would certainly not let the Major down, not when he believed in him so much!

Joe returned to his tiny cabin in the Corporals' terrace where he changed into casual clothes for he had some time to himself. While he dressed in loose pyjamas, he relived the scene in the Colonel's office, recalling with a degree of surprise that he had grown or the Colonel and Major had shrunk; he seemed to be taller than both of them! Chuckling to himself at the irreverent thought, he headed off to his favourite spot above the cantonment where he liked to come and sit under the peepul tree, and ponder over the way his life had blossomed since that day in Dublin when he decided to enlist. Few members of the European community ever came here, so the bench had come as a surprise, having appeared since his last visit.

'Just wait until I tell Moti,' he muttered to himself, and smiled at the thought of her. Moti was such a joy, as true a pearl as her name translated to. She had come into his life soon after he had been made a Corporal, and brought him relief in the one area of his life had was a continuing problem for him, his as yet unfulfilled sexuality. He had moved into his tiny cottage, and had taken on a pair of 'untouchables' as servants, Ishwar and Sita, who would deal with all the household chores. At the back of the cabin was a small hut and cooking area where the two could live close at hand. They had been there two weeks when Joe saw two small children and an older girl squatting in the dust near the cooking fire. When he questioned his servants, they admitted that the trio were their children, but they hadn't told him for fear of being turned away. Joe knew that people like this lived near the poverty line, as they were at the bottom of the Hindu caste system, so he was more sympathetic than angry. The older girl had kept her eyes lowered during the conversation, but Joe could see she was about sixteen or so, with a sweet face half covered by the end of her sari.

Two days later, Sita came to see him as he relaxed after tiffin,

'Sahib,' she began, making namaste. He returned the greeting,

'What is it Sita?'

'My daughter, Moti, Sahib…'

'Yes Sita, what about Moti?'

'She needs to find work; she is sixteen and we cannot afford to keep her. The Sahib lives alone; he needs a woman.' Joe looked at her, trying not to look shocked. Sita went on hurriedly,

'She is a virgin, Sahib, but knows all she needs to. I have asked her, and she is willing. She prefers the Sahib to an older man who she may not like. It is not easy for us Sahib, she cannot marry outside her caste.'

Joe thought the matter over carefully. After his initial shock, he considered it more rationally. After all, these people were more pragmatic about relationships than Europeans, and their marriages usually arranged. If Moti did not marry, what would her future be; a nautch girl in Kotepore? He had seen them, young girls debauched at an early age; he had often been offered their services but had declined. This arrangement was commonplace, and otherwise she would be offered to someone else, he had no illusions about that. And it would solve a pressing problem for him!

'Sita, what if I choose to marry one day?'

'Never fear, Sahib. As long as you promise not to cast Moti aside without thought, she would accept it. There will be no children,' she asserted quietly.

When she had gone, Joe was still bothered by the somewhat sordid note to the arrangement, but accepted the pragmatism of Ishwar and Sita, prepared to sell their oldest daughter so that they could feed their two smaller sons. He had long discovered that even 'untouchables' favoured boy children over their girls.

That night, Moti came to him. She stood shyly before him, her head uncovered, and her sweet features revealed for the first time. Joe spoke to her in Urdu, trying to soothe the frightened look in her eye, and in truth he was as inexperienced as she!

'Moti; your name suits you, you are like a pearl.' Moti's eyes opened even wider, and looked like a creature caught fast in a gin. Silently she unwound her sari, letting it slip to the beaten earth floor. Her black hair fell in profusion over her small breasts, slipping past her neat buttocks. She took Joe's hand, and led him to his cot, where she did indeed prove that she knew what was needed.

Joe awoke the next morning with a feeling of contentment, and found Moti gone. She came in soon after, carrying his chota hazri on a lacquer tray. Her sari once again covered her face, but her eyes could be seen, and in them Joe detected a smile. He breathed a sigh of relief; it was going to be alright!

Moti had grown into his life since then. Quiet and unassuming, she carried out her domestic duties efficiently, and her nocturnal duties joyfully. She did not intrude into her military life at all, but was happy to listen to Joe when he confided his thoughts to her in his rapidly improving Urdu. He felt that with Moti, his happiness was complete.

Joe got up from the bench, intending to walk home. The sun was almost at its zenith, and sweat sprang from his brow as he left the shade of the peepul tree. He decided to take the path that kept to the shade of some trees. It was slightly longer than a direct descent, as it wound to the brow of the hill before curving downwards towards the cantonment, but the shade was welcome, and he was in no hurry.

The path would take him by the gate of a convent, occupied by an order of Irish nuns. Joe had discovered its existence some time before, but avoided going near it at first, fearful of invoking sad memories. He had finally decided some three years before, that he needed to move one, and had walked that way often since then. He rarely saw anyone beyond the massive cast iron gates, which shut the convent off from the outside world. Through the gates he could see a carefully raked gravel drive bordered by flower beds, always a riot of colour. Gravel paths led off the main drive, disappearing out of sight. The convent served the community as it ran a small hospital, and a school for the children, but the entrance to these was at the back of the building; and the front entrance seemed to be simply for show, and Joe had never seen the gate or the imposing front door open. He was not surprised to see the place deserted in the torrid noonday heat, and was about to pass by to return to the tree shaded path, when a voice with an unmistakable Irish lilt floated across the shimmering air,

'Kate, Kate. Where are you girl? Come in from that sun or you'll dry up like a prune!'

'Kate!' The earth and sky tilted before Joe's eyes, and his mouth went dry and his pulses raced. 'Kate!' An image swam in the dancing sunbeams, an image of a tall, graceful woman with tumbling red-gold curls, and his own blue eyes; Kate, his mother. The world settled as a prosaic voice answered,

'Don't call me Kate; an I'll come when I'm ready!'

'Please yourself madam,' returned the first voice, 'but at least wear your bonnet!'

Joe held his breath as he waited to see if 'Kate' would appear. He could hear footsteps crunching on the gravel out of sight, and they seemed to be coming nearer. He stood by the massive gate post peering through the ornate cast iron swirls, when at last a diminutive figure came into view. Joe nearly laughed out loud as a girl of about sixteen or seventeen approached, for anyone less like the Kate of his memory could not be imagined. This one was short; indeed the top of her head would scarcely reach his shoulder. She was dressed in Victorian fashion of a white muslin dress draped over a modest crinoline, which showed off a neat figure with rounded limbs.

Brown hair, tied back with a ribbon at the back of her head, fell in a cascade down her back, without the hint of a curl. Her face had no pretensions to beauty, the mouth being slightly too wide and the nose slightly too long, but it could be attractive in animation. At the moment, however, the expression was stormy, and her lower lip rolled forward mulishly. The sun bonnet was being mutilated between two small hands, as their owner muttered to herself; Joe could make out a few broken phrases,

'….do this……come here, go there…….so boring!'

Her perambulations had brought 'Kate' almost opposite the gate, when a slight movement caught her eye. She looked up startled, and spotted Joe peering through the gate. Fright made her say with acerbity,

'What are you staring at?'

'Why ma'am,' replied Joe soothingly, 'I was just wondering if you had lost your companion, and thought I'd offer to help with your conversation!' The girl looked thunderously at him, but then the humour of the situation struck her, and her lower lip quivered slightly.

'Yes indeed; I fear I am known for talking to myself. Sister Ursula says it is the first sign of insanity, but I am so used to my own company that I developed the habit too long ago to change now!' She came closer to the gate to get a better view of Joe, and asked,

'Well, what are you really doing here, and who are you?' Joe drew himself up to his impressive height, doffed his sun helmet and swept a deep bow,

'Sergeant Joseph Harrington, at your service; and I am here because I heard a rumour that there was an angel to be seen in the Convent.' Not to be outdone, the girl drew herself up to her diminutive height of five feet two, and then dropped into a deep curtsey,

'Miss Catherine Lynch; and you must be Irish!' Joe's mouth nearly dropped open, as he knew that his voice held no trace of an accent; he had worked too hard on it to have doubts! Miss Catherine Lynch laughed at his expression,

'I know a touch of the blarney stone when I hear it. I am Irish too!'

'You don't sound Irish?'

'Well no more do you! I was born in this country, but my parents are from Ireland.'

'Lynch? Where have I heard that name before? I've got it; a bench down yonder path; Mrs. Philomena Lynch?' Catherine gave him a strange look,

'Yes. She was my mother.'

'I'm so sorry; I should have realised. Is it very recent?' Catherine sighed,

'My mother was ill for a long time, but she didn't tell my father until it was too late. I don't think anything could have been done though. He brought her here, for the nuns have a reputation for healing. She died just before Christmas.'

Joe didn't know what to say, and the glaring sun was making his head spin. Catherine was still clutching her bonnet, so Joe said quietly, 'and we'd both better get in the shade soon. May I see you again?'

Catherine looked up at him and he could see tears glistening on the ends of her lashes. Now that she was closer, he could see that she had grey eyes, deep set, and fringed with long, sweeping lashes, enlarged by the trembling tears; her finest feature. She nodded,

'I will come out at the same time tomorrow; perhaps a little earlier.' She glanced around nervously,

'Reverend Mother is very strict; I shouldn't be talking to strange young men, even through a gate!' Joe put his hand to his breast and said solemnly,

'But Miss Lynch, we have been introduced!' She gave a gurgle of laughter which dispelled the tears, and clapping the bonnet inelegantly on her head and tying an untidy bow under her chin, she put her small hand through the gate, and shook Joe's fingertips,

'Goodbye Sergeant Harrington; till tomorrow,' and with a parting shot, 'It's a pity you are not an officer!' she was gone.

Joe smiled to himself as he walked down the shady path, a welcome relief after the glaring sun, which had given him a headache. 'Little minx' he thought to himself as he descended the winding path that ended at the cantonment. Taking a perimeter path to avoid the bungalows of the senior officers, he arrived back at his tiny cottage where Moti waited for him. Stripping off his sodden pyjamas, he stood in the courtyard while Moti poured a chatti of water over him; the water was luke warm but refreshing for all that. He rubbed himself dry with a coarse towel, and knotting a lungi round his waist, entered the cabin to enjoy some tiffin. The chiks were rolled down over the windows, and Moti had thrown water over them to increase their cooling effect. All the while, Joe had been chatting to Moti in desultory fashion,

'Phew but it's hot today. Soon the memsahibs will be gone to the hills and many of the sahibs too. I hope I get the leave I applied for; it will be good to go to the hills with Swales Sahib. By the way, Moti, we will be moving soon; I've been made a sergeant; what d'you think of that?'

Moti's eyes flew open at the last statement, but Joe kissed the tip of her nose affectionately. She rarely said anything, but he had long since learned to interpret her expressions, and this one was fearful!

'You, Ishwar and Sita will be coming too!' and then smiled at the look of relief. It was not until a while later, while dozing in post-prandial somnolence that he thought again about Miss Catherine Lynch. She would be interesting to get to know; he recalled her lively humour and the idle banter that they had shared. Also, he was curious; if her mother died at Christmas, why was she still at the Convent, and where was her father? With such thoughts running through his head, he fell asleep.

That evening, he had his supper with the Swales, and the trio lingered at the table. Occasionally the two men would stroll to the mess set aside for non-commissioned officers, but in truth they preferred a cosy chat round the table. Joe told them the good news about his promotion, and Adam opened a bottle of wine to celebrate. The two men then fell to discussing the latest book by an author new to both of them, Charles Dickens. Two of his books were in the latest parcel from England, and Adam and Joe were equally fascinated by their insight into the world of the poor. Not for the first time, Joe reflected on the divide between rich and poor the world over, and he said as much to his friend. Adam puffed on his cheroot reflectively before replying,

'I fear you are right, and yet, there are rich men who use their wealth for good works; but not too many of them, eh Joe?'

The conversation turned to the subject of their summer leave. The trio had planned to travel to Kashmir and explore the lakes, but Adam reluctantly admitted to Joe,

'I'm afraid we will have to change our plans,' and he put his arm affectionately round his wife, 'we have recently learned that Louise is with child. We do not want to take any chances with her health, so I plan to take her to Musoorie for the hot season. I'm sorry Joe; you'll have to find someone else to go to Kashmir with you?'

Joe was too pleased for his friends to be disappointed for himself, and he said so firmly. Besides, he said mysteriously, he had a project in mind that he would be able to carry out that very summer. Then he changed the subject before they could ask too many questions by telling them about the young lady he had met that very day. Louise looked at him sharply when he spoke of Miss Catherine Lynch, but made no comment. Not for the first time, Joe thought what a restful person she was, and how lucky Adam was, and how he wished he could find someone as compatible for himself; of Moti he did not think at all.

An hour before midday, Joe was once more outside the Convent gates. He could see two gardeners watering the gravel of the drive, and raking it over with long handled rakes, forming swirling patterns. They were dressed in simple dhotis and cotton shirts, and Joe envied them their cool garb; he had never mastered the art of tying a dhoti, and would not have had the courage to wear one if he had! He was hoping that Miss Lynch would appear before the sun got too hot, when his wishes were granted. As the gardeners moved out of sight, the young lady appeared, slightly out of breath,

'I thought I wouldn't be able to come. Sister Ursula just wouldn't stop talking! She'd asked me to do the chapel flowers, and said a dozen times if she said it once, how pretty they were. Huh; I hate arranging flowers and I'd just thrown them in the vases!' Joe smiled at the tirade, and gazed at the expressive face; no, she wasn't beautiful, but the constantly changing expressions gave her face a certain piquancy, a gamin quality. Finally, her grumblings died away, allowing Joe to get a word in,

'I've been wondering since yesterday; have you been here all the time since, er, Christmas?' She nodded then sighed,

'It's a long story, but my father works, worked for the East India Company. He and Mama came here when they were first married as he had no prospects at home; in Dublin. They were very happy, and I can remember being very happy as a child. We moved around a lot, and two years ago came to live in Lucknow. It was there that Mama fell ill. I was never told what it was, but I believe it was consumption; I'd read about it in 'Jane Eyre'; d'you know the story?' Joe nodded, 'well, she got thinner and thinner, though she tried to hide the worst of the symptoms, but I'd hear her coughing in the night. One day Papa came home and found her in bed, coughing up blood! He brought her here, and as I told you, she died just before Christmas. My father was devastated. He shut himself away for three days after the funeral, and when he came out, he looked terrible!' Joe's heart stirred with pity, and wondered what came next. Catherine continued,

'Papa told me he couldn't bear to stay in India, and he planned to wind up his affairs as quickly as possible and go back to Ireland. He didn't ask if I wanted to go. He just left me here while he went to sort things out in Lucknow.' She paused in her narrative, and gazed sightlessly beyond Joe, towards the grove of trees where the bench had been constructed,

When she was still to get up, Mama liked to be carried to that spot where she could see the cantonment and Kotepore; she loved the view. Sometimes Papa would be with her, and others it was just the two of us.' She sighed deeply, but bravely went on, anxious to finish the tale,

'When Papa returned from Lucknow, I told him that I didn't want to leave India; I was born and grew up here; and I have friends in Lucknow and other places; there was nothing for me in Ireland. I hoped he would change his mind and stay, but he just said, if that is what I wanted I could stay, but it must be in the Convent! I begged to be allowed to stay with friends in Lucknow, but he would not listen. It was then I realised that he didn't really care about me, only Mama, and just wanted to get away as quickly as possible. He left money with the Convent for my keep, and then he was gone!'

Joe listened to the prosaic voice recounting the final stages of the tale, and felt profoundly sorry for her, for she had not only lost her mother, but her father too, in the cruelest way possible; he chose to leave her! But she would have none of his pity; her chin came up, and she insisted roundly,

'I wouldn't mind so much if I didn't have to live here, it's so tedious. Our life is governed by bells, and I am expected to go to chapel three times a day!' Joe smiled sympathetically at her indignation.

'I help in the school with the little ones, which I like, but I'm not allowed out for I've no chaperone, and none of my friends I had in Lucknow have invited me for a visit. It's like being in a prison!'

Joe thought for a while,

'I have friends in the cantonment and some of them are married. I know one such couple in particular. I could ask Mrs. Swales to write to Reverend Mother and invite you to tea?' And then teasingly, 'that's if you don't mind having tea with a mere Sergeant!' Catherine clapped her hands in delight,

'Oh would you, please. Just to get out of here now and then!'

'It'll have to be soon as they leave for the hills when the hot season starts. I'll ask Louise this vey evening.'

By then the sun was scorching overhead, and they parted, promising to try and meet again the next day.

Joe related the story of Catherine's parents to a sympathetic Louise, who immediately offered to help, just as Joe knew she would. She promised to write the very next day,

'I'll have to think of a reason why I should know Miss Lynch, but leave it with me!'

Joe made the journey up the hill every day for a week, but to his disappointment, Catherine did not appear. He waited in a fever of impatience for a reply to Louise's invitation, which had been duly dispatched. Finally, at the end of a long week, she received a reply. She sent a note to Joe, who responded instantly,

I'm afraid it's good and bad news, here read it for yourself.'

Joe took the note, written on heavy white paper with an impressively embossed heading, and faintly scented with incense; he read,

Dear Mrs. Swales,

Thank you for your kind invitation for Miss Catherine Lynch to join you for tea. Unfortunately, Miss Lynch has recently left for our sister convent near Simla, where our convalescents pass the hot season. We considered it advisable for Miss Lynch to spend some time away from this Convent where she so recently suffered a bereavement. She will return in October, and I am sure she would like to respond to your kind invitation.

Yours sincerely,
Reverend Mother Theresa.

'Do you believe this, Louise? It's very sudden; d'you think they had seen her talking to me?'

'It's possible, Joe,' replied Louise, gently, 'but it is also feasible that the reason is genuine, and the Reverend Mother does say that she can come in October!' With that, Joe had to be content. But at least he had something to look forward to!

Louise discussed the situation with Adam when he returned from duty.

'He seems very smitten with Miss Lynch,' suggested Louise.

'I don't know,' replied Adam, 'he wasn't very complimentary about her looks or her height. And he said she was rude about him not being an officer! What are you laughing at?'

'You men are so blind! Of course he was smitten; he just doesn't know it yet!'

Two weeks later, his leave confirmed, Joe set about putting his plan into action. He still intended to travel northwards towards the cooler regions, but he intended to do so as an Indian! He had first thought of it soon after they had all settled in Kotepore when he had begun to visit the Raja's palace in Kotepore regularly.

His first visit there had been as part of Colonel Deluce's escort when he had paid a formal call on the Raja. On that occasion, Joe had sat in the courtyard gazing about him with interest, and wondering if Prince Saeed was in residence. On the second visit, again on escort duty, he had been summoned from the courtyard to the Prince's presence deep in the palace. His eyes had widened as he had taken in the opulence of the room, which had made the Prince laugh. The two found that they had much in common, even though their backgrounds couldn't have been more different; the one born to wealth and grandeur, the other from a hovel in Ireland. They could not explain it, but there was a bond between them that could not be denied. After that occasion, Joe had been invited along to hunting trips, though only intermittently, as the Prince was often away. But on these trips, Saeed insisted on Joe being dressed in a similar manner to himself, Joe was more than willing, as the materials of the robes were of much better quality than anything than he could afford, and he soon got used to them all, even the turban! The also conversed mainly in Urdu or the more refined Hindi that Joe was now learning, and their conversation was wide ranging. One day, Saeed looked at his companion riding easily in his Indian garb, his red hair hidden under a turban and a tulwar stuck in his sash,

'You know Joe, you could pass for an Indian; even your eyes could proclaim you as a northern Pathan; many of them have blue eyes!'

The casual remark had an effect that the Prince had certainly not intended. As his command of the languages improved, Joe also studied the mannerisms of the native people he was surrounded by. Joe vowed that one day he would travel incognito, and try to find out what it really felt like to be an Indian.

With Moti's help, Joe made his preparations. His face was tanned, and with a turban would appear dark enough, but his body skin was very pale. So he sat in his tin bath while Moti sponged him all over with diluted walnut juice. The result was somewhat patchy, but as it would mostly be hidden under clothes he decided that it would pass muster. He had already purchased an outfit in Kotepore market, comprising baggy trousers, tunic and waistcoat, all of which had seen better days. Leather sandals for his feet and a wickedly curved knife completed the ensemble. Moti showed him how to tie his turban, and he practiced assiduously. The biggest problem was his hair, and he vowed to keep his head covered at all times when in company.

Throughout all of the activity, Moti had gone about her tasks without comment. Joe noticed her abstractions but in his anticipation of the coming adventure, took little notice for she was normally a quiet person. But in the night before his departure, Moti made love to him with unusual passion, and at the end of it lay on the crook of his arm weeping silently.

'What is it little one?' asked Joe gently, 'I won't be gone long, you'll see. Sita tells me you are all to go and visit your Uncle in Lucknow. You'll enjoy that!' Moti made no reply, but her tears dried as she drifted off to sleep.

Joe was bothered by her weeping, as it was not like her to be emotional; he had gone away before after all. Then he forgot about her in the excitement of the morrow, and mulling over his arrangements, he fell asleep.

Joe left early next morning by dak-ghari with his Indian outfit rolled up in a light blanket. This small bundle was the only luggage he took, and his money was secured about his waist in a belt worn close to the skin; the same belt that Kit had shown him how to fashion so long ago. He headed northwards, travelling by dak-ghari for four days, staying overnight in dak-bungalows. On the last night, he woke refreshed, and he rose early, donning his Indian clothes, and rolling his European wear tightly into the bundle. The turban took a while to get right, but fortunately Pathans favoured a rather casual style, but he decided it was time to try his disguise out on the couple who ran the bungalow. Climbing out of his window, he made his way to the front of the building. A dhoti clad figure was lethargically sweeping the front porch, and catching sight of Joe, he shouted angrily,

'What are you doing here, you ignorant coolie, off with you!' Joe smiled to himself and set off.

Going north all the time in search of coolness, Joe travelled the way itinerant Indians did, with but a blanket to roll himself in at night, and a few rupees in his pocket to buy food. He shared the simple fare of the country folk, curds and dal and a handful of rice or chapattis. He felt fitter than he had for years, and not once on his travels was his true identity discovered. He had taught himself to squat on his hunkers for hours on end, and to talk with his hands as much as with words. He enjoyed the camaraderie of the road, and the conversation by the evening fires with the scent of wood smoke and manure rising in the still air. He learned to share his bidis, passing them round the circle of one time companions, each cupping the burning tobacco within their palms. The talk was often about the pilgrimages these travelers were making, many to the origin of the Sacred Ganges high in the hills, and Joe decided to go along with the crowd. For added security he gave his name out as Jhoti which he soon learned to answer to readily.

After wandering northwards for three weeks enjoying the cooler weather, it was then necessary to turn back south as he to be back in Kotepore by the middle of August, just in time for the worst of the monsoons, he thought ruefully. As he neared the province of Oudh, the talk round the camp fires changed in character and began to cause him some disquiet. It was all about the 'angrezi-log' and the way they were taking over the whole country. The word 'annexation' was used more than once, always with bitterness. Joe became more nervous than he cared to admit and began to avoid company for fear of being unmasked, though it had not happened as yet. He needed to discuss his findings with someone, for there were disturbing similarities with the situation in the outstation; and after all, those aggressors had also come from the same area he was travelling in now!

After careful consideration, Joe decided to change his plans. He had intended to make his way slowly back to Kotepore, following the course of the Ganges, but instead he would make for the mofussil as fast as he could. He knew that Major Willoughby and his wife were spending the hot season with the Ferguson's and Mr. Willoughby in their summer residence in the foothills. He should, if all went well, see the Major and still get back to Kotepore before his leave ended. With that in mind, he travelled mainly at night, and spent the hottest part of the day resting in the shade. He was in the mofussil when the first rain fell, and he spotted a group of small picanninies run out from their huts, laughing as the rain beat down on them. Joe smiled at the memory of Kit and himself in Bombay when they had run out to join them!

At last he reached the Ferguson's plantation, and discreetly got directions to their summerhouse. He reached it a week later, coming across the small bungalow in a valley. Walking boldly up to the front entrance he stood with legs astride and waited for a reaction. Two figures appeared on the verandah; one was Nancy Carter and the other a houseboy he didn't recognise. The houseboy shouted at him,

'What do you want? Food? Get round the back!'

Why is it thought Joe that an Indian cannot stand in his own country without being tacitly being accused of being up to no good? Sighing, he replied in Urdu,

'I have a message for Major Willoughby. May I see him please?'

'No you may not. If you have a message, give it to me and be off!'

Nancy had listened quietly to the exchange, gazing steadily at the tall Pathan. Then he raised his head for the first time and looked at her directly. Her lip quivered slightly, and she turned to the houseboy,

'I think you'd better fetch Willoughby-Sahib.' The houseboy glared at Joe, but did as he was bid, muttering darkly under his breath about 'thieving Pathans'! James appeared on the verandah shortly afterwards, brushing his moustache for he had been enjoying a rum punch with his father and Lucy,

'What is it Nancy? Samee says that there is a Pathan with a message, what can he want?' Nancy waved her hand in the direction of the Pathan, an enigmatic smile on her lips.

'Well?' demanded James, 'd'you speak English, fellow?'

'I speak very good English, Sir,' Joe replied with his best upper class parody.

'Good God,' expostulated James, and he strode down the verandah steps towards Joe. He peered closely into his face and then swept off the untidy turban.

'Good God,' he repeated, 'Joe. What on earth are you doing here, and what is the meaning of this..this..charade?'

'It's a long story Sir. Could I have a drink, I've come a long way today?'

For the first time, James saw the exhaustion in the younger man's face, and nodded.

'It'll keep.' Then turning, he shouted, 'Samee!' The houseboy reappeared, his mouth dropping open at the sight of Joe's chestnut hair and distinctly British appearance, notwithstanding the native clothes.

'Take the sahib in and give him anything he wants. I'll be with the memsahib when you are ready.'

Joe followed the houseboy, who grumbled all the while of the perfidy of British sahibs who deliberately set out to fool humble servants. He spoke in his own language until he remembered that Joe had used fluent Urdu to address him and he lapsed into sulky silence.

After a bath and a change of clothes followed by a long cold drink, Joe felt ready to face the Major with his fears. He found him sitting on the verandah, Lucy seated beside him. Her stomach seemed to be slightly swollen, and Joe realised that, like Louise, she was expecting a child again.

'Sit down Joe, and tell us what you have been up to?' Joe glanced anxiously at Lucy, a look intercepted by James,

'My wife is conversant with all Regimental matters, Joe.' Thus gently reprimanded, Joe recounted how he had decided to travel as an Indian, just to see if he could, and to see what it was like being an Indian,

'And did you?' asked Lucy, 'Oh yes,' said Joe.

'Go on,' urged James, aware that that alone had not caused Joe to travel all this way, and on foot!

'You remember the incident at the outstation not long after we came to Kotepore?' James nodded, 'how could any of us forget!'

'The bandits I overheard talking by the fire talked of their anger at their country being taken over. I didn't understand all that much then, but that seemed to be the gist of it. And then they spoke of the surprise attack, and I came to you. I have heard more of this talk as I travelled back to Kotepore, more and more as I got closer to Oudh. I got worried in case I was discovered. I hadn't before; I just thought if it happened it would be put down to eccentricity; but when I heard this kind of talk, I felt that these men might use their knives to prevent me carrying tales.'

James mulled over Joe's story, while the younger man sat quietly. He was not worried that he wouldn't be believed, but did expect some more questions.

Then James said,

'D'you know of Robert Clive, Joe?' Joe thought,

'The Clive who beat the French at Plassey?' James gave a snort of laughter,

'I should have known you would know who I was talking about; you never cease to surprise me! There was a prophecy made that the British Raj would crumble one hundred years from that battle. It is now 1854. The Battle of Plassey was fought in 1757!'

Later that evening, Joe was introduced to Richard and Esme Ferguson, and Charles Willoughby. The older Willoughby looked very frail, with yellowing skin and age spots on his hands. He peered at Joe from under beetling white eyebrows, but Joe had the distinct impression that he was not really aware of him. They all insisted that he sat down to dinner with them, and he was made to feel very comfortable among them by being included in the conversation. At least Joe felt that he could deal with most topics after his many years of debating with Adam! When he finally excused himself on the grounds of extreme exhaustion to take himself off to a bed for the first time in weeks, he left behind a buzz of conversation. They all agreed that young Joe Harrington was indeed a remarkable young man, given his unpromising start in life, which made James feel rather smug at having discovered, and then nurtured such a paragon! After that, the conversation turned to the news that Joe had taken such trouble to bring to his Major. James made it clear that it could not be ignored.

'I'm not too surprised at Joe's story; there has been trouble simmering for some time. Governor-General Dalhousie has been riding rough-shod over many Indian Princes, and his policy of annexation is bitterly resented.'

'But James,' countered Richard Ferguson, 'there has been a lot of good done too; after all, it is the British who got rid of suttee and the thugs!'

'True, but there are many Indians who would say that we had no right to interfere with their customs!'

But what about the rights of the poor Indian widows, who had to throw themselves on their husband's funeral pyre?' asked Lucy, indignantly, 'some of them were little more than children forcibly married to old men!' James smiled at his wife's vehemence, but could only agree with her sentiments.

'But,' he went on, 'Dalhousie is talking of annexing Oudh on the grounds of gross mismanagement, and if he does, we are in for trouble, mark my words. More than two thirds of our sepoys come from Oudh, and they have grown in numbers since the Regiment arrived; there must be three times as many of them as there are British troops by now as we are just not getting the replacements we ask for.'

'Good God man,' protested Richard, 'they have taken our salt; they cannot possibly turn on us now!' James smiled grimly, 'I hope you are right!'

Joe rested for three days, and feeling much refreshed, set off for Kotepore. He traveled more easily now, as James had loaned him a horse, with the instruction to hand it over to his groom when he got back; and then he handed him some food with grateful thanks for the information. The evening before he left, Lucy found the opportunity to talk to him alone,

'I have not been able to thank you properly for what you did for me when, er, before my wedding to Major Willoughby; or for your discretion afterwards!'

'You did thank me,' reminded Joe, 'and he was an evil man; I had to do something.' Lucy nodded and pressed his hand.

'Well, I won't ever forget it, and if there is anything I can do for you, please ask.'

Within a week, Joe was back in Kotepore to the full fury of the monsoons. But at least he had his memories of the journey to look back on and October to look forward to! He reached his cabin, dripping from head to foot,

'Moti, Ishwar, Sita!' he called. Sita appeared, wringing her hands together,

'Sahib. You are returned,' she said unnecessarily.

'Sita, where's Moti?'

'She's gone, Sahib.'

'Gone? Gone where?'

'She is in Lucknow with my brother. She has decided to stay there.'

'Why Sita?'

'The Sahib will marry soon; Moti thought it best if she stayed in Lucknow.'

'Sita? That's nonsense. I am not going to marry!'

'What about the memsahib in the Convent?'

'The who? But..but...I've hardly spoken to her, and I've no thought of marrying anyone! Tell her so, Sita!' But Sita merely shook her head and went about her business. Joe was stunned. What nonsense was this? He liked Catherine Lynch and had felt sorry for her confined as she was to the Convent. He looked forward to seeing her again; but marrying; he wasn't about to marry anyone!

It was October before Joe found out how Moti had learned of his meeting with Catherine. He was waiting anxiously for Adam to bring Louise back from the hills, when Ishwar brought him a crumpled note that smelled faintly of the early violets that used to cling to the banks of the lake at Clonarty. Ishwar muttered,

"It's from the memsahib.' He turned to go, uncomfortable inside the sahib's house, preferring to go about his tasks out the back, or attending to the quaintly named 'night soil'.

'Wait a minute, Ishwar,' said Joe, 'how did you come by this?' Ishwar scuffed his bare feet on the floor, and looked acutely uncomfortable. Finally, he managed to admit that his brother-in-law's cousin was a gardener at the convent, and had passed the note to him from one of the house servants, another cousin, who attended to the lay residents, including the memsahib Lynch. Then Joe understood. The brother-in-law's cousin must have seen them talking together at the Convent gate, and the word had got back to Moti. But what a lot of fuss about a simple meeting!

'That'll do Ishwar,' and the servant departed thankfully leaving Joe turning the letter over in his hands.

He missed Moti; not just in his bed but around the house; her quiet presence had been part of his life since he moved into the cabin. He missed her when he returned home for tiffin and had now to throw a chatti of water over his own head; he missed her when he sat reading his favourite book from Adam's parcel and she longer curled up at his feet, or rubbed the day's tension out of his shoulders; he missed her when he needed to rant against the injustices of the British way of life and had listened with her head on one side but never interrupting. Dammit; he missed her!

And all for a chit he hardly knew, and who he would not admit even to himself had occupied his thoughts far too much since he had last seen her in May. Sighing, he opened the note, and read a few lines in an untidy, childish hand,

'Dear Sergeant Harrington,

I am sorry I didn't get a chance to say goodbye before I left. I had a perfectly tedious time in Simla. It was just as boring there as it is here. I am just DYING to go visiting. Please don't forget to ask your friend if I may come to tea. I am sorry to ask you like this, but you might have forgotten. I hope you passed a pleasant summer?

Yours sincerely
Miss Catherine Lynch.
PS I shall try and stroll in the garden before midday'.

Joe smile at the letter and could just imagine the vehement little face uttering the words 'boring' and tedious'. He could understand; being immured in a Convent was no life for a lively young woman; how old was she he asked himself? He wasn't sure; not more than sixteen or seventeen he thought. There was no telling when Adam and Louise would return, and Louise in the later stages of pregnancy would need some time to recover from the journey before starting to send out invitations to tea!

But there was another person who would give him a sympathetic hearing he was sure; Mrs. Willoughby. She had returned with James some two weeks earlier, having a shorter distance to travel. He had already been summoned to the Major's office to repeat his story to Colonel Deluce and the other senior officers; a singularly nerve wracking experience! He was due to see the Major again this very evening to discuss a project that the Major had in mind, and he could use the opportunity to ask for a meeting with his wife.

'Come in Sergeant,' directed Captain Forsyth, 'the Colonel and Major are expecting you.' Doffing his shako, Joe entered the room and stood smartly to attention,

'At ease Sergeant. Take a seat.' Joe perched gingerly on the high backed chair in front of the Major's desk. The desk seemed to reflect the man who sat behind it, everything laid out with military precision; blotter, pen, knife, a small bronze statuette of the Duke of Wellington mounted on a rearing horse acting as a paper weight. The Colonel began,

'We have discussed your report at some length, Sergeant Harrington, and both of us consider that you were correct in bringing it to the Major's attention. There is now the problem of what to do about it! The Major has already been investigating the situation through our agents in Kotepore and Lucknow; in fact this began shortly after his return. Joe was surprised; he had not realised that they had been so concerned!

'It is confirmed that there is some unrest, but we cannot ascertain the full extent of it. It is thought that the Rohilla Raiders who were blamed for the attack at the outstation may well be used again in further riots.' Joe could not but wonder why he was being taken into their confidence; he soon found out!

'The Major tells me that you can pass for an Indian, a Pathan, and for the weeks you travelled so, were able to discover these stories?'

'Yes Sir.'

'I won't go into the reasons for doing this, but suffice to say, we are very grateful to you.'

'Thank you Sir.'

'Are you willing to do so again from time to time; go into Kotepore and listen to the opinions of the locals?'

'You mean, act as a spy?'

'There is nothing wrong with that, Sergeant. We need a reliable source of information. Our paid agents are not only unreliable, but we suspect give us false information. Your investigation could well save lives! What d'you say? Or would you like some time to think about it?' Joe thought for a moment,

'I'll do it Sir.'

'Good man. The Major here said we could rely on you. It'll mean an increase in pay which I'm sure will come in useful. The Major will brief you; we thought perhaps a regular foray once a month.'

'Very good Sir.' Joe snapped to attention, and turned about face smartly. He reached the door to find the Major right behind him,

'Come into my office, Sergeant, and we'll discuss details.' The two of them agreed that Joe would adopt a regular character, Jhoti the Pathan, an itinerant pedlar, and would establish a presence at random intervals. When he felt the time was right, he would start probing gently. James finished by saying,

'I'm not completely happy about this, Joe. I don't trust the Raja at all, and I am not sure what he would do if he discovered your identity, and of course, we could not admit to sending you out; you'd be on your own!'

'I know Sir, but I do believe I can do it, and safely. Sir?'

'Yes Joe?'

Could I possibly have a word with Mrs. Willoughby?'

'Yes of course, but can I not help?'

'Er, no Sir It's rather, er, personal.'

'Why,' thought, 'the boy's blushing!'

'Call by after dinner. Mrs. Willoughby keeps early hours at the moment.'

'Thank you Sir.'

Joe called by that evening to the Major's bungalow set high on the hillside, and reached by its own short drive from the roadway. From the front garden could be seen the lights of the cantonment, and beyond, the lights of Kotepore. By day, the view was equally spectacular as the river could be seen lined with sheeshum and neem trees. Lucy Willoughby was at home indulging in an evening glass of milk before retiring; her advancing pregnancy making uncharacteristically lethargic. She greeted Joe cheerfully enough, and commiserated with him when she learned that he was on his way to piquet duty.

'What is it Joe? My husband told me that you wanted to speak to me.'

She was easy to talk to that Joe launched into the tale of Catherine Lynch and her frustrations with Convent life.

'She is desperate to go out and about,' he continued, 'but the Reverend Mother won't allow it unchaperoned. She seems entirely friendless. I wondered if you could invite her to visit you, I am sure that will be acceptable. Mrs. Swales did invite her last May, but she was sent to Simla for the hot season, and now she's back but Mrs. Swales isn't!'

Lucy listened to the rush of words, noting the wistful tone of Joe's voice.

'You care for this girl?'

'No….no….nothing like that! I just want to help her!'

Lucy smiled to herself. She was a romantic by disposition, and is spite of Joe's protest, she was delighted to help with what seemed to be a burgeoning relationship.

'I think the best thing would be a tea party for A Company non-commissioned officers and their wives, and invite Miss Lynch. I would say that I am acting on behalf of Mrs. Swales. What d'you say, Joe?'

'That would be perfect, Mrs. Harrington. That is, if it isn't too much trouble right now, for you….as you are?'

Lucy laughed at his rising colour,

'I feel perfectly well; just a little tired at the end of the day. Leave it with me, Joe, and I'll write to the Convent. The Reverend Mother sounds a bit of a dragon, but I suppose she must be careful with such a young lady in her care!'

After further thanks, Joe continued on his way to piquet duty, feeling more light hearted than any time since his return in August to find Moti gone. The picquets, including his friend Bear, found their Sergeant in exceptionally high spirits, and were delighted with a hand out of cheroots when it was time to hand over to the next watch!

Next day, Joe bounded up the hill to the Convent gates an hour before midday. He took care to peer round the gate post before he took up station, but there was no sign of any gardeners. The flower beds were bare of flowers as they had been cleared for the new season, and the roses had been ruthlessly trimmed with odiferous piles of manure placed around their roots. The day was cool and overcast and gathering clouds threatened a shower of rain. Joe looked anxiously up at the sky as he waited in a fever of impatience. Just as he was giving up all hope of seeing Catherine that day, he heard a patter of feet on the gravel path, and in the next moment, the young lady appeared at a brisk trot, looking towards the gate with a worried frown. She was exactly as he remembered her, though this time she was not crushing a hat between her hands! Her brown hair was piled on top of her head which made her appear to be a little older, and her dress was a decorous grey serge rather than frivolous summer muslin; but her features were just the same, even to the mutinous roll of her lower lip when she thought he wasn't there. But when he stepped out from behind the gate, she gave a whoop of delight,

'Sergeant Harrington! I thought you weren't here! I hoped you'd get my letter but I couldn't be sure. Oh, how are you?'

'I'm well; and you? You sounded so….?'

'Desperate is the word! It was so lonely in the hills. The Convent was close to Simla, but it could have been in Timbuctoo for all the difference it made to me. I still had to look after the little ones, and go to chapel!'

Joe smiled at the spate of words, seemingly saved up for a long time. When he finally managed to get a in word, he told her about the planned tea party and the invitation that would be sent. She clapped her hands delightedly, looking absurdly young suddenly, in spite of the elegant hairstyle. Then she frowned worriedly,

'I'm sure Reverend Mother can't have any objection if Mrs. Willoughby is an officer's wife?'

And so it turned out and a week later, a carriage arrived outside the Willoughby bungalow, and deposited a very nervous Miss Catherine Lynch, accompanied by a maid servant and a driver. She was introduced to Mrs. Willoughby by the hovering Joe and stammered her thanks for the kind invitation. Lucy wondered what a handsome young man like Joe could see in this seemingly plain little creature, but by the end of the afternoon, Catherine had relaxed enough for her natural animation to shine through. She kept the company amused with tales of convent life, and had them all chuckling with her wicked mimicry.

Joe enjoyed every minute of the tea party. The sun shone warmly and they were able to sit in the garden. Adam and Louise had returned in time to attend, and Louise sat with Lucy discussing their respective pregnancies. The other wives sat chatting in relaxed fashion, and a few children ran around the garden, chased by their harassed ayahs. The other Corporals and Sergeants looked vaguely uneasy, as though wondering what the event was in aid of, and they gradually made excuses for having to cut their stay short, and left their wives to their chatter with much relief!

But suddenly it was time to go. Like Cinderella, Catherine knew when her time was up, and that if she didn't return promptly then she would, like as not, be confined more strictly! She sighed as Joe took her round to say her farewells. She thanked Lucy prettily for her hospitality and Louise for her earlier invitation.

'Don't worry,' Louise assured her, 'I'll repeat it soon!'

'Oh thank you,' sighed Catherine.

Joe escorted her to the waiting carriage. As he handed her up, he kissed the back of her small hand and looked up into her face,

'Soon,' he said, 'I'll see you again soon.'

Catherine nodded, and as the carriage pulled away, twisted in her seat to wave as they went up the hill to the Convent, until they went out of sight behind some trees. Joe waved too, and then turned back to the garden to thank Lucy for her help.

'You're very welcome,' assured Lucy, 'I've enjoyed it too. It has given me a chance to get to know some of our neighbours a bit better, especially Mrs. Swales here. We've discovered that our babies are due quite close together!'

Joe took his leave then, surprisingly thinking about Mrs. Willoughby rather than Miss Lynch! In an age of Victorian modesty, her candour about her condition was refreshing, and he considered, not for the first time, that the Major was a very lucky man.

Following the tea party, Joe was not able to visit the Convent for a week. He had warned Catherine so she would not be concerned or disappointed, but he did not tell her the reason. During that week he was due in Kotepore as his alter ego, Jhoti. He prepared his disguise alone as he did not want anyone else to be involved, especially his servants, as he knew them to be tattle mongers! He was also beginning to feel uncomfortable with them, in fact had done so since Moti had left him, and knew that he should apply for a Sergeant's bungalow and leave them behind.

He did not bother to stain all of his torso, as he didn't plan to be away long, but he tied the turban carefully to hide his distinctive hair, and looked in his bedroom mirror critically. When he was finally satisfied, he lifted his bundle of goods to sell in his guise as pedlar.

He spent two days in Kotepore, finding a lodging in the poorest quarter. He eased himself into his role over a supper of dal and chapattis, and found that he was instantly accepted. He spent the second day trying to hawk his wares around the bazaars of Kotepore, with indifferent success, and towards evening, bade his landlord farewell with a promise to return soon. The man spat a stream of betel juice to land by his left foot, and shrugged. He was an ugly brute with two missing front teeth, and an unpleasant leer, But he had swallowed Joe's story of being an itinerant pedlar without question.

Joe arrived back at the cantonment, and slid by the picquets with being seen, a fact he was not entirely happy with! Reaching his cabin without detection, he stripped off his disguise and a thorough wash door with several chattis of water, to get rid of the odour of the slums!

The next morning he reported back to Major Willoughby, and was congratulated for his efforts,

'Give it two or three more visits so that you are fully accepted, and then start to really keep your ears open!'

Joe was rewarded with being allocated a Sergeant's bungalow set on the lower slopes of the hill, and he took on new servants, only too glad to say goodbye to Sita and Ishwar, and their constant reminder of Moti. His new servants, another married couple were only to glad to fulfill their duties and otherwise keep to themselves.

Between forays into Kotepore as Jhoti the pedlar, he managed to see Catherine most days through the gates of the Convent, learning more about each other with each meeting. Twice, Catherine had sallied forth, once by invitation to the Swale's for tea, and the next to a Sergeant's wife who had taken to her at the Willoughby tea party.

But gradually it dawned on Joe, that these meetings were not enough. He wanted to meet her openly; to watch the myriad expressions that chased across her face; her happy, gurgling laughter. He discovered that she had a passion for books that matched his own, and was as widely read, and she confided to him that there had been times when losing herself in a book was the only way to keep the deadly boredom at bay!

Then one day he reached the Convent gate to find that there was no sign of Catherine; and in her place was Ishwar's brother-in-law's cousin, standing on one leg with the other wrapped round his long handled rake, and holding a note: it smelled faintly of violets.

The note seemed to have been written in haste, judging by the smudges, and Catherine said that their meetings had been reported to the Reverend Mother and she had been treated to a long lecture on the impropriety of such behaviour, and how she must have lost all respect, and so on and so forth! But the outcome was that she was forbidden access to the garden for an indefinite period and all visits banned until her gaoler (underlined) considered that she had learned her lesson. Underneath the writing was a small smudge that could have been a tear, and Joe was deeply touched by her obvious unhappiness. He cursed the restrictions placed on he as if meeting through a solid cast iron gate could possible allow them any degree of intimacy, or the tea parties for that matter.

Next day, after a sleepless night of tossing and turning on his cot, his resolve hardened, and he sat down to write a letter. It cost him much scratching of his head, and several sheets of precious paper, but at last it was done. In beautiful copperplate, it begged an appointment with reverend Mother Theresa at eleven o'clock the very next day, in order to discuss Miss Catherine Lynch, currently residing at the Convent of the Sacred Heart. Joe read it over three times before pronouncing himself satisfied, and he went to find Ishwar in the Corporal's section to have his letter delivered. He paid Ishwar generously to ensure that the note reached the convent, and instructed him to wait for a reply; all day if necessary!

It was evening before Ishwar sought him out in the Sergeant's quarters where he found Joe sick with anxiety. A shout of triumph told its own tale; the request had been granted.

Strangely, he suddenly missed Moti more than he had ever done, not thinking of the incongruity of it; he would have voiced his fears out loud and she would have listened gravely with her head on one side. Instead, he spent the evening with Adam and Louise, too agitated to be alone. He asked Louise over and over if the Reverend Mother would think him too forward in asking to see their ward in the Convent; had he done the right thing in writing; and would he be forever barred? Finally, Louise laughingly called a halt; then she asked him gently,

'She will probably ask what your intentions towards Miss Lynch are; what are they Joe?'

'Why, I like her very much; she's such fun to be with and we have so much to talk about; and she's locked up in there all the time!'

Are you sure that is all?'

'Of course!' Louise smiled, 'be sure before you go!'

She shifted herself awkwardly as she was close to term, and Joe took his leave soon afterwards. Louise confided to Adam that she felt that the next morning would bring it all to fruition. Adam had learned long ago not to argue with his spouse; she knew too much about the nature of the male of the species!

Promptly at five minutes to the hour of eleven, Joe stood before the main gate of the Convent. He was resplendent in his best uniform, his boots polished to a high gloss, and his hair under the shako pomaded to a polished chestnut glow. It looked as deserted as ever, but he did not feel inclined to creep to the back entrance. He pulled a large iron ring attached to the end of a chain and a loud bell rang above his head. A turbaned figure emerged from the large wooden doors of the Convent's front entrance, and trod imposingly down the gravel drive. He unlocked the gate, and pushed open the right hand side, which swung slowly open with a loud creak. The bearer made namaste and bade Harrington Sahib to follow him, and in solemn procession the two trod up the gravel drive to the front entrance. The door was massively constructed of teak, but it swung open with well oiled silence, and Joe found himself in a darkened hall. The bearer made namaste again and disappeared through a baize door on the right. Joe stood irresolute, his shako under his right arm, and wondered what to do.

Suddenly, a cough at his elbow startled him, and a tiny sari clad figure made namaste to him. Beckoning, the small maid servant showed him into a parlour and bowed herself out. It was just on eleven o'clock.

The room was overstuffed with furniture in the best Victorian tradition. A dusty aspidistra stood disconsolate on a jardinière; and small tables scattered about carried numerous tracts and religious objects. Under a glass dome, a hoopoe strutted, its crest erect, and under another a mongoose remained frozen in the act of seizing a cobra behind the neck. Joe looked with distaste at the exhibits and looked around him for somewhere to lay his shako. He could not find sufficient space of any of the tables, so sitting gingerly on the edge of a high backed chair; he balanced the shako on his knee.

At that moment, Reverend Mother Theresa entered. Joe leapt to his feet, his colour rising and his shako rolled across the floor and came to rest at the nun's feet. Regarding him steadily from beneath her wimple, she picked up the errant shako and handed it into Joe's nerveless grasp.

'Do sit down Sergeant Harrington,' she said, 'and tell me what you wanted to see me about.'

Mother Theresa also sat down, but in the dim light of the parlour, Joe found it difficult to discern her features, particularly under the coif and wimple of her order. He did get the impression of deep grey eyes with a suspicion of a smile in them, and emboldened, he began,

'It is about Miss Catherine Lynch, Reverend Mother.'

'So I gathered from your note. How did you come to meet Miss Lynch?' Joe decided that complete honesty might serve him best, and went on,

'We met by chance when I was walking past the main gate,' the wimple seemed to nod approval, 'she was in the garden and we struck up an acquaintance.'

'That was not wise, Sergeant Harrington. She is a young lady; just seventeen; entrusted to my care by her bereaved father. It is not an easy task, you understand?' Joe nodded, but persevered,

'But we saw no harm in it; there was the gate after all!' again the wimple nodded. But then came the question he had been dreading; the question that had kept him tossing and turning all night,

'What are your intentions towards Miss Lynch?' But then the reply came easily after all,

'I would like to marry her.'

Mother Theresa looked at him steadily. It seemed all of a sudden that it was lighter in the parlour for he could see her face properly for the first time, and he was sure that he could detect sympathy there.

'Are you able to support a wife; you are very young?'

'Oh yes, Reverend Mother. I have spent little of my army pay except for my accommodation. I have also been given extra pay for duties as a clerk; I feel that I can support a wife comfortably.'

'Miss Lynch's father gave me full authority to act in his daughter's interest, considering the difficulties of communication between Ireland and here. However, he did indicate the sort of man that he considered suitable for his only daughter. Someone well established in the East India Company, or perhaps an officer,'

'But I love her!' interrupted Joe, desperately.

'Young man,' said Mother Theresa sternly, 'what has that got to do with it?'

Joe was silenced. His tormentor went imperturbably,

'However, I have already made enquiries about you from your Colonel, and you appear to be held in high esteem; for a sergeant!' Joe held his breath,

'Have you asked Miss Lynch?'

'No. I thought I should speak to you first.' This time there was definite approval from the wimple. The nun indicated a grille set in one wall of the parlour,

'I will be saying my office in there. You may have a few moments with Miss Lynch.' Rising, Mother Theresa prepared to take her leave. Joe jumped to his feet, and his shako fell once more. A smile twitched at the stern mouth, and then surprisingly she said,

'Miss Lynch has not been ......happy. We had hoped for a vocation.....but no matter.' And she was gone.

A few minutes later, Catherine came in, shyly holding out her hands. The formal atmosphere in the overcrowded room made natural conversation impossible and the two exchanged commonplaces for a moment or two.

The getting desperate last they be disturbed, but conscious of the grille, Joe whispered,

'Did you know I was coming today?' A nod.

'Did you know why I was coming?' he shook her head.

'I came to ask the Reverend Mother if we could be married.'

Startled grey eyes looked up at him, and she blushed a vivid scarlet. Joe smiled at her carmine stained cheeks,

'That is if you want it too?' her head went down and the shoulders heaved slightly. Joe was alarmed; was she crying? Was it such a dreadful thought for her?

'I'll…I'll go if you'd rather,' he stammered, 'and we'll say no more about it.'

Catherine's head lifted at last, and Joe could see she was brimming with laughter,

'Oh Sergeant Harrington; Joseph; Joe; of course I'll marry you!'

Joe took his leave soon after in a daze of happiness. Moti had been right after all; she had known him better than he knew himself! Miss Catherine Lynch with her willful smile and her diminutive stature had wrapped her small hands very firmly round his heart. He could not imagine life without her!

A month later they were married in the small Convent chapel. It was a private ceremony, with Adam Swales standing by the nervous bridegroom. His wife was not with him, having been delivered of a healthy baby girl two weeks before; but she had sent him off with a smug, 'I told you so!'

Catherine's personal maid attended her, and two small Convent orphans were dressed in European clothes to act as flower girls, the little Indian faces looking incongruous above the frilly dresses. Catherine was dressed in a bell shaped crinoline, with her hair streaming in a glossy brown river down her back from a simple circlet of rosebuds gathered that very morning from the very rose beds that had witnessed their courtship. She looked demure as she walked up the short aisle to her waiting husband-to-be, but as she reached him, she gave him an enormous wink, which made him want to shout with laughter! But he managed to control himself as the priest started the nuptial mass, the words invoking memories of a life he thought he left behind long ago, but of course, Catherine was a Catholic. Behind the fretted wall were the serried ranks of the sisters, and the principals of the wedding ceremony could hear them sighing at the romance of it all.

Then it was over, and they emerged into the sunshine, the front door flung wide for them. A wedding breakfast awaited them, courtesy of the Willoughby's, at the Sergeants' Mess, and in a moment the bride and groom were seated in state in a carriage. Adam shook Joe's hand warmly having already claimed a kiss from the bride. Reverend Mother had emerged briefly to hug Catherine, and instruct Joe to take good care of her. As she turned away, Joe could swear he could see a tear drop glinting in the sunshine; but he couldn't be sure. Then they were bowling along the road that led from the Convent to the cantonment, winding down the hill, carrying Catherine to a completely new life.

At the crossword where the Kotepore road forked away from the cantonment, it appeared that the entire Indian contingent had gathered to greet them; sepoys, syces, bearers, grass-cutters, sweepers, ayahs and many more. Joe had not realised until then how much these people liked him for the care that he had taken to learn their language and their customs. The pair in the carriage were cheered to an echo and showered with marigolds.

Lucy Willoughby had been safely delivered of a sturdy boy within two days of Louise, so could not attend the wedding breakfast; but had made the necessary arrangements before her confinement. Joe missed the two women who had played such an important part of his life, but knew that there would be plenty of time to thank them both later. When the feasting was over, they were sent on their way with many congratulations.

The Swales had given them one more gift; a short stay in the best of the Lucknow Hotels! There would not be time to reach it that night, so their first night would have to be spent in a dak-bungalow en route, but Adam had also arranged that they would be the only guests that night.

When Joe returned to his bungalow briefly to change for the journey, he found a large brown package on his bed. Mystified, he picked up the accompanying note. It came from Prince Saeed Khan, and congratulated him on his marriage and wished him a fruitful wife!

'How on earth did he know about it?' said Joe aloud, but then shrugged; he shouldn't be surprised as the Raja's spy network was a lot better than the British one! But he had thought that the Prince was away as he hadn't seen him for over three months. The package contained two sets of garments; a tunic and trousers for him in emerald green, and a sari and choli for Catherine in azure blue; the fabrics were exquisite to the touch. Joe mentally thanked the Prince and resolved to try and see him on his return from honeymoon.

Honeymoon; at the very thought of it his pulses raced. He had been celibate since he had said goodbye to Moti back in May, and he could not wait to hold his new wife in his arms that night.

The carriage that had brought them from the Convent waited to take them to the dak-bungalow. It was still full of marigolds so it felt like climbing into a golden sea. Then they were off with small children shrieking with delight as they raced alongside the carriage. They turned round to wave at the assembled guests, and to his delight, he spotted Louise at the door of her bungalow, her baby daughter in her arms. He waved vigorously and she blew them a kiss. Further up the hill stood another figure who he knew must be Lucy, though she was too far away to make out her features and again he waved and the distant figure waved back. The sentries at the cantonment entrance drew themselves up to rigid attention as the carriage swept through, and they were on their way to their future.

'Are you happy?' asked Joe, turning to his bride. She had changed into a travelling costume in dove grey that matched her eyes, as did the chic little hat perched atop her hair that had been swept up since the wedding ceremony. Joe preferred it loose, but didn't say so; but looked forward to loosening all those hair pins later! They chatted amicably as they bowled along the road, Joe marveling anew how easy they were in each other's company. He could not understand why it had taken so long to realise that he loved her!

Later that evening they prepared for bed in the dak-bungalow. True to his promise, Adam had ensured their privacy, and even the couple who looked after the place and departed after serving the dinner, with promises to return the next morning. From a distance they could hear night birds shriek and jackals bark, their sounds almost drowned out by a chorus of frenzied crickets, but the noises did not intrude on the sense of peace that they shared.

Joe took his young wife in his arms and kissed her softly. It was the first time he had done so, as the Reverend Mother had kept Catherine immured even more securely after their engagement. He felt her lips tremble as he gently parted them, and he began to kiss her more passionately. She did not resist, but there was no answering urgency. Joe drew back, a sense of doubt overriding the clamour of his body; she was, after all a product of the Victorian age, bereft of her mother at a crucial time of her life and closeted in a Convent full of virginal nuns!

'Catherine my love?'

'Mm?'

'Do you know what happens between man and wife?'

'We will live together now.'

'Yes; but at night?'

'Joe,' she blushed, 'I may lie with you now?'

'But do you know how a child is conceived? You do know that Mrs. Swales and Mrs. Willoughby had both recently given birth to infants?'

'But Joe; that is a natural consequence of marriage, and doubtless we too will have children. Why all these questions? Please kiss me again; I like it very much, and then we can sleep for I am very tired!'

Joe was aghast as he realised that his suspicions were well founded There had been no-one in Catherine's life to prepare her for married life. But she must have noticed the activities of the pi-dogs that roamed the streets wherever you went in India? Perhaps she had thought that man was a different type of animal, and thought, like the Virgin Mary, all women had Immaculate Conceptions? He felt defeated and suddenly very tired, all ardour having fled in the face of such complete innocence and ignorance!

Joe awoke in the middle of the night with Catherine curled up beside him swathed from neck to toe in a voluminous nightgown. An idea began to stir in his head. He could not think of a way to tell her himself what was expected of a wife, nor could he think of anyone else to do it before they returned from their honeymoon. But who was it who wrote 'a picture makes a thousand words?'

The next day they set forth again, the dak-keepers returning in good time to prepare breakfast. Catherine chased her new husband out of the room while she dressed for the day, leaving her hair loose under the chic hat, at Joe's request. The carriage was half way between Kotepore and Lucknow when Joe called to the driver to halt. Helping Catherine down from the carriage, he took her by the hand and led her along an overgrown path. Mystified, she followed him to a ruined temple out of sight of the road. Joe had discovered this place during his first year at the cantonment when he had set out to explore the whole area. Now was the right time to share his discovery.

The whole temple was covered with carvings; the first one nearest the entrance showing a man and a woman, both naked and gazing at each other in languorous fashion. Catherine gave a little gasp then looked at them with pursed lips, as if only just realizing what the male and female forms were really like! She slowly followed Joe as he moved round the room, the carvings showing the couple reaching for each other, becoming entwined and finally the man entering her. Further on, the possibilities of the love act were explored in seemingly endless variety, until at the end the two figures were once more separate, enigmatic smiles of both of their faces!

Catherine did not utter a word through the whole of their passage through the temple, though her colour came and went. Nor did she flinch away from any of the carvings but examined each carefully. At the exit she turned for one last look, and then stepped out into the sunshine. From some way away a hoopoe called and nearer at hand a group of 'seven sisters' birds ran around hysterically at the intrusion of visitors. Joe was beginning to feel anxious as the silence between them stretched out. At last she spoke,

'That's what you meant last night, wasn't it? I….I…didn't know. I've not even seen myself since I entered the Convent; the nuns always bathed in a robe and they made me do the same. Is it the same for everyone….I mean….all men and women?'

'Yes my love, the same the whole world over.'

'I do understand now and I will try to….to…be a wife to you Joe. But please be patient with me.'

'I know. But I think you will get to like being together like that when you get used to it. You liked being kissed last night, didn't you?'

'Yes.'

'Well, we'll start with that and you'll see, everything will be fine.'

'Yes Joe.'

There was constraint between them for the rest of the day, as though the sword of Damocles was hanging over them. Joe prayed that the coming night would put everything right between them, for he loved his new wife so much, but at least she knew what to expect now!

Later there was the distraction of arriving at the hotel, where Joe signed the register with a flourish as Sergeant and Mrs. Harrington; that at least brought a smile to the white face. If the receptionist wondered what was wrong between the handsome soldier and the white faced girl by his side, reputedly on honeymoon, he gave no sign.

At last the long day was at an end. They had pretended to eat in the ornate dining room where the vigorous activity of the several punkah wallahs made the room positively cold; Catherine must have been cold for she kept shivering. If only she did not look as if she was her way to her execution, thought Joe grimly.

'Don't be frightened,' he whispered into her hair as they were finally prepared for bed. Catherine was once again swathed in her cotton nightdress buttoned right up to her chin, and Joe was uncomfortable in a night shirt worn for only the second time in his life. The top of her glossy brown head only reached his shoulder, and her head was buried in his chest. He picked her up effortlessly and laid her on the bed. She lay with wide open eyes, though her gaze was unfocussed. Her hands were balled into fists so Joe gently prised them open and kissed each small palm. Then he kissed her forehead, her eyelids, her cheeks; soft, butterfly kisses that were as yet undemanding. Gradually the tension left her body, and Joe saw a teardrop tremble of the edge of the sweeping lashes. He nibbled her earlobe, and heard a giggle.

'You taste wonderful; mm, I'll never go hungry with you around me!' Another chuckle. Encouraged, Joe kissed her lips, softly, softly, and was rewarded with them parting of their accord. He felt himself grow under his night shirt, and prayed for the self control he would need to treat this girl gently; this night could set the pattern for their marriage. He kissed her again, responding to her slowly increasing ardour with his own. Gently he began to unbutton the top of her nightdress; the buttons feeling tiny in fumbling hands; how many buttons were there? He was about half way down the nightdress when a small hand stayed him. He held his breath, but she was taking over the task for him, her fingers moving with a surer touch. Then she raised herself up and in one swift movement, the nightdress was off.

'Now your turn,' she muttered. Joe complied, and smiled at her startled look at his manhood. It was going to be alright. Two sighs hovered in the air above two entwined figures as Joe and Catherine became one.

Chapter 9

Joe sat in a state of contentment, puffing on a cheroot. It was January 1857, and he had been married for two years. He sighed deeply as he rocked gently on the back porch of his Sergeant's bungalow, with its pots of marigolds adorning the edges on the small plot surrounding it, and thought over the last two years. His young wife had been an endless source of delight, with her ready laugh and cheerful disposition. Initially she had simply been overjoyed at being released from the 'prison' of the Convent, as she described it, but as she had grown accustomed to her freedom, she had blossomed into an enchanting partner, ready to share every aspect of his life. They visited the Swales whenever they could, where Catherine enjoyed spoiling little Christina or indulging in feminine chit chat with Louise, while Joe and Adam put the world to rights. On other occasions, the Swales would visit them, leaving Christina in the care of her ayah, and the four would linger over supper.

Periodically, Lucy Willoughby would hold a tea party for the non-commissioned officers and their wives, once baby Charles had been weaned as she had much enjoyed the first occasion when she invited Catherine from the Convent. As before, Lucy and Louise got on very well, while Catherine met more of the ladies of the cantonment and made new friends. She was especially fond of Nancy, even though she was Lucy's maid, as Lucy herself treated her more like a friend than a servant!

At long last, Catherine was able to visit her old friends in Lucknow that she had been separated from since she had been confined to the Convent by her father. Patricia Day and Charlotte Morris had been her friends ever since the trio had met in boarding school in Calcutta over ten years before, and had been inseparable throughout their schooldays, though Catherine had know them as Pattie Booth and Charlotte Henderson.

At the end of that time, though, they had been separated as their families were scattered all over India. But then, Catherine and her parents arrived in Lucknow where her father joined the local office of the East India Company, and had made the acquaintance of Peter Booth and Richard Henderson. Over tiffin that first day, they discovered that their daughters had all been to the same boarding school in Calcutta. When he arrived home that evening, Catherine's father asked her if she knew of girls at her boarding school called Patricia Booth and Charlotte Henderson and wondered why his daughter threw herself at him with a crow of delight and hugged him tightly.

'Oh Papa, they are my best friends in all the world, and now they are in Lucknow?' Her father smiled indulgently,

'Well their fathers are working with me at the Company office, so I assume so. I'll check for you tomorrow.' Within days, the friends had met up in Catherine's house, by invitation of her mother; the three of them disappearing into Catherine's bedroom to catch up with their news.

Their friendship deepened, and the trio shared all of their secrets, Pattie being the first to shyly own up to meeting a 'wonderful young man' by the name of Christopher Day. He had recently joined a local newspaper as a 'cub reporter', and the two had bumped into each other in the busy streets of Lucknow. Their friendship, and then their courtship had progressed, with the blessing of their parents, and within a year, the couple had announced their engagement. Catherine and Charlotte had been Pattie's bridesmaids at her wedding in the Catholic Church, and had shed tears when the newly-weds drove away in their carriage, convinced that their three cornered friendship would be at an end.

But it was not so, and the three now got together in the Day's bungalow, where they had no need of chaperones as they were visiting a respectable married lady, a title that made them all giggle. But then Catherine's mother fell ill, just after Charlotte announced her own budding courtship with a junior clerk at the East India Company Office, John Morris. There was little time for confidences between the three of them, as by Christmas, Catherine and her parents were in Kotepore in the hope of a cure for her mother's illness. She was forced to follow Charlotte's love affair by letter, and later that same year, her wedding to John.

But all that was in the past, the three young married women met after their long separation, when Joe took Catherine to Lucknow while on a short leave, and the three couples met at the Company's social club for a meal together. The ladies were only too anxious to leave the men to their cheroots and final drink, and took themselves off to a lady's lounge to catch up all of their news.

They also attended a few functions at the Residency, where East India Company employees and their wives were invited, along with their guests. Joe and Catherine usually stayed with Pattie and Chris, as the four had found that they enjoyed wide ranging discussions.

'Yes indeed,' sighed Joe; the past two years had certainly been full of new experiences and friendships. Then he chuckled as he also recalled his wife's occasional tantrums; her Irish temper flaring when she couldn't get her own way. She would stamp her small foot, and beat his chest with her fists, until laughingly he would seize her wrists, and lower his head to kiss her. Then the dust really flew and Joe was treated to some very unladylike language!

But in the peaceful times, their household ran smoothly and efficiently. Catherine was used to be in charge of servants, having had to take on that role after her mother had begun to fail. They had taken on a maid, Maya, to help Catherine with her toilette and wardrobe, but the girl was more of a confidante. Joe had considered taking on a bearer for himself, when a knock at their door revealed a gap toothed young Hindu with protruding ears, for all the world like a young, brown version of Kit, even to the corrugated lines of worry on his forehead!

'What is it?' asked Joe, brusquely, startled by the apparition.

'Sahib,' said the young man, wringing his hands together nervously, 'my sister's cousin is your memsahib's maid, and she told my sister that you needed a bearer?' Joe frowned; he had casually aired the thought to Catherine the previous evening, and here was an unlikely looking candidate on his doorstep the very next morning! He had forgotten the efficiency of the Indian method of communication!

It was the memory of Kit that urged Joe to take on this unlikely looking servant, who went by the name of Ghopi, but within a short space of time, he had become part of the household and Joe couldn't remember a time when he wasn't there to respond to his shout of, 'chuldi, chuldi, Ghopi, chota hazri!' first thing in the morning, when Joe was due on duty and running late!

If there was a cloud at all on their cosy life, it was the lack of a baby to add to their household, and more than once, Catherine had wept on his chest as she longed for an infant of her own. But he had assured her that she was still very young, and there was plenty of time after all.

As Joe mused it was well that he did not know that his contentment was to be short lived!

Joe had continued with his forays into Kotepore as 'Jhoti the pedlar' intermittently during his married life. With the permission of Major Willoughby, he had confided in Catherine about his 'additional duties', as he did not wish to lie to her. The Major had understood, as he felt the same about his own wife, but he pressed on Joe the need for absolute secrecy from her. Joe assured him that Catherine would understand. He usually stayed a few nights in his usual lodging, and as he had grown more confident in his role, had tried to foment a little unrest of his own round the cooking fires in the back streets to little effect. That is, until recently.

During his last trip to Kotepore as Jhoti, he had settled at his customary cooking fire, and greeted familiar faces. As he looked around, he noticed four or five strangers that he had never seen before in any of his visits. He listened cursorily to the conversation that went round the fire, accompanied by much hand gesturing. The word 'annexation' was used several times, with obvious anger by the strangers, and there was muttering around the fire and heads were nodded in agreement. Joe joined in with the muttering, but as soon as he could, he rose and stretched, and then ambled back to his lodgings. He had only stayed one night, but thought that this was serious enough to report back with all haste. He reached the cantonment the following evening, and immediately went to the Major's office where he found him still at his desk. The tale was soon told, and

James thanked his protégé absently; this latest news fitted in with what the Colonel and he were discussing only the night before.

'That's all for now Joe. I believe we will need to send you perhaps more frequently for a while, to see if what you saw and heard happens again, or fades away as before.' Joe pulled a wry face, thinking of Catherine's reaction to more frequent absences, but knew that it had to be done. He saluted the Major, and went home to tell Catherine the disquieting news.

As he feared, Catherine was more than a little displeased, as she was planning all sorts of trips during the coming weeks; and when reminded that it was the price to be paid for marrying a soldier who was obliged to follow orders, simply responded with,

'Hah'

James sought an appointment with Colonel Deluce the following morning, and the two men discussed Joe's report at some length. James reminded the Colonel of the unrest caused by the annexation of the Province of Oudh the previous year, caused by the lack of a direct male heir and the refusal of the East India Company to recognise an adopted son. This policy known as the Doctrine of Lapse, had been introduced by the Governor-General of India, Lord Dalhousie and was much resented by local landowners, or taluqdars who lost land in the process. But, the two men reminded each other, the resentment and unrest had died away over a period of time.

But James was more unsure this time, echoing Joe's own disquiet, and informed the Colonel of the decision to send Joe into Kotepore more frequently for a while. The two men then fell to discussing more wide ranging issues in India, and James was privately pleased that the Colonel chose him as his confidante, even though knew that he was being groomed to take over the Colonelcy when Deluce retired.

The two men were further aware that they were due to receive a consignment of the new Enfield rifles, first issued in 1853. These were a vast improvement on their present ones, but were reputed to use cartridges that were covered in greased paper as they were a tighter fit. The instructions were that the sepoys would be required to bite off the end of the cartridge to release the paper, and rumours abounded as to the nature of the grease. Some said it was made of pork tallow, which would offend the Muslims, and others that it was beef tallow, which would offend the Hindus. The two men sighed over the potential for trouble when their rifles turned up.

In March of that year, Joe had two pieces of news, both of which would have dire consequences on the course of his life. The first was an occasion for joy, when Catherine shyly confided in him that she thought she was pregnant. In time honoured fashion, an anxious Joe asked,

'Are you sure?' Catherine was not apparently, but had questioned Louise about early symptoms and the ladies had agreed that the signs were good. Joe hugged his wife cautiously, which made Catherine inform him tartly that she was not made of glass!

The next piece of news was more disquieting, when Joe was once again around a cooking fire in Kotepore. More strangers were angrily relating to the crowd the dreadful treatment received by an Indian stationed near Calcutta called Mangal Pandey. This hitherto loyal soldier was so annoyed at the behaviour of the East India Company, and declared he would rebel against the British. He had shot at his Sergeant-Major and then at a mounted Lieutenant, but only managed to wound the horse! Other sepoys present were ordered to arrest him, but refused, all except one who restrained him single handed. Pandey was now in prison awaiting court-martial, and probable hanging. The group once again was stirred up, and suggestions were made on what they could do to follow Pandey's example. More than one volunteered to meet with sepoys stationed at Kotepore and incite them to rebellion. As before, Joe quietly left them to return to his lodgings, and the next day reported this latest unrest.

James had already heard of the 'Pandey incident' from official dispatches, but was more than a little disturbed at the speed with which it reached the back streets of Kotepore, until Joe reminded him of the efficient nature of the 'bush telegraph' when someone's brother-in-law's cousin twice removed had just returned from… and so forth. James nodded in agreement, and suggested that Joe return to Kotepore in a few days time.

Joe could only agree when directly ordered by his Major, but he knew that Catherine would not be pleased. She was hoping to visit the Day's in Lucknow to tell her friend Pattie the good news about her pregnancy. As he predicted, Joe was soundly scolded and told in no uncertain terms that he was being selfish in the extreme in preferring to dress up and go on a jaunt to Kotepore in preference to escorting his wife to see her dearest friend!

With every excursion into Kotepore, Joe became more and more alarmed, and informed Major Willoughby so. In early April, the fireside talk was of the hanging of Mangal Pandey and suggestions that his death should be avenged. Later, he heard that that another sepoy, Jemadar Ishwari Prasad, had been ordered to arrest Pandey but he had refused, and others followed his example. He too was hanged and his regiment was stripped of its uniform disbanded for their disobedience. The badmashes were working up the populace to fever pitch, and Joe felt that it was only a matter of time before they infected the sepoy barracks at the cantonment. He knew that the Major and the Colonel were also increasingly disturbed by his reports.

Then at the end of April came the most troubling news of all. In the town of Meerut, not far from Delhi, ninety Indian soldiers of the 3rd Bengal Light Cavalry were ordered to drill with their new Enfield Rifles, and were issued with greased cartridges. Of the ninety men, all but five refused the cartridges. By early May, these men were court martialled and sentenced to ten year's hard labour. They were stripped of their uniforms and shackled. But the later news had not yet reached the cantonment.

The next day the eighty five had been released by the rest of the sepoys, and many British men, women and children were slaughtered in the town of Meerut. The Indian Mutiny had begun.

James sent for Joe as soon as the news of the refusal of the sepoys to use their new Enfields in Meerut reached the cantonment. He told Joe in confidence what had happened and told him that he should go back to Kotepore,

'But,' said James, 'it may well be more dangerous this time if there is unrest in the streets of Kotepore; I won't order you, Joe, you must decide for yourself.' Joe thought carefully for a moment. There was Catherine to consider, now that her pregnancy was confirmed; she would not be pleased with him leaving her yet again. But if trouble flared at the cantonment, wouldn't it be better to be forewarned so that the women could be protected or sent out of harm's way?

'I'll go, Sir. But I would be grateful if someone could make sure that my wife is looked after, as she is, er, in a delicate state of health.'

James smiled at this unexpected coyness from Joe, knowing that he had grown up in an Irish village where the woman seemed to be constantly pregnant!

'Of course, Joe. I'll ask my wife to call on her as she is pregnant!'

When Joe arrived home, he found his wife in an agitated state, with her maid fussing round her ineffectually. Across the floor lay shards of chinaware in a pool of milk and tea; clearly some brouhaha had occurred! Dismissing the maid, he squatted down beside Catherine, who looked at him and burst into tears,

'What is my love?' asked Joe anxiously, thinking something had gone wrong with her pregnancy.

'Oh Joe, I want to go and see Pattie in Lucknow for a while. Everything is going wrong here, and you are always going away!'

'Oh Catherine love, now is not a good time to be going anywhere. But I will take you as soon as it is safe to do so!'

'What do mean Joe, why isn't it safe?' Joe was annoyed with himself as he had been sworn to secrecy, so he diverted her with asking,

'What happened here my love? Why all the mess?'

Catherine launched into an agitated tale about how she was feeling sick again and had rung for a cup of cha. Her maid, Maya, had come into the room with a tray, when a cobra had slithered by Maya's skirt closely followed by a mongoose, which generally lived beneath the bungalow. The cobra had then slithered across Maya's feet, again with the mongoose in hot pursuit. The maid had screamed and thrown the tray into the air from where it had crashed to the floor.

Joe's lips twitched as he envisioned the scene, but he said, seriously,
'But what happened to the cobra and mongoose?'

'The mongoose killed it and took it away; but Joe, it was frightening!'

'I know, little one,' said Joe, gathering her into his arms, and whispering into her hair,

'What a gurrh burrh; I will call Maya back to clear up this mess. That will make you feel better.' Joe thought it best not to talk of his impending trip until the furore had died down!

Later, as they shared their evening meal in the glow of lamplight, Joe thought how her burgeoning motherhood had given Catherine a glow, a beauty she had not possessed previously. He told her so, but instead of basking in his admiration, Catherine told him tartly that it did not encourage him to fulfill her dearest wish and take her to Lucknow for a visit. Joe took a deep breath,

'There is a compelling reason why I cannot take you right now; I have been ordered back to Kotepore tomorrow.' Catherine looked strickened, which made Joe feel even worse having lied to her about being ordered to go. A tear trembled on his wife's eyelashes, and she rose without another word, and left the room, leaving him to finish his meal alone. Joe threw down his napkin and got up from the table, unsure whether to follow her, and possibly make matters worse, or leave her to think over the situation on her own. Expediency won, and he settled for pacing the floor as planned the next day. Later, her stole into their bedroom to find Catherine in bed, and apparently asleep. He leaned down and kissed her cheek softly,

'Goodnight my love, I will be gone when you wake up, but I'll be back just as soon as I can.' Catherine did not stir.

The next morning as the sky began to lighten, Joe slipped out of bed, dressed quickly in his Jhoti garb, and quietly tiptoed out of the room. He made his way to the servant's hut outside, and called Ghopi out in muted tones, giving him instructions to look after the memsahib, and not allow her to leave the cantonment whatever the provocation. He already knew that a doolie was due to leave the cantonment very soon, and did not wish to miss it.

The next morning, the Colonel and James were once again ensconced together. Colonel Deluce looked grave, as he handed James a dispatch that had arrived that morning, apparently having been delayed along the way if the date at the top was to be believed! The consignment of Enfield rifles, received some two weeks before and awaited further instructions, had largely been forgotten in the face of a series of more disturbing pieces of news, but this was the dispatch that should arrived with the rifles. There was a brief manual on how the rifle was to be used, and the instruction to muster the troops, British and sepoys, as soon as possible, issue the rifles, and begin practice sessions with them.

The two men were silent as they absorbed the news, believing that this direct order could not have come at a worse time; but they were obliged to follow instructions or face disciplinary action sometime in the future. James spoke first,

'This is not the best time for this,' he said with a wry smile, 'but given the recent news, perhaps we should try to deal with it a bit more tactfully!'

'What have you in mind, James?' asked Deluce.

'I note in the manual, that the paper cartridges are to be greased using the supplied tallow, but if we get some of our privates to grease them with ghee before issue, it should put the sepoys' minds at rest.' Colonel Deluce thought about the suggestion, looking for possible pitfalls, but finally,

'That could work, if handled properly. The sepoys cannot object to ghee. James, I want you to direct operations. Instruct the privates in your Company as soon as possible, and we should be able to have a full parade tomorrow morning early, and all of the troops can be issued with the rifles.'

James did as he was bid, and a dozen privates were sent to the armory to collect enough cartridges for a practice session and to set about the task of greasing them with ghee.

The following morning, A Company led the way onto the parade ground, and the British contingent lined up in good order with much shouting from Sergeant Majors. Each Company in turn were issued with their Enfields, and given a demonstration of how to use their new rifles.

Then the sepoys were marched in, and lined up in ranks opposite their British counterparts. Major James Willoughby strode across the parade ground, flanked by Captain David Wells and Lieutenant Carless. The three came to a halt in front of the sepoys, and James addressed their Jemadar,

'Have your men form lines to receive their new Enfield Rifles, Jemadar.' The Jemadar saluted smartly and with dead pan features said,

'We cannot use these rifles, Sir, for we have been told the cartridges are greased with pig and beef tallow.' James heart sank; the very thing that he feared. Somehow the news of the Meerut uprising had reached their own sepoys,

'Do not worry Jemadar, I know of your concerns, and I have ordered ghee to be used.'

'Very well, Sir.' He turned to face the sepoys and shouted,

'Satvinder Roy, take your men to the British private with the rifles, and take one each, chuldi, chuldi.' Satvinder Roy stepped forward and saluted,

'We cannot, Jemadar, for you told us not to already.' He stepped back. The Jemadar frowned,

'Sorry, Sir; they have heard bad stories and don't want the rifles.'

Lieutenant Carless listened to the interchange with increasing impatience. His temper had not improved over time and heavy drinking had only exacerbated it. He spoke to James,

'Major Willoughby. Are you going to tolerate this insubordination?' And stepping forward, he strode to Satvinder and seized his arm, attempting to drag him to where the rifles were stacked awaiting distribution. Sepoy Roy pulled his arm away sharply and the swing of his arm pushed Carless' helmet off his head, to tumble to the ground. Enraged, Carless drew his sidearm and pointed it at the hapless Roy, who fell to his knees in front of him. James quickly reached Carless and struck up his gun hand,

'That will do, Carless. Sergeant Major Willis, come here if you please.' A figure detached itself from the ranks and joined the officers.

'Take Lieutenant Carless to the guard room, Sergeant Major, and I will attend to him later.'

'Sir!' and taking Carless' arm, he strode away towing the incensed junior officer. James issued a similar order to a second Sergeant Major and ordered him to escort Sepoy Roy and take him to his office, where he would see him as soon as possible. He then ordered the Jemadar to lead his men to their barracks, and inform them all that they would not be using cartridges greased with tallow. Finally, the British troops were ordered to the firing range where they were to commence practising with their new Enfields. The parade ground rapidly emptied, and James breathed a sigh of relief. He would have to have a repeat the performance tomorrow, but hopefully the sepoys would be fully informed by then.

He dealt with Sepoy Roy first. He found the man in his office shaking with fear, obviously expecting a severe punishment, even hanging if the stories from Meerut were to be believed! James looked at him, and spoke gently,

'Sepoy Roy, I have heard good stories about you and that you are a loyal soldier?' The Sepoy looked up at him with a worried frown, but stayed silent.

'Do you know of me, Sepoy Roy?' The sepoy whispered,

'Yes Sir; that you are a fair officer.'

'Well, Sepoy Roy. I knew you were worried, and I ordered ghee to be used on the cartridges, so you do not have to worry. Look at me, Sepoy,' the shaking figure did as he was told, looking James in his face, 'I would not lie to you.'

'No Sir.'

'You may go, Sepoy. But I cannot tolerate any more disobedience. You will return to your barracks and tell the other sepoys what I have said. I expect you all on parade tomorrow morning with no further fuss.'

'Yes Sir.' And the sepoy saluted with a much relieved expression, wheeled about and marched out of the office.

James then faced the more unpleasant task of disciplining Carless, who would be incensed at being admonished in front of sepoys, who he considered little better than the 'untouchables'!

He found Carless pacing the guardroom, watched by his anxious escort. As James entered the room, Carless spun round and opened his mouth to speak; James did not give him the opportunity,

'Sergeant Major; kindly wait outside.'

'Yes Sir!'

'Now Lieutenant Carless. What did you think you were doing attacking Sepoy Roy like that?' Carless' mouth dropped open. He had not expected such a question.

'I....I... wanted the man to obey orders, Sir.' The 'sir' was said grudgingly.

'Carless', pursued James. 'you could have precipitated a much bigger insurrection that one sepoy; d'you understand?' Thoroughly confused now, Carless stammered,

'No...n.no, Sir!'

'Next time I am dealing with a situation, Lieutenant Carless, you will wait for orders, or face much greater disciplinary action. You may not understand, but you will do as you are ordered. Do I make myself clear?' A thoroughly chastened Simon Carless mumbled an apology and left the guardroom. James was acutely aware that this episode would simply exacerbate the hatred that Carless nurtured for him, but he had no time to deal with it right now. He would, however, ensure that the Lieutenant had nothing to do with the issue of the Enfields the next day!

Joe awoke to find himself with a splitting headache and surrounded by gloom. He sat up and nursed his head in his hands, trying desperately to remember where he was, and what had brought him to this place? Slowly, painfully, memory returned, and he groaned out loud at the realisation that he was in prison and a general uprising was probably taking place. Even as he sat nursing his sore head, the people he held most dear were in the gravest danger, and he was powerless to help them.

He had entered Kotepore to find the place seething with excitement. Going first to his usual lodgings, he had been greeted with,

'Hah, Jhoti, have you heard the news?'

Later by the cooking fire, he heard tales that varied from sepoys being held down and forced to swallow a greased patch, to all eighty five Meerut sepoys being treated thus, and were even now awaiting transportation across the 'kala pani'! Both of these were forbidden by their religion and would disgrace the sepoys for all time. Joe tried his best to curb such wild exaggerations, but his efforts earned him several black looks from the scattering of strangers fomenting unrest, so he to desist for fear of reprisals. These badmashes had been active for some time trying to stir up hatred against the British, and Joe was only too aware that they were succeeding!

It was not until the middle of the next day that he heard the news that caused him the most disquiet. He had been sitting with a group of coolies, when a fellow started up with the usual tale of sepoys being forced to eat cartridge papers, when a fellow on his right wagged his head and broke in with,

'Huh. That is nothing. In Meerut where eighty five sepoys were treated so, and then they were all marched off in shackles and locked up. They are even now waiting to be court-martialled at the orders of Burra-General-Anson!'

'When was this?' asked Joe, as casually as he could. The Indian waved his hands vaguely,

'One, two weeks; how should I know? I heard it from my wife's uncle who lives there!'

'When will they be court-martialled?' was answered by another shrug.

Shortly afterwards, Joe left the cooking fire, and sauntered back to his lodgings, his mind in turmoil.

'Does the Colonel know of the court-martials? I am sure he would have told me! Why didn't Meerut not inform other cantonments?' He was so deep in thought that he failed to hear the sound of approaching horses; but it was brought to his attention by a shout,

'Hey mind out there!'

A small troop of horsemen trotted by bearing lances, and Joe noticed that they wore the livery of Prince Saeed; so he was back in Kotepore? Joe had not seen him for many months and had not known that he was back; no matter, this was no time for socializing!

But what should he do next? The news from Meerut needed to be reported quickly, along with the information that the talk around the fires was becoming much more belligerent. But should he probe a little more first? In spite of the general feeling of indignation, Joe sensed a reluctance to take the final step into wholesale insurrection. Perhaps the citizens of

Kotepore were waiting to see what other districts would do; each frightened to act alone!

Joe decided that before he returned to the cantonment, he needed to find out what Raja Ajit was planning. It was known that he had been building up his private army, a rissal, for years, and Joe assumed that he planned to use it when the time was right; and that time could be now! He would need a change of clothes if he hoped to penetrate the rissal's headquarters in the precincts of the Rajah's palace in Kotepore, as they wore a distinctive uniform; long white tunic over baggy trousers sashed in scarlet, with matching scarlet turban. His own shabby pedlar disguise would stick out like a sore thumb, and he would be thrown out before he got very far! The rissal soldiers were armed with lances and tulwars and Joe had seen them on visits to the palace carrying out manoevres on the maidan, and he had been impressed!

Getting into the outer courtyards of the palace wasn't difficult as there was a number of people milling about, but as he approached the soldiers' quarters he had to be careful, as there were sentries posted at every entrance. He lingered about the courtyard, apparently stopping to talk to others here and there, but in reality, watching the coming and going of soldiers, or palace officials. Finally his chance came to act as dusk was falling and flares and lamps had yet to be lit. A maid servant went by to fetch water from the well, her sari clad figure swaying gracefully as she supported a heavy chatti on her head. She undulated by one of the sentries who seemed to know here, as he responded with a lecherous leer. She reached the well and made great play at having difficulty with the winding mechanism. The sentry lounged over to her nonchalantly, and very soon had his arm round her waist as he helped her draw up the bucket.

Joe's teeth gleamed momentarily in a smile; soldiers seemed to be cast in the same mould regardless of their race! He wasted no time and slipped through the unguarded entrance to find himself in a dark passage. He moved cautiously along it, pressing himself close to one side, but he met no-one. The passage finally opened into an inner courtyard where several cooking fires were being used to prepare the evening meal. Perfect; with their minds on their stomachs, they would not be vigilant; and why would they expect a visitor in the fastness of their barracks?

Joe retraced his steps along the passage, and explored a few of the doors that opened from it. As he expected, the rooms were mainly sleeping areas, with rows of charpoys ranged along the walls. In the third room he tried, he found what he was looking for; on one charpoy was flung a uniform, complete with turban; its owner doubtless lounging comfortably in the courtyard waiting for his evening meal clad in casual clothes. There was no-one else in the room, and it was the work of a moment to lift the pile of garments and return to the passage. He stiffened as he heard voices approaching to the entrance through which he had just come, but they passed by the entrance without glancing in. Breathing a sigh of relief, he tried some more rooms until he found one that appeared to be a store room, and stripping off the shabby Pathan outfit, replaced it with the splendid palace uniform. He stuffed the discarded clothes under a pile of sacks and then peered out of the store; still no-one in sight. He stepped out briskly, walked up the passage, this time openly, and entered the inner courtyard, which was bustling with activity.

He seated himself cross-legged by a group who had obviously eaten, and lit up a bidi. Drawing on it deeply, he passed it companionably to the man on his right, who took it and drew on it in turn before handing it back. Conversation flowed round the fire,

'When do the court-martials take place?'

'Soon; it is said within two days.'

'What will happen to them?' The first speaker shrugged,

'Who knows what the angrezi will do. At the very least they will be stripped of their uniforms and lose their pensions.' Another voice chimed in,

'How can the angrezi treat them so after many years of loyal service? They must have know that the cartridges would cause offence.'

'We must all rise together. There are few enough of them, but we must act together. What say you?' The question was put directly to Joe, who had seated himself in the shadows and remained silent until then,

'I agree; the angrezi must be taught a lesson. They cannot keep trampling on our beliefs and caste forever!'

There was a chorus of approval. But Joe noticed one or two of the group looking at him with sideways glances, no doubt querying whether they had seen him before. But he was relying on the sheer size of the army, and the number of courtyards like this one, and many soldiers sitting round them who had not met before.

After a while he relaxed, confident that they were no longer suspicious. He carefully watched the ebb and flow of soldiers, and finally got up, and followed a trio through an archway and into another courtyard. But after listening to more chit chat round the fires, finally concluded that that the soldiers did not yet know what was expected of them, but were all waiting on the news of the court-martials in Meerut. But after that? He could not wait to find out.

The evening was nearly over and the soldiers would soon be returning to their quarters and their charpoys. He had not heard an outcry, so assumed the theft of the uniform had not been discovered; but it would be too dangerous to try and replace it, with so many men disappearing into their sleeping quarters. He decided to leave by another exit and find a change of clothes elsewhere, but when he tried the exits to the streets of Kotepore, he found them all locked for the night. He realised that he would have to resign himself to a night in the barracks and find his out first thing in the morning. He curled up in the corner of a courtyard behind some dense bushes and prayed that he wasn't sharing his accommodation with a scorpion or a snake!

He slept fitfully and awoke as the early morning mist was starting to lift. He rose and stretched, thinking wistfully of his comfortable bed in his Sergeant's bungalow, with Catherine curled up against him. He was lounging nonchalantly when the first soldier emerged bleary eyed from the nearest sleeping quarter; the man nodded to him briefly. He carried a jug of water, clearly intent on relieving himself. Joe followed at a cautious distance, and as he had hoped the soldier made his way through the courtyards and out of a gate opening onto a patch of open ground, obviously the local latrine if the prevailing stench was anything to go by. Joe got his bearings and with a cheery wave to his unwitting guide, set off to make his way back to the cantonment.

The uniform was a problem; safe enough in Kotepore itself where soldiers of the rissal were a common enough sight, but he would need to change before reaching British lines. Fortunately he had a few rupees with him, and decided to purchase a change of clothes as soon as the bazaars started to stir.

By mid-morning he was ready to go home, feeling rather satisfied with himself. Not only had he found out about the happenings in Meerut, but had penetrated the very heart of the rissal barracks. The uniform was safely tied in a bundle and could come in useful for a future occasion. As the previous day, his preoccupation prevented him hearing the sound of horses approaching until they were very close. He looked up startled, straight into the face of Prince Saheed. The Prince was mounted on a showy chestnut stallion, and he looked down into the face of his friend. Recognition was instant; he was the one person who was used to seeing Joe in a turban and the blue eyes were unmistakable! He snapped out an order, and two of his men sprang from their horses and seized Joe's arms. He struggled, and at a gesture form the Prince, one of his captors hit him on the back of his head with his tulwar. The Prince looked sadly at the slumped form of his friend, and shook his head; the cavalcade moved off.

Joe felt the back of his head gingerly, and winced when he found a swelling at the base of his skull, just under the turban. Peering round in the gloom, he found a chatti of water in the corner of the cell, and soaking a strip of cloth torn from his turban, bound the swelling with it.

When the throbbing died away sufficiently, he explored his surroundings; the work of a moment. He was in a square cell, some ten feet wide, with a stout door in the middle of one wall, and a small grille set high on the opposite wall. The only furniture was a small stool and a pile of rotting straw. He stood on the stool and managed to peer out of the grille. The fitful light outside suggested that the day was not yet over as he could not believe that he had been unconscious all night! Of his bundle there was no sign.

He heard footsteps approaching and jumped off the stool, causing a stab of pain at the back of his head. The door swung open, and a coolie entered with a tray of food; a small pile of chapattis and some dal. He was escorted by a soldier with his tulwar at the ready, so Joe decided against precipitate action. He took the tray and tried to question his visitors,

What time is it? Where am I? May I see the Prince?'

The pair maintained a stony silence and backed out the door, which shut noisily behind them, leaving Joe to his gloomy thoughts which matched the gloom of the cell. How long did the Prince mean to keep him locked up? Depression weighed down on his and his head throbbed anew. How could he have been so stupid after all he had achieved, and not hear the horses approaching? Complacency; sheer, unadulterated complacency! He had been so busy congratulating himself on the success of his mission that he had brought disaster on himself; and possibly on the entire cantonment. His self-criticism made his throb even worse, so abandoning it, he laid down in the noisome straw, falling into a fitful sleep, punctuated by dreams of the neat bungalows in flames and their occupants running for their lives. The leading figure was Catherine who held up her arms to a giant figure in a scarlet turban who raised a tulwar high above his head and then brought it down; he jerked awake in horror at the memory! He was bathed in sweat.

The night seemed endless as every time he fell asleep he suffered the same nightmare and the same awakening. If he stayed awake, he was conscious of the varied animal life in the foetid straw, and he was bitten all over by the time a fitful light came creeping through the grille. The cell must face east, he thought inconsequentially, for the light seemed stronger than the previous evening; the cell must face the cantonment!

It seemed like many more hours later that his gaoler returned with more food; some curds and sliced mango. This time he ate in order to keep up his strength for the coming day. The gaoler stood over him while the soldier with the tulwar remained vigilant. When Joe told him that he needed to relieve himself, the man gave a gap-toothed leer and pointed to the corner of the cell. Joe decided to wait as long as he could as he had no wish to add to the odours already present, but the man merely shrugged and pointed to the door. Joe emerged into a subterranean passage, and escorted by the soldier he was led through a maze of passages, finally emerging into the blinding sunshine of a paved garden. The contrast to his cell could not have been greater as the setting was sumptuous. A fountain plashed into a pool full of golden carp, and planted about with exotic blooms; a bougainvillea scrambled over a trellis and roses added a heady perfume to the air.

Breathing in deeply to get the stink of the cell out of his nostrils, Joe followed the guide through an archway into a diwan-i-khas, a small private audience chamber. Seated on an ornate golden chair was the Prince, his chin resting on his fist as he looked at Joe as he entered; he frowned as he approached and made namaste. Ordering the sentry outside, the Prince returned his gaze to his prisoner; the silence lengthened, but neither spoke, then at last, and in English, Prince Saheed said,

'My father would kill you of he knew you were here.'

There was no response to that, so Joe remained silent. The Prince went on,

'It has come; that which my father has waited for so long.' Silence again, and then,

'Why did they all come here? The British, the French, the Portuguese squabbling over India like jackals over a tiger kill? And the worst of them all were the British; they thought that they were so clever when Clive beat the French at Plessey! At first, all they wanted to do was trade, they said; but it wasn't enough and they spread their tentacles into every corner of our land. Soon they had their soldiers here too. Then they had to interfere with our customs; said that they were uncivilized; hah! We were civilized when the British were still running about naked!' He stopped then, and looked at Joe,

'Of course, you know all this. I thought that you, of all people would understand how we felt?' Joe could only look back helplessly, as the Prince held out his bundle that contained, unmistakably, a rissal uniform. The Prince got up from his gilded throne and paced about the room liked a caged tiger, talking in a bitter tone,

'My father has hated them all his life. He watched while they infiltrated into Oudh; building their cantonments. The Honourable East India Company, bah! Just a bunch of brigands; and they claim that thuggeree was barbaric! And then they ignore our custom of adopting a son when there is no direct male heir, and annexed Oudh!' He swung round abruptly,

'What right did they have?' Joe shrugged helplessly; the Prince glared at him, but then subsided, slumping back into his chair,

'Of course, what could you do? We are all pawns in their vast game, are we not? My father has long resolved to throw off their yolk once he was powerful enough, but he knew that he could not do it alone; kill a few and they would be replaced. He sent me to study the British and explore their weaknesses; and I did! Do you know what is their greatest weakness Joe?' Joe shook his head.

'It is their monumental arrogance; They cannot believe that they could be wrong. But this time they are; oh yes, this time. But my father made a small mistake; he could not foresee that I would grow to like some of them; one in particular; though I always thought that he was different. Why do think that he has sent me away so much?' The Prince paused again; Joe thought that he had aged ten years since he had last seen him,

'This time they have overreached themselves, and done what we could not do ourselves and united the Muslim and Hindu; and upset their own sepoys; their ever loyal sepoys; and all to a cartridge!' The Prince laughed mirthlessly,

'Over a cartridge! How could they be so stupid? Do you know what happened at Meerut?' Joe shook his head,

'They were all court-martialled, all eighty five of them, when was it, ah, Friday! The very next day they were stripped of their uniforms and shackled.'

Looking at Joe's shocked face, he repeated,

'Yes, shackled, in front of their comrades. These proud men, most of them Brahmins; so stupid! They were sentenced to ten years hard labour and marched away. The next day the sepoys rose up.'

The Prince got up again and strode over to Joe, looking at him deep into his eyes, and spoke softly now,

'It has begun. From Bombay to Madras, from Delhi to Calcutta; in the Punjab, Bengal, Rajputana; and Oudh; the British will be driven out and India will become Indian again.'

Joe was appalled, his mind racing as he took in the words; what did he mean by 'rose'? Did it mean that they had taken over Meerut, or worse? The Prince was speaking again,

'Whose side are you on, Joe? Now is the time to make your choice.'

'I…I don't know, Prince. I know what you said was true, but…but,'

'Ah yes. But after all you have the same coloured skin, do you not?'

'That isn't fair!'

'Not fair! That is, oh, so British. Not fair; Joe, just look!'

The Prince thrust his arm out and laid it alongside Joe's. There was little to choose between them for colour. The Prince drew a bejeweled dagger from its ornate sheath and drew its tip across both forearms until blood flowed and mingled in a thin stream,

'Now tell me the difference between us!'

Joe found he had no words to refute anything that the Prince had said. The British had no right to steal the lands from Indian rajas who had held it for generations, any more than they had had the right to take their land from the Irish. At last he spoke quietly and humbly,

'But what has happened in Meerut?'

'Ah yes, Meerut. The imprisoned sepoys were released by their fellows, and then they turned on the British and killed them all. Then they went to Delhi to release the last of the Moghul kings. My father has been waiting for such a happening, as have many other districts. Now we will all rise up. But you must stay here Joe. There will be much bloodshed, but after it is all over you can make your choice; either live here under Indian rule; become a Talukda; or leave and go back from whence you came!'

'But Prince; my….my wife?'

'I'm sorry Joe. There is nothing to be done. As I said, my father will kill you if he sees you, so I cannot let you go just yet.' He took Joe's arms and gripping them tightly, shook him,

'Think about it Joe, you are Irish in spite of that uniform you wear; or sometimes wear,' waving at Joe's present garb with a wry smile, 'my soldier out there is loyal to me. Keep your head covered and you should not be recognised by anyone else. But for now, you must remain locked up.' He gazed steadily into Joe's eyes, his own brown eyes awash with tears. He embraced Joe once, and then pushed him away,

'Goodbye, I hope it won't be for too long.' He called for the waiting sentry outside the door, who led Joe away and back to his cell.

As the door closed behind him, he began to plan his escape. Clearly the sepoys of Kotepore were to rise up with the help of the rissal, if they hadn't already done so! He closed his mind to that disturbing thought. Whether or not all the British men, women and children had been killed in Meerut, he had to work on the assumption that it was planned for Kotepore cantonment. His hideous nightmare of Catherine being threatened by an upraised tulwar suddenly became a possibility, or worse, a probability!

He calmed himself in order to think rationally. It was obvious that Saeed did not want others in the barracks to know about him. The only people he had seen were the gaoler, a weedy little fellow, and the rissal sentry, a strapping Sikh who had doubled as his guide. If that was all he had to deal with, then he might have a chance of getting out. Presumably they would feed him again, and he must be ready for them when they came with his meal. How long? He had gone to the diwan immediately his chota hazri, but how long had he been there? It was difficult to judge, but the sun seemed to be high according to the light entering the grille. Yes, tiffin should not be long in coming!

He examined his cell carefully; not much help there, except perhaps for the stool. He picked it up by one leg; it seemed flimsy enough, and struck it sharply on the floor. Sure enough it broke up, leaving him clutching the leg; not much of a weapon, but it would have to do. But then he remembered the thugees, referred to by the Prince. He had read that they used a weighted scarf to strangle their victims. He tore off another strip from his turban, and knotted some earth in one corner. Not a heavy weight, but it too would have to do. He practiced flicking it until he felt that he had the action right.

Just in time, for he heard footsteps outside the door. He moved quickly behind the door, so he would be initially hidden as it swung open. It opened slowly, and then he heard an exclamation from the other side and the next moment the gaoler stepped inside. Joe brought the leg of the stool sharply on the back of his head, wincing in sympathy as the man slid to the floor. He moved into the doorway, and was relieved to see only the Sikh outside; only, dear God; the man seemed ten feet tall! He dropped the leg of the stool and advanced on the sentry. The Sikh's teeth bared with delight in the magnificent set of whiskers, and he dropped to a semi-crouch. He must have been warned not to injure Joe as he made no attempt to reach for his tulwar, 'thank God' breathed Joe in relief. The two circled warily, Joe with his weighted strip in his right hand hidden at his side. He suddenly flicked it out and the weighted end flew round in an arc round the Sikh's neck, and Joe grabbed it; then he side stepped to get his knee into the bigger man's back. He had both ends of the strip twisted together now, and he continued to twist. The Sikh grabbed at the tourniquet slowly cutting off his air, but to no avail. Though Joe was desperate to get away and get to the cantonment, he kept up the steady pressure until he felt his adversary slump, and then fall to the floor. Still he held on, in case he was feigning his collapse. But he did not want to kill the man; just keep him quiet for long enough to escape. He dragged the unconscious Sikh into the cell, and laid him alongside the gaoler who was gradually coming round. Joe removed the Sikh's turban, apologizing to the man for the sacrilege, and used lengths of it to firmly truss the pair, and gag them. He hoped that someone would find them, but not too soon!

Joe stepped back out into the passage cautiously, but there was no-one in sight. He tried to remember the route through the passages as he had no wish to come out in the garden where the diwan was, but needed to get away from the palace as soon as possible. As he moved away from the cell, he began to move more quickly, as there was only the Prince and the sentry who knew that he had been locked up, and he was still dressed in his Indian clothes. He finally found a part of the palace that he recognised from previous visits and within ten minutes was heading out of Kotepore. The sun beat down brassily so it seemed that it was only early afternoon as he had hoped. The streets were deserted; was it because of the heat or for a more sinister reason? In spite of the heat, he ran as fast as he could in the direction of the cantonment.

Chapter 10

Major James Willoughby looked down at the bed in which lay Colonel Gerald Deluce. But he found it difficult to reconcile this desiccated husk of a man with the Colonel he had spoken to only that morning. The Colonel he knew had an upright stance and always moved and spoke with precision. The face could look stern when the occasion demanded it, but the mouth under the stiffly waxed white moustache could break into an attractive smile. The hair, white to match the moustache, was always brushed to snowy perfection, neatly parted in the middle. His only vanity had been to wear it slightly long at the neck where it curled thickly in spite of his years.

The man in the bed seemed strangely shrunken and breathed stertorously through his nose. One side of the face had slipped so that one half of the moustache drooped, while the other stuck up ludicrously. The hair looked sparse and unkempt.

'Oh Colonel,' whispered James softly, 'you could have chosen a better moment to suffer a seizure.'

That evening, the Colonel had slid sideways off his chair causing temporary panic among the officers gathered together for an urgent meeting. A stretcher had been called for and the meeting had broken up in disorder. Another would have to be called in the morning as a matter of urgency. For that very afternoon a despatch had arrived from Meerut describing the dire situation there, and the slaughter of innocents. James sighed; if only the Meerut officers had seen fit to handle the situation over the new rifles and their cartridges in the way that they had, perhaps it could have been avoided. After all, their own confrontation had quickly subsided when James had dealt with sepoy Roy with consideration rather than disgrace.

The news from Meerut could easily precipitate the crisis that they had worked so hard to avoid, for he had no doubt that Raja Ajit Khan was fully informed, and had probably been so for several days. It never ceased to amaze him the speed at which the Indian community disseminated news without the sophistication of the telegraph!

The other problem taxing James' mind as he gazed at his mentor and friend as well as Commanding Officer, was the matter of seniority. He knew that he was being groomed to take over the Colonelcy, but it had not been ratified as yet, and it should be the most senior of the Majors who should now step in as Acting Colonel, and that was Major Conroy. James liked the man, but he really wasn't up to handling this situation. It may be that no-one was, but dear Reginald Conroy was a bumbling oaf, grown even more so since his marriage to Lucy's twittering Aunt. 'Dear God,' he groaned, 'how Enid would revel in the role of 'Colonel's Wife'; what a gurrh burrh, what a great noise she would make of it!'

James reached a decision, and moved accordingly. Leaving the Colonel in the care of his aide, he made his way to the mess where all the officers were now seated, their faces grim as they reflected on the news from Meerut. James quietly seated himself in the Colonel's chair, a move that seemed to be wholly accepted, even with a fleeting look of relief on Conroy's face. 'Thank God,' he thought, as dissension about command was the last thing they needed right now.

'Gentlemen,' he began, 'I have to tell you that the Colonel has not regained consciousness from his seizure, and Surgeon Anderson is gravely concerned about his condition. We cannot wait for him to recover before we make decisions as the situation is too serious.' He paused to give his audience time to digest the news that the Colonel was extremely unlikely to be capable of leading them in the near future, and more probably, would never do so again. He went on,

'Yesterday, we were in the process of discussing the urgent evacuation of our families. Now it would appear that this needs to be acted upon with greater speed than we had first thought, even if lodgings are difficult to be found in the hills. We must encourage everyone to share if need be for the short term!' He looked around as he spoke and noted one or two junior officers looking uncomfortable at the thought of their wives haring accommodation with perhaps wives of other ranks!' He smiled grimly to himself; if only that was all they had to worry about! He went on inexorably,

'You should all have heard of the events in Meerut by now. It all began on 24th April and we know that General Anson was informed and it was he that insisted on a full court-martial on 9th May, which caused the later uprising and massacre. I cannot for the life understand why the Meerut establishment could not deal with the situation in a similar manner to us; they must have known that the cartridges greased with tallow would cause offence!' A young subaltern from B Company spoke up,

'Sir, we did hear about our incident, and that you reprimanded Lieutenant Carless; was that necessary? I heard that his shako was struck off by a ...a...' His voice tailed off as he saw the expression on James' face. But James thought very carefully before answering, as he know what the subaltern was getting at; Carless had been struck, albeit accidently, by a native, and that was inexcusable in many British eyes!

'How long have you been in India, Mortimer?'

'About six months, Sir, but I don't see...'

'No, you don't. The situation was precipitated by Lieutenant Carless. The sepoy in question has served with the Regiment since we arrived in Kotepore; a good deal longer than you,' the subaltern looked uncomfortable, 'he did not act out of a spirit of disobedience, but due to deep felt religious belief. It would have been akin to asking a Christian to spit on a wafer!'

'But surely it's not the same: these men are heathens!' James sighed for he clearly had not got his message across,

'I'm sorry you don't understand, Mortimer, but you'll just have to take my word for it that I acted for the best, and with the Colonel's full agreement. Any more questions?' There were not, and James told the assembled officers that they were to return to their Companies and have all married Officers and other ranks to prepare their wives to leave for the hills within a day or two, and to take the minimum of trunks with them.

The meeting broke up with a babble of noise as officers argued the pros and cons of James action, and their impending precipitous flight. Not all agreed with the urgency of the situation, believing that Meerut was too far away to concern them. James made his way to the Colonel's bungalow to be told by his bearer that there was no change, and the Army-Surgeon-Sahib had recently called. The man looked ill at ease and kept looking over his shoulder, making James query,

'Anything wrong, bearer?'

'Oh no Sahib,' wringing his hands in agitation. James was too tired to follow it up,

'Send a message to my bungalow at any time in the night if there is any change in the Colonel-Sahib, for better or worse, d'you hear?'

'Yes Sahib.' The bearer watched James go down the Colonel's front path and into his own, where his wife waited in the doorway to greet him. The bearer's face was impassive.

Catherine was bored. Joe's departure that morning had irritated her beyond measure, and she had been seething with resentment ever since.

'Why don't they ever tell us anything?' she muttered to herself more than once, 'that's the trouble with men; they think we're incapable of understanding anything! Hah!'

It was later that day, as she lay dozing after tiffin that she experienced a strange sensation in her belly. It wasn't nausea, those days were long gone, and it wasn't unpleasant. She lay perfectly still trying to analyse it, gripped with a strange excitement at the butterfly fluttering inside her. Suddenly she laughed out loud,

'Of course,' she clapped her hands with glee, 'it's the baby!' It just had to be this strange entity growing inside her, and she laughed again with relief, and thus reassured, fell asleep. But by chota hazri the following day, she was longing to share her experience with someone, and he wasn't there! Resentment stirred again, and she finished her breakfast in a state of high dudgeon!

Shortly afterwards, Gopi brought her a letter. The young bearer had a worried frown on his face, but he said nothing as he handed it over, making a hurried namaste before leaving her to peruse it. It was from Pattie in Lucknow, urging her to come and visit as soon as possible;

'There is talk of a last dance at the Residency before everyone leaves for the hills. Charlotte is to come as well and then we could make up a party for a picnic in Cawnpore see Rachel there too! Oh do come.'

The letter went on in similar vein, and by the time she had finished reading it, Catherine had made up her mind to go whether or not Joe returned that day.

'If he can leave me just when I felt the baby move,' she told herself irrationally, 'then I will go and find someone who is interested!' She rang her handbell vigorously, bringing Gopi at a run. She ordered him to arrange a carriage and escort for the journey to Lucknow, leaving first thing the next morning. Gopi's mouth open and he stammered,

'But Memsahib, Harrington-Sahib said that…'

'That will be all Gopi. Just do as I say, I will speak to Harrington-Sahib about it.'

'Yes Memsahib.'

Later that same afternoon, Lucy Willoughby called. Though prompted by James to do so, she was more than happy to oblige as she was fond of Catherine and found it no hardship. James had said,

'I promised to keep an eye on Joe's household while he was gone but I know I will be busy all day, and I have a feeling that Mrs. Harrington will be none too pleased at being left alone!'

Lucy soon discovered that Catherine was indeed 'none too pleased at being left alone' as she poured out her woes into a sympathetic ear,

'And what is going on,' questioned Catherine, 'why will they not tell us anything?'

'There is some sort of crisis to do with a sepoy who refused the new cartridge. James says that it will soon blow over but we should be prepared to leave for the hills very soon. I have already done most of my packing, so I don't have much left to do.' Catherine sighed,

'If there's a crisis, why did Joe leave me?'

'He is a soldier, my dear, and must do his duty,' answered Lucy quietly,

'Well he promised me that I should visit my friend, Pattie Day, in Lucknow. So if he isn't back by tomorrow morning, I shall go on ahead.'

'I should wait for your husband, dear,' replied Lucy, preparing to take her leave, 'surely you will be leaving for the north with the rest of us?'

'I don't know; I did want to see my friend before we go!'

Lucy left shortly afterwards; concerned, but not overanxious about Catherine. In true Victorian fashion, James had played down the seriousness of the situation, as had all the husbands who knew anything about it. Consequently, though the wives were being encouraged to prepare themselves for their annual migration, they did not really understand the true urgency of their impending flight.

Lucy's visit did nothing to improve Catherine's temper; indeed it merely served to increase her determination to go early the following morning. Gopi reported that he had made the arrangement as ordered, but with tears in his eyes, begged her not to go before Harrington-Sahib returned. The bearer wrung his hands in distress, but Catherine was beyond reasoning and dismissed him.

Early the following morning, accompanied by a syce, Catherine left for Lucknow. The day started warm and sunny, but promised to become very hot. Gopi made one last attempt to deflect her from her purpose, but to no avail, and the carriage swept out of the cantonment. Catherine paid no attention to the lack of activity on the road, nor did she see the black looks that were cast at her from the few Indians who were about!

Shortly after Catherine had left for Lucknow, James made his way to the Regimental offices. He had slept fitfully and his eyes felt gritty. His wife had slept easily beside him, in blissful ignorance of her husband's concerns, making him feel thankful and irritated in turn. Once in the night, James had heard his son cry out, but before he could move, the patter of feet from the ayah making her way across the wooden floor sounded through the stillness; then he heard the soothing sounds of Meeta singing softly to him in Urdu; the child slept. Outside, pi-dogs barked and nightjars shrieked. He tossed and turned, but still sleep evaded him; what was it that prayed on his mind? He finally fell into a fitful doze early in the morning and woke to bright sunshine. The fears of the night receded with the new day.

Midway through the morning, the door of the Colonel's office opened slowly to reveal Major Conroy's face blinking owlishly at him,

'Ah there you James,' he said unnecessarily,

'As you see, Reggie.'

'Busy?'

'Just getting on top of the Colonel's paperwork before we leave for the hills.'

'James?'

'Mm?'

'I wondered; that is, Enid said; that is, with the Colonel ill; perhaps......?'

James heart sank. It had come as he expected it to; obviously inspired by Enid, Conroy was going to claim his rightful place. Before Conroy could gather his courage to finish, there was a brisk knock at the door,

'Come in,' called James. Captain Forsyth entered, and ignoring Conroy, he addressed James,

'Sir; I thought you should know straight away; the telegraph lines have gone dead!'

'When did this happen?'

'The telegraph operator isn't sure, but he tried to send a message a few moments ago and found the line was dead. He said that there had been no incoming messages at all during the morning, so it could have been since last night.'

'Thank you Forsyth.'

'Very good Sir.' James passed his hand over his face; what did this mean? Had the lines come down by themselves, as had happened at regular intervals in the past, or was there a more sinister reason?

'Sorry Reggie. What were you saying?'

'Ah, oh, nothing; I'll leave you in peace.' And Major Conroy hurriedly left the room. James smiled grimly; responsibility did not look so attractive all of a sudden!

Before James could send out a detail to go out and track down the break in the telegraph wires, more disquieting news came in. There seemed to be a sudden severe shortage of doolies, palanquins and carriages necessary to transport the ladies and their belongings to their summer dwellings. They were normally available for the summer migration, so where had they all gone?

James spent and hour or two by the Colonel's bedside towards late afternoon as the worst of the sun's heat was dying away. Gerald Deluce looked just the same as the previous day and James wondered if he was aware of his surroundings at all. He sat by the sick man's bed and poured out his worries,

'There is definitely trouble brewing, Sir. You can feel it in the air. The sepoys attended morning parade, but they looked slipshod, as if they didn't care anymore; and they looked sullen, all of them. Then the telegraph lines were cut; God but it makes you feel isolated. Then the carts and carriages have vanished; where have they gone? Whatever happens, we must get the women and children away, even if they have to walk!'

James finally reached his bungalow late in the evening. He had not taken a break all day, even after tiffin, and he felt drugged with weariness. Another worry that nagged at him like a sore tooth was the continuing absence of Joe. His brief had been to try and counteract the story of Sepoy Roy and also to assess the effect of it; the work of a day. But Joe had gone early Saturday and it was now Monday evening and even allowing for the short distance of travelling, he should have been back long before now! With that on his mind, he asked Lucy,

'Did you get a chance to call on Mrs. Harrington?'

'Yes, I called on Sunday. She was talking of going to Lucknow, but I believe I persuaded her to wait for Joe.'

'My God! Are you sure that she hasn't gone? Didn't you tell her we are all leaving for the hills very soon?'

'No, I can't be sure that she hasn't gone. I've been too busy today with the last minute bits and pieces, and yes, I did tell her we are all going to set out for the hills. But what is the problem; is there still a crisis? You haven't said any more about it!'

'Yes; the situation is still very tense, and the only place you ladies should be going is the hills, not gallivanting off to Lucknow!'

'I couldn't order her to stay, but I'm sure she will be sensible.'

'I hope so. I must find time to check in the morning; I am sure Joe will be back by then!'

'Where is he James?'

'He had to carry a message into Kotepore for the Colonel,' answered James, vaguely,

'Then why has he been gone so long?' As James was wondering the same thing himself, he didn't have an answer for her. What should he do if Joe wasn't back in the morning? Insist that Catherine go with them and leave a message for him? But what if he was in danger; shouldn't he try and do something to find him? The previous night finally caught up with him, and James nodded off in his chair, a glass of brandy pani slipping out of his flaccid hand, only rousing himself to go to bed at Lucy's urging.

Tuesday dawned, the sun promising to be hotter than ever. Normally, they would all have been looking forward to their coming journey, but this time the preparations were overlaid with anxiety. Even the wives, kept in ignorance about the situation, caught the contagion of alarm and bustled about gathering last minute necessities. Only the children seemed blissfully unaware and ran about uncaring in the rising heat.

The search for transport had borne some fruit, and a motley collection of doolies and carts harnessed to tired looking nags stood in the parade ground, their drivers lounging against the wheels, stolidly chewing betel and spitting red streams into the dust. There were not nearly enough carts to go round, and shrill dissensions rose, as harassed husbands tried to persuade stubborn wives to take only what was strictly necessary.

'I'll bring the rest on later,' was an argument that fell on more than one pair of deaf ears!

James had had enough as midday approached. At this rate they wouldn't get away until evening, and he had planned to leave first thing in the morning! He decided to see how the Colonel was and make sure he had been made ready for the litter that would carry him to Simla. There was a brooding stillness about the place that disturbed him, which he put down to his overwhelming sense of responsibility for all these people.

On the way he decided to pay a long overdue visit to the Harrington bungalow. He felt guilty as he realised that he had not seen Catherine out and about that morning, but had done nothing about it. He knocked, and a frightened looking Gopi opened the door.

'Is the memsahib at home?'

'No, Major Willoughby-Sahib.'

'Where is she? Down by the doolies?'

'No, Major-Sahib. She went to Lucknow.' Gopi looked terrified at the anger on James' face,

'What!' he thundered, 'you let her go?' he was being unfair and he knew it, for what could a bearer do, but anxiety made him irrational,

'When did she go?' he roared at the cowering Gopi, almost on his knees with fright,

'Yesterday, Major-Sahib; very early.'

'Very well,' said James, subsiding a little, 'you'd better wait for Harrington-Sahib and tell him so!'

'Yes Sahib; thank you Sahib; sorry Sahib.'

James strode away in a temper, guilt fuelling his anger. If he and the Colonel hadn't sent Joe into Kotepore, then he would be here now, and his wife would not be on the road to Lucknow. Trying to calm himself, for there was nothing to be gained by regrets, he waved to his wife as he passed their bungalow. She was dressed in shirt and pyjama trousers with a silk scarf over her blond hair, opting for comfort in travelling rather than Victorian elegance! Charles in his sunbonnet and light shirt also waved. James smiled for the first time that day,

'That'll give them something to talk about; the Major's wife gone native!' he chuckled to himself.

He let himself into the Colonel's bungalow, frowning at the absence of a bearer. The chiks had been rolled down and the bungalow was in semi-darkness, pleasantly cool after the brassy heat outside. He paused in the hallway with a frown; where were the servants? Then it occurred to him that apart from Gopi, he had not seen any servants moving about the cantonment all the way up to his destination. Surely there should have been a constant coming and going of them with their eternal chatter, carrying bits and pieces for packing.

Shaking off a feeling of impending doom, he went into the Colonel's bedroom, pausing a moment to allow his eyes to adjust to the gloom. As he stood there, he noticed something else was missing; the room was absolutely silent, in spite of the clamour of crickets outside. There was no sound of laboured breathing from the bed, or the swish of a punkah; normally a constant in their daily lives. Then he let out an oath as he caught sight of the ornate hilt of a dagger protruding from Gerald Deluce's chest.

James stood aghast for a moment as the implication of the murder sunk in, then he turned and ran outside. Spread out in a panorama below him, the tragedy of Kotepore cantonment began to unfold. From the sepoy barracks figures were running, tulwars held high above their heads, a cry if 'Din! Din!' sounding in the overheated air. Across the bridge that divided them from Kotepore town ran more figures, dressed in white and sashed in scarlet; the Raja's rissal. They reached the sepoys like two rivers meeting, and the confluence surged towards the parade ground with its milling mass of British soldiers, women and children. Even in his moment of desperation, James noted that there was not one Indian left in the parade ground; even the doolie drivers had vanished.

Like a tableau, the parade ground figures seemed frozen as they stared at the rapidly approaching mob brandishing their fearsome weapons. Seconds stretched eternally and the figures remained frozen; then a woman screamed. Instantly, all was panic as women ran to pick up their children. One small child lurched into the path of the running sepoys; he tottered briefly on unsteady, chubby legs, and then sat down. His mother arrived at the same moment as the leading sepoy and without pausing in his stride, he raised his tulwar and brought it down; mother and baby died together in a bright spurt of blood. The die was cast; a British Memsahib and child had been killed; it was mutiny; it was a fight to the death!

The act of butchery unfroze James as the screams had unfrozen the British in the face of approaching death. There was little he could do for the milling multitude below, and he hoped that they had the sense to make for the nearest barrack block and barricade themselves in as quickly as possible. In the meantime, there were still some British on the hill, including, dear God, Lucy and Charles! He ran from the Colonel's drive, drawing his pistol as he went. Already some sepoys and rissals had split away from the main flow and were systematically working their way through the bungalows. He could see a screaming woman running out of a Sergeant's bungalow chased by three white clad figures. She was cut down as she reached the road. Behind her on the verandah slumped two small figures as flames started to lick through the wooden structure, as flaming torches were used to good effect.

James reached his bungalow near the top row, but he could see no sign of his wife or Charles. He had not seen her running away, so assumed she was hiding.

'That would not save her,' he thought grimly, 'if the mutineers plan to fire all the bungalows!' He shouted desperately,

'Lucy, Lucy, where are you? We have no time to lose!'

He ran from one room to another, shouting, until two frightened faces peered out from a wardrobe in the master bedroom.

'James; oh James,' sobbed Lucy, throwing herself at his chest. James soothed her, noting that the Indian clothes, and scarf hiding her bright hair might help her get away. The child, though, would be another matter, with his white blond hair.

'Come,' he said tersely, 'keep your head covered. If we get separated, make your way to the barracks.' Privately, James did not hold out much hope of making it to the foot of the hill, let alone the barracks, but he wasn't going down without a fight. If it had not been for his wife and child, he would have gone out and faced them head on! There was a movement outside the bedroom window, and a brown, turbaned face peered in. James raised his pistol as a voice said,

'Don't shoot, Sir, it's me!' James' hand shook as he lowered the pistol, 'Good God, Joe, where'd you spring from?'

'It's a long story, Sir. No time now,' replied Joe, climbing in the window, 'Sir, where's my wife, where's Catherine?'

'She's, er, gone to Lucknow. Yesterday, or was it? Yes, it was yesterday, early!'

'Ah,' said Joe, enigmatically, 'I think we should get away from here! We could get Mrs. Willoughby and your little lad into the woods up there,' waving his arm at the crown of the hill, 'I don't think they'll expect any of us to go that way. There is always the Convent!'

'No. There's safety in numbers. We must join the others in the barrack blocks and organise their defence!' Joe shrugged; he was not about to argue with his Commanding Officer, and anyway, discovering Catherine gone, he had lost the sense of urgency to do something.

Joe and James went into the drawing room where windows overlooked the hill, and peered out cautiously. The number of flaming bungalows was increasing rapidly and climbing up the hill as the sepoys and rissal did their grisly work. At intervals, screams proclaimed hidden British women and children being flushed out and murdered; the two men shuddered at the awful sounds, angry at their helplessness. The Joe suddenly remembered,

'Sir! Shouldn't Nancy be here, too?'

'She was down in the parade ground, getting the carriage organised; oh God!' Joe looked at his long time hero and had the irreverent thought,

'Why; he's as confused and helpless as I am!' and he felt a hundred years older than yesterday! Then,

'Sir; if we just try and make a run for it, we'll have to fight our way through. I'll try and make a diversion; I'm still dressed as Jhoti, and you try and get your wife and son down to the barracks.' It was a desperate plan, but neither of them could think of a better one! Before he left, Joe found a strip of cloth for the little boys head in an attempt to hide his blondness. The child gazed solemnly at him with his thumb in his mouth, then shoved the impromptu turban with an experimental finger, but otherwise left it alone. Then the men gathered some cloths and piled them in the drawing room. Joe put a large dollop of ghee in the middle of the pile and applied a match. Thick smoke rose rapidly making them all cough, and they retreated from the drawing room in some haste. The Willoughby's moved to the back of the bungalow ready for flight, while Joe stepped out on the front verandah; he raised his tulwar and screamed in Urdu,

'No-one in this one!' and ran from the bungalow to a nearby Major's dwelling. The ploy worked, and the sepoys, who had been running towards the Willoughby home, saw the smoke and heard Joe's shout, and veered off to join him.

James peered out of the back window and saw the backs of the running figures, all moving away. He climbed out and helped Lucy out, then lifted his son up into his arms for a brief hug of reassurance. James stood still for a moment as tried to decide on the best route to the barracks. It looked hopeless; there seemed to be sepoys or rissals everywhere! As he stared at the shifting scene, James could see one possible escape route; a footpath ran from top to bottom of the cantonment, skirting all the bungalows and emerging beyond the barrack blocks. He could see that Barrack Block A seemed to have been occupied, from the amount of activity round it, but the rear seemed to be unguarded; there was a small door on that side.

'Come on,' he whispered to Lucy, giving her a swift reassuring kiss; then they moved off with James clutching his pistol. The billowing smoke from their bungalow gave them a degree of protection, as they moved down the perimeter path in a semi-crouch; down past the officers' quarters, where the pretty gardens had been trampled they crept. Down, past the neat rows of sergeant's and corporal's cottages where still forms, some decapitated by the razor sharp tulwars made them avert their eyes. Down, until they reached the shelter of the main barrack blocks. Tenser than ever they moved cautiously, but there was no-one behind B Block; but James was anxious to reach A Block where the majority were sheltered. They reached the end of B Block where ahead of them lay a gap between the buildings. James peered round the corner of B Block; there was confusion in the parade ground as isolated pockets of soldiers were fighting their way to the shelter of the barracks. Even in their extremity, James noted with some pride that their years of training had paid off, and tight squads of men were moving in a concerted body towards the door. Making the most of the diversion, James told Lucy that they must make a dash across the gap,

'Take Charles,' he whispered, though they could not have been heard above the tumult, 'in case I need to defend us.' She nodded and swallowed. She had conquered her hysteria and was determined to show what the daughter and wife of a soldier was made of!

'Now!' hissed James and they ran. They had almost reached safety when a shout told them that they had been spotted. Sepoys detached themselves from the melee and ran between the blocks to get to them. The fleeing trio reached the door, only to find it locked. James pounded on it desperately,

'Open up for God's sake; it's Major Willoughby, Hurry!' There was the sound of bolts being drawn,

'Hurry!' urged James under his breath. Shoving Lucy behind him, he drew his pistol and fired at almost point blank range at the nearest sepoy; he fell, tripping the one immediately behind him. It gave them the moment they needed, and as the door opened behind them they almost fell into the building. The door slammed shut again.

James comforted his wife and son for a moment, then encouraged Lucy to take Charles to where women and children were huddled together. Only then did he look around him; it was like a scene from Dante's 'Inferno'. The building was full to overflowing with men, women and children, many if a state of hysteria. The cots usually occupied by the private soldiers were filled with the wounded; but there were not enough to go round and many of the less grievously injured lay groaning on the floor. The most common injury was tulwar slashes, and some of them were horrific; almost severed limbs poured their life blood to the floor while comrades stood near them, unable to stem the flow. James noted with satisfaction that Surgeon Anderson had survived and was even now moving among the injured, binding up the worst of them with the help of impromptu orderlies.

Barrack Block A was a simple rectangular building, with tall windows on all sides, opening onto a verandah, and a door set in the middle of each wall. Cooking and washing was usually done outside, so apart from store cupboards, the only furnishings were the cots and lockers of the usual occupants.

'Should be easy enough to defend,' thought James, noting with satisfaction that there were already soldiers at each window, firing into the parade ground. In his absence, Majors Edward Colby and Robert Harding, his erstwhile companions, had organised the defenses, while Major Conroy was solely occupied with patting his wife's shoulder to little effect, as she was sobbing pathetically.

'Thank God you're here,' said Robert fervently, 'we didn't know what had happened to you or your family!'

'How many do we have in here?' asked James.

'I don't know yet; there was a lot of confusion out there; still is! Though this block was the nearest, some made for the others; and quite a lot were still in their bungalows.'

'I know,' said James grimly, 'I saw most of them being slaughtered! My God! How could we miss the signs?'

'They just seemed to melt away,' broke in Edward, 'one minute the doolie drivers and bearers were hanging about; but the next, they weren't! Who would believe they would turn on us like this!'

'There's no point worrying about it now,' said James, 'these people,' waving his hand round the room, 'are our immediate concern.'

James had another look around him; he noted that Lucy had placed their son on a pile of bedding in a corner of the room where, worn out by all the excitement he had curled up and was sound asleep. Lucy was currently engaged in calming the hysteria of several of the women, and was diverting them into helping Anderson, and generally trying to reduce the confusion that reigned in the room.

'Good girl,' muttered James, with a moment of pride at his choice of wife. He crossed to a window overlooking the parade ground. The open space was littered with bodies, both Indian and British, and here and there, a crinoline stuck up in the air pathetically. All the bungalows were now ablaze, though the ones on the lower slope were already dying down. James scanned up the hill, past his own bungalow now ablaze, to where the Colonel's was just beginning to smoulder. He made a silent farewell to his father's life-long companion, and his own friend and mentor since he had joined the Regiment, a callow youth of sixteen. Perhaps it was as well he had collapsed when he did rather than have his heart broken by the tragedy that engulfed the Regiment. And wasn't it better that he had died swiftly with a dagger to his heart than dying slowly, snoring his breath away for days, weeks or even years to come?

With that in mind, he thought of his father away in the mofussil with the Ferguson's. Was he safe or had the tumult reached them yet? But there was no use agitating himself with such questions; he must concentrate on the task in hand. He was a measure comforted at the thought that John Carlton was close by, and would know better than anyone of the unrest that could come their way!

He scanned the area outside again, trying to guess where Joe could be. He wasn't overly concerned about his safety for had he not proved his resourcefulness, time and again? The Indians were milling about on the far side of the parade ground, using the Regimental Offices to shield themselves from the deadly Enfield rifles that the British soldiers used to great effect; they might not have wanted to use them, but they were fully aware of their power! Some of the sepoys had broken into the offices and there were excited shouts when they emerged, throwing piles of paper into the air; all the Regimental records went wafting upwards in the overheated air currents. They did not attempt to attack the barracks.

Suddenly, the tumult grew, and before the outraged gaze of the defenders, Sepoy Satvinder Roy was carried shoulder high across the far side of the parade ground. Behind him was shouldered another sepoy carrying aloft the severed head of a British officer, its mouth stuffed with cartridges. From the blond head, it was apparently Carless, his identity soon confirmed by the shouted insults across the square. He had not been a popular officer, but this insult was too much to take. Subaltern Mortimer, who had been raised as a sharpshooter on his father's estates, and could pick off a running rabbit at a hundred yards, raised his Enfield and steadying it on the shoulder of a private, fired. The bearer of the head died instantly. Snatching another rifle, Mortimer loosed off another shot, and Sepoy Roy tumbled into the dust.

Screams of rage followed the deaths, and there was a concerted rush for the barracks. It was greeted by a volley of Enfield fire, and then it was beaten off with the loss of two British soldiers, a child and a dozen attackers. They then retired behind the offices, where it all went quiet for a while.

It was getting on for mid-afternoon, though the hard pressed defenders felt that it had been hours since the attack began.

The afternoon wore on, and an anxious James wondered what the Indians were waiting for. There was sporadic shooting, and at one point during the long hours of daylight, a woman rushed out of a bungalow, her clothes in flames. She must have remained hidden, until the heat of the flames proved too much to bear. A sergeant from C Company looked at her and let out an anguished scream,

'Daisy! Daisy!' and before anyone could stop him, he dashed for the door, and wrenching it open, ran across the parade ground, jumping over bodies as he went. The startled sepoys did nothing for a moment, but then, almost casually, one put out a foot and brought down the running sergeant. He went down and in another moment a dozen tulwars fell. The scarlet jacket could be seen briefly, and was then seen again, the blood no less bright than the jacket. The woman's screams died away, and husband and wife were reunited.

James used the waiting hours to improve the defences of the barracks. He had the doors barricaded to prevent anyone else dashing out for whatever reason, and to prevent attackers rushing in. He then had the windows screened to prevent the enemy from seeing inside too easily and picking them off. Finally, he had the officers take an inventory of their provisions of food and water and weaponry. They were well stocked with rifles and ammunition for the soldiers of A Block, in contravention of orders, preferred to keep their weapons to hand instead of locked away in the armoury.

'Thank God for that,' was James' unspoken comment.

There was also a quantity of food, though no-one had any inclination to eat at present. But of course, there was no way of knowing how long they would be 'confined to barracks'! Their biggest problem was water. There were several large chattis at one end of the end of the room, but how long they would last between such a crowd, and with the weather so hot during the day. Already, several visits had been paid to the supply. Perhaps during the hours of darkness, they could try and creep out to the well at the rear.

But James' biggest worry, which he chose not to share, was that there seemed little hope of rescue. The telegraph lines were down, and even they had not been, they could not get to the telegraph office. So there was no way of informing anyone of their predicament, and the nearest large cantonment was Lucknow, a day's travel away. And of course, if Meerut had been overrun, and now themselves, was the whole of India in revolt? He could only play a waiting game; take each hour, each day as it came, and perhaps decide on a breakout if matters became desperate.

Again, he was conscious of the fact that their women and children were an inhibiting factor. Without their presence, he knew he would have opted for a concerted breakout and a dash for the countryside. But it could not be done, for who would defend their weaker members if they were all killed?

Night fell, and still there had not been another attack. Lookouts were posted at every window, relieved at regular intervals. The block was kept in darkness to enhance their vision of the exterior, but the Indians had no such inhibitions, and out of range of the deadly Enfields, spent the night in roistering and singing.

Inside the barrack block, there grew a sense of unreality. That morning, they had felt safe and secure, cocooned in comfort and surrounded by servants all apparently willing to do their bidding. By the evening, their secure world had been turned upside down; the events leading up to the terrible happenings outside completely out of their control. Not that the British memsahib could hold herself entirely blameless for the catastrophe that had overtaken them. Apart from a few enlightened ones, like Lucy Willoughby, who had tried to adapt to the Indian way of life, most had brought Victoriana with them as they landed on Indian shores. They filled their homes with oversized, overstuffed furniture; they insisted on afternoon tea and dressed in their absurd crinolines! When the weather got too hot to bear them, they simply took to the hills and indulged their habits there! They treated all the Indians that they met, whether high or low born as rather primitive children who needed to be converted to Christianity and taught British manners. They did not understand them at all!

Even in their current extremity, they continued to behave as if they were in their drawing rooms, and tried the utmost to maintain their class divide; a caste system as rigid as any the Hindu had devised. Only Lucy Willoughby, a Major's wife was perfectly comfortable cosily chatting to Louise Swales, a sergeant's wife, comparing notes about their toddlers born within days of each other. Lucy was dressed in the shirt and pyjamas of the hill women and Louise in the sari of her maternal relatives, and they were more comfortable in them than any of the other women in the overheated atmosphere. The rest of the ladies, jammed together in their crinolines, shawls and mittens, spent their time making sure they did not sit with women of inferior class. The officers' wives drew themselves to one end of the room in order to avoid contamination by the wives of rankers or non-commissioned officers. Enid Conroy was in a terrible dilemma. She wanted to sit with the wife of another Major, and indeed of the acting Colonel, but that would mean being close to Louise, the wife of a Sergeant. Worse still was the presence of Nancy, safe inside after all, and chatting amiably with the other two ladies as though all three were of the same station. Isobel Harding and Cristabel Colby were cosily seated and clearly ignoring her, so she was reduced to sitting with Reggie and complaining all the while about the overcrowding!

To add to their discomfort, the barrack was supplied with facilities for the hundred or so men, who used it in the form of large pots, screened off at one end. The private soldier was not particularly fastidious, and the pots were usually emptied in the morning and evening by sweepers. Now, several hundred were crammed in together, both male and female, and there were no sweepers on hand. The stench rapidly grew appalling; and it was in the cool of the night. Their minds did not want to imagine what it would be like the next day as the sun rose!

James spent an uncomfortable, hot night, considering the odds against them. He had lain down by Lucy and little Charles, but had been unable to even doze, so giving up the struggle he went to the window and looked out. The glow from several fires came across the parade ground, lighting up the many bodies, the flickering flames giving them apparent movement! But then he realised with a shudder that they were, indeed, moving; doubtless being visited by the carrion eaters of the night. He turned away in disgust. He mused to himself,

'How many do we have in our care? We arrived in India with nigh on six hundred on strength. Disease and retirement has reduced that to about five hundred, as we thought the sepoys could make up the shortfall, God help us! Allowing for men on leave and those slaughtered, there must be three hundred in this barrack block, with perhaps a hundred and fifty women and children. My God, we are crammed into a space designed for a hundred or a hundred and fifty at the most!'

Ranged against the, he knew, were some fifteen hundred sepoys and like as not, the same number of rissal soldiers. But that was at the last count, and the Rajah may have increased them by now. James sighed, feeling helpless and hopeless in the face of such overwhelming odds.

A scuffling noise at a side door distracted him, and he moved hurriedly to that end of the room. There had been no movement from the Indians, he was assured by the lookouts. He heard whispered voices outside, English voices! He had his men hurriedly remove the barricades and opened the door to a dozen refugees, including three wounded men and two women. These had taken shelter in another block, but found themselves isolated when they realised that most of them had gone to Block A. They had hidden themselves as the sepoys swept through their block, and then waited in sweating fear until they felt that it was safe to creep the short distance between the blocks.

Later, when the moon had set, James organised a party to make an attempt at reaching the well. The sounds of revelry had reached a crescendo, and James could only hope that the sepoys were less scrupulous about posting sentries; what had they to fear after all? They opened the rear door and several men, all volunteers, slithered out. The well lay twenty yards away, and the leading man reached it safely, crawling all the way on his belly. James placed marksmen at adjacent windows with loaded Enfields at the ready to guard the safety of the twenty men stretched in a line and passing empty chattis from hand to hand, and the filled ones back. The worst moment occurred when the winding mechanism started, and to the straining men, it sounded as loud as a scream; they all held their collective breath, but the roistering went on without interruption. Later, James was to realise that the attack was less well organised than he had first thought and had been precipitated by their planned migration beginning earlier than usual!

The chattis continued their double journey until every one was filled. Then the overflowing pots were carried out carefully, and disposed of away from the block and the well. The volunteers then crept back to the door thankfully, to receive thanks and praise from their commander. The door finally shut behind the last man with a collective sigh of relief.

The night ended with wounded men groaning and babies crying. Few had slept well, if at all, and everyone had been plagued by heat and insects. Across the parade ground there was little sign of life; James gathered his officers around him,

This is the moment to break out if we are going to. A concerted charge could roll them up, then we can get the women and children away; make a break for the hills. What d'you say Harding?'

'It could work.'

'Colby?'

'I don't know. We are greatly outnumbered.'

'Conroy?'

'We cannot do it man! What happens to these people if we fail?'

'What happens to them if we stay here?'

At least we are sheltered here until we are relieved!'

'And who will relieve us? No-one knows what has happened here!'

The argument waged back and forth, but then it was too late. The sound of galloping horses brought them all to crowd round the windows. Crossing the bridge from Kotepore was a cavalcade, sunlight glinting off lances and tulwars. Reinforcements; but for the Indians, not for them! Leading the troop of white clad soldiers was Raja Ajit and his son, Saeed.

The troop pulled up beyond the office building; clearly the Raja had been warned of the danger from the deadly Enfields! Shouts sounded across the still morning air. Those with a smattering of Urdu recognised that the besiegers were being reprimanded for their hangovers.

'If only we had sallied forth, I'm sure we could have rolled 'em up!' thought James, regretfully. Then a figure walked across the square, carrying a white flag.

'How well they have learned from us,' observed James grimly to Robert, watching beside him.

The figure reached A Block and stood for a moment uncertain. It was a sepoy and he was clearly nervous of his mission, his nervousness increasing as a growl from outraged British throats swelled around him. James silenced them tersely, and then called out to the frightened sepoy,

'What is it?' he called out in Urdu, 'chuldi, chuldi!'

'Ah Sahib. I have a message from his highness Maharajah Ajit Khan.'

'Promoted himself,' muttered Edward by James' other side.

'Where is it?'

The sepoy shuffled along the verandah, fear sweating from every pore. He had a piece of white vellum, which he handed to James through the slightly opened window, and beat a hasty retreat backwards. There were howls of derision when he fell off the edge of the verandah, and then scrambled to his feet and scuttled back to his comrades! James read the note,

Angrezi soldiers. We mean you no harm. We merely wish to reclaim what is rightly ours. Oudh has fallen, Delhi has fallen, Lucknow has fallen. Surrender now and you will have safe passage to a port where you may take ship. If you refuse you will all die. Indicate your willingness to surrender with a white flag.

Raja Ajit Khan

The letter shocked James to the core. Delhi and Lucknow fallen! What hope did they have? But he did not trust the Raja; he could not rely on his word to spare them. And if Oudh was indeed inflamed, then there was no protection for them. He said as much to his Majors; the only voice of dissension was Conroy. He was overruled!

'Ready men!' came the order. The Enfields took careful aim. The Raja and his son were out of range, but some sepoys and rissallers had moved incautiously closer, expecting the white flag at any moment.

'Fire!' A volley rang out, then another. Howls of rage greeted the salvoes, and with shouts of 'Din, Din' there was a concerted charge on the block. It was beaten off. The enemy regrouped and charged again; it was repulsed. Each time there were casualties inside the block though not as many as among the attackers.

After a third unsuccessful attack, the sepoys and rissallers drew off, and squatted comfortably out of range to wait for the sun to rise to its zenith. Soon the parade ground was swarming with flies which settled on the bodies. They began to swell as the sun rose higher, and to smell, their stench adding to that of the overflowing pots. Tempers frayed in the block. The Indians attacked again and were repulsed.

Watching from a vantage point high on the hillside, Joe had a grandstand view of all the events. After heading off the attack on the Willoughby bungalow, he had carried out diversions for other unlucky souls trapped in their bungalows. Few made it to safety, however, as they relied on a quick dash down the hill rather than the flanking movement that James had used with his wife and son. As that first long afternoon had worn on, he had made his way to the top of the hill towards the Convent. He found the beautiful teak bench hacked to pieces in a frenzy of destruction, the brass plaque glinting in the late afternoon sunshine. He picked it up and slipped it into his pocket.

Joe reached the Convent gates; they stood wide open as they had done on the day of his wedding, but today there were no ecstatic cheers, or Indians throwing marigold garlands round the necks of him and his bride. Today there was a brooding silence. He walked cautiously up the drive, expecting to hear shouts of 'get round the back you ignorant coolie'. But there was no shout. The main doors also stood wide open and sprawled across the entrance was the body of the man who had led him to see the Reverend Mother.

'So, they even attack their own kind,' muttered Joe to himself. He crept through the dim passage and peeped into one room after another. All was confusion and destruction, with furniture overturned and smashed, fringed curtains ripped to pieces and horsehair stuffing bursting out of the plump sofas. At last he reached the chapel where he had been married. They were all there; Reverend Mother Theresa had her arms around two young novices and had buried their heads in her voluminous habit so that they could not see death approaching. But she had faced it. Her eyes were wide open as she had looked her attackers straight in their eyes as they had raised their tulwars. The other sisters were close by, many in the attitude of prayer.

'Why? What had these gentle creatures done? They had helped these people over the years; cured their sick; taught their children. Why?' Joe shook his head; when the killing rage began, it knew no bounds!

He heard a soft rustle in the shadows and his hand leapt to the dagger in his belt. The sound came from behind the altar, so soft that it could have been a mouse. He moved silently on sandalled feet, making his way to the altar. As he reached it he lunged behind it and dragged out a terrified girl; the diminutive sari clad figure who had shown him into the parlour that day so long ago. She did not seem to have grown much since then! Terrified, tear drenched eyes implored him for mercy.

Joe squatted on his haunches and spoke gently to the girl in Urdu. To his questions, she said that she had seen them coming; not sepoys or soldiers, but badmashes from the bazaars who had robbed the chapel of everything of value. She had hidden under the altar cloth and had narrowly escaped detection when a thief pulled it off. But he had been too busy stuffing the rich silk fabric into a pack to notice one small person crouching in the shadows.

Joe nodded at her and dried her tears with gentle thumbs. So that was it; he had thought it strange that the Raja should order an attack on the Convent; he was known to hold the Reverend Mother in high esteem; one of the few Europeans that he had any respect for! No; these were opportunists, seizing the chance to loot and plunder under the cloak of the uprising. He turned away in disgust, and led the child back out into the sunshine. She had soon lost her fear of him and confided that she lived with her parents who had served the Convent for many years, and she could find her way home safely now. Joe watched he scamper through the flower beds, trampled by many running feet. Where would the killing end?

By the time Joe returned to the cantonment, dusk was falling and the main action seemed to be over for the day. He decided to remain at large as he could do little to help with the defence of the barrack block; his would be just one gun among many. Whereas out in the open, he could try and find out the enemy's intentions. Strange how quickly he had accepted the Indians as 'the enemy'; it was not so long ago that they had been his friends. He looked into his bungalow in passing and found a frightened Gopi hiding in the shadows amidst the wreckage that had been his home. The bearer's huge, terrified brown eyes reminded him of the child he had rescued from the Convent!

'Oh Sahib, oh Sahib,' wept Gopi, 'what have they done? What have the done?' Strangely, Joe felt in no danger from Gopi, but he gently told him to take himself off and cease to be associated with a Ferenghi,

'Oh Sahib, don't send me away. What will I do?' After a brief discussion, Joe sent the bearer into Kotepore to do some ferreting out of information. He gave him a handful of rupees and told him to return to the bungalow on the next day, then they would see what to do next. Joe then asked,

'Did you see the Memsahib leave?'

'Yes Sahib, she took a carriage to Lucknow. I begged her not to, but she wouldn't listen. She had a letter, Sahib.'

'Very good, Gopi. Go now and be careful.'

'Yes Sahib.'

Joe waited until the sepoys and rissallers had lit their cooking fires and begun to make merry before he went down the hill to mingle among them. Though not in uniform, there were many others dressed like him, acting as servants and cooks. As the evening wore on and many became overcome by drink or bhang, Joe was able to question them freely. What he discovered he found very interesting, and he stored it all away for use in the very near future! Later, when the revelers had lapsed into incoherence and then sleep, he went back up the hill, and climbing a tree, wedged himself in a fork between bole and a large branch, he fell into a fitful sleep.

In the early hours of the morning, Joe awoke to find himself being examined by two black, boot button eyes. They belonged to a squirrel which was furious at finding his private domain invaded by a large human. Joe apologised gravely and prepared to climb down from the tree. The squirrel cocked his bushy tail at him and scampered back into its hole, the three black smudges on his back showing clearly in the rays of the early morning sun. Joe recalled that the marks were supposed to be the hand print of the Lord Krishna himself!

Joe settled himself in a vantage point where he could watch the parade ground, and as he expected, a cavalcade arrived from the direction of Kotepore, clattering across the bridge that separated town and cantonment. The Raja and his son reined in behind the office block, and Joe was an interested spectator to the delivery of a message by a sepoy carrying a white flag. While they waited for a response, father and son sat easily on their horses but without apparently communicating. Rumour had it that they did not agree about the present action, and their attitude towards each other seemed to bear this out!

As he watched, Joe tried to remember everything he had learned about the Khan's history. They had begun as Taluqdars of the Nawab of Oudh, four or five generations before. They had flourished by the use of armed retainers, and a certain talent for acquiring both wealth and land. The current Raja's grandfather was the first to use the title, and his son had carried it forward. The family had always been fiercely nationalistic, and had resented the incursion of the Ferenghi from the very start. They had tolerated the gradual building of the cantonment only by direct order of the Nawab, who had caustically reminded them that the title of Raja was by Royal permission, a privilege that could easily be withdrawn!

Raja Ajit's father had learned to live in reasonable harmony with the intrusive Angrezi, the most avaricious of all the Ferenghi, but his son had not. With one or two exceptions, like John Carlton and Reverend Mother Theresa, he hated them all! He had tried to imbue his son with the same intense hatred, but he made the serious mistake of sending the boy to study in England. The young man learned enough about the English to know that, in common with the rest of the world, there was good and bad in all of them!

But the final insult was the policy of annexation; hated in principle by the rabid Raja, and now very much resented in fact. When Oudh had been annexed, the Settlement Officer, Thomason, sent to examine the situation, decided in his limited wisdom that the land belonged to the Taluqdar tenants! That the decision was incorrect according to ancient Moghul law, or Oudh law or even just plain common sense, made no difference to the pompous Thomason. No wonder these people felt that they had had enough!

Joe remembered his last meeting with Prince Saeed before the attack started, recalled the tears in his eyes as he had given him the choice; join them or fight them,

'You were so wrong, Prince,' murmured Joe to the Prince far below him, 'it wasn't a matter of colour, but of loyalty. If this was my country and my people, I would have joined you, like the Fenians in my own land of Ireland. But these soldiers that you fight took me in; I have eaten their salt, so I cannot fight them now. I am sorry, Prince. Perhaps this will all pass and we can be friends again one day?' Joe put his head on his arm and wept softly for the friendship he believed he might have lost forever.

Then his head snapped up in alarm as a volley of shots rang out; the British had replied. All day the battle rage; the sepoys and rissallers made one, two, three assaults and were repulsed. The heat rose and the sun became a burning golden disc. Even from high up the hillside the odour of corruption reached Joe's nostrils as the bodies strewn across the parade ground turned black with the swarm of flies. He could only imagine the conditions inside the crowded barrack block!

The attackers rested through the heat of the day, merely making random charges to ensure that the British soldiers did not get any rest. The Prince and his father had long since departed. Towards evening, there was a fiercely pressed, massed attack from all side of the block. Heart in his mouth, Joe watched as waves of sepoys reached the windows and one or two even threw themselves inside. For a tense moment, it appeared that the block would be overwhelmed, but the defences held. Joe could hear screams from within the building, even above the battle cries of 'Din, Din' from the attackers.

The besiegers at last retired and as darkness fell, lit their fires. But as Joe kept vigil, the scurrying figures around the fires seemed to dwindle in number. There was no drinking and revelling this time, but there was a lot of noise made for all that! Sometime in the darkest hour of the night, the last of the Indians disappeared in the direction of Kotepore, unbeknownst to the defenders, enduring another night in the barrack block. They spent a restless night and made another foray to the well, not realizing that the need for secrecy was past. By this time, Joe was curled up in a corner of his cottage waiting for the first light of dawn. He had known about the withdrawal; had known since the previous night when the sepoys had discussed the plan in his hearing. He had also learnt that the sepoys had been ordered to kill the Angrezi by the end of the day or leave them for another occasion. They had a more important appointment to keep!

As the sun rose to the east of Kotepore, lighting up its minarets and spires, the weary sentries in Barrack Block A rubbed their eyes as they looked across the parade ground. A solitary figure in Indian dress, but with bright copper red hair was hoisting the Union Jack back up to its proud position on top of the flag pole in front of the Officers Mess. The figure looked at the flag for a long moment before he saluted it, and then turned to wave at the blockhouse. James, hurriedly summoned, was heard to exclaim,

'By God; it's Joe; it's Sergeant Harrington!'

It took a few more moments for them all to realise that they were not suffering from delusions, and that their tormentors were nowhere to be seen; just the solitary figure of one of their own! The cautiously spilled out onto the verandah, Joe approached and saluted his commander,

'Good morning Sir! Yes, they've really gone. By now they're on their way to Delhi to proclaim the last Moghul as their true ruler.'

James narrowed his eyes at that!

'Delhi? Has it really fallen?'

'I'm afraid so, Sir, but I have more to report.'

'I will have your news, Sergeant. But first we must deal with this.' James swept his arm over the appalling scene in the parade ground,

'If you are sure they won't be coming back, we must arrange burials for these poor souls.'

Already the barrack block was emptying, as soldiers were followed by women and children, blinking owlishly in the early morning sun, and averting their eyes from the carnage as they picked their way to the far side of the parade ground. Most offered up silent prayers that they too had not joined the unfortunates on the ground.

Close inspection showed that though the bungalows had been burnt out, most of the main stores and the other three barrack blocks were intact. The first priority of the recently besieged was to wash and then to eat, and then it was time to organise burial parties. The cemetery was some distance from the cantonment, so James made the decision to have a mass grave dug behind the barracks for security's sake. The Regimental Chaplain had survived the assaults and conducted the service. Many of the soldiers had lost their wives, and wives their husbands. A number of children were among the dead, and the sight of tiny figures being lowered into the ground brought distress to them all. Lucy and Louise stood close together holding their own children close to their breasts as they wept, the tragedy bringer them closer together than before. It was sad to note that the same could not be said of other officers' wives as they soon fell to squabbling again about carts and carriages!

James decreed that they would set out at dawn the following morning. He told his officers sternly to inform their soldiers and their womenfolk that they may be forced to flee during their long journey northwards and that they must be ready at dawn with the minimum of luggage! For the coming night, they would have to share the barrack blocks, and soldiers were to assign one of them for the exclusive use of women and children!

While preparations were underway, he called a council of his senior officers and asked Joe to pass on his important information. There were some dark looks at the indignity of being thus addressed by a mere Sergeant, but James told them testily that this was no time for such niceties!

'Go on, Sergeant Harrington,' he urged.

'Well Sir. I spent the first night of the attack listening to the sepoys and the soldiers of the Raja's rissal. Also, my bearer spent that night and much of yesterday in Kotepore. Between us, we have a fair picture of the situation.'

'You bearer?' questioned Conroy, peevishly, 'a black man? Is he to be trusted?' Joe did not reply to the slur on Gopi's character but went on; Conroy subsided with a sniff when he got no support for his view.

'It appears that the attack at Meerut was broken off fairly quickly, the mutineers making off towards Delhi. The station was well manned by British troops, but there was no pursuit. The sepoys in Delhi were incited to rise and there was more killing of civilians. The Red Fort is in the hands of the mutineers and Mohamed Bahadur Shah has been proclaimed leader, and is the rallying point of the mutineers. It seems that Cawnpore and Lucknow are under threat, but are still under British control. But the countryside is inflamed!'

'What about the rest of India, or is it confined to Oudh?' asked Edward.

'Apparently it is mainly Oudh and Bengal but I have no news of other regions; but I believe they are waiting to see what happens here.'

'Well gentlemen,' interposed James, 'you have heard the worst at the moment. We cannot rely on relief from other cantonments, even Lucknow, as they will be busy taking care of their own people. So we must take care of ourselves. We have choices; make for Lucknow and risk meeting a large force of mutineers on the way; or break for the North as we had planned to do. If the Sergeant is right, we should be clear of trouble spots within a day or two and get our families safely to the hills. Then we can return and present ourselves to Sir Henry Lawrence in Lucknow; or General Anson, but we can decide that later in the light of further intelligence.'

Vigorous debate broke out, during which Joe asked to be excused, and could he please speak with the Commander alone when it was convenient. Permission granted, he went quickly in search of Adam and Louise.

He found Louise talking to Lucy, but she turned and enfolded him in a hug, tears starting from her eyes. In turn, Lucy hugged him, though Nancy merely gave him an enigmatic smile. Joe picked up Charles and Christina in turn, and buried his face in their chubby necks. In the midst of his tears, he murmured,

'Thank God these little ones, and you two, are safe; and Adam; I saw him at the burial party!'

'I'm so sorry about Catherine,' said Lucy quietly, 'I should have kept a closer eye. I do hope all is well. It is possible she fared better in Lucknow?'

'If she is not,' replied Joe bitterly, 'it is my fault! I would go to Kotepore when she begged me not to. I did no good there; I couldn't even warn the cantonment of the attack, and if I had stayed, she would not have gone!'

'Yes, said Louise acerbically, 'and she might have been one of those cut down in the first attack, Joe, there is no saying. She might be perfectly safe; indeed safer than here!'

Later, when James finally emerged from the council with the decision made to his satisfaction; they would head north, he found Joe waiting for him,

'Yes Joe?'

'Sir. May I have leave to go to Cawnpore to find Catherine? I won't be much help with the column, just one soldier among many, and I would be worried about her all the way. Please, oh please; Sir?' His voice broke, and he lowered his head to hide the ready tears.

James looked at the ravaged face. He knew that if he refused, the young man would probably go anyway; and how could he refuse such a request, for he remembered another impulsive young man who had disobeyed his Colonel's orders in Ireland! And did not this young man have an even more compelling reason to go? He put his hand on the younger man's shoulder,

'Go then, Joe. But why Cawnpore? I thought she had gone to Lucknow?'

'I found a letter in the bungalow. It is from her friend in Lucknow and they were going to go together to Cawnpore to see another friend. If she is not there, I can go on to Lucknow. Thank you Sir.'

'God go with you, Joe.' James almost missed the bitter reply,

'If any harm has come to her, it will be the God Kali who will go with me!'

By early the next morning the column was ready. The parade ground had been cleared of its grisly litter, and the remaining doolies and carts were piled high with baggage. Haltingly, nervously, the drivers and bearers crept back, and abasing themselves before their British master, they pleaded for forgiveness,'

'Oh Sahib,' they wailed, 'we feared for our lives if we stayed; we had to flee!' With them came the maids, the grass cutters, the cooks and the sweepers.

Thankfully they were taken back, as the tender British had forgotten how to fend for themselves. As dawn broke over Kotepore, the cavalcade set out, the women and children in the middle of their escort of scarlet clad soldiers; Enfields loaded and bayonets loosened ready for action. They would not be caught unawares again. It was 16th May, a week to the day when eighty five sepoys had been court martialled in Meerut.

Joe saw them go. Sadness weighed heavily on him; how many of these people would he see again? He had embraced Adam and Louise, who had wept again,

'Find her,' she urged. Lucy too embraced him, and James shook his hand, long and hard. Many of his fellow soldiers slapped him on the back and wished him luck. None envied him the task he had set himself; few expected to see him again!

By the time the dust of the column had started to drift back to earth, Joe was ready to leave. He had prepared himself for a long period in disguise by getting Gopi to dye his hair and all untanned parts of his torso with walnut juice. Only his eyes glowed blue in his lean, ravaged face. Shouldering his Brown Bess, for the Enfield was not a sensible choice of rifle for a supposed Indian, he set off followed by Gopi. The diminutive bearer carried a pack containing two blankets and a few provisions. Around Joe's waist was his money belt, containing, apart from a precious store of rupees, a small miniature of Catherine and a shiny brass plaque. He did not look back.

Chapter 11

'Good God Cathy! What are you doing here?'

'But…but Pattie,' said Catherine almost in tears, 'you wrote to me; twice!'

'But that was ages ago. Do you mean to tell me that you have only just got my letters?'

'Well; one came about a week ago, and I was planning to come then; but there were problems; and….and then another one came yesterday; so I decided to come after all! Oh Pattie, don't say you aren't pleased to see me?'

'No of course not, my dear girl. It's just that when you didn't reply, and I have to tell you, I was a bit miffed, I assumed you weren't coming! But where's Joe? Don't tell me you came on your own; and at a time like this?'

'It's a long story, Pattie. Do let me rest awhile; I seem to have been travelling forever. Then I'll tell you what happened.'

Pattie looked at her young friend properly for the first time, and saw signs of fatigue in the white face, and her red-rimmed eyes.

'Yes of course, my love.' She rang a small hand bell and directed her maid to take Catherine to the spare bedroom where she could refresh herself, and lie down for a while,

'Chris isn't home yet; he spends all his time at that infernal newspaper; says there is something happening every minute of the day! I usually have some food with him when he gets home; if you're hungry then, you can eat with us.'

Catherine nodded; too tired to think about being hungry. She followed the maid to a room elegantly furnished in chintz, and washed her hands and face, before having the maid loosen her corsets so that she could lie

on the invitingly cool looking bed. She drifted off to sleep, worn out with the events of the day.

She had set out that morning so sure of herself, and full of righteous anger at Lucy Willoughby, Louise Swales, Gopi, and anyone else who had tried to dissuade her from leaving Most of all, she was angry with Joe.

The day had started warm and promised to get hotter. Already the thought of spending some days in Lucknow amidst the bustle of the busy town was losing its appeal. If only he hadn't gone; a touch of forlornness overlaid the anger. By mid-morning she was regretting her decision, and by tiffin, when she was more than halfway to Lucknow, she wished heartily that she had not been so foolish. But by now it was clearly more sensible to continue than go back. Well, she would stay for the shortest time that decency allowed, and when Joe arrived, she would not bear a grudge; she would allow him to apologise for deserting her, and then return!

The carriage had reached a dak-bungalow, and the driver asked her in a surly manner if she wished to take tiffin there. She said that she would, as the sun was beating down uncomfortably, even striking through her large parasol. Her head swam with temper and tiredness, for she had not slept well the night before. She swept into the dak-bungalow, wrinkling her nose in distaste at the smell. She ordered tiffin from another surly Indian, and elected to eat outside in the shade of a peepul tree; the 'travellers' friend'. She was puzzled at the offhand manner with which she was being treated, though not unduly worried. Even so, she was used to the native population treating her with politeness, even downright servility, but the atmosphere around her today was odd to say the least. She ate the meal that was brought to her, and asked for some water to refresh herself; it was brought grudgingly by a woman in a white sari who gazed at Catherine in an insolent manner. She began to feel decidedly uncomfortable and called on the driver to move on.

'But Memsahib,' he said churlishly, 'the sun is still hot and the poor beast will not be liking it!' As Indian drivers were notoriously indifferent to the suffering of their unkempt nags, this was clearly an excuse. But

Catherine decided not to argue, but sat fanning herself under the peepul tree until the man rose reluctantly, scratching himself, and calling for the escort to bestir itself.

Catherine was feeling very sorry for herself by now, and wondering why on earth she had got into a temper with Joe and embarked on this rash journey when he had specifically asked her not to? She well remembered her father's voice from her childhood, when she stamped her tiny foot in rage, and he had laughed at her red face,

'Oh Katy child, that Irish temper of yours will get you into trouble one day!'

'Don't call me Katy,' she had screamed at him, but he had merely laughed all the more, and swung her high into the air. And her mother, who was fond of quoting old adages, would rub her daughter's aching tummy after a surfeit of mangoes,

'Well Cathy dear, you've made your bed, and now you must lie in it!'

Catherine sniffed sadly at her memories.

But what was happening to India anyway? Why was there all this trouble? This wasn't the India she had grown up in and loved. She remembered the ayah of her childhood, a rotund Hindu lady whose soft expansive bosom had been the receptacle for many a childish tear. It had seemed then that the native population loved the British residents and she had never felt herself to be an interloper. But now there was agitation on all sides, doubtless the fault of the Raja Ajit Khan. Catherine had met him once and didn't care at all for his cold features. She much preferred his son Saeed; he and Joe were such good friends, and she recalled seeing them together dressed in similar fashion; even looking alike with their chiseled features and their heads swathed in turbans, the only difference being the colour of their eyes! She sighed deeply and hoped things would calm down before the baby arrived!

The journey seemed endless. Catherine was dressed in her smartest travelling outfit, which was getting a little tight for her in the fifth month of her pregnancy. There seemed to be a brooding atmosphere that followed her along the road, which made her feel more and more uncomfortable. She could have cried with relief when she saw the spires and minarets of Lucknow come into view. From a distance with the sinking sun lighting it up, Lucknow looked beautiful; a vision of azure and golden domes, colonnades and cupolas, façades and pillars all rising above the bright green of the undergrowth. But Catherine could not appreciate it fully for her body ached with fatigue and she was experiencing a return of the nausea that had plagued her in the early months of pregnancy.

The carriage drove through the Mariaon Cantonment at a brisk trot; all seemed to be as usual, with elegantly dressed memsahibs taking an early evening stroll with small children decorously holding their hands under the eagle eyes of their ayahs. Everywhere, smartly clad aides bustled about clutching sheets of paper. They left the cantonment behind and clattered across the Iron Bridge over the River Gumti, past the Residency whose three storied building was set in smooth lawns and bright flowerbeds and shaded by massive mohurs and feathery neems, and peepuls with their long pointed leaves, and the elegant sheeshums. There was certainly a stir and a buzz about the place, but nothing dramatic. Catherine began to think that her unease was misplaced; to be sure she was making a gurrh-burrh about nothing!

Finally, the carriage plunged into the teeming streets of Lucknow town, the driver clearing his path with a strident voice and liberal use of his lash. He too was anxious to finish the journey and forget about the bad tempered memsahib he had been carrying all day. Once rid of her, he would make his way to his brother's house where he could share the family meal and a smoke of the hookah. The Day's lived in the heart of the town as Pattie's husband Chris believed that a journalist should be able to keep a finger on the pulse of Indian affairs by living among them, not in the cloistered atmosphere of the Residency or the cantonment!

Much later, Catherine heard voices and assumed that Chris had come home. The dim light in the room showed that it was very late, but she could not rouse herself to greet him; her whole body felt drugged with fatigue. She drowsily listened to the disjointed voices,

'Oh God,' came Chris' deep tones, 'you mean she came here alone…. have to stay until…..there's been trouble at Meerut…' Then came Pattie's lighter voice,

'You should have seen…distress….row with Joe….we'll see in the morning….' Catherine slept.

'Good morning, Catherine my dear.' Chris greeted her cheerfully as e sat over chota hazri the next day, a folded paper propped up in front of him.

'I must say I was surprised to hear that you had come for a visit!'

'So Pattie said; I hadn't realised that her letters had been sent so long before.' Chris chuckled,

'That's Pat for you, she never puts a date on her letters! She'll be along soon for chota hazri; I'll ring for some tea for you. You're looking well; Pat said you looked very tired last night, and so she didn't want to wake you for supper.'

'Yes; I felt that I had been travelling forever, not just one day! Chris?'
'Yes my dear?'

'What is happening? Joe doesn't tell me much; just says that there is some agitation. But when I drove here yesterday, I got the distinct feeling that there was something seriously wrong, but when we drove through the cantonment and the Residency, it all looked; well, normal. What is going on?'

'I'm sure Joe didn't want to worry you unduly, especially in your delicate situation. There is some unrest among the sepoys. It should blow over pretty soon, you'll see. But in the meantime, I think you had better stay here, unless Joe comes for you.'

'Chris; you are as bad as the rest. Now you are saying 'don't worry'. Why do you men treat us like imbeciles, or children?' Chris looked hurt, but managed to evade the issue by gathering up his papers and preparing to leave,

'Sorry to dash off; we hope to start printing early today and I've a despatch to get off to London. Bye my dear; tell Pat I had to run; she shouldn't be long; she'll tell you the rest of the news.' He gave Catherine a quick peck of the cheek and then fled.

Catherine was working herself up into another temper when the door opened to admit her lifelong friend and confidante. She knew from long experience that Pat was not at her best until she had had at least two or three cups of her best Darjeeling cha, so she managed to stay quiet.

While Pat sipped her cha with her eyes tightly shut, Catherine studied her. She had a round face, emphasized by the light brown hair, parted in the middle and drawn around her ears into a bun at the base of her neck. Her hair was inclined to vigorous curls, and by the end of the day, tendrils had invariably escaped, giving her a shaggy look. She had soft hazel eyes, somewhat myopic so that she had a habit of screwing them up to see properly. Sometimes, she reminded Catherine of a bedraggled owl! But she loved her dearly; dear Pattie. She hadn't changed since they had been in Convent School together in Calcutta; how many years ago was that? Goodness, it must be at least ten. Pattie was two or three years older, and had already attended the school for a year when Catherine had started, nervous of the nuns in their habits, heads tightly coifed, and stern voices admonishing the girls to imitate the saints like good little Theresa. Catherine had felt overawed, but Pattie had given her a sweet and held her hand. The friendship had been forged in that moment. Later Charlotte had joined them, and the threesome had earned something of a reputation for mischief, which they gleefully cultivated!

'Dear Pattie' surfaced at last. Opening her eyes after her third cup of cha, she said very firmly,

'Now, I want to know everything. I want to know why you've run away from that handsome husband of yours; and mind, I want the truth! This is Pattie, remember; I knew you when you were in smocks and patched stockings!'

Catherine could not help laughing, and thus instructed, told the whole tale. It sounded rather pathetic in the cold light of day; how she had promised not to leave, and then had felt the baby move and longed to share the experience with someone, and that someone hadn't been there. Surprisingly, though she was childless as yet, Pattie seemed to understand. She explained,

'I started a baby, Cathy, and then lost it. Oh it was months ago; but I remember how I felt, and if Chris hadn't been here with me, I'd have felt ten times worse. Now, what is to be done? I think a short note to Kotepore; tell Joe where you are, as in spite of everything, he will be more worried than angry!'

'Yes I know,' and suddenly Catherine burst into heartbroken sobs. Her friend looked at her with a quizzical expression,

'That's it. Cry it all out and then we'll do something about it!'

Later, the friends discussed the situation. Being in the middle of Lucknow and married to a journalist, Pattie was far more *au fait* with the situation than even the military in their cantonments. She was able to tell Catherine more about the problems by the annexation policy, and the issue of the hated cartridges than she had ever heard from Joe.

'On Sunday, there was a mutiny of sepoys in Meerut,' explained Pattie, 'Apparently there was some killing of women and children and then they all took off to Delhi to raise the sepoys there.'

'Why Delhi?'

'It's where the old Moghul Emperor sits like an ancient spider in his Red Fort. He's something of a figurehead according to Chris.'

'I thought things had quietened down when that man, who was it? Of yes, Jackson, was removed by Calcutta?'

'Yes, it helped. And the new man, Sir Henry Lawrence is certainly more sympathetic in his dealings with Oudh. But the damage had been done; Oudh was annexed the Maharaja deposed, And now Thomason is telling the Taluqdars that the land doesn't belong to them but their tenants. And lots of them have their own armies, rissals, mostly little better than dacoits.'

'D'you think there'll be more trouble?'

'It's possible. Chris says we must be ready to move to the Residency and hope they can accommodate us if the need arises. But we must wait and see. I think we should stay in today; just write your letter and let's hope it gets delivered sooner than the last two!'

'I will,' said Catherine, but in any case I left word with his bearer where I had gone.'

'Good!'

All that day, the young women stayed in the house. They had plenty of gossip to catch up on, and the day passed quickly. Several times that day there was the sound of running feet and shouting. They looked anxiously through the chiks, but did not venture outside. Twice, Pattie rang for a servant only to find that they had all gone out to see what was happening, which in itself was a disturbing development!

That evening, Chris came home earlier than usual and he looked very grim,

'Delhi has fallen! God knows how many civilians have been killed. I believe we have a full scale mutiny on our hands!' he studied the two young women looking back at him anxiously. He said slowly,

'I think I should get you two to Calcutta. I don't believe it will spread that far, but if it does, we can get a ship out.'

Catherine sat down abruptly, the room spinning about her,

'I...I can't! Joe won't know where I am. I can't leave him!'

'Chris, aren't you being a bit hasty?' interposed Pattie, alarmed at her friend's white face, 'and how would we go? If it is as bad as you say, surely we would be safer in a large British community?'

'Delhi was supposed to be safe. Meerut had as many British soldiers as Indians,' he replied bitterly, 'we'll sleep on it, but I think we should go.'

That night, Chris argued long and vigorously with his wife, but she was obdurate.

'Catherine won't leave; that is obvious. I wouldn't in her position! And I won't leave her. She is expecting a baby and I won't leave her with a crowd of strangers.'

'She'll be perfectly safe in the Residency, or with one of the families in Mariaon; you girls know lots of the wives there! She won't be among strangers.'

'No!' Chris tried one more argument,

'The military telegraph lines are cut between here and Kotepore; I tried to send a message to that cantonment during the day, but I didn't want to tell you. So Kotepore might have suffered the same fate as Meerut, except that they have more sepoys and local rissals than Meerut! Joe may not come at all.' He heard the rapid indrawing of breath from his shocked wife, but then, very firmly,

'No!' Chris gave up.

Catherine became very worried towards the end of the week, and if Pat had not restrained her, she would have hired herself a carriage and gone back to Kotepore,

'But something's happened, Pattie, I know it has, or Joe would be here by now.'

'That's as may be, but Joe can take care of himself, and he'll not thank me for letting you traipse across country again. You must know that you were very lucky to arrive here safely!'

Catherine did know, but it did not stop her fretting, which earned her another scolding,

'Come on now; not eating is not going to help Joe, and certainly won't help that baby of yours!'

'But it's the not knowing that's the worst!'

Having the telegraph lines down made it feel as if Kotepore was the other side of India. By the weekend, they know that Commander-in-Chief Anson had been informed in Simla and was preparing to set out for Delhi as soon as he could get his army in train. They knew that Cawnpore was still safe, though General Wheeler was trying to fortify it, 'just in case'. They knew that there had been sporadic outbreaks all over Oudh, Bengal and Rohilkand, and they knew that Lucknow was seething with unrest, though Sir Henry Lawrence had managed to contain it so far. But like Wheeler in Cawnpore, he had started to fortify the area round the Residency.

'The job's impossible,' insisted Chris, 'it's too close to the town and too scattered. He'll never do it. We must just hope that it won't be needed!'

His hopes were dashed, however, when halfway through the following week, he was attacked on his way home from the newspaper offices. The Day's were very popular in their area, but the badmashes were out inciting trouble wherever they could. A group of them had caught sight of the alpaca clad figure hurrying through the streets, and one particularly evil looking character in a soiled dhoti had picked up a stone and thrown it. The stone missed, but it was followed by several more; Chris was struck on his forehead with a large missile and he feared that he would pass out. He knew that would be his end as the sight of his falling body would rouse the ever lurking blood lust. His house was in sight and had the sudden agonizing fear that he was bringing danger to the women inside, but as he reached it, the door opened and his house boy stood on the porch step with a large tulwar in his hand. With the other hand, he reached out and pulled the lurching figure of his master into the house and faced the crowd. In the time honoured manner of all bullies when confronted with a true adversary, the badmashes melted away with a few, last, half-hearted stones.

Inside, Chris was helped to a chair by his wife while Catherine dispatched servants for hot water and bandages, and very soon the 'wounded soldier' was swathed heroically in a white bandage and sipping a whisky-pani.

'That's it,' he said, through gritted teeth, for his head throbbed, 'tomorrow I am taking you two to the Residency.' There was no argument.

Later that evening, Chris spoke to their house servants, and he had a special word of thanks for the house boy, Arwin, whose prompt action had saved the situation. He thanked them all for their long and loyal service, and paid them handsomely,

'It is best that you go from this house. There is trouble to come, of that I am sure, and it will not go well for you to be known as servants of Angrezis.' He made namaste to them all, and shook the house boy firmly by the hand.

Early the next morning, the trio had chota hazri and prepared themselves for the trek through the streets of Lucknow. Chris eyed their frilly morning wraps,

'D'you have dresses like that, without those ridiculous birdcages you put under them?' Catherine pouted at that, but Pattie said,

'Why Chris?'

'I've got hold of a couple of bourkas. I think that you would both be safer in Indian dress; at least not obviously British.'

'What about you then; you are still recovering from yesterday?'

'Don't worry; I intend to travel incognito as well; there's no better disguise for a bandage than a turban!'

After chota hazri, they gathered their baggage near the front door, and Chris peered out cautiously. There were, as yet, few people astir, and he wanted to be on his way before the streets got crowded. Fortunately, the Day's were used to moving home and renting their lodgings, so their luggage was modest. Even so, they were obliged to to leave quite a few of their possessions behind, with little hope of ever seeing them again. Catherine had not brought much with her either, so was also 'travelling light'.'

'Ah there he is,' said Chris, thankfully as he spotted Arwin threading his way towards them. The house boy led a small procession, made up of a coolie pushing a hand cart, and three palanquins, each carried by a quartet of coolies.

'Right girls; put these on.' Chris held out two dusty looking bourkas and both Pattie and Catherine made a moue of distaste as they donned the all enveloping garments over their light muslin dresses. As directed, they had dispensed with the 'bird cages' and shortened the dresses by the ruthless application of Pattie's dressmaking shears. They settle the face flaps so that they could see where they were going.

'How do Muslim women stand these things over their faces all the time?' muttered Catherine.

'Shush,' whispered Pattie, 'those coolies are looking at us very strangely.'

Perhaps it was the tense atmosphere of yesterday that made them anxious, but one or two of the coolies were indeed giving them dark looks. Swallowing nervously, the young women settled themselves in two of the palanquins, while Chris directed the loading of the cart. Arwin quietly reassured him that he had hired the fellows some distance from the house, so they shouldn't know that their passengers were British. Chris nodded without speaking, but when it was time to go he wrung the house-boy's hands once more in gratitude. Strange how some of the population wanted to murder them, yet others were ready to risk their lives to help them!

The journey through the streets of Lucknow was uneventful. Catherine peered through the shabby curtains, but all she could see were a few bazaar traders setting out their wares for the day. She saw no Europeans at all. Soon they were on the road that led from the town, jogging through parks and past the Imambarra with its towering minarets. The palanquin bearers began to pant as they trotted up a slight incline, and as they reached the top, the brass studded gates of the Baillie Guard came into view, wide open. The gates were surmounted by a stuccoed arch and flanked by two smaller arches; remnants of an old city wall. There was activity here, with soldiers guarding the entrance, and others bustling about their various duties. With other British people around them, the trio were able to emerge from their palanquins, the ladies throwing off their bourkas with a sigh of relief. The coolies glowered at them, but there was nothing they could do now, especially as Chris paid them off generously. But he persuaded the collie pushing the handcart to stay with them by offering him extra money.

Entering the Residency area, the three of them gazed about in wonderment. Everywhere there was activity and bustle. All around the grounds there were coolies throwing up mounds of earth and piling up sandbags. The formal gardens were being uprooted and trees cut down to make it easy for gun placements to be set up. Catherine could have cried when she remembered the elegancy of the Residency grounds when she had attended the military balls, and she jumped as a flame-of-the-forest tree crashed to the ground nearby, spilling its scarlet cups onto the ground like giant drops of blood. She shuddered.

They were accosted by an officious looking Captain who brusquely asked them where they had appeared from. Chris explained that they had been driven from their home in Lucknow. The Captain nodded,

'You are not the only ones. There are a number of civilians coming in from plantations and outstations; it seems that the trouble is more widespread than thought at first. Better report to the quartermaster and get yourself on the list for rations. No-one knows how long this might last!' And he hurried away.

'Mind yourselves!' A shout made them jump, and they found a limbered gun bearing down on them, drawn by a pair of bullocks. Fortunately the beasts were plodding along in their own ponderous fashion and they had plenty of time to move. Catherine began to feel very lost and alone, in spite of the presence of her friends,

'Oh Joe; where are you? Please come for me,' she silently prayed.

'Come on,' Chris was saying, 'let's find out where we can stay. If this emergency dies down, we'll try and return to Lucknow; I get nervous with all this military activity!'

They finally tracked down the quartermaster, who dutifully wrote down their names on one of his numerous bits of paper. Chris was heard to mutter,

'God help us! Was there ever a soldier who didn't love to make endless lists!'

'Oh hush,' whispered Pat, 'or he'll not help us find accommodation!'

The quartermaster scratched his head,

'Let's see; what did you say your name was Miss; oh sorry, Mrs.,' as he caught sight of Catherine's swelling abdomen.

'Mrs. Harrington. My husband is with the Kotepore Regiment.'

'Ah! Soldier's wife, eh. Rank?'

'Sergeant.' The quartermaster appeared to lose interest.

'Wives of non-commissioned officers and rankers are in the basement of the Residence.'

'Basement?' queried Catherine, despairingly.

'That's it. We'll be full to bursting by the time this is over. The cantonment is to be called in soon, and I've yet to find room for the officers' families. Now if you'll excuse me,'

'What about us?' asked Chris, 'we're not military.'

'Ah yes; there are houses over there,' waving, 'you could see if they'll take you. Now, if you'll excuse me, I must go,' and tucking his sheaf of paper under his arm, he strode off with upright carriage peculiar to a long–serving soldier.

Chris sat his charges down on a fallen tree while he tried to track down some accommodation. In spite of the bustle, he did not believe that the place was anywhere near full up yet, and sure enough, he was back within a short space of time with the news that one of the permanent residents was prepared to take them in. Very soon they were introduced to a buxom woman who announced herself to be Mrs. Appleton. She was the wife of a Company Servant, which was why she was a permanent resident. It was a charming little bungalow, though it seemed to be too small for all of them. Mrs. Appleton confided that her husband had gone on a trip into the mofussil to take stock of some indigo plantations that traded with the Company, and she was 'fair sick with worry about him.' Catherine felt an instant empathy with her and confided her own worries in return. The motherly lady instantly took Catherine under her wing and clucked over her condition.

'I've born and raised three of my own,' she told Catherine, 'though they've flown the nest, bless'em.'

It was arranged that Pattie and Catherine would lodge with Mrs. Appleton, who was soon telling them to call her Sue, 'for I never could abide formality,' and her three chins shook at the very thought!

'Where will you go, Chris?' questioned Pattie anxiously.

'Don't worry about me; I'll find a corner somewhere. There isn't room here, but it will put my mind at rest if you two are settled.'

'You are planning to go back to your paper!' accused Pattie. Chris looked uncomfortable,

'I'll be fine. While I was searching for lodgings for you, I talked to some others who lived in Lucknow; they say that there has been very little trouble, and my attack was an isolated incident.'

'Why can't we go back to the bungalow, then?'

'Please Pattie; stay here, just in case. When the 'all clear' sounds, we'll all go back.'

Sue listened to the exchange, and interposed at this point,

'Your husband's right, dear. The men get on a lot better if they don't have us to worry about!' Pat gave up, and Sue earned a grateful glance from Chris. Pattie and Catherine followed their hostess into a small bedroom, charmingly furnished with a bed and dressing table.

'I'll have a charpoy put in here before this evening, never fret. It's a bit small, but it's all I've have!'

'Don't worry Mrs. Appleton; oh sorry, Sue, Catherine and I have shared a room before, at school.'

'Well, I'll leave you to get settle. Your husband said he would bring your bits and pieces presently.'

The next few days passed, with a growing feeling of unreality. The weather grew hotter and hotter, and for much of each day, Pattie and Catherine lay on their beds panting under the swishing punkah. Every morning and evening, Chris knocked on the door and was entertained to chota hazri or evening tea by the irrepressible lady of the house. She was a kindly soul with a heart as large as her expansive bosom, and her guests soon discovered that she was a bit of a favourite with the soldiers of the 32nd Foot Regiment, stationed in Lucknow. They came to confide their troubles to 'Aunt Sue' as they called her, and enlivened the day for the newcomers.

Pattie was glad of the diversion, for it stopped her worrying about Chris, who persisted in going to his newspaper every day; claiming that it was vital for residents to remain informed. Catherine, too, welcomed the company which prevented her from pining too much for Joe. But as the days wore on, and there was no news from Kotepore, she grew more and more restless, and during the hottest part of the day, lay with wide open eyes on her bed. The heat made her peevish, and she snapped at Pattie when she tried to jolly her out of her misery. Finally, in despair, she snapped back,

'Well suppose something has happened to Joe; you are carrying the only memory of him you have left; do you want to lose it?' As soon as she had said it, Pattie wished she could take the words back, for Catherine's eyes widened to great, grey saucers with shock,

'Oh Pattie; oh Pattie,' she sobbed pathetically, and buried her face in her hands. Pattie looked at the head bowed in grief, and then she sat down and putting her arms round the heaving shoulders. The next moment, Catherine flung her arms round her neck and cried till she thought her heart would break.

'Hush dear,' murmured Pattie, 'I didn't mean it, Hush do; you are not doing yourself any good.' Eventually the sobs died away, and Catherine sat up, red faced with heat and crying. The sobs died to the odd hiccup, until she managed a watery smile. The outburst seemed to help her recapture her spirits, and she made an effort to appear cheerful, so that soon she was chatting to the visiting soldiers and listening to their troubles, and offering to write letters for those who could not do it for themselves.

Pattie sighed with a relief that was short lived. News had finally come from Kotepore, delivered by messenger as the lines were still down. The despatch told of the attack on the cantonment, and the desperate battles that were fought. Chris, who had brought the news, and thought it best to pass it on quietly to Pattie, said,

'It appears that Colonel Deluce was murdered, and Major Willoughby has taken command. They were due to escort the women and children to Simla, but that was a week ago. I am sure if Joe survived, he would have been here by now or he would have sent word. For God's sake, don't tell Catherine in case I am wrong, but I fear he may have perished!' Pattie nodded, feeling desperately sorry for her friend.

Preparations for a siege went on inexorably; mounds of round shot were everywhere, neatly thatched against the searing sun. Foodstuffs came into the compound purchased from local bunnias, who rubbed their hands in glee at the unexpected bounty, and convinced that they would get it all

back very soon. Valuables were buried secretly at night to save the trouble of protecting them, and day by day the tension grew with the temperature.

Chris was finally forced to abandon his precious newspaper. He had gone to it as usual one day, only to find it surrounded by a yelling, stone throwing mob. Two typesetters narrowly escaped with their lives by creeping out of a rear entrance. Chris, who now habitually dressed as an Indian with loosely tied turban, escaped notice. He had hung around hoping to rescue something from the mob, but when the inevitable tongue of flame began to lick the front porch, he resigned himself to a total loss of all the files within, and trudged despondently back to the Residency. Pattie was much relieved, though not for long, as Chris volunteered his services to a gun post.

On 23rd May, all British were ordered in from outstations, and on 30th May, the Mariaon Cantonment was attacked and fired, and the entire population was moved into the Residency. The trouble again seemed to have been contained, but Sir Henry was not prepared to take any chances.

Catherine and Pattie met Sir Henry often as they strolled around the Residency grounds in the comparative cool of the evening. Catherine thought that has face looked haunted, and learned from Chris that he had lost his wife some three years before, and since then he had lost all *joie de vivre*. He was tall and thin, with slanting oriental eyes. He suffered from a lung complaint, which made his face look more cadaverous than ever, but he always smiled distractedly at the two young women, doffing his hat with gentlemanly punctiliousness. They were not treated with the same manners by the memsahibs that moved into the Residency after the cantonment had been abandoned. These high nosed ladies persisted in dressing in sprigged muslin over enormous crinolines, white gloves, and carried frilly parasols. They picked their way fastidiously round piles of ammunition or horse fodder, as if they had been placed there specifically to inconvenience them!

About a week after the attack on the cantonment, when the Residency seemed to be full to bursting, there was a knock on the door of the Appleton bungalow, It was early evening, and the three ladies were taking tea together while waiting for Chris to come off duty,

'Ah,' said Pattie, 'that must be Chris now, though it's a bit early. Perhaps we all take a walk tonight Cathy?' She disappeared and Catherine and Sue heard the murmur of voices which then got louder as if raised in anger.

'Can't be her husband,' commented Sue, 'I've never heard them raise their voices to each other.' She heaved herself ponderously to her feet and followed by Catherine, went outside. They found a Captain standing on the doorstep flanked by two ladies, meticulously dressed for evening visiting, and fanning themselves with elegant painted fans. They were clearly mother and daughter and unmistakably of military origin. The Captain clicked his heels together at the appearance of Sue, and doffed his shako. He had blond curls and a sweeping blond moustache that reminded Catherine of Lieutenant Carless, whom she cordially detested.

'Good evening ma'am,' he said in a nasal drawl, 'just like Carless', thought Catherine with a shudder.

'These ladies have been assigned to your house. I was trying to inform this, er, young woman here, but she has chosen to be obstructive.'

'But Captain,' answered Sue, getting flustered, 'I already have these two young ladies; I really have no more room.

'There has been no official request for you to house these, ah, two. They will have to find somewhere else to reside.'

'Just a minute,' argued Pattie, hotly, 'Mrs. Appleton in not under military jurisdiction. She has kindly offered to share her accommodation with us.'

'Young woman,' said the Captain, curtly, 'This is an emergency and the army has jurisdiction over everything!' He turned his back on Pattie and Catherine and waved to two hovering orderlies, carrying a quantity of baggage. Within minutes, a bewildered Mrs. Appleton watched as her young guests belongings were firmly removed from their bedroom, and the two uninvited guests installed. They introduced themselves as Mrs. And Miss Dunwoody, and thereafter completely ignored their unwilling hostess. They had brought their own cook and servants who took over the kitchen as if it belonged to them.

In the meantime, Pattie, seething with rage, muttered to Catherine,

'C'mon. we are not taking this lying down! We're going to the Residency if we have to accost Sir Henry himself!' Sadly, they did not manage to get near Sir Henry; if they had they might have had some sympathy. But they got no further than the nearest office inside the entrance. An aide, as high nosed as the Captain they had so recently encountered, icily informed them that they had no rights to such salubrious accommodation when better born ladies were homeless. He consulted his lists ostentatiously, having enquired after their names,

'Ah yes, Mrs. Harrington; I understand you are a Sergeant's wife, and you, Mrs. Day, your husband is a journalist.' He managed to make Chris sound as lowly as a sweeper, 'you have both been assigned to the basement; you had no business moving in with Mrs. Appleton.'

The friends made their way back to the bungalow to tell their erstwhile hostess and friend the sad news. They found her sitting on her front porch in her rocking chair, looking totally bewildered by the turn of events. She was suitably shocked about their new accommodation and promised to take up cudgels on their behalf. But just as she finished speaking, she suddenly gave a squeak of excitement, and launched herself out of her rocking chair and towards the Baillie Guard at a speed surprising in one of her bulk. Catherine and Pattie watched her go with their mouths open.

'Arthur, Arthur!' came a shriek across the intervening space. They saw a spare figure dressed in grey alpaca being enfolded in a voluminous embrace. They grinned,

'Mr. Appleton?' suggested Pattie.

'Mr. Appleton,' agreed Catherine. The new arrival took their minds off their predicament momentarily as they were introduced to Mr. Appleton by his ecstatic spouse. He was as thin as his wife was stout, with lugubrious features. But then she bore him away to find out what had been happening to him, leaving the pair standing on the porch.

'Well,' said Pattie, 'That's that! I think we had better find our new dwelling. I hope Chris finds us; I wonder what has been keeping him?'

They picked up as many bags as they could manage, and made their way back to the Residency building, where they were shown how to penetrate the basement. A flight of stone steps led down to the subterranean regions that had formerly been used as store rooms, and now housed the wives and children of the 32nd Foot. The place was vaulted like a wine cellar and inadequately lit, and even more inadequately ventilated. It was packed with families, mostly moved in since the cantonment had been overrun, and everywhere children cried, or ran around screaming. Catherine vowed to spend as little time in there as she possibly could. They finally found a small area that wasn't already occupied, and made themselves as comfortable as possible. They had been issued with two meagre palliasses which they spread out, trying to ignore the curses from their nearest neighbours, learning some interesting vocabulary in the process. They tucked their bags away as neatly as possible, but Catherine looked at the area that they must call home for the foreseeable future, and shuddered.

'Come on, Pattie, let's get out of here.' Pattie looked dubious,

D'you think our things will be safe?'

'What can we do? We can't guard them all the time, and I won't stay down here all the time.' Pattie nodded and they made their out into the humid evening air. The barking of dogs sounded in the still air with startling clarity, and Pattie looked at the rising moon,

'I hope the rains come soon. If it gets any hotter, it will be unbearable down there. Ah! There's Chris.' She waved.

'What happened?' demanded Chris, 'I went to Sue's, but she was vague, full of excitement over her husband! And there was these two supercilious females ensconced in the parlour!'

Pattie sadly recounted the events of the evening. Chris pursed his lips,

'I'll see what I can do tomorrow, but the Residency is full to bursting and the memsahibs from Mariaon are behaving as if they own the place. Would you believe it; they are still going around leaving calling cards! I think it will all change soon. The town is getting more and more restless and all sorts of rumours are flying around. Tomorrow we are to start driving stakes in ditches around the main buildings!'

At the end of June came the terrible news that Cawnpore had been overwhelmed and everyone in it massacred. The occupants of the Residency were stunned. Many of them had friends or family there; and just couldn't believe that they had all been killed! On 28th June, as the Chapel held a service, attended by smart ladies in white gloves, the Baillie Guard was closed and the first shower of rain fell. The Residency held its collective breath, but the natives were quiet, and no more rain came down.

Next day, after Catherine and Pattie spent an uncomfortable night in the basement listening to babies crying, women squabbling, and occasionally screaming, they emerged into daylight blinking owlishly.

'Oh Pattie,' said Catherine, 'we can't stay there!'

'We have no choice, Cathy. All we can do is spend as much time as possible out of it.' They had been told by one helpful inmate of the basement, where they could get chota hazri, and they set off to find it; at least they would be fed!

Later, they met Chris for their evening walk round the gardens.

'There is to be a foray,' said Chris to his eager listeners, 'there's a strong feeling that Cawnpore needs to be avenged. Gubbins is insistent that there aren't that many real soldiers out there, and Sir Henry has agreed to lead a force, but his heart isn't in it. It will go out at dawn.' Pattie had been watching his face as he spoke, and then said quietly,

'You're going too?'

'Yes.'

'Oh Chris, you're not a soldier.'

'They need every man that can be spared. Lawrence must leave enough to guard the Residency, so every able bodied man is needed; soldier or not,' Catherine listened to the exchange and then moved away to let them talk in peace. Suddenly she missed Joe with a searing pain that left her gasping. She sat on a pile of round shot until the spasm passed, tears running down her face,

'Joe, Joe, where are you?'

After her outburst with Pattie, she had resolutely put aside her fears for Joe, and concentrated on the infant that was growing inside her and she had managed to forget her loss for hours at a time, sometimes a whole day, but it was not easy with Pattie and Chris being together so much. And this evening the agony was almost unbearable. It had been so long, surely he must be dead? But inside her, a flame of hope still flickered; it refused to be extinguished.

Next morning, at dawn, a small force set out to meet the rebels at Chinhut. The Commissariat seemed to forget the Napoleonic maxim that an army marches on its stomach, and they set out hungry. Nevertheless they set out with their heads held high, drums beating and scarlet jackets crossed with belts of white, pipe clayed perfection. A group of Sikh Sowars in blue jackets rode out, pennants fluttering, and after them came the volunteers, including Chris with a borrowed rifle. He kissed his wife and hugged Catherine, swallowing the chunk of bread that Pattie had managed to find for him,

'Don't worry my pet,' he whispered, 'we'll thrash the pandies and be back in time for tiffin, you'll see!' Pattie smiled through a mist of tears and watched him go.

'What's that he called them?' asked Catherine, 'pandies?

'Mm; Chris says it's after the first sepoy that mutinied; you remember, he was called Pandey?'

The avenging force marched through the scorching heat, and when a rest was called, discovered that no food had been brought along for them! They were tired and hungry; and then they encountered the enemy. The 'small force' they expected outnumbered them by some ten to one, and was well armed. It was hopeless from the start. Lawrence was not an able soldier and was outmanouvred and outgunned and worst of all, outsoldiered! He finally retreated with all speed back to Lucknow, leaving Colonel Inglis to try and retrieve what he could of the situation. Their precious howitzer; indeed their only howitzer, had been lost.

Catherine and Pattie spent the day in the basement. Neither had slept much the previous night, Catherine through discomfort on the lumpy palliasse, and Pattie through worry. And as they dozed, they missed the first bout of firing that the Residence had experienced. They woke in the early afternoon to hear that their brave soldiers had been routed and were even now fleeing for their lives; as many as had survived!

All that evening and night, they straggled back. The walking wounded supported comrades and the few able bodied carried the sorely hurt, but there were pitifully few of them. Pattie spent the hours of darkness by the Baillie Guard, with Catherine dozing beside her, impervious to the brusque instructions from the sentries to 'get back where they belonged.' As the sun showed as a golden rim on the horizon peeping over the Martiniere School, whose boys were dispersed throughout the Residency, she saw him come in. Chris was limping from a musket ball in the fleshy part of his thigh. He had fashioned himself a crude crutch, and his face was filthy and drawn with pain as he staggered through the crack in the gate left open, watched by anxious sentries on constant lookout for a rush of pandies lurking out of sight. Chris was the last one through.

Pattie flung her arms round him as he lurched, and would have fallen without her support. Catherine took one arm and together they supported a sagging Chris,

''Ere, let's be 'aving 'im.' A cockney voice floated through the semi-dark, and two stalwart privates took hold of Chris and bore him away to the Hospital followed by two weary women, both with tears of relief running down their faces.

The next day saw the removal of the small force stationed at the fort of Machi Bawan. The ammunition stored in it was blown up, a display of pyrotechnics that first shocked and then awed everyone in the compound. The great gates of the Baillie Guard were drawn to and sealed. The Residency of Lucknow prepared for total siege acknowledging that God alone knew how long they would have to defend themselves before help arrived.

Chapter 12

The heat rose steadily as Joe and Gopi trudged along the road that led south from Kotepore. They wrangled in half hearted fashion as they walked,

'Gopi,'

'Yes Sahib?'

'If you persist in walking two paces behind me, don't you think that observers might find it hard to believe that we are the brothers we claim to be?'

'It is so, Sahib.'

'Then walk next to me; now!'

'Yes Sahib?'

'It is not the custom for a brother to address another as Sahib. Is that not so?'

'It is so, Sahib.'

'Then call me Jhoti, if you value my life!'

'Yes Sah…Jhoti.'

Joe sighed. This journey was already fraught with danger without Gopi causing problems over his attitude towards him. If the sepoys he had overheard were to be believed, then the whole of Oudh and Bengal, and probably Rohilkand as well was up in arms, and anyone of obvious European appearance must be an immediate target for the disaffected element in this part of India. He also fretted about where he should head for. Everyone seemed to be sure that Catherine had headed for Lucknow, but the letter she had received while he was still with her, spoke of the friends immediately setting out for Cawnpore. But perhaps that journey had not been possible and they were still in Lucknow? Cawnpore was further away, so perhaps he should check Lucknow first? His head buzzed with tiredness and too much sun.

Squinting upwards, he noted that the sun was almost directly overhead, and he decided that they should spend an hour or two in the shade; it would not help the situation if he were to expire with sunstroke! Besides, he and Gopi had reached the point when he must make the decision, as close by there was a fork in the road. One fork headed directly south and would take him to Lucknow within a few hours. The other veered off south west, and would take him to Cawnpore, but on foot that journey would take two or three days.

Squatting Indian fashion under a banyan tree, he discussed the situation with Gopi,

'Tell me,' he asked, 'when did the Memsahib decide to leave for Lucknow after all?'

'It was on Sunday, Sah…er…Jhoti,' he replied, 'it was after the other letter came.'

'Other letter? You didn't tell me about another letter!'

'I am telling you now!'

'Yes Gopi; go on.'

'It came just after chota hazri, and the Memsahib rang the bell and told me to hire a carriage for the very next day. She seemed very cross, er, Jhoti!'

'Why was she cross?'

'I do not know. She didn't tell me!' Joe had to laugh at that. Of course she didn't tell him. But what was in the letter to make her decide to go after all, when she had promised to wait on his return. He sighed again, the age old masculine complaint creeping into his mind; 'women; there was no understanding their thought processes; they were entirely illogical; why couldn't they think like a man?' Now there was no saying where she was! But his mind was made up; he would go to Lucknow, it was nearer after all! With the decision made, he fell into a doze, and dreamed of his reunion with Catherine, and the scolding he would receive; his moth twitched with humour as he slept!

The pair dozed with their arms resting loosely on their knees. Anyone passing by would have taken them for friends, or indeed brothers, travelling together. Both were dressed in baggy pyjama trousers and muslin shirts;

Gopi forsaking his beloved dhoti to highlight their similarities. Both their heads were bound with turbans and sandals protected their feet. In Joe's belt was stuck a fearsome looking tulwar, while an old fashioned 'Brown Bess' rifle rested under one brown hand. Gopi was armed with a dagger, and wore crossed bandoliers of cartridges. They looked the image of a pair of disaffected Hindus looking for some hated Ferenghis to attack!

The worst of the day's heat passed, and though still very hot, Joe and Gopi rose to their feet and adjusted their bundles in readiness for moving off. The sound of horses' hooves came from the direction of Lucknow as the pair knuckled sleep out of their eyes, and squinting against the harsh light, Joe could make out a carriage moving at a spanking pace towards them.

As it drew closer, he could see that the carriage held a red faced European, clad in the universal uniform of a Company servant, the alpaca suit; this one in light fawn but discoloured by sweat stains. In the back of the carriage sat two women, their similar features but age difference proclaiming them mother and daughter The older women was correctly if unsuitably clad in black satin over an enormous crinoline. A matching hat perched atop an elaborate coiffure; a hat more suited to the fashionable streets of London, rather that the oppressive atmosphere of India in May! The lady was of ample proportions and the heat of the day had made her perspire freely, so that the black satin was stained under the arms. Her face was vermilion and she ineffectually dabbed at her forehead with a scrap of lace. Her daughter was more suitably clad in white muslin, though her crinoline was equally voluminous. She shaded her brown curls with a parasol, though she found it difficult to hold while clutching her mother fiercely. The trio seemed to be in abject terror, as though chased by demons, and it was certainly unusual to see a ferenghi driving the carriage himself, and through the heat of the day. The animal was lathered in sweat and his flanks heaved in distress at the pace at which it was forced to move.

Joe quickly summed up the situation and surmised that the trio was fleeing from sepoy attack. They probably lived in a small outstation, the husband trading for the Company. Whatever the reason for their precipitous flight, here was a heaven sent opportunity to investigate, as they were coming from the direction of Lucknow!

Without a second's thought as to his appearance, Joe stepped into the road and raised his hand in salute.

The trio in the carriage, Mr. and Mrs. Monkton and their daughter Hannah, had that morning sat down to chota hazri, secure in their placid existence. Oh yes, they had heard vague rumours about trouble among the sepoys, but what had that to do with them? Were they not good to their servants and did not the servants love them in return? So they reasoned. That very morning they had planned a shopping expedition to Lucknow to purchase last minute supplies before setting out for their small summer property in Musoorie. As they had prepared for their shopping trip, their maid who had been with them for many years, and indeed had been Hannah's ayah, had stood before them, ill at ease and twisting her hands together,

'What is it Alpa?' asked Mr. Monkton.

'Oh Sahib, Memsahib; I am thinking you should not go to Lucknow today.'

'Why ever not? It is important that we make these purchases. What has got into you today?' demanded Mrs. Monkton.

'I am thinking you should not go!'

Alpa left the room, and later could not be found when she was called; furthermore, all the servants seem to have vanished, including their carriage driver. It was then that unease crept into their minds, and the alarming tales began to be believable. By then the day was getting very hot, so they decided to wait until the cool of the evening before setting out for Lucknow; if indeed they went to Lucknow! Soon after midday, Hannah, who had been sulking on the verandah under the shade of an awning, saw a mob of armed Indians moving along the road, and then turn into their drive.

'Papa,' she screamed, running into the bungalow. One look at the approaching mob had Mr. Monkton grabbing his wife and daughter's hands. He had been making quiet preparations for such an emergency and the carriage stood ready, with the horse tethered and resting under the shade of a jacaranda tree. Stuck in his belt was a loaded and primed pistol. Pushing the females in the back of the carriage, Monkton seized the reins and whip, and hit the animal smartly on the rump.

The carriage set off at a canter straight up the drive, taking the Indians by surprise as they expected to find the family sleeping through the heat of the day. The carriage was through them before a tulwar was raised, and howling with rage, they chased the retreating wheels for a hundred yards or so. But the excessive heat and the futility of their action soon drove them back, where they vented their spleen by sacking the Monkton bungalow and then firing it. Then satisfied with their labours, the attackers went on their way, watched from the undergrowth by the servants; too frightened to intervene, though they had no animosity towards their employers. Had the Monkton's heeded their warnings they would have been safe, they told themselves!

As it was, they were fleeing along the road compelled to get away from immediate danger. It was then that a solitary figure had stepped into the road in front of the blown horse. The figure, dressed in typical Indian fashion had a tulwar stuck in his belt. Another Indian lurked under the cover of the banyan tree. Monkton reacted instinctively and raising his pistol, he fired at almost point blank range. Joe was spun round by the force of the ball passing clean through his left shoulder. He grunted with pain and fell to the ground. From his prone position, through a haze of pain, he saw the carriage go another twenty yards, when three sepoys sprang from the undergrowth and seized the horse's reins, dragging the carriage to a halt. More sepoys appeared, yelling at the tops of their voices. Monkton used his discharged pistol as a club, but to no avail. Joe saw the tulwars make short work of the family, mother dying a second or two before her daughter, the white muslin shockingly stained with their blood. Husband and father had no time to grieve before he joined them. The sepoys moved away, their grisly work done. The horse stood still in the shafts, head bowed by exhaustion, but agitated by the smell of fresh blood; but after a while, when no-one commanded it to move, it began to crop the parched grass by the side of the road.

Gopi stepped from the shade of the banyan tree, aghast at the turn of events. The retreating sepoys had not spared a glance at the crumpled figure in the road. Gopi approached fearfully but saw straight away that his master was alive, but bleeding badly from the shoulder wound. He leaned over him and whispered tentatively, though the road was no deserted,

'Sahib; Sahib, are you hurt?'

'What a bloody stupid question Gopi; I'm bleeding like a stuck pig!' Joe tried to sit up, but the pain of his shoulder made him fall back with a grunt. Already he felt dizzy

'Bind up my shoulder, Gopi. Quickly man before I bleed to death!'

Shaking, Gopi tore off the end of his turban and bound it tightly round the wound. Through gritted teeth, Joe guided him,

'That's it; make a pad of it' press on it. You've got to stop the bleeding. Aaaah! No; go on; press down; don't mind my shouting; press; damn you!' Then he fainted. The young bearer kept pressing until he was sure that the blood flow had slowed. Then he bound up the gaping hole carefully. There was no-one in sight, and he cast around his mind desperately for a solution to the problem. He was so used to being directed at every moment of the day, that he found it difficult to decide for himself what to do. His master's breathing came raggedly through his parted lips, and his skin under the walnut juice had taken on a grey pallor. Gopi did realise that unless he acted soon, his master would die.

He sat back on his heels. Memory stirred. They had passed a village not long before they had stopped for tiffin and a break from the relentless sun. In a village there was often a woman skilled in healing. But how to get his master there? The Sahib was a big man, and Gopi was not. He was skinny, in spite of the good living he had enjoyed with the Harrington's, so there was no question of him carrying the Sahib the half mile or so that separated them form the village. His forehead corrugated with effort; but of course, the carriage! He rose from his heels and walked cautiously over to the vehicle, slewed across the road and still bearing its grisly burden, the three bodies already covered by loathsome black flies. But Gopi was not squeamish, simply not very strong. Bracing against a wheel to stop it rolling forward, he dragged the three bodies out and left them in a tumbled heap by the side of the road. He thought vaguely of the British obsession with a 'decent burial', but he felt nothing for these total strangers; his master came first.

Turning the horse and carriage carefully, he led the reluctant animal back to Joe's huddled form. The next problem was how to get Harrington-Sahib into the carriage. Gopi reached under his arms and tugged, but all he got for his effort was a groan. He was just too heavy for him. Still no-one around, so squatting down again, he shook Joe urgently by the uninjured shoulder, hissing,

'Sahib; Sahib; get up. Look, I will help, but get up!' He shook his master again,

'Whassamatter….? Mumbled Joe, but his eyes opened, and he groaned aloud.

'Gopi, what are you doing? Leave me be. It can't be time for chota hazri; I've only just closed my eyes!'

'Sahib! Get up! The sepoys are coming; your house is in danger!'

It worked; Joe's eyes flew open and he struggled to get up. Seizing his chance, Gopi wriggled under his good shoulder and heaved; Joe was on his feet and swaying, with Gopi staggering under the burden. One lurching step followed by another, and they were at the carriage,

'In you get Sahib!' With much groaning and swearing, Joe heaved himself up with Gopi's help, and then collapsed across the seat in a dead faint. Gopi got in too, and straddling the supine body, urged the horse to a trot. Within minutes, the village appeared in view. It was like hundreds of others flung across this part of India, merely a collection of crude huts surrounded by water tanks; very low now in the fag end of the hot season. Pi-dogs roamed, ring tailed and yellow eyed; while a hump-backed cow paused a moment in its cud chewing to survey the new arrivals. Small children tumbled out of the huts, brown eyes enormous in their round faces, pot bellies above sticklike legs. They stood and stared in frank curiosity, fingers in their mouths. Gopi was used to that; curiosity was a national characteristic after all! Adults began to appear and finally an ancient crone who looked as if she could be a healer. Gopi got down and addressed the old woman with a respectful namaste. Her seamed face peered at him from under the veil of an orange sari, and she moved her toothless gums in her sunken jaws,

'Old woman. My friend, er Jhoti, has been hurt by an Angrezi gun. He is likely to bleed to death. Can you help him?' The crone stared at him with boot button eyes, mumbling. Gopi held out a small handful of rupees.

'Save him and there will be more!' She jerked her head at the hut behind her, and spoke to two younger men, apparently her sons. They lifted Joe out of the carriage, none too gently in spite of Gopi's scolding, and carried the inert form into the hut, laying him on a crude charpoy.

They then went out leaving the crone and Gopi with his master. His colour had deteriorated even during the short carriage ride, and Gopi was seriously worried that he wouldn't survive through the night. The old woman unbound the wound and looked at the hole made by the ball. Fresh blood welled up instantly. She nodded to herself, and directing Gopi to press down again, she disappeared into the sunshine. She returned a few moments later, carrying what appeared to be wet clay, which she slapped onto the wound, having removed the remnants of the improvised bandage. Very soon the clay hardened, and she grunted with satisfaction. She settled Joe more comfortably on the charpoy, and raised his head to allow him to sip from a chatti of water. He slipped in and out of unconsciousness, but Gopi was sure he was unaware of his surroundings. He muttered under his breath, and leaning close, Gopi listened, fearful that he would cry out in English, but the muttered words were all in Urdu!

For two weeks, Joe's life hung in the balance, and Gopi never left his side. He was ever fearful that Joe would give away his true nationality, and he did once or twice cry out in English,

'Catherine, my Catherine, where are you?' But fortune smiled on him and Gopi was alone with him at those times. Gopi would start talking to him in Urdu, and the diversion worked, and the mutterings changed to that language. Now and then, Joe cried out in a language Gopi did not know, for why should he recognise Erse? And if he didn't why should anyone else? It could be one of the myriad Indian dialects"

Two days after the ambush, the wound turned bad. The woman who called herself Gita, removed the clay poultice, and sucked on her gums as she looked at the wound. The flesh round the hole was puffed and angry and yellow matter oozed out of it. She went out of the hut and returned with a concoction of leaves, which she slapped on and bound into place. Once again, Gopi kept vigil; two, three days passed and the wound grew worse. Livid blood vessels pulsed from the shoulder and the whole area swelled up until Gopi thought that it would burst. Joe's body burned with fever, and he tossed his head restlessly. He fought Gita when she changed the dressings every few hours, and she shook her head at Gopi's anxious questioning. He fought Gopi when he tried to raise his head to drink. Then, slowly but surely the swelling began to subside and the furnace of Joe's skin began to cool, until one day Gopi put his hand on his forehead and found it clammy to touch, a healthy sweat glistening there. The livid blood vessels disappeared back into the flesh of his shoulder, and when Gita removed the poultice there was an area sticky with exuded matter. Gita washed it away and underneath was a depression big enough to put a finger in, but it had healthy flesh around it. Joe slept deeply and naturally that night for the first time, and Gopi slept too, secure in the knowledge that his master would not die after all.

During this time of crisis, Gopi did not once think about the quest that they had been on, but now he did. But what could he have done alone? And he would not have left the Sahib in the midst of strangers who might have turned him out to die as soon as Gopi's back was turned! Gopi never questioned his own loyalty to his master; he would no more have considered betraying Joe as he would his own father. He had been raised to be a bearer; it was his dharma, as serving this man was clearly his dharma. He had managed to remove the money belt from Joe's waist when he and Joe had been alone in the hut, and it now rested uneasily around his own skinny waist.

He would be very glad to leave this place, though there had been no overt hostility. But these people lived close to subsistence level, and he and Joe were an added burden on their food reserves, though he had paid them for it. What if they were to decide to investigate where the trickle of rupees were coming from?

It was when Joe was well on his way to recovery that Gopi found out how wrong he was about Gita and her sons, and he felt ashamed of doubting these simple folk. He had returned from a trip to relieve himself in a nearby field and when he entered the hut, he found his master lying in a shaft of light. The sunbeam played on Joe's head where the turban had been removed for comfort and half an inch of coppery red hair showed where the dye was growing out. Gita was washing Joe and must have seen the true hair colour, and of course, his beard was growing too! Gopi had not thought of that and looked at Gita in alarm. She straightened up as he entered and looked at him long and hard for a moment,

'He is good to you, this Angrezi?' Gopi did not even try to talk his way of it,

'Yes he is. He speaks our language and tries to understand our ways.'

Gita nodded and went on with her washing; the matter was not spoken of again.

Even when the danger was past, Joe was left as weak as a kitten and was forced to endure a period of convalescence. As he returned to his senses, he was depressingly aware that time was passing, but he was also depressingly aware that he was of no use to anyone, least of all his wife, until he grew stronger. He patiently lay and let Gita and Gopi administer to him until he felt strong enough to try and get up for a short period every day. Day by day he slowly gained strength. The next big hurdle was to go out of the hut, though the scorching sun hurt his eyes and drove him back inside. The hot season was nearly over, and they all waited patiently for the rains to break. One of Gita's sons, he could never tell them apart, fashioned him a stick, and with its help, and Gopi hovering around him, he was able to take himself to a nearby field to relieve himself, saving Gita that unsavoury duty! Slowly, slowly he walked a little further every day in the cool of the evening. He incessantly asked Gopi,

'Any news?' But Gopi shook his head. Though they were near the Kotepore to Lucknow road, any passing travellers had little time to bother with such a mean collection of buildings. Gopi was secretly thankful as he wanted the Sahib to regain full strength before he went chasing after the Memsahib again. She did not deserve it, after all, he reasoned, having disobeyed her husband, unlike a good, Hindu wife.

And while Joe slowly recovered, the uprising spread. It had quietened for a while, after the drama of Meerut and Delhi; but it had still grumbled and simmered all this time like Joe's festering wound, until like the wound, it had boiled over again!

In Cawnpore, General Sir Hugh Wheeler began to fear for the safety of his lively station. It was a straggling town, set in the dusty Ganges Plain and would be hard to defend. Wheeler though to keep things calm by forbidding all celebrations, even going to church, or firing guns in honour of the Queen's birthday; but all that achieved was to set everyone's nerves on edge! He was not too fearful, yet, for his own wife was an Indian lady and caste-fellow of Nana Sahib, Raja of Bithur and the adopted son of the last Peshwar of Poona. But though Nana Sahib considered himself more 'British than the British', he was deep in debt and was angry with the British for refusing him the pension his predecessor had received.

Wheeler decided he should select a site to defend in case of need, but he chose very badly. Two barrack blocks that had served as a hospital, one with a thatched roof, and overlooked by unfinished buildings, were set aside. A parapet and a gun placement were built, very badly, and some food moved in. The nearest well was some distance away and in the event of attack, would be exposed to enemy fire.

There were many false alarms, which set everyone nerves on edge, but it was getting more and more certain that Nana Sahib would attack,

which he did, having first informed them of his intention! On June 4th the rumble of wheels and heavy limber could be heard through the stillness of the night. They all moved into the barracks and waited. On 6th June, the siege of Cawnpore began.

While Sir Henry Lawrence in Lucknow continued his preparations for defence, and Catherine Harrington waited anxiously for news of her husband, the British in Cawnpore endured hell on earth. Short of food and plagued by heat and flies, lacking sanitation and water, they endured day after day of torment. Women, children and soldiers died; of gunshot, of sunstroke, of round shot, of disease; they died.

One of those who suffered in Cawnpore was Charlotte Morris, Pattie and Catherine's friend and one time school chum. The same Charlotte who had urged them to visit so that they could picnic together! But that was in another existence. This one consisted of days filled with sunstroke and starvation, discomfort and distress. She endured with a stoicism of which the British woman is often capable of in times of crisis. She endured by keeping herself busy as she could. She had lived in a neat bungalow next door to her parents who were part of the military establishment. Charlotte and husband John had found Cawnpore to their liking, and had moved there some two years previously from Lucknow. Her parents were among the first to die, theirs and other bodies tipped unceremoniously down an unused well, their corruption adding to the prevailing stench. Her father had died at a makeshift wall by a shot that had passed straight through the parapet. Her mother had run to him, to succumb to the next shot.

Charlotte was forcibly restrained from running to them as well. And she had spent the day watching their bodies turning black under the broiling sun.

After that, Charlotte busied herself ministering to anyone who needed her; she comforted children who had lost their mothers, cradling small bodies to her unfulfilled bosom. She comforted wives who had lost soldier husbands and soldiers who had lost their wives. She helped in the makeshift hospital, where she saw her husband, John brought in, having been co-opted as a soldier during the emergency. He sat with him through the night, and held his hand to ease his passing as dawn broke over the beleaguered barrack blocks. Then one night, the thatched roof of the hospital was fired on by an incendiary from an enemy battery. She performed heroic deeds helping screaming women, children and wounded out of the burning building, many with clothes aflame. Most of the precious medical supplies were destroyed, and when the charred remains of the building finally cooled, at least forty blackened bodies were discovered. If only they had known, beneath the second barrack block was an enormous cool cellar, that could have sheltered them; but it was not known about until even their ghosts had ceased to haunt the battle scarred walls.

Joe sat in a peepul grove and pondered his course of action. For some days now he had tentatively tried wielding his tulwar, cursing at his continued weakness. He could only be thankful that it was his left shoulder that had been wounded, and he was right handed. But even so, his muscles felt flaccid and feeble and incapable of sustained action. He continually berated himself for being so stupid in stepping out in front of the carriage, with its clearly terrified occupants, without even thinking of his disguise. He could only wonder why, since the start of the troubles, everything he had done had just seemed to make matters worse! He had been supposed to find out what was happening in Kotepore, but had been captured. His absence had caused Catherine to flee to Lucknow or Cawnpore, and on the way to rescue her, he had been shot! His low spirits were compounded by his bodily weakness and the awareness that too much time had passed while he lay on his charpoy as a result of his own stupidity!

As he sat fanning himself with a large peepul leaf he heard the sound of tramping feet. Up the Lucknow road marched a ragged band of men, though a certain orderliness suggested that they sepoys. He kept his eyes lowered so as not to draw attention to himself and watched them from under his eyelids. They halted at the village and asked for food and a place to stay for the night. Dusk was close and no Indian would turn away a traveller in need. Very soon cooking fires were lit in an open space near the tanks and the twenty or so men were squatting comfortably by them, drawing on bidis.

The overheated air danced and swam above the fires, and Joe wondered how they could sit so close. But here was a perfect opportunity to learn some up to date news. Sidling up the nearest circle he sat cross-legged and listened in casual fashion to the chatter. They were the usual motley band of disaffected soldiers bragging about their conquests in the manner of soldiers since time out of mind. Joe had to struggle to keep an impassive expression on his face as he heard tales of atrocities being bandied about; a child spiked on a lance as it ran screaming from its murdered mother; a woman decapitated as she knelt in prayer. Joe wondered how many stories were actually true, but then he remembered the Kotepore cantonment, and could not quite suppress a shudder. As casually as he could, he asked,

'But where do you go now?'

'Hah! We are going to join the glorious Nana Sahib who is about to defeat Wheeler-sahib at Cawnpore.'

'But why is the Nana Sahib attacking Wheeler-sahib? I thought that Wheeler-memsahib was a caste fellow of the Nana Sahib?'

'Where have you been, ignorant sweeper?' said one hulking sepoy with a half healed cut down his right cheek; a sabre slash, thought Joe.

'Nana Sahib was just playing with the Angrezi. Why should he care about the memsahib? She has defiled her caste consorting with one who is not Hindu!'

Joe thought rapidly as the speaker scratched his round belly and spat a stream of betel stained spittle into the fire, where it bubbled and hissed evilly. If Nana Sahib had invested Cawnpore, even though he was reputed to be a friend of the British, then matters were serious indeed. He probed further,

'If Nana Sahib is winning against the Angrezi, why do you go there?'

The British are to be offered a chance to leave by boat for Allahabad. It is being said that Nana Sahib is letting them go and that cannot happen!' And the hulking sepoy nudged his friend and they both guffawed, displaying teeth stained by betel; it looked like blood in their mouths. Suppressing a shudder, Joe asked deferentially,

'May I journey with you? I have been ill and missed a lot of fighting, and would like to see the end of the Angrezi.'

'Come if you wish fellow. Come and wonder at our prowess. After we have killed them all in Cawnpore, we will return to Lucknow and kill them all too. Soon, all of India will be rid of these usurpers!'

Later, in Gita's hut, Joe told Gopi of his decision to go to Cawnpore,

'If what they are saying is true, The Residency in Lucknow is still open and unharmed, but Cawnpore is under attack. I will go there first, and if the memsahib is not there, I will go to Lucknow.'

'Sahib?'

'Mm?'

'Why did you say 'I'. Am I not to come too?'

'Gopi; you have done enough for me already. You saved my life out there on the road. Stay here with these people. They are your people. And I have seen the way a certain young lady has been looking at you from behind the veil of her sari! And she has no brothers and sisters, which would mean a fine inheritance for you.' But Gopi looked shattered, his brown eyes filling with tears as he pleaded to be allowed to accompany his master. Joe sighed,

'It is not a matter of allowing you Gopi. I just thought you might have had enough of me and my troubles. But sleep well; the sepoys to leave before dawn to travel before the heat of the day. And Gopi.'

'Yes Sahib?'

'No more Sahib. It must be Jhoti!'

'Yes Sahib.' Joe gave up.

With the moon still up, the group of sepoys rose, scratching and grumbling. A small chota hazri of cold chapattis and they were on their way, followed by Joe and Gopi knuckling sleep from their eyes. Before the sun began to beat down brazenly, they had put several miles between them and the village.

Joe had made his farewells to Gita the night before, thanking her for her care of him and her medical skill. He was aware that she knew his true identity and added thanks for not betraying him. She studied him carefully and then her seamed face broke into a smile,

'Angrezi,' she said softly, 'my people were here before the Ferenghi came, and will be here when you have all gone. This trouble is no more than a gurrh-burrh; what is it to do with me?' Joe smiled back at her pragmatism as he pressed her palms within his own, and then gave her a purse that jingled satisfyingly. She smiled back toothlessly and broke into a cackle. His grin grew broader until he laughed with her.

Two days later, towards evening, they arrived at Cawnpore. They had crossed the Ganges and then veered south to cross the smaller Ganges Canal. Marching along the Bithur Road, they could see the barrack blocks of Wheeler's entrenchment on the right. Joe sucked in his breath in horror at the sight. One block was blackened and roofless, pockmarked with round shot and bullets. The other was equally scarred, though as yet unfired. Round the entrenchment ran a crude embankment, no more than waist high and looking incapable of protecting anyone. Even as they marched towards the Nana Sahib's forces, Joe saw defenders being picked off snipers as they crouched behind the inadequate shelter.

'How can anyone survive that hell-hole?' he asked himself. There appeared to be only one well and that was in clear view of the besiegers so that water must be in short supply, and the hot weather was at its most enervating. Joe was stunned; he had not expected anything as bad as this! Why on earth hadn't Wheeler chosen the Magazine which would have been much easier to defend?

The small band of arrivals was welcomed by the forces of Nana Sahib, and they settled down for the night. Rumours were rife that matters were due to come to a head, and the hated Angrezi would have to capitulate soon. Though some of those round the fire expressed a grudging admiration for the fortitude of the defenders, they all agreed that with the hospital destroyed and food running low, the Angrezi would have no choice but to give in. The new arrivals all nodded; it was as they had been told. Very soon they could expect their revenge to be complete; it was the hundredth anniversary of the Battle of Plassey!

Two days later, on 25th June, a half-caste woman carrying a child was sent to the British entrenchment with terms for surrender. The Nana Sahib was anxious to bring the battle to a conclusion, for disturbing rumours about a rescue force massing at Allahabad began to circulate. Accordingly he wrote to Wheeler, opening with,

'To the subjects of Her Most Gracious Queen Victoria…'

The message went on to promise safe passage to Allahabad to all those who were not involved with the acts perpetrated by the hated Dalhousie.

General Wheeler read the letter over and over, heartsick at the thought of capitulation. His spirits were already low having witnessed the death of his son, Godfrey, his head blown off as he had chatted to his mother and sisters. So Wheeler was now inclined to hold out until relief arrived.

'Relief from where?' questioned Captain John Moore, a sentiment echoed by others. All that sweltering day the argument raged back and forth, tempers as heated as the air. The messenger, still holding her child, was sent back to beg for more time, and finally towards evening it was agreed that they should talk with the enemy without committing themselves.

All that day, Joe had listened to the buzz of speculation and rumour; he had watched the woman and child go to the British camp and later return, her hands held upwards in a gesture of non-committance. Later, he saw three men leave the entrenchment, the leading one wearing the insignia of a Captain.

'Why not General Wheeler?' he asked himself.

The negotiators sat down together and thrashed out the terms of the agreement. Sidling as close as he could until he was cuffed away, Joe managed to hear enough to tell him that matters had been arranged as foretold by the sepoys he had travelled with. The British were to give up their big guns, but would keep their small arms. In return they would be given carriages to take the women, children and wounded to the river, where boats would be waiting.

'Surely they can't refuse?' Joe asked of the scar faced sepoy. He merely grinned,

'Of course they can't. Then we'll be waiting for them!'

'But the Nana Sahib wants them to leave; I heard him say so this morning.'

'Do you want them to escape?' hissed the sepoy, bringing his face close to Joe's, 'that is not what you were saying when you asked to walk with us!'

'No, of course not. But if the British come in force they will want revenge if we kill their women.'

'Then we shall be waiting for them. Go back to your village if you have no stomach for the fight. Kali is on our side; we cannot lose. These Angrezis have made you soft; made you forget your Gods. See this,' and he held out a wooden crucifix. Joe recognised it instantly; it had once adorned the end of the Reverend Mother Theresa's rosary, 'this is what their God has done for them!' Gripping it between his two hands, he snapped it in two and tossed the pieces at Joe contemptuously. With a final disgusted glare, he strode away.

'I must find a way to warn them,' muttered Joe to himself as he picked up the pieces of the broken crucifix. The face of Mother Theresa swam before him, as did that of her murderer. Not a sepoy at all, just a cold blooded killer.

The negotiations seem to have broken up, and the three scarlet jacketed figures strode away. The leader from both sides agreed the terms shortly afterwards, and Nana Sahib wanted the evacuation to start immediately. Captain Moore, who had conducted the negotiation, fell into a rage and threatened to blow up the entrenchment and everyone in it if they could not have some time to prepare. Shocked at the display of temper, Nana Sahib relented and agreed to wait until dawn.

That night, Joe tried to make his way to the entrenchment, crawling on his belly. But the moon was up. And he had not gone far when he was challenged by an Indian sentry and nearly shot for his pains! He would have to seize the opportunity the next day once the evacuation had started.

In the entrenchment, the British slept as they had not slept for three long weeks in the absence of the incessant bombardment. They were even able to draw water from the well in safety rather than send men out in the dead of night, and who still were targeted by their vigilant besiegers. They wanted to trust the Nana Sahib; anything was better than enduring the hell on earth for even one more day. Charlotte, sleeping with two small heads in her lap, had offered up a prayer for their safekeeping. For herself, she had had enough of being crowded into inadequate shelter with so many other women and children; she was tired of trying to keep herself decent when it was impossible to even relieve oneself with the danger of getting shot; tired of seeing children blown to pieces before her eyes. Surely God could not ask any more of them?

At dawn the next day, the evacuation began. Elephants and palanquins, doolies and bullock carts appeared. The British emerged from their refuge blinking in the bright morning light. Children looked around them, eyes enormous in their ravaged faces. Women had hurriedly sewn their treasures into their clothing, where they clinked among the stains of ordure. They all began to scramble into the conveyances, though the mahouts chose to make it more difficult by refusing to make their elephants kneel.

Joe stood with Gopi, watching the process with anguished eyes. He could not do anything without revealing his identity, but he crept as closely as possible so that he could scan every female face, a difficult task in the midst of the melee. In his hand he had secreted a piece of paper in which he warned the reader to beware of betrayal by a group of sepoys, though he did believe that Nana Sahib was genuine in his offer. He waited for the opportunity to pass it on to someone in authority, but all such were busy organizing the procession. At last it moved off.

Once away from the entrenchment, there was no turning back. The British had left behind their artillery and were strung out. The mob of besiegers lined the route, jeering and catcalling, some even daring to spit at their one time overlords. But there were some who wept at the sight of their former masters and mistresses, and rushed forward to beg for forgiveness. Joe capered alongside jeering with the rest. He recognised the Captain from the day before, and coming as close as he dared, appeared to trip, reaching out for the man's arm as he did so. The Captain cursed and tried to push him off, but felt something pressed into his palm. The next moment, Joe had melted into the crowd, where an anxious Gopi waited for him. They watched as the Captain casually glance at the piece of paper in his hand, and frown heavily at the message. He glanced about him, but would not have recognised Joe in the milling mob, the contact was too fleeting.

The procession reached the river, where the Ganges flowed between high brown banks. About forty large boats awaited them, thatched against the broiling sun, which even now was making its presence felt. They were fully provisioned. The refugees moved in a double line of sepoys, many reaching out to old comrades, assuring they would leave without harm. Joe stood back, scanning the sepoy lines for the ones he had travelled with. He spotted scar-face, moving to a position further up the bank. He had a group of five with him, and they all carried rifles. Desperately Joe looked about him for Nana Sahib to warn him. He finally located him on the bank overlooking the ghat, and surrounded by his retinue. From the arguments that had gone on the previous day, Joe knew that some of his own retinue did not share the Nana's liking for the British, and would be delighted to have trouble started elsewhere and everything to then get out of hand. But he had to try. He had not seen Catherine, but in the choking dust of the journey to the river, it was quite possible that he could have missed her. If he failed there was likely to be more bloodshed. Wriggling between straining bodies, followed by an eel like Gopi, he made his way towards Nana Sahib. Suddenly the crowd shifted, and he fell to his knees, right in front of his quarry. Looking up, he stared into a pair of restless black eyes, set in a corpulent pockmarked face. The black eyes stared back at him,

'What do you want?'

'Sahib,' said Joe, abasing himself in front of the Mahratta warrior,

'Among your rissal are badmashes who are plotting to fire on the British.' The face darkened in anger,

'How do you know this?'

'I heard them plotting last night and they are along the river back at this moment with their guns at the ready.'

The Nana Sahib sighed, then turned to the hawk faced man behind him,

'Go and see if this is true. Post lookouts and if badmashes try to make trouble, bring them to me.'

The hawk faced man bowed and moved away, but as he went, Joe looked into his hooded eyes and saw hatred there; could he be trusted to carry out the Nana's wishes?

Joe could do no more, and he wriggled back the way he came, anxious to remove himself from a potential 'lion's den'. He reached the top of the ghat where the refugees were beginning to descend and climb into boats.

Suddenly he saw a face he recognised, though only just! Charlotte Morris was standing in front of him holding a small boy and girl by their hands. She was waiting her turn to descend, looking bedraggled and bewildered. Joe could only guess at what she had endured since the siege began, but noted her ragged and stained clothes, and the purple shadows under her eyes. There was no time to lose and he sidled forward until he was alongside her,

'Charlotte! Charlotte,' he said quietly. She looked about her searching for the speaker.

'Charlotte; it's me, Joe; here, under the turban!' and he smiled at her. Charlotte stared at the grinning, blue-eyed Indian next to her, scarcely able to believe it was the husband of her friend Catherine. Hurriedly now, for the crowd was beginning to push from behind,

'Is Catherine with….' Even as he spoke, Joe was elbowed aside by a Corporal, making the mob of watching Indians hiss with hate, Desperately Joe tried to get back to Charlotte, but she had been swept down the ghat and on to the beach. Then she was handing her charges to the boatman before climbing on board herself. The embarkation went on; five or six hundred of the original thousand who had entered the entrenchment, believing that their torment was about to be over, gazing longingly at the provisions piled in the boats to sustain them on their journey to Allahabad. Joe went on searching the crowds, looking for a diminutive figure with long brown hair. Time and again he thought he saw her from behind, convinced that a fall of brown hair was hers, until the owner of the hair turned round.

It was all so Indian; unhurried, muddled, casual; the women and children, the seriously wounded, the walking wounded, and finally the fit men all piled into the boats. The sun shone and birds called to each other from the trees that came down to the river on the far bank. Voices shouted instructions to each other; the atmosphere was almost lighthearted. The fighting was over; for now at least. Joe narrowed his eyes against the glare of the rising sun. Were there shadowy shapes in those same trees that sheltered the birds? They must be very still as the birds were not alarmed; he could see the bright plumage of a flock of parrots and black mynahs called to each other.

The there was the sound of a bugle; just one or two tentative notes. The soldiers looked up in alarm and reached for their rifles. The birds rose shrieking from the trees as the boatmen spilled from the boats and made for the shore, spurred on the crackle of gunfire from the British Enfields. Return fire broke out from both sides of the river, pouring into the boats, so dense that it must surely have been prearranged? Cannon sounded from the reeds where they had been hidden from sight and within minutes the thatch on the boats was aflame.

Screams rent the air as the occupants of the burning boats flung themselves into the water. Charlotte, in a boat as yet intact, clutched her two charges to her. The little girl cried piteously,

'Oh why are they firing at us? Didn't they promise to leave off?' and she sobbed hysterically.

Wheeler was cut down and fell face down into the water; Captain Moore followed him. Sowars spurred into the water after their quarry, cutting and slashing with their vicious tulwars. Children were slaughtered, their brains dashed out by iron tipped clubs; were set alight by flaming brands thrust at their skirts.

Joe stood on the ghat helplessly, hopelessly watching the carnage. The sepoys and sowars were in a killing frenzy, and he could only scan the melee desperately searching for Catherine in the hope of coming to her aid if he spotted her; he did not see her.

One boat managed to break free and drifted off downstream where it was assaulted at every sand bank. Joe could see scar face in the thick of the fighting, a triumphant leer lighting up his evil features. All the boats were constantly attacked by snipers as they slowly drifted with the current.

Abandoning his search for his wife, Joe made for where the Nana Sahib had been standing in the hope of begging him to stop the massacre. He was too late; Nana Sahib was in a livid rage at the slaughter that was being perpetrated against his express orders, and was screaming at his retainers. They sullenly moved to do his bidding, and the firing gradually petered out. Little more than two hundred men, women and children were herded on to the beach and then onto the bank.

Charlotte stood on the beach looking totally bemused. Her senses reeled as the scene took on an unreal quality. It had all happened so fast; one moment a grinning blue eyed Indian was claiming to be Joseph

Harrington, and then she was on the boat with her charges, reaching out eager hands for the piles of food but being told to 'wait until they were underway', as though they were off to a picnic! Then the scene had shifted into chaos and pain. She stared at the turgid waters of the sacred Ganges, reddened by the blood of some four hundred British victims. Bodies floated face down and drifting slowly in the current. Many more were sprawled on the shore in grotesque attitudes. Nearby, a small boy lay as though asleep, the back of his head staved in by an iron tipped club, but his face unmarked and innocent as a cherub.

One of her small charges had vanished, little Jeremy. She had looked after him for a full two weeks after his mother had been shot through the breast desperately trying to reach the well to get water for her fretful infant. Mother and baby had died from the same bullet, leaving Jeremy, alone and forlorn. Now he had gone, one of the victims that profaned the sacredness of the sacred river! The little girl, Fanny, was sniffling by her side, her face streaked with tears as she buried it in Charlotte's skirts. Slowly, quiet fell on the scene; even the birds were silent.

At the Nana Sahib's orders, the survivors were herded along the river bank; the men separated from the women, never to be seen again. Charlotte, with the other women and children trudged along in the rising heat, completely cowed and surrounded by jeering sepoys. Past the bridge they went until a 'Bibigarh' or 'Lady's house' came into view. It had been built by a British officer for his native mistress, and was an attractive, if small residence. Two rooms, some twenty feet by ten, whitewashed and overlooking a small courtyard, were surrounded by a garden perfumed by rosebushes. In the centre of the courtyard was a well. The women and children were crowded into the rooms and guards set over them.

Joe followed, shadowed by the faithful Gopi. His mind felt torpid with the horror that he had witnessed, but he doggedly followed the women. He had the notion to try and see Charlotte again, though how that could be accomplished his befuddled brain could not work out. The milling mob reached the Bibigarh and as the women were hustled through the door from the garden, Joe thought he caught a glimpse of a fall of brown hair. Were his eyes deceiving him yet again? He rubbed them, but too late; the brown haired woman had vanished. He was determined to stay around and try and check again to see if Catherine was among the women, and even if not, try to help Charlotte.

For two days, Joe lurked near the Bibigarh trying to accomplish his purpose, continually urged by Gopi to 'come away', that the 'memsahib was not here' or 'could not possibly be here', until Joe lost his temper with him and told him to 'go away if he didn't want to help in the search'. Gopi sulked. Joe was in the grip of an obsession compounded by extreme fatigue after his wounding and shock. For two days, they squatted outside the Bibigarh listening to the sounds of women and children crying as they tried to make themselves comfortable as they could on coarse bamboo matting; crying as they were fed small handfuls of lentil porridge by sweepers; crying as all hope of rescue vanished.

Gopi decided to take matters into his own hands, and leaving Joe squatting by their small cooking fire and smoking a pungent bidi, he went off to find out what fate the Nana Sahib had in store for these bedraggled survivors of the Cawnpore Cantonment. Judicious questioning among the Nana Sahib's rissal convinced him that there was no immediate danger as the Nana Sahib intended to hold the captives as hostages against possible British reprisals. Satisfied, the bearer returned to Joe, rocking gently n his haunches and seemingly lost in dire thoughts of his own.

'Sah… Jhoti,' whispered Gopi urgently, 'the Nana Sahib will not harm these memsahibs as he plans to use them as hostages. And it is said that Havelock-Sahib is coming this way from Allahabad. He should be here very soon!'

Joe started at the name, and looked at Gopi in perplexity,

'Havelock? You mean 'Holy Havelock'? Good god! Then there is a chance for these memsahibs. But he needs to be told that there is no time to lose. The Nana Sahib may mean them no harm, but who knows what the badmashes may get up to; again! We must go, Gopi, and tell him; now!'

All depression and lethargy thrown off, Joe jumped to his feet and gathered up his small bundle. He muttered to himself as he worked,

'If you are in there Catherine, hold on; I'll be back as soon as I can with the entire British army if necessary!'

Before leaving Cawnpore, Joe and Gopi returned to the scene of the massacre. It looked eerie and desolate in the moonlight, and the smell of corruption hung like an evil miasma over the stretch of river by the Sati

Chowra Ghat. But Joe needed a scarlet uniform if he was to approach Havelock and be believed. They searched the beach area until they found a body about the right size and not too hacked about by tulwars. Joe noted that it had belonged to a lieutenant and wondered grimly what the penalty was for impersonating an officer? Rolling the scarlet jacket and white trousers into his bundle, he bade a silent farewell to the ghosts of the massacre.

Travelling by night to avoid the worst of the day's heat, Joe and Gopi reached the outskirts of Allahabad a few days later. They had passed the remains of the garrison of Fategarh two days earlier, unaware that the survivors of that unhappy place had been sent to join the ladies in the Bibigarh at Cawnpore! When they got near enough, Joe changed into the dead Lieutenant's uniform and prepared to enter the British camp. He had no fear that his charade would be discovered; many years of studying the quirks of the Kotepore officers had left him in no doubt that he could play a 'perfect officer'. Judicious questioning led him to Brigadier Havelock's headquarters, and he asked an aide if he could see the great man himself.

While he waited, he thought about 'Holy Havelock' as he had been unkindly dubbed. He knew that the man was in his sixties having been held back from promotion by lack of funds. He was said to be a fiery Baptist and a powerful believer in temperance, hence his soubriquet 'Holy', but Joe had also heard that he was a reasonable man.

'Come this way,' said the aide, interrupting his reverie, and led him into Havelock's presence. Joe drew himself up rigidly to attention,

'Lieutenant John Harvey reporting from Cawnpore, Sir!' Havelock eyed him somewhat suspiciously with piercing eyes under a shock of white hair. His sour expression was far from encouraging,

'Cawnpore? A messenger has not long reached us to say that it has fallen and that there are no survivors?'

'Yes Sir. It has fallen, but there are survivors. Some two hundred women and children are being held by the river.'

Havelock's eyes narrowed,

'How did you come by this information?'

Joe looked into the older man's face. The direct gaze from those piercing eyes compelled honesty,

'Sir. I am from Kotepore cantonment, under Colonel Deluce.' Havelock nodded in acknowledgement, 'the Colonel was using me to investigate the situation in the Raja's Palace as he didn't fully trust the Rajah of Kotepore.' Again a nod; the Brigadier had obviously studied all the local trouble spots! Joe continued, describing the evacuation of Kotepore and his won journey to Cawnpore in search of his wife.

'But Kotepore was overrun several weeks ago?'

'Yes Sir. I was badly wounded en route and only survived through the ministrations of a villager. I reached Cawnpore just before the evacuation and witnessed the massacre by the Ghat. But there were survivors. I don't know where the men were taken, but the women and children were taken off to a Bibigarh.'

Havelock considered this new information,

'Well Lieutenant. It seems we must act with all due despatch. But we must not be too precipitate otherwise we could make matters worse. Write a full report and leave it with my aide.'

Clearly dismissed, Joe saluted smartly and left the room. He could do no more for the present, so he went in search of Gopi who was sitting outside the headquarters in obvious fear of his life.

In spite of his reservations about Joe's credentials, he did indeed act with all despatch. He telegraphed Lawrence in Lucknow that Cawnpore had fallen and that he intended to move out with a rescue force. Within four days he did so.

With monsoon clouds rolling ominously overhead, Havelock bared his head and led his men in prayer for the success of their mission,

'We must avenge the dreadful fate of these British men and women,' he intoned. A slight man, no more than five feet five in his stockinged feet and clad in a plain frock-coat, he was not an inspiring figure. But he ruled his men with a rod of iron. There would be no malingering or falling out in his column. A soldier would have to prove he was close to death before he would be allowed any relaxation!

Led by a skirl of pipes from the 78th Highlanders and the Band of the Madras Fusiliers, they marched out bravely; a motley collection of some twelve hundred men, including a fair sprinkling of untried teenagers. Among them marched Lieutenant John Harvey and his bearer, the Lieutenant savouring the sweetness of real authority for the first time in his life, and praying that he would not disgrace his position, or be exposed as an imposter!

They marched as the monsoons broke about their ears, turning the road into a steaming quagmire. They waded knee deep through mud and slush, through a landscape resounding with the boom of monsoon frogs and the chittering of crickets. They passed the ruins of villages and dak-bungalows; they passed bodies, both brown and white skinned, half gnawed by wild pigs. The devastation around them created a feeling of foreboding among the marchers. For Joe there was an eerie sense of *déjà vu* aside from the landscape; the sense of desolation and death could have been Ireland in the height of the famine. He shuddered as they passed a group of huddled bodies in a field, where bloated vultures eyed them glassily as they passed by, before taking off languorous flaps of their great wings.

Then they reached Fatehpur where they came across a force of rebels under Tantia Topi; the Nana Sahib's military adviser. The rebels were deploying to attack a small force of irregulars under Major Renaud when Havelock's column reached the place. The battle was short and sharp, the Enfields proving their worth with their superior range and fire power. The rebels fled, leaving much treasure and Tantia Topi's personal elephant. The British were jubilant and a triumphant cheer rent the sodden air; the first stroke of vengeance had been delivered!

'D'you see that?' shouted an excited ensign, 'we showed those pandies!'

'Pandies?' asked Joe, perplexed. The Ensign eyed him curiously,

'Yes; that's what we call 'em; after the 'Pandey' who was the first to be hanged for insurrection; didn't you know?'

Joe muttered some reply and moved away, 'My God,' he thought, 'what a strange immortality!'

The British troops rested awhile at Fatehpur, and then prepared to move on to Cawnpore, anxious to rescue the women and children. They assembled at dawn and the Brigadier bared his head and led them in prayer. Joe looked about him amazed; he had heard the men complaining about 'Holy Havelock' and his 'Bible bashing', but there was not one man who had not doffed his shako and bowed his head; and many of them in fact knelt to listen to the prayer. Joe felt a thudding in his breast; this day might prove that Catherine was in that hell hole of the Bibigarh, or he had been on a wild goose chase all along. That she might have died in the entrenchment or at Sati Chowra Ghat he did not consider at all. Havelock's voice cut through his thoughts,

'By God's help we will save them or every man will die in the attempt.' A cheer went up at that; then they marched off into the pre-dawn darkness to where a force of ten thousand men with heavy guns awaited them.

They made a brisk pace and then stopped, gasping with fatigue and heat to break their fast at Maharajpur, just outside Cawnpore. Havelock passed the order through the ranks, wounded and baggage to be left where they were as they expected to engage the enemy very soon.' Men straightened up and donned their packs; checked over their Enfields, wincing as the sun scorched barrels seared their fingers.

The Highlanders bore it stoically, but in their woolen kilts and coats, more than one burly soldier slid out of ranks with sun-stroke. They were left where they fell.

The land was flat, an area of paddy fields punctuated by the odd clump of palms, so they could see a long way ahead. Thus they saw the enemy waiting for them some distance away, festive in the sunlight and playing English tunes discordantly. Incongruous among the jolly music, seven big guns pointed their snouts at the British as they faltered,

'Oh my God!' breathed the youthful ensign who had marched alongside Joe, treating him as his mentor as well as superior. Now his face had gone deathly white, and he desperately prayed in a loud whisper. Joe gave his elbow a reassuring squeeze,

'Steady now. Hold your head up and fix your eyes above them.' The ensign swallowed and tried to follow the advice; certainly his spine stiffened.

'Good lad,' said Joe bracingly, 'what's your name?'

'Richard, Sir; Richard Masefield.'

'Right Richard. Stay close to me.' Richard nodded fervently!

Havelock made his deployments swiftly before the men could become demoralised at the sight of the massed forces ranged against them, still beating out their frivolous tunes. The Madras Fusiliers were sent to the right and left in a flanking movement through some mango groves. A tiny squad of cavalry was sent forward to distract the enemy while the burly Highlanders were prepared to be sent forward, straight at the guns. On the edge of the infantry, his hand firmly under Richard Masefield's elbow, Joe waited tensely.

'Charge!' The sound of drums beat through the scream of case and grape shot, as the Indians sent withering fire into the solid line of Highlanders. In spite of marching twenty miles under a scorching sun, the line did not falter. Great holes appeared in the ranks but they went on. As they came within rifle range, their Enfields rang out. Still they went, and incredibly, the enemy began to break before the inexorable advance. The sight of the huge skirted British soldiers bearing down on them was too much, and they turned and fled.

Pipes skirled and drums beat out as impassioned Highlanders with revenge in their savage breasts, reached the Indians who were scrambling to escape. Bayonets flashed in close quarter fighting, and rifle butts beat on turbaned heads. Joe found himself in the thick of it, wielding his bayonet with the rest, memories of the massacre at the Ghat spurring him on. The fight was bloody and brutal, and soon appeared to be over with pandies streaming up the Great Trunk Road.

But Nana Sahib was made of sterner stuff, and rallied his men. Besides, he had a greater reason to fear a British victory; he knew what awaited the rescue force in the Bibigarh! Another great gun was drawn up and a milling crowd of Indians waited for the exhausted British, but they appeared to be diminished in number!

The Highlanders with Joe and Richard in their midst, stood with heaving chests surrounded by the debris of battle, and groaned aloud as they saw the renewed force ranged against them. They could see a gorgeously dressed figure spurring from point to point among them, and a growl went up when Joe informed them that it was the Nana Sahib himself. More than one Enfield rang out, but he was out of range.

The great gun bore round until it faced them directly. They felt too stupefied to move, but suddenly Havelock was among them, fearlessly spurring his horse in direct view of the Indian gunners,

'Come on men,' he shouted, 'another charge wins the day!' pressing alongside his father, young Harry Havelock waved his sword above his head and shouted to the soldiers ot follow him. He galloped forward, straight at the at the gun muzzle, which gaped at him like the door of hell. Forward they went in a cheering dash. The enemy was astounded.

The advance was littered with dead and dying but still they came on. The enemy broke once again and began to flee in earnest, led by the Nana Sahib, galloping up the road Bithur where he could hide in his palace.

As they neared the great gun, Joe felt his Richard falter in his stride, and without turning he called out,

'Come on lad. Nearly there!'

The battle round the gun was fierce and bloody, with the Highlanders determined to prevent the escape of as many as possible in their quest for vengeance. So it was a while before Joe looked for his youthful companion. He was nowhere to be seen. Retracing his steps, he moved through a welter of bodies, brown and white, until he found the boy soldier. He was resting the body of a huge Highlander, a great hole torn in his chest. He was still alive but breathing bubbles of blood. Joe knew that his lungs were destroyed and that it would not be long for the lad. Sorrowing for a young life coming to an end, he squatted by him and raised his head gently,

'Lieutenant,'

'Yes Richard?'

'Am I going to die?'

'I fear so.' The boy sighed and then coughed.

'We did it, didn't we?'

'We did that, lad.'

Strange. I've been so hot all day, but now I feel so cold.'

It was the last thing he said, and Joe, holding his hand, felt the life slowly fade away. The eyes flew open and his face, unmarked by battle or age, suddenly looked absurdly young. Joe closed Richard's eyes and laid the boy's hand down. For the first time in years, he felt the urge to pray, but found that he had forgotten the words. Stricken, he did not hear a horse snort nearby. Then a familiar, dour voice said,

'God bless the boy, he died bravely.' And 'Holy Havelock', with a tear in his eye, pressed his hand onto Joe's shoulder and moved away, weaving among the wounded and dying, muttering encouraging words where he could. Joe watched him go. He felt an enormous respect for the man; a respect that he reserved for very few among the British officers he had met, and then he understood why his men prayed with him.

Darkness was falling and their baggage was five miles away. Exhausted men slept where they could, praying that it would not rain in the night.

Somehow, Gopi found Joe, and proudly unwrapped a parcel of food which was promptly shared out. He had also brought Joe's bedroll, so compared to many, he passed a reasonably comfortable night. Given the choice, he would have preferred to press forward to Cawnpore, only two miles away, but he understood Havelock's reasons for waiting for the morning. Nevertheless, he fretted about the prisoners immured in the Bibigarh, conscious of the band of fanatics round the Nana Sahib, any one of them capable of exacting vengeance on the helpless. He could not know that it was already too late to worry, had been too late as they scored their first victory at Fatehpur. It was as well that they didn't know the horror that awaited them and were able to sleep the sleep of exhaustion. They would not sleep as well again!

They roused themselves cheerfully next morning. The picquets reported no alarms in the night and the atmosphere was lighthearted. They were convinced that they would find the Bibigarh with all guards fled and the women ready to throw themselves on the necks of their rescuers. To a man they volunteered to be the first to enter Cawnpore. Havelock, as sour faced as ever was having no such levity. He detailed Captain Henry Ayton to lead the advance force of one hundred men of the 84th Foot. They cheered at being chosen, and prepared to move out. Havelock beckoned to Joe,

'Lieutenant Harvey.'

'Sir?'

'Go with Captain Ayton as you know where the Bibigarh is situated. Captain Ayton.'

'Sir!'

'Watch out for rebels. We have reports of Indians streaming out of Cawnpore, but don't take any chances. There may well be fanatics among them. And Captain, don't risk the ladies and the little ones; they have suffered enough.'

'Yes Sir. Permission to move out.'

'Permission granted.'

They marched into Cawnpore, hot and dusty, tired and footsore, but triumphant for all that, and heads were held high. They marched along the canal until the Ganges came into view. Away to the right but out of sight was the Sati Chowra Ghat, bit they were not thinking about that. Joe led the way, his heart beating fast, seized by a sudden premonition of doom. He shivered; was it simply the small monsoon cloud passing in front of the sun? Turning left before they reached the bridge they saw the Bibigarh ahead of them.

An eerie silence hung over the pretty whitewashed building. As they drew nearer they caught a whiff of a stench; an evil miasma that was almost tangible reached out to them. Joe stood stock still. Memory heaved and strained inside his head; this same smell from the mists of time had come from a simple clod cottage in Clonarty, and the world spun around but then steadied again.

'Lieutenant Harvey! What is it man?'

'Don't go in there. For God's sake, don't go in!' But it was too late. A soldier came out retching. He leaned over a rose bush and heaved and strained as though he would never stop. It was the only sound. Not a bird called; not a pi-dog barked; even the crows were silent. A tough old sergeant pushed past and disappeared inside, followed by others unable to contain their curiosity any longer. In they went and soon reappeared with the same white faces and retching stomachs. Finally, Joe prepared himself for the horror of the Bibigarh. He had to know!

The first thing he saw was bloody handprints all around the white washed walls; small ones low down, larger ones higher up, Congealed blood lay inches think. Looking up, he saw a child's body swinging from a meat hook, flanked by two women lashed to two pillars, their throats cut. His bemused mind took in further details, small toys, frilly parasols all lay in tumbled abandon on the floor. Several severed limbs lay about, and the worst horror of all, a pair of infant shoes, their owner's feet still in them. It was then that Joe finally broke, and he retreated to the outside where he heaved and gulped in the tainted air.

Reason began to return and he wondered at the very small number of bodies he had seen. There was blood enough for the two hundred that had come here, but where their bodies? Wandering dazedly through the garden, noting tulwar slashes on the trees as though victims had dodged behind them to escape. Then he heard a shout from the courtyard. A group of men were leaning over the well in the centre, openly crying. The well was full to the brim with the dismembered bodies of the two hundred women and children who had survived the siege; the horror of Sati Chowra Ghat only to face a worse horror at the Bibigarh.

Later they learned that five men with razor sharp tulwars had done it all.

Chapter 13

Catherine lay on her sweaty pallet, her body wracked with pain. How long had the torment gone on? She could not remember. Voices whispered at her and spoke encouraging words, but she was too exhausted to take them in. Her body had been wasted by long weeks of poor food, the growing infant taking more than its share; growing big and boisterous as she grew weak and wan. Now it was impatient to be born, and she had tried so hard to help it; but now she could do no more. She could hear voices again, whispering; one of them sounded like Pattie,

'Must fetch the doctor.......won't last.......too weak.......'

'Pattie,' she called weakly.

'I'm here Cathy dear. Take my hand; it won't be long now.'

'Pattie; you'll look after my baby, won't you? I don't know where you'll find milk, but you must…must!' The soft voice rose, strident now as the pain seized her again, drowning her mind in a flood of agony, throwing her gasping on the shores of delirium. The spasm passed, and the voice was weaker now,

'Pattie; what day is it?'

'It's 25th September, Cathy love.'

'Mm.'

'The relief force is here; you must hold on, d'you hear me Catherine; the relief force…' But Catherine had lapsed into unconsciousness again. The two women, Pattie Day and Cristobal Lewis, looked at each other with anguish. She could not last much longer, as her weakened body was slowly ceasing its efforts. Pattie said,

'I'll try once more to get the doctor. They can't refuse, surely?' Cristabel shrugged,

'It's not their fault; they're taken up with relief; and wounded are pouring in all the time and the hospital is overflowing.' Pattie nodded; it was all so true. Three times they had begged Dr. Darby to come, but each time he had looked up, his face haggard with exhaustion, and promised to come as soon as he could, but that nature would take its course anyhow.

For once it was quiet in the subterranean room of the Residency. Most of the inmates had ventured outside to watch the relief column arrive, in spite of bullets whizzing about and the continual clamour. Only a few of the women were resting inside, especially those with small children, fearful of the dangers still lurking outside. It would be calamitous indeed to lose a child after enduring so much for so long!

One woman rose and came to see how Catherine was getting on. She looked with compassion at the young woman's shadowed eyelids and sunken cheeks,

'She'll not last the hour,' she stated, her voice resonant with doom. Pattie turned on her fiercely,

'Don't say that. The baby's just a bit too big for her, that's all!' The woman shrugged and went on her way. Pattie followed her outside to try once more to fetch the doctor without any great hope of success. As she emerged blinking into the bright daylight, a great cheer went up; the first of the relief columns was in sight.

In the basement, Catherine lay in a state of semi-consciousness. She no longer felt any pain; rather, she felt strangely at peace with the world. She was aware that Pattie had gone, but Cristabel was holding her hand. Dear Cristabel. They had got to know her well since they had moved into the basement, and she had been a staunch friend from the first. David Lewis, her husband, was a gunner on the Gubbins battery, and was a regular visitor to see them with gifts of sugar and tea, and even occasionally, a little brandy. All of these gifts were shared out by Cristabel as she knew that Catherine did not have her husband to support her, and Pattie's husband, as a civilian, did not come by these little treats. She smiled; it was these little things that had kept them all going, but now her resilience had gone, and she would join Joe, wherever he was. She frowned to herself; how long had they been besieged? Pattie had said it was 25th September; dear God, it was nigh on three months! So long? They had expected to be out and 'back to normal' in next to no time. Her drifting thoughts swam back to the day when Chris had limped back through the gate from the chaos of the Battle of Chinhut.

Chris groaned as the pain in his leg grew in intensity. His anxious nurses waited helplessly for the doctor to come, brushing away the flies from the gaping wound as best they could. The hospital, set up in the Banqueting Hall was full of men, wounded and dying, and their screams echoed under the high ceilings. There were cries of 'water' on all sides, and as they waited, Catherine and Pattie took it in turns to offer a dipper to anyone in dire extremity. The doctor had then appeared and took them to task for their efforts,

'Don't give them anything until we know what has to be done; you could kill a man with a stomach wound! Catherine's eyes filled with tears at the brusque tone, but Pattie was not so easily cowed,

'They could die anyway while they waited, so what harm would a drop of water do?' The two stood glaring at each other over Chris' body until a groan from him reminded them both of the reason for the doctor's presence. Muttering all the while about 'damned interfering females,' Dr. Darby prodded and probed in the gaping hole making Chris' eyes almost start from his head until he fainted clean away. Darby grunted with satisfaction as he lost consciousness, and moving with sure movements, extracted a lead bullet a moment later, which he dropped into Pattie's nerveless hand,

'Take that; I've no doubt he'll want it for a memento. Bind up his wound with a strip of your petticoat and then get out of here. A hospital's no place for women; especially in her condition,' jerking his head at Catherine, who had not uttered a word throughout the proceedings. He strode away to attend to his next patient, followed by a grinning orderly who winked at them as he passed.

Pattie was livid at the callous treatment they had had, especially Chris, and she grumbled as she bound up the wound tenderly as instructed with her sacrificed petticoat. However, they did not leave for several hours, as Pattie held Chris' flaccid hand, willing him back to consciousness, and Catherine did not want to return to the gloomy basement alone.

They returned to the hospital the next day, and the next, to be greeted with sour looks from Darby, but he didn't send them away. During the course of a week they had witnessed the worst there was to see in a hospital, and thought they were inured to all the horror. During that time several amputations had been carried out without the aid of chloroform to dull the pain. The victim was given a quantity of liquor until he reached a state of maudlin contentment, when four or five orderlies would throw themselves on the hapless patient while the doctor made the first incision. It was usually over before the echo of the first scream had died away among the iron bedsteads, crammed into every available space. The patient usually died, either from shock or from the gangrene that was prevalent in the insanitary conditions.

Chris' wound had seemed to heal, and then one day they arrived to find him running a high fever; the wound had started to fester. Catherine was ministering to a young soldier several beds away when Darby arrived to examine Chris, but soon a full scale argument could be heard throughout the lofty room,

'You will not remove his leg,' shouted Pattie.

'Young woman. Any fool can see the leg is infected. If I do not remove it, he will die,'

'If you do remove it, he will surely die!'

Two pairs of eyes glared at each other over Chris' flushed body, their tempers matching his heat. The entire room seemed to be holding its collective breath while several grinning orderlies had paused in their duties and patients forgot their own pain in the excitement. It was Dr. Darby who finally broke,

'Have it your own way, you ignorant female,' he shouted, 'if he dies, it is on your head!' And with that he marched away, yelling at an orderly to 'jump to it if he didn't want to be put on a charge.' A little Martiniere schoolboy who had been pulling the punkah nearly jumped out of his skin as the steaming doctor went by, and pulled the punkah so vigorously that the foetid air actually moved a little!

One of the orderlies came over the now trembling Pattie, who seemed about to burst into tears. Catherine had come over to comfort her, to no avail.

'Here,' said the orderly, thrusting a bottle of rum at her, 'use this.'

'But,' protested Pattie, 'how can he drink this, he's unconscious?'

'It's not for drinking. Wash the wound with it. I've seen it work before; it's worth a try, eh?'

'It was certainly was worth a try,' observed Pattie, a week and a half later, 'and it did work!' She gazed fondly at her husband, whose fever was quite gone and the flaming redness round the wound had subsided, He was on the road to recovery.

'What worked?' asked Chris, puzzled. Pattie smiled again,

'Just a drop of rum from a friendly orderly did more for you than that sour puss of a doctor; who was all ready to remove your leg!' It was the first time that Chris was aware of this, and he questioned Pattie further, so relieved that she had fought for him.

She told him how his life hung in the balance, as every day she washed the wound with rum, and bound it with her rapidly disappearing petticoat. But his fever had mounted and the flesh round the wound puffed up round the hole. But one day when she changed his dressing, she noticed that the swelling seemed to be subsiding, and his temperature dropping. Over a week from the crisis, Dr. Darby had grudgingly pronounced that the infection was on the mend. But he refused then, or ever, to admit that he had been wrong, but over the weeks of the siege, Pattie and Catherine saw him perform miracles among the sick and wounded with little medicaments at his disposal, and formed a grudging respect for the man.

In between their sessions at the hospital, the friends had developed some sort of routine for themselves in the basement. They had met another young woman, Cristabel Lewis, who seemed to be a fellow spirit, and between themselves existed in reasonable heart. Every day, they were issued with basic rations that were adequate, though hardly exciting; gun bullock meat that was extremely tough, and a handful of gram, lentils or rice. They cooked flour into chapattis on primitive cooking fires made from bricks stacked together, coughing as the smoke wreathed around them, before making its own way out of the dungeon.

Cristabel's husband came down every day and kept them informed of the happenings in the Residency, at the same time pressing on them small packets of spices to flavour the stringy meat stews, or some tea in a screw of paper. Outside there was a ceaseless bombardment, as if the pandies were determined to defeat them by wearing away at their nerves. The bombardments had claimed an early victim, and one they were all most reluctant to lose; Sir Henry Lawrence himself. David Lewis told the three of them about it with tears in his eyes as they all sipped at their weak tea.

'He'd been resting on the upper floor of the Residency, see, while his staff prepared to move to the lower floors the very next morning, as they did think it might be unsafe! They were right, by God! A shell came right through the window and burst right by him. They moved him to Dr.Peyrer's verandah at the hospital, but there was nothing to be done. You can hear his screams all over the compound. You are better off down here at the moment, believe me!'

Two days later, David told them that it was all over, and the great man was at peace. The whole entrenchment mourned. More than anything else, the man had inspired hope; how would they manage without him?

There was much speculation on a successor. David considered that Gubbins would wrest the job from all comers. But none of them could forget that it was Gubbins who had virtually forced Lawrence to move against the pandies at Chinhut with such disastrous consequences. And many suspected him of hoarding the best of the food in his house, a fact borne out by David's frequent gifts. But his swarthy Welsh face would break into a grin and he would mutter,

'I won't hear a word said against him!'

But finally they heard that Major Banks was named as successor by Sir Lawrence before he died to be in charge of civilians, with the stalwart Colonel Jack Inglis in charge of the military. The entrenchment breathed a collective sigh of relief.

All of these stirring happenings helped Pattie bear the uncertainty over Chris' health, but as he slowly mended, she was able to pass on tidbits of gossip that David had brought to them. It all helped to endure the discomforts of daily life.

The heat slowly increased until they were forced to lie gasping during the midday hours, praying for the onset of the monsoons. The cavernous basement was poorly ventilated and almost unbearable by noon. The three young women preferred to risk a pandey shell rather than shelter down in the 'hole' as they came to call it.

Then the monsoon rains broke in earnest, turning the compound into a quagmire. From being hot and dry, now they were hot and wet. They never felt completely dry, their clothes steaming on their backs as they moved lethargically about. Anything put down and left for a while became mildewed, and the floors and walls of the 'hole' constantly wept with moisture.

Then there was the smell. Early in the siege, many animals had been slaughtered as they couldn't be fed, and their bodies hastily buried in the unyielding iron-hard ground. Those that couldn't be buried were flung over the wall near the slaughterhouse, where they slowly putrefied. The rains simply made matters worse by washing out shallow graves, exposing bodies, both animal and human. The graveyard itself was a vulnerable place for enemy fire, and a large grave was hurriedly dug every night to receive the day's quota of unfortunate victims.

And they died. All over the compound they died, men, women and children. They died of bullet wounds, in spite of the barricaded windows; they died of wounds turned gangrenous in the unsavoury and insanitary hospital; they died of dysentery and cholera.

Those that didn't die were plagued by flies; great black flies that swarmed in clouds around them; settling on their food and crawling into their eyes and mouths. They were plagued by enormous pursy spiders that inhabited every room. They were plagued by the constant throbbing noise of monsoon toads that intruded above the roar of guns. They were plagued by prickly heat and boils and agues from being constantly damp. But most of them endured with true British stoicism.

Chris was finally strong enough to leave the hospital, hopping about on a crutch fashioned by a carpenter found by David Lewis.

'How does he do it?' marveled Pattie, 'I'm sure if I asked him for a piano to while away the hours, he would find one; and claim that 'he just came across it'!' Catherine grinned at her,

'But Pattie, you can't play the piano!'

When he was strong enough, David carried Chris off to the Gubbins Battery as he couldn't stay in the basement which was solely for women and children, particularly at night. The Battery was in constant action and Pattie fretted that her husband would yet be snatched from her. But every able bodied man was involved in defence, so there was no help for it.

Then a new and frightening method of warfare began; mining! It was first discovered by a woman in Catherine and Patties' section of the basement. It was late evening and the place seething with activity as the residents prepared for the night. One woman had been dozing, her head pressed against the wall, when she suddenly sat bolt upright. Shouting to those around her for quiet, she pressed her ear to the wall. The crowd of women held their breath as she listened, holding gentle hands over children's mouths to keep them quiet for a moment. The woman turned to her audience, and simply stated,

'Them's digging out there!' She rushed from the room and returned soon after dragging some soldiers behind her. They too pressed their ears to the wall and nodded at each other. Then, in the insufferable manner of men, they left without explanation. It was David who supplied the answer the very next day, saying briefly,

'Mining!'

From then on, the whole compound was on constant alert against tunneling. Ex-miners from the mines of Cornwall were pressed into counter-tunneling in a desperate effort to prevent a breach occurring. In all the weeks of effort on the part of the rebel tunnellers, they never managed an effective breach, though not for want of trying! There were some minor breaches, the first coming as a shock, as they had all been enjoying a sudden lull in the constant bombardment, and were making the most of. The absence of noise was wonderful after so long, and the basement emptied as its occupants swarmed outside.

But their joy was short lived. A devastating blast rent the air, followed by shrieks of 'Din! Din!' as unseen pandies began to charge through a pall of yellow smoke that rolled around the compound. Women seized their children and rushed for shelter while men scrambled to arms.

For several hours the din continued unabated, batteries on both sides belching round shot at each other. Finally it was over around four in the afternoon and the dust and smoke began to disperse. No-one moved for a while, unable to believe it was all over, but then they tentatively emerged. Pattie was one of the first out, peering anxiously about for a sight of

Chris. Cristabel followed close behind and then Catherine. As reached the entrance of the Residency she felt the baby kick sturdily. She held her stomach protectively, a surge of maternal feeling coursing through her body,

'Steady baby,' she laughed, 'you nearly had me over!' The trio picked their way over rubble and debris. Catherine grabbed her friends by the arm and pointed,

'Look!'

'What is it?' asked Pattie, as Catherine pointed urgently, 'there's nothing there!'

'I know,' whispered Catherine, 'that was where Sue Appleton's house was!'

Towards the end of July, a message was received that Cawnpore had been retaken. Their delight was short lived as they learned that the entire garrison had indeed been slaughtered, and the full horror of the Bibigarh became known. There was a brief wave of drunkenness among men who had had themselves under iron control until now. Pattie and Catherine grieved afresh for their friend Charlotte when they knew the full tragedy of her end, recalling happier days from their shared girlhood adventures. Cristabel wept with them.

'Oh God,' said Pattie, 'and to think we were talking of picnics. Picnics, for goodness sake!'

August dragged on and the rain continued. But when it didn't rain it was hot and humid; and then their rations were cut. They had been adequate, just; tedious but adequate. Tobacco ran out, so the men suffered, all reminisced sadly about the sight and smell of freshly baked white bread! The coarse whole meal flour that they used for chapattis caused irritation of the bowel and constant diarrhoea. That in turn caused problems with the lack of sweepers whose unenviable task had been to clear away the quaintly named 'night soil.' Now they had they do it for themselves!

Through it all, Catherine's pregnancy advanced. That far off day when she had first felt the butterfly fluttering inside her, which had precipitated her flight to see Pattie, and so to this hell hole, seemed a lifetime ago. Her belly was now swollen and rounded and the baby kicked with a vigour that made the other mothers in the 'hole' exclaim that she was surely carrying a brand new soldier,

'Not if I have anything to do with it,' said Catherine indignantly!

While she and Pattie had stayed with Sue Appleton, Catherine had taken the opportunity to fashion some comfortable gowns. In the absence of crinoline hoops, her sprigged muslin gowns had hung somewhat shapelessly, so she had cut out panels from three of them, and inset a length from another. As she had studied herself in the mirror of Sue's tiny spare bedroom she had been pleased with the effect; the front of the gown falling straight from under the bust, allowing plenty of fullness for the growing infant.

'Mm,' Pattie had commented, 'you'll start a fashion among the less than slim among us!' and the pair had giggled together, thinking of their rotund hostess.

The panels had been a great success, though the three dresses were now looking very shabby with constant washing, but at least they were comfortable and reasonably cool. During her daily visits to the hospital, which she continued even after Chris had been discharged; she thought that her condition was not obvious at first. Later, she had thought to stop her visits for fear of embarrassing herself or the patients, but she found that they liked to talk to her about their own families. Soldiers would talk of 'when the missus was expecting a nipper' with tears in their eyes. After the dire news from Cawnpore, where many of the wives had lived, she avoided them for a while for fear that her condition might invoke sad memories, but they were soon asking Pattie where she had got to.

'It helps them talk about their loss, you see,' said Pattie gently. Catherine nodded, and returned to her daily visits; in fact these were the only thing that made the noise and squalor filled existence bearable.

When the rations were cut, Catherine began to fear for her baby's life for the first time. Up to that point, she had dutifully swallowed the nauseous meals they had concocted between them for the sake of the baby. But now, there was simply not enough to sustain her let alone a growing infant. She had anxiously questioned Dr. Darby, by now a firm friend and admirer of the stoical young woman,

'Ah lassie,' he had replied sympathetically, 'don't you worry about the baby, it will take all it needs, never fear. It is you who will suffer, you'll see!' Catherine thanked him, mindful that Dr. Darby's own wife had been pregnant when he had left her in Cawnpore.

But he was right, and as she ate less, Catherine's body became thinner almost by the day. Her arms and legs, previously rounded, were now stick-like, and her cheeks fell in. Her belly protruded almost grotesquely from the bony frame. Strangely, she did not seem to worry about herself once she was assured of her baby's health. In vain did Pattie try to persuade her to take a larger share of their rations.

'It's all right Pattie. The baby's fine, you see. I know you'll look after him for me.' Pattie grew exasperated, but could not shake the almost ethereal calm her friend had developed.

'Don't worry,' said the all knowing David Lewis, 'It's quite normal in late pregnancy for a woman to turn inwards like that. It's nature's way of protecting the new born.' His wife looked at him in amazement as they were as yet childless, and demanded,

'And how do you know so much about it?'

'And aren't I the eldest of thirteen!'

Catherine let the talk flow over her, for she was convinced by now that Joe must be dead, and she was going to join him as soon as the baby was born. In the night, with the distant boom of pandey gunfire barely intruding in the subterranean room, she would lie awake feeling the baby moving within her. Around her were the grunts and snores of sleeping women and the fretful wails of hungry children, but she would wrap her arms round her belly and talk to the child inside her, and tell him all about his father. She was convinced that she carried a boy-child who would look just like his father, so she dreamed of the child's features as he grew through life.

'And such a handsome father,' she whispered into the darkness, 'with such bonny eyes, like the crystal blue of the sky in the middle of an Indian winter; and so tall and strong, but oh so gentle.'

He surety of Joe's death had come slowly to Catherine, but after so long, she could not believe any more that he had survived. Now it was a relief to accept rather than brood on it any more. And Pattie's words in the Appleton bungalow had taken root after all; she was carrying the only reminder of Joe that would ever be.

At the end of August, a message finally arrived from Havelock.

'I can only say,' it stated, *'do not negotiate, but rather perish sword in hand.'* The message also vowed that he would be with them within twenty or twenty five days.

The defenders were stunned. They had been looking out for their rescuers since the beginning of August, scanning the skies nightly for signal rockets. Hope turned to despair; another three weeks on top of the two months they had already endured; sturdy soldiers bowed over their guns and wept.

That evening, David and Chris visited the women in the 'hole'. For the first time since she had met him, Catherine saw David without a smile on his face, his dark Celtic features brooding and sombre as he said,

'I doubt there'll be enough food to last another month.

'But the message said twenty days,' protested Pattie,

'He was saying that since he retook Cawnpore.' Pattie was silenced. The gathering that evening was sunk in gloom until a woman, known for her Presbyterian leanings, raised her voice in a rousing hymn. Soon the stirring words of 'Onward Christian Soldiers' reverberated round the ceiling of the Residency basement.

Next day, rations were cut again. In Cawnpore, Colonel Neill, who had been left in charge by Havelock, was wreaking terrible revenge on any captured Indians, while Havelock himself was on his way to them. He was supposed to be close, but with the noise of the pandey guns, it was difficult to tell if it was so. And Lucknow was still surrounded and completely cut off. They suffered yet another major assault, their fourth, and somehow withstood it.

The hospital again filled to overflowing, though Catherine no longer visited or tried to help. She had been strictly forbidden by Dr. Darby, who told her sternly,

'I haven't time to stop an amputation to help you give birth, so go and don't come back!' Catherine pouted at the brusque words, but in truth she was glad to be out of there. She was sick of the smell of gangrene and ordure, of sweat and of blood and vomit. She had once thought of herself as a lady, cut off from such unpleasantness. Well, she had endured them for long enough and the men who looked forward to her visits would have to make do with Pattie, who was much better at it anyway as she was less emotional and more practical. She would miss the little Martiniere school boys who lived in the hospital, and who were put to good use as punkah wallahs and miniature bearers. She would miss their peaked little faces, but nothing else!

Within a day of her departure, she had her first visitor in the basement. Her particular favourite among the Martinieres, a cheerful ten year old called Hal, penetrated the gloom and sat with her for an hour passing on all the news from the hospital. She thanked him and gave him a precious sugar coated biscuit that David had presented her with the evening before. The boy's eyes lit up at the sight, but he carefully broke it in three equal pieces before eating one portion, the other two being for 'me friends, miss.' He came every day after that, often with two or three others in tow.

Then their spirits were cheered by the news that Delhi had been retaken, and the King who had been a figure head for thousands of disaffected sepoys was a prisoner of the British; his sons summarily executed. And Havelock was definitely close; some said he was at Alambagh, the palace and pleasure gardens of the kings of Oudh some way to the south of them. Wiseacres shook their heads and said the best way forward was to cross the river and skirt the enemy entrenchments.

The besieged almost held their breath with excitement as they could hear the sound of gunfire from the south on the evening of 24th September. The pandies were unaccustomedly quiet, and Chris and David dragged their wives away to take a look from the roof of the hospital, vowing that they would see friendly fire for once. They tried to persuade Catherine to go with them, but she shook her head. She had felt strange all day; restless yet lethargic. Her eyes were circled by purple shadows, and her long brown hair hung lank and oily; she had not bothered to roll it up that morning. Pattie peered at her,

'Are you all right, dear?' Catherine gave a wan smile,

'Of course, I'm just very tired. This child,' patting her stomach, 'doesn't give me much sleep at night. I'll rest a while. You go and tell me about it when you get back.' Pattie gave her a quick hug and hurried out with Chris, following the laughing Lewis's up the stone stairs. They scrambled up to the roof of the hospital, to find it crowded with like minded people. An officer came up and warned them that there were still enemy guns in action and to get the women below. He was ignored.

To the south, flashes of light told of action at the Alambagh and a cheer went up. Chris and David whirled their wives around feverishly, earning them a protest of 'take care or they'll be off the roof'! Everywhere there were people hugging each other and shedding tears of relief.

After an hour or so, Pattie returned to Catherine, to find her friend lying on her pallet, her face screwed up with pain.

'Is it the baby,' whispered Pattie.

'Yes I think so.'

'When did it start?'

'Soon after you went. I thought I had a backache and tried to sit comfortably, but then I had a strange feeling across here,' and she rubbed her swollen abdomen.' Pattie nodded confidently, but inside she was full of anxiety. She had had no experience of childbirth and she didn't like the look of Catherine's peaked, white face. Well they would just have to do the best they could. Dipping a piece of muslin in a chatti of water, she wiped Catherine's face, earning a grateful smile.

The others returned then, laughing as they clattered down the stairs. When Chris and David learned what was happening, they backed away hurriedly with promises to send messages of any progress on the relief.

Pattie asked Chris to get a message to Dr. Darby and try to get him to come and check on their friend; he nodded agreement before clattering back up the stairs with David, excitedly discussing the relief, and how long it should take them to arrive. They delivered their message to the hospital and then returned to the roof to share a long hoarded cheroot and await developments.

All that night, Catherine laboured. Pattie and Cristabel rigged up a crude screen to give her some privacy, but so many of the women came to offer unsolicited advice, that in the end they removed it. Towards dawn, the waters broke and one amateur midwife assured them that it wouldn't be long now. There was still no sign of Dr. Darby, though Cristabel and Pattie had gone in turn to the hospital. The doctor had told them tersely that he had too many wounded to attend to, and the baby would have to birth itself 'as they have always done!'

'But she is so weak,' pleaded Pattie, who still had not quite forgiven him for wanting to remove Chris' leg so their relationship was somewhat prickly, but she did detect some sympathy in the haggard face.

'I will come when I can, but….' And he waved his hand helplessly over the iron bedsteads crammed together in the foetid room. Pattie nodded and turned away, defeated.

Morning turned into afternoon and Catherine seemed to be sinking into a coma. She no longer had the strength to push, and it began to look as if the baby would die with her. One woman offered the advice of 'a good pinch of pepper; one good squeeze and it would all be over!' Pattie looked at her, bleary eyed; it was crazy enough to work, but where would they find pepper? She rubbed her eyes and told Cristabel that she must get some air. Cristabel nodded but suggested that she shouldn't be away too long. Heartsick, Pattie stumbled up the stairs to a noise filled exterior. It seemed that the world and its neighbour milled around the compound in total disregard of stray bullets whizzing around. She saw Chris on the hospital roof and waved to him; he hurried down to her,

'They're crazy, Havelock's men; they're coming through the streets, by God! Have you heard anything like it? There's fire pouring at them from houses on either side and they're being cut to ribbons. Come and see!'

Pattie mutely followed him onto the roof and gazed at the scene which was just as Chris had described it. Scarlet jacketed figures could be seen running through the narrow streets, firing as they went. As she watched she saw three, no four drop in their tracks. She just couldn't take it in. The relief force was nearly with them and her friend, her best friend was dying, and there was nothing she could do about it. She began to cry hopelessly, helplessly; great gulping sobs wracking her emaciated frame. Chris looked at her, startled, not understanding such grief in the midst of the prevailing excitement; then he remembered and gathered her into his arms,

'Has she…er….gone?' Pattie shook her head numbly, and choked out,

'Not yet, but it cannot be long.'

'Poor little Catherine. So near!' They stood quietly together and watched the soldiers nearing the gate. The defenders suddenly realised that the Baillie Guard was still tight shut against incursion, and rushed to remove the barricades. Even as they frantically laboured, a horse appeared by the arch of the gate, and scrambled over the wall to resounding cheers.

'Good God!' shouted Chris, 'will you look at that!'

The leading horse was followed by others scrambling anyhow over the remnants of the wall, while gangs of men clawed at the gate trying to shift sandbags, rubble, baulks of timber, bits of furniture; all that had been piled against it over the past three months. The horsemen were followed in turn by the Highlanders, who scrambled over the wall with wild whoops, loosing off their guns as they came. The excitement around the gate reached fever pitch as the rescuers were embraces by the besieged and whirled about in a frenzy of gratitude.

Pattie felt totally divorced from the prevailing atmosphere of carnival, and stirred in the circle of Chris' arms. She could feel his limbs trembling with barely concealed excitement, and knew that he longed to join the milling throng below.

'I'll go back and relieve Cristabel,' she said quietly. Chris looked down into her tear streaked face and kissed her tenderly, wiping away the tears with gentle thumbs. He helped her down from the roof and watched her vanish into the Residency entrance before he hurried off to the Baillie Guard Gate. He arrived at a run and let out an involuntary cheer at the sight of the Highlanders pouring over the ever increasing gap in the wall. One burly jock grinned at him as her passed by.

Chris watched them for a while, noting the miscellany of uniforms, Havelock's original force having been swollen by numerous reinforcements. As he stood in a fever of excitement, he noticed one soldier wearily traversing the wall followed by a diminutive bearer. There was something vaguely familiar about both the soldier and the bearer. The light was beginning to fade, but at last he had it; he was looking at Joe Harrington and his bearer Gopi!

'Joe!' The yell quivered in the evening air, and in spite of the prevailing noise, several bystanders looked up startled. It also had the desired effect and the weary soldier peered in his direction.

'Over here, Joe. By God it's good to see you. Oh man, we thought you were dead!' By this time Joe was by his side and pumping Chris' hand vigorously. Then he seized his arms fiercely, croaked out,

'Chris; is she here; Catherine, is she here?' And he shook Chris roughly.

'Hey take it easy Joe. Yes she is here….my God!' Chris' face turned white and he stared at Joe.

'What is it? You say she's here, so what is the matter?'

'I'm sorry Joe. It's the baby; she grew so weak. Pattie's with her; she doesn't think…..'

'Take me to her; now!' Chris did not argue just turned and made for the Residency. Joe followed on his heels, just pausing long enough to thrust his rifle and pack at a bemused Gopi. As he followed Chris, Joe saw, but did not take in the battle scarred Residency that he had known so well. The elegant flower beds and trees all gone, and everywhere buildings were pockmarked and walls collapsed in a welter of rubble. The Residency was hardly even recognizable so devastated was the structure. But Joe saw none of it as his gaze was fixed on Chris' back. Down the stone stairs they went, penetrating the gloomy basement, almost empty but for a small group of people on the far side.

Catherine lay on a rude pallet, her swollen belly mounding grotesquely. On either side of her knelt Pattie and Cristabel, heads bowed as if in prayer. Joe heard Chris mutter,

'Oh no; I think we're too late!'

'Cath…er…ine!' The despairing cry rang round the cavernous room and the kneeling figures looked up, shocked. The supine form at their knees gave a shudder. With a few strides, Joe reached Catherine's side, nearly knocking Cristabel over in his haste; she hardly seemed to notice. He gathered his wife to his chest, rocking her in a paroxysm of grief. The onlookers averted their gaze from so much raw emotion, and Pattie got up and crossed to Chris' side. Cristabel nodded briefly to them and slipped away to find David, feeling distinctly unneeded.

Catherine's eyes fluttered open and she found herself looking into her husband's anguished ones, their bright blue dimmed by grief.

'Joe,' she whispered with a tremulous smile, 'have I died? I knew I would see you then.'

'No my love. You haven't died, and I am here now, and you are not going to die. Come acushla; one more try and the baby will be born. Do this for me.' Pattie turned at that and stretched out her hand in supplication.

'Ah Joe; she's had enough. It's been so long and she's so weak!'

Joe turned to her with a glare,

'Leave be; this babe must be born or she will surely die.' Pattie stepped back, startled by his ferocity; but then looked on in amazement as the girl on the pallet gave a compulsive heave. Her belly tautened, and Catherine strained, her face screwed up with the effort,

'Quickly now,' hissed Joe to Pattie, and she fell to her knees to see the head start to emerge Chris went away quietly, unnoticed by the trio.

'Easy now,' softly to Catherine, 'wait for the next pain and don't fight it when it comes. Ah; now!'

The baby slid into Pattie's nervous grasp and lay in a welter of birth blood.

'Wipe its mouth,' instructed Joe, and Pattie complied. She did not stop to think that she should be in charge of the birthing. Joe seemed to know exactly what he was doing. As Pattie dealt with the baby, wrapping it in a square of muslin that had been prepared for the task some time before, Joe hugged his wife and soothed her perspiring brow; murmuring love words in Urdu. She did not even have the strength to put her hand up to his face, but smiled gently at him at the miracle of his arrival at such a moment. Finally she whispered,

'Is our son alright?' Joe glanced up startled; he had not even thought to look! He heard Pattie chuckle,

'You have a daughter, and she is beautiful.' She handed the small bundle to Joe, who seemed perfectly capable of handling such a delicate package. Joe held the wrapped infant so that Catherine could see her just by turning her head. She was beautiful, with the clear skin and perfect features of the full term baby. As the three of them watched her, she opened her mouth and gave a lusty yell, and Joe soothed her with Urdu endearments, murmuring 'dil ki aziz' or 'heart's sweetness'. Catherine's eyes closed and she fell asleep to the sound of her husband saying,

'Why little one, you are just like a flower about to open, my little rosebud.'

But Catherine's last thought before she faded into the first real sleep she had had for many weeks, was,

'But I did so want a son!'

Pattie moved Joe so that she could settle Catherine more comfortably and clean her up somewhat. Strangely she felt no awkwardness in his presence as she carried out such intimate tasks. They had all been through so much that the need for modesty seemed unimportant, even trivial. After all, Joe was her husband and had brought her through the birth when she had been unable to. Completing her tasks, she patted the baby's cheek, hugged Joe carefully and left him to enjoy his wife and daughter in perfect peace. There was no-one in the room at all. She reached the stairs and looked back; Joe had settled himself by Catherine and with the baby on one elbow and his wife's cheek on the other, he drifted off to sleep. She emerged into the evening's tumult and went to find Chris and join in the celebrations.

Chapter 14

The occupants of the basement returned late that evening, laughing and chattering with exuberance in their joy at their relief as they clattered down the stone stairs. As they saw the tableau near the far pillar, they quietened down somewhat, the women nodding with satisfaction at Catherine's successful delivery, but more than a little curious about the presence of the man in a Lieutenant's uniform. What was Catherine doing in the 'hole' with them if he was her husband?

Cristabel and Pattie came down with them, and gently shook Joe awake, and whispered to him that he must find quarters elsewhere, but he could return in the morning, but 'not too early' he was told sternly, as the women needed some privacy first thing in the morning. As Joe slid his arm from under Catherine she sighed gently but did not wake. Pattie found a basket as an improvised bed for the tiny infant, and then settled down for the night themselves, worn out by the day's activities.

Sometime in the night the baby woke to demand sustenance, but Catherine slept on, seemingly drugged with weariness. Cristabel and Pattie did not know what to do as they were loath to wake their exhausted friend. But one of the women nearby came with a smile and some advice. She had been given a little packet of sugar by one of the rescuers and she dissolved some in a little water. Dipping a clean piece of muslin in the sugar water, she offered to the baby to suck, and within minutes the tiny scrap was asleep again. Pattie thanked their rescuer profusely, only too aware that they had a lot to learn about the care of babies!

As soon as he decently could the next morning, Joe was back to find Catherine awake but still very weak. She smiled a pale, wan smile and held her arms up to him. Joe knelt by her side, and gathered her in his arms, wrenched to his core by the feel of the slight frame; remembering how she used to complain at her gently rounded form. She, who had yearned for the ethereal look of the infamous Caroline Lamb, mistress of the even more infamous Lord Byron! Joe used to laugh at her, claiming that he likes his women to be a 'decent handful', earning him a playful dig in the ribs. He kept his thoughts to himself.

'Morning a chara. You're looking wonderful today; but where's my beautiful new daughter?' Catherine smiled lovingly at him,

'Pattie's making her a cradle; look,' and she pointed across the gloomy basement. Sure enough, Pattie was busy with a small knot of women, all chattering and laughing together. From the cooing sounds, and the 'oohs' and 'aahs' he assumed that the baby was being much admired. He took the chance to have a precious moment of privacy with his wife, clearly a rare commodity in the stinking, overcrowded basement.

'Pattie told me that you came in with the relief force?' said Catherine, her voice still very weak.

'Mm, I'll tell you all about it when you get stronger; it's a long story. Oh Catherine, I thought I'd lost you more than once over these past weeks.'

'Me too, Joe. When you didn't come to find me at Pattie's I thought that something must have happened to you!' The two were silent for a while, caught by the miracle of their reunion. But their precious privacy was shattered by Pattie who called out excitedly,

'Will you just take a look at this; was there ever such a grand cradle, fit for a princess!' The 'cradle' was a wooden box donated by a resident who had used it for her meagre possessions, but gladly sacrificed for the little one who had taken on the status of their mascot. Now it was decked with a soft blanket and delicate Kashmir shawl.

'The shawl and blanket are a gift from Mrs. Bagley, dear,' whispered Pattie. Catherine nodded, mutely. Mrs. Bagley's baby son had died of cholera some weeks before, and she had not spoken of it since. That she had given his shawl and blanket was generosity indeed. But Pattie chattered on in her usual garrulous fashion,

'Mrs. Bretby said she'll come over in a moment and help you start the baby on her feeding. Joe, I'm sorry, but I'll have to turn you out again.

It's difficult enough to be private down here, and husbands usually visit in the evening!' Joe nodded. He had to attend to his duties anyhow, but he was dismayed at the thought that he couldn't visit Catherine whenever he wished.

'I'll try and find somewhere just for us, sweetheart,' he muttered fiercely to his wife. She shook her head,

'There isn't anywhere. The place is bursting at the seams. But won't we be leaving now?' I thought we'd been rescued?' Joe was silenced by the pathos in her voice. Far from being rescued, the new force had yet to find a way to bring out all the women, children and the wounded through Lucknow, which was still being held by rebel forces. He stood back, relieved of the necessity of answering by the arrival of Mrs. Bretby, who was the nearest thing to a midwife that they had in the 'hole'.

'Pity she didn't find time to help last night,' thought Joe grimly, as he kissed his wife and took his leave, promising to be back later. But he had one or two private duties to attend to before he addressed his military ones!

As he emerged from the basement, the heavens opened in a short, sharp shower. Looking across from the Residency towards the hospital through a curtain of water, he was appalled to see a continuous stream of wounded still arriving; a veritable snake of men entering at the Baillie Gate and making their way tortuously to a supposed haven. He ran through the deluge across the compound to peer inside the hospital. On the wide verandah, in the huge downstairs room, once an elegant ballroom, anywhere there was the smallest space, bodies lay. Many groaned aloud and begged for water; others lay ominously still. Others less wounded tried to help their companions. One private lay in a pool of blood, a shattered leg lying at a grotesque angle; he croaked at Joe,

'You the doctor for Gawd's sake?' Joe shook his head, helpless at the enormity of the problem. Their arrival yesterday had cost them dear.

Hardening his heart against the misery around him, for there were figures attending to the wounded, albeit slowly, he went in search of the stores. He was no stranger to starvation, and he knew he could still lose Catherine and his daughter if she didn't receive some decent nourishment, and very soon. He had been shocked to learn that very morning, that a vast 'swimming pool' of food had been discovered. Apparently it had been laid down by Lawrence who had died before informing anyone of its existence and location. There had been dark mutterings among the garrison soldiers, with whom he had spent the night and early morning that the notorious Gubbins must have known about it and had said nothing. One look at the robust appearance of Gubbins and his wife gave credence to the suspicion!

Joe found the quartermaster with the inevitable list in his hand, gazing at his new found treasures. Joe explained that he needed an instant increase in rations for his lady wife who had recently given birth, and was suffering from severe malnutrition. The quartermaster scratched his head with his pencil, and said 'no, he couldn't authorize anything that. Anyone could come and claim to be in need of extra sustenance and where would he be then? It was more than his job was worth to do such a thing without a chitty from a doctor. If the Lieutenant would such a chitty, he would be only too pleased to oblige!' Joe sighed at the working of the military mind, and retraced his steps to the hospital.

He tracked down Dr. Darby in the midst of attending to a bullet wound, and winced in silent empathy as the bullet was probed for. He waited patiently until the doctor handed over the task of bandaging to an orderly, and turned to him with a testy,

'Well, what is it? Can't you see I've got patients to attend to?'

'Yes, and I apologise for interrupting you, but my wife has just been delivered of a baby but is desperately weak and needs good nourishing food. I need a chitty to authorize it.'

'Heavens above man. I haven't time to write chitties when men are dying around me!' The doctor turned away in exasperation. But Joe was not so easily put off; the memory of Catherine's white face and the feel of her emaciated frame stiffened his resolve.

'And my wife is as likely to die as one of your patients if she does not receive care now!' he uttered through clenched teeth. 'D'you want a mother and baby's death on your conscience?' Darby glared at him out of red-rimmed eyes, but then he sighed and took a crumpled piece of paper out his pocket,

'What's your wife's name?'

'Mrs. Catherine Harrington.'

'Good God, man. Why didn't you say so! Woman of a million that little lady of yours! So she came through it then? Her friend was very anxious; what did she have?'

'Yes she came through it, but only just. That's why she needs extra food. Oh, and she had a girl.' Darby nodded,

'Hunger is a severe strain on a breeding woman. Well, here's your chitty, but don't feed her too much too soon. Take it slowly, and try to get her to eat little and often. And good luck to you both. Get her to come and see me when she's strong enough.' Joe promised he would, and set off for the stores again. The same fussy little quartermaster was still making lists. He examined Joe's chitty suspiciously, turning it over a few times as if he would find contrary orders on the back. Finally, apparently satisfied with the doctor's signature, he wrote out an authorization for one Mrs. Catherine Harrington to be given double rations. In a surge of generosity, he pressed a small loaf of bread on Joe that had come in with the relief troops, and wished him luck.

On his way back to the Residency, Joe pondered on the problem of his identity. He had arrived as Lieutenant John Harvey of 94th Foot, though Havelock knew him to be from Kotepore, and here he was claiming Mrs. Catherine Harrington as his wife. He had to hope that the prevailing confusion would allow him to quietly revert to his own identity and consign John Harvey to oblivion. Somehow he needed to acquire a Sergeant's uniform, which should not be too difficult with so many deaths! But that could be left to later.

He left the parcel of food with Pattie, and Dr. Darby's instructions. Pattie nodded and confided that Catherine was sleeping,

'The best thing for her!' Joe could only agree. Then he went in search of a niche for the two of them, but soon gave up on what was clearly a hopeless task. The compound had been full even before the new arrivals, with women even occupying the old Thug Gaol! Now that the relief force had arrived, men lounged everywhere.

As he wandered, he saw that men were still straggling in through the Baillie Guard Gate even now. God alone knew how they had survived the night in hostile territory and he wondered how many had perished in the dark alleys that had run from the lane they had trod in their desperate dash. Of the two thousand who had set off the previous morning from the Alambagh, some five hundred had fallen, dead or wounded. Joe shook his head, a bad business and the route through the city badly chosen. He recalled the famous poem about the Charge of the Light Brigade in the Crimea, a few years ago; how did it go?,

'Theirs not to make reply
Theirs not to reason why
Theirs but to do or die'

It was three evenings later that Joe finally got tired of seeing Catherine in short snatches. He longed for time alone with her and their new daughter, and a chance to talk together without an incessant audience. It was a pleasant evening, an earlier shower of rain giving way to a balmy softness in the air. He had picked his spot well, a heap of rubble that had once been a house and sheltered from stray sniper fire; though in truth that was not such a problem now that the enclave had been enlarged. Joe had scooped out a hollow in preparation, and now was ready to install his wife into the nest for a few precious hours.

Preceded by Pattie carrying Catherine's palliase and pillow, he carried the slight form of his wife up the stone stairs, through the entrance hall of the Residency and out into the compound. Catherine breathed deeply, glad to be out of the foetid air of the basement. The rainy season was slowly drawing to an end so the compound was not unpleasant with the onset of cooler weather,

'Oh, it's good to be out of there!' she sighed deeply. Cradled in her arms, the baby slept peacefully.

Pattie laid the palliase down, and helped Joe settle Catherine into the hollow he had fashioned. Then she lectured him,

'Don't keep her out too long; she's still very weak!' Joe grinned at her,

'And what do you think she's going to do out here, dance a jig?' Pattie gave him a playful dig in the ribs, kissed her friend and departed to find Chris, glad to be 'off duty' for a while. Joe sat down next to his wife and put his arms round her thin shoulders. He examined her critically. The great purple shadows under her eyes were fading and her cheeks were less sunken after three days on improved diet, but it would be some time before he face and body regained its rounded contours he was used to,

Though she had never had pretensions to beauty, Catherine's face owed much of its attractiveness to the liveliness of her character. Joe recalled when he had first seen her at the convent, lower lip rolled out and a frown of annoyance creasing her forehead; even then he had been fascinated by her animation. Since then he had seen her exhilarated, happy, sad; a whole gamut of expressions that would chase each other across her face and he loved them all! Now her eyes appeared sunk in her head and her nose stood out beakily and her cheeks were hollow and her lips almost bloodless. But to Joe she had never seemed so dear and lovely, for he had so nearly lost her. Catherine stirred against his shoulder and murmured drowsily,

'Joe; we haven't chosen a name for our baby yet. I was so sure it would be a boy that I didn't think of any girls names.' Joe pondered,

'When I first saw er, I thought of the roses in my grandfather's garden back in Ireland. She had that curled, closed look that a rose bud has with all the beauty to come. Shall we call her 'Rose'?' Catherine turned the name over in her mind,

'Don't you want to name her for one of her grandmothers? Philomena or Kate?'

'No. She is unique. A brand new person. And she should have a brand new name.' He looked down at his sleeping daughter. She was cosily wrapped, her eyes screwed up tightly. One tiny fist was tucked under her chin, and her lips were slightly pursed as though she was about to blow a bubble. Joe touched her cheek with a gentle finger tip, marveling at the silky smoothness of her skin. In the fading light it was difficult to see the colour of her hair, but Joe thought he could detect a faint blush of auburn in the down that covered her head.

'So, my little Rose. How do you like your name, eh?'

'Mm. Yes, I like it,' murmured Catherine, 'we must get her baptized as soon as possible, Joe.'

'Yes my love, though I don't know of a priest in this place. I'll see what I can do.' The couple sat quietly a while, savouring the time alone together, 'alone by God' thought Joe with a smile to himself with the compound seething with men bustling about their business, or squatting in groups and puffing on cheroots. Fires were lit, and flares gave sudden bursts of light against the darkening sky. The danger of pandey snipers had been with them so long that Catherine had forgotten what it was like to see lights at night, and she was fascinated by the sight. Occasionally a soldier clanked by, but gave no more than a cursory glance at the trio in the shelter; so used were they to seeing people find a home wherever they could. Catherine broke the silence at last,

'Joe?'

'Yes my love?'

'Why are you wearing the jacket of a lieutenant, and not even of your own regiment?'

'It's a long story.'

'Tell me!' So Joe began to tell her, starting right back to the day he returned to Kotepore cantonment to find it under attack, and no sign of her. He related the barest outline of the events, not wishing to distress her with details, forgetting that after long weeks of siege, she was more than used to terrible sights. She interrupted briefly to enquire after friends at Kotepore. Joe was able to reassure her that Louise and Adam Swales were safe, as was their little daughter, Christina. Yes, Lucy Willoughby and little Charles were also safe, as was Nancy Carter.

Having satisfied her curiosity, Catherine allowed him to continue. He went on to describe the departure of the rebels and the decision to depart for the hills,

'D'you think they will have got there safely?' enquired Catherine, somewhat drowsily.

'Mm; yes they should. The more I hear of this uprising, the more it is clear that it was unplanned. There would have been a lot of hot air expended round cooking fires, but when things got out of hand at Meerut it took everyone by surprise, including the Indians. Provided they moved swiftly, I believe the Regiment would have had little trouble with natives en route. The majority of 'em don't wish us any harm; just want to get on with their own way of life. But let me tell you about one who saved my life!'

So he continued with his leaving Kotepore with Gopi to find her in Lucknow, and the unlucky shot that nearly put an end to him there and then. He told her of Gopi's struggle to get him to the village and of Gita's nursing that saved him when the wound turned bad. Finally he reached the part of his story when he had decided to go to Cawnpore after all,

'It's difficult to remember now why I was so determined to go,' he explained, 'but it seemed the right thing to do at the time. We got there just as the final tragedy was about to unfold. Oh God, Catherine, I don't think I'll ever forget it! By the way, did I tell you, I saw your friend Charlotte by the river?' Catherine shook her head,

'How was she? Did she look frightened?' Joe shut his eyes, remembering the heat and the smells of that long distant day. He recalled Charlotte standing there, her clothes in tatters, and smelling of urine and worse, two little waifs clinging to her hands, eyes enormous in their pinched faces.

'She looked fine my love. Not frightened at all. And she was looking after two little ones; you know what Charlotte was like, always looking after someone!' Catherine nodded with a reminiscent smile.

'Go on; what about the uniform?' So Joe continued the tale; how he had taken the uniform to gain access to Havelock's headquarters,

'You see, acushla, I still wasn't absolutely sure whether you were among the women that were marched off to the Bibigarh. I wanted to bring help as quickly as possible, and this uniform was the best fit I could find. So behold, Lieutenant John Harvey of 94th Foot!'

'Why John Harvey?'

'I always choose a name close to my own so I soon get used to answering to it; Joe Harrington; John Harvey; Jhoti; see?' She nodded.

'Joe, what happened at the Bibigarh? We heard so many dreadful stories; they can't possibly be true?'

'What did you hear?'

'That all the women and children were butchered by tulwars and dumped in a well! Joe, the Indians can't have treated women and children like that?'

'You must remember acushla, that this is total war. It was horrific but I think it happened out of panic. The Nana Sahib knew we were coming and probably gave the order out of pure fright. I have since heard that the sepoys he sent to do it refused, and the ones that carried out the actual massacre were badmashes of the worst kind. And it has to be said that our forces are capable of brutal behaviour too! Let us not talk of such things any more, sweet.' For Joe was remembering the well at Cawnpore and the weeping men who emptied it of its gruesome contents. The bile rose to his throat as the memory rose of long moments when he had stood watching, steeling himself to look for anything that could identify his wife, until his nerve had shattered and he had turned away to vomit in a nearby bush. After that he had been unable to watch any more, and so had not known until he arrived in Lucknow whether his wife was alive or dead. He knew that he would never completely banish the sights from his mind, but for the sake of his sanity and for the future of himself and his marriage to this dear person, he must bury the images as deep as possible. He changed the subject,

'Now it's your turn. D'you feel up to it? I still don't know what happened to you since you left Kotepore; and why?' Catherine sighed,

'It all seems so long ago. You see Joe, I felt the baby move and I wanted to share it with someone! All the rest followed from that. Poor Gopi, he tried so hard to stop me. By the way, is he alright? I haven't seen him since you got here?'

'Oh yes. He's found himself a berth in the native quarters. Things are a little strange for him without a bungalow to look after!' Joe chuckled,

'You're quite right to say 'poor Gopi', I don't think he's had a moment's peace of mind since all this started, with both of us behaving irrationally all over the place! Anyway, go on, what happened after you reached Lucknow?' Catherine obliged, though it all sounded very tame after Joe's saga. She told of the reasons they moved into the compound, and moving in with Mrs. Appleton, and the subsequent move into the basement. Joe bristled at the high handed way she had been treated but Catherine shushed him,

'Joe, her house was demolished by a pandey shell and they were all killed; I was safer underground!' She went on to talk of the hospital and the sights she had witnessed there. Joe marveled at her fortitude, and remembered Dr. Darby's words, 'a woman in a million.'

'That reminds me. You've made a conquest of Dr. Darby; he wants to see you when you feel strong enough.' Her lips curved in a reminiscent smile,

'It wasn't so when we first met, let me tell you! He didn't want us at the hospital at all, and he and Pattie had more than one set to, especially when he wanted to take Chris' leg off when it turned bad! But he's a good doctor and he has so much to contend with, and no bandages and medicaments to deal out. Are things any better since you came?'

'I don't think so; we had to leave a lot of our baggage, so we brought may wounded but nothing to treat them with.'

At that moment the baby stirred, her eyes fluttering open and giving her father a cross-eyed look. Her face screwed up ready to cry.

'Here,' said Joe, 'give her to me.' He took Rose from Catherine and cradled her against his jacket, handling the tiny scrap with ease. The memory of a sprite with red-gold hair rose in his mind, but now the image did not hurt as this new little sprite nudged her way into his heart and sat there comfortably alongside the spirit of Nuala.

Looking down at his wife, he saw her eyelids drooping and was relieved to see Pattie making her way towards them with Chris in tow. The journalist walked with a pronounced limp and was as gaunt as the rest. He was dressed in the same alpaca suit that he had entered the Residency in three months ago, and his hair was unkempt, hanging over his collar in rat's tails. Next to him, Pattie looked neat in a much washed dress that hung limp without its crinoline. Her rebellious hair had escaped from its pins as usual and stood about her head like an aureole, highlighted by the flares. Joe watched their approach with affection; they really were such dear friends. Pattie looked anxiously at Catherine, and took Joe to task for keeping her out for so long.

'Don't scold Pattie, there's a dear. It's so lovely to be outside. If it wasn't for the chance of rain, I think I'd prefer to sleep out here.'

'And feed your baby in the open?' Pattie looked positively shocked. Catherine laughed at her friend's scandalized face,

'Those things don't seem so important any more. Oh Pattie, Chris, we've chosen a name for our little one, or at least Joe did; Rose. What do you think?'

'Lovely my dear, now let's get you back to bed.' Joe pulled a face, but did as he was told. Rising from the ground stiffly, he handed the baby to Chris who immediately panicked, and lifted his wife into his arms,

'We'll do this again as often as possible, my sweet,' he murmured against her lank hair. Catherine nodded.

In the years that followed, Catherine would remember those evenings above all else; long after she had forgotten the filth and the squalor, the hunger and despair. The heap of rubble became their meeting place whenever weather and duty allowed, though it was altered and adapted to make a cosy den for them all to catch up on the news. The others would join in, Pattie and Chris, Cristabel and David. Catherine watched them all in drowsy contentment, marveling at the differences between them and how well they all got on in spite of those differences. There was Chris with his thin, aesthetic face and lank brown hair flopping over his forehead, which he would push away impatiently with lean brown fingers. David was the complete opposite, dark haired and stocky. He belied the popular image of the dark and dour Welshman and always had a ready smile that lifted the corners of his luxurious moustache and lit the depths of his black eyes. He spoke with a lilt so that the sound lifted at the end of each sentence; and was prone to bursting into song at the slightest provocation. Then there was her own darling Joe, the best looking of them all. His face with its strong lines and planes seemed to have aged since she had last seen him, though that could have been due to the dark dye that still stained his hair. His face was deeply tanned and his brilliant blue eyes peered out from a mass of fine lines that radiated from the corners. He had lost some weight too and his limbs were lean and knotted with muscle. All three men talked volubly with much hand waving, puffing vigorously on cheroots, the smoke rising in the still air to mingle with the fire that had lit in the centre of their circle.

The talk, enlivened by quantities of brandy or rum purloined by the indefatigable David ranged from the cause of the mutiny to the probable outcome of it all, each man having his own fixed opinion, often disputed by their wives. In an age when women were not supposed to have opinions of their own, it was remarkable to find a trio prepared to hold their own in a discussion, and even more remarkable to find three men willing to allow them to do so! But, thought Catherine to herself, none of them are English! Her own Joe was Irish, Chris' family came from Scotland, and David was an ex-miner from the coal valleys of Wales. All agreed that it was the British or rather the English who had brought about the situation by their pig-headedness and their unwillingness to understand the feelings of the peoples they had thought to conquer. David asserted that the future was bleak for British in India, but Chris fiercely opposed him,

'You must know them better than that! The British do not lose anything they have acquired. Why even now they'll be throwing up their hands in horror at the massacre stories in their cosy drawing rooms, and preparing to send more troops to suppress the rebellion. It'll all be a memory within a year!'

'I agree,' interposed Joe, 'and I don't think they'll leave it to 'Johnny Company' anymore; its days are numbered. The poor Indians will never be free again.'

'How can you call them 'poor Indians' after what they did in Cawnpore and here; and your own Kotepore?' asked Cristabel indignantly,

'Ah, you see, Cristabel, they never asked the British to come here, did they?'

'But Joe, we've done so much good, haven't we?' David listened to the interchange. His wife was English to her very core, and never would understand what Joe was saying. Sometimes he wondered how they fitted together so well, with Cristabel's ethereal blond looks belying an unshakeable belief in the rightness of the English way of life. He himself was as rabid a Welsh patriot as Joe was an Irish one; nevertheless, their marriage had been a happy one, and he yearned for the day when he could take her to the Welsh valley he called home.

They also discussed Havelock's situation. He had been in command when Cawnpore was retaken and had fought his way here towards Lucknow, but had learned by reading a newspaper that he had been superseded by Major-general Outram.

'Can you imagine it,' Joe told them, indignant on behalf of the man he had grown to respect, 'to go through all that and then be told that someone is put in over you; and not even the courtesy of an official despatch. I have to say he took it very well. It also must be said that Outram behaved impeccably and insisted that Havelock should have the honour of taking Lucknow!'

'That was truly a generous gesture,' agreed Catherine quietly.

'Yes, but it didn't work. Outram meant well and tried to restrain himself from interfering but couldn't always help himself. Then the men got confused and didn't know whose orders to obey! In fact, it was Outram who suggested the route that we should take through Lucknow because he had been resident here once. Trouble is, though the route was direct, he forgot that it was overlooked all the way by houses that were bound to contain snipers. It would've been much better to skirt the river; we would not have lost so many men.'

It was Catherine who finally asked the question on all their minds,

'But when will we leave? I thought the relief was meant to get us all out?' The other fell silent. In her placed post-natal state, Catherine had not really paid much attention to what was going on, and no-one had been willing to disillusion her; much better to let her build up her strength for feeding Rose and putting a little colour in her cheeks. At last Joe replied, choosing his words carefully,

'That was the idea. But when Havelock and Outram broke through, it was at enormous cost to our soldiers. And they didn't drive off the rebels, just forced their way through them. With so many injured and so many women and children to defend, we cannot break through safely.' Catherine was silent for a moment, a tear gathering in the corner of her eye, and then,

'Oh Joe; I did so want to go home!' Joe was nonplussed for a moment,

'But acushla, we have no home just now.' He felt rather than saw the others move away and silently blessed them for their tact. Pattie was cuddling Rose, and took her away with them so that Joe could gather his wife to his chest; he rocked her as he did their tiny daughter,

'It'll end soon, you'll see. And it is not so bad now. Chris was telling me that you couldn't sit out like this before, even of it didn't rain for fear of snipers. The enclave is enlarged and the hospital extended and there is enough food to go round. When the next column arrives, they will be able to do the job properly.' Catherine listened to him, weeping all over his handsome gold-laced jacket until she managed to blurt out,

'I'd forgotten about our bungalow. Oh Joe, we'll have nowhere to go after all this, and I did so want to go home,' and she wept afresh, all the pent up unhappiness of the past months rising like a spring flood, and overflowing at least. Joe said no more, but shushed her gently until the tears died away to broken sobs, and finally to intermittent hiccoughs. And then there was silence. Joe gently eased a finger under her chin and lifted her face so he could see her properly. She had fallen asleep, worn out by her distress, her closed eyelids looking bruised and swollen, and the imperious little nose wet with tears. Reaching into his pocket Joe found a kerchief and gently dried the tears and kissed the tip of her nose.

'Come acushla, it is time you went to bed. May the time come soon when we can share a bed again for I miss you sorely at night.' There was no reply from his sleeping wife, and he lifted her as easily as ever. She had slowly regained her strength to walk unaided, but Joe did not want to wake her; she needed the healing power of sleep more than anything else right now.

Catherine did not mention the relief again, nor did she cry until the day they left Lucknow, but then they were tears of joy!

As September died and October began, the long beleaguered residents of the Lucknow Residency were able to emerge from the dark depths of the basement or from innumerable houses where they had been crammed together; too terrified to venture outside for fear of sniper fire. They were able to stroll about in the October sunshine and exchange visits as though the siege and all its suffering did not exist. Stout matrons, their multiple chins much reduced, escorted their daughters about taking care that they were not too much exposed to the rude and licentious soldiery! More than once, Joe had to stop himself laughing aloud as a gaggle of women, their crinolines much crumpled and stained, pick their way carefully among the gangs of coolies clearing rubble into some sort of orderly heap. Tattered parasols were hoisted against the sun, and dirty white gloves pulled over hands that bore evidence of manual work for the first time in their pampered lives. He marveled afresh at the resilience of the Victorian woman, determined to bring their drawing room manners to the most unlikely of settings!

The garrison had shaken down to their new arrivals, with Outram now in command. Inglis, who had done as well as he could after Lawrence had perished, was given the command of the Residency itself, and Havelock took charge of the buildings on the perimeter; an uneasy command as it was the closest to the pandey lines and exposed to constant fire. But the main enclave had been enlarged and the hospital expanded with the aid of tents. There were still no medicines or bandages, but at least there was room to move about among the beds without treading on sick and wounded men. All they needed now was news of further relief on its way that would take them out of it all for good!

Joe had been given duties with the Sikh sowars, which suited him very well. He spent his duty hours in the company of these tall, fiercesome looking Sikhs, with their smart blue coats, impeccable turbans and stiff moustaches and beards. Gopi had a charpoy in their barrack room, and was constantly being teased about his diminutive stature and lack of facial hair. He took it all with a shake of his head and a slow smile, but he was happiest when the Sahib was there, as the Sikhs held back when he was around!

The siege entered a new phase with the defence being mainly involved with the renewed threat of mining. Thwarted of the usual targets with the perimeter much enlarged and the compound out of musket range, the pandies threw themselves into tunneling with renewed vigour. David found his skills as an ex-coal miner much in demand, and he spent much of his day underground,

'Wouldn't you just know it,' he grumbled, 'just when the weather improves and it's safe to walk outside, I get sent to the bowels of the earth! I joined the army to escape all that!'

In the tunnels, he found himself in the company of other miners, mainly tin men from Cornwall. One of their number was a strange character by the name of Thomas Kavanagh. He was a civilian clerk who had distinguished himself more than once during the siege, but now flung himself into counter-mining with enormous enthusiasm, and earned himself the respect of men whose way of life had been below ground. More than one pitched battle was fought in the guttering light of tallow lamps and candles, but they kept the pandies at bay.

Only Chris was at his old post at the Gubbins battery, and it was he who kept the others up to date with the news. One evening, in their den, he was able to report that another relief column was on its way led by Sir Colin Campbell.

'Ah well,' sighed the irrepressible David, 'I'm sure there's room for a few more!'

'It's nothing to joke about,' scolded his wife, 'it would be too much to bear if they make the same mistake. We seem to have been locked up in here forever. Little Rose will be able to walk out of here if we wait much longer.' Joe grinned at Cristabel's remark and gazed fondly at his daughter sleeping peacefully in Catherine's arms. She was a contented baby, as if she knew that her parents had enough to contend with without a fractious infant to cope with.

'It needs someone to guide them in next time,' suggested Chris, 'so they leave the way open for the evacuation.'

Joe looked at him enigmatically, but said nothing; indeed he had been quiet all evening. An icy chill of fear worked its way along Catherine's spine, but she too said nothing. What she wanted to say could not be said in front of the others for she did not trust her emotions.

Her chance came the next day. Joe had an hour or two free at midday, and leaving his sowars to sleep off their tiffin, he went in search of his wife. He found her outside the Residency with young Hal and a girl of about fifteen in tow. He doffed his shako and made an elegant bow, making the youngsters giggle,

'Madam, would you care to take a turn with me in the rose garden?' Equally politely Catherine dropped a curtsey, and gazing around at the devastated landscape totally devoid of even a blade of grass, replied,

'Thank you kind sir, but I would prefer the sunken Italian garden.'

By this time, Hal and his companion were doubled up with mirth. Normally, they were much in awe of the tall, handsome lieutenant, but the interchange put them at their ease.

'Well acushla, will you walk with me?' repeated Joe.

'I'll just Rose in her cot, if Harriet here will mind her for me?'

'Oh Mrs. Harrington, I'll put here to bed for you and stay with her.'

'Thank you my dear. Your arm Joe.' And the pair set off for a stroll around the enclave, marveling at the pace at which it had been tidied since the relief had arrived. Houses that had been destroyed during the constant bombardment had been piled into neat heaps of rubble ready to be used to reinforce the perimeter. It was such a pile that they had made their own. They walked for a while in companionable silence, until Catherine remembered what had been on her mind since the previous evening.

'Joe,'

'Yes dear?'

'Yesterday, when Chris mentioned a messenger should try and reach Campbell, I saw the look on your face. You mean to try and go outside again?' Joe stopped walking and looked down into his wife's troubled face,

'I'm doing no good here. Davy is doing sterling work underground and Chris has his niche at the battery. But me; I'm not needed with the sowars. They have their own officers. Oh Catherine, don't look at me so! It's a fact; they didn't know what to do with an odd soldier from another regiment, so they put me there because I'm supposed to be 'good with the natives.' Catherine listened to the bitter speech and tried to understand, but it was hard,

'But Joe, I've only just found you again!'

'I'd be in no danger, you must know that. The only time I got injured was from an English bullet!'

'Joe, I know you're restless shut up in this place, but we have been here much longer.' Joe detected a note of pique in her voice, and tried to explain,

'It's not just being shut up; I do sympathise with what you have been through, but I feel so useless!' Catherine sighed.

'Please promise me you won't go out.' Joe prevaricated,

'Havelock and Outram may not want me,' and swiftly changing the subject, 'will you just look at that!' 'That' was a bungalow, one of the few left intact. It had suffered an explosion nearby sometime during the siege, and its verandah and one end of the building had collapsed sideways, giving it the appearance of being inebriated. Notwithstanding the damage, a group of memsahibs were determinedly taking a post tiffin cup of cha; their wicker chairs propped up with a miscellany of items including a Bible, little fingers crooked at just the right angle, and the conversation muted and genteel, they could have graced the sweeping lawn of a great English mansion! Joe's lips twitched as he punctiliously doffed his shako. The burra-memsahib guarding her trio of delicate young ladies was soothed by the sight of the handsome lieutenant with his wife on his arm, and really inclined her head,

'Good afternoon Lieutenant. A pleasant day is it not?'

'Yes indeed ma'am.' Joe preferred not to introduce himself or Catherine as he was conscious of his dual identity and did not want names to get back to the lady's military husband and so with a nod he donned his shako and moved away, ignoring the frown on the burra-memsahib's face. He chatted to Catherine, carefully avoiding their previous topic of conversation. Catherine had her answer, and she made Rose's imminent feed an excuse to return to the basement.

Next day, Joe went in search of Havelock, out on the eastern perimeter. For the first time he was aware of the constant crackle of musket fire and the whine of bullets, 'so this is what they had to endure all those weeks,' he observed to himself as he approached the building appropriated by Havelock for his headquarters. Looking around he saw squads of soldiers aided by coolies hard at work, trying to plug a gap in the perimeter wall. The enlargement of the enclave meant that several places were vulnerable to attack, and it was a matter of urgency to fill them in as fast as possible.

A few moments later he was shown into Havelock's office, where the Brigadier was frowning over reports. He looked up as Joe entered and smartly saluted.

'At ease, Lieutenant Harvey,' he said absently. Joe waited for permission to state his mission.

'Harvey; you're supposed to understand these fellars? Why don't they give up, eh? Delhi's fallen, Cawnpore taken, Agra safe. What do they hope to achieve keeping us penned up like this?' Joe chose his words carefully,

'This uprising was a long time coming, Sir. In spite of their losses, as long as they do keep us penned up as you say, they feel they have us in their power, even if it is only here. After all, Sir, it is what we would do!'

'Eh, eh? What's that you say. Yes, but.....' Joe silently finished the thought, 'but they're only natives!' As long as the British continued to think of the Indians as ignorant savages, then they would have trouble defeating them. Havelock changed the subject,

'By the way, Harvey, I've news of the Kotepore Regiment.'

'Indeed, Sir!' responded Joe, eagerly, 'are they safe?'

'Yes. The despatch says that they reached the hills safely with their families, and the soldiers under Colonel Willoughby returned in time to take part in the relief of Delhi. They are there now helping in the clear up operation. As soon as we get out of here, you can rejoin them. By the way Lieutenant, did you find your wife?' Joe looked into the face of the man dubbed 'Holy Havelock' who was supposed to be so rigid and devoid of human emotion, but he only saw kindly concern.

'Thank you Sir, I did. Quite safe.'

'Good, good. What is it you wanted to see me about?'

'Sir, you may remember That Colonel Deluce used to send me to gather information for him, as I could pass as a native?'

'Spying you mean?' Joe detected an acerbic note of disapproval in his reply, but continued,

'Just to keep informed of the current situation. I wondered if I could offer the same service. Or perhaps carry a message to Campbell advising him of the best route to enter.' Havelock bristled, his startling white eyebrows drawing together in a heavy frown,

'Are you saying that the previous route was wrong, eh?'

'No; that is….'

'Well Lieutenant, you are right, of course. We did no good to these people here, trapped for so long. And I prayed long and hard for guidance! Well, I have no need for a messenger; we have natives going out all the time. And I have no need for a spy, but thank you for your offer. I will remember it if I need such a person.' Joe knew that he was being dismissed, and somewhat ignominiously. He turned to go with the thought, 'at least Catherine will be happy!' As he reached the door, the vinegary voice stopped him momentarily,

'Perhaps Outram can use your services.'

'Yes Sir.'

Joe did not immediately see Outram; he felt sore and ill-used by Havelock's use of the word 'spy', and was disinclined to hear it again from Outram. Nevertheless, he chafed with impatience as the sunny days of October turned into the cooler days of November. Catherine did not raise the subject again but was obviously relieved that he had seemed to have dropped the idea.

Chris kept up a stream of information gleaned from Gubbins' house. Part of Outram and Havelock's forces had been left at the Alambagh, and they were in contact with Campbell's forces. Then they heard on the 9th of November that Campbell was on his way from Cawnpore, and was due to join up with Hope Grant across the Sai. The defenders held their breath, for rations had been cut again, and hope had begun to turn to despair. But Campbell arrived at the Alambagh on the 12th. He led a force that was as motley a collection of troops as any that had been thrown together in the uprising. Apart from the ever patient foot slogging infantry, there were Highlanders; most of them Gaelic speaking and fiercely loyal to Campbell. There wild looking Sikhs in flowing fawn robes, and fierce Punjabis intent on loot. There was even a detachment of sailors under Captain William

Peel, son of a former Prime Minister. Their camp followers were so taken aback at the sight of them that they deserted almost to a man, leaving only the lowliest sweepers and doolie drivers. But this force fought through with little opposition and lifted the spirits of the besieged once again. But as before, the problem was how to reach the Residency while leaving the way open to evacuate the women, children and wounded.

Joe followed the progress of Campbell and Grant avidly, and felt that the time was right to offer his services once more. This time he approached Outram.

He found him closeted with his officers, and was obliged to state his business to them all. When Outram heard him offer to carry a message through the enemy lines, he gave a loud guffaw,

'How do you propose to pass as a native? Look at you; blue eyes, red hair?' Joe's hair had been growing steadily out of its dye, but he answered firmly,

'I have done it before very successfully. The hair is no problem under a turban, and as for the eyes, the colour is not unknown among northern Indians. It is only the Europeans who think all Indians look alike!' Outram bristled at the tone of the remark, and Joe cursed himself for his stupidity at antagonising the man. However, Outram responded mildly enough,

'I cannot allow an officer to put himself at such a risk. I need to be satisfied that you could carry it off successfully!' Joe could hardly believe his ears; he was to be given the chance to go after all. He did not for a moment consider that his disguise would not be accepted.

He hurried away to find Gopi, and on the way to the sowar barracks found Chris at the Gubbins battery. He explained his intentions, and then,

'Chris; try not to tell Catherine unless she directly enquires after me. She is used to me doing strange duty hours.' Chris frowned,

'I can't lie to her, Joe.'

'I'm not asking you to. She knows what I have in mind; in fact she's known for some time. It is something I must do; for the first time I can do something constructive for these people.' Chris still looked troubled, but said no more; but shook Joe vigorously by the hand and wished him luck.

Later, an aide leaving Outram's office noticed an Indian lurking outside. The fellow was dressed in a motley collection of clothes; baggy trousers and muslin tunic. A sash was tied round his waist and held a fearsome looking tulwar. The turban was exceedingly filthy and the aide thought he had a furtive look about him,

'What are you doing here? Do you not have duties to attend to?' The Indian made namaste and pleaded to see the Burra-Sahib Outram.'

'What do you want with the General? He is having his dinner.'

'I must tell the Burra-Sahib in person; I have a message for him.' The aide was troubled, but with messages arriving all the time, he could not risk turning away a genuine messenger. But he still didn't like the look of this one, he had the appearance of a badmash! He went inside and reported to Outram, who looked out of the window at the figure, lolling against a pillar in the casual way of the Indian. There was something about the man that bothered him,

'Very well, I'll see him. But you'd better be on hand.'

'Very good, Sir.' The Indian was called in and stood before Outram, wringing his hands in agitation at being in the presence of such an exalted being.

'What is it?' asked Outram testily. As he spoke, the Indian straightened up and took on a soldierly stance. He removed his turban and saluted smartly, apologizing at his lack of shako.

'Good God, Harvey. I'd never have believed it. There's nothing more to be said. We must make the necessary arrangements at once!'

Later that evening, with Gopi in attendance, Joe slipped over the perimeter wall, and was instantly swallowed up in the dark streets of Lucknow, the message stowed safely in his turban. In the middle of the following day, a signal flag was raised at the Alambagh to indicate to the watchers in the Residency that the message gad been delivered safely. The relieving force now knew the route that they should take to avoid the narrow streets that had been Havelock and Outram's undoing.

On 14th November the defenders could hear the sound of gunfire as the relief force moved out. The rebels were first driven from the picturesque Dilkusha Park, where the browsing herds of deer fled at the sound of heavy guns. From there the rebels were ousted from the Martiniere School, and the advancing force headed for the canal, garrisoning as they went. Joe was in the thick of it all, guiding and advising at each step of the way. By the 16th they had reached the palace of Sikanderbagh and were preparing to pound it into submission.

To the long besieged in the Residency, the sound of gunfire was music to their ears for the second time in four long months.

Yelling 'Cawnpore, remember Cawnpore,' the attackers overwhelmed the Indian defences and moved on to the Shah Najaf Mosque. To their horror, they found the Mosque full of gunpowder ready to blow up at any moment! At last they reached the Mothi Mahal, a palace close to Residency, where they met by Outram and Havelock.

In the Residency basement, Catherine sat on her pallet and cradled Rose. Everyone else had gone outside to keep in touch with developments. Presently she heard familiar footsteps on the stone stairs; Pattie come searching for her,

'Why are you down here? They are beginning to come in! You'll never believe it, Cathy love, but there are sailors among them, complete with pigtails! Ah; what is it?' For Catherine did not reply, but gazed with enormous smoky grey eyes, then,

'And will he be with them this time? *Why* did he have to go?'

'Hey. You should know your husband better than that by now. He's a soldier. And you know as well as I do that there was no-one else as fitted for the job.'

'But what if he is killed?'

'Cathy! Am I hearing you properly? We could all have been killed at any time during the past few months merely walking to the hospital. You nearly died having Rose, Joe got shot by a fleeing Englishman, and Chris could have died from his wound! There is no reason to suppose Joe is in any more danger now than before!'

'But Pattie, he *promised* not to go.'

'Did he? Did he really?' Catherine subsided at the fierce look on her friend's face. They had been too close for too long, and she couldn't pretend,

'Well no; but I *asked* him not to go!' Pattie did not bother arguing anymore, but grasped her friend's arm,

'Stop sulking down here, and come and see if he is safe.'

Carrying Rose, Catherine followed Pattie up the stairs to find Cristabel standing with David and Chris. David turned to them and said,

'Isn't that a grand sight?'

There was Sir Colin Campbell, and they pressed forward to see the great man, made famous by his exploits in the Crimea. It was passing strange, thought Catherine that all great men seemed to be so small, and she giggled at the impious thought. Sir Campbell was an unprepossessing figure, with a thatch of untidy, gray and curling hair. His Highlanders adored him, though some of their pet names for him were less than complimentary! The most famous of them had been gained in the Crimea where he had thrown his troops against cavalry in an extended front instead of the recommended hollow square. The manouvre had been successful, earning him the title 'the thin red line tipped with steel!'

Now Sir Campbell stood, flanked by Outram and Havelock, both of whom had been wounded near the Mothi Mahal. Havelock was nursing his delight at receiving the news that he had been conferred a knighthood for his services in India. The original garrison mustered in front of the commander of the relief, every able-bodied man, both brown and white skinned, and Campbell stared at them as if he couldn't believe his eyes. Five hundred gallant defenders paraded with not a decent uniform or suit of clothes between them, soldiers and civilians alike; faces drawn with long experienced hunger and feet bound with cloth from the clothes of long dead comrade. Nor did they forget that two hundred of them lay wounded in the hospital. Chris and David stood to attention with the rest.

'Good God,' Sir Colin muttered to Havelock, 'how have they sustained themselves in this state.

'Now you know why we were so keen to get to these people,' replied Havelock, 'when we saw the state of the perimeter and the Baillie Guard Gate, we just made the quickest entry we could.' Campbell grunted in reply and then gave the order,

'You have two hours to get the women, children and wounded out of here!'

The assembled audience of women he had referred to looked stunned by the news. Now that that the moment had come for them to actually leave this place, they suddenly discovered all sorts of reasons why they shouldn't! Thoughts of loved ones left in the cemetery, thoughts of precious possessions, thoughts of braving the pandies outside suddenly became overwhelming.

Suddenly Catherine found Rose plucked unceremoniously out of her arms and thrust at Pattie, the outraged infant letting out an indignant yell. Catherine was swung off her feet and encircled by a pair of strong arms that she knew so well. A familiar voice whispered in her ear,

'Forgive me a chara, I had to go, and as you see, I am safe returned.'

She smiled tremulously, fighting tears of joy,

'Put me down you great oaf! Look, you've made Rose cry, and she never cries!' Joe laughed aloud, and swung her round again, much to the amusement of the onlookers. Pattie and Cristabel stood watching him with gentle smiles, Pattie soothing Rose with an expert touch. Then Joe became serious,

'Collect anything you need, but keep it to the minimum. We leave again as soon as possible. We must be separated once more, briefly, for the men are to cover the retreat. Go now.' And he gave Catherine a pat on her behind, sending the three young women back to the basement for the last time.

A cacophony of sound assaulted their ears as they descended, as women tried to decide what to take and what to leave. Most of them had few possessions, but were loath with any of them. Children ran about unchecked for once, and got under everybody's feet. Catherine was soon prepared. Her dresses had long since disintegrated, and she only had the few baby clothes that Mrs. Bagley had given her, so her bundle was pitifully small. Pattie and Cristabel were in a similar state, so the thankfully left the babble behind and regained the fresh air. Pattie helped Catherine fashion the Kashmir shawl into a sling to carry Rose and leave her hands free. Rose lay in her improvised cradle placidly taking in the new view of the world with eyes that rapidly becoming as bright blue as her father's.

'Little precious,' cooed Pattie, 'I've never know such an undemanding infant before.'

'Get on with you Pattie,' laughed Catherine, 'you've never knew any babies at all!' Pattie was indignant,

'But I've heard a lot about them, how noisy and smelly they generally are. This little one makes me inclined to try again for one of our own', and she looked momentarily sad at the memory of her lost baby so long before.

They looked around for their menfolk, but only Chris could be seen; he hurried over to them,

'David has been recalled to his unit. The 32nd are to cover the retreat. Campbell said that they had fought long and hard and to them must fall the honour of seeing their charges out. For myself, I'd have thought they'd had enough of fighting! Oh, and Joe had gone to see if he is needed with the sowars, but expects to be back.' Catherine was too happy at his safe return so didn't take offence at his absence now!

The made their way to the gate to find total confusion reigning. The 'gently bred' ladies were bellowing as stridently as any fish wife, refusing to leave without their possessions; all of them. One woman was arguing volubly to be allowed to take her piano? A harassed soldier was trying to explain that the evacuation had to be done quietly with the minimum of noise, but he faced an uphill battle.

Then they were all informed; they were to be reprieved. Too many women had declared that they just couldn't *possibly* leave at such short notice! The long-suffering Sir Colin agreed to a twenty four hour delay, though he was heard to mutter, 'I thought they'd be glad to leave this place!'

That evening, the three couples retired to their 'den' to discuss the day's stirring events. David and Chris questioned Joe closely about Sir Colin; they had heard so much about him. Joe laughed,

'And it's all true! He's quite a man, is Sir Colin Campbell. His Highlanders adore him, but that might be because he's the only one who can understand their Gaelic! I've heard that if they want to see him any time, they can; even in his bath! At least they put an end to the excesses going on in Cawnpore.' Chris gave a warning cough, but Joe chose to ignore him,

'I know that what was done against those innocents can never be condoned, but Neill took it out on any and every Indian he came across. He made them lick up the blood, and encased Muslims in pig skins and Hindus in cow hide before executing them!'

'That's enough,' said David urgently, 'these three have had enough.' Joe looked at three white faces,

'I'm sorry,' said Joe, tightening his hold on Catherine's waist, 'but there has been great wrong done on both sides. A strange man, Neill. All those terrible actions to the Indians, but he was the only one who thought to bring sweetmeats for the children of Lucknow. Pity he was killed before he could deliver them.

'You said Campbell put a stop to all that?' asked Pattie,

'Yes, he realised that the ones being punished could have had nothing to do with the massacre, so he ended all reprisals. A stern man, but a just one; I've got a lot of time for him.' Those who knew Joe well knew that that was praise indeed!

At that moment, the object of their admiration was sitting at dinner at the Gubbins' residence, where Mrs. Gubbins had laid out her best glass and silver ware. The food was beautifully prepared and served, fresh meat, vegetables, truffles and other delicacies. It was the sort of food the hungry members of the enclave had been dreaming about for as long as they could remember. The Gubbins' guest gazed at the repast, and fully aware of the starvation that had been endured, refused to eat a morsel of it, but sat in stony silence throughout the meal,

'Why,' he asked his hosts, 'do you eat so well when the injured in the hospital are denied the basic necessities?' Mrs. Gubbins dissolved into tears, wondering at the ingratitude of a so-called 'great man' when she had tried so hard to please him!

The following morning saw a scene of indescribable confusion by the gate. The intervening hours had been put to good use, with every vehicle not damaged by the bombardment piled high with household possessions. Catherine, Pattie and Cristabel laughed until their sides ached at the sight of a group of very rotund ladies obviously wearing every stitch of clothing they possessed.

'Thank goodness we don't have a lot to worry about,' observed Cristabel pragmatically, 'I don't think this is a picnic we are going on!'

'Look, there's Hal and Harriet,' said Catherine, waving, 'I shall miss those two, especially Harriet, she was so good with Rose.'

At last the column set off. It passed the Baillie Guard Gate, the gate that had been closed for so long. The names of each group were called out as they went forward to make sure no-one was left behind. Protected and shielded by the relief force, they moved forward, a long line of bullock carts, doolies and horse drawn carriages. There was constant gunfire setting their nerves on edge; they were not to be allowed to forget for an instant that they were moving through enemy lines, and that they must be quiet at all costs.

'How do they expect quiet?' hissed Pattie, walking behind Catherine. Ahead a bullock cart got jammed in a narrow street, and there was much swearing by the native driver until he could get the ponderous vehicle through the narrow space. The column stretched, full of grumbling women and fretful children, unable to understand why they were continually shushed by their parents when they were *free* at last!

They reached the grounds of the Sikanderbagh, where they were fed, with the dead of the previous day's battle around them. Children ran around excited by being given white bread, while rumours spread that 1,857 rebels had perished, which had to be a good omen!

Then they were hurried on to the safety of Dilkusha Park, where they could be more easily defended. Long before they reached their final destination, the three women were totally exhausted. Unused to walking any distance and still weak from the effects of malnutrition, there were many who would not have reached the safety of the park had it not been for the troops who lined the way. These kindly men despised the imperious memsahibs riding comfortably in their carriages, but three weary but persevering young women roused their finest instincts. They were passed from one to another; helped over pot-holes and lifted over obstructions. Rose was taken from Catherine more than once and carried for some distance before being returned to her. They knew that their rescuers acted solely out kindness was brought home to them when a young private observed too loudly to his mate,

'If that's what siege does for 'em, you can keep 'em; not much as lookers, are they?'

The trio were stunned for a moment, and then laughed out loud until hushed by a harassed looking lieutenant. They apologised and hurried on their way.

Catherine moved like a zombie, her feet aching and blistered in their inadequate sandals. The pause at Sikanderbagh had helped lift them for a while, but then they stumbled onward.

At last they reached the park, where preparations had been made to greet them. Tents were erected and tables laid with food; more food than they had seen for many a long, weary week. Catherine felt too tired to appreciate it, and retired to the nearest available tent to feed Rose. Pattie found her there presently, fast asleep with Rose asleep on her breast; she settled the pair more comfortably. The tent looked tiny, but it was theirs. With Cristabel squeezed in as well, and Rose wedged between them, the threesome slept for nearly fifteen hours.

The Residency was finally evacuated by November 22nd by the remaining troops, the last to leave being Outram and Inglis; though not quite! Captain Waterman of the rearguard had fallen asleep with exhaustion and woke to find everyone gone. The eerie silence and desolate scene totally unhinged his mind after all he had endured, and though he escaped, he had to be invalided home; a broken man.

Only two days later, Havelock died of dysentery in the arms of his son, and was buried at the Alambagh. He was mourned by men closest to him and by Joseph Harrington of Kotepore, who observed to his wife when he was finally reunited with her, that Havelock was one of the few officers who he had any respect for!

There was a period of rest in Dilkusha Park where they were able to recoup their sadly depleted strength. The Park was lovely, full of dappled shade. They all seem to have forgotten what trees and flowers looked like after so long, and laughed aloud at the antics of the ubiquitous squirrels, and exclaimed at the beautiful deer that soon became bolder and approached them to be fed. Children ran about clutching crusts of bread and shrieking with delight; the atmosphere was almost carnival. Then they were moved to the Alambagh.

Reunited with their men, the three friends were happy again and prayed that the situation would continue as long as possible, though Catherine and Cristabel knew that their husbands would have to leave them again to report to their units as soon as the families were safe in Allahabad. But that was the future, today was for relaxing and talking and laughing without constant gunfire. Today was for eating well and being together and night!

Finally they were moved out again, moving along the road to Cawnpore; a name and place so emotive that they dreaded what they might find there,

'Never fear', reassured Joe, 'there's no trace of the massacre left. Catherine and Pattie remembered their dear friend Charlotte, and regaled Cristabel with anecdotes of her so that she must have thought her a saint!

The road was muddy after a recent shower of rain, and the column was several miles long. As usual, when the British marched, they were surrounded by innumerable servants; passing strange when so many of their countrymen were bent on destruction! The soldiers of the rearguard at the Alambagh turned out to wish them 'God speed', and to press on them gifts of eggs and bread, sweetmeats and milk that the trio did not know what to do with them all. At the last moment, a laughing David arrived with a phaeton that had once been an elegant and graceful vehicle. Now it was a ramshackle affair, with mismatched wheels; but it was a vehicle and pulled by a moth-eaten nag. David laughed anew at their expression and asked if they preferred to walk, 'no, no' they assured him, and were handed into the carriage as though they were going to a ball! They sat perched atop a carriage more suited to Rotten Row than an Indian track after the rainy season, but it lurched along with the nag in the shafts looking as though it was about to expire at any moment!

All through the day soldiers went past them; sailors from the Shannon in their blue and white outfits, and Highlanders marching to the skirl of their pipes. The men of the 32nd Foot who had so long defended Lucknow, were easily recognised by their rags, but their spirits were high and they exchanged quips with the three riding high above them.

They rested that night, unable to pitch tents and thankful that the weather was dry and warm; in the morning they moved on again. They had forty miles to cover before evening and there would be no time to exchange pleasantries.

In the distance they could hear gunfire but did not know the reason for it as thought the enemy had been left far behind. Later that day as they halted briefly, Joe came up on horseback from the sowar lines. His face was grim,

'It seems that Windham in Cawnpore is being attacked by Tantia Topi' There is a rumour that the bridge of boats into Cawnpore has been fired but we won't know until we get closer; but Windham's a good man.' Then he was gone.

The column kept moving, though Campbell had gone on ahead, He found Windham in the old Wheeler entrenchment, having been put to flight by Tantia Topi's forces. Campbell was furious because all the stores and baggage he had left had been destroyed by the rebels, but his own arrival had seemingly turned things around, and the Indians fled, leaving the bridge intact.

The column arrived that evening, and preparations were immediately made to evacuate them to Allahabad, as Tantia Topi was still lurking in the vicinity.

'Will we ever be safe?' asked a weary Pattie of Chris, but he had no answer for her. Both Joe and David were on guard duty, and he bore the brunt of three querulous females alone!

The very next day they were ready to go, when the final 'bombshell' struck, All the soldiers had to remain behind to engage and defeat the troops of Tantia Topi and the Nana Sahib once and for all. David and Joe came to their wives in the early hours of the morning,

'See you in Allahabad a chara,' whispered Joe against Catherine's hair, shining again with washing and improving health. She nodded against his gold lacing, too full of emotion to speak. Nearby she could hear Cristabel sobbing, and she was determined not to give way this time.

'Take care of the little one for me, and I'll be back before you know it.' She nodded again, raising her mouth for a kiss. The long weeks and months of deprivation swept over them and both were shaken by a wave of longing. Joe looked deep into his wife's eyes. Then he let her go to lift her into the phaeton. He took his daughter from Pattie and cradling her for a moment, passed her to the grieving but dry eyed Catherine. A moment later, Cristabel and then Pattie were lifted in. Chris shook hands with Joe and David,

'I'll mind them for you,' he said, his voice husky with emotion.

The column moved off.

Chapter 15

'Well Davy my friend; there they go!' Joe sighed as the last of the column of men, women and children disappeared down the road to Allahabad in a cloud of dust. But there was no time to feel sad at the loss of their wives for the sound of bugles and drums called them to order. Waving a cheerful farewell, David Lewis hurried off the find his unit of the 32nd Foot, the men of the 'ragged Regiment' as Campbell called them! Joe moved off to find his detachment of sowars, their blue coats making them easy to spot from a distance.

Orders were being issued as an artillery bombardment of the bridge of boats began. Nana Sahib with his shrewd military adviser, Tantia Topi was determined to punish the cheeky British who dared snatch their prisoners from under their very noses. The British retired behind the town walls as the rebels attacked in great numbers.

Joe found himself at the rear with his sowars, as Peel's sailors began a counter bombardment. The wall held strongly, resisting the rebels until Campbell was ready to counter attack. Joe waited until the order came to advance, and with lances glittering in the sunshine and harness jingling, he led his unit of sowars forward. When they were clear of the wall, he steadied them, and fixing his eyes on his target, a battery on top of a slight rise, he extended his sword arm forward and yelled,

'Cha…rg….e.' The sowars began to gather speed with Joe as the tip of a speeding arrowhead. He saw the battery get closer and closer, and the rebels around it start back in alarm. Then they were among them; no room for musket work here, it was hand to hand fighting all the way. The lances of the sowars had been used to deadly effect, and now they wielded their tulwars, so sharp they could cleave a man right down his length, or sweep a man's head from his body. The fight was short, sharp and bloody and the enemy was put to rout.

Taking a moment to look around him, Joe that the tide of battle was flowing their way and everywhere, rebel troops could be seen taking flight. He led his men from one strong point to another, assisting in rolling up the enemy, and sending back captured guns and ammunition carts.

There was a great roar from his left, and leading his men in that direction, Joe found General Mansfield on the point of overcoming the Nana Sahib himself. From a nearby vantage point, Joe saw him flee, surrounded by his retinue. From deep within him, Joe felt for the first time that the uprising was over.

Later they found the Nana Sahib's treasure hidden in a well in Bithur as the chased the Indian leader from his domain.

That night, Campbell's men celebrated their victory in Cawnpore, but it was a somewhat muted affair, for none of them could forget the events that had taken place there. Joe decided that now was the time for him to leave. Havelock had told him that the Kotepore Regiment was in Delhi, and with Catherine safely on her way to Allahabad, there was nothing else to keep him here. Besides in the prevailing confusion of different units fighting alongside each other, it was time to lose 'Lieutenant John Harvey' before he became too firmly established. He relied on his equivocal position to cover his tracks.

He had entered Havelock's garrison as a Lieutenant of the 94th Foot who had otherwise all perished at the Nana Sahib's orders by the Sati Chowra Ghat, close to where they were now encamped. Havelock knew that he had come from Kotepore, but had probably not informed anyone else of that fact. Outram and Campbell knew him merely as an unattached soldier helping out with the sowars.

With all this in mind, he sought out Campbell that very evening, and informed him that he felt that he should rejoin in Regiment in Delhi. He was deliberately vague about identifying the Regiment, and as he had suspected, the harassed commander had no time to probe further. He did, though, question the wisdom of travelling while the countryside was still inflamed, but was reassured when Joe said he would adopt the native disguise he had used when they first met outside Lucknow. Campbell thanked him for his efforts and sent him on his way. He had nearly left the room when a terse voice commanded him to leave his name and that of his Regiment with an aide so that a commendation could be sent to his Colonel. Joe swallowed hard, saluted and left hurriedly. Fortunately there was not an aide to be found so he hurried away to find Gopi, and bid David farewell.

Before midnight, the pair slipped away, the borrowed uniform bundled up with his bed roll, and ready to be discarded as soon as possible. They left an encampment secure in the knowledge that they had for the moment put their chief protagonist to flight.

The first person Joe saw as he entered the Kotepore Regiment's headquarters in Delhi was Adam Swales, who looked at him open mouthed. A moment later Joe was hugged fiercely and then his hand pumped up and down briskly,

'You're a sight for sore eyes; where'd you spring from? Where've you been all this time? Still dressed like a native I see!' Joe laughed and rescued his mauled hand, rubbing it with affected grimaces of pain,

'One thing at a time! It's good to see you too. I must report to Major Willoughby; or is it Colonel now? And then I'll tell you all. Gopi, stay with Sergeant Swales until I get back.' Adam watched the broad back retreating down the corridor with an absurd grin on his face, 'God but it's good to see that head of red hair again!'

'Come on Gopi, I'll see if I can find a room for your Sahib in this rabbit warren.'

Colonel Willoughby, for his promotion had been officially ratified, stood with his back to the window overlooking an ornate courtyard in the heart of Delhi, and surveyed the dishevelled figure in front of him. Like Adam, he was absurdly pleased to see the younger man, but was aware of his new position in front of the hovering aide, Captain Forsyth.

'Well, Sergeant Harrington, it has been a good few months since you left us. Were you successful in your mission? Just a moment,' and turning to Forsyth, Willoughby gave him an errand. As soon as he had left the room, he strode across to Joe and pumped his hand vigorously. Joe felt that his hand was going to go numb with all the manhandling!

'Well, don't keep me in suspense, man; Catherine, did you find her?'

'I did, eventually. She was in Lucknow, but I was, er, delayed on the way by an unfortunate bullet that nearly put an end to me, had it not been for an old Indian woman and her healing skills!' Willoughby looked horrified'

'I'd have thought that your disguise would have been more effective?'

'It was a British bullet,' observed Joe, drily. 'I was some time recovering, and by the time I did the siege was under way. In the meantime, I diverted to Cawnpore in case she was there,' James' head came up at that,

'So you were there when….?

'Yes,' said Joe quietly, 'but thank goodness Catherine was not; but I ended up with Havelock's forces and went in to Lucknow with him.'

Willoughby was silent for a moment, sifting papers about his desk until he found the one he had apparently been searching for,

'You have just explained a despatch that has been puzzling me. It is from Brigadier-General Outram, and he has sent a commendation for a Lieutenant John Harvey of the Kotepore Regiment, who distinguished himself in the relief of Lucknow, passing through enemy lines to deliver a vital message to Sir Campbell's forces. Perhaps you can explain who this person is, Joe, as you were there at the time!' Joe searched his commander's face and found what he was looking for, a glint of humour in the green eyes. Nevertheless, the mouth under the gingery moustache did not smile. There was silence in the room for a while as Joe marshaled his thoughts,

'It seemed to be the right thing to do at the time,' he said, apparently inconsequentially, 'it was after the massacre by the Ganges when the besieged from Cawnpore had been promised safe passage by boat. I had to get to Havelock to tell him that there were women and children locked up in that terrible Bibigarh. It was the only uniform I could find to fit me and…' He got no further, for James was openly chuckling now,

'My God, Joe, but you're brazen. You ought to be court-martialled for this. But how can I punish an officer so highly thought of my Outram? Apparently Havelock himself suggested the commendation before he died. How on earth do you do it? How do you gain admiration of all you come across?' Joe began to feel embarrassed by the fulsome praise, but was delighted to see James tear the despatch across once and then twice more.

'I think Lieutenant John Harvey had better catch a nasty dose of dysentery and sadly pass away very quickly, don't you?' Joe nodded fervently in agreement.

He was sent away to find a new uniform and a billet in the myriad rooms of the mansion in Delhi that Willoughby had commandeered for his men. He was also told to report back the next day to render a full account of the events he had witnessed in Cawnpore and Lucknow.

'By the way, Joe, are you a father now?' Joe blushed,

'Yes Sir. Thank you Sir. I have a daughter; we've named her Rose. Oh, but Sir, Catherine nearly didn't survive the birth; it was so bad in Lucknow, you won't believe!' And Joe caught a sob back from his throat.

'Gently lad. Leave it all till tomorrow.' Joe nodded, saluted and left quickly before his remembered grief could overwhelm him.

That evening, two men took their ease together, wholly comfortable with each other. The room was small, but well furnished with rattan chairs softened by plump, silk covered cushions. Fretted windows overlooked another of the mansion's innumerable courtyards, though little could be seen of it at this late hour. The room was lit by an oil lamp, the light glowing through a brass shade, fretted like the windows, and casting curious shadows round the room.

The light softened and blurred the outlines of the two men, their long legs stretched out before them as they lounged in the chairs, but it was sufficient for their purpose for they were deep in conversation.

The light showed Adam's face, much the same as it had been when he had left his loving home so many years before, a callow and dreamy youth. Age and the Indian sun may have dried and tanned the skin, but the essence of the man was still the same, the dark hair flopping romantically over his intelligent forehead, the brown eyes soft and introspective. Long experience of his fellow man, both high and low born had not changed the essential goodness of this man or destroyed his faith in human nature; Adam Swales would be the same romantic dreamer to the end of his days.

The light also softened the outlines of Joe's face and smoothed out the radiating lines from the corner of his eyes, and the lines of suffering etched either side of his firm nose. Joe would carry the marks from his experience at Cawnpore to the end of his days! Like Adam, his basic nature had not been changed by his experience in the ranks of the British army, the 'scum of the earth.' He was still eager to learn, to absorb information and experience like a sponge, to take everything he could from it all, and where possible, share it with kindred spirits. His favourite of all those spirits was sitting in front of him and they were busy exchanging their experiences during the months since they had parted.

'What was the journey north like?' asked Joe, 'I only know that you reached the hills safely, Were you attacked on the way?'

'No,' replied Adam, 'but the first day or so we were on edge, expecting the worst. Colonel Willoughby kept sending out scouts and keeping double guard at all times, day and night. But it was soon apparent that the attack we suffered was not general. Very soon we were passing through villages where the looks we got were the same as always. What was even stranger, the servants who had all vanished the morning of the attack kept reappearing; must've trailed us, and rejoined when they thought it safe to do so. It proved that they'd been frightened into deserting. Christina's ayah came to us with tears in her eyes and begged to go with us; what could we do?'

'And then?'

'Ah. When we got to Simla, that's when the fun started! Not with the rebels,' seeing the look on Joe's face, 'the women! You should have seen some of the expressions when officer's wives were told they had to share with wives from the ranks until more suitable accommodation could be found. My God, I thought we were in for another mutiny there and then; among the memsahibs!' Adam's eyes streamed at the memory, and Joe joined in, his fertile imagination conjuring up pictures of Enid Conroy assailed by the lower class of 'common law' wives.

'So what happened next?'

'Colonel Willoughby beat a strategic if cowardly retreat! He'd already sent a despatch to Anson to inform him of the situation, and to get his position ratified. But then we had the news that Anson had died of cholera *en route* from Agra. But, Sir Henry Barnard had taken over, and he ordered us to join him at Delhi as fast as we could. So leaving Mrs. Willoughby with the unenviable job of sorting things out in Simla, we marched south with all speed. Mind you, with the temperatures soaring with every mile we travelled, it was not quite as fast as we hoped.'

'All this must have happened while I lay in that village recovering from that wretched bullet wound?' Adam nodded, having had Joe's saga already that evening.

'We got to Delhi and joined the camp on top of the ridge overlooking Delhi, you know Joe, the one to the north?' Joe nodded, picturing the scene,

'That's a strong position; how long did it take to recapture the city?'

'You'd think so, but though we had a good view of the city, we could also see rebel reinforcements arriving across the bridge of boats. By God, they had the infernal cheek to sing our songs as they marched in. They even sang 'God Save the Queen!' Can you believe that?' Joe could only grin at that.

'But,' went on Adam, 'it was no joke. It was like a furnace up there on that ridge, and a lot of the men weren't used to the hot weather. Colonel Willoughby encouraged us to rest through the hottest part of the day in light clothes. But I saw other Regiments who were ordered to wear jackets at all times! There were even some in brass helmets! And then cholera visited us again. You know Joe; I'm of the opinion that we are largely to blame for it, or at least our own waste! I've noticed before that camps that keep their latrines away from living areas have much less disease. But we were all thrown together on that ridge. We couldn't even bury our dead properly.'

'But didn't you attack the city?'

'We bombarded it, but there was no organised attack at all. We could even see the rebels carousing in the streets in a state of drunkenness half the time. Hodson pressed for attack, but Barnard didn't seem to be able to make up his mind. One was planned, but no-one told the piquet officer to stand down his men.' Adam shook his head at the memory! 'And all the time men were dying of cholera and sunstroke. There was a feeling that dying in battle was preferable to sitting and waiting for disease to strike! Colonel Willoughby kept our morale up by keeping us busy in the cooler hours, but you could almost feel the spirits of the men on the ridge sinking day by day.' Adam paused to light a cheroot, and call for another brandy-pani for the two of them. Then puffing vigorously, he continued,

'Then on the anniversary of Plassey, the rebels attacked, they must've known the legend as well as we did! That was a battle, let me tell me and a close thing; but we won, thank God. But it was not without its disasters; the rains started and Barnard died of cholera! Old Archdale Wilson was put in to replace him; not a man to inspire confidence!'

'Isn't it strange,' observed Joe, 'that the British soldier is probably the best in the world, but is so often let down by his commander?'

'You must remember,' returned Adam, 'that an officer just has to have enough money to buy promotion, he doesn't have to be a good soldier!'

'I wonder if that will ever change. It just seems so unjust; Havelock is one of the best commanders I have ever come across, but he really was too old for the job, having had to wait years for his command.'

The two old friends grumbled awhile on the iniquities of the British system of promotion, fortified by several brandy-panis, supplied by an eager Gopi, glad to be back in his customary role. He had even rediscovered his favourite garment, a dhoti. Joe had to smile at his beaming face when he brought in the drinks, white teeth gleaming in the dim light. He had left off his turban and his black hair was dressed with coconut oil which glistened in the lamp light, and smelt very strong!

'So what happened when Wilson took over?' queried Joe.

'Morale lifted a little, but we still weren't getting anywhere. We'd heard about Cawnpore by then, which upset a lot of men; many had friends or relatives there. Then of course there was Lucknow. But then John Nicolson arrived! What a man he was, full of drive and vigour, and so resourceful! Even his detractors allow him that! He came with a large number of reinforcements having fought a few pitched battles along the way; and best of all, he won them! You know Joe; they were the first wins we had since the uprising began! So you can understand the effect on morale he had. By this time, inhabitants began to desert from Delhi, which was another boost; their own rats were deserting!' He paused again to sip from his brandy glass,

'Go on,' urged Joe, 'you can't leave it there!'

'We finally got the orders to launch a full scale attack, but not until 14th September. We'd been bombarding at close range to breach the walls and on 13th all the commanders were called in for a briefing. Wilson was nominally in charge but everyone knew that the driving force was

Nicholson. It's my belief we would still be sitting up there on that accursed ridge if it had been left to Wilson. We also had Campbell and Hope Grant; good men, both,' Joe nodded, 'I've met them. Go on.'

'Our Regiment was assigned the Kashmir Gate and were due to go in with the second wave. We spent the night before preparing ourselves; writing letters and the like. I believe that most of us expected to perish the next day, but strangely, no-one seemed to be afraid. We'd lost a lot of men to disease already, including Major Conroy; though I'm sorry to say, he was not much missed. We were supposed to attack at dawn, but the rebels repaired the breaches, so the sun was well and truly up before we set off. I can't tell you much about the battle to be honest; it was just one long blur. I remember we threw up scaling ladders, and then we were in. There was noise and confusion; but I was wounded early on; a slash across the left arm.' Adam rubbed it reminiscently, 'but I hardly felt it at the time; just noticed the blood running across my hand. Then we were in those narrow streets and there was fire from the houses; men were dropping all around! Then suddenly, we were mixed up with Campbell's men. The order came to press on to the Jama Masjid; you know the place Joe? It's clear across the city and already we were exhausted.

But we fought our way through, expecting reinforcements from Nicholson coming through the Kabul Gate. It was then that it all went wrong! Nicholson had been killed trying to take the gate, and the Jama Masjid was sandbagged against us. We had to retire to the Kashmir Gate and wait out the night.' Adam took another break, noting briefly that he should have become book writer after all this story telling, but Joe begged him to finish the tale and not leave him in suspense.

'You may not believe it, but things seemed to go our way after that! If the Indians had pressed home their advantage, we would all have perished at that gate. I heard that Wilson wanted to call a halt, but was overruled. It took us two days, but we took over the city.' He smiled bleakly for a moment, 'but we lost some good men in the attempt; one of them was Major Colby. He was greatly missed by his Company, let me tell you! But there were others,' Adam listed those that he and Joe had known well, and the two fell silent for a while in memory of lost friends, then Adam took up the tale again, now drawing to its close, he told Joe,

'The most amazing thing is that half the men were blind drunk! They'd broken into a liquor store near the Kashmir Gate and before the officers could stop them, were imbibing freely. They remained in that condition all the next day. Whether it gave them the courage to go on, we'll never know. But the rebels did not seem to realise and take advantage. But in the end we won, and then we took the fort. The King and his sons had fled, but the old King surrendered a week later. His sons stayed in hiding as they knew they were implicated in the worst atrocities. Hodson was sent to capture them, which he did, but then, to my mind, he behaved shamefully; he shot the three of them himself!' Adam grimaced with distaste, 'and he made them strip first; you know what Indians, especially high born ones, think of that!' Joe nodded, shocked that a British Officer could behave in such a barbaric fashion, but had he not encountered such before? But Adam was speaking again,

'But that was the end of the uprising here. The next week or so saw terrible looting and outrages against the people of Delhi, many of whom didn't even support the rebellion,' Adam sighed, 'I suppose it was inevitable after all the atrocity stories the men had been fed, and all that time on top of the ridge; but after all, our own experience in Kotepore was bad enough. Many of the Regiments are gone now; you know about Campbell and Grant yourself. But we were ordered to stay and restore some sort of law and order, and Colonel Willoughby keeps things very tight. But it's nearly over now.

Joe mused over Adam's tale, not so different to his own after all. He had experienced the horror of Cawnpore, but could not agree with the behaviour of Neill afterwards. Horror and violence are not cured by more horror and violence. It must all end if the country was to get back to some sort of semblance of normality.

He said as much to Adam, and they went more time exchanging information of their time apart, midnight becoming early morning before they stumbled to their beds. One look at the bloodshot eyes told Gopi that it was more than his life was worth to wake the Sahib before mid-morning at the earliest!

A bleary eyed Joe reported to Captain Forsyth at eleven the next day, to be told to come back when he looked decent. Beside, said the Captain, his mouth wrinkling in disgust, the Colonel had been called away until the next day. Thankfully, Joe took himself back to bed.

After making a lighter night of it with Adam, a fresher looking Joe reported to the Colonel's office the next day. He was instructed to sit down at a desk and write his report, and the Colonel would see him in due course. Wondering if he was in some sort of disgrace from the Colonel, Joe seated himself across the room from Forsyth. He could feel the aide's gaze on him, but couldn't interpret his expression. He took up a pen and dipping it into the ink well, began to write. Soon he was immersed in the account, brought back so vividly by telling it to Adam. He reached the moment when he was about to enter the Bibigarh; suddenly the scene was fresh in his mind again. He could even smell the appalling stench that hung over the place like a miasma. Sweat started out on his brow and his hand began to shake; he heard a voice as though from a great distance,

'Harrington; what is it man? You look sick, for God's sake.' A shadow fell over the desk as Forsyth leaned over him to see what was wrong. As he read the words glaring out of the whiteness of the paper, the Captain fell silent. He moved away and poured a stiff whiskey into a tumbler and pressed it to Joe's rigid mouth.

'Drink this,' he said tersely. Joe obeyed, and as the spirit went down, he was able to unclench his jaw and the fists bunched in his lap. Putting his head on the desk, he began to weep; convulsive sobs reaching up from his very depths. Forsyth gazed at him for a long moment, compassionately, and then went in search of Adam.

Later, Adam told Joe that he had always believed the prim and proper Captain Forsyth to be incapable of human emotion! But the writing of the story had exorcised Joe's soul. The act of setting it down in writing, even more than the act of relating it, had helped him live the experience again, and in doing so, put it behind him forever. He would never forget it, but he could now live with it.

His report finished, and good tiffin inside him, Joe waited to see Colonel Willoughby. He was finally told to enter, so in he marched, resplendent in his new uniform, shako punctiliously under one arm,

'Ah; there you are Harrington.' Said James, inconsequentially,

'Sir!'

'At ease Joe!' smiled James as Forsyth disappeared, 'settling in?'

'Yes Sir.'

'Well don't get too comfortable; we'll be moving out again soon. We've been ordered to join Campbell southwards. There is to be a campaign to clear up pockets of resistance.'

'Why is he confiding in me?' wondered Joe, and 'do the officers know?' As though he had spoken aloud, James answered him'

'That's where I was yesterday, though I understand you were in need of a little extra time to sort your report out.' The words were spoken without reproof, and Joe relaxed.

'I've also read your report; you write a good hand, Joe.'

'Thank you Sir.'

'When you returned, Joe, I had been turning over a project in my mind for some time. I have now reached a decision, though it has not been easy. You actually helped me make the decision by your actions in Lucknow as a Lieutenant!' Joe now felt thoroughly alarmed, but James went on, standing by the fretted window gazing sightlessly at the untidy courtyard below. Joe could see over his shoulder a rather drunken looking statue in the middle of a disused fountain.

'You must know that the system of promotion of officers depends on the purchase of commission?'

'Yes Sir.'

'However, in time of crisis, it is possible to circumvent the system and promote officers on merit. I think what we have could be called a crisis!' He paused for a moment to marshall his thoughts, 'it is also possible to promote from the ranks.' Joe could not believe what he was hearing; promote from the ranks? Could it be possible that he…a Sergeant could be…. no….., but James was continuing,

'We have sustained heavy losses in the battle for Delhi and from disease during the weeks before. I am desperately short of officers. I have decided to promote you and Sergeant Swales to the rank of Lieutenant.' James fell silent and waited for the words to sink in. He smiled at the dawning incredulous look on Joe's face, his jaw actually dropping open. For the first time in many a year, Joe was lost for words! Then it was as though the sun came out from behind a monsoon cloud; joy radiated from the intense blue eyes and he was clearly fighting the urge to reach out and pump his superior officer's hand. James defused the tension by reaching out his own hand but then winced at the force with which Joe seized it. Then he sounded a cautionary note,

'I'm not really sure that I have done you any favours, Joe. It will be easier for Swales, for he is known to be of gentle birth, whereas you….. He left the statement unfinished, for Joe to add quietly,

'Whereas I am from a peasant farm and Irish at that!'

'There are those who admire the way you have improved yourself, but that will not stop the majority of the Regiment's officers disapproving of your elevation. I, too, will be castigated for promoting you. Are you strong enough to take it, Joe?' He got his answer in the steady gaze.

'I thought so otherwise I would not have entertained the thought for a moment. But you maintained the character of Lieutenant for a long time, so you must know how to conduct yourself! Perhaps it is as well we are moving, it'll give them something else to think about. Go now and send Swales to me; oh and Joe, don't tell him, I've a mind to see his reaction myself!' The Colonel was treated to a beautifully executed salute as the newly created Lieutenant Joseph Harrington spun on his heel, and left the room at a brisk march.

Having delivered the message to Adam, and resisting the temptation to drop a hint, he suddenly felt an overwhelming urge to be on his own. Borrowing some casual clothes from Adam's room, he took himself off to wander through the streets of Delhi, trying to remember it as it had been before the uprising. Then the streets had teemed with traders and other people hurrying and scurrying on all sides. Now, though there had been some return to normality, the streets were relatively quiet. He carefully kept to the wider thoroughfares having been warned to stay away from dark alleys. There were too many stories of soldiers disappearing in the meaner streets, never to be seen again. There were clearly badmashes about who would be delighted to put an end to an accursed angrezi.

Presently he found himself at the red fort just as the sun was sinking behind him, throwing the crenellations into sharp relief. His mind teemed with thoughts, and leaning against a wall, stained with the ever present betel juice, he allowed those thoughts free rein. A Lieutenant! Small wonder Colonel Willoughby hadn't felt inclined to punish him for impersonating an officer! But what an exceptional man; Joe had no doubts that if Conroy had been in charge, he would be languishing in a guard house awaiting punishment, flogging, probably, and then reduced to a private for evermore. But, smiled Joe at the thought, Conroy would not have had the intelligence to work out who the mysterious John Harvey was! Mustn't think ill of the dead, he scolded himself, but his grin grew broader. Poor Reggie; what a way to die, his life flowing out of him in his own stinking effluent instead of gloriously in battle. If one had to die, that must be the way for it to happen.

A chill wind got up, for it was nearly Christmas, bringing himself back to his surroundings. A few Indians moved about, eyeing him in frank curiosity; he called to them in Urdu and they grinned, and went on their way.

Lieutenant! A chance to feel real power, to carry real responsibility. There was no doubt in his mind that he could cope with the situation, and at least he would have Adam for mutual support. But he also had no illusions about it either. The likes of the late and unlamented Carless would have plenty to say about it, but the majority of the officers would think that their Colonel had taken leave of his senses. Never mind; he was used to isolation as he had not had anything in common with his fellow soldiers for a long time, and was content with his own company, or more lately, with Catherine's and of course, Adam. Well, in the fullness of time, he was sure he would show them all what he was capable of.

The sun was disappearing beyond the city walls when he finally straightened up and retraced his steps back to headquarters. There he found an impatient Adam striding up and down the courtyard waiting for him.

'Where've you been?' he asked urgently, 'I've been waiting to talk to you and you disappear off again!' He looked aggrieved and Joe was immediately contrite,

'Sorry Adam. I just wanted to be alone for a while; to take it all in. I don't think I could have trusted myself to speak before!' Adam forgave him. Leading the way back to his room, considerably larger than Joe's, they both bellowed for their respective bearers, who arrived at a trot, alarmed by all the noise. They stared open mouthed at their sahibs, who, in the few moments since they had called, had suddenly thrown off all restraints and were jumping up and down clutching each other's arms! The sight of the two Hindus staring from the doorway set them off in paroxysm of mirth. At last the two men were able to gasp out,

'Whiskey-panis, chuldi, chuldi,' sending the bearers scampering away convinced that their sahibs had finally been driven out of their minds by their experiences!

Later, Joe and Adam went to the Sergeant's Mess, aware that by the next day the new promotions would be listed, and they would have to face the gauntlet of the Officer's Mess. The other sergeants were bemused to be offered drinks 'on them', and a vast quantity of ale was swilled down parched throats. The men were bored with Delhi and were eager to return to Kotepore and familiar surroundings, or get back to the fighting. They had all indulged in some looting immediately after the city was retaken, but now it was strictly forbidden on pain of severe punishment; and furthermore, there was not much left to loot! So they were all ready for a relaxed evening of drinking at someone else's expense.

They all shared an excellent meal of a variety of curries and dal and were replete to the point of discomfort. Eventually Joe and Adam took themselves off to a chorus of good wishes. As they left they gave instructions for the men to have another round or two on them. Arm in arm they set off for Adam's room and settled to another cosy chinwag.

'Will you write and tell Catherine?' enquired Adam. Joe mused for a moment,

'No; I've a mind to see her face when I appear in a Lieutenant's jacket again. She'll think I have gone mad with it all.' And his teeth gleamed in a broad grin,

'But I must write and tell her where I am, but warn her not to write until we are settled again. Have you heard from Louise since you have been here?'

'Yes indeed. Even when we up on the Ridge, the Colonel ordered that letters to Simla could all go in the Regimental despatches; he had left a small force there just in case trouble did spread there after all. Louise told me about all the skirmishing that went on over the rooms.' He smiled reminiscently, 'she found a small bungalow for herself and Christina with two other sergeant's wives and says she is reasonably comfortable. Her last letter complains that it is very cold. I'd forgotten that none of them are used to being there in the winter; they are usually back in Kotepore at this time of year. She said that some hill men came by with some shaggy coats to sell. They smelt appalling, apparently, but are very warm. She bought one for herself and Christina, as did Mrs. Willoughby, but most of the other officer's wives turned their noses up at them; seem to prefer shivering!'

'Adam?'

'Mm?'

'Have you seen or heard anything of the Khan's? The night before they left Kotepore the talk was of their joining the King in Delhi.' Adam pulled deeply on his cheroot,

'It is possible. When we first camped on the Ridge we could see into Delhi very clearly, and more than once I thought I could see those white outfits with scarlet sashes; pretty distinctive even from a distance. But then all the sepoys took to throwing away their uniforms and wearing white, so it was difficult to tell. In the final push, I couldn't say who we were fighting, but the Khan's were not among the prisoners taken, that I do know. It doesn't mean they weren't there; there was time to get away before the end, and it was the King and his sons who were being chased all over the place. Rumours abound, and the talk was of them joining the Rani of Jhansi. I know you were close to Saeed, but if he has thrown in his lot with the rebels, it is unlikely you will ever see him again.

Joe sat quietly, digesting the information. A memory rose unbidden; Saeed with his forearm laid alongside his own, and drawing blood to show that they were the same after all. And then, brown eyes awash with tears, saying 'goodbye, I hope it won't be for too long'. Well it had been; too many weeks and months had passed since then, and an aeon of experience. But for all that, Joe missed him sorely and in spite of all the terrible events, still counted the Prince as one of his closest friends. He sighed deeply; these thoughts he could not share with Adam; he doubted he would understand. The evening ended after too many brandy-panis. This night would be the last of their old life; the next day would see them rise as Lieutenants, and all the problems that would bring.

The next morning found Joe and Adam peering at the listings outside Colonel Willoughby's office. They drew in their breath sharply; they would be together under Major Harding. Various other names were displayed as well, many of whom Joe did not recognise, reminding him more than anything just how many of their Regiment had been lost during the retaking of Delhi. Adam confirmed this, and identified a few recently arrived from England,

'And it shows' he grumbled tersely, 'full of their own importance and ready to tell us how we were all wrong in the way we handled the Mutiny, and full of righteous wrath against the natives; all of them!'

At that moment, Major Robert Harding appeared and ushered them into his office. They stood rigidly to attention as he eyed them up and down. Robert had just spent an hour with James, his erstwhile friend and now senior officer. For the first time since they had met, they were at total variance with each other, as James told him of his decision to promote two Sergeants.

'But James,' he protested, 'I could just about understand Swales; he is at least of gentle birth even if his family is impoverished; but Harrington! Good God, I was there when you brought him in from the back of beyond, stinking of poverty and death. And I am not the only one; there'll be a riot over this, you mark my words!'

Then he looked at James' face for the first time; it wore a cold shuttered look, his green eyes like chips of ice. His tone was clipped as he replied,

'Then I rely on you to make sure that there is no trouble over this. I have given the matter long consideration and have reached my decision and I do not care to be questioned. But I will say just this, Harrington has the keenest mind of any soldier in this Regiment; officer or not, and is certainly better educated than some I could mention!' Harding gave up. He had no illusions about the effect that this promotion would have, but accepted that argument was futile. The only good thing about it all was the two were being moved from their familiar A Company to one where they were less well known.

It was no accident that James had chosen his old friend Robert Harding to take on the onerous task of training two new lieutenants. He knew that though Robert might disapprove, he was completely loyal, and would do his best to force the transition on his company. He softened the blow a little,

'We have orders to move out within the week. Campbell is moving out of Cawnpore before Christmas and we are to meet up at Fategarh with the intention of opening up the route to the Punjab. Being on the move will give the men something else to think about rather than their Commanding Officer finally being driven mad!'

So now, Harding surveyed his new officers with less than enthusiasm. He may disagree with James, but he did know the worth of these two; both were widely read and *au fait* with events in India. But Swales was a dreamer, more ready to philosophise about a situation than take action over it. Whereas Harrington, for all his peasant background, had a shrewd brain and a capacity to assess a situation rapidly and accurately; and then act. He sighed and then spoke,

'Colonel Willoughby has put you two in my Company. I will be honest and tell you that I disagree with the decision, and will be looking for any excuse,' he paused to glare at the pair standing rigidly to attention, and repeated, 'any excuse to send you two back to the ranks, where you belong. Understood?'

'Yes Sir,' they chorused. Harding grunted, and proceeded to outline their duties as lieutenants in his company. If he intended to frighten them, he failed to do so, as they both considered their duties as sergeants far more onerous, and wondered how officers managed to fill their hours in peacetime! No wonder junior officers seemed to have a habitual air of boredom. Doubtless the reality would be very different? Harding finally dismissed them to go and see about their uniforms, with a warning that they had two days to present themselves fully accoutered as the Regiment was due to leave Delhi very soon. The two saluted smartly and left the office feeling as mangled as a muslin shirt after the administrations of a dhobi-wallah!

'Phew!' exclaimed Joe as they walked down the corridor, 'if that's the welcome we got from our Major, the rest should be easy.' Adam grinned but did not reply.

They found a derzee in the back streets of Delhi and promised great rewards if he delivered miracles for them. Two evenings later, they stood before a full length mirror in one of the mansion's many rooms. It was extremely ornate and spotted with age, and in the dim light allowed into the room through the fretted windows, it was very difficult to see themselves properly. But that did not dim their enthusiasm in the slightest. First of all they tried on their everyday uniforms; scarlet jacket, not unlike the common soldier, except for the gold frogging and epaulettes. But instead of cross straps in white, pipe-clayed canvas webbing, they had one leather cross strap on the right shoulder, passing over the breast and ending in a housing for a sword, yet to be purchased. The tails of the jacket were stiff with gold thread and made the wearer stand very upright. The pristine white trousers were a perfect fit, and showed off their shapely legs. These tucked into knee length boots in gleaming black leather. The outfit was topped by a brand new shako, finished with a loop of gold rope and a stiff cockade on the left.

The two strutted and cavorted in front of the mirror, admired by the dutiful Gopi, and Adam's bearer, Dara. They assured their sahibs that they had never seen anything so magnificent, and surely the Burra-Sahib Willoughby would be struck dumb with admiration!

Then it was on to the mess outfit. Similar to the everyday outfit but even more gold lacing; the scarlet of the jacket front almost disappearing behind row after row of gold frogs that took at least ten minutes and much swearing by the bearers to fasten,

'God, Gopi,' protested Joe, 'are you trying to strangle me?'

'No Sahib. Please to keep still, Sahib. Ah; it is done.' Sweating profusely, Joe gazed at the gorgeous apparition in the dingy mirror,

'Just wait until Catherine sees me in this; she will be so proud,' he muttered as a wave of longing to see his wife and daughter swept over him; he brushed it away. The sooner this business was over, the sooner he would see them again.

Finally it was time for the ball dress, the main feature being a 'bum freezer' jacket. The cropped style looked positively indecent to him, showing off his physique in more ways than one. He said as much to Adam, who laughed at his innocence and murmured about 'cod-pieces'.

'It seems I have a lot to learn, Adam,' Joe remarked, more soberly now.

'Don't worry old friend, we'll learn together.' In a wave of affection, the two men hugged each other, and Joe counted himself truly fortunate to have such a good friend in Adam. He had long admired and respected James Willoughby of course, but his rank precluded him from being a close friend as was Adam.

All the parading could not put off the moment any longer; that evening they were due to dine in the Officer's Mess at the personal invitation of

Major Harding, to meet their fellow officers. The next day they were due to move out.

Dara and Gopi helped their sahibs with a bath and close shave. Joe also had Gopi trim his hair so that the last of the black dye disappeared. He surveyed himself in the cheval mirror,

'Mm. What d'you think Adam; a moustache might give me more presence?' Adam hooted in derision, whereupon Joe threw his towel at him, causing a startled Dara to nearly draw the razor he was wielding across Adam's throat!

But the horseplay could no longer disguise their trepidation, and donning their mess uniform and shaking each other by the hand, they prepared to make the journey across the courtyard to the Officer's Mess. They could hear laughter as they stepped out into the darkness and skirted the inevitable dried up fountain. A shiver ran down Joe's back; surely the night wasn't that chilly?

The mess was installed in one of the main rooms of the mansion and was very large and airy; a vast open space with a ceiling supported by regularly spaced pillars. There was an abundance of fretwork and decoration, and costly silk hangings adorned the walls. A number of cane chairs and tables filched from other rooms were dotted about, and most of these were occupied by groups of officers from all four companies. A pall of smoke from cheroots and cigars hung in a cloud under a variety of lamps and chandeliers and eddied about where the punkahs moved the balmy air. A hubbub of voices and laughter filled the room as Joe and Adam mounted the two steps from the courtyard and entered the ornate double doors.

As the men seated nearest the door saw the new arrivals they fell silent and nudged their neighbours. The silence spread like a ripple on a pond until it completely filled the room, and every head turned towards the newcomers. Straightening their shoulders, Joe and Adam strode into the room, bowing politely to the assembled officers. Joe saw the scene in startling clarity; the red faces of those who had been there a while; the sweat standing out on the foreheads of the overworked khitmagars; a boil on the back of the neck of Major Jackel. Suddenly he was not nervous anymore; these were only ordinary officers after all, he had talked with generals! Smiling at the assembly, Joe and Adam sat down at a vacant table.

A khitmagar sidled over to them and spoke in a theatrically loud whisper,

'What can I be getting you sahib?'

'Whiskey-pani; chota-pegs,' replied Joe, smiling broadly now. The whole affair was taking on an element of farce. The walls of silence beat about them as the khitmagar shuffled out with his brass tray held high.

On the next table sat a quartet of lieutenants. The one with his back to them was Marcus Mortimer, recently promoted from Ensign; the same Mortimer that had brought down sepoy Roy with one deadly bullet. He reminded Joe of the late and unlamented Carless, with the same blond curls in attractive dishevelment, though he lacked Carless' clear cut profile as his chin had a disastrous tendency to recede, but he spoke with the same high pitched whine. He sat with his favourite cronies, Anthony Lethridge, Vincent Muirhead and Tarquin Nelhams; but it was he who finally broke the silence by observing to them,

'I say, d'you notice the smell in here?' he raised his aristocratic nose, emphasizing his unfortunate chin, and sniffed ostentatiously,

'Is it… a privy…or…no, it's an Irish bog! Hard to tell the difference, wouldn't you say?'

His friends squirmed uncomfortably but gave half hearted laughs, which encouraged Mortimer to further comments. He loudly declaimed on the folly of raising men above their stations and how their esteemed Commanding Officer must be suffering from sunstroke. Joe and Adam incensed him further by paying him not one jot of attention, while the rest of the Mess gradually got bored with the tirade and got on with their interrupted conversations. They may have tacitly agreed with Mortimer, but he was going too far when he denigrated Colonel Willoughby.

Finding that he was losing his audience, Mortimer became even more strident in his invective, threatening to write to Canning in Calcutta to protest the appointment. At that moment, Colonel Willoughby strode into the room, halted when he heard the high pitched whine, and then came soft footed to stand behind Mortimer's chair, much to Joe and Adam's amusement. Mortimer was waxing lyrical as to the contents of his letter to Canning but noticed at last the looks of horror on his friends' faces. He swiveled sharply to find the man that he had been insulting standing at his ease behind him, his arms folded and an unpleasant smile playing about his mouth. His voice was silky smooth as he addressed the discomfited Mortimer,

'You are really most inventive Lieutenant. Report to me tomorrow with a draft of your letter to Canning; I am most impressed!'

Willoughby passed on to his own table with a brief nod of acknowledgement to Joe and Adam, where he was joined by his Majors. The quartet of lieutenants left soon after, led out by a red faced Mortimer.

Later that evening, Major Harding introduced the two new lieutenants to the other officers of C Company. They were greeted with a distinct lack of warmth, but no overt hostility.

The first hurdle was over.

Three days later they left Delhi. It was Christmas Eve.

Watching the milling multitude crossing the Bridge of Boats to form up on the opposite bank of the River Juma, Joe was reminded of his first experience of travelling in India some ten years before. Then he had been amazed at the sheer number of servants that it was considered necessary for a body of soldiers to move about. He was amazed yet again!

The scarlet jackets of the Regiment were almost lost in a teeming torrent of bearers, sweepers, grass cutters, water carriers, doolie and ghari drivers, mahouts with their elephants and other sundry persons who all had some designated duty or other. He shook his head and chuckled at the absurdity of it. Here they were, off to do battle with rebel forces, and the rebels' own countrymen were helping them towards their destination. There was really no fathoming the Indian mind. Doubtless, Gopi would mutter of 'dharma' or observe 'jo hoga, so hoga,' or 'what will happen, will happen!' He had definitely forgotten how noisy the whole affair could be, mahouts shouting 'hup, hup' to get their large charges to rise ponderously from their knees; there was the crack of whips as gun-bullock drivers urged on their clumsy beasts straining in their yolks, bells hanging round their necks adding to the clamour; there were simply Indians everywhere screeching at each other, and British soldiers shouting at the Indians; in short, a cacophonous bedlam!

During the intervening years since their arrival from Bombay, Joe had grown used to travelling in lighter fashion, particular during the past few months, and travelling with Havelock had certainly been a streamlined affair. His musings were rudely interrupted by a loud, raucous voice,

'Jump to it Lieutenant Harrington, see that those men form up; chuldi!'

Joe sighed and 'jumped to it'; it was Captain Alistair McBride.

Following the retreating back of Major Harding down the corridor of the Regiment's offices, two days earlier, Joe and Adam had been extremely nervous. It was the morning after their introduction to the other officers, and they were wondering what was in store for them. They had met Harding on the way, and had been greeted with a curt nod, but he had otherwise been uncommunicative. Entering the office, they found all the Company officers assembled as news of their impending departure had spread, and they expected to receive their orders.

The chatter ceased abruptly as Adam and Joe appeared; it would seem that they had been the topic of conversation. The Major introduced them to their Captains,

'Swales, you are assigned to Captain Timoney, and Harrington, you are with Captain McBride. They will brief you as to your duties. Gentlemen, be seated.' The officers sat down around a circular table, and the plans for departure discussed at length.

As he listened, Joe covertly studied the man from whom he would receive direct orders. His heart had sunk when Harding had announced his decision; why could it not have been the other way round? Captain Timoney was generally held to be a quiet, reasonable man, but McBride was another matter entirely. A minor Irish aristocrat, and a Protestant, he was as rabid a hater of Catholic Irish peasants as Joe had ever met. The man was also well aware of Joe's background as he had been with the Regiment when he joined it in Dublin. His hair was a bright, carroty red and the powerful Indian sun had turned his face a permanent brick red. Cold eyes of an indeterminate shade of muddy brown peered out from under bushy eyebrows. He was inclined to corpulence, and rolls of flesh hung over his tight collar, and strained the gold frogs of his scarlet jacket, which clashed violently with his complexion. Even during the briefing, he was glaring at Joe, his hostility plain to see. He probably would have tolerated Adam, with his gently-born background, but Joe knew that he could expect no mercy. The only difference between him and Lieutenant Mortimer was that he had the sense to keep his thoughts private rather than blab them aloud for the Colonel to hear. Joe wondered uneasily if he had asked Harding to have Joe assigned to him; he shuddered at the thought!

The general briefing over, the Major left them. The meeting broke up. And Captain Timoney greeted Adam affably before carrying him off. Alastair McBride leered at Joe standing stiffly to attention before him, and slowly circled the rigid figure. Joe's flesh crawled when McBride was out of sight behind him; he could hear his breath rasping in his throat, and a wave of foul exhalation swept past his ear. He could feel himself start to tremble and knew that it was what McBride wanted. Joe clenched his teeth to stop himself shaking; God, but this was worse than facing a charge of enemy sepoys! Eventually the corpulent Captain appeared again; leaning forward so that Joe got a blast of his foul breath full in his face, he hissed,

'So; you think you're an officer, you ignorant little bog-trotting turd!' He went on to cast aspersions on his parentage, the morals of his mother and grandmother, his appearance and the state of his uniform; the diatribe went on and on as Joe admitted to himself that the man was certainly inventive! But he stood rigidly to attention, determined not to give the Captain any excuse to reprimand him. Finally, McBride ran out of ideas and breath; panting heavily he sat down and collected himself to deliver the threat that had been hanging in the air since his invective had started,

'I intend to break you, d'you hear? You'll not last a week in that grand uniform; any excuse and you're finished!'

Since then, McBride had been as good as his word, and had had Joe running around every minute of the day, and the night, the more onerous the duty, the better. All the previous night, Joe had been on piquet duty, the Captain claiming that the duty officer had been taken ill, and there was no-one else. Having been busy all that day, Joe had gritted his teeth and fought to stay awake, aware that he was being watched like a hawk. The night had seemed endless.

Then in the morning, the Regiment had turned out in preparation for its departure from Delhi. As ordered Joe formed his men up, trying to ignore the waves of fatigue that swept over him, making his eyes feel as though they were full of grit. The men were grinning, but without animosity; they seemed to dislike the Captain as much as Joe did and were entirely co-operative, 'it's strange,' thought Joe, 'you'd think they'd resent one of their own being promoted.' But it was clearly not so. Joe just didn't realise how much he had endeared himself to these men over the years. Though he had grown beyond them in learning and sophistication, he had never grown too grand to speak to them in their own terms. His innate talent for mimicry enabled him to respond to the broadest of Cockneys, the soft spoken Yorkshire men or the lilting Welsh, not to mention his own countrymen whose numbers were greater than the rest. So the men of his detachment entered into a secret conspiracy to defeat the obnoxious Captain McBride, and they responded to orders from Joe in a way that drew commendation from Major Harding who was passing by, and drew a scowl from the surly captain.

At last they were off, the head of the column a full half mile in front of the rear guard. Almost asleep in the saddle, Joe walked his horse alongside his detachment, not noticing the soldier on the end of the line surreptitiously was holding the drooping rein to ensure that the animal did not stray. Captain Alastair McBride was not going to disgrace their brand new Lieutenant, not if they could prevent it!

Christmas Day was spent travelling, the only concession to the festival being an al fresco service held by the Regimental Chaplain. Even the sermon was curtailed, much to the men's relief, when Colonel Willoughby told the harassed Chaplain to 'get on with it as they had an appointment at Fategarh!' They met Brigadier General Campbell at Bewar and together they occupied Fategarh on 2nd January 1858.

The town was packed with ten thousand troops. Some had come from other parts of India; mostly reinforcements sent from the Punjab by John Lawrence, brother of the gentle and much lamented Sir Henry Lawrence of Lucknow. Others had come from Burma and Ceylon, Mauritius and China, Crimea and even England. The great milling multitude packed the streets and house of Fategarh and formed a vast tented city around it.

Escaping the eagle eye of McBride for a brief moment, Joe met up with Adam on the edge of the organised chaos that was the British army. The two compared noted as to their experiences as Lieutenants, and Adam acknowledged that Joe clearly had the worst of it. Andrew Timoney, he asserted, was the best of fellows, and as long as he carried out his duties, left him alone. Joe sighed.

'With any luck, McBride'll get carried off in battle; I'm not sure I can take much more! I've a mind to plead with Colonel Willoughby to let me be a drummer again!' Adam grinned at the rash threat, but commiserated. He hoped that McBride would not push Joe too far after all they had achieved together. But for now, they had a few precious off-duty moments together and he didn't want to waste them.

'I've had a letter from Louise from Simla just before we left,' confided Adam, 'she says that they've had snow; Louise has never seen it before! And as for Christina, she was so excited that she promptly fell in it, and then howled because it was cold!' Joe grinned as he conjured up the scene, thoughtfully fingering his upper lip. Adam peered at him in the fading light, and then gave a shout of laughter,

'You old devil; you're growing a moustache!' Joe looked sheepish,

'I know; I just thought it might…'

'Give you more 'presence'?' suggested Adam slyly'

'And I didn't want to be recognised; some of these men knew me as Lieutenant Harvey before I actually promoted! Stupid really, when you see the numbers here; I had no idea!' and changing the subject,

'If I could only have a few days free, I could see Catherine and Rose in Allahabad.' Adam looked thoroughly alarmed,

'Joe, you won't try it?' Joe laughed at his expression,

No of course not; it'd be just what McBride is waiting for. But they seem so close and you know, Rose is three months old already and I've already missed so much time in her life.' Adam nodded, empathizing with him as he missed his wife and daughter just as much,

'It was Christina's third birthday on Christmas Day! Have you heard from Catherine, Joe?'

'No, there was no time before we left so I didn't expect to hear. I did write to her with all that has happened since we parted at Cawnpore and sent it via a bunnia who was travelling south, but God knows whether she will get it or not.'

After rushing to get to Fategarh, they then proceeded to kick their heels there. The original intention had been to harry the rebels into Rohilkand, and then 'roll them up'. But orders streamed from Canning in Calcutta contradicting each other day by day. First, Campbell was to stay where he was as Oudh might become inflamed again; then they must return to Cawnpore and await more reinforcements; then they must relieve Outram, still holding off the rebels at the Alambagh outside Lucknow.

The men got restless and disenchanted, 'sitting on their backsides' at Fategarh while others gained glory and plunder all around. One such was Major-General Sir Hugh Rose, recently arrived in India the previous September. He immediately distinguished himself with his dash and decision. A dandified and polished exterior covered a core of steel, and Rose was determined to finish off the campaign as quickly as possible. Not for him the ponderous 'sea' of men on the move; he favoured 'flying columns' that engaged the enemy as often and as quickly as possible, usually in vastly superior numbers. So while Campbell sat in Fategarh, Rose campaigned all around him, moving from Mhow in the south to the aid of beleaguered Europeans in Sauger, then east to Gathakot, finally throwing himself at the fortress city of Jhansi, stronghold of the legendary Lakshmi Bai, its beautiful and warlike Rani. The men sitting around in Fategarh heard all the stories and sighed!

'We're moving at last!' An excited Joe ducked into the tent he shared with Adam. It was nearly the end of February, and they had been stuck in Fategarh for seven long weeks. Seven weeks of unadulterated misery for Joe as he struggled to avoid falling foul of his hostile Captain. McBride had tried every trick he could think of to trip Joe up, even to sending him contradictory orders that were impossible to carry out. But again and again his own detachment came to his rescue, often intercepting messages and acting on them independently. The baffled Captain, not known for his intelligence, increased his efforts, but to no avail. But Joe was weary and 'hag-ridden'. He had developed a nervous tic in his left cheek, and it was only the intervention of a merciful bout of dysentery that laid McBride low for a week that prevented him from giving up altogether.

Even when McBride wasn't chasing, Joe had to endure the ceaseless sniping from Mortimer, and others of like mind. Mortimer had not spoken out again after an extremely painful interview with his Colonel, but he reserved his venom for more selective company. Joe was becoming adept at avoiding him, but his own equally poisonous Captain, but he was getting so tired! Perhaps the news that they moving out would give everyone something else to think about.

The ponderous army crossed the Ganges and headed for Unao, following the same route to Lucknow as Havelock had done so many months before. But Havelock had travelled fast and light. This great winding procession of elephants, camels, horses, carts, palanquins, doolies, gun-bullocks, pack horses and beef cattle, and men with their own army of servants! Moving at the pace of a demented snail they finally reached the outskirts of Lucknow at the beginning of March, determined to retake the city. By now, Campbell had twenty thousand men but faced one hundred thousand rebels.

Entering the Dilkusha Park on the heels of the kilted Highlanders, Joe could see rebels streaming out of it and fleeing towards the city. By the 5th march they retook Chinhut, haunted by the ghost of poor Henry Lawrence in his ignominious defeat, and headed for Outram who was moving out of the Alambagh. They reached Sikanderbagh, where the bones of the soldiers killed the previous November still littered the ground. Joe shuddered and observed to his Sergeant that it was impossible to tell whether the bones were British or Indian; the Sergeant echoed his own thoughts,

'It maikes yer fink, don't it?'

Then they assaulted the Begum Kothi Palace; a difficult place of courtyards and walls. In the vanguard was the infamous Hodson, who had personally executed the Moghul Princes of Delhi. Joe, with a detachment of Kotepore veterans supported a group of Highlanders under Forbes-Mitchell as they rushed through a series of linked courtyards. The rebel defenders seemed remarkably reluctant to fight, and the British assaulters sensed victory. Ahead of him, Joe could see Hodson limping from a leg wound. They were confronted by a stout door and Forbes-Mitchell despatched a couple of Highlanders for gunpowder. Around him, Joe could hear mutterings from the soldiers close behind Hodson,

'Keep close to 'm, 'e can sense booty from a hundred paces!' Joe's lip curled with disgust; is that all they could think about at such a time? He heard a shout from Hodson demanding that they force the door lest the pandies escaped.

A concerted rush carried them to the door, which gave way before so many stout shoulders. As it swung open the crackle of musket fire could be heard, and Hodson fell, fatally wounded. The rest of them swept through and within a short space of time the Begum Kothi palace was in their hands, one of a very few casualties being Hodson. Then the plundering began.

Joe gathered up his men, who muttered mutinously and led them away.

That evening, the recaptured Martiniere School, Colonel Willoughby congratulated his officers for their exemplary conduct since the campaign began.

'We are to take part in the assault on the Kaiserbagh and then on to the Residency itself. It has been a festering sore in our side that the rebels have held Lucknow for so long, and we will avenge all the souls that suffered and perished there.' He paused for a moment, and then went on sternly,

'It has come to my notice that as each palace and mosque is taken the British Army has begun to sack them. It is hardly surprisingly when some of their leaders set them a bad example. Sadly, it is rumoured that Hodson himself was engaged in such activities when he was killed.' Joe looked up startled as he had been there, and Hodson had died even before entering. But he held his peace, wary of drawing attention to himself with McBride just two seats away. Major Harding was not so reticent,

'Oh I say! The man's a hero' I heard that he died before even entering with his wife's name on his lips!'

'Be that as it may, Robert,' went on Willoughby inexorably, 'there is plundering going on, and it *is being* initiated by officers in many cases. If I hear of any officers of the Kotepore Regiment being involved they will be punished; make no mistake!' He glared round the table to emphasis his message.

If Joe had been sitting opposite, rather than on the same side as McBride, he would have been very disturbed by the gleam in the man's dun coloured eyes, and the nod that he exchanged with Mortimer. That night, for the first time in days, Joe's evening was undisturbed by his Captain, and he was able to relax with Adam, gathering strength for the next day's assault. He was too tired to question his good fortune, too grateful to be suspicious.

The advance of the British was slowed down over the next few days as the Kaiserbagh was systematically bombarded by heavy artillery. But with the British surrounding the palace in the Sikanderbagh, the Martiniere, the Begum Kothi and the Shah Najaf Mosque, it was simply a matter of time before they achieved their goal.

On the 14th March the Kaiserbagh was taken and once more the Kotepore veterans were in the vanguard. It had been a torrid day and the stench of corpses hung over them. The soldiers moved forward in a state of high excitement, firing on the retreating rebels as they went. By evening it was all over and the looting began. White statues were plastered with blood and bayoneted sepoys lay in the exquisite flower gardens. Priceless hangings were thrown about and slashed with tulwars, and pictures and mirrors were smashed to the ground in a frenzied orgy of pillage and plunder. Joe found himself alongside Adam, and using the flat of their swords, began to beat back their men. It was not easy to control men with the red glow of battle in their eyes, but slowly they managed to bring them to order and march them out of the palace.

Bone weary, Joe lay on his bedroll in a small room in the Martiniere where they had been billeted. He found it difficult to sleep as the day's events rolled behind his eyes and he was worried by the looting that had occurred at the end of the battle. Had he got all his men out, or were some of them due for disciplinary action? His fevered brain worried at the thought as a pi-dog worries a carcass in the street. Just as he was drifting into sleep, he heard the sound of footsteps outside, and also low voices. One of them was McBride. He groaned aloud; what had he done or failed to do that had brought his Captain to his billet? His tired mind could not find an answer. Then McBride entered followed by Harding, his round face full of concern. It was the Major that spoke,

'Get up Harrington.' Joe did so as fast as his tired body would allow and sketched a salute, forgetting his state of undress. Harding frowned,

'Captain McBride tells me that you were seen taking part in the looting this evening, Harrington. I must say I am very disappointed in you.' Joe's mouth dropped open,

'But Sir….I wasn't…..I was trying to stop….!'

'Silence!' roared McBride, 'you'll have your say in good time.' Harding frowned,

'Yes, well. Get on with it Captain.' McBride pushed past Joe roughly, unbalancing him so that he fell against the wall. Compressing his lips, Joe watched his tormentor throw his bedding about and upend the bedroll, shaking it vigorously. A chain made of thick gold links slid onto the floor where it lay winking dully in the faint lantern light. The three men formed a circle round the damning evidence; Joe's eyes narrowed,

'So,' he thought, 'he's done it at last.' Harding frowned more heavily,

'Get dressed Harrington. The Colonel will hear of this immediately.'

Ten minutes later, James Willoughby was disturbed by a vigorous knocking on his door; he sighed.

It had not been a good day for him and he was preparing to retire. His bearer had just knocked to say that his camp bed was prepared and would the Colonel-Sahib like a chota-peg before retiring. The Colonel-Sahib had said he would, and the man had pattered away leaving James to his thoughts. These were focused on his father and his aunt and uncle who were God knows where. James had not heard from them since the uprising began the previous May, and the worry was beginning to seriously affect him. As soon as the women and children had been safely installed in Simla, he had sent his most loyal bearer, armed with many rupees on a journey to the mofussil, urging the man to report as soon as he had news. The bearer had returned and reported that the Ferguson's plantation, bungalow, stores and workshops had all been gutted by fire, and that there was no sign of the sahibs and memsahib. Acting on his own initiative he had also gone to the Carlton estate that marched alongside, but had found the same scene, except that the bungalow had been spared the torch. Of Carlton and his Hindu wife, there was also no sign. But, assured the bearer, he had not seen any bodies. Shaking his head vigorously to stress his point, he repeated,

'Definitely, definitely no bodies, sahib; I am telling you this and it is so!'

James had only been partly comforted. Perhaps they had fled into the mofussil, and perhaps they were altogether. If that were so, Carlton would take care of them. But if not? This was what was agonizing him. He had sent his bearer back to the area recently, but had been disappointed with 'still no news sahib.' With this on his mind, and a day of fighting and reports of looting, James was not in a good mood when the knock came upon his door,

'What is it,' he called out testily. The trio entered, led by Robert Harding followed by Joe, with a smug looking McBride bringing up the rear. It was the last of the three that caused James to narrow his eyes,

'What has he been up to, I wonder?' came into his mind. The three saluted and Harding reported on the search and finding of the gold chain. The tale told briefly sounded damning even to Joe's ears. Harding could see that James was tired, and wished to bring the matter to a close as quickly as possible. But in his heart he couldn't help the thought,

'Breeding will out, and I did warn James after all!' There was silence for a moment, and then James questioned Joe first,

'Did you take the chain, Lieutenant Harrington, in spite of my strict injunction?' Joe's head had sunk to his chest with dejection, but the tone of James' voice brought his head up and hope stir in his breast. How could he doubt this man whom he knew to be fair and just. He would get to the bottom of it. He lifted his chin, squared his shoulders,

'No Sir.' There was a snort of derision from McBride and his lip curled disdainfully. He was quelled by a glance from James.

'Very good Lieutenant. Wait outside.'

'Yes Sir.' Joe saluted, spun on his heel and left the room. Inside, James looked from McBride to Harding and back again. He noted that Harding seemed relaxed but McBride started to fidget. Almost conversationally, he asked the Captain,

'What made you search Harrington's room?'

'I'd heard that he'd taken the chain. I knew he must have hidden it.'

'Who told you he'd taken it?' McBride began to worry. The interview was not going quite as he expected, and with his limited intelligence, he had not thought beyond the need to plant damning evidence in Joe's bedroll. He had considered that his word as an 'officer and a gentleman' would be believed before that of a 'jumped up peasant from an Irish bog'. Like his co-conspirator Mortimer and the hapless Carless before him, he had a profound belief in the superiority of the British aristocracy and treated all others like so much dirt beneath his well polished boots. So now he could only bluster earning him a straight look from James, who repeated the question with a hint of steel in his voice,

'Who told you he'd taken it; who is your witness?'

'It was Lieutenant Mortimer, Sir.'

'Where did he witness this theft? I assume you questioned him?' Again McBride had to think frantically,

'Er, in the Kaiserbagh; er, yes, that was it, the Kaiserbagh!'

'Very good.' James went to the door where his bearer was hovering,

'Send a message to Lieutenant Mortimer that I wish to see him; chuldi, chuldi.'

'Sah!' the bearer pattered away. There was silence in the room as James studied the flustered Captain, his normally florid colour rising by the minute and not entirely due to the sultry night. Then Mortimer came in, apparently the worse for drink. James addressed with a voice as smooth as silk,

'Captain McBride tells me that you witnessed the theft of a gold chain today. Is this true?' Like McBride, Mortimer had to think very fast. The last time he had fallen foul of his Colonel had been an unnerving experience and he had no wish to repeat it. He had been told in no uncertain terms, of the penalty of undermining the authority of a superior officer, and warned that commissions could be forfeited and their holders sent home in disgrace. The plot to disgrace Joe had been hatched and carried out very simply as neither of them had thought for a moment that their word would not be believed. But he was not going to get himself into trouble for McBride. Besides there was a small matter of other treasures hidden in his own belongings that would not bear inspection. The slow workings of his mind finally bore fruit, and he looked his Colonel straight in his eye and said,

'I'm sorry Sir. I have no idea what Captain McBride is talking about; I didn't see any such thing.' Like a pricked bladder, McBride's corpulent body seemed to collapse in on itself and his face turn even ruddier.

'God,' thought Harding, 'the man will have an apoplexy any minute. James simply said,

'Thank you Lieutenant; you may go.' Mortimer hastily vacated the room, watched by an increasingly cheerful Joe, as he saw the expression on the Lieutenant's face! Turning to McBride, in a voice as cold as ice, he said,

'Wait outside Captain McBride.' The man was so unnerved that he forgot to salute and left the room with his head bowed. There was silence in the room for a moment, and then Harding spoke tentatively,

'Sorry to disturb you with this, James, but I thought that you should be aware of this situation immediately; we can't let this sort of thing go unpunished.' James looked at his long time friend profoundly disturbed.

'What are you saying, Robert; you still believe McBride?'

'Of course,' replied Robert, sounding bemused, 'the man is a gentleman after all!' James shook his head in disbelief,

'Can't you see that the story was fabricated from start to finish; he'd clearly put the chain in the bedding himself, or got Mortimer to do it.'

'But James,' a bewildered Robert asked, 'why should he?'

'Oh Robert, Robert,' replied James sadly, 'can you not see what has been going on under your nose?' Then changing the subject, 'whose idea was it to put McBride in charge of Harrington?'

'The man volunteered. I knew it would be difficult getting the men to work with the two of them, especially Harrington. I had thought Timoney would do it, but McBride offered, so I took up his offer. Why?'

'And you agreed, even though he's an Orangeman? Robert, I knew these appointments would be unpopular, but still considered them right for a time like this. I asked you to take them on because I thought you would be loyal enough to back me. No; don't answer that for a moment!' he said abruptly as Robert opened his mouth to interrupt, 'I thought even you would realise that someone like McBride would only volunteer his services out of spite and for no other reason. I've watched him put that young man through hell these past weeks and hoped you would notice and act. I didn't interfere thinking it best sorted out among yourselves. But I would have done so if it had gone on much longer. I was forced to reprimand Mortimer as I actually heard what he said and couldn't ignore it, but knew that it would merely increase his bitterness. Did you hope Harrington would fail too, Robert?' Harding looked uncomfortable,

'James, I …….dammit James, the man's not a gentleman!'

'And McBride is? What constitutes a gentleman? I believe it is not an accident of birth but the way he behaves. Well?'

'Yes, but.' Robert sighed, 'I suppose you could be right. Harrington has never done anything like this before.'

'Robert, I intend to go to bed. You must sort this out. But be very careful how you do it; Harrington did not take that chain!'

James left Robert in the office alone with his uncomfortable thoughts. Now he knew why James had been Colonel and not him; it took an exceptional man to hold things together in these troubled times.

He had to admit that he preferred the quiet life; preferred to let others take the painful decisions. To make matters worse, he had recently lost his friend and confidante during the battle for Delhi; he'd never realised before how much he had depended on Edward Colby's good sense; God how he missed him! Well; he had been left the job of resolving this affair. He squared his shoulders; he could not simply accuse McBride of engineering the whole thing; that would go completely against the grain, and would stir up even more enmity against the younger man; however,

'Captain McBride, Lieutenant Harrington!' bellowed Harding, pleased with the assertive sound of his voice. The two entered carefully avoiding each other's eyes. Harding addressed them,

'I have considered the matter carefully, and feel that there is insufficient evidence against Harrington to take the matter further.'

'But Sir,' blustered McBride.

'Enough,' roared Harding, his nervousness making him shout louder than he intended, 'if I start an investigation, there is no saying how long it will take, and what it might find!' The threat was unmistakable and McBride subsided.

'Furthermore, I feel you have more than done your duty in guiding young Harrington here, Captain McBride, and I propose to give you a rest and relieve you of your duty.'

'But Sir, I really don't mind cont…..'

'That will do Captain.'

'Very good Sir.'

Joe could hardly believe his ears. Not only had he been exonerated but had also been released from the evil clutches of McBride. He knew who he had to thank for it, and it wasn't the Major who was now speaking again,

'Now, before I retire, I want to see you two shake hands.'

McBride moved in front of Harding and put out his hand to Joe. With his back to the Major he gripped Joe painfully tight and silently mouthed,

'I'll get you Harrington. We've a few battles to get through, so watch your back. I've plenty of time; but I'll get you!'

Joe lay on his bedroll, no nearer to sleeping than he had been before Harding and McBride had dragged him off to see the Colonel. His body shook as if with ague, and he felt closer to tears than he had ever been since he had bade farewell to Ireland nigh in ten years before.

McBride would never, must never know how close he had been to breaking his spirit. Even Adam, close friend though he was, did not know. When Sean O'Hara had taken the name of Joe Harrington and had become part of the British Army, he had vowed that there was nothing he could not do if he put his mind to it, and so it had been. He had learned to speak English in a variety of fashions, to read and write more efficiently than most of the officers, and was more widely read. He had learned to deal with his uniform and to be a drummer boy, a private, a corporal and sergeant. So that when he had been offered the chance to be an officer, a role he already masqueraded, he had seized it without a qualm. He had known it would be difficult and that acceptance from other officers would not come easily, but he did believe that he would prove himself given time.

But McBride had worn him down until he had been close to giving up.

'Perhaps it has been a useful lesson,' he observed wryly to himself, 'teach me not to think I am infallible! But', he reflected, 'there was the loyalty of the men who did their best to help thwart McBride's plans. Without them, I would certainly have given up long ago. And that would have meant letting the Colonel down who just this night had proved that he still believed in me.' With that comforting thought, and without dwelling on McBride's threat, he fell asleep.

He awoke next morning, heavy eyed and unrefreshed, to find Gopi with a tray in his hands. He was looking very worried, and said,

'Why did the Sahib keep shouting in the night? Every time I came in to see what you wanted you told me to go away! What is it that I have done?'

'Sorry Gopi; must've been a bad dream. What have you got there?'

'Chota-hazri Sahib, your favourite; curds and honey isn't it? There is to be an attack on the Residency sahib.'

'How on earth do you come by your information? Though it makes sense; get it all over and done with! What else have you heard?'

'Well sahib, I heard yesterday that Outram Sahib was going to take the Iron Bridge, but Burra-sahib Campbell stopped him, and the Firuz Shah, Kunwar Singh and the Begum escaped; and they took the Prince.'

Joe considered the news; it was bad indeed as these three could form the core of further resistance. Then he voiced his next thought aloud,

'Why the hell did Campbell stop Outram?' Gopi answered in puzzled fashion,

'How should I know sahib; he did not think to tell me!' Joe gave a shout of laughter and the worries of the night receded a little. But Gopi had not finished,

'It is said that Rajah Ajit Khan was in the Kaiserbagh but escaped into the Residency.'

'Good God; are you sure?'

'No sahib, but I heard it from…'

'Yes, yes, I know; your cousin's wife's brother-in-law!' Gopi looked hurt and served his breakfast in injured silence. While he was eating, Adam came in and Joe took the chance to relate the events of the night before, though he left out the threat that McBride had mouthed at the end. Adam whistled,

'I never believed the man would go so far! But at least he will be off your back now; I'd a notion that you were close to breaking point, Joe.'

'Mm. By the way, Gopi here tells me that Ajit Khan was seen in the Kaiserbagh. D'you know if that's true?'

'No, I've not heard that. If it is, we might meet up today as we are to storm the Residency.' And he wondered why Joe laughed!

When they reported for duty, however, they were informed that the day would be spent consolidating their position. It was a strange feeling for Joe not to be jumping at every moment of the day to McBride's contrary demands. Somehow, in the inimitable fashion of the ranks, the men already knew that he had been relieved of the McBride, and he was treated to sly grins and congratulations wherever he went. Major Harding gave him the briefest of curt nods, but Adam was of a mind that it was due to embarrassment. He didn't see McBride at all for which he was duly grateful. That night he slept more deeply than he had done since being made a Lieutenant; maybe he was going to make it after all!

Next day, the 16th of March, the Kotepore Regiment was lined up to support Outram in storming the Residency. The sun was high in a brassy sky and a group of officers were running sweaty fingers under their high collars. Joe examined the area that he had last seen the previous November. The pandies had considerably strengthened it since them, and why not; they had all the labour and the time they had needed. Colonel Willoughby was scanning the area with a small brass telescope, and as the eyeglass swept across the roof, he gave an explanation of surprise. Even without a telescope, Joe could see what had startled him; surrounded by his rissal in their white sashed with scarlet, stood Rajah Ajit Khan and his son Saeed.

Next moment came the order to open fire, and the group vanished from the roof. The Kotepore soldiers advanced, enfilading the Residency with a storm of fire from their Enfields. Already the return fire was dwindling, and within half an hour the battle seemed to be over. The Khan's and their rissal seemed to have completely vanished.

Wandering about the enclave when it had been cleared awoke memories that Joe shared with Adam. He searched for the pile of rubble that had been their meeting place, but it must have been used for rebuilding the scarred walls. He took Adam down into the basement, empty and echoing, and showed him where the women and children of the 32nd Foot had lived for five months and where his daughter had been born. Adam was lost for words, a rare event for him!

Later, C Company were ordered to clear part of the perimeter near the Stone Bridge, west of the Iron Bridge which was now in British hands. They approached cautiously for there were still pockets of resistance. Joe kept a wary eye on McBride, walking some ten paces away on his right, and intercepted an evil leer. Clearly McBride wanted him to suffer in anticipation of an attempt on his life! As they neared the bridge they heard the clatter of hooves coming from the direction of the city. Turning, they could see a tight formation of horsemen rapidly approaching, the main body of them dressed in white sashed with scarlet. C Company parted to line both sides of the road, and the front road dropped to their knees and raised their Enfields, The officers held them steady as the riders came up at speed.

'Aim. Fire!' A double row of Enfields crackled, and several white clad bodies hit the ground. The second row of British soldiers took aim, though the rissallers were almost on them,

'Fire!' The Enfields spoke again and more bodies crashed to the ground, terror stricken horses galloping for the bridge and the safety of the Mariaon Road. Then the horsemen were among them and striking out with their tulwars. The British defended with their bayonets breaking ranks to engage in hand to hand fighting. But it became clear that the pandies were simply seeking to escape and had no stomach for the fight.

Joe was engaging one large horseman and had side stepped to avoid a sweeping blow from a vicious, razor sharp tulwar, then suddenly the man was gone. A large chestnut horse reared in front of him, and he looked up into the face of Prince Saeed Khan. The Prince was dressed as gorgeously as ever in peacock silk tunic and leggings tucked into glossy black boots. A cloth of silver turban was topped with an aigrette with an enormous ruby. Beneath the turban, the Prince gazed down at Joe, sadness written in the eloquent, liquid brown eyes. The Prince had been mounted on a chestnut horse last time they had encountered each other, but then Joe had been dressed as a native and trying to get to Kotepore cantonment. Now he was in the regalia of a British officer, a fact noted by the Prince and acknowledged by a wry smile. Now it was the Prince who was the fugitive, the uprising over for him and his father's dreams of an India free of the British yoke in tatters around him.

The Prince raised his tulwar in a mocking salute, touching the handsome aigrette. Then his eyes widened in alarm, and leaning forward, he brought the tulwar down in a sweeping movement. Joe just had time to step to one side as the tulwar whistled past his left shoulder, so close he felt the wind of its passing. He heard a scream of pain, as a hand carrying a pistol fell to the ground at his feet. Joe turned and saw McBride, clutching his mutilated wrist as he fell to his knees, his life blood pumping onto the dusty ground. Sickened, Joe raised his eyes to the Prince, who murmured softly in Urdu,

'Your choice in allies is passing strange, my friend.' Then he was gone, spurring across the Stone Bridge with his father and the remnants of their escort. The soldiers of C Company took stock of the dead and wounded scattered about them. British losses were few, three dead, with McBride about to join them in spite of a tourniquet hastily applied by a burly sergeant. Joe looked down at the puce, hate filled face and could not find it in himself to feel any regret. The man had made his life hell for many weeks, and had been cut down in the act of trying to murder him. No, he would not mourn his passing.

The pandey losses were heavy, with a dozen killed outright by the Enfield volleys, and several more were wounded. These were roughly bound and taken off to the Residency hospital, still used for the purpose since the original siege.

Major Harding congratulated his Company on the prompt way they had responded to the emergency, and then made his dispositions.

'Captain Timoney.'

'Sir?'

'Lieutenants Swales and Harrington will assist you. Post piquets on the Bridge. You will be relieved in due course. I will be reporting this incident to Colonel Willoughby and will return presently.' Then very quietly,

'Lieutenant Harrington.'

'Sir?'

'I saw how McBride died. It will go no further.'

'Yes Sir!' Joe was immensely relieved. As far as he was concerned he simply wished to forget McBride and all that he had stood for. Yes, this way was the best. McBride had died in battle defending the bridge and that was the end of it.

A week later, the fight for Lucknow and the surrounding area was over. British losses were light, some hundred and twenty officers and men killed, and five hundred wounded; a mere bagatelle compared to the carnage at Delhi. But as a result of bungling and incompetence by the leaders, including the redoubtable Campbell, one hundred thousand rebels had streamed away from Lucknow, determined to carry on the fight. Among them was a figurehead, the young king of Oudh, under the protection of his mother, the Begum. Another was the Maulavi of Faizabad, one of the original instigators for the rebellion. A man eaten with hatred of the British and all they stood for in India. The situation was summed up for them all by an embittered Harry Havelock, still mourning his father's death in this very place,

'Our magnificent force was capable of crushing everything; it could overtake nothing!'

Chapter 16

'Morning Sahib. We're going home!'

'Wha….wha?' A bleary eyed Joe peered out of his muslin drapes and groaned as Gopi opened the shutters and let in the bright, brassy sun of an April morning.

'For God's sake, Gopi, close that shutter. And what did you say?'

Gopi grinned and did as he was bid. By the state of the whiskey bottle on the table, his Sahib and Swales-Sahib had made a night of it. He repeated,

'We're going home Sahib.'

'Where did you hear that? And what do you mean by 'home?'

'I heard it….'

'Never mind that bit.'

'I mean go back to Kotepore. Burra-Sahib Campbell is to go to Rose-Sahib at Jhansi and Colonel Willoughby-Sahib is to look after Kotepore again.' Joe shook his head at his bearer, not bothering to argue with him. He had long since ceased to wonder where he got his information from. He could only imagine that some officers treated their servants as if they did not exist, and matters of great importance were discussed openly as tiffin was being served, or over evening chota-pegs. The soft footed khitmagars would lose no time in passing on these nuggets of information. But, he acknowledged to himself with a wry smile, it wasn't every sahib who was privileged to receive these nuggets as most were considered unworthy! He chuckled at the thought of the high and mighty Mortimer considered to be too lowly to be given such valuable information by the natives he so despised!

A week had passed since the last of the pandies had been cleared out of the Residency and Lucknow; a week of rest after the battles in the overheated air. The Kotepore Regiment had settled into their billets in the Martiniere School and wondered where they would be sent next.

For Joe, the relief of being free from his torment wrought by the unlamented McBride had wrought miracles to his jaded spirits. He was clear-eyed again with the nervous tic gone from his cheek and his shoulders squared once more. He moved about his duties with a brisk step, ignoring the rising heat that was beginning to sap the energies of his comrades, especially as midday approached.

It could not be said that he and Adam had been fully accepted, but at least now there was no overt hostility. Even Mortimer confined himself to venomous glances whenever they met, which Joe found easy to ignore. When he and Adam entered the Officer's Mess now, the talk no longer faded into strained silence, but neither were they greeted affably, as were others as they entered. Conscious of the need to not disgrace themselves, they drank very little in the Mess, but preferred to retire to one of their rooms after dinner and down a few whiskey or brandy-panis in a more relaxed atmosphere. It was also cheaper that way, for they only had their officer's pay to settle their mess bills, unlike the majority of the officers who were of independent means. It had not taken them long to discover that there was more to being an officer than simply ordering men around!

The previous evening they had both had a particular reason to celebrate, hence the hangover that stopped Joe enjoying the bright morning! As Gopi moved round the room, tutting over the state of the uniform jacket flung carelessly over the back of a chair, Joe mulled over the events of the night before; he and Adam had both received letters.

Joe had sent off many short notes to Catherine keeping her informed of his movements, at the same time tacitly telling her that he was still alive! He had not expected replies as he had told her they were constantly on the move, so he had been overjoyed when a crumpled missive was handed to him by an impassive Gopi, who explained that the letter had arrived by a disreputable looking saddhu, and it had cost him more than a rupee or two in contributions to his begging bowl. Joe had grinned and promised to reimburse him before carrying the letter off to the privacy of his room.

It had clearly been written many weeks before, shortly after Christmas in fact, and had travelled all the way up to Delhi before finding its way down to Lucknow. Doubtless it would have found its way back to Allahabad if he had not been able to intercept it. It was dirty and crumpled but as soon as he opened it and saw the familiar writing, an image of Catherine busy at her desk rose in his mind. He could see her clearly, forehead creased in concentration, the tip of a pink tongue just visible in the corner of her mouth. She would write swiftly and then pause, gazing into space while she marshaled her thoughts, and then she would dash off some more lines. She wrote as she spoke, and he could hear her voice, slightly breathless as she tried to tell all her news at once. Strangely, he did not picture her as he had last seen her, hair still lank and uncared for, face still peaked from hunger and the demands of the baby; ah, the baby! He read the letter over several times,

'Dearest Joe,

I began to write this on Christmas Day, but then had to stop as it was too painful. Last Christmas was such a happy time for us! I don't even know if you will get this, but I thought I'd write anyway as it helps bring you closer. Allahabad is like Lucknow when we first arrived. We were put with some 'charitable ladies' who looked down their noses at our rags as if we should have put on white gloves to visit them. They twittered about 'all the sufferings you poor dears had to endure,' and then scolded us gently for not dressing for dinner. You can imagine how that made us feel. The three of us were billeted separately, but Chris was wonderful and found us a tiny bungalow where we can all be together. He has found employment with a local newspaper and it is his wages that is keeping us in food. They gave us a small allowance when we arrived, but when Cristabel and I chose to leave the 'ladies of mercy who had so generously taken us in' they washed their hands of us!'

Joe's jaw tightened at the shameful treatment his wife was receiving but it also made him feel so inadequate. He could not even help her when she needed him! At least he could send some money to the address she had written, but this missive was weeks old. He bowed his head and read on,

'In spite of everything it's lovely being with Pattie and Cristobel again. They spoil Rose shamefully. She will miss them dreadfully when we have to part! Oh Joe, Rose is so good. It thought that when we were in Lucknow, somehow she knew she had to be quiet because of the situation; that somehow she understood. But she's just the same here. The other day she smiled at me, really smiled. One interfering old biddy said it was wind, but I knew better. Her eyes really lit up. I'm not sure of their colour yet. Some days they are so blue like yours, and other days they seem grey like mine. Oh Joe, I miss you so. Do be careful. We get very old news of events so I don't even know if you are in action, but I am sure I would know if you were in danger. Please, please be careful! I know I shouldn't say this to a soldier, but I can't lose you now!'

The letter went in similar fashion, finally closing with endearments, and by the end of it Joe felt wrenched in two. Certainly a mixed blessing, but on balance, he was very glad to have received it.

That evening, he and Adam compared letters, Louise's had been more recent, written a mere four weeks before, and she wrote of warmer weather coming to the hill station,

'I think even the children were tired of snow, and the spring is lovely,'

she had written. Apparently they were all thoroughly bored with each other and talked longingly of their bungalows in Kotepore cantonment,

'though how could they have forgotten they were all burnt, I cannot imagine!'

The ladies were also forgetting, she had gone on, that with the hot weather coming it would be impossible anyway!

The two men discussed every aspect of the situation, as frankly they had forgotten it too. When would Adam get to see his wife and daughter again? Likewise for Joe; he confided that he had found it almost unbearable that Catherine was so close and he could not go and see her! Memories of their time together in Lucknow had almost been too poignant to bear!

The talk turned to less painful topics, the two men stretched out in comfortable cane chairs, puffing on a hookah they had found in a deserted corner of the Kaiserbagh. Plumes of smoke wreathed about their heads as the level of the whiskey sunk lower in the bottle. Dara and Gopi had long since been dismissed, and they had gone off laughing and chattering at the strange ways of the sahibs.

'What d'you think will happen now, Joe? You seem to read the Indian mind better than most.' Joe puffed contentedly for a while, and then

'Most of the Indians would be glad to see all this finished and life return to normal. Haven't you noticed that the bazaars of Lucknow are operating as if nothing has happened? They would have cheerfully slit our throats if it had gone the other way! But the really rabid revolutionaries; they'll be licking their wounds and getting ready for the next round. I suspect the terrible trio of Nana Sahib, Tantia Topi and the Rani of Jhansi will get together. My God, if they do, they will be formidable indeed!'

'I've heard a lot about the Rani; that she's as beautiful as she is warlike?'

'Did you know that I'd met her?'

'No, but it wouldn't surprise me; you seem to have met everyone of any importance in India. Go on Joe, tell me about her.'

'I'd been invited on a shoot as companion to Saeed. I don't think Saeed ever told his father just how lowly I was and we took good care to keep out of his way. Anyway, this hunting party was a big one and the Rani was the personal guest of Rajah Ajit, and she turned up with an enormous retinue. She was covered from head to foot in a bright golden yellow sari, as it was Basunta; you know, first day of spring. All I could see apart from a pair of magnificent eyes were her hands, painted with henna and loaded with rings and bracelets. I was smitten I can tell you, but of course, I was a mere impressionable lad at the time. She travelled on an elephant and we headed out to shoot muggers. I was nowhere near the front so the best shooting was over before I got there, but I heard the bearers say that she had got the biggest bag. Quite a woman!'

'I'd heard that she was involved with a British officer back at the beginning of the mutiny?'

'Yes; I heard those stories too. But it ended when some British families took refuge in the fortress. They emerged at the promise of safe passage and were all murdered!'

'I wonder that they trusted her; her late husband was as anti-British as any of 'em after being annexed.'

'Well, we'll never know. Now she's thrown in her lot completely with the mutiny. If only Campbell hadn't let so many of them escape. No use going on about it, I suppose, but it's a fact!'

The two men continued to chew over the situation to take their minds off their missing loved ones. Their voices grew slurred and maudlin, and they made outrageous plans for their leaders until the last of the whiskey had gone. Gopi and Dara timed their return to perfection and helped their semi-conscious masters to their charpoys, grinning widely, Dara displaying a generous gap in his front teeth that caused him to speak in a sibilant whisper, as he did now, observing to Gopi,

'Iss it not strange that the angressi inflict such pain on themselves, and their heads will have such terrible pain tomorrow, isssn't it?' Gopi wagged his head in agreement, but they also knew that they wouldn't change their masters for any other, Indian or British!

The summons to a conference later that day came as no surprise to Joe, having been informed that morning by his all-knowing bearer. They sat round an enormous table that had once served as a refectory table of the Martiniere School, and now comfortably seated all the officers of the Kotepore Regiment. At the head sat Colonel Willoughby flanked by his Majors, with Joe and Adam taking lowly positions at the far end. Joe found it the perfect place to sit as he could see Willoughby's face, which was not possible for the Majors. James addressed them,

'Gentlemen, I spent almost the whole of yesterday with Brigadier-General Campbell. Governor-General Canning has ordered Campbell to advance into Rohilkand, while Sir Hugh Rose is busy in Oudh.'

'Where exactly is Sir Hugh, Colonel?' enquired Harding,

'The latest report puts him outside Jhansi, but Tantia Topi is expected there at any moment!'

'Who are we to assist?' came from Major Jeckel,

'Neither,' said Willoughby, tersely. His assembled audience waited with bated breath, though one of their number simply smiled to himself, then,

'We're going home!' A babble of voices broke out round the table which James made no effort to silence. He leaned back in his chair with a half smile playing round his mouth as he watched his officers exchange comments. He shook his head to any questions, waiting for the gurrh-burrh to die away, and then he explained,

'Campbell feels it is important that the British presence in Oudh is re-established as soon as possible. We have been in Kotepore for many years, and he thinks we will do more good there that running around with him or Rose.'

'What about the Rajah of Kotepore?' put in Major Mandus of B Company.

'He is known to have joined the Rani of Jhansi along with his rissal. It is thought that the residents of Kotepore were not involved with the uprising.' Joe heard a suppressed snort from Mortimer off to his left, and a *sotto voce* comment to Lieutenant Muirhead sitting beside him,

'Can't trust those niggers; string a few up and show 'em once and for all who's master!' Joe eyed the poisonous Lieutenant with ill-concealed dislike, and tried to concentrate on what was being said at the other end of the table. The flip-flap of the punkahs hardly disturbed the heated air and he found it hard to keep his eyes open in the enervating atmosphere.

'Our brief is to rebuild and repair the cantonment. The barrack blocks were intact when we left, but we have no way of knowing if they are still undamaged. With the hot weather and then the monsoons to come, time is not on our side, but it is hoped that the remaining mutineers will be captured before long.'

'What about our families?' asked Tom Sinclair, Major of D Company, who so far had not opened his mouth. Suddenly the whole table was hushed as they waited for James to speak.

'I am aware,' said James carefully, 'that it is nearly a year since we last saw our wives and families. But it makes no sense to bring them back yet, particularly as there is still fighting going on. And the accommodation will be limited until we have repaired the bungalows.' There was a collective sigh from the assembled audience. But then James smiled broadly, his eyes dancing as he had saved the best till last,

'However, I have agreed with Brigadier Campbell that it is not necessary for the entire Regiment to be in Kotepore at all times.' There was absolute silence once more,

'So.o.o I've decided to release one quarter of the Regiment to travel to Simla in turn; in other words, one Company at a time.' As the officers took in his words, broad grins broke out on all sides, even among men who had no dependents in the hills. The chance to get away from the battle area and relax in the pleasant summer weather in the hills was exceedingly welcome to these war weary men.

'But who will go first?' asked Captain Timoney tentatively.

'I thought the only possible way to decide would be by ballot. Captain Forsyth here has written on four slips of paper the numbers one to four. The Majors will draw in turn while the rest of you pray for success!' James grinned mischievously; he had pondered the problem of choice for some time, and believed he had made the right decision.

While the officers chattered amongst themselves while waiting on the appearance of Forsyth and their fate, James thought back to the day before. He had pleaded with Campbell long and hard to release one quarter of their strength at a time, as the Brigadier was not at all happy with the idea. But James put forward the most cogent argument of all, the morale of the men. They had been involved with the Mutiny from the beginning and were battle weary. They needed some relaxation if they were to function properly again. He had then promised that he, personally, would not leave the district until he was fully satisfied that it was quiet. Campbell had capitulated at that, and James had hugged the knowledge to himself, only too aware that his Regiment needed this morale booster after their experiences through the uprising.

'His Regiment,' he smiled to himself as he understood at last just what had kept Gerald Deluce 'in harness' for so long. He had, like James, come into the Colonelcy at a relatively young age, and had adopted the same paternal attitude that James now felt towards the men under his command. His musing was interrupted by the arrival of his aide with the slips of paper; he placed them in his shako.

'Who's to go first, Sir?' James waved his hand helplessly, 'let 'em decide among themselves!' Jeckel looked around at his peers, and nervously suggested,

'Shall I; A Company y'know!' The others shrugged and then took the slips in the order suggested. The junior officers held their breath; on those slips was written their fate.

'Karma,' muttered Joe to Adam, but his heart beat fast; if Harding drew number one, he would see Catherine so much sooner. He saw Mendus scowl and throw down his slip,

'Dammit; last!' James commiserated.

'Never mind; you'll have the honour of escorting them home! But I'm happy to say I will be honoured to take any letters with me.' The broad smile on his chubby face said it all as he waved his slip,

'First, by God!' and he beamed round at his juniors. Joe and Adam pumped each other's hands, while Mortimer looked on with a scowl; he was in D Company and had just learned that his Company was third!

Two days later the Regiment marched towards Kotepore for the first time in nearly a year. They had left behind Hope Grant garrisoning Lucknow to ensure that it was not retaken. Campbell was preparing to move out against the Maulavi of Faizabad and Kunwar Singh who had besieged a small British force at Azamgarh, away to the south east. They had marched with the news that Sir Hugh Rose had delivered a crushing defeat on Tantia Topi in the face of enormous odds. He had then gone on and overcome Jhansi, firing the ancient city with many of its inhabitants. Taking advantage of the British habit of looting, the Rani escaped with Rajah Khan and his son. The Kotepore men marched with light hearts at the news, and also the knowledge that they did not have to deal with any of it; they were going home!

The road from Lucknow approached the cantonment round a long sweeping bend, and the vanguard came to an unplanned halt as it reached the point where the cantonment could be seen. The column behind pressed forward until the entire Regiment spilled out of ranks on either side of the road, and stood gazing at the place they had called home for some ten years. One old private summed up their feelings,

'Blimey, I never thought I'd be pleased t'see the old barrack blocks again!' as he wiped away a tear.

The four barrack blocks were intact. It was clear that when Ajit Khan had ridden away with his coterie, there had been no further action against the buildings. Over the admin block, the Union Jack hung limp in the still, overheated air, faded by the sun of the previous summer, but proudly intact. It was as Joe had left it on that fateful May day eleven months previous.

Up the hill, the remnants of the bungalows marched, burnt out, every one. From the Colonel's bungalow at the top of the hill, to the neat Lieutenant's row at the bottom, gaping and blackened timbers showed.

Once orderly gardens were now indistinguishable from the surrounding rampant growth, and the graveled paths that had been watered and raked daily had all but disappeared. Men who lived in these comfortable homes with their families wore a mask of grief; but one and all knew that they had been lucky to survive to see this view again, and that thought did much to cheer them.

During the following week there was feverish activity. The entire Regiment squeezed into the barrack and admin blocks after chasing out the white ants and snakes that had taken up residence in their absence. A detachment sent into Kotepore resulted in a veritable army of coolies arriving at the crack of dawn each day, ready and willing to set about the task of resurrecting Kotepore cantonment. They all earnestly entreated the sahibs not to blame them for what had happened, and that it was the Rajah who had ordered them to desert the sahibs.

James gave strict instructions that there was to be no reprisals of any sort, which was obeyed, though with reluctance by a few. Work started very early each morning and went on very late, with a long break in the middle of the day due to rising heat. After the first week, James declared himself satisfied with the safety of the cantonment, and gave the order for the first Company to be released.

Before he left for Allahabad, Joe climbed the hill to the woods on the crown. The teak bench was as he had left it, smashed to pieces on the ground. Continuing on his way he came to the convent gates which still stood agape with the gardens now overgrown. There was an eerie silence as he strode up the drive to the front entrance, memories and images jostling in his head; the day he first met Catherine, the visit to Reverend Mother Theresa to ask for her hand in marriage, her stern face breaking into a benevolent smile as she blessed his suit. But then he recalled his last fateful visit to this very spot, the doorman sprawled across the doorway. He rubbed his eyes; no-one here now, just the cawing of crows in the trees. There was a flash of green as a flock of pigeons fled across a corner of his view. He entered and peered into rooms either side of the corridor which seem to have tidied by someone. Finally he reached the chapel which he entered with some reluctance. But instead of Mother Theresa's body, smiling in death and with her arms round two novices there was an atmosphere of peacefulness. The bodies were gone and the chapel looked as it was ready for a priest to begin Mass. Without knowing what he was doing, he approached the altar and knelt before it, his hand performing the Sign of the Cross. The Lord 's Prayer crept unbidden into his mind and he thought he spoke the words out loud. Then another voice joined in; he turned without surprise to see a slight, sari-clad figure beside him. The child, now less of a child after an interval of a year, gazed at him unblinking from enormous kohl ringed brown eyes.

She took his hand and led him from the chapel and out of the convent to a hut at the rear. A woman and a man squatted there, the woman cooking chapattis. The pair made namaste, and the woman waved for Joe to sit. He did so, squatting comfortably in the Indian manner, and talked awhile in Urdu. The young girl never took her eyes from his face as her father explained what had happened since he had left,

'We buried the holy-lady, and her spirit waits for the angrezi saddhu to say correct prayers for her,' the old man said proudly, 'it was not good what was done here. It was badmashes, not the soldiers of the Rajah. They came to steal. We have looked after the convent for the holy-lady so that her spirit should find peace.' Joe nodded; it was as he had thought.

Joe shared their simple meal of rice and dal, and left them to their self-appointed task of caring for the convent, He supposed that one day more nuns would arrive from their Mother House, but in the meantime the place was in good hands. Now he felt free to find Catherine and his daughter, and his heart beat faster at the thought. He hurried down the hill to say goodbye to Adam and send his good wishes to Louise in Simla. The friends embraced and went their separate ways, Adam with C Company marching up the road to the north and Joe in his Indian garb, heading south on foot with Gopi; bound for Cawnpore and Allahabad.

The journey was uneventful, the most disturbing aspect of it being the number of corpses he found hanging from trees. Joe studies the remains and recognised that they were, in the main, simple farmers such as the people in Gita's village; Gita who had saved his life. On one group of burned out bungalows was scrawled, 'avenge your murdered countrywomen.' He stood for a period, deep in thought, while Gopi fidgeted, anxious to be gone. In their Indian garb they could easily be targets for the avengers! He tried to rouse Joe tentatively and received the full force of his blazing wrath,

'This is the work of newcomers, Gopi. What do they know of Indians and what led them to their desperate action?' Gopi crept away and left Joe to his angry ruminations. He had never understood his sahib; never understood the nature of the man who could not help but see both sides of the conflict, as he had done while growing up in insurrection torn Ireland.

Eventually he calmed down and they continued on their way, travelling mainly by night, the midday hours being spent under the shade of peepul trees where they could be found. Soon after midnight on the third day, they reached the outskirts of Allahabad. Joe decided to camp there for the rest of the night. And enter in the morning.

They were up very early the next morning, and Joe dressed himself in the full splendour of his Lieutenant's uniform. He conjured up a vision of Catherine's face when he presented himself at her bungalow, and he chuckled richly at the thought. But first he had to present himself at the military headquarters as he had a despatch to deliver for Colonel Willoughby. James had handed it to him on the morning of his departure, wishing him 'bon voyage' and the very good wishes for his wife and daughter. Joe had looked at his mentor and friend over many years, and could not find any words. James had understood and had simply nodded while shaking his hand, reminding him to be back in good time!

His mission done, Joe made his way through the bustling streets of Allahabad. He was amazed yet again at the normality of the scene. It was hard to believe that just up the river at Cawnpore, terrible murders had been perpetrated and neighbouring Lucknow besieged for months. Even now, desperate battles were being waged as the rebel leaders fought to regain ascendancy. But here in Allahabad, the bazaars were teeming with bunnias shouting to attract custom or busy haggling over the price of mounds of mangoes, ornate daggers or ridiculous slippers, reminding him poignantly of Kit. He shook his head to clear the feeling that this was another life to the one he had lived for close on a year.

At last he reached the address that had been on Catherine's letter. It was a small, unprepossessing bungalow, with a narrow verandah running round the perimeter. The windows and front entrance were shaded with split bamboo chiks, rolled down and soaked with water to bring relief from the rising April heat. He stood in front of it, Gopi fidgeting behind him as he straightened his jacket, smoothing down the tails over the pristine white trousers. Sweat broke out on his forehead as the uniform was not really suitable for the temperature, but he would have suffered much more to impress his wife! Gopi stood on one leg, and watched his sahib in bemused fashion, 'all this for a woman' was his irreverent thought, and his teeth bard in a private grin. Next minute he was told to 'jump to it' and announce their presence.

'Yes sahib,' he said sullenly, and he went up the steps onto the porch, searching in vain for a door pull. In the end, he resorted to rapping imperiously on the door frame, and then he retired from the scene to let Joe brave the arrival of the houseboy. He duly appeared in the doorway and stiffened to attention at the sight of the magnificent apparition in front of him.

'Is Mrs. Harrington at home?' asked Joe politely, while his palms sweated profusely.

'Yes sahib. Who shall I say is asking for her?'

'Just direct me to her. I wish to surprise her.' The houseboy fidgeted at this departure from routine, but his anxiety was allayed by the pressing of baksheesh into his palm. Joe stepped inside a small hallway, and then into a room indicated by the houseboy who then pattered away on slippered feet. Joe adjusted his uniform yet again, as he faced an arch screened by vertical split bamboos. Beyond the screen, a punkah-wallah pulled a cord in languid fashion using his toes. Joe could hear a gentle voice singing a soft lullaby and he recognised it as one that his mother Kate had sung to him so many years before.

He gently parted the screen so that he made no sound, to see his wife seated on a cane chair; alone in the room save for the child on her knee. Joe had time to gaze his fill; he saw that she had recovered her looks and her health since he had seen her last November, four months earlier. Her face had filled out so that her cheeks were smooth again, and the purple shadows banished from her eyes; her features were finer drawn than before, but it suited her. Her hair had recovered its gloss, and was dressed for coolness, with a knot fastened high on her well shaped head. Her diminutive frame had filled out somewhat, but the months of starvation still robbed her of the comfortable roundness she had used to bewail, though feeding her daughter had given her a fullness in the bosom that Joe found extremely attractive! She was dressed in a simple, sprigged muslin morning gown with ruffled sleeves and a lace fichu over a half crinoline. Clearly she had done business with the derzees of Allahabad.

As for Rose, Joe was instantly captivated. The intervening months had taken away the tiny dependent baby, with little in the way of character, and replaced it with an enchanting infant. Her hair had grown to a gleaming brown cap, touched with a hint of auburn which swirled round the crown of her well shaped head. Sturdy limbs peeped out from a muslin dress, and as Joe watched, chubby arms reached out to clutch her mother's hair and pulled tendrils from the neat coiffure. The child chuckled as her mother took her hands away from their destruction and kissed the knuckles, before bouncing her on her lap again, singing a song to match the action.

Joe must have made a movement causing Catherine to look up. She saw him framed in the arch and her eyes grew huge with shock, their grey almost smoky in the filtered light through the chiks.

'Joe….JOE!' her voice rising to a scream. Then she was up, nearly dropping Rose who wailed in protest. Recovering her daughter in a firm grasp, Catherine was across the room and in Joe's arms before he had time to take a step forward, so that the bamboo screen fell around their ears. Joe's arms held his wife and daughter in sure embrace as he murmured endearments into her fragrant, shining coiffure. Rose bore it for a while and then she began to squirm with indignation. Joe released them both and stepping into the room he took Rose from Catherine, holding her under her armpits. He brought her up to eyelevel so that he could see her features properly for the first time. Great, grey eyes rimmed in blue gazed back at him. Her features were rounded and as yet it was difficult to tell who she favoured; yet Joe imagined, perhaps hopefully, that he saw a little of his mother, Kate in the angle of her cheekbones.

'She's beautiful, larla,' said Joe, using his favourite Urdu endearment, meaning darling, 'but no more than her mother. God but I've missed you.' Rose finally got bored with the scrutiny, and reaching out. She caught one end of his now luxuriant moustache and gave it a fierce tug. Catherine's hand flew to her mouth as Joe gave a shout of laughter, and he gently shook his daughter in mock anger. Then he and Catherine sat down on a chaise longue, with Rose set between them. They sat silent for a moment, just gazing at each other, but then both spoke at once,

'Joe, when did you….'

'Sorry I couldn't give….' Then they both laughed. Catherine quickly cut in,

'Joe, tell me all that's happened since we waved goodbye in Cawnpore.'

So he told her of the journey to Delhi and finding the Regiment there. As he spoke, Joe completely forgot his wish to surprise Catherine with his uniform, but long before he reached to point of his promotion, Catherine started to frown at him, and then interrupted,

'Joe, I know you were dressed as a Lieutenant in Lucknow, and why; but don't you think it a little foolish now! If I'm not mistaken, that's a Kotepore uniform?' Joe raised her chin and kissed her softly on the mouth,

'I'm sorry, acushla; I did so want to impress you; I know how you like consorting with officers.' Catherine gave a rich chuckle, and then got serious again. But Rose, thoroughly bored with all the talking, tried to get off the chaise longue and fell onto her nose. She had to be picked up and cuddled, and then Catherine set her on the floor and gave her an ivory rattle which kept her amused banging Joe's knees. Joe then managed to finish his story and told an enthralled Catherine how he had earned the right to wear the uniform. Her eyes grew larger and larger as she took in what Joe was saying. She knew enough about Victorian life in general, and the military in particular to understand the magnitude of his achievement, and she was briefly silenced. Joe told her something of the difficulties and hostilities he had faced, but he knew he would never tell her of the full extent of the damage that McBride had done to him. He finished his saga with Colonel Willoughby releasing the Companies in succession and his luck at being among the first.

'Our new Company was lucky; oh Catherine, I was so longing to see you after I got your letter that you wrote after Christmas.'

'My letter! I wrote all the time! I must have sent a dozen in all. But I didn't know how lucky I would be in getting any of them to you, not even knowing where you were. Never mind; I wrote as much for me as for you; it helped bring you closer somehow.'

'Tell me all that has happened to you now,' urged Joe, 'you said in that letter that you didn't like living with the Regimental ladies?' Catherine gave a moue of disgust,

'Oh Joe, you wouldn't believe how supercilious they were. I expect the officer's wives were treated alright, but they treated us like errant children.

But they pretended that they felt sorry for us. Cristabel was treated the same way, so as soon as Chris found this place, we moved out. It wasn't easy, because Allahabad is full to bursting, just like Lucknow when you arrived!' She chuckled reminiscently; this bungalow was luxury compared to that!

'It's been lovely since then, though we were a bit crowded.'

'Were?' queried Joe,

'Yes. David found a billet for himself and Cristabel, so we are more comfortable. But they still come when they can. It is possible that the 32nd Foot will be posted soon, but we're hoping that it won't be for a while. David is talking of leaving the army, and India, and taking Cristabel back to Wales. He says that coal mining must be better than this!'

'Where's Pattie and Chris?' asked Joe, realizing that in the euphoria of their reunion he hadn't noticed them missing.

'Chris works at the local newspaper, but comes home for tiffin and a rest midday. Pattie went to the bazaar; we don't have much money, so we do the shopping ourselves.' Joe's jaw tightened,

'You said something of that in your letter. I'll settle with Chris. I've some back pay, which is very generous since I was promoted. You won't want for anything again, I promise you.' Catherine smiled at his vehemence.

'Oh my love; lack of money was nothing compared to living with those….those…' words failed her for a moment, so she settled for 'old biddies. It's much nicer living here. Oh!' She was diverted by the sight of Rose who had taken advantage of her mother's attention being elsewhere and was pulling the trailing edge of a lace cloth. The cloth covered a small round table covered in knick knacks, which were in imminent danger of being pulled down over the baby's head. As one of the objects was a brass paperweight, instant action was needed. Joe swooped and rescued the lace cloth from the infant's grasp, just as a voice outside the room heralded the arrival of Pattie.

She swept into the room having been forewarned by the houseboy and hugged Joe, who had to hastily pass Rose to Catherine. She then surveyed him from head to foot, exclaimed at the uniform and the moustache, and demanded to know how he came to be here. He began his tale again, only to be interrupted by the arrival of Chris, his slight frame as casually dressed as ever in a crumpled alpaca suit, and still limping heavily. He pumped

Joe's hand and slapped his back and exclaimed at the uniform. Joe finally managed to finish the tale without further interruption. Rose had had enough of adult chatter by this time, and Catherine bore her off to be fed and put down for a nap, while Pattie rang for the houseboy to bring them tiffin, Joe took the opportunity to thank them for looking after Catherine and Rose, and tried to press some money onto Chris, who became very embarrassed and said gruffly 'not to be so foolish, and that it was no more than Joe would have done for Pattie.'

Joe then left them to see his daughter before she slept. He entered Catherine's bedchamber as she was fastening her bodice. She handed the sleepy baby to Joe while she tidied herself. He buried his lips into Rose's neck and smelt the baby smell of her. He gazed at Catherine over the baby's head and whispered softly,

'Feeding suits you, larla. You always bewailed a lack of fullness,' and he gently touched her swelling breast, bringing a rosy blush to her cheeks.

'You cannot know how much I've missed you, acushla.' Joe's voice grew husky with longing, and Catherine's heart beat faster behind her lace fichu.

'And I you, my love. But we must rejoin Chris and Pattie.' Joe grinned cheekily and muttered,

'I'm sure they'll understand!' but Catherine gave him a playful slap on the hand reaching for her generous contours again. She took the baby from him, the little head lolling, and laid her in a wicker cradle, draping a muslin net over it against the mosquitoes that claimed the lives of so many European children. Softly, husband and wife kissed their daughter and left her to her dreams as they walked hand in hand back to Chris and Pattie waiting in the shaded room for tiffin. Later, they all retired to get some rest during the hottest hours of the day. But in truth, Joe and Catherine slept very little as their intense longing was finally assuaged, after the long, weary months of abstinence. The handsome uniform was forgotten and discarded in disarray on the floor.

The month of Joe's leave passed all too quickly, but at least they would not have to part, as Catherine was determined to travel back with him.

When he protested that the cantonment would not be ready for families, she merely replied that she would find lodgings in Kotepore town,

'For,' she said sweetly, 'you said yourself that the populace was friendly enough and it was the Rajah who was set on rebellion!'

'I wish you wouldn't turn my own words back on me,' grumbled Joe; but in his heart he was delighted. The only real worry he had was the effect of the hot weather on Rose, but Catherine said very firmly,

'If she's to thrive in India, she needs to get used to it Joe. The only way to escape would be for you to take us north, and there is no time, is there?' Joe could only agree, and it did seem that the baby did cope with the heat here in Allahabad, and Kotepore would not be any worse. By the end of his leave period it was mid-May and the heat was searing at midday. But Rose seemed to manage to sleep through the worst of the heat and was active in the long evening hours and in the early morning. She remained as healthy as a native baby, so Joe stopped worrying.

He had met up with David and Cristabel again, and many of his leave evenings were spent as a sixsome as they sat on the verandah of the bungalow and discussed the affairs of the world as they had done in their 'den' in Lucknow. Joe told them of the retaking of Lucknow and that their 'den' had vanished, which saddened them briefly, but Cristabel observed that she would prefer that no-one else used it so perhaps it was as well that it had been dismantled!

During Joe's absence from the cantonment, news came to him via Chris that events were moving on with the winding up of the Mutiny. The Maulavi of Faizabad had been driven into Rohilkand. Kuwar Singh had lost his stronghold at Jagishpur and was desperately trying to flee across the Ganges. He had had a hand shattered by a cannon ball, and had lopped it off to throw into the sacred waters as an offering to the Hindu Gods. Perhaps they heard him, for he turned on his oppressors and inflicted a crushing blow on them. But old and dying, it was to be his last throw!

Meanwhile Sir Hugh Rose was busy again against the Rani of Jhansi and her allies, Tantia Topi and a nephew of Nana Sahib, Rao Sahib. Rose advanced towards Kalpi and the Rani, where she lay in wait for him with a plan for his defeat, but Tantia Topi, overconfident with the numbers at his disposal, and in his belief that the British could not stand the searing heat, he met Rose at Kunch. There, Rose inflicted a crushing defeat on the rebels, losing a tenth of Tantia Topi's losses. But he still had to face the Rani, six miles away at Kalpi, where she had a stronghold made up of a line of temples. She had been joined by the Nawab of Banda and together with Rajah Ajit Khan and Rao Sahib, they made a formidable team.

The friends discussed this latest news, and Joe's opinion was sought as he was acquainted with the Rajah. Joe responded,

'The Rani has quite a reputation as a military leader. In fact, I've heard her described as 'the best soldier among them'. Trouble is, in the male dominated company she's in, her tactics will probably be ignored. I can't see Rajah Ajit listening to a woman!' Catherine glared at him, but he smiled at her,

'Not my words, acushla, I've the greatest respect for *your* tactics!' Their friends laughed at Catherine's outraged expression as she threw a cushion at Joe's head, which he had to duck.

'When do you think it will be over?' asked Cristabel, 'it seems to have gone on forever.' Chris answered her,

'I think that it is over, Cristabel, but the likes of the Rani and the Rajah won't admit it. It would be a very different story if the rest of India had joined in, but it was very localized.'

'But why?' asked his wife, 'surely other Indians were as discontented as the ones here in Oudh?'

'Yes,' replied Chris, 'but it is the story of India in a nutshell. They lack unity with their innumerable castes. The army here in Bengal are mainly high-caste Brahmins and have little in common with the low-caste sepoys in other areas such as Madras. In the Punjab there was some dissatisfaction, but John Lawrence held it in tight control, and was even able to send sepoys to fight the pandies here!'

'I've had enough,' stated David firmly, 'as soon as this is over I'm leaving the army and India for good. Cristabel has no family here, and we'll make some sort of a life in Wales. It's got to be better than waiting to be murdered in our beds.' Joe listened to him and then put in,

'I don't think that this'll happen again. Victoria's government has learned its lesson and will more than likely take direct control. There is talk of railways being built which will make troop transport easier. But more than anything they must now realise that they can't just trample over people's religious beliefs and get away with it.' Chris snorted derisively,

'Joe, Joe, still the romantic! I agree with a lot of what you say, but the great British aristocracy will never accept that they can't ride roughshod over anyone they choose!'

'Maybe you're right, but I'd like to believe that they've learned from their mistakes. I must feel that as I have been promoted, haven't I?'

'But by all accounts that's down to one rather exceptional member of the upper classes?' Joe had no answer to that, remembering the likes of Carless, McBride and Mortimer. Perhaps Chris was right and the British government would learn nothing from this whole sorry episode. But one thing he was very sure of though, the British would tighten its grip on a hapless India which would never allow it to shake off its domination!

But then it was time to go. Gopi found a dak-ghari to carry Catherine and Rose and their meagre belongings. Joe reported to the barracks the day before their departure, and received a bundle of despatches for Colonel Willoughby. They set off before dawn, determined to put many miles behind them before the sun would drive them to seek shelter.

Rose was still asleep when she was lifted from her cradle and kissed tearfully by Pattie and Cristabel, who grown to dearly love the lively infant. Joe shook hands with David and wished him luck for his future in Wales, though he himself had no wish to copy him. But he was saddened by the thought that he would likely never see these two dear people again. Then he said goodbye to Chris and Pattie, while urging them to come and stay in Kotepore whenever the wished. Once again, Joe thanked them for taking care of his loved ones, earning him an abrasive remark from Chris,

'Just get going, old chap, before I get really angry with you!' Joe grinned, kissed Pattie, and settled Catherine in the dak-ghari with the sleeping baby. He intended to ride home this time as a British officer, and for safety had hired a small escort. They looked back once at the group waving from the verandah of the bungalow, and then a corner of the street hid them from view. It gave Joe the feeling that they had turned a corner of their lives. The events of the past year would be put behind them. They had emerged, if not unscathed, but had a delightful daughter as a bonus.

He was now an officer determined to prove his worth, and in Kotepore, their new home was in the process of being built. He looked down at Gopi walking alongside clutching his stirrup, and said in Urdu,

'What is my dharma now, Gopi?' The young Hindu's teeth gleamed in the torchlight,

'Jo hoga, so hoga, Sahib.' Joe gave a shout of laughter which startled the broken down ghari-nag so that it broke into a brief trot!

Hugh Rose defeated the triumvirate of Indian leaders at Kalpi, though not without being close to defeat himself. The sun was his greatest enemy with more men falling with sunstroke than fell in battle, But he prevailed and recaptured trophies gained by the rebels at Cawnpore.

In Rohilkand, Campbell was being outmanouvred by the forces of the Maulavi. His efforts were carefully documented by William Howard Russell, a correspondent for 'The Times'. The journalist was caught up in the thick of the fighting at one point, and nearly died at the hands of fanatical Rohilla ghazis dressed in green turbans and cummerbunds, he had fallen from his horse directly in their path, but they thundered over him leaving him bruised and battered but alive. Later, the ghazis were all killed, but Campbell's forces were close to exhaustion, and men were falling with heatstroke. One old soldier gasped out to Russell,

'I've been eighteen years in service and never known hardship like this!' Russell looked for him later, but found him dead. But just as their morale reached rock bottom, the Maulavi was murdered by one of his own allies, an Indian nobleman who decided the time was right to change sides, and curry favour with the British by turning his coat.

It was thought to be all over, and stations all over Oudh rejoiced, including Kotepore, where Catherine Harrington and her daughter had settled into a small but comfortable residence on the very edge of the town, close to the bridge connecting it to the cantonment. Her husband came home after a particularly hot and trying day supervising the reconstruction of the bungalows, and told her the story of the last battle of the Mutiny.

'We thought it was finished and the Central Indian Force was being disbanded; you know, Rose's lot?' Catherine nodded, as Joe had been set against the decision as being too precipitate.

'Tantia Topi attacked Gwalier; the Maharajah had thrown in his lot with us, but not his army! They flocked to Tantia Topi, though what they hoped to gain at this late stage I just don't know. Well, they threw him out, the Maharajah and declared the Nana Sahib the ruler. They were all there, the Rani, Tantia Topi, Rao Sahib and Rajah Khan; oh, and Saeed.' He gave the last name almost in a whisper, and Catherine noting the distress on his face, rested a light hand on his shoulder. He went on in a monotone, as though reading from a despatch,

'Rose hastily got his force together again, and marched against them. Time was not on his side with the rains due any day. He met them at Kotah-ke-serai, and engaged the Rani. She led her army dressed as a cavalry soldier, and was flanked by the Khan's. She was seen to be hit by a bullet in the side, though she rode some way before falling from her horse. Ajit Khan was also hit and died beside her, and Saeed was wounded. I've since heard he died of his wound.' Joe paced the room, 'he never believed in the rebellion, Catherine. I know that; I've always known it. He never said so out of loyalty to his father, but I saw him in Kotepore when it all started; I saw it in his eyes. Oh God, we are all victims of karma I suppose. He knew he couldn't win, but he had to follow his father to the end. His father sent him to England to learn about the enemy, but Saeed learned all too well; it was there he realised just how strong the British are!' He bowed his head and Catherine thought that he wept. To ease the tension, she asked quietly,

'What happened to the others, Tantia Topi and Rao Sahib?'

'They escaped again,' replied Joe bitterly, 'those two will always escape!'

He wasn't quite right about that as Tantia Topi was hanged nearly a year later. Rao Sahib managed to reach Mecca, where he died in abject poverty some years later. But it did not matter; the Mutiny was finally over.

Chapter 17

The years following the Great Revolt were years of consolidation and reconciliation for the inhabitants of Kotepore and their neighbours in the cantonment. Years when distrust and fear were steadily replaced by a return of trust and confidence in each other.

The cantonment was completely rebuilt, with the layout redesigned and roadways widened to make it easier for carriages to move between the bungalows, something that had definitely been lacking in the previous plan. James Willoughby also decided that the original design placing the Colonel's bungalow at the apex of a triangle, with the lower ranks spreading below should be replaced with a mixture of ranks on all the levels. Some die-hards tut-tutted at the innovation, but within a year or so were sagely nodding their heads, and maintaining that they believed all along that it would improve Regimental relationships!

The pattern of command in Oudh and Bengal also underwent radical change. The British could never be brought to admit that colonization was inherently wrong, and therefore the Mutiny was a shock to their complacency rather than their arrogance and self-confidence. Their faith in the Victorian march of progress was still very strong, and no-one 'back home' could see any reason for the British Raj to ever come to an end. But of course, mistakes had been made, and it was determined that they would not be made again. The 'disease of mutiny' had struck at the Bengal army, without contaminating the armies of Bombay and Madras, so it was the Bengal army that must suffer the cure. The Kotepore Regiment saw their sepoys of Brahmin origin replaced by Ghurkas from the slopes of the Himalayas, Sikhs from the Punjab and Rajputs from Rajputana.

All around Oudh the soldiers of the East India Company were paid off or absorbed into the British regiments. The biggest change was that the disparity of numbers was corrected, and there would not be more than two Indian soldiers to every one European, unlike the days before the Mutiny when the ratio had reached in some cases, eight to one! Lastly, the formidable artillery of the old Indian army was disbanded; their gunners were just too good at their business!

As those with a sound grasp of Indian affairs had predicted, the East India Company disappeared and the government of India passed to direct rule from London. In 1858, the Board of Control was replaced by the Secretary of State for India, who had cabinet status and was advised by men with expertise in Indian affairs. In India, the Governor-General became a Viceroy, and was a Crown appointment. On 1st November 1858, the Queen's Proclamation of Crown Rule, issued in eighteen different languages, was read out all over India. It was received with varying degrees of enthusiasm. Some Indians felt happy at the demise of 'Johnny Company', feeling that it was becoming overly concerned with profits. Others felt the British 'noose' tighten still further. Many were simply glad that an amnesty had been granted to all who took part in the rebellion, apart from the notorious Tantia Topi, thereby preventing any further bloody reprisals being meted out to the guilty and innocent alike. But the vast majority of Indians simply shrugged their shoulders and got on with scratching a living as best they could. Their lives were bounded by the unpredictable rains and hot seasons, rather than the British Crown. The Mutiny and the aftermath made no difference to them whatsoever!

In Kotepore, the amnesty had one startling and unforeseen result. Saeed Khan, who had been wounded at the battle that took his father and the Rani of Jhansi, had not died as was widely reported. His few remaining loyal soldiers had spirited him away from the battlefield, and put the story about, fearing for his life if it had become known that he had survived. Once the amnesty had been announced, a litter bearing the injured Prince arrived in Kotepore, and it was borne in state through the streets to the palace.

Joe heard the news the same day, and had to turn away from the men he was working with to hide the tears in his eyes. He had not known until that moment how much he had grieved for the friend he thought he had lost.

Colonel James Willoughby, as representative of the British Government visited the Prince on his sick bed. With the authority granted to him by Viceroy Canning in Calcutta, he informed the Prince that he would administer the town and district of Kotepore, with the neighbouring cantonment having an advisory role. The Prince acknowledged the tact in the term 'advisory' as he knew better than anyone that he would never be allowed to act autonomously again. Nevertheless, he thanked the Colonel for his visit and responded gravely that he hoped they could work together in harmony.

Joe visited him the next day, and gazed down at his injured friend with joy in his eyes. Prince Saeed put out his left hand to grasp Joe's, and said,

'Well my friend, it would seem that our roles are reversed! And I see you are now an officer; I thought that it would not be possible for you?' Joe sat of a stool by the Prince's bed and the two shared their stories from the time Joe had been incarcerated at the Prince's orders.

'You must tell me some time, how you managed to escape,' smiled the Prince, 'but now tell me how you come to b e wearing that smart uniform.' Joe complied, and also questioned the Prince about his feelings about the Mutiny. As Joe had expected, Saeed had strongly argued against it which led to his estrangement with his father, even though he loyally stayed with him throughout. It was, he said, his own father's action in sending him to Britain that had caused the rift,

'You see Joe,' he said, waving the arm in a handsome emerald silk sling to match his turban, 'when my father sent me to the English school, I was told to search out any weaknesses in 'the enemy'. What my father forgot to ask was, 'what were their strengths'! I knew from those days that the British would never lose their grip on India; there was too much at stake. Was it not Napoleon who said that the English were a nation of shopkeepers? To lose India would hurt their pockets far too much. But my worst sin of all from my father's point of view, I even grew to like them, especially one; though of course, he wasn't English at all!' He smiled at Joe again, and they clasped arms again, happy that their friendship had survived as well as themselves!

'And we have both been promoted,' laughed the Prince, 'you to Lieutenant and me to Rajah. But that's life, isn't it?' The two men were comfortable together and knew they could look forward to learning more about each other during the years of peace to come.

For James Willoughby the end of the fighting brought about a relief from the nagging worry about his father, the Ferguson's and John Carlton with his Indian wife. Even as he waited patiently to journey northwards to Lucy and his son, Charles, he received a letter from his wife. Her father-in-law, and the others, had arrived in Simla at last, but she reported, his father was exceedingly frail. Lucy also reported that John had written to him several times to put his mind at rest, but none had reached him. She gave a brief outline of the trials the group had been through, but said that he could find out the rest when they all met up again.

John was able to fill in the details some time later. It transpired that Carlton had had warning of the uprising, for his house servants were intensely loyal, especially as many of them were caste-fellows of his wife, Dharshi. He had fled from his home with his wife and son, taking as little baggage as possible, and travelled to the Ferguson's. He found them blissfully unaware of the events about to overtake them, and had only managed to convince them of the need for haste when they had seen fire in their fields glowing against the night sky. They had all fled together, heading north to the hills, living simply in dak-bungalows as they went, never staying in one place for very long. But they were forced to have frequent rests as James' father was very frail. As they moved further away from Oudh they began to feel safer, and they finally reached the foothills of the Himalayas. John told James that he had sent messages from every place they stayed, and was only sorry that none had reached their destination to put his mind at rest. He also said that he would have returned to Oudh to try and help as much as he could, but realised that the others were just too dependent on him to leave them to fend for themselves. James could only thank him for his consideration.

The winter had been long and hard, though they had cautiously descended the slopes in search of warmth. By this time, Lucknow had been relieved and Carlton had decided to bring his charges back to Kotepore, but Charles Willoughby had fallen ill with pneumonia. He had fought bravely for his life and, John believed, it was only the thought of not seeing his son again that made him pull through. By the time he was fit enough to travel, John had realised that the air in Simla would be better for him than the torrid heat of Oudh. And, he correctly surmised, the Kotepore families would be there. Charles had travelled the many miles in a litter, but was still desperately weak, Lucy urged her husband to come as soon as he could if he hoped to see his father again.

By this time, work was progressing well at Kotepore, though the expected rains could bring it to a halt at any time. It was also very clear that further trouble was highly unlikely in the district, though battles still raged around Jhansi and Gwalior, but that was far away. So James decided to head north with as much speed as he could, and arrived in Simla at the beginning of July to a rapturous welcome from his wife and son.

James held the boy aloft and told him that he had grown apace and if he went on at this rate he would be measured up for a uniform in no time! Charles laughed with delight and then told his father, who he absolutely adored, that he was doing his drill every day. James put him down and ruffled his golden hair, and held out his arms to a smiling Lucy. She came to them swiftly and the two remained tightly enfolded until an urgent tugging at his sword belt brought them back to reality. It was his son demanding attention. James held the boy between them as he anxiously questioned Lucy about his father, young Charles' namesake. She nodded gravely, her brown eyes sombre in her tanned face,

'The pneumonia has left him very weak and he has difficulty breathing. I do believe it is only the thought of seeing you again that is holding him to this world.' James gently pushed his son to Lucy, promising to spend time with him later, and moved towards the house. The boy looked at his retreating back, and clutched his mother's hand tightly,

'Is it Grandpa, Mama?'

'Yes my pet. Grandpa's very ill, and your Papa is very worried about him. We will see to your tea now, and you can see Papa again later.'

James entered the sick room where his father lay beneath crisp white sheets, in startling contrast to his yellow, papery skin. He seemed to have shrunk since James saw him last, and his hands were like claws clutching the sheet. His eyes were closed and sunk into his head, the lids stained with purple. He had been propped up on several pillows, but even so the sound of laboured breathing filled the room. James' heart wrenched in pity and the image rose in his mind of his mother as she lay in similar state soon after their arrival in India. With a shock he realised it was a full ten years earlier.

'Papa,' whispered James, and then more strongly, 'Papa, I've come a long way to see you, and I've heard you've had many an adventure since we were together last.' He winced at the false bonhomie in his voice, and cursed himself for being a ranting fool, 'adventures' by God!

The bruised eyelids fluttered open, revealing washed out eyes like a muddy English pond on a winter's day; eyes that had once been as bright green as James' own. They peered at James, red-rimmed and rheumy,

'Is that you, m'boy?'

'Yes Papa.' James came to the bedside and knelt so he could take his father's hand. It felt like a bundle of dry sticks, the skin like desiccated parchment.

'It's been a long time. Where have you been, eh, eh? I don't know what your mother would have said.' The voice quavered querulously, almost like a petulant child. James' heart broke for this old man, who could not understand why his peace had been shattered; why he could not have been left to finish his life pottering round the Ferguson estates. He stayed there kneeling until the eyelids closed again, and his father slept in the swift, light manner of the old. The laboured breathing filled the room again with its grating rasp. James left the room quietly.

In the parlour he found John Carlton and his aunt and uncle seated in comfortable chairs indulging in a sherry. John rose swiftly to his feet and strode across the room to shake James' hand.

'Good to see you again. By God there's been some water under the bridge since I saw you last in the mofussil!' James nodded, and turned to his aunt to kiss her cheek. She patted his shoulder affectionately and watched as he greeted his uncle and accepted a glass of sherry. Questions flew as they tried to bring themselves all up to date about their respective experiences. Presently Lucy came in dragging a shy and reluctant Dharshi. The young woman had grown easy in the company of the Ferguson's and the elderly Charles, but the arrival of James had thrown her into a panic again, even though he was no stranger. She was a beautiful young woman with enormous kohl rimmed brown eyes. She was dressed in a blue silk sari, and she had drawn the end over her face, so that little more than her eyes showed. In the parting of her black hair could just be seen a red tika. John came to her side and drew her further into the room, holding her protectively to his side,

'It's alright, janee,' he whispered to her, 'we are among friends here; there is no need to hide yourself away.' But Dharshi could not be comfortable in the room, and after a while, she slid out again in a gliding motion, her graceful body swaying. John watched her go, half amused, half exasperated,

'She just can't bring herself to throw off the habits of purdah,' he explained unnecessarily.

Dinner that night was a subdued affair, with the knowledge that Charles was slipping away casting a pall over them all. Even the joy of seeing Lucy and little Charles again could not relieve James' heaviness of spirit. Before he retired that night, he looked in on his father again, but he was in a fitful sleep, so he slipped out again.

In their bedchamber, he and Lucy spoke in hushed tones. In spite of their long separation, James did not feel in the least inclined towards lovemaking and he tried to explain it to Lucy, his eyes pleading for understanding. It was there in full measure, and they lay together under the muslin net murmuring together about the future. James told her about the rebuilding of Kotepore, and how he had changed the design of the officer bungalows, at which she raised an eyebrow but otherwise made no comment.

It was in the early hours of the morning, when the air still had freshness to it, when there was a gentle knocking on the door. Lucy's Hindu maid put her head round the door, and said softly,

'Sahib, Memsahib, Samee thinks you should come to Willoughby-Sahib chuldi, chuldi!' Lucy and James rose swiftly, and only pausing long enough to throw dressing gowns over their nightwear, hurried from their room to Charles' bedside. The houseboy, Samee, looked distinctly relieved but apologised for rousing them.

'It's alright Samee,' reassured James and approached the bed. His father's breathing had grown more laboured since the afternoon, the tendons of the wasted throat straining with the effort.

'Papa!' said James urgently. His father's eyes opened and he looked his favourite son full in the face. A claw-like hand lifted and touched his cheek, and Charles smiled a gentle smile. James bent low over him as his father was speaking so quietly he could barely hear the words,

'You're a good boy, my son; take after your father, eh? Go for a soldier, eh?' He coughed and struggled for breath. James urged him to save his strength but he went on,

'Gerald's alright; if…if only he wasn't…..such a dull……dog.' The voice trailed away as a last despairing breath sounded, then stopped. A beatific smile spread across his face,

'Lettice!' and he was gone.

James closed the sightless eyes, and placed the hand he had been holding on his father's chest, setting the other on it carefully. He felt Lucy's hand on his shoulder, and looking up, saw her eyes bright with unshed tears. He touched her hand with his cheek, and the two stayed quietly like that until footsteps outside heralded the arrival of others. Esme entered first, followed by Richard with John bringing up the rear, knuckling sleep from his eyes. James stood to let them approach the bed.

'He so longed to be with Lettice,' said Esme, her voice quite calm, 'I cannot feel sad for him, but I shall miss him. He has been part of our lives for many years now.' Her husband nodded and gripped James' arm in commiseration. He too would miss the old man in his cream alpaca suit and panama hat; would miss the astringent comments he had about everything and everyone; except this second son of his.

Next day, funeral arrangements were made and Charles Willoughby was laid to rest in the Anglican Cemetery. As the chaplain intoned the words of the funeral service, James remembered with surprise that his father had not known that his old friend and companion in arms, Gerald Deluce, had perished nearly a year before, and he felt glad. No need to distress his father with details of his demise, and they were surely now reunited.

That night James and Lucy came together again, the long abstinence bringing a special joy to their union, as though they were loving each other for the first time. Afterwards they lay with Lucy's golden hair spread across James' chest and spoke of their love, their marriage and their son, and then at last, of James' father. Sometime in the night, Lucy told him that the Ferguson's planned to return to England; that they had no wish to start again in India,

'For their estate was completely destroyed you know?'

'Mm yes, I did know; but surely now that peace has returned?'

'No, they say not. They are quite wealthy and much of their money is safely invested in Calcutta, so they will be comfortable.'

'We'll miss them though.'

'Poor little Dharshi, James; she seems terrified of you!'

'I can't imagine why? Have I such a fierce look or a terrible reputation?' Lucy gurgled with laughter, but then,

'Their son is here with them. He's a delightful boy and has hit it off with Charles already.'

'Mm, Amar isn't it?' asked James sleepily.

'Yes.'

'It won't be easy for the boy, with mixed parentage. I wonder how he will get on as he grows.'

'John seems determined to raise him as an Indian; says he must know his heritage, But I have to agree with you, he will always wonder which world he belongs to.' Presently the voices faded away as they drifted off to sleep, with James feeling that the hurt of his bereavement was already being healed with the love of his wife.

Catherine Harrington, installed in her own small bungalow on the edge of Kotepore was completely happy for the first time since the day she left for Lucknow over a year before, In spite of the torrid, humid heat she hummed to herself as she went about her daily tasks. In common with the Indian population that she lived amongst, she rose early while it was still full dark, and tried to rest during the hottest hours of the middle of the day.

Some days, the brain fever bird would call at noon and the temperature would rise still further, until she felt that he head would burst. On such days, even the normally contented Rose would become fretful and out-of-sorts. But these days passed and at long last the rains came.

The first downpour brought out the usual crop of picanninies to dance in the deluge, and Catherine smiled at them as she stepped outside with Rose in her arms. The baby put out her pudgy hands and chuckled as plump raindrops splashed off her palms and into her face; soon she and her mother were wet through, their muslin dresses plastered to their skin which showed through pink and glowing. Then Joe arrived, all work suspended for the day. He stood amazed at the sight of his wife and daughter laughing in the rain; then an enormous bubble of joy welled up inside him and throwing back his head, he laughed with them. Rose reached out for him and the three of them danced up and down, splashing the little pot-bellied boys who didn't know quite what to make of the mad angrezis. All too soon the shower was over, and a gaggle of drab seven sister birds scuttled out onto the front lawn, scolding each other and the intrusive humans. Great monsoon toads crawled from beneath the bungalow where they had sheltered from the fierce rays of the sun and squatted obscenely in puddles, croaking out their seasonal chorus.

The months since their return from Allahabad had passed swiftly, and as the rains died away, Rose had her first birthday. By then she was crawling swiftly across the floor; so swiftly that one day she caught the tail of a startled mongoose as it stalked a snake through the front parlour. Catherine stood transfixed, terrified by the snake and the mongoose's sharp teeth, not knowing whether to risk precipitating an incident by trying to drag her daughter out of harm's way. The mongoose turned sharply but saw nothing more threatening than a small human, he made a sudden movement that released the captured tail and was gone, leaving a round eyed Rose gazing after it and clapping her hands with delight.

By Rose's birthday, Catherine knew that she was pregnant again, and traced the conception to their passionate lovemaking in Allahabad. Joe escorted her to the Regimental Surgeon, who scolded her for the closeness of the two pregnancies, especially after Joe had admitted to her low state after Rose's birth. They were lectured on the dangers of such immoderate behaviour until Catherine's cheeks were stained a rosy red, and they both felt like errant schoolchildren. After reducing the pair to a state of suitable chastisement, Surgeon Anderson relented, and said that Catherine was to be cosseted throughout her pregnancy. The most violent exercise she was to indulge in was the lifting of a book or a pen, but no more. Catherine pulled a face at that, but cheered up a little when told that she may, indeed must, walk a little every day. Also, a sustaining diet was a vital necessity.

They left Surgeon Anderson's room feeling thoroughly taken to task, but then they looked at each other and burst into a fit of giggles, laughing helplessly and clutching at each other until the door to the surgery opened to reveal Anderson putting his nose out to see what all the noise was about. They hurried away.

In spite of their mirth, Joe felt that the advice was sound, and Catherine found herself being spoilt as never before in her life. Part of her reveled in the cherishing, but underneath it all, she was bored, and longed to be bustling about again. She did manage to catch up on some reading, and her correspondence had never been so up to date! And then Louise Swales came back.

Adam had been about since their own return, but had been busy with his duties, as had Joe. But Louise was her special friend, particularly with Pattie stuck in Allahabad. There were enough bungalows finished to house the wives as they returned, but Catherine was happy where she was. Louise found her household more comfortable than the raw new dwellings beginning to march up the hillside once again, and was to be found at the Harrington household more often than her own. She thoroughly agreed with the cosseting, having heard the story of Rose's birth, and abetted Joe's determination to keep his wife healthy.

Louise exclaimed over Rose, and brought along her Christina, who at three going on four, was ready to be enchanted by a younger infant. Many an hour did the two women spend having a comfortable 'coze'. They read companionably together, and were able to discuss literature with their husbands in the evening.

The days following the rains were delightful; warm but not too hot, and the air had a freshness about it they had almost forgotten. Catherine found the winter more comfortable as her pregnancy advanced. As travel became possible, Chris and Pattie spent several short visits with them. The Mutiny seemed to have belonged to another life, and the rebuilding of the cantonment was followed with interest, as though it was something that they had all wanted to do, rather than born out of necessity.

On one of their visits, Chris shyly told them that he had written a book based on a diary he had kept in Lucknow and he had sent it off to a publisher in Calcutta. He had received a letter that was highly encouraging and a sum of money! They were all delighted for this quiet, self-effacing man and said so over a celebratory bottle of wine. Even Catherine was allowed a sip! Chris went on to say that he had plans to start a newspaper of his own in Delhi.

'Surely it's too soon; there is still much rebuilding to do,' questioned Joe. Chris shook his head at that, brushing his floppy brown hair out of his eyes in a familiar gesture,

'No. Now is exactly right, while the rebuilding is going on. It is always best to be first in the field!

In February 1859, Catherine gave birth to a seven pound boy, perfect in every respect. Anderson, who had attended her, told Joe that she was tired but otherwise had come through the birth well. The baby boy cried lustily, as Catherine held him to her breast with tears in her eyes. He had a shock of black hair and waved his fists about as though angry at his entry into the world. Joe looked down at mother and baby, holding Rose in his arms,

'Look poppet, you have a baby brother.' Rose, not at all sure she cared for the attention that this baby brother was receiving, decided to join in the bawling, whereupon Catherine told Joe rather peevishly to take her away. Joe was startled, but put it down to tiredness. He took Rose out and spent some time with her, reading a story to lull her to sleep before returning to his wife. He found her already asleep, the baby on the crook of her arm, the ayah keeping an eye on them. Feeling somewhat surplus to requirement, he went away.

The new arrival ruled the household from the first, his doting mother organizing her life round his imperious demands for food. Once he had lost his new-born redness, he was a handsome child, with a vigorous head of dark hair, and eyes that changed from baby blue to a deep brown. Joe thought he saw his father in him and hoped he would be blessed with a sunnier temperament. It was difficult to tell as yet as he spent so much time with his face screwed up and bawling lustily for his mother's breast.

Joe began to worry that Catherine was so besotted with her son that she was pushing Rose away from her. More than once he saw the hurt in the child's eyes as Catherine gave all her attention on the new baby. He was wary of interfering until one day he took his daughter in to see her brother, asleep and snuffling in his cradle. In spite of the rebuffs from her mother, Rose adored the little one, and she went on tip toe to touch the soft crown of his head. At that moment Catherine entered and seeing Rose bending over the cradle rushed over and slapped her hand away.

'Be careful, you'll hurt him!' Then she saw Joe's face, taut with anger. He said quietly, but with a touch of ice in his voice,

'She was doing no harm; just touching him. Can't you see she adores him?' Catherine pursed her lips but did not reply, nor did she take Rose in her arms. Joe picked up his daughter and swung her high in the air,

'Come little one, it's time for a story. What would you like today?' The child soon recovered her smile lost with her mother's slap. She buried her face in her father's neck and breathed in his ear,

'Yours.' Joe smiled. The little one was not to know that they weren't his at all, but her great-grandfather's!

He took the child to her room and called for her ayah, Nilmini, to prepare her for bed. He waited quietly in the nursery thinking over the incident with his wife and Rose. He had known she had longed for a son when she first became pregnant, and perhaps she had been a little disappointed when Rose was born, but it had been a hard birth. But she had adored Rose, hadn't she? He hoped that this overprotectiveness towards the new baby would soon pass, but it seemed to him that it was intensifying by the day. He remembered his own unhappiness as a boy, when he had worshipped his father and yearned for a kind word from him, so he knew just what Rose was going through but felt powerless to help.

He musings were interrupted when a tiny figure rushed at his knees clamouring to be lifted, and he put his worries aside in the pleasure of relating the story of 'the Princess and the Giant.' Long before the tale was finished the head on his shoulder had drooped. Looking down, Joe extracted a pink thumb from between her soft lips and lifted her into her cot. Kissing her gently he tucked the covers round the slight body and arranged the muslin drapes. He stood awhile gazing sightlessly into the cot, pondering the best course of action.

But though Joe was a man of immense courage in many spheres, he could not face discord in his household, and he could well imagine Catherine's face if he accused her of neglecting her first born. And he was an Irishman, with an Irishman's innate optimism; of course things would improve with time, and could he not provide all the love and affection that Rose needed until they did? He conveniently forgot that other child who had his mother's intense devotion, but yearned for one, just one kind word from the father he adored. And did not that child have to wait many a long painful year to have his wish granted? So Joe took refuge in the old adage, 'leave well alone', and so he did nothing. And so the pattern was set that would persist through Rose's childhood and then into adulthood.

In the meantime, the little tyrant who was setting the household on its ears had yet to have a name. Not for him a casual conversation in a heap of rubble when 'Rose' had been agreed on. Names were put forward, considered carefully, and discarded. Patrick was tentatively offered by Joe, and immediately rejected,

'But it's so Irish!'

'But we are Irish, both of us.' But that merely earned a moue of annoyance. Catherine in turn offered some 'high born' English names, Claud and Humphrey being the two that amused Joe the most,

'How can you saddle a little scrap with a name like that?'

'That 'little scrap' happens to be your son and heir, and it is important that he should have a good name. It could make such a difference later on.'

'Exactly how is being labeled 'Humphrey Harrington' going to help him?' Joe asked with heavy irony. That did at last make Catherine's lips twitch at the sound of it, and the touch of humour helped ease a situation that was becoming heavy with tension. In the end, it was Rose who resolved the dilemma when she prattled in infantile fashion after a trip to the Swales and a story she had heard. In the midst of the prattle, Joe could make out 'wobert'.

'That's it! A right royal name, and not English or Irish either!' he added hastily at the look in Catherine's eye,

'Robert, mm, as in Robert the Bruce!' Catherine said it a few times and as Joe held his breath, nodded,

'Yes, I like it. Robert Bruce Harrington.' And as Joe drew a sigh of relief, added a parting shot,

'And woe betide anyone who calls him 'Bobby!'

But then she got rid of the ayah. She was a good hearted soul and Rose adored her. Past the first flush of youth, she had raised a family of her own before coming to the Harrington household, and her soft rounded bosom was very welcome to a lonely little girl when her father was kept at his duties and unable to see her to bed. Nilmini would sing her Urdu lullabies to soothe the child to sleep.

'But she left Robert crying for a full fifteen minutes, *and* she had the temerity,' added Catherine to a protesting Joe, 'to tell me that I was spoiling him! It does no good to leave a child screaming in this heat!'

'Was he hungry?' asked Joe, trying to defuse the situation,'

'No, but what has that to do with it? He was distressed. Anyway, I sacked her, and that is that!'

Joe was concerned as he knew that the ayah would find it difficult to find another position at her age, but Catherine was adamant; she would not keep on such an unfeeling person. Joe foolishly pointed out that Rose adored her and had cried herself to sleep that very evening, That argument elicited a stamped foot and a toss of the well shaped head,

'And what does a child not yet two know about it?' Joe gave up, but made it his business to seek the help of Lucy Willoughby, who seemed to have taken on the task of looking after the welfare of all the Regiment's females, British or Indian.

The aftermath of the dismissal gave rise to a situation that would have been amusing in its irony if Joe had not been so close to it to appreciate the humour of it! He was aware that Catherine had advertised for a new ayah, and he returned home one evening to find one of the applicants leaving his bungalow with a small child in tow. The slight figure in a white sari seemed vaguely familiar, but the sari drawn across her face made it difficult to be sure. As he mounted the steps to the verandah, the woman looked up and two enormous kohl-ringed eyes gazed into his,

'Moti!' The eyes grew even larger, like a frightened gazelle, and then the sweeping lashes came down to hide them. Moti stood quite still.

'Moti, I didn't know you were to come. Won't it be…that is…..will you…?'

'Sahib,' Moti made a graceful namaste, 'I need to work.' The eloquent gesture towards the watching child said it all.

'But where is the child's father? It's not…?' Moti shook her head shyly, and Joe could see that the child was too young to be his and breathed an inward sigh of relief; that would be a situation fraught with danger!

'I was married, Sahib, after I left your home. He was a shoemaker in Lucknow.'

'Was, Moti?'

'He was killed in the fighting.' That silenced Joe for a moment. The British had been so incensed over their losses that they tended to forget the Indian ones, which were, after all, so much greater.

'I must work, Sahib,' and the brown eyes looked straight into his for the first time, 'the past is past.' She turned to go, and Joe was struck afresh by the quality of calmness evoked by the gentle sway of the graceful back. A poignant memory of those early days in Kotepore rose unbidden; calmness seemed to be a quality sadly lacking these days! Quashing the disloyal thought before it could grow, he entered the house to be greeted with two pieces of news; they had a new ayah and they were moving back to the cantonment, as their present accommodation was too cramped!

Moti soon became part of their lives as though she had always been there. She seemed to please everyone, even the fractious Catherine, who gradually relaxed as the burden of the new baby grew easier. Joe could only wonder how she had managed Rose in the terrible squalor of Lucknow under siege; but found her second baby so difficult to cope with in a well-ordered house in Kotepore? But Moti soothed the infant when he cried, singing softly to him until he calmed in her aura of peace. And as Robert stopped fretting, so did his mother.

Rose adored her from the first and soon stopped crying for 'Nil-Nil', her name for the departed ayah. Moti played finger games with her and her own child Ashok, and sang to them both in Urdu. Seeing them together, Joe was struck by how close they seemed to be in age, but it was only much later when he had pieced together her story, he learned just how right he had been in his guess.

After she had left him, Moti had married a widower from Lucknow. Her father, Ishwar, had paid the man well for her loss of virginity, for Joe had been a generous employer. Her husband, Murthi, had lost his first wife in childbirth but her death may well have been hastened by ill treatment. Moti did not say these things openly, but Joe could read much into her silences. She did not care for her husband and was constantly berated for her lack of fertility; he was not to know that Moti was taking her own precautions, fearful of suffering the same fate as her predecessor. But she did become pregnant just as the trouble broke out, but she was saved from Murthi's brutality, as he joined the rebels in the street and vented his anger there rather than at home.

Moti's parents joined the household at this time, as their employers had fled into the Residency, which only served to increase Murthi's temper, and he took to beating her. She was in the late stages of pregnancy when the news came of a relief force on its way, and Murthi rushed off in a fever pitch of excitement, to fight the 'cursed angrezi'. As he left, Moti started her labour.

On 25th September, as Joe was battling his way through the narrow streets of Lucknow to reach his wife in labour with Rose, Moti was in labour with Ashok. The women and Joe survived, Murthi did not. It was Moti's father who suggested her son's name, Ashok, after a great warrior king, for 'wasn't the boy's father a great warrior?' Moti smiled her gentle smile, and agreed.

Life became hard after Murthi's death, Moti said. He had not been much of a provider, but now they had nothing. Ishwar did his best by going out begging every day, and her mother, Sita, insisted on Moti having the best of any food to keep her strength up for feeding Ashok. Ishwar had gone out one day on hearing rumours of strange soldiers in skirts, causing Joe to smile at the description of Campbell's Highlanders, but had got in the way and had perished, leaving them even more destitute. Strange, thought Joe, they were starving inside the Residency and apparently outside as well!

Sita soon followed Ishwar into death, leaving Moti to do her best to survive by begging. She would gladly have died herself, but was desperate to give her son a chance to live.

She managed to keep them going by begging, and as the town quietened, managed to get a job as ayah to a low-caste Hindu family. Her wages were low, but she had a roof over her head, and food to eat.

Then she heard that a British family living on the edge of the city needed an ayah. She staked all on the chance of better paid employment, and politely but firmly told the Hindu couple that she was leaving. She had dressed herself in her cleanest white sari, and holding her son with one hand, and her bundle with her other, she had set off into the unknown yet again. She had not known until she reached the bungalow and heard the name of the memsahib, just who it was who she hoped to work for, but it was too late to turn back. And, as she had already said, 'the past was past' and she had her son to think of. The memsahib seemed to like her, and so she had become part of the Harrington household again.

Catherine added an element to the tale when she told Joe of the interview,

'I don't know what impressed me so. She just stood there with her eyes fixed to the ground, holding the child by the hand. I hadn't wanted an ayah encumbered with a child of her own, but there was something about her; I can't explain it? But she's a good choice, isn't she Joe? And Robert seems to thrive under her care!'

Joe fervently agreed, silently adding, 'and your daughter loves her too, or haven't you noticed?' But such thoughts sprung to mind less frequently as Catherine returned to the laughing girl he had known and he hoped that the megrims following Robert's birth were gone for good. He had questioned Anderson about the causes of his wife's post-natal mood but the army surgeon was more used to treating war wounds than ladies in a delicate condition, and could not offer any help. Robert was certainly thriving and now that his demands for food were less strident, he did show a sunnier side to his nature. Rose adored him, and under Moti's watchful eye, played with him for a while every day.

The family moved to a bungalow in the cantonment about half way up the hill. On their terrace were assorted captains and lieutenants, and Major Harding. At both ends of the curving row were sergeant's and corporal's quarters making for an interesting mix of ranks. Each bungalow was slightly different to its neighbour, as were the gardens, and already the individual tastes of the owners were showing themselves. Coming into the scheme as late as they did, Joe and Catherine had little choice left, but were delighted with their allocation, sited where the bend was most marked giving them a broad expanse of front garden. And to Joe's delight, in the middle of what would be lawn was a well established jacaranda tree that had somehow survived the firing of the original bungalows. The tree was one Joe had long admired and to find it sitting in the middle of his own garden he felt to be a good omen.

But next door to them, much to Catherine's alarm was Major Harding and his wife, Isabel. Catherine still felt insecure in her position as a lieutenant's wife, knowing as she did of military snobbery, and indeed, knowing a little of what Joe had gone through. Although he had made light of his experience, she well remembered his drawn features when he had come to find her in Allahabad. She had plagued Adam until he had enlightened her a little, and she had felt an unladylike satisfaction at the death of the odious McBride. But to find herself in such close proximity to Joe's Major made her extremely nervous. The lady herself did not help matters, coming as she did from the 'old school' that believed in an officer being born a gentleman, and for some time she ignored her brash new neighbours.

However, she was a kindly soul at heart, and liked to sit out before the hot weather got under way, and watch little Rose playing in the garden while Robert slept in a wicker cradle, guarded by Moti against dangerous insects, snakes and the myriad other hazards that could strike a defenceless child. Furthermore, Isabel Harding had lost her closest friend Frances Colby, who had returned to England following her husband Edward's untimely death in the battle for Delhi.

After two weeks, the lady made a momentous decision, and sending for her houseboy, had him deliver a missive written on elegant cream paper, subtly scented with sandalwood. It ran,

Dear Mrs. Harrington,

I note that we are now neighbours and would like to invite you to an 'at home' on Thursday next at three o'clock.

Yours
Isabel Harding

Catherine received the invitation with some trepidation, and immediately went in search of Louise Swales on the terrace below to seek some advice. Louise was highly amused,

'My dear Catherine, Adam has been a lieutenant no longer than Joe, so why should I know more than you about 'at homes' and the like?'

'I don't know; I just thought. Oh Louise, d'you think I should go?'

'Of course you should. Apart from anything else, you said that your parents entertained before you lost your mother? And this could help Joe, y'know. Adam says that they still aren't fully accepted in the mess. He said only the other day that he didn't believe they ever would!'

Catherine's indignation on behalf of their husbands asserted itself, and she raised her chin at that, and she decided to go, come what may! Louise gave her just one piece of advice,

'Just be yourself. All these fancy ladies spend their time putting on airs and grace; it can't be comfortable!' Catherine chuckled, and feeling much better about it, accepted the invitation with a carefully written note delivered by her houseboy. But then she began to fret over what to wear!

On the day of the 'at home', Joe kissed her as he left for duty in the morning, wondering aloud if she would be too grand to speak to him when he returned home. Grinning, she cuffed him playfully, but as soon as he had gone, had her entire wardrobe out for inspection. Rose sat in the middle of piles of muslin and lace, crinolines and stays, while Catherine pestered her maid to press this dress and then that. Rose's eyes grew rounder and rounder at the chaos until at last the outfit was chosen and the rest consigned back to the wardrobe from whence they came.

The morning dragged on and not even time spent with her baby son could take Catherine's mind off the coming ordeal. She tried to eat a light tiffin, but found she could not swallow, and then tried to rest, but the flip-flap of the punkahs drove away all thoughts of sleep. So finally she rose and looked at the dress laid out in readiness, changed her mind and had her entire wardrobe out again. By three o'clock, the entire household felt that it had been through a particularly powerful mangle, so limp and exhausted were they. But in the midst of it all, Catherine stood smiling; now that the moment had come she felt perfectly calm and capable of anything!

'Anyway,' she informed her audience of her maid, Rose, Ashok and Moti holding baby Robert, 'my father was a gentleman, even if he was in trade!' Her audience nodded solemnly.

She was dressed in a simple sprigged muslin dress of palest blue over her day crinoline. The neckline was scooped, and finished with a row of darker blue rosebuds. The colour suited her fair complexion, and lent colour to her grey eyes. Her brown hair was dressed by her maid into her favourite chignon, allowing a few tendrils to escape and soften the imperious nose, which she absolutely hated. She considered it beaky, whereas in reality it gave her face a distinction it would otherwise have lacked. She pulled on soft shoes with a cleverly designed heel to give her an extra inch or two. On her gleaming coiffure she tied on a wide-brimmed straw hat, for she suffered from the glare of the sun and did not wish to spend the afternoon screwing up her face against its strong rays. It was possible that 'at home' meant 'in the garden' at this time of year! At last she was ready and sinking down, she gingerly hugged Rose, while warning her against squashing her skirts.

Watched by Moti, Rose and Ashok, and preceded by her maid, Simbi', Catherine swept out of her front door, down the steps of the verandah, along the front path and turned left before sweeping up the front path of the house next door, up the steps to the verandah and halted before the front door to let her maid tug on the bell pull; somewhat unnecessarily as a houseboy stood ready to receive guests.

Matching hauteur with hauteur, Simbi announced the arrival of Memsahib-Harrington. The houseboy bowed and ushered Catherine inside where she felt her palms suddenly dampen inside her white lace gloves. Inside the drawing room was a collection of woman that she knew well by sight, but had never met socially before. Isabel came forward and effected introductions, to which Catherine responded like an automaton. Isabel must have been impressed as she told her husband later on that 'she was *just* like a lady, y'know!'

The ladies did not know quite how to treat Catherine. She was after all the wife of a lieutenant, but one who was, well, not really an officer, as they had delicately put it to each other before she arrived. A blond woman with a vapid prettiness simpered at Catherine,

'Oh Mrs. Harrington, *so* nice to meet you at last. I've heard *so* much about you and your *so* clever husband!' Catherine smiled equally vapidly and replied,

'I'm afraid you have the advantage of me, Mrs. …er…I'm afraid I haven't heard of you at all!' A low chuckle in the doorway stifled the reply of the simpering blond, as Lucy Willoughby swept unannounced into the room. She embraced her hostess and then came straight over to Catherine. Leaning forward for the requisite touching of cheeks, she whispered,

'Well done! I had meant to be early in case you needed support, but I can see you have no need of my help!' Catherine blushed at the praise, though she was angry at herself for rising to the bait offered by the vapid blond who had since turned away to sharpen her claws.

The afternoon turned out to be a success after all. The blond woman, who she discovered to be the wife of the odious Lieutenant Mortimer, and known for her waspish tongue, was not popular in the close community of officer's wives. The other ladies preferred to take their lead from the Colonel's wife, who clearly accepted Catherine Harrington. So she was fêted as she had not expected to be, and her opinion sought on such weighty matters as the new colour for sprig muslin recently discovered in Lucknow, or the exact angle that the latest style of bonnet should be worn; Catherine thought she would die of boredom as she was more used to discussing much interesting topics with the men of her acquaintance. Lucy, watching her closely, read her mind like a book; and sympathised. But there was no escape from her social duties, and if Catherine wanted to help Joe, she must learn to hide her ennui. Mentally noting that she must advise Catherine on their next meeting, Lucy took her leave and gave Catherine a genuinely warm hug.

During the years that followed, Catherine was hard put to say whether she had enjoyed life more as a sergeant's wife or as an officer's. Certainly there been more freedom in the former, with less expectations as to how she should behave or dress, but in the latter she had an entrée into a more

cultured world, and was able to accompany Joe to soirees and balls in their Mess, or in Lucknow.

Joe had the same dilemma. His pay as an officer was better than a sergeant, but so were the demands on it. His household was larger than before; a lieutenant could not make do with an old couple to do his laundry and other menial tasks. Studying the list of servants, from his own bearer, Gopi, the personal maid, Simbi and of course the ayah, Moti, right down to the humble dhobi-wallah, punkah-wallah and inevitable sweeper. He would sigh histrionically and say,

'Do we really need all these, Catherine? Do we really need a cook's assistant?' And Catherine would explain the function of all these people patiently as if to a retarded child; and then add sweetly,

'And don't forget your horses and your syce; mayhap they could go?' Whereupon Joe would throw the offending accounts into the bureau, and storm off in high dudgeon to the sound of his wife's chuckle.

'God, but life was simpler as a drummer boy!'

Then there were the mess bills! Though he and Adam were as circumspect as they could be, there were a certain number of mess appearances to be made. The once-a-month mess night, for instance, when the officers would throw decorum to the wind and indulge in wild games which invariably left someone with a broken head or sprained ankle, and all of them with raging hangovers, could not be avoided. Not if they were to be accepted, and acceptance was not easily won. It took many years and many changes of junior officers coming fresh out of England for their past to be forgotten and their credentials no longer questioned. But it all cost money, and for men of no independent means, too much money. Small wonder Joe put his head into his hands regularly and wondered if he would ever be free of debt!

But there was a brighter side to it all. Like Catherine, he enjoyed the social functions where conversation was more stimulating than that to be found in the lower ranks. He could converse freely with James Willoughby at last, with no questions asked, and so could make an accurate assessment of the man he had for so long admired; only to find he admired him all the more. Now that he was an officer, Joe could understand the courage of the man in *making* him an officer. How easily it could have backfired and precipitated a full-scale insurrection.

He was also able to visit his old friend Rajah Saeed Khan freely, with no need for subterfuge. An officer in Victoria's army was considered more than socially equal to a Hindu Prince! He and Catherine were privileged to witness Saeed's wedding two years after they had all resettled in Kotepore. The bride was a Rajput princess from a family that had constantly intermarried with the Khan's over the years.

In deference to her bridegroom's improved status after the Mutiny, the bride travelled to him, a progress requiring several weeks of tortuous journeying across the width of India. Eventually her entourage arrived, and Her Royal Highness Princess Shushila was seen, or rather not seen, in a ceremonial howdah on top of an elephant riding through the streets of Kotepore. The town was packed for the festivities, with people travelling from miles around to be fed at the Prince's expense. The guest list ran into hundreds and the Royal coffers creaked at the strain. It was fortunate that the bride price was generous and would go a long way to paying for the wedding!

Saeed himself was strangely detached from it all. He had discussed the whole affair with Joe some weeks before, and confessed that he had become westernized enough to want to choose his own bride, but not enough to overcome tradition. His Princess had been chosen by his father many years before, and his advisors naturally assumed that the arrangement would be honoured. It was so utterly unthinkable that he should go back on the promise made by the generation before his, that he did not even mention it.

Joe was becoming worried about his friend. The time since the Mutiny had wrought subtle changes in him that were disturbing. The clear cut features were becoming blurred by a surfeit of good living and too little exercise. He even preferred to go hunting on the back of an elephant rather than ride his own horse these days! And behind it all was an inertia that was the most disturbing of all. It was as if the Mutiny and subsequent settlement had robbed the young Rajah of the urge to do anything.

'After all,' he reasoned, when Joe asked him, 'it is not as if I can change anything even if I wanted to!' His staff ran his affairs efficiently, even if a portion of his money found its way into their pockets, and the neighbouring cantonment in the person of Colonel Willoughby took all the serious decisions. All he had to do was spend his State pension and the revenue from his vast estates prised from the taluqdars. Even in this matter of his wedding; all he had had to do was….nothing….and it happened!

On the morning of the wedding, Joe dressed in his full dress uniform, so smothered with gold lace that his wife observed that he outshone the sun! With dress sword clanking at his hip, he handed his wife, dressed in her finest crinoline of white satin, so wide it looked like a huge bell, into a carriage to take them to the palace. Colonel Willoughby would be there, escorted by his senior staff, but Joe would be there by personal invitation and his heart swelled with pride.

The British officers might think that they looked very fine, but they were completely outshone by Indian guests. There was a plethora of silks and satins in bright colours at every turn, so that the eye could scarcely take them in. In the palace courtyard, a small band played to the assembled multitude in a atmosphere scented by marigolds and jasmine from the many garlands draped from every wrought iron balcony.

Catherine was taken inside to where the bride was being prepared for her wedding. She had been housed in a pavilion, which stood in lieu of her home, so that the groom could journey to her, even if for a matter of yards rather than miles! Inside the pavilion, all was noise and confusion as high caste ladies squabbled over some minor point of precedence. In the midst of it sat the bride, looking lost and alone, and absurdly young. Catherine was touched and tried to get near the child, but was shooed away by an aunt. As a caste-less person, Catherine was not really welcome here, and it was only the Rajah's express command that allowed such a happening.

The doll-like figure of Shushila had been dressed in all its finery, the hands and feet dyed with henna and the nails painted with gold-leaf. The sari was of scarlet silk, the skirts wide in the Rajput style. Her face was covered by a veil of marigold and jasmine buds. Her husband-to-be would wear a similar veil so that they could not gaze at each other until they were truly wed. The sound of the bridegroom's procession could be heard outside, and Shushila's head jerked up, and for a moment the veil of buds parted and Catherine looked straight into a pair of enormous terrified eyes. She closed her own eyes for a moment for a moment and tried to transfer reassuring messages to the tense figure, as taut as a fawn ready to take flight. Perhaps it worked, for the tension seemed to ease, and the girl slumped until her mother admonished her to get her head up and behave like a Rajput princess!

The crowd of women then surrounded Shushila and escorted her outside where they waited in the entrance to greet the bridegroom. The bride was handed a garland to put about his neck in token of acceptance. As the Prince's party approached, the cacophony of flutes and horns startled a flock of pigeons, which rose in a green cloud from the lawns around the pavilion. At last Saeed stood before the bride, towering over her, resplendent in an achkan of his favourite emerald green. The matching turban and the achkan were stiff with jewels, mainly emeralds, with a fair sprinkling of diamonds. The magnificent aigrette was topped with the biggest emerald Joe had ever seen, and a matching one topped the ceremonial sword of solid gold. Like his bride, Saeed's face was obscured behind the veil of buds, and Joe would have given much to see the expression in his eyes,

After a long drawn out note, the music stopped, and the bride raised the garland. Saeed lowered his head, and Shushila accepted him as her husband by placing the garland round his neck. There was a sibilant sigh from the assembled audience; there were some at least who thought the Prince might yet back out from the arrangement. But now it was done. The marriage had yet to take place, but both participants were now committed to it.

The music struck up once more and the two parties mingled as they surged into the pavilion for the feast. The groom's party would be fed first, and then the bride's, with the overflow being accommodated on the spacious lawns recently vacated by the pigeons. The British party retired at this point, for they were without caste, and would defile the wedding party if the were to eat together, 'a sobering thought,' observed Joe as an aside to James as he turned to find Catherine. James grinned and agreed, but there among their party who found the idea of being rejected from the feast humiliating. Perhaps they had not learned the lessons of the Mutiny after all!

Later that evening, the British party returned to witness the actual marriage ceremony in the durbar hall of the palace. All that afternoon they had heard the music and revelry from across the river as several bands vied with one another to make the most noise. As darkness fell, lights appeared all over Kotepore, and were reflected in the river so that the town seemed to float in mid-air. Then fireworks were set off, streaking away in a blaze of crimson, green and turquoise. It was time to go.

The durbar hall was packed to capacity and stiflingly hot. Joe eased his finger under his high collar, surreptitiously trying to loosen the top hook. The air was perfumed, but now it was incense, sandalwood and the sharp odour of patchouli. The British were afforded the honour of chairs, though Joe would have happily joined the Indians seated cross-legged on the cool marble. But at least from his vantage point he could see over the sea of turbaned heads. Catherine spread her wide skirts with a shushing sound and looked about her with interest; like her husband, she had never witnessed a Hindu wedding before. She was the only observable female other than the bride as the rest were behind the purdah screen, and she was well aware of the enormous concession that had been made for her.

A priest appeared and a hush fell over the crowd as they watched him light the sacred fire. The overpowering scent of incense rose in the still air, which mingled with the pungent smoke given off by aromatic salts flung into the fire from silver platters. Then Saeed and Shushila stepped into a circle of rice flour around the fire. The bride looked tiny next to her groom, whose sturdy figure was enhanced by the finery. Joe felt a wave of sympathy for them both; at least he had been able to choose his own bride, and he gave Catherine's hand a squeeze which she returned with an enigmatic smile; doubtless she was thinking the same as him!

The couple exchanged their vows, promising to live according to their creed, to beget sons, and so it went on. Then the bride's sari was knotted to the end of Saeed's sash, and together they took the seven steps round the fire that bound them together forever. Saeed intoned the words of the ancient Vedic hymn,

'Become thou my partner as thou hast paced all seven steps with me. Apart from thee I cannot live. We shall share alike all goods and power combined. Over my house thou shall bear full sway.'

Then the couple were blessed by older members of their households, though in Saeed's case that meant one ancient uncle who had to be supported by two retainers. Then the bride was led away to remove her finery and eat at last. Unlike the guests, she had fasted for a full twenty four hours. Saeed was carried off to feast by the men. As he passed Joe, he invited him to join him in an undertone, quirking a quizzical eyebrow at Catherine by his side as he did so. Joe understood; tolerant he may be, but he couldn't flout custom on such a day. Joe nodded imperceptibly, and then lined up with the other officers to take formal leave.

Having escorted Catherine home, he gratefully shed the restricting 'bum freezer' jacket that had left an angry ring around his neck, and re-dressed in silk achkan and white pyjama trousers; both gifts of the Rajah. He topped it off with a handsome turban tied by Gopi and pinned on an aigrette, though a much more modest affair than the Prince's. Catherine watched the proceedings through narrowed eyes, one small foot tapping an impatient rhythm on the polished wooden floor. Joe tried to explain as he dressed,

"Tis the Rajah himself asked me.'

'I didn't hear the invitation!'

'No, well, he didn't want Colonel Willoughby to hear. The official part is over, after all.'

'So why are you invited?'

'Catherine, larla, you know Saeed and I have been friends for many years.' Catherine did know, but had no intention of admitting it, or making things easier for Joe. How dare he go off just as she wanted to talk about the affair while it was fresh in her mind. But Joe was not to be diverted, so kissing the averted cheek, he ran off with a cheery wave, leaving Catherine to stamp her foot in temper, which disturbed a snake curled up in the corner. She ran from the room, muttering,

'Trust him to run off and leave me in danger!' rolling out her lip and looking ridiculously like a seventeen year old again.

She did not see Joe for two days, but thankfully he had no duties!

Two years after Robert's birth, Catherine gave birth to another son. He arrived unexpectedly early, for which Catherine was very grateful. Another fortnight and she would not have recovered in time to travel to Musoorie for the hot season. No longer did Catherine insist that children had to learn to cope with all India had to throw at them, not since the advent of Robert in fact! Now the family processed northwards every May and returned in late September.

The household had been in the process of packing when the first pain caught her unawares, and she sat down abruptly in a trunk half full of muslin dresses and gave a sharp squeal. Moti glanced up from her packing in surprise, and then she nodded and helped Catherine out of the trunk and onto her bed. Anderson was not needed for which Catherine was grateful for she could not get used to a man's presence at such a time. The labour was short and quite painful, but by the time Joe returned from work, it was all over.

He was met by an excited Rose, who ran down the path to greet him. He swung her high over this head as she babbled the news into his ear so that he almost dropped her. Squealing with mock fright, she repeated,

'Papa, Mama's been making a lot of noise but is quiet now an I've another baby brother an can I have a baby sister next time?' The whole thing was said in a breathless rush without pause, but this time Joe managed to make sense of it and rushed inside with a shout of glee. There was Catherine, propped up in bed, and looking absurdly young against the white, frilly pillows.

Cradled on the crook of her arm was a tiny head with a fuzz of silvery hair. Seated on the bed next to her was Robert, very puzzled about all the fuss and bother. He was not at all impressed with this so-called baby brother who didn't look in the least bit capable of playing with him. Quashing the almost forgotten memory of Rose being ejected from the sight of the new baby Robert, he bent down to kiss his wife. Easing back the shawl, he gazed at the crumpled red face of the newborn. He was much smaller than Robert, but of course was much earlier. Seeing that Catherine was sleepy, he left Moti in charge of mother and baby, and carried off Robert, for once resisting Catherine's protests,

'Let him be, he's not doing any harm.'

This time the baby was named with little fuss, and was dubbed Daniel after Joe's grandfather, with Catherine again sternly forbidding any shortening to 'Dan'. Robert soon picked that up and would race round the room, shouting 'Dan, Dan', but then got the biggest shock of his young life when his father tapped him sharply on his bottom, *and* his mother didn't intervene beyond frowning heavily! Robert rushed at Joe's legs, beating them and crying,

'I hate you. I'm going to fight you when I grow up!' Joe promptly suggested that he didn't wait that long and obligingly dropped to his hunkers and put up the boy's fists. Robert's eyes glowered for a moment, and then his innate sense of humour took hold, and instead he put his arms out. Joe swung him aloft, joined a moment later by Rose. With a child on each shoulder, Joe left his wife in peace to feed her newly named Daniel.

He was a quiet child, unlike his vigorous older brother, though without a suggestion of sickliness, in spite of his premature arrival. He was as fair as Robert was dark with his father's sapphire blue eyes and his hair had a hint of red in it, though the fuzzy down had little substance as yet. As he grew, he tended towards introspection that bordered on secretiveness that reminded Joe strongly of his sister Eileen. She had had that same shuttered look that was not so much unfriendly as an apartness. He too would grow to love all living creatures, and they in turn would come to him for succour, his favourite being a mongoose, injured at an early age and nursed back to health.

Two years later, they had another boy. This one also had blue eyes and a crop of red-gold curls, the only one to inherit his colouring in full. Gazing at this latest addition, Joe was reminded forcibly of Nuala and was glad that the infant was a boy in spite of Rose's disappointment. They called him Thomas, or as Joe preferred, Tomos. Strangely, his name quickly became shortened to Tom, without any objections from Catherine. Perhaps she was just worn out?

She told Moti earnestly after the birth that enough was enough and she did not want to spend her life looking like an elephant, ceremonial howdah and all! Rarely for her, Moti laughed, covering her face and peering through her fingers at her mistress. Then she smiled her enigmatic smile and whispered gently in Catherine's ear, at which her eyes opened wide, but then she too smiled and nodded. There would be no more children.

Their financial circumstances grew worse and worse, until Joe seriously considered taking out a loan with the local bunnia. He knew he should not, and very likely he would be in the fellow's clutches for the rest of his life, but what was he to do? His mess bill was due any day, and not to pay was too heinous a crime even to consider it.

He had been promoted to Captain, as had Adam, the year before, but it did not seem to help, the bills just piled up higher and higher. The demands of four children and a large household just grew out of control. He would not tell Catherine of his decision as he knew she would disapprove, and foolishly he did not consider asking her to economise, not after those earlier fights! In fact, he had sold his horses and dismissed his syce long ago. It was agony for him to watch his fellow officers out on the maidan trying out the game they had recently taken up, polo.

Almost grinding his teeth with frustration, he watched their fumbling attempts to control their horses and hit the ball with their mallets; he knew he could do it so much better. And he had to endure the sniping of the likes of Mortimer taunting him for his penny-pinching ways.

James Willoughby saw his torment, but felt powerless to help. Joe would resent his interference in his household and an offer of financial help would be proudly spurned.

Joe arrived home and shouted to Gopi to pour him a chota-peg,

'No dammit, a burra-peg. Chuldi, chuldi.' Gopi hurried to do his bidding as the Sahib in this mood would have a very short fuse and he had no wish to be at the end of it!

Swallowing the large whiskey-pani in one long gulp, Joe sent for another, and scowling, went to find Catherine to inform her that he was going into Kotepore, but he did not say why! He did not even take time to greet his children. He found her seated at their bureau, frowning over a letter. The look on her face jolted him out of his own ill-humour, and dropping to his knees by her, he said,

'What is it, acushla? You look as if you've seen a ghost!'

'Not seen one; read about one. Here, take a look at this.'

'This' was an imposing letter headed by the words,

'McMahon, McMahon and Cuthbertson, Solicitors.'

The letter went on to inform Catherine that her father had died in Dublin the previous year, and had left his entire estate to his beloved only daughter. The estate was valued at some ten thousand pounds, and McMahon, McMahon and Cuthbertson awaited instructions from Mrs. Harrington as to how they were to transfer the monies.

Joe sat on the floor with a thump, his head reeling with the significance of it; all their problems solved, his troubles extinguished by the dry dusty language of the letter. He shut his eyes as he felt a tear well up, and firmly quelled it. Then he heard Catherine's voice as though from a great distance,

'How *dare* he, how *can* he? He didn't want me when I needed him, and now he thinks he can throw money at me, and all will be well!' Joe's head reeled at the illogicality of it,

'But…but he's dead! Perhaps he wanted to make amends in the only way he could. And after all, you didn't want to go with him.' That unfortunate thought earned him a storm, a veritable tirade of abuse,

'How could he go and leave me in that convent? Me, his own daughter, and just when I'd lost my mother! He's just an unfeeling brute; I don't want a penny of his damned money!' and she flung the offending letter across the room.

White to his lips, Joe got to his feet and retrieved the letter. He was angrier than Catherine had ever seen him, and strangely it had the effect of calming her. Uncharacteristically she sat quietly and listened to what he had to say,

'Do what you like about this, but just think before you throw this gift back in a dead man's face. There are two sides to what happened all those years ago. You lost your mother, but he lost his wife, and I can imagine how that felt having nearly faced it myself! So he was wrong to leave you, but he did his best to protect you, didn't he? We are deep in debt, and I had planned to take a loan to pay some bills, but it is unlikely that I will be free of the bunnia if I do; but I still can. If you don't want this,' holding up the letter, 'put it into a trust fund for your children. But think carefully over this, Catherine. This will make a big difference to our lives!'

With that he left her sitting at the bureau, looking small and defenceless suddenly. He resisted the impulse to go back and take her up into his arms and beg forgiveness. But for once he would not. For once she must see that her Irish temper and impulsive active could be the ruin of her family. As he passed through the door, he had to smile to himself; she wasn't the only one with an Irish temper in the bungalow!

Chapter 18

Joe eased his long legs out in front of him and sighed deeply. He had had several whiskey-panis and was feeling very sorry for himself. As he saw it, his finances were in ruins as was his marriage. He should have acted years ago, long before things had come to this pass, and now it was too late. In his maudlin state he catalogued his crimes one by one.

First and foremost there was the matter of Catherine's father. He had always tried to see things from both sides, and though he had never met William Lynch, he had more than a measure of sympathy for the man. If Catherine had died in Lucknow, might he not also have wanted to turn his back on the country that had taken her from him? He should have said so to his wife and perhaps it would have eased her bitterness; but he hadn't.

Then there was the matter of the household expenses. How could Catherine have known how desperate things were, when he didn't confide in her? Those petty skirmishes they had had in the past were no more than that, when she had countered his suggestions of economy with her tart reply that he get rid of his horses. He should have sat down with her and gone through it. Perhaps they could have saved the situation even then.

Ready tears of the depressed drunk rose in his eyes, and he brushed them away angrily. What was the matter with him? Was this the Joe Harrington who had faced up to each and every one of life's challenges with a stout heart and a ready smile?

And then there was Rose! Though Catherine was no longer overtly hostile to her oldest child and only daughter, she clearly favoured her sons, with Robert the obvious favourite. He considered his children one by one and tried to understand.

At seven, Rose had outgrown infant prettiness and now had more character than beauty. Her face was oval, with a high intelligent forehead and her mother's imperious nose, as yet softened by childhood. Her eyes were her best feature and would fascinate as she grew older, with their clear light grey rimmed by a blue border. They tended to reflect the light and colour around her, so that on a sunny day, their blueness was in evidence, but in the evening the grey seemed to expand giving her eyes a smoky look.

Robert, his oldest son, looked more and more like his own father, with a shock of dark hair that would not be tamed, and one dark curl that always fell onto his forehead. His dark brown eyes were wont to smoulder if he could not get his own way, and he was capable of a violent temper. But he could be loving and would defend his sister and younger brothers against all comers; a veritable tiger lurking within his thin chest! In spite of inheriting his grandfather's sombre nature, his gentler upbringing did much to temper it.

Daniel was as different from Robert as he could be. His hair was silvery fair, complimenting his sapphire blue eyes. When Joe had wondered aloud at the origin of his fairness, Catherine had said in a surprised voice,

'Why, it's just like my mother's! I used to yearn for hair that colour instead of my own indeterminate shade,' and she had touched her glossy brown hair that Joe so admired. The comment came as a bit of a shock to Joe, as he had never known her family. He had always felt that she had been formed complete at the age of seventeen, just waiting to meet him in the Convent of the Sacred Heart. If it had not been for her old friends like Pattie and Charlotte, the illusion would have been complete; but then it was the same for her, as she had never know his family either!

Daniel may have his maternal grandmother's hair colour, but Joe was sure that he had his sister Eileen's nature. Ever quiet and secretive, he gave nothing away of his inmost thoughts. Not for him the shouting and tantrums of his brother when thwarted, Daniel got his own way, but subtly.

Finally he thought about the last of the brood. Two year old Tom was simply enchanting. With his red-gold hair and blue eyes, his nature was as sunny as the infant Nuala had been. His limbs were chubbier than any of the others, and he padded around on sturdy feet with ankle and wrists still bangled with baby fat. He had been late getting to his feet, and Joe hoped that he would shed the excess dimples before too long.

But none of his broodings could explain Catherine's attitude to Rose. Joe loved them all equally, so he just didn't understand it. Perhaps it was always so between mothers and daughters, but remembering his own mother with Little Eileen and Nuala, and Louise Swales with Christina, he didn't believe it to be so. He should not have kept silent for so long, allowing the child to be become progressively more hurt. Now, Rose did not turn to her mother for affection but was quiet and biddable in her presence. Only with Joe did she behave naturally.

It was full dark when Joe realised that he had sunk a full bottle of whiskey, 'which will not help my money worries,' he observed to himself morosely. He heard the shushing if silk skirts and a creak as Catherine settled into a rattan chair opposite him. He did not look up.

Catherine regarded him dispassionately for a while, noting the disorder in his dress, unusual for a man normally so fastidious in his habits. She also noted the almost empty bottle of whiskey on the low, rattan table beside him. He had not even gone through the motions of ringing for Gopi to bring him whiskey-pani but had taken it neat. She knew that he drank more than he should on mess nights, but he had never been in such a state at home.

She too had suffered since they had parted earlier, the letter lying crumpled on the floor where he had flung it. At first she had been shocked by what he had said, and then very angry. How *dare* he speak to her like that; how *dare* he suggest she was wrong to feel about her father as she did. But then she started to think about his words properly. Had she let her hurt over her father's departure from India blind her to his hurt over losing his wife? She thought about her feelings for Joe, and how she would have felt if he had died in the Mutiny. She still remembered her despair when she thought he had, and it was only Pattie who had dragged her out of it. Would she have fled from India? And would she have abandoned her children in the process? No, of course not; but they were very young and would have come with her so there was no need for choice. But she had been older and had made a choice. Perhaps she had no-one to blame but herself?

The process of healing began at that moment of realisation as she had sat slumped at the bureau. Presently she had picked up the crumpled letter and smoothed it out carefully. Re-reading it more thoroughly, she also noted that her father's effects were also bequeathed to her, including some family portraits, and a packet of letters address to her from her father; why had they never been sent?

The she recalled Joe's other words, spoken so bitterly. What had he said? Bills unpaid, debts? Her temples throbbed and she rang her bell for Simbi. The maid appeared looking concerned. Catherine suppressed a wry smile; there were no secrets in a house full of servants. They would all know that the Sahib and Memsahib had had a major disagreement, and had tactfully stayed out of the way!

'Ah, Simbi. Where is Harrington-Sahib?'

'He's on the verandah, Memsahib,' the maid tentatively offered.

'Has he had dinner?'

'No memsahib.'

'Ah.' Catherine read into the girl's reluctance the unspoken information that Joe had been drinking.

'Simbi, lay out my blue silk and prepare a bath. Make it a cool one. Oh, and find my cologne; I have a headache. That is all.'

Simbi disappeared and Catherine rose from the bureau, feeling intensely weary all of a sudden. Her skin felt sensitive, even the soft muslin feeling rough against it; her whole being cried out to be soothed. She had the notion that this evening could see the end of her marriage, or a new beginning.

As she passed from the drawing room to her bedroom and began to remove her day clothes with Simbi's help, she thought about the years since Joe had 'rescued her' from the convent. She had thought him her knight errant, and had admired his tall, good-looking body and the handsome face with its polished chestnut hair and intense blue eyes. But those girlish romantic notions had given way to adult passions after their marriage. She blushed as she recalled her ignorance on her wedding night and smiled reminiscently at Joe's patience. As she stepped into the bath, she conjured up the images in that ruined Hindu temple that had taught her more than most Victorian girls would ever know. She had been shy then, but willing to learn, and their relationship had deepened and become richer with each passing year. Until when? She tried and failed to pinpoint the time when things had started to change.

After the siege; the birth of Rose, or Robert; when he had become an officer? Perhaps the strain had been greater that either of them had realised. No; there was not one single moment. But through it all, their relationship in bed had been satisfying. Especially since Moti had relieved her of the strain of childbearing. No use probing any more she decided. What was more important was that it did not degenerate further.

Climbing out of her hip bath and feeling much refreshed, she allowed Simbi to envelop her in a fluffy towel. Then seated at her dressing table, she had her hair brushed out until it crackled with static. Simbi polished it with a strip of silk until it gleamed in the soft oil light. She shook her head at Simbi's question,

'No; leave it loose, Simbi, the Sahib likes it that way and we are not entertaining.' If Simbi wondered why she had chosen her best silk evening gown if they were not entertaining, she gave no sign. Waiting until her mistress had touched her eyelids and lips with a little colour, she helped her into stays and numerous petticoats, and finally into the evening gown. Blue was Catherine's favourite colour, and this one was in a deep shade like the sky on a star strewn night. It brought colour to her pale cheeks and a depth to her grey eyes. She touched her wrists with the stopper of a perfume bottle, and taking a deep breath, she moved towards the door. She paused there for moment,

'Simbi.'

'Memsahib?'

'Are the children in bed?'

'Yes Memsahib.'

'Ask Moti to make sure they stay there.'

'Yes Memsahib.'

'Oh, and Simbi.'

'Memsahib?'

'Tell Gopi we are not to be disturbed. I will ring for dinner when we are ready.'

'Yes Memsahib.'

Catherine swept out onto the verandah, where the panorama of Kotepore was spread out across the river, no less bright than the starry sky above. The noise of night creatures did not impinge on her thoughts, so intent was she on the task in hand. She seated herself in a rattan chair and looked across at her husband.

The silence stretched as Catherine tried desperately to find the right words to open the conversation. Joe was no help at all, sitting slumped in his chair with his legs splayed out and his hands hanging loosely between them, a glass almost falling from his flaccid grasp. His head was bowed, the mop of tousled chestnut hair glowing in the light of the oil lamp hanging above him. For the first time in their relationship, Catherine felt a tug of pity for this man. He had always seemed so big and invulnerable, or was it simply his height that gave him that illusion? Then the words suddenly came, and she said softly,

'Why didn't you tell me we were in debt, Joe?' Without looking up, his voice slurred, he muttered,

'I thought I did!'

'But I didn't take it seriously, did I?' Her tone did not imply blame, rather a query, then,

'Joe, I have been thinking about what you said; about Papa. I've never tried to see it from his side before. I...I...wish I had.' Her voice became husky as she tried to put her emotions into words, to reach through the alcohol fumes that swirled between them,

'I tried to imagine, to remember how I felt when I thought I had lost you when I was having Rose. I wanted to die then, Joe. I wanted to be with you, and I didn't really care about the baby, just assumed someone would take care of it; Pattie, or Cristabel. But the point is, I just didn't care! Perhaps that's why I feel I can't really get close to her, perhaps I feel guilty about it?' Her voice faded away and she desperately willed Joe to respond. Had he heard her, or had the whiskey fuddled his senses totally?

Slowly, slowly his head came up. His eyes were red-rimmed, the blueness lost in the shadows cast by the overhead light. A suicidal moth flew past his head to immolate itself on the lamp. He brushed it away angrily. At least it was a positive action, a return to life, thought Catherine.

'I'm......I'm glad you have understood at last.' And his head drooped again. Catherine's control snapped at that, and she stood up so sharply that her chair crashed backwards off the edge of the verandah. Dropping to her knees by Joe's chair, she took his glass and set it on the table by the bottle and took his arms, shaking him roughly until he looked up again.

The eyes were dull and unseeing, and to her dismay a tear stood in the corner of one of them. He mumbled thickly,

'S'no good. Can't pay the mess bill…drummed out of the Regiment… reduced to ranks b'God.' Catherine realised he was too far gone in drink for coherent thought, so she stood up again. Reaching for a small hand bell, she rang it vigorously until a startled Gopi came running out of the bungalow.

'Take that bottle away and bring some coffee; hot and strong!'

'Memsahib.' The bearer disappeared, and Catherine retrieved her chair and sat down to wait. She was appalled at Joe's state. Unused to men in this state, she didn't know how to deal with it, but she was determined to settle their differences this very night, fearing that if they were left, they would go on festering and slowly destroy their marriage. And she was very, very sure that their marriage was worth saving.

Gopi reappeared bearing a round, brass tray on which was a coffee pot and two cups. He put it down carefully and poured out the thick, dark liquid. Catherine peremptorily waved away her own cup. Gopi nodded and suggested deferentially,

'If the Memsahib wishes; I have done this before?' Catherine looked up startled and then laughed,

'Yes, I suppose you have.' She sat back and watched Gopi's quick sure movements as he lifted Joe's head and the cup to his lips. The bearer looked tiny next to Joe's bulk, but he handled him with a deftness that spoke of much practice! The amusement she felt helped relieve the tenseness inside her, and she waited patiently for the coffee to take effect. Joe was busy cursing Gopi to hell and back again, using words that Catherine did not know existed. Her eyes opened like saucers, and then she couldn't contain herself anymore and threw back her head to laugh out loud in very unladylike fashion. The peals of laughter rang out round the verandah and frightened a jackal that had been slinking through the undergrowth at the edge of cantonment and sent him fleeing back to the open countryside.

Joe pushed the cup out of Gopi's hand, spilling its contents down his shirt front, and burning his chest. With one more explosive oath at the pain, he sat up and glared at Catherine,

'What the hell is going on, and what the devil are you laughing at?' Catherine waved Gopi away and returned to the side of Joe's chair. Sinking down, so that here bare shoulders and arms seemed to rise from a midnight blue sea of silk, she touched his arm gently,

'We need to talk Joe, and you had taken rather too much whiskey!'

'You could say that, and why not?'

'Joe, will you listen?'

'What is it?'

'I don't know whether you heard me say it before, but I've thought a lot about Papa.'

'I heard,' he said curtly.

'I...I agree it would be wrong to refuse the money. And there were some letters too. I.....I'd like to read them.' He regarded her steadily,

'It's your decision; your money.' She began to feel angry then, but desperately suppressed it; the ground was just too fragile,

'It's not my money, Joe, but ours. What use is money to me if you go under, I just didn't know, and wish I had listened before, but it's not too late to pay the debts now!'

Joe's head drooped again and came to rest on top of Catherine's scooped neckline. To her alarm, she felt hot tears drop onto her bare skin; seeming to burn its way into her heart. Her arms came around his shoulders, and she soothed and petted him as she would one of her small sons. She murmured endearments and all kind of nonsense she could not afterwards recall, but it seemed to work. The effect of the whiskey was slowly overcome by the coffee and the release of emotion long suppressed. Catherine's knees began to ache, and she suspected that she would have trouble moving, but presently the shuddering of her husband's shoulders ceased and he was quiet.

He raised his head and she could see that his eyes were calm, though red from drink and weeping. Then she said, prosaically,

'Would you like dinner now?' It was Joe's turn to give a brief shout of laughter, and lurching to his feet, almost oversetting his wife in the process, he reached for the bell and nearly dislodged the clapper with the violence of his ringing.

'Sahib?' said a startled Gopi, who arrived so quickly that he must have been lurking close by,

'Gopi, my wife and I will take dinner now!' Gopi's eyes gleamed in the lamplight,

'Yes, sah!'

Joe held out his crooked arm, and groaning with aching knees, Catherine tucked her small hand inside the elbow, they processed into the dining room. That night, they did without any wine for they had matters to discuss that required their full concentration.

Joe went to see Colonel Willoughby the next day to discuss a delay on the settlement of his mess bill. James was delighted to hear of the Harrington's windfall, though Joe had kept the full account of the previous night to himself. It was agreed that the mess account would wait for the period of time needed for the transfer of funds from Dublin to take place. But then James probed further,

'I knew you were having difficulty in meeting your commitments; how did you plan to solve it?' Joe prevaricated, until James said baldly,

'I trust you weren't thinking of falling into the hands of a bunnia? You know, of course, that is definitely the road to ruin. I would hope,' he said more gently, 'that you would have come to me first!' Joe had the grace to look abashed, but simply grinned sheepishly before taking his leave. Trust Willoughby to know exactly what was going on, and what a generous man he was!

The Swales were also delighted for them, and in their usual gentle fashion, not in the least overcome by envy. Though Adam's pay was the same as Joe's, with only Christina in their nursery they kept a smaller household, and Adam was not drawn towards horses and polo! So he had just about kept his head above water. Like James, he had sadly watched Joe struggle in the quicksand of debt, but had been powerless to help.

Joe and Catherine decided to settle some of the money on their children against possible future disasters. Catherine suggested making Rose's allocation less,

'She's a girl and will marry, so will have a husband to take of her.' But Joe was adamant,

'She may not want to marry; why should she not have the same freedom to choose as the boys?' Their difference of opinion almost precipitated the first row of their euphoric new relationship, but Catherine wisely decided not to argue further. Her feelings towards Rose were still a problem as yet unresolved as she didn't know herself why she felt the way she did. Perhaps she had touched the root of it on the night of their reconciliation, or perhaps there was too much of herself in the child; but whatever it was, she was no nearer finding a way to change it!

The family debts were cleared, lifting an enormous cloud from Joe's head, and he was able to buy two polo ponies and at last join the matches on the maidan.

They also made another purchase in the form of a bungalow of their own in the hills. They chose the friendly town of Musoorie over the more fashionable and ultra-Victorian-English Simla. It was a lovely place, horseshoe shaped and surrounded by fruit trees. They would have preferred to buy a bungalow on the shores of one of the spectacular lakes of Kashmir, but the residents there had resisted the advance of the avaricious Victorians and forbidden them to own any land or property within their borders. The cunning angrezis managed to get round this sanction eventually by having houseboats constructed to float permanently on the lakes; but that came much later. The Harrington's enjoyed visiting Kashmir, but were happy to stay at a local hotel and hire a string of horses to go sightseeing.

Long before the Mutiny, railways had been slowly but steadily pushing their way across India; but since the Mutiny, they had taken off like a spider's web. On the eve of the troubles there had been a mere two hundred miles of track. But ten years later there were nearer four thousand miles and within twenty years, close to eight thousand. There was method in all this industry beyond the simple urge for internal improvements; an India laced by railways could be penetrated more swiftly in times of trouble, should they arise again. For the British migrating northwards in May and southwards in October, the railway was a godsend. Whole families would set off in plush accommodation with their army of servants travelling in much less comfort further back, with all that was necessary for their comfort down to a leather covered chamber pot to give easement en route!

Soon after Catherine's inheritance had been transferred to the Kotepore bank, a small trunk arrived with her father's effects. In it were two portraits of her parents, and for the first time, Joe could study his in-laws, even if posthumously. Philomena Lynch had been a striking looking woman with silvery blond hair and her daughter's grey eyes. The portrait showed her turned slightly away from the painter, so that her face was in three quarter profile, and Joe could see the origin of the imperious nose. William Lynch, known as Liam in his lifetime, had much darker hair, much like his daughter's brown shade. The artist had captured a humorous gleam in the eyes, and Joe felt sorry that he had not known the man. Full side whiskers joined a luxuriant moustache, so little more of his features could be seen, though a hint of a generous mouth peeped through the growth. Catherine told him that the portraits had always hung side by side wherever they lived, and they did so again in their Kotepore bungalow.

Apart from a few other knick-knacks, the other content of the trunk was a packet of letters. The first was dated just before William Lynch had left India and the last just before he died; he had never sent any of them.

The letters traced his life from the time he had said goodbye to his daughter; and in each one he begged for her forgiveness in leaving her, but spoke of his anguish at the loss of his beloved Philomena. They went on to describe his financial success in London where he had set up a business selling Indian muslins, carpets and the like, hardly interrupted by the uprising. Another letter described his anguish when he had learned that his daughter had perished in Lucknow, and later his joy in discovering he was wrong. Before Catherine could even wonder at his knowledge, he explained that his agents in Lucknow had kept him informed before they had to take refuge in the Residency, and resumed their reports when they released to do so. He had known of Joe and of her children.

Catherine read them all, one after another, with tears streaming down her face. More than once, Joe looked into the room, but went away quietly until she had need of him. The last letter was the most poignant and written just one month before he died. By that time he had retired and returned to his beloved Ireland and his native city of Dublin.

'I know I have not much longer as I saw the physician recently. It is fitting, for like your mother, I have cancer. My dear, there is but one regret in my life,

that we could not be reconciled before I die. But I have left it too late. Why did I not send all the letters I have written; why did I not come back for a visit? I don't know. Afraid that you wouldn't see me perhaps? You and I share a certain stubbornness, my dear. At least I can leave you the means to make your life easier. I hope when you hear of my passing, you will soften enough to accept it, for I am sure your large household will need it. I hear that your husband is a self-made man, but an officer's pay is not generous.

God bless you, my child. Never let your stubborn pride interfere if there is love.

Your loving father.'

Catherine never showed her letters to anyone, not even Joe; and he did not ask. How well her father had known her after all! The healing process that had started on that fateful night gathered pace, and the ache in her heart over her father's imagined defection vanished completely.

Even Saeed remarked on Joe's improved spirits next time they met. In defiance of custom, Saeed insisted on inviting Catherine as well as Joe, and often their children, to take tea with him and his family in their private gardens. The pavilion that had housed the Princess before her wedding was now a retreat for their growing family, and the lawn where a myriad guests had bustled, now boasted a fountain and flower beds. Even when the weather was hot, the plashing water and pergolas dripping with quisqualis kept the air cool. Stately peacocks strutted among the marigold beds, the males displaying to the drab females.

The women and children were gathered at one end of the garden with attendant ayahs keeping a close eye on their small charges. The Rani Shushila found the relaxation of purdah too uncomfortable as yet, and compromised in Joe's presence by sitting as far away as possible. Catherine was amused, and though she preferred mixed company, tolerantly sat with her youthful hostess. The gazelle-eyed girl had given way to a poised young woman, proud of her promptness in providing an heir to the throne. Catherine found her conversation far more interesting than she expected, and far so than that of the cloistered cantonment women. Shushila was studying the Mahabharata with the aid of her munshi and was happy to share her discoveries with such an interested companion.

Lolling back against exotic silk cushions, Saeed congratulated Joe on his improved health, as the Rajah had assumed that Joe's pallor had been due to illness. Joe patted his taut belly muscles and commented,

'Ah, it's all due to taking up polo. I've recently bought a handsome little bay stallion with an amazing turn of speed.' The Prince laughed and admired Joe's energy, for the spring season was advancing apace, and very soon the cantonment would make its annual pilgrimage.

Joe could not return the compliment for his friend was looking decidedly unhealthy. The once glowing skin had a pasty look about it, and the edges of his fine features were blurred. Beads of sweat clustered in a line under the edge of his turban, though the garden was relatively cool in the late afternoon shadows. His rotund belly strained against the silk achkan, and even now he shifted uncomfortably on the soft cushion as he reached for a sticky sweetmeat.

'What you need, my friend,' suggested Joe, 'is to take up polo. It'd do you the world of good!' Then cunningly,

'You always claimed to be a better horseman than me; why don't you get up a palace team and challenge us?'

'You arrogant angrezis! You think you invented polo, do you not? I must tell you that the Afghans were playing it since time out of mind; only they used a goat's head instead of a ball!'

'I know that Saeed; but what do you think?' Saeed chewed his lower lip reflectively but wouldn't commit himself. Instead he sighed histrionically and changed the subject,

'I've had to get rid of my chief minister!' Joe raised an eyebrow in question, 'corrupt!' said Saeed dramatically. Joe's eyebrow became quizzical,

'I know, I know,' said Saeed sighing again, 'I should be used to it. If you ever decide to leave the army, Joe, come and work at the palace; I need someone, just one person, I can trust.'

'Why don't you keep a closer eye on them; it would give you something to think about.'

'Really Joe, it simply isn't done!', Saeed delivered with a perfect parody of an upper class English drawl. Joe laughed, but privately considered that he had hit the nub of the matter. The Rajah had nothing to do, with no responsibilities to think about he was dying of sheer boredom. His father had been engaged in training his rissal, but Saeed's soldiers were purely decorative. As he had said, it was not done for the Rajah to sully his fingers with the day to day running of the palace or the vast estates. He had done his duty and made love to his wife energetically enough to beget two sons already, and Joe thought, another on the way. Hunting trips seem to have lost their savour, so what else was there?

He steered the conversation back to polo, and Saeed began to ask questions about the rules, the number of men in the teams and the ideal quality of a polo pony. Joe was beginning to feel he was making progress, when Catherine came to remind him that they needed to return to the cantonment as he was on duty that evening. Saeed heaved himself to his feet and took leave of his favourite guests. On the way out of the garden he repeated the statement he had made half in jest earlier,

'I mean it Joe. If you ever leave the army, there's a job for you here!'

Joe was to remember those words three years later and wondered if Saeed had the gift of prophecy. When they were first said, he had no thoughts of leaving the army, and had assumed he would spend the rest of his working life in it. He had grown to love India and knew that Catherine considered it her home. The Regiment seemed to be settled in Kotepore, though individuals may come and go as they finished their years of duty.

They had been three contented years with India at peace, though troubles had broken out in Afghanistan from time to time, but their Regiment was not involved. Their only brief was to keep the peace in their part of Oudh, and make sure the ruling house of Khan did not overstep the mark.

Joe and Catherine loved the festivals of the Hindu religion and were invariably invited to the palace to join in or simply to observe. The children loved Holi, where the populace gleefully threw coloured water at each other, turning themselves into walking rainbows. But their parents preferred Diwali when a myriad oil lamps were lit to show Rama the way home the way home from his period in exile. The girls of Kotepore made their own lamps and carried them to the river where they were floated. The girls held their breath for if their lamp stayed alight as long as it was in view, they would have good luck all year. When Rose was old enough, she was allowed to join in. her face was serious as she knelt by the river, with Moti keeping a close eye in case she fell in. The little lamp set off surrounded by many others and was soon mingling with them, making it impossible for her to pick out her own. The girls all clapped, their shrill voices cutting across the water where Joe and Catherine stood with the royal party. The bobbing lights made a beautiful sight as they were caught by the current, and started on their journey to where the river met the mighty and holy Ganges. Saeed explained to his guests that they should take the chance to clear up outstanding debts or quarrels, and don new clothes, as Diwali marked the end of an old year and the beginning of the new.

'I intend to buy a new pony,' he laughed at Joe, for he had taken up the challenge of polo and looked much better having done so.

It was just after Diwali which followed Rose's tenth birthday, that Joe received a note asking him to attend Colonel Willoughby in his bungalow at his convenience. He was surprised; an invitation to visit the bungalow meant that it was not to do with duty, as that would have taken place in the admin block; but nor did it seem entirely social. He presented himself an hour before tiffin as suggested, and was ushered into the drawing room by Samee. Lucy Willoughby was in the room hearing her son, Charles, read. Joe noted that it was a book by Charles Dickens, 'A Christmas Carol', and smiled, as Dickens was his favourite author. He said as much as he came in for he was on easy terms with the Colonel's wife and son. He then asked if he could see James. Lucy rose and smoothed her day dress with elegant brown fingers; she was a lady who was not afraid to go out in the sun!

'I'll get him for you. I know you are expected.' She went out with Charles, her skirts shushing on the polished floor. The punkah flapped idly, though it wasn't particularly hot. An early shower had left the air with a crispness that was refreshing and added savour to the scent of roses wafting from the garden.

James strode into the room and invited Joe to be seated. He tugged at a bell pull, summoning Samee to give him an order to bring drinks.

'I expect you're wondering why I've asked you to come here, and on your own?'

'Yes Sir.'

'Come on Joe. After all these years, and here in privacy, for goodness sake call me James!'

'Yes, er James.'

'Besides,' said James somberly, 'I will not be your Colonel much longer!' Joe's jaw dropped in shock.

'Yes. This is strictly classified, you understand?' Joe nodded, dumbstruck at this unexpected news.

'I've had a letter from England. Me brother's died.' Joe tried to commiserate, but a waved hand cut him short,

'Don't. I hardly knew him. We didn't get on particularly well as youngsters and I've not seen him seen him since I left for Ireland. My father used to refer to him as 'that damned dull dog!' He smiled briefly at the memory, and went on,

'Trouble is, Gerald, that's me brother, fathered a parcel of girls. There was a boy, but he died in infancy. Fact is, the estate passes down the male line. There's no way out, an' I've got to go home.' He gave a mirthless laugh, 'strange how it's still home after all these years!' Joe kept quiet, understanding that there was more to come, after all, none of the news so far impinged directly on him. But James was not to be hurried,

'Lucy and I have discussed it. Fact is, her parents are getting frail and she's not seen her brothers and sister since she left England, and so she's happy to go. And me; I've got no choice. But there's more than one kind of duty, eh Joe?' He nodded.

'Anyway, it's not your problem, and so why have I sent for you? Fact is Joe; I don't know what will happen to you when I leave. You've done very well for yourself since you became an officer; probably the best Captain I've got.' Joe started to thank him, but was again waved to silence.

'It is true. But there are those who still say it should never have happened, even if they keep their thoughts out of my hearing. You may think that you and Swales have been accepted, and to a large extent you'd be right. But I know that you won't go any further, and for someone of your talents that would be very wrong. In a just world, you should progress to Major, Colonel and perhaps beyond! Perhaps one day it will happen, but not yet, and not for you. I don't think Swales will worry as he lacks ambition, I believe.' Joe could only nod again, it was a fair assessment of his friend.

'Well it's up to you. Unless you commit some heinous crime, you shouldn't lose your captaincy, but it could be the right time to think about leaving the army.' Joe was stunned into silence, an unnatural occurrence for him! He muttered,

'But what will I do?'

Though the question was largely rhetorical, James chose to answer it,

'There could be openings in the Civil Service, perhaps in Delhi or Calcutta where your fluency in Urdu and knowledge of the British way of doing things could be valued. I have given you advanced notice of my intentions in case you wanted a reference. I'll need to know before I leave. Joe stood up, still somewhat stunned by the news which would turn his life, and that of his family, upside down.

'Thank you for telling me. I must think on this, and discuss it with Catherine. Before I go, in case I don't get the opportunity again, I'd like to thank you for everything. I didn't really understand in those early years, just what you did for me!' James grinned at him,

'It's been a good few years, eh Joe? But when I first saw you with your mother, I somehow knew you had far to go, given the right chances. The Indians would say 'karma' would they not? If it hadn't been for the famine I wouldn't have been in Dublin and you wouldn't have wanted to leave Ireland. Food for thought if nothing else! At least you've grown since then!' They both laughed at that, as Joe topped James by at least two inches. But when they had first met, Joe thought him a giant in his handsome uniform. Looking closely now, he saw the signs of age in the other man. What was he now; late forties perhaps? Difficult to tell as James kept himself fit and avoided the worst excesses of the mess, but his brown hair was edged with grey, and a network of fine lines radiated from the corner of his eyes. The two men shook hands solemnly, an undercurrent of emotion spontaneously turning the handshake into an embrace.

Joe left the Willoughby's to their tiffin. As he left, Joe encountered the ayah with their youngest child, another boy, born the spring after their return from Simla following the Mutiny. The lad had James' green eyes and brown hair, and his thoughtful nature. He had been called Edward after James' erstwhile friend who had been killed in Delhi during the Mutiny. Joe ruffled the boy's hair in passing, feeling sad that he wouldn't see him or his older brother grow up.

It wasn't until he was on his way to his own bungalow that he remembered Saeed's words of three years before. He had laughingly repeated them from time to time as he sacked one finance minister after another; but was he really serious?

Chapter 19

All too soon it was time to go. Lucy Willoughby stood in the middle of the bare room, part of her home for the past ten years. After the terror of the Mutiny, she had thought that she would never feel comfortable in India again, but that feeling had passed with the passage of time. The bungalow had been built for James and her and furnished totally at her direction. James had been too busy at the time with Regimental affairs, so she felt that it was wholly her creation, and she grieved that she had to leave it as though it had a life of its own.

Chiding herself for these foolish thoughts, she looked about her. Bare patches on the walls showed where pictures had hung, and scuff marks bore the scars of furniture continually rubbing, In this home had been born her second son, conceived, she was sure on the night of Charles Willoughby's funeral, giving a twist to the old saying 'a life for a life'. A pity that they had already used the name Charles, for it would have really been a fitting tribute to the old man! James had tentatively suggested Gerald after his old Colonel, or Hilary after her father. Of his brother, Gerald, he did not think at all. But then, James remembered his dearest friend for so many years, who had sadly perished in the retaking of Delhi, so the child was christened in the smart new Regimental chapel, Edward Gerald Hilary Willoughby. A very grand name for a very small person, observed James, wryly. But he was the first new born to arrive in the rebuilt cantonment, and because of that became something of a mascot, and loved by all the men, officers and lower ranks alike.

And now the Regimental mascot was leaving. Brushing the clinging cobwebs of memory away, Lucy left the room. She had only come to check if it had been cleared properly, and had stood like a maudlin fool for a full twenty minutes. This would not get things done! Outside she could hear the wailing of the female servants. They had been doing that for the last two hours, as though they accompanying a funeral procession, and Lucy was getting tired of it; but she was also touched.

None of the servants would suffer financial hardship when the Willoughby's had gone, as James had settled a generous sum of money on them all, so Lucy had to suppose that they would really miss them,

'Well,' she informed the stationary punkah, 'I will miss them too.'

She went through every room in turn, and found everything cleared satisfactorily. The bulk of their belongings had gone, securely packed in huge trunks and they should meet up with them in Bombay. The journey across India was likely to evoke memories of the earlier one when they first arrived. She shuddered briefly as an unwelcome image of Carless rose in her mind, and then the last sight of him, or rather his head, being carried around the parade ground ten years before. No use to think of the past, and the rushing arrival of her sons woke her thankfully out of her reverie,

'Mama, Mama. Papa's waiting for you,' they shouted in unison. Lucy braced her shoulders; this was going to be the hardest part of all.

Lined up outside was the entire household from the cook to houseboy, from her maid to the lowliest sweeper. Carefully passing from the highest caste to the lowest, to avoid giving offence and defilement, she shook them all by the hand and pressed a small gift into each waiting palm. It was still strange to think that these people had served them over many years, but not one of them would eat with them. No; she would never truly understand, no matter how hard she tried!

Her sons followed her along the row of weeping faces, with James bringing up the rear. The only ones not crying were her maid, the ayah and Samee, who would accompany them to the west coast. The other escorts had been separately hired. At least it would be quicker than last time, with much of it covered by the railway. In another year or so and the sea journey would be quicker too, with a canal being driven through from the Red Sea into the Mediterranean.

The Willoughby's finally got into their carriage to take them the short distance to the parade ground. Lucy had grumbled at riding for such a few yards, but James had reminded her for the need for 'correct behaviour';

it just would not *do* for the departing Colonel and his lady to arrive on foot. They were to be fêted for one last time. The carriage swept between the two barrack blocks, their freshly whitewashed walls dazzling in the morning sun.

The entire Regiment was drawn up in serried rows, waiting for inspection. Solemnly, flanked by her sons, Lucy followed her husband up and down the rows. The men looked resplendent in their parade uniform; the pride of Victoria's Indian Army, and Lucy's heart swelled; for was she not the daughter of a soldier as well as the wife of one? James had a word with them all, acknowledging them one by one by name. Lucy herself knew most of them by sight but was impressed with her husband's feat of memory. They came to C Company where Robert Harding stood waiting. James embraced him briefly, as the two old friends had taken a more emotional leave the previous night. Then he moved onto Joe, and congratulated him on the job he was to take up with the Rajah shortly. Responding to the wink with a gleam in his eye, Joe solemnly thanked him. Like his Major, he had also taken his own farewell with James the night before.

At last it was over, and they climbed into the carriage again.

A month after the Willoughby's departure, Joseph Harrington became a civilian. His family also took a sad leave of their bungalow and moved into a fine house close to the palace. It was not very far from the small bungalow that they had taken on their return from Allahabad, but much more spacious. The house was built round a courtyard, with a large pool and fountain in its centre, and surrounded by lawns and flower beds. Around the edges, raised flower beds allowed hanging plants to tumble earthwards to meet the rampant flowers growing upwards, their heavy scent filling the air. Pipes had been cunningly let into the walls and were connected to the river flowing nearby, and by means of a donkey driven pump, could spray water on the flower beds. Opening from the courtyard were innumerable doors, all carved and fretted in imitation of the Palace of the Winds in Jaipur. Catherine grumbled that she would never find her way around the seemingly endless rooms, but the children loved it instantly, chasing each other through rooms and corridors shrieking, even the usually quiet Daniel. Their shrill voices sounded through the fretted windows on all sides.

'Isn't it beautiful, larla?' said Joe, enfolding Catherine to his unfamiliar alpaca suit, and resting his chin on her gleaming coiffure. 'Not bad for a simple country boy born in a sod cottage?' Catherine did not reply, but noted to herself that as Joe got older and more successful, he also became more comfortable with his past. In their early years together, she had found it difficult to get him to speak of his years in Ireland at all. But he was right, their new house was beautiful, and already felt like home. Or perhaps that was because their entire staff had come with them, and even now, a grinning Gopi was approaching bearing a tray of cha.

Joe soon settled to his new duties, and was too busy to miss his army years. Nor did he have to give up his polo, but simply switched sides to the palace team! The job as chief Finance Minister was an enormous challenge, as he had to master the intricacies of the Rajah's affairs, and then set about discovering where the biggest abuses were taking place; and then stop them. Saeed had said to him, half in jest,

'Perhaps we should hire you a food taster, or can you trust your khansamah?'

Joe was startled, but assured him that his cook had been with them many years, but perhaps an increase in pay might not go amiss! At least he could afford it now, with his money troubles a thing of the past; his present salary was three times that of an army captain!

Catherine soon settled into her new home and was not lonely, for all her friends came visiting, 'oohing and aahing' in envy over their beautiful accommodation. The first to come was, of course, Louise. She exclaimed at the house, declaring it to be a miniature palace, and laughingly dubbed it 'Chota Mahal' or 'Little Palace', and the name promptly stuck. Woman like, Catherine reveled in the compliments, but had to admit that it was none of her doing, the palace was as they had moved into it!

Their most unexpected of visitors was Nancy Carter. The same Nancy that Joe had befriended many years before and who had become a maid to Lucy Willoughby. Her position as maid had largely been a complimentary one in a country bursting with servants willing to work for their keep and little else. Catherine had been friendly with her on and off for years, and time had wrought changes in the once brash Northern girl. Many a private, corporal and sergeant had trodden a path to the Willoughby's door, begging for a chance to 'walk out' with their maid. She had refused every invitation, and Lucy had never pressed her for a reason. She was treated more like a companion than a servant, and had grown more reclusive with the passing years, until she was rarely seen outside the Willoughby bungalow and its gardens. The boys treated her as one of the family, never questioning her presence and calling her Aunt Nancy. Lucy had offered a passage for Nancy to go with them to England, and was very surprised when she refused. She told Lucy that she had no wish to return to the country where she had suffered so much and would stay where she was. In her husky voice which had never quite lost its Manchester accent, she said,

'I'm sure I'll get work an' I've saved a tidy sum. You've been more than generous to me.'

James and Lucy would not hear of her seeking another position, only too well aware the sort of pittance she would be offered. James settled an annuity on her, overpowering her protests with the threat that they would force her to travel with them if she didn't accept. Smiling at the empty threat, Nancy gave in and expressed her grateful thanks. She moved out some days before the family, unable to bear the heartbreak of a deserted bungalow and found herself a small house on the edge of Kotepore, not fifty yards from Chota Mahal.

Shyly she called on Catherine when she knew Joe was from home, and thereafter came on a regular basis. Their mutual liking deepened as they grew to know each other again, and Catherine soon ranked Nancy alongside Louise Swales and Pattie Day as her special friend. The children soon got used to her quiet presence in the house, and though Nancy made no special effort to engage them, they were often to be found sitting next to her and discussing all manner of topics. Of them all, Rose was the closest to her, finding she could talk to Nancy as she could not to her mother.

It was a year after the Harrington's had moved into Chota Mahal and Joe was working all hours of the day and sometimes night; and Catherine was getting bored in her well ordered household, that she and Nancy began an enterprise that was to change their lives. Later, they decided that it was

Tomos who was the impetus behind the project, and he was more than willing to take the credit.

Catherine and Nancy sat sitting at peace with each other, working at their stitchery. Catherine was smocking a soft muslin shirt for Tom, working a pattern of herringbone with small delicate stitches she had learned years before at the convent. Embroidered shirts could be bought for next to nothing in the bazaars, but Catherine enjoyed it, and was happy to have the time to indulge in it. Nancy was working more prosaically on a petticoat flounce. The two women made desultory conversation which somehow turned to the subject of marriage and families. Catherine thoughtfully licked the end of a length of peacock silk before threading it, and asked,

'Did you never want to marry, Nancy? I'm sure there must have been many a man delighted to have you for his wife?' Nancy smiled enigmatically,

'That's true, but I never fancied any of 'em. 'Sides, it was mostly because there was a shortage of white women!'

'You're a terrible cynic, Nancy! But did you never fall in love?' The smile grew even more enigmatic,

'There was someone once.' Catherine waited, and then grew impatient,

'Well?' Nancy shrugged,

'He married someone else, so that was that!'

Before Catherine could probe further, her curiosity thoroughly aroused, there was a patter of feet on the marble floor, and Tom ran in clutching his favourite book. At five, he had shed much of his baby fat, though his face was still appealingly round. He stood between his mother and her friend and studied them carefully. Then having reached a momentous decision, he gave Nancy a seraphic smile and plumped himself next to her on the small couch. He handed her his book,

'Please Aunt Nancy,' he lisped. Nancy went very still and Catherine gave a sharp intake of breath as she knew that Nancy had never learned to read. She wondered how she could recover the situation as tactfully as she could, but underestimated the resourcefulness of her friend. Nancy calmly put her sewing down on a low carved table nearby and took the book from the child. She opened it and studied the pictures with interest; but then firmly closed it again.

'But you know this old book inside out, Tom,' Tom gazed at her, his face beginning to pucker comically, but she went on,

'But you haven't heard,' and Nancy launched into a long, involved fairy tale that Catherine could only imagine she had heard read to one of the Willoughby boys, but whatever its origin, it kept Tom enthralled to its very end. He sat tucked right up to Nancy, his blue eyes as big as saucers and fixed on Nancy's face; he sucked his thumb and pulled on one chubby earlobe as he listened intently. When Nancy had finished, he flung his arms around her in a swift hug,

'Oh thank you,' he lisped before pattering out again.

'Where did you hear that?' Catherine asked. Nancy shrugged,

'Charles and Edward were always being read to an' I've got a good memory.' She was silent for a moment, and then,

'But I've always wanted to read; just never had the courage to ask anyone.' She picked up the book that Tom had abandoned. It was printed with large words under pen and ink sketches, and Nancy traced the letters with her fingertip,

'I've learnt most of the letters by listening to Mrs. Willoughby when she taught her boys, an' I've got an idea of the sounds they make. But when I try to put them together to make a word, that's where I get stuck.'

'Here,' said Catherine, 'let's see what we can do with this page.' The two women settled together side by side on a large couch and soon became absorbed in the lesson. Catherine took Nancy through all the letters of the alphabet and encouraged to make the right sounds. Both she and Joe had helped their children learn to read at an early age, and even little Tom had begun to cope with short words, so she was well used to the process of learning. Before long Nancy was sounding out simple words in Tom's book.

So absorbed were they that they failed to hear the arrival of Joe, hungry for his tiffin and ready for a post-prandial nap before taking up cudgels with the palace administrators once more. He stopped short at the entrance to the drawing room, unaware that Nancy had become a regular visitor,

'Nancy Carter, if I'm not mistaken! It's good to see you; I'd heard that we were near neighbours.' Man-like, he did not notice the alarm on Nancy's face as she jumped to her feet, muttering about 'time to go; outstaying welcome…..'

'Nonsense,' said Joe, striding across to the bell pull. 'Stay for tiffin; I'm sure Catherine would enjoy your company!' Catherine chuckled, but didn't enlighten Joe to the cause of her amusement. She saw the agitated Nancy out, and returned to find Joe looking puzzled,

'Is it something I said? I didn't intend to chase her away; I haven't seen Nancy for a very long time' looking well, isn't she?' Catherine mused,

'Mm, she has lived nearby since the Willoughby's left; and visits regularly, but always when you are out. I wonder.....? her voice tailed away and Joe quirked an eyebrow at her, but Catherine kept her suspicions to herself, and Joe was too tired to pursue it. But Catherine was as sure as she could be that she had discovered who Nancy had fallen in love with all those years ago; and if she was not mistaken, still had a fondness for. Strangely, she did not feel threatened by the knowledge.

The reading lessons progressed apace, and Nancy moved off children's books and onto more adult reading. The satisfaction she felt at mastering the skill gave her enormous satisfaction, and she said so to her tutor,

'It would've been nice to learn years ago, but I'm so glad to've done it at last. Just think of the soldiers' children. I'll wager they'd like to learn.'

The same thought hit both women simultaneously,

'Why don't we....'

'It'd be wonderful...' Then they laughed, and Nancy tried again,

'Why don't you start a school? I could help, but I couldn't teach 'em.'

'Nor can I Nancy; I'm not a teacher. You were easy and really wanted to learn.'

'Begging your pardon,' said Nancy firmly, 'you *are* very good at teaching. An' I'll bet there's lots of littl'uns who really want to learn. I know I'd've given my eye teeth to learn when I was a sprog in Manchester!' Catherine acknowledged the probable truth of it, having heard Joe expound on it at great length. She said thoughtfully,

'I'd have to ask the new Colonel for permission to set it up. We can throw it open to anyone as we have no need to charge.'

'Begging your pardon again, but you must charge summat, even if it's a few annas. If it's not paid for, it's not valued. That's how soldiers will see it.' Catherine did not argue further as Nancy knew better than she the workings of the private soldier's mind.

On the principle that 'there is no time like the present', she sent a brief note to Colonel Braithwaite at the cantonment, who had arrived to replace James Willoughby six months before. His appointment had caused much bad feeling, as Major Harding had been Acting-Colonel in the interim, and by all accounts, doing a good job. But Braithwaite had simply turned up out of the blue, carrying the endorsement of his position from Calcutta. Rumour had it that he was a pompous, fussy man, and he appeared to be universally disliked. But, thought Catherine charitably, any stranger would find it difficult to penetrate that closely knit community. She also heard that his greatest sin was that he didn't like polo!

Dressing in her neatest gown, and trying to look like a school marm, Catherine was carried through the cantonment by carriage a week later. Though she had been to see friends since their departure, she still found it strange being a visitor rather than a resident. The feeling persisted as an aide handed her down from the carriage by the admin block. He informed her that Colonel Braithwaite was expecting her and would she kindly follow him.

She was ushered into the Colonel's office, and asked to sit while the Colonel finished a very necessary piece of paperwork he was engaged on. Catherine had the distinct notion that it was a deliberate ploy to make her feel like an intruder; a feeling reinforced when the Colonel ostentatiously sanded the document and sent for an aide to deliver it. He finally addressed her directly for the first time,

'Sorry about that. Affairs of the Regiment don't you know. Very urgent.' He folded his hands and waited, the very picture of a man overwhelmed with important matters, but prepared to be polite to a 'little lady' who clearly didn't understand that a Colonel's time was precious!

Suppressing her irritation, Catherine outlined her proposal to open a school to teach the children of the soldiers of the Regiment, the rudiments of reading, writing, Geography and History, or anything that might be considered useful. The Colonel looked shocked,

'My dear Mrs…?' he consulted the note on his desk, 'Harrington. Why is such a school needed?'

'To give them chance to gain some learning hitherto denied them.'

'And who do you propose should finance this….this….whimsy?'

'This is not a whimsy. Why should these children be denied the chance to improve themselves? And I am not looking for financial help; in fact I am not looking for help at all. I merely wished to extend you the courtesy of informing you, as my proposal affects the Regiment. But if you are not interested, I will waste no more of your so valuable time. Good day!' With that Catherine rose, pulled on her white gloves, picked up her reticule and swept out of the door so rapidly that she nearly fell over the aide who was listening outside. He grinned at her somewhat sheepishly.

Catherine was trembling with rage by the time she got home to report to Nancy. She strode up and down the drawing room in a most unladylike fashion, her wide skirts swinging sharply from side to side, and endangering many ornaments scattered about on occasional tables. Nancy watched her in amusement, listening to the tirade,

'How did a man like that get to replace a man like James Willoughby? You should've seen him Nancy, sixty if he's a day, and short!'

'You can't blame him for his height, or lack of it,' observed Nancy mildly. Five foot two Catherine merely snorted and went on remorselessly,

'And his face was all red, especially his nose. I'll wager he's fond of his port! Pompous ass; suggested the school wasn't necessary. I'll wager he hasn't even noticed that there are children about the place. Well I told him; didn't need his money. We'll do it on our own; so there!'

'What will Mr. Harrington say?' queried Nancy, nervously. I've a little to spare but…'

'Joe won't mind; it's my mon… Well anyway, he won't mind. He believes in education for everyone. The only problem is, can that idiotic little man stop us?'

'I don't know; if they're Regimental children?'

'I'll ask Joe. He'll know!'

Joe didn't know, but thought an independent school should be open for anyone to attend. He had listened to Catherine's much edited account of the interview and felt saddened that the Regiment had such an unworthy successor to a man like James.

Saeed was considerably more helpful than the Colonel, and found Catherine and Nancy a suitable site. He thought that the school should not be too close to the palace as the children they hoped to attract might be intimidated. And it shouldn't be too far from the cantonment, but not too close. Finally, the choice fell on a piece of flat land on the cantonment side of the river, but shielded from it by a grove of sheeshum trees. Perfect.

Joe was dragged in to design the schoolhouse. He protested feebly that he had never actually been to school. His objections were ruthlessly overcome, and he was told to sketch a suitable plan.

The crude sketch was given to the palace architect who wrinkled his nose scornfully; he was used to things on a much grander scale! When the drawings were complete, a veritable army of coolies set to work clearing the site, and baking straw stiffened bricks for the walls. Within a remarkably short space of time, the Kotepore Elementary School began to take shape.

Meanwhile, Catherine took it upon herself to collect the materials that would need. She turned to the one person who would know what was needed, Chris Day in Delhi. By this time, he was editor and publisher of a prominent newspaper in Delhi with a very healthy circulation. His account of the Mutiny had been a best seller, and the Day's were now very comfortable indeed. Since then, Chris had contented himself with writing short stories and long editorials, and had gained a certain notoriety for his pithy articles that poked not-so-gentle fun at the British and the British Raj. He was currently working on a full length novel based on the life of a British boy whose parents had been killed in the Mutiny, and who had been raised by his ayah to believe he was Indian, only to discover his real origin much later. The novel attempted to portray a character torn by being part of two worlds and not belonging to either. Reading excerpts from it, Catherine had been amazed at the insight into human nature that Chris evidently had.

But for now, she needed his help in finding the books and other paraphernalia necessary for the setting up of an elementary school. The sort of books she had used for her own children were a good basis, but of course, she would need many more. And the scholars would need slates and chalk.

She was not privileged to see Chris' face when he received her letter, which was as well, or she may have given up on the spot. Pattie was far more excited about the whole thing, and said so, to be told tersely,

'Romantic fools!'

But Chris did as he had been bid, and by the time the shell of the school had been completed, a large crate arrived at the Chota Mahal. Apart from the items requested, there was a large bill which made Catherine swallow hard, and an enthusiastic letter from Pattie, who vowed she would rush to help if the numbers of children applying got out of hand! Catherine told Nancy of it and observed wryly,

'We don't know yet if we'll get any!'

'Cold feet?' asked Nancy, though not unkindly. Catherine nodded, but her depression vanished as she opened the crate. Inside were stacks of primers; books for the early readers, progressing readers and proficient readers. Nancy's eyes gleamed; she would try some of them out herself! There were history books, Geography books, and joy of joy, a globe, packed in segments to be put together by the aid of pegs. There were Bibles and religious tracts and even some hymn books, all of which brought a smile to Catherine's face as she knew Chris' opinions on religion!

At last all was ready, and Joe accompanied Catherine and Nancy to the school he had designed. Outside, in a parody of a guard of honour, stood two rows of coolies who had worked on the construction. They all stood with one leg wrapped round their spades or mallets, smoking bidis and grinning expansively. They didn't understand the enterprise, but the angrezis wanted it so, and they had provided. Joe looked round the simple room with its rows of benches ready for small behinds to descend on them, book shelves crammed with books and the globe in all its glory. He was amazed.

'Why it's just like the one I once saw in a village near Clonarty where I grew up,' he whispered, the memory poignant in his mind. He had only seen it once, and here it was, reproduced!

The problem of potential customers was discussed in a family 'council of war'. Catherine was in favour of a head-on approach, with a small hand bill sent to every soldier with a family, but Joe tactfully pointed out that most soldiers could not read themselves. Catherine countered with the suggestion of a personal visit to the barracks which Joe vetoed by saying that this was trespassing, and the Colonel could prevent it very easily; it could even cause trouble for the men. Catherine fumed for a while, but was not easily put off,

'That man has probably forgotten about it by now. And if he did recall my visit, would probably think me incapable of carrying it through as a mere woman!' Joe smiled at the outraged sniff, and said playfully,

'Ah, he doesn't know you my love. If he did, he'd be shaking in his shoes!' She tossed her head at that, but then Joe became serious,

'I've been doing a bit of investigating on your behalf, and Adam has been more than helpful in keeping his ear to the ground. Your assessment of the Colonel seems to be very accurate. He is a fussy, pompous little man, and apparently he was furious when you vowed to go ahead with the project without his permission. The only thing you can do is to open it to all comers and hope it attracts the customers you want. After all, there are very few British children other than the military.'

'I'm happy with that; it was always meant to be for anyone who wants an education.'

Nancy had kept silent up to now. She still felt uncomfortable in Joe's presence, but had been forced to see more of him during the planning of the school. Now she interjected quietly,

'Have you ever noticed that if you don't want summat to get out, then it's all over the cantonment in a minute. All we need to do is whisper in an ear or two that the school is here, an' the Colonel doesn't like it....!' Joe gave a shout of laughter and resisted the temptation to slap her on the back in comradely fashion,

'By Jove Nancy, you're right; it just might work!' And it did.

Clutching their small coins in sticky fingers, ten children appeared on the day the school opened, and within a month there were thirty. They did not all attend every day, and Catherine decided philosophically that it was no use planning a programme. So each lesson was a 'one off' with a topic that would stand alone. Geography became a firm favourite and the children liked to trace the route to England. Most of them had been born in India and had never been 'home' as they called it.

Reading was learnt by a progressive method. Each day there was a period set aside when the pupils divided into groups and started work on the books from Delhi. With their haphazard attendance, they soon fell into different grades, so one type of book was never overloaded. While Catherine took care of their minds, Nancy took care of their bodies, as the daily charge included a meal. They suspected sometimes that it was the only decent meal the children had, the way they attacked it voraciously!

By the end of May it was time to close the school until after the rainy season in October, and Catherine and Nancy pronounced it a resounding success. The books were carefully packed away in tin trunks to protect them from white ants that seemed to love anything made of paper, and locked the door with a satisfied sigh. Catherine dusted her hands and declared,

'I feel I've earned my holiday this year. Come with us, Nancy, after all, you used to go with the Willoughby's.'

'Ye….s, yes. I'd like that.' So she did for that year, and every one after, until Nancy Carter was as much part of the Harrington household as she had been of the Willoughby's.

All this enterprise did not interfere with the Harrington's social life, as school opened very early in the morning, and finished after tiffin. A post-prandial nap revived frazzled tempers and the afternoon could be devoted to visiting.

Rare but very welcome visitors to the palace were the Carlton's from the mofussil. John Carlton preferred to spend his time overseeing his expanding empire, and his wife Dharshi was shy and retiring by nature, so was perfectly happy with this arrangement. But periodically he would drag her unwillingly to Lucknow or preferably to Kotepore, to attend to his business affairs. When in Kotepore, they stayed with Rajah Saeed, who had taken his father's place in John's affections. There too, he met Joe and Catherine, and found that they had a lot in common. John missed his old friend, James, but he discovered that his young protégé was a fascinating character to talk to.

Soon after Christmas, 1869, the Carlton's arrived for a two week stay, this time with their son Amar in tow. They were all in the palace's private garden, with the women as usual at one end with Shushila and Dharshi trying ot explain to Catherine the finer points of tying a sari. She shook her head in incomprehension, so the Indian ladies grabbed her arms and bore her away for a demonstration. The children were all in the garden, watched by hovering ayahs. Amar was lording it over the rest as the oldest by a clear two years; he was fourteen to Rose's twelve years. He had the younger boys enthralled by stirring tales of hunting trips with his father in the mofussil, and claimed to have bagged four tigers already. Robert was inclined to be scornful and said so, which nearly precipitated a bout of fisticuffs; but the protagonists were firmly separated by Moti, who chided the boys for their unruly behaviour in the presence of their parents.

Joe smiled at the shrill chatter from the other end of the garden, and then turned back to the masculine conversation.

'I've heard what your wife has achieved, Joe,' said John, 'and I'm most impressed. It is rare that anyone cares about education for the masses!' Joe admitted that part of the impetus had been his own experiences in childhood. Saeed put in,

'What are your plans for Amar, John? I've heard you are against sending him to England and school there?'

'Are you surprised after your own experience at Eton? You're quite right though. I had intended to keep the boy here and manage it myself, but Dharshi says that he must experience both sides of his birthright. Where we are situated, he will only get the Indian side.'

'Won't that lead to confusion?' put in Joe, 'here he knows who he is and what he is?'

'I thought so too, but I'm coming round to Dharshi's way of thinking.'

'So,' said Saeed, 'will it be Eton or Harrow?'

'Neither. Even without your experience of Eton, I'd heard enough to put me off both of these unnatural places! No, I've found one in the West Country which should let the boy develop in his own way, and not take too much notice of the colour of his skin!' Joe looked up sharply. It really was ridiculous this business of colour. Looking at the three of them, Carlton was easily the darkest, his face the colour of mahogany from long days spent in the fields. He too was bronzed in spite of his red hair, and Saeed was a relatively light skinned Indian, probably heavily laced with Aryan blood. Yet he was classified as 'black fellah' by the more ignorant of the British. And John's son Amar, was no darker than Robert sitting with him, but would be taunted with 'darky-whitey', if he had had the misfortune to live in the cantonment. He shook his head as the conversation moved on to the knotty problem of caste, for Dharshi had raised the boy as a Hindu. John was saying,

'Remember all the problems your father had sending you over the Kala Pani, Saeed? It seems that the holy-men take a more pragmatic view of it all now that so many Indian families are sending their sons to England to be educated. It seems that purification on their return will do very nicely!' Saeed smiled, but had never forgotten that long and dangerous overland journey.

'I don't know whether I will send my sons over when the time comes. Perhaps I will send them to Mrs. Harrington's school, eh Joe?' Joe chuckled at the thought of three gorgeously clad Princes sitting among the Regimental urchins. While John and Saeed discussed the relative merits of school over private tutor, Joe gazed at the youngsters across the lawn. Rose was sitting apart, the only girl except for Shushila's latest baby, a fat little princess cradled on her ayah's knee. But it was not the only reason that Rose was sitting apart. She had her eyes fixed on Amar's face and was drinking in every word he uttered. In lordly manner he totally ignored his adoring audience, but just once looked across at the girl, and gave her a sweet smile; and then looked away again. All colour seemed to drain from Rose's face and she seemed on the point of fainting.

'So,' thought Joe, 'my little girl has found another male to admire,' and surprised himself with a stab of jealousy. But then he told himself,

'Good God; she's only twelve!'

Just then, three sari clad figures entered the garden giggling. The third of the three hung back, reluctant to move any further, but she was dragged along by the other two. It was Catherine! The children jumped up and surrounded her laughing. Tom nearly created a catastrophe by tugging at the end and unwinding the whole affair, but the situation was rescued in time, and the sari admired by all, especially Joe, who suggested she wore it more often. Catherine blushed. Then he looked again at Rose, who was a normal twelve year old again, chasing round the garden hotly pursued by Robert with a frog!

The years passed inexorably. In January of 1870, Joe realised that he had reached the venerable age of forty. He rose in a temper that deepened with each passing hour. He scowled at his staff, and snapped at Gopi when he poured a pre-tiffin sherry. He wasn't sure whether his temper was due to the fact that he was forty, or that everyone seemed to have forgotten his birthday altogether! Catherine had seemed preoccupied that morning, muttering about a difficult child at the school who she hoping to get rid of, until he could have shouted at her.

So the long day wore on. He had to work late, one trivial problem after another keeping him at his desk longer than usual. Was it his imagination or was his secretary being more inane than usual? Then he had had enough; the secretary came in with yet another piece of paper and received a snarl for his pains.

'No more today; I'm going home!'

'Yes Sahib.'

He stood up and stretched. He had adopted Indian dress over the last few years, finding it far more comfortable than the alpaca suit, the traditional uniform of the Civil Servant. But even in pyjamas and achkan, he felt hot and sticky, in spite of the season being winter. Suddenly he yearned for a bath, a stiff whiskey-pani and dinner; in that order.

Moments later he strode through his front entrance to be greeted by Gopi, grinning from ear to ear. He found himself almost dragged into his bedchamber where a bath stood waiting in the nearby dressing room, and a clean outfit spread on the bed. 'That's better,' he thought, but told Gopi to change the proffered outfit for a simpler one.

'Too grand for an evening in,' he muttered as he sank into the scented bath, cheroot clamped between his teeth. He let the trivialities of the day steep away, and called drowsily,

'Does the Memsahib know I'm home?'

'Yes Sahib.'

'Then why the devil doesn't she come and say hello?' But the question was a rhetorical one. He scowled; not even his own wife remembered. He stood up and took a towel from Gopi.

'Thought I told you I wanted something else to wear!' Gopi chose to look stupid,

'The dinner gong, Sahib, it has gone.'

'Oh very well.' Grumbling, he donned the dark blue achkan fastened with small sapphire buttons, and wound with a sash of silver. He stood in front of the mirror, sucking in his stomach,

'Not bad for forty?' he asked the reflection, which nodded in agreement.

As Joe entered the drawing room, he heard the popping of champagne corks. They were all there; Nancy, Saeed and Shushila, John and Dharshi, and surprisingly, Amar, back from school. There was Chris and Pattie from Delhi, with a small son in tow, Chris looking as untidy as ever. There were

Adam and Louise with Christina, looking very grown up suddenly. Other officers and their wives who were more recent friends made up another half dozen; and they all raised their glasses,

'Happy birthday!' Came a chorus.

Catherine was by his side, pressing a glass into this hand. She kissed him fondly. Then Rose reached up to kiss him, at fifteen nearly as tall as her mother. She breathed in his ear,

'He's home, Papa. Isn't it wonderful?!'

The boys came in turn and solemnly shook his hand, but he wasn't having any of that, and firmly hugged them all. Then he greeted everyone else in turn, tears standing in his eyes. It was a good party, and well worth the hangover next morning.

———m———

It took Rose a further four years before Amar was brought to realise that he loved her. It was not an easy courtship, as the Carlton's habit of staying in the mofussil for months on end made contact between then difficult. But succeed she did.

They married in Kotepore, twice. The first was a civil ceremony by the British Commissioner recently appointed to Kotepore. The second was a Hindu ceremony reminiscent of Saeed and Shushila's wedding years before. Joe wasn't sure about his beloved daughter embracing an alien religion, while Catherine was absolutely furious about it. But playing the devil's advocate, Joe persuaded her to accept it.

'We've always believed in tolerance, acushla; we can hardly go back on that now!' There was no answer to that, so as they sat watching, Rose followed Amar round the sacred fire, tied to him by the end of her sari.

After the couple left for their honeymoon up in the idyllic mountains and lakes of Kashmir, Joe suddenly felt depressed.

'We need a holiday,' stated Catherine, in a voice that brooked no argument. Joe waved a feeble hand,

'My work at the palace?'

'It's time you had a vacation. Saeed won't mind, you know that, and your staff will be positively delighted!'

'Your school?'

'Extended holiday; though Nancy could take it over; she's observed me for long enough; she must know the lessons off by heart!'

'The children?'

'Children, hah!' She made it sound like an expletive, 'Robert's eighteen and even Tom is fourteen, and we've an army of servants. I thought it was mothers who worried. Don't you want a holiday with me?' The pathos in her voice caught him until he realised she was smiling. But she was right; what was the matter with him?

'Where shall we go?'

'Where do you want to go?'

'Ireland!'

Chapter 20

Though it took some weeks to make arrangements, but the very thought of a vacation acted as a tonic to Joe's jaded spirits. And when Rose and Amar returned from their honeymoon, his spirits took another lift when he saw a contented glow in his daughter's eyes.

The pair were full of the sights and sounds of Kashmir in general, and Srinagar in particular. It was still early in the year, so there had not been many visitors, which suited the honeymooners very well indeed.

'But weren't you cold?' asked Tom ingenuously, and he couldn't understand the laughter that greeted the question, or Amar's answer,

'We really didn't notice!'

But preparations went on apace and at last it was time to leave. Passages were booked on one of the brand new British India Steam Navigation ships that would take them across the Arabian Sea to the Suez Canal and thence to the Mediterranean. Joe was intrigued by the idea of taking a ship across land, but Catherine was distinctly nervous at the very thought of going to sea! They had decided, prudently, to time their arrival in England to coincide with spring, for blood thinned by years in the heat of India would find the dank chill of an English winter hard to bear!

All problems had been overcome just as Catherine had predicted. Saeed had readily agreed to the long vacation, insisting that Joe's efforts in countering the abuses to his finances would more than cover the cost of a deputy. Nancy had valiantly agreed to run the school until it was time to close for the summer season. She was a little nervous of coping with the advanced readers, but Adam solved that problem by offering to put in an appearance for an hour or two each day. He was as dreamy as ever, but had taken his faithful old pipe out of his mouth long enough to remind Joe of the lessons aboard ship,

'If I could cope with a parcel of soldiers in the hold of a heaving ship, when none of 'em wanted to learn, then I can cope with this little lot!'

'None of 'em wanted to learn?' queried Joe, rather hurt by the accusation; but Adam laughed,

'I didn't have to teach you; you just soaked it up like a sponge!'

But the hardest problem to overcome was the matter of ladies' fashion! Catherine was thrown into a panic at the thought of arriving in London unsuitably dressed. Joe's innocent enquiry as to why she couldn't wait and see until she arrived, and then have a few dresses 'run up' was treated with withering scorn, and she went into a huddle with Louise and Nancy, the trio poring over fashion magazines. Sadly the magazines were several months out of date, but even so showed that fashions had changed dramatically of late. The crinoline had reached noble dimensions by 1860, but then had slipped round the back to enhance the roundness of the female form, and by the end of that decade had developed into a bustle. Since then the bustle had slipped downwards and turned into a train. Catherine took some of the pictures to her favourite derzee to have a few outfits made up. She was about to order them in silks and muslins but then remembered the weather would be cooler where they were going. She asked Joe,

'But won't it be spring when we arrive?' Joe guffawed,

'An English spring is like our winter, my dear, trust me!' So Catherine had the dresses made in the finest velvet instead.

At last the day came for their departure. Saeed came to see them off complete with an escort of splendidly attired Sikhs who were to deliver the Harrington's to Lucknow, where they would board the train for Delhi. Shushila hung back behind him, clutching her sari across her face, her eyes wide with embarrassment. But Joe was not going to let her get away with that, and lifted her off her feet in a bear hug, much to Saeed's amusement. He kissed her on both cheeks then set her down. She stepped back hurriedly, those same cheeks aflame, and fumbled for her sari, but not before Joe saw a shy smile. Saeed returned the compliment and embraced Catherine before shaking Joe's hand and clapping him vigorously on the back. He encouraged them not to rush back as he, Saeed, would keep a close eye on his affairs. Privately pleased that Saeed looked in much better shape these days with his interest in polo, Joe thought that he probably would, but he said slyly,

'But it simply isn't *done* old boy!'

Rose came forward next and hugged him warmly. Amar had brought her to Kotepore to see them off, but would have to return forthwith. He was in the process of learning about his inheritance, and his father had wisely insisted that he start at the bottom. It was not the privilege of field workers to get extended holidays!

'Happy sweeting?' whispered Joe in Rose's ear.

'Oh yes, Papa,' she breathed in reply, 'we'll miss you, but don't hurry back. You and Mama have needed this holiday for a very long time.' Joe let her go to say goodbye to her mother and was surprised to see that she had grown a good inch or two taller than Catherine; when had that happened? He must have been walking around with his eyes shut! He observed the pair of them as they embraced briefly, noting the identical profiles. Catherine's hair was darker, and Rose's eyes bluer, but really there were very alike; was that the reason for their coolness towards each other? He had never fathomed it, but with Rose now a woman grown, there was nothing to be done.

Here was another surprise; Robert stepped forward for a hug and Joe found himself looking the boy straight in the eye,

'Good God,' he muttered, 'have you all grown six inches overnight?' Robert laughed,

'No Papa, it's you that's shrunk!' Joe had been right about Robert with his sombre nature inherited from his grandfather; a loving home and upbringing had suppressed the darker side of his nature and brought the lurking humour to the fore. The humour was much in evidence now, gleaming in the depths of his dark eyes, as he brushed an unruly curl black curl out of his eye and made way for Daniel.

His second son clutched him warmly, as if in panic at the impending departure. His silvery hair formed an aureole in the early morning sum, while his eyes matched the blue of the sky.

'I've got a handsome family,' thought Joe proudly, for here was Tom, red-gold curls tossing. He had grown gangly of late; all arms and legs like an awkward colt. His hair was darkening and would doubtless end up the colour of a polished conker, just like his own.

The boys clustered round Catherine now, Rose and Amar standing back, an enigmatic smile playing round Rose's mouth. Even Tom was taller than his mother and she disappeared in the midst of them as the three heads bent over hers, black, silver and red-gold.

'Chup!' said Saeed firmly with a downward sweep of his hand, 'you'll miss your train at this rate.'

Into the carriage, the ghari-wallah discarding his bidi, and then they were off. Craning backwards, Catherine and Joe waved until the carriage turned the corner outside Chota Mahal and they were lost from view.

'Where was Nancy?' asked Joe curiously.

'We said our goodbyes earlier,' explained catherine, 'she said she hated public farewells,'

She didn't say goodbye to me,' said Joe, piqued. Catherine shrugged but did not reply. Privately she was pleased. Joe was the least vain man she knew and had no idea that Nancy nursed a secret love in her heart, and she had no intention of enlightening him. 'Leave well alone' seemed an excellent tenet to follow.

They boarded the hissing, clanking monster that steamed and belched its way to Delhi with the Harrington's and their mountain of luggage. They paused there to spend a few days with their friends Chris and Pattie, but much as they loved their friends, they were eager to be on their way, so they boarded the next stage to carry them towards Bombay.

The next morning, Joe drew the blinds back in their comfortable sleeping compartment and gave a snort of laughter. He called Catherine to come and share the view. Along the edges of the fields, keeping precisely parallel with the track, the entire Indian complement of the train was squatting to accomplish their morning evacuation. The sight of so many full moons caused Joe and Catherine to explode with laughter, which resulted in a violent knocking from the compartment next door, where an aging couple was still trying to sleep. They subsided giggling as the train moved off again, leaving a field well fertilized by the comfortably eased passengers.

Bombay was familiar to Joe as they travelled through it. It could have been yesterday rather than the nearly twenty five years since Joe had last seen it. There was the hill to the north overlooking Back Bay, with its lush vegetation. To the south were the old Portuguese fort and the godowns packed with all manner of goods awaiting shipment to the west; indigo and cotton, spices and tea, jute and rice. Leaving Catherine to sort herself out in the hotel, Joe wandered the streets. In the harbour, a different breed of ships rode at anchor. These steam leviathans were impressive to look at but lacked the grace of the three and four masted sailing ships that had brought them here. But at least they were not dependent on the vagaries of the weather. Here and there sails could be seen, but would they too disappear in time?

He stood by a corner and a scene jumped into his mind; a young Prince gorgeously dressed, trying to control a rearing stallion and receiving abuse for his efforts. Even after the passage of time, Joe blushed for the ignorance and arrogance of the Englishman involved. Looking across the streets he could almost make out a running figure carrying a pair of outrageous slippers with curled up toes, and encrusted with glass beads and gold braid,

"Ere Joe, look at these!' he blinked hard but the image was gone. At his elbow, one of the ubiquitous traders held out samples of his wares,

'Here Sahib, look at these.' Joe brushed him away, uncharacteristically rude. The bunnia shrugged, used to arrogant angrezis, and he spat a stream of betel-stained saliva at the retreating back.

They boarded the four hundred foot British Indian Steam Navigation Company ship early next morning. It towered over them like an Indian palace, the many fretted windows replaced by rows of portholes. Above it all reared three funnels from which black smoke was already curling lazily into the still air. Their luggage had preceded them on the heads of a string of coolies, their shrill voices adding to the prevailing din. They had thought themselves used to the noise of Indians *en masse*, but in the confines of the harbour, the cacophony reached clamorous heights.

'At least it's cooler than last time I was here,' observed Joe, wryly, as they watched with great interest an altercation between a nattily dressed Sikh and a Hindu coolie concerning the whereabouts of the Sikh's luggage. Insults concerning each other's parentage, religion and mode of dress were hurled back and forth. The argument was settled by the appearance of another coolie carrying the missing luggage, at which the Sikh transferred his temper to the new arrival. He straightened his turban, brushed his luxuriant moustache and then strode away, straight into a pile of dung thoughtfully deposited by a passing camel!

The voyage passed swiftly and pleasantly. Joe was much amused to find them described as 'POSH', one of the select breed who favoured the shady side of the ships during their cruises, and were therefore placed 'Port out Starboard Home'. They had had no idea when they booked their passage as they were more than used to the sun, but were fascinated to see the lengths to which fair skinned Victorian ladies would go to avoid the merest kiss of the sun.

Nevertheless they met some interesting companions to while away the days, and the lengthy dinners at the captain's table. Most of the passengers were sightseers returning from expensive cruises in the Far East and spent much of their time complaining about the primitive sanitation, even in high class hotels. They exclaimed over Joe and Catherine's immunity from it all and would not believe that they didn't suffer from 'gippy tummy' as they delicately described it.

The sea was kind to them, in spite of the earliness of the season, and before long they reached Suez. From there they entered the Suez Canal that would carry them the hundred miles from the Arabian Sea to the Mediterranean. Captain Timothy entertained them with a few statistics the night before they docked in Suez.

'Napoleon Bonaparte first thought of the idea, but was told that the Red Sea was three feet different in height from the Mediterranean, so abandoned the notion. But it was eventually begun in 1859 to the design of a French engineer, Ferdinand de Lesseps. It took ten years to complete at a cost of twenty million pounds; and eighty million cubic yards of soil was removed. It is thirty feet deep and three hundred feet wide at the top, the bottom tapering to two hundred and sixty two feet. There are locks, and it passes through several lakes in the course of its ninety nine mile journey.' Listening to the clipped voice reciting the details of the canal, Joe couldn't help wondering if it was part of a modern day Captain's brief to learn all these facts and figures for the edification of his passengers. He smiled at the thought, which the Captain took to be appreciation of his efforts, and he bowed to them before leaving for the bridge and the more onerous duty of docking his large ship.

Joe found the canal completely fascinating, and spent much time hanging over the ship's rail looking at the bank. Strings of camels could be seen, pacing the steamship, and snorting in aristocratic disdain at the intruders. Sometimes he saw intrepid Victorian travellers in neat khaki 'bush outfits' complete with pith helmets, and clinging precariously to their mount's strange hump. One morning a huge explosion had the entire complement of first class passenger rushing to the rail on the promenade deck to see a ship ahead of them being blown apart. The Captain reassured them that they were not under attack; the ship had run aground and was a hazard to other shipping in the narrow confines of the canal, and was being removed in the most efficient way possible.

All too soon they reached the other end of the canal at Port Said. The whole party went ashore for a few hours sightseeing, and then again at Alexandria just along the coast. Then they were properly into the Mediterranean and shivering in the unaccustomedly cool air. The steamship moved steadily through the placid waters of the enclosed sea, passing the enormous profile of Crete rising out of Homer's 'wine dark sea' early one morning. Their next sighting of land was Malta, followed by the southern coast of Sicily and then Sardinia. Catherine was fascinated by following the route in actuality that she had so often traced on the schoolroom globe. She looked forward to passing through the Straits of Gibraltar and thence into the Atlantic Ocean. She confided as much to the Captain one night over their meal,

'I fear you will not think so when we reach the Bay of Biscay,' warned Captain Timothy, a sentiment endorsed by seasoned travellers at their table. They shuddered expressively at the thought of the Bay in April, leaving Catherine in a state of high anxiety. Joe told her not to fret, for she would in all probability have the best sea legs of them all!

He was right, for as the steamship fought its way northwards through the worst storm of the whole voyage they found themselves in solitary splendour in the dining room! Sensibly they dined lightly and alone and then went out to the promenade deck to view the elements do their worst. They were glad of the warmer clothes they had purchased before leaving India, but even so found it too cold to linger long on deck. Joe stood with his arm round Catherine as they watched twenty foot waves come at the ship and break to rush down its length. The sea was a turgid grey-green, the waves topped by dirty foam, whipped away by the northerly gale, not at all like the Arabian and Mediterranean Seas they had left behind. For the first time, Joe was glad they were aboard a steamship and not a sailing ship otherwise they could have driven southwards, miles off their route.

But eventually the storm disappeared behind them and the sun came out almost apologetically, giving them a watery smile. The sky cleared and the wind died to a zephyr as they glided by a headline near Brest, and turned into the English Channel. A fellow passenger stood near Catherine and Joe at the rail and pointed out famous landmarks to them; there was the Isle of Portland with the up and coming resort of Weymouth behind it; there was the great sweep of sand around Bournemouth followed by the Needles on the end of the Isle of Wight. Then they were round the island and sweeping into the Solent heading for Southampton, the steamship sounding its whistle with a 'Woop! Woop!' as tugs took up the task of easing the great ship into its berth. The voyage was over.

Catherine watched Joe's face as they edged closer to the quay, but of course this wasn't his home. Southampton was as strange to him as it was to her, but it was the nearest he had been for a very long time; but his face was impassive and gave nothing away. But his thoughts must have been many miles away, though, as he started violently when the gangway crashed down. Than all was bustle and confusion, as somehow they transferred themselves and their luggage to the Railway Station; their first destination in England was to be London.

Once again, Joe left Catherine to her unpacking as he went on a nostalgic trip to Clerkenwell. He hadn't told his wife about it as he wasn't sure what he would find; there was no way of knowing if the old inn where he and Kit had stayed all those years before still existed, and if it did, the people they had known still alive!

He hired a hansom cab and gave the driver the name 'The Spotted Cow'. To his relief, the man chucked his horse into action, and they were off. He looked about curiously, but London seemed as noisy and dirty as when he had left it. In some streets, cadaverous women still sat nursing emaciated babies and pulling on bottles of gin. He shuddered,

'So much for progress,' he muttered to himself. He paid off the driver outside the hostelry and stood awhile surveying it. It looked much the same, slightly shabbier perhaps, and the sign had obviously had had a coat of paint or two over the years. Plucking up courage, he entered.

The appearance of a well set up man in an elegant frock coat and neat cravat caused a mild stir, but interest soon waned and the business of drinking continued. The interior had been smartened up, and now sported many horse brasses and other ornaments arranged tastefully above the bar. Shiny brass spittoons were arranged at intervals around the room, and the floor was covered by a good inch of sawdust. Obviously the inn was very much a going concern.

A young man took his order, Joe remembering in time not to ask for whiskey-pani. Settling for a glass of ale, he wondered how he could find out what he wanted to know. Just then an elderly woman came into the taproom from a side door, and began to gather up dirty tankards. Joe eyed her narrowly, until convinced it was who he thought it was, Ma Baker. He waited until she was close to him, and said softly,

'Ma; Ma Baker!' She looked up sharply and wrinkled her eyes at him, as though short sighted.

'Come on Ma; don't you know me?' The woman fumbled in her pocket and fetched out a pair of steel rimmed spectacles; she put them on and peered at him again. Joe smiled and said,

'Take off twenty five years, about ten inches and a lot of pounds; and I came here with Kit Barnet!' She peered again,

'Kit? Little Kit? Then you must be......?' on a rising shriek, 'Joe!'

She recollected herself in time to set the mugs down safely before giving him a voluminous hug, tears welling in her eyes. The other customers gave them interested glances, which did not slow down their drinking elbows in the slightest.

'Where'd you spring from? Where's Kit?'

'He's dead, Ma; been dead many a year!'

'Ah. I allus wondered what happened to the pair of you. 'Ere, come in the back and tell me all about it.' He followed Ma out of the door she had entered from and found himself in a familiar kitchen. Flitches of bacon hung from the rafters, and a great cauldron seethed on the range, just as he remembered, He sighed comfortably, and they sat down in front of the hearth. Joe was glad of its warmth, as he was finding the chill of an English spring hard to get used to.

'Now!' said Ma. He told her the highlights of his years away, carefully editing the details of Kit's death, but waxing lyrical about his own advancement, marriage and children. Ma demanded that he bring Catherine to see her, and received a firm promise to do so.

She then told her of her doings, including the death of Barney some ten years before,

'It were that old leg of 'is. Took bad with gangrene it did. I couldn't make 'im go to the surgeon; he'd a mortal fear of 'un after losing the leg. Well it turned bad until he died of it.' She had run the inn since then with the help of various underlings.

'But it's not the same,' she sighed, 'I miss the old devil an' 'is leg tapping up an' down the cellar steps.'

It was three hours and an enormous feed before Ma Baker would let him return to his wife. She was impressed with his improved girth, but clearly felt that he could glide perilously back into malnutrition if she didn't do something about it!

They spent three weeks sightseeing.

'Just like vulgar trippers,' sighed Catherine contentedly. Joe had sent a letter off to the Willoughby's address in Yorkshire, and while they waited on a reply, 'did' all the sights. They marveled at the Tower of London, whispered to each other in St. Paul's Cathedral, watched a balloon ascent in Hyde Park and wandered round art galleries, and gasped at the realism of Madame Tussaud's waxworks. By the end of three weeks they were absolutely exhausted, but as excited as a pair of ten year olds. But a letter arrived from Yorkshire; James and Lucy would be delighted to see them and they were welcome to stay as long as they wished.

April gave way to May and England put on its best dress to show off to them as they journeyed north by train. Spring bulbs vied with blossoms on the trees in making the brightest splash of colour, and rows of hawthorns looked as if they had been dusted with snow, so dense were their flowers. The weather turned noticeably colder as the train chugged straight up the centre of England, and Catherine shivered,

'How do they stand it, living here all the time?' Joe laughed,

'But this is springtime! I could have brought you here in winter. I've heard the trains get stuck in snow drifts sometimes!' Catherine shivered anew. But the scenery was certainly spectacular, the hills and mountains they passed reminiscent of the lower slopes of the Himalayas, or the hill country round Simla.

Eventually the train pulled into York with a loud hiss of steam. Craning out of the window, Joe could see James and Lucy standing on the far end of the platform; Lucy distinguishable by her golden head; but James, he realised with a shock, had gone completely white.

The journey from the station to Bensham Manor was filled with non-stop chatter, so that the visitors hardly had time to look around at the impressive countryside.

'Never mind,' thought Joe, 'we'll get a chance while we are here,' for there was so much to say.

'How is….?'

'Is the cantonment….?'

The questions and answers tumbled over themselves, but then suddenly they were there, sweeping up a broad drive lined with stately elms. The house could be seen as they emerged from the trees, built of grey stone, as craggy as the moors surrounding it. There had been a house on the site for centuries, but this one had been built in the Reign of Queen Ann, and was impressive with its massive symmetry. Three stories rose in perfect balance, the windows on the ground floor being huge, while those at the top were no more than dormers. At the exact centre of the building, a double stairway curved elegantly up to a massive wooden front door.

As the carriage pulled up, the door opened ponderously, and a butler stood waiting to greet them, awesome in his dignity. Black frock coat and white gloves adorned a figure as stiff and unyielding as the granite from which the house had been built.

'Good day Sir, Madame, Sir, Madame,' as the foursome ascended the sweep of the left hand stair.

'Don't be fooled by the exterior; he's got a heart of gold,' whispered Lucy to Catherine, though Catherine privately thought that he must keep it well hidden!

Over the next few days, the main impression that the visitors had of the house was the large number of people it seemed to contain. After seemingly endless introductions had left their heads reeling, Lucy took pity on a bewildered Catherine and carried her off to a bedchamber to explain. As Catherine moved about, removing an elegant little hat that had perched at a dashing angle over one eyebrow, Lucy sat back on the enormous four poster bed, and begun,

'When we arrived here from India, Gerald's widow, Elspeth had been running the estate efficiently. In fact we had the distinct impression that that she had been doing so for some time before his death! Of course, it had been her marital home and she had raised six girls here. There was a son, but the poor little thing died in infancy. Well, as James saw it, he couldn't possibly throw them out, even to the Dower House across the estate. We all had a long talk about it, and James suggested she stay. After all, the house is big enough, God knows!'

'But does it work?' queried Catherine, 'after all, two women running things; isn't it awkward?'

'It might be with anyone else but Elspeth. She fought the suggestion at first, probably for the reasons you just mentioned, but in the end agreed to give it a try. I couldn't help but see the relief on her face. She had still got three girls unmarried, and it would not have been easy to launch them from the dower house. Anyway, to cut a long story short, we came to an amicable arrangement about who should do what, and so far it's worked. And if things get on top of you, there is always a quiet corner where peace can be found!'

'But you said Elspeth had three unmarried daughters, but I'm sure I met many more than that; and some young men too?'

'Yes, that's so, for the foolish young women fell in love with younger sons; very unreasonable of them! So here they are while they save up for a home of their own. I am so glad you're here, Catherine, we can escape from it all for a while!'

Catherine was stunned by it all. She had not expected to walk into such a ménage, and she wondered how Lucy coped with it. Lucy, who was used to being chatelaine of her own castle! No wonder there were lines of strain around her eyes, and James' hair had turned white! She said as much to Joe as they were resting together after luncheon, sprawled on a huge four poster bed. Joe lay on his back gazing at the swags of crimson velvet above his head.

'Poor James,' he said with feeling, 'but it's like him to insist that Elspeth stay in the house. He explained something of it over a glass of Madeira. Said that if it hadn't been for the entail laws he wouldn't have come back at all, as he knew Elspeth was capable of running the place. But there you are. The law says that the estate must go to the male heir only. Of course,' he murmured innocently, 'I agree with the law; how can a woman have the intelligence to run….' He didn't finish the sentence as a veritable virago hurled itself on his chest and began to pummel him. In his attempt to defend himself, the virago's bodice became loosened, and one thing led to another, so they didn't get much rest after all!

Dinner that night was a lavish affair, with the table laid for twenty persons. The party consisted on James and Lucy with their sons Charles and Edward, now twenty one and eighteen respectively, their two guests, Elspeth and six daughters, three husbands, the local vicar and three hopeful males trying to woo the unmarried daughters. Catherine's head reeled with the effort of trying to remember all their names, so she gave up, staying close to Lucy and Elspeth as pre-dinner drinks were dispensed by the formidable butler. He was, as Lucy described, 'a treasure' as he handled orders with consummate ease and an aplomb that had to be admired.

At dinner, Catherine found herself seated between James and the vicar, who she had been told was Reverend Alan Forman. He was in his late forties, with a high domed forehead and bushy side whiskers. Pale grey eyes peered out from beneath eyebrows, which gave a slightly cross look, which was at variance with his mild mannered speech, She thought that she intercepted one or two languishing glance cast at Elspeth seated the full length of the table away, but thought perhaps it was her over active imagination. But a little judicious questioning elicited the information that he was a bachelor of long standing, so perhaps after all?

At the far end of the table, Joe sat between Lucy and Elspeth, and was thoroughly enjoying himself. They were both intelligent women who delighted in the cut and thrust of good conversation, and their discussion ranged from world events to literature and back again.

Along both sides of the table sat the younger generation, Elspeth's children and 'hangers on', and Charles and Edward Willoughby. The older boy had shot up since Joe had seen him last, until he topped his father by a good inch. He had his mother's golden hair, cut neatly with a centre parting, and then curling romantically either side of his intelligent forehead. He also had his mother's brown eyes, an attractive combination in the lad as well as his mother! Joe caught snatches of banter from that area of the table suggesting that Charles was very much a lady's man as he flirted shamelessly with the oldest of his unmarried cousins. His brother Edward was quite different from his ebullient older sibling. He had his father's combination of brown hair and green eyes, but his was a retiring nature. He had hardly uttered a word throughout the meal, though Joe thought he caught him gazing soulfully at the youngest of his cousins, a sprightly young lady, inaptly named 'Peace'. There was nothing peaceful about the seventeen year old with bright blond curls and violet blue eyes, which she used with effect on every male in her vicinity, including, Joe noted with amusement, himself!

The lengthy meal finally came to an end with a wonderful confection capped with a mélange of fruit, and waistcoat buttons and stays cried out to be eased. The ladies disappeared in the direction of the drawing room to enjoy some tea, while the menfolk were left to their port and brandy and cigars. Ruthlessly excusing them from the younger set and the vicar, James picked up a decanter of port and brandy, and bore Joe away to his den; a cosy room lined with books and two shabby but comfortable armchairs. James poured two generous snifters of brandy and produced two large cigars from a carved wooden box, clearly Indian in origin. He lit their cigars then sat back in his chair with a sigh,

'At last,' he said, 'some peace. I know Lucy will be doing the same for Catherine, so let's take the chance to catch up on all the news. I've enjoyed your letters, Joe, but it's not the same as a face to face chat; for a start, I can't ask questions! Tell me first, how is the Regiment?'

Joe did his best, but admitted that he didn't keep in close touch any more. He did say that the appointment of Colonel Braithwaite was the worst thing that could have happened for their morale, and touched briefly on Catherine's experience when trying to set up her school. James already knew that his old friend Robert Harding had retired to England, ostensibly for his health, but in reality to his inability to work under Braithwaite. James looked saddened at the thought of 'his' beloved Regiment let down by such a bumbling fool!

'But rumour has it that he will be promoted out of harm's way very soon,' said Joe, 'he's supposed to be going to transfer to administrative duties as a Major-General; and not a moment too soon!'

The talk then turned to Joe's work with Rajah Saeed, a much happier topic. Then they discussed the school, which prompted the thought from James that it should have been done years before. Then it was the turn of the children and the recent wedding of Rose and Amar.

Both the brandy and port were sinking low in their decanters when the talk finally turned to James' life since he had left India.

'Y'know Joe,' James murmured, his voice slightly slurred, 'I thought I'd miss the Regiment terribly, but running an estate is not so different.' He chuckled, 'I can still say 'jump to it' and get obedience. Elspeth had done a good job with the help of the estate manager, but the fact is such men don't take kindly to working for a woman, be she capable or not!' Joe smiled in memory of his conversation on that very subject with Catherine earlier; and its outcome, as James continued,

'We must ride out tomorrow. I try to ride every day; keeps me fit, y'know, 'patting his flat belly, 'and of course there's hunting in season. It's not such a bad life, though the house is a trifle crowded, as you've noticed! But we were used to that in India after all, with all those servants! I've even got used to the climate, though that took a while!'

The conversation came to an end with Joe and Catherine's plans once they moved on from Yorkshire.

'Ireland is it?' questioned James, gently. He blew a smoke ring as he stubbed out his cigar, and drained the last of his brandy,

'D'you think that's wise? Memories have a habit of playing you false, and there's been trouble recently; though you might ask when there hasn't been trouble in Ireland! But the Fenians are very active at the moment, and there's Parnell causing trouble with his Land League.' Joe listened politely to the end, but then replied,

'I know that all you say is true and I have followed the political situation on Ireland from news sheets over the years. I also know my childhood home is probably no more, but I've got to go; just once.' James nodded in understanding, and then added,

'I'll show you something tomorrow that will surprise you; and it's all down to a lad called Sean O'Hara.' He saw Joe start, and surmised correctly that he hadn't thought of his former name in many a year,

'Better get used to it again Joe; it's who you'll be looking for is it not?' For once Joe had no answer.

Next morning James mounted Joe and Catherine on two of the extensive stable's occupants. Joe was up on a handsome bay with a white blaze down his forehead, and one white sock. Catherine was given a spirited little chestnut mare. She was dressed in a dashing new riding habit, topped with a curly brimmed bowler. The look of admiration in both men's eyes did wonders for her ego! Even Lucy exclaimed at the chic ensemble.

They trotted out together until they reached a long, wide sweep of bridle path filled with soft earth. They gave their horses their heads and the four of them thundered along at a brisk gallop. Afterwards, they walked the horses as James led them round the estate, pointing out small hamlets and the variety of crops in the fields that were being experimented with. Whenever they passed someone, James stopped for a word, and as in his former life in the Regiment, he knew them all by name, details of their families, ailments and aged parents! No wonder his men always adored him, thought Catherine.

Almost at the end of their tour, they came across a large blockhouse, not unlike a barrack block in design, though smaller in size. James dismounted and invited the rest of them to do so. Lucy was smiling broadly but did not want to spoil her husband's surprise by saying anything. James led the way inside where the visitors could see a dozen beds ranged along both sides of the room, each with a locker and a tall boy beside it. At the far end of the main room was another one, the open door revealing cooking facilities. Obviously the blockhouse was a self contained unit, but what was its purpose? But then Joe and Catherine's eyes were drawn to a plaque above the large double doors through which they had entered; it bore the legend, 'The Sean O'Hara Home for Irish Orphans'! The words swam before Joe's eyes as he tried to focus properly until they became clear again. Catherine knew that he had had that name before coming to India, but she was as puzzled as he. Eventually a chuckle broke through their musings,

'This is all down to you, Joe. When I left for India all those years ago, I was determined to do something for the numerous orphans that the famine had caused. D'you remember two servants from that house in Dublin?' Joe nodded, still looking dazed, 'well I left them some money, and with my father and brother's help, brought twelve orphans here to learn husbandry. When they were grown, they were given the chance to return to Ireland or stay. Since then, they have been a succession of such children, all given the choice to return to Ireland, stay here as land workers, or be given money for a passage to America or Australia. I have to say, most of 'em chose America!'

'I....I....don't know what to say,' and Joe turned away as tears flooded his eyes; he was wholly overcome by the generosity and foresight of his friend and mentor who had tried to help his own beleaguered countrymen. He heard Catherine's low voiced question,

'Are the good servants still here, James?'

'Sadly no. They died within a year of each other some ten years ago. But they were replaced by equally caring people.'

'Where are the children now?'

'They're out and about round the estate. They spend a year at a time learning different skills. When they reach sixteen they move on. This block is only for boys, the girls stay at the house and learn domestic duties or farming skills, it's up to them.'

Joe finally mastered himself, but could not trust himself to speak and simply grasped James' hand.

'Don't thank me,' said James, his own voice somewhat husky with emotion, it was Gerald and Elspeth who did it all.'

'But it was *you* who thought of it,' countered Joe, finding his voice at last, 'I always knew you were an exceptional man, and this is but the final proof. James waved the sentiment away, as overcome as Joe.

They stayed a full month, but even that did not seem long enough to see and do all they wanted. They visited local sighs, and spent a few days in York; just the four of them, which was a welcome break from the busy mansion. Lucy was move to exclaim,

'Elspeth is wonderful, but she's not exactly restful!' Indeed, for all her diminutive size and figure rounded by seven pregnancies, she was a veritable dynamo. Even in the evening when the rest of them leaned back in relaxation, watching the young ones perform on the pianoforte, or playing games of Spillikins, Whist or Fox and Geese, Elspeth would be busy with her fingers, sewing or tatting, or doing delicate crochet work for her latest grandchild. No, not a restful figure!

'Must be a feature of short women,' said Joe wickedly, earning him a sharp slap on the wrist from his wife's fan. They were at a dance in the assembly rooms, and Joe privately thought that their ladies were the best looking in the room

The visit was over all too quickly and sadly Joe and Catherine took their leave. James told them that as soon as Charles and Edward were old enough to take over the estates, he and Lucy would go on their travels, like his parents before him, and perhaps would come to see them in India. He did not mention that both sons were talking of joining the army, but only time would tell. Catherine took an affectionate leave of Lucy, a woman she had long admired, but now had grown very fond of. Elspeth and her entire brood, down to the newest infant gathered to see them off, and the round of hugs and kissed seemed to go on interminably. But at last they were waved off down the drive of elms, taking a last look at the elegant Queen Ann house as the carriage turned into the roadway beyond.

They travelled to Liverpool by carriage, staying overnight at an inn along the way and embarked on a small steamer to take them across the Irish Sea to Dublin. Joe began to feel more and more nervous as his final destination approached; what would he find, how would he feel? Unanswerable questions. Part of him cried out to leave well alone, and take a train from Liverpool back to London, and forget about Ireland. He said as much to Catherine, who promptly agreed, worried at the haunted look on her husband's face. Perversely he decided to go on.

The seagulls were shrieking over Dublin Harbour, just as they had the day he left. He remembered the words that had sounded in his head, 'Sean O'Hara's dead; Joseph Harrington lives' over and over. But just who was coming back?

They stayed in a hotel in the fashionable part of Dublin, well away from the slums. This part of the city was unfamiliar to Joe, so it did not touch him in any way. But what did touch him was the hear English said with an Irish lilt, or even the spoken Irish language.

'I'm going out,' he said to Catherine.

'D'you want me to come?' He shook his head and left the room. Catherine watched his retreating back with a worried frown. In Bombay and then London he had done the same, and all had been well; but this was Ireland and Dublin! But she could not bring herself to interfere. This was his chance to slay his dragons, and finally put his past to bed forever, and he had to face the task alone. Tomorrow she would ask him to take her to her father's grave, but today was his. She sighed and concentrated on unpacking. She seemed to have gathered more and more outfits wherever they had stayed and her luggage seemed to have expanded almost out of control.

Joe wandered through the streets, not at all sure where he was going. At some point in his rambling he found himself under a sign that said 'Henrietta Street', and recalled Mrs. Markham who had him picked up and brought into her kitchen when he had been close to collapse. He eyed the elegant facades with their fanlights over the front doors and the wrought iron railings where the steps led down to the servants' basements. It came slowly into his memory, the freezing cold night when he had stumbled along here, exhausted and hungry, and had fallen down some kitchen steps. He could not identify the particular house, and wondered if the handsome lady who had ensnared the younger James Willoughby still lived here?

The thought did not entertain him long and he wandered further and came across the Liffey. Fishing boats still bobbed up and down, but alongside them now were more steam ships at their moorings than sailing boats. He crossed a bridge, and found himself entering the slum district. Was it on that quay that he and his father stood to register for Public Work? He couldn't be sure. He wandered through the slums where single rooms in squalid tenements housed whole families.

'Nothing really changes at all!' he thought as he looked about him and inhaled the foetid air. He was accustomed to extreme poverty; had grown up with it; saw it every day in Kotepore, Delhi or Bombay; had recently seen it in London and York; but Dublin seemed to crown them all for the sheer scale of it. The squalor, the filth, the smell all reached absolute heights here in the land of his birth; or had he simply forgotten?

His smart jacket and trousers were attracting a great deal of attention as he walked, and looking down he found himself surrounded by a mob of children. Emaciated faces peered out from beneath tangled hair, bellies distended by malnutrition, and sticklike arms ended in claw-like hands. Those hands now reached out beseechingly. One head was red-gold beneath the dirt, and the old-young eyes a cerulean blue. Trying not to inhale the foetid air too deeply, he fumbled in his pocket he pulled out a handful of coins. He tried to dole them out, but gave up as he was being jostled so flung them down in the mire. He strode away as fast as possible. What was the matter with him; had he grown fastidious in his old age?

They spent the next day tracking down the cemetery where William Lynch's remains had been laid to rest, and it was Catherine's turn to be nostalgic and melancholic.

But then it was time for the final journey. Joe hired a carriage, and early the next morning they set out from Dublin, moving southwards at a smart pace. He observed to Catherine that the road was much better than the one he used to trudge back and forth to his work; perhaps it too was a product of those days?

It was a lovely day; June was well advanced and the air was warm and balmy.

'Just like spring in Kotepore," sighed Catherine contentedly. She looked about appreciatively, noting the distant mountains and the massed wild flowers that lined the road. 'How far is it?' she asked, as much to rouse Joe from his reverie as the wish to know.

'About ten miles, but we should see Kilgarth first.'

They drove in silence for a while, the beauty all around catching Catherine's breath; she had not known that the Irish countryside was so lovely!

Presently, Joe spoke in a voice devoid of feeling,

'We should be going past Kilgarth by now.' All around them were fields where sheep grazed contentedly. One black face ewe looked up at them as they passed by, her half-grown lamb running in panic to its mother.

'Perhaps you've mistaken the landmarks; it's been a long time,' offered Catherine tentatively. Joe did not answer.

They swept around a bend, and there before them was a small lough, glistening in the sunshine. Behind the water, a hill rose gently, a stream running from a spring high above them, feeding the lough. Nearer them as the land fell away eastwards, the bright green of the grass proclaimed a marsh, and the scars of old turf cuttings were clearly visible. The sides of the hill rippled with bright green wheat, the tips already turning light gold in the hot sun. Above the wheat stretched an area of bracken, and beyond that a stretch of turf was starred with flowers as though dusted with icing sugar. At the top of the hill stood a clump of trees, and Catherine thought she could make out the chimneys of a large house behind them. She whispered softly,

'Why, it's beautiful, Joe.' But when she looked at Joe's face, she knew something was dreadfully wrong. Hi voice sounded strangled,

'This is it; this is Clonarty.'

There was not a trace of a house or cottage to be seen; not a hearth, not a stone; nothing. The road swept on through the cultivated fields and then skirted the bog before disappearing over the brow of another low hill as it continued south. Catherine looked into her husband's bleak face, and her heart stirred with pity for him,

'Are you sure?' he got down from the carriage and absently helped his wife down too. He walked away and eyed the lough, noting the willows still growing down to the edge. His eyes followed the line of the hill. This was it; there was no doubt in his mind at all. Up there circled by the stand of trees was Danforth House, but of Clonarty and Kilgarth, and doubtless Colkenny as well, there was no trace. The landlord had grasped the opportunity offered by the famine, and cleared the land. The land that had been farmed by O'Malley's, O'Hara's and Murphy's since time out of mind had disappeared under the acres of sheep grazing and rippling, alien wheat. He felt sick inside.

He looked about him trying to conjure up the cluster of cottages, his own on the edge of the group. Each of them would have their pile of pig manure outside, and barefoot, ragged children would be playing. Time romanticized the memory, and he forgot the squalor and the stench, no better than that of Dublin. He only remembered the sunshine and the soft sweeping mists. Those ragged children would have played tag on the slopes of the benign hill, and then tumble into their cottages to eat potatoes boiled in their skins and tossed in buttermilk, the sweet-sour taste bringing his taste buds to life. As Joe stood, lost in memories, a man walked down the hill, following the sparkling stream. He was short and thickset, dressed in a rough fustian jacket and trousers held up by string. A bowler hat perched precariously on top of a thatch of brown hair, and a dew drop was stitched to the end of his bulbous, pitted red nose. He strode towards Joe and Catherine, a shillelagh balanced on one shoulder; he shifted it to rest on the ground and addressed them aggressively,

'What are you about? Don't yer know yer trespassing?' Joe looked at the man in a daze,

'O'Leary; is that you?' The man grunted,

'O'Leary? Who're yer talking about? It's O'Shaunnessy; if it's anything to you.'

'Trespassing?' queried Joe, 'I used to live here!' O'Shaunnessy looked puzzled. His intellect was not powerful, but the strangers' mode of dress, and Joe's clipped English speech proclaimed 'upper class'; so what did he mean 'lived here'?

'What are you meaning, ere? Up at the Big House? Is it so? Before himself perhaps?' That was it; the stranger was just trying to confuse. But no, the stranger was speaking again,

'I lived right here,' and leaving the road, he strode through the wheat decisively now. Then he stopped and stood with his legs astride,

'Right here,' he repeated. O'Shaunnessy snorted,

'No-one's lived 'ere for over twenty five years, 'n I've been agent for most of 'em. I suggest you look elsewhere. Good day to you now; you should be on your way.' He didn't really know what to make of Joe and the lady with him, but decided that discretion was definitely the better part of valour, though the man was probably touched in the head! Unable to help himself, he touched his forelock, and hefting the shillelagh back onto his shoulder, and strode away up the hill on bowed legs.

Joe watched the man go with sombre gaze. He looked at the beauty around him and as he did so, a cloud swept across the sun and a swift shower of rain fell on them. It was a soft Irish shower, not the vigorous deluge of Indian rain; a mist not a monsoon. He stood there blinking away the tears and knew that he had not found what he had come looking for. James had been right; he had come searching for Sean O'Hara, but he had died at this very spot, outside the sod cottage in which had lain his mother and brother. It was Joe Harrington who had stood up and faced the world, who had learned that places and possessions were not important, it was people that mattered. Loved ones like wives and children, and good friends like the Willoughby's, the Swales' and the Khan's, they were the most important things in the world.

It was Joe Harrington who turned and strode to his wife and held his arms out to her. She came into them as she always did. He rested his chin on her shining hair and gazed speculatively up the hill,

'Catherine larla,' not so strange that it was the Indian endearment should spring to his lips rather than the Irish one,

'Yes Joe?'

'Let's go home.'

'Oh yes please Joe.'

The man lay in bed, the noises of the household muted in his ears. How long had he lain here? Four days, five, a week? His tired mind could not remember so he gave up the struggle. In all that time he had not been left alone.

Usually it was Catherine who sat by his bed holding his hand, her eyes reddened with weeping. Why did she cry? Or perhaps it was not weeping, just tiredness, as she seemed to be there every time he opened his eyes. When had her hair become touched with grey? He felt a little aggrieved that she had grown older without telling him. There wasn't much grey, just wingtips of silver dusting the temples. He knew that his own hair was completely white, in the manner of red heads; but at least he hadn't lost it like Adam, who was left with the merest fringe which gave him the look of a tonsured monk. He had told him so the last time they had spent an evening together, but Adam had not risen to the teasing, and had merely remarked,

'Losing hair or turning white; it really doesn't matter old friend. It just means that we are both getting old!'

Joe stirred, trying to ease his aching buttocks. That was the problem with lying in bed for days on end like an invalid; it made his bottom sore! He must tell Catherine when she came in. Where was she? Just when he wanted to talk to her she wasn't there. He wanted to ask her if he was an invalid. The figure seated across the room was unfamiliar. Why wasn't it Nancy or Louise, who were usually there if Catherine wasn't? He felt petulant, like a querulous old man. There, that was the second time he had used the expression. How old was he? He stirred his sluggish brain to work it out. Today was special; he'd heard them talking about it; New Year's Eve. Tomorrow would not be just a new year, but a new century! That was it; it was December 31st 1899. Soon he would be seventy. A tear of self-pity stood in the corner of his eye as he realised that he wouldn't be around to witness the twentieth century.

What changes would there be? Victoria still crouched on her throne. She'd had a Jubilee; when was it; 1877? She should have given way to her son long ago, but it was said that she hated him, blaming him for causing her husband's death, the irreproachable Albert. If she'd loved him so much, why hadn't she named him King instead of a mere 'Consort'? And she talked of India as 'The jewel in the Crown', but had never bothered to visit; not one royal toe had stepped ashore from one of her grand ships.

He peered again at the figure seated quietly reading from a small book. From the veil and wimple he decided that she was a num from the convent on top of the hill. He had been right about that; soon after the Mutiny was all over, a new set of nuns had arrived from the Mother Convent in far away Limerick. The Reverend Mother had been just like Mother Theresa; perhaps they were all of a breed, with a stern exterior hiding a soft heart? The new band of God's missionaries had attacked their work with a zeal that left them all breathless, and had opened a brand new hospital within a year of their arrival. Perhaps the sister sitting so calmly with him was a nursing sister? Was he so ill then?

He tried to grin to himself, but grimaced as the pain in his chest made it difficult to breathe. When had that started? Wasn't it during the last hot season when he and Catherine had gone to their favourite spot in Kashmir? They had followed the prevailing fashion and had had a houseboat built and moored it on Nagin Lake. They had spent several peaceful weeks there, alone except for the usual bevy of servants. Then one day he had decided they should go pony trekking as they had done when the children were young. Catherine had foolishly said that he might be little too old for it, a remark he had treated with the contempt it deserved, and had made the arrangements. Two days later they had been climbing steadily towards the Apharwat Peak. They had passed the Alpather Lake where ice could be seen floating, even though it had been July, and the scenery was simply spectacular. They had been about half way up when Joe had experienced a shortness of breath and had turned to Catherine to suggest a short rest. She had been about to make a tart reply about him being 'fit for his age' when she had caught sight of his grey complexion and hastily agreed. After their rest, she had insisted that they turn back for Gulmarg, claiming it had all been too much for her. He had thankfully agreed and they had returned to their houseboat for the rest of their time there. He had not told Catherine about the pain in his chest; like a flower opening it had been, expanding and growing.

But that had been months ago! He had felt fine since they had returned to Kotepore in October, and resumed their usual social life. He had retired long before and there was no need to overexert himself. Even polo was enjoyed from a spectator's chair these days, though he believed he could still show these youngsters a thing or two! Then suddenly it was Christmas and this particularly special New Year. They had all come.

Rose and Amar had brought their brood from the Carlton Estate. Amar had been running it for the last seven years since John had died, closely followed by Dharshi. Who was it that said mixed marriages never worked? That one certainly had, and he strongly suspected that Dharshi had become suttee in her own quiet fashion, and left the world with the minimum of fuss.

How many children did Rose have now; four, or was it five? He must get Moti to have a quiet word with her before she ruined her health with constant childbearing. But Moti had gone too; swept away by India's periodic curse, cholera. It was a hot season a few year before. She had stayed behind as she had taken to in the latter years.

'I am used to the hot weather,' she would say when Joe pressed her to come to the hills or the houseboat with them. So she had stayed behind and succumbed to the cholera that had raged through Kotepore while they were away. Ashok had fought it off with the resilience of youth, as little Moti could not. By the time they returned, she had been burned at the nearby ghat and her ashes scattered on the river to become one with it when it met the Holy Ganges.

Ashok had been a young man then, and Joe had given him enough money to set himself up in business, He had a suspicion that Moti would not have allowed it, but he wanted to help the boy. He had taken it with tears in his huge brown eyes, so like his mother's,

'Thank you Sahib, You have been like a father to me.' Touched, Joe had replied,

'I hope so Ashok; after all you were born on the same day as my Rose, so you have been like another son.' He had done well, young Ashok; though not, of course, so young any more. He was over forty now with a round little Hindu wife and a parcel of children of his own. He had not turned out a badmash like his father, and his business of buying handicrafts from all over India and shipping them to England where the fashion for such goods was waxing strong had made him very wealthy.

But the cholera that had taken Moti had also taken Gopi. Gopi, who had been with him since he first trekked across India. Gopi, who had taught him to squat comfortably on his hunkers and smoke bidis, cupping the thin cigarillos in his palm; and who had taught him about dharma and karma. But while Joe had grown up and out, Gopi had stayed short to the end of his days, with his gleaming smile and black hair glossy with coconut oil, thin legs exposed by his dhoti. He had stayed behind with Moti, for whom he had nursed an unrequited passion; had caught cholera with her and had died with her.

Wasn't that the same year that he had received a letter from Lucy in the wilds of Yorkshire, informing him that his friend and mentor, James Willoughby had died. So many deaths that year that he had unable to bear it and had been snappy and irascible for weeks on end, until Catherine had lost her temper and told him sharply to remember his loved ones who were alive, and would likely leave him if he went on much longer. That had shaken him out of his depression; she had always known how to handle him!

Joe stirred again in the bed. Where was Catherine? He was feeling peevish and the stupid nun did not seem to notice his discomfort; indeed she seemed to have fallen asleep for her breviary had slipped to the floor.

He could the sound of male voices now. Perhaps it was Robert come to visit. They had all been here at Christmas when he had eaten too much of the rich curries and side dishes, and had felt the dull ache of indigestion and the return of the searing pain in his chest which had then travelled down his left arm. He had lost consciousness then, waking up to find himself in bed with Catherine weeping all over his nightshirt. His voice testily telling her to leave him alone had startled everyone, crowded into his bedchamber, for he could see them all behind Catherine, peering and sighing.

Robert; there was a son to be proud of. Joe had sent him to Calcutta to study at the University. After he had graduated he had entered the Indian

Civil Service and had risen rapidly. Indians were beginning to take over, which was as it should be, but Robert had done well in the meantime.

He had argued about it with Saeed, who insisted that the European was a better organiser and administrator than the Indian, and it had been Joe who had defended the Indian side. He insisted that they hadn't had a chance to prove themselves since Clive had taken over. Even though he loved this country, he couldn't shake off the feeling that he and his kind were intruders.

'You mark my words,' he had told Saeed, 'your people will rise again one day and kick us all out, you'll see! Like that fellow; what's his name? The one who's gone to South Africa to practice law and is busy fighting for the rights of the coloured people there? Gandhi, that's it!'

But then Saeed had become more English than the English of late. He had, in the end, sent all three sons to school in England, though like John Carlton, he had chosen the school in the West County, rather than Eton where he had suffered so much. The three in turn came home enthusing about cricket and polo and very little else. Why, it had been Saeed who had encouraged the big Christmas party. When Joe had protested that he wasn't even a Christian, he had laughed and said,

'Any excuse for a party, old boy!' just like any upper class snob.

But, thought Joe sadly, after a few years of improvement, Saeed had let himself go again, and was now thoroughly corpulent, his face puffed and pasty. Joe had told him recently that he was heading for a seizure; ironic that it was he who had succumbed! That would appeal to Saeed's rather cruel sense of humour!

More voices, but when would they come? He had a sudden desperate urge to see Catherine, but striving to keep calm and breathe evenly, he thought about his other children.

Daniel the dreamer; the one who most shared his love of literature. He had gone to Chris Day in Delhi to train as a journalist. Chris was famous now; his 'Tales of India' was reputed to be found by the Queen's bedside. Certainly Chris had had no need to work for many years, but before he retired, he had trained Daniel who had followed him as editor in due time. Chris' own son had not been at all interested. Daniel had made a name for himself too, but as a poet. Joe couldn't imagine where he had got the talent from, but had scribbled rhyming couplets from an early age. Perhaps it was from his Irish heritage, like that other poet who'd been making a name for himself; Yeats wasn't it?

Daniel had been here for Christmas, but Joe didn't know whether he had returned to Delhi. He hoped not, for he had a particular fondness for this son. But then, he had a particular fondness for them all! But how could he know anything when he lay here helpless as a child and no-one to attend him.

The only one who had not been home for Christmas was Tom. He had been a harum-scarum young man; in and out of scrapes. But then he had startled everyone by joining the army. He had been sent to England to train and had returned dressed in the 'khaki' that had replaced the bright scarlet of Joe's days. He had not liked the colour, declaring it drab and mud-coloured. Tom had winked and said,

'But that's the idea, Papa; stop us making such easy targets!' Then he added wickedly,

'But it doesn't hide the blood like the red!' earning a frown from his father and a squeal from his mother. He had gone to the Sudan and distinguished himself in the fighting there after the world had been shocked by the loss of Khartoum. Then he had returned to Kotepore and spent some time in skirmishes in Afghanistan, where the British were bedeviled with the thought of a Russian invasion. Finally he'd been called up with half the Regiment to fight against the Boers in South Africa.

'Don't worry Papa. It's only a bunch of farmers; it'll be over by Christmas!' He had gone as a Captain but had confided to Joe that he hoped to return a Major.

'At least he'll be promoted or not out of merit and not the ability to pay,' Joe had thought proudly, remembered James Willoughby's words so many years before. At least that had changed. He had left in October and there had not been a word since.

The pain in his chest was getting worse, and a sudden panic caused the breath to catch in his throat. The nun started, took one look at her patient and hurried from the room; she had been asleep for five minutes.

Joe gazed out of the window. The edges were scalloped and fretted with pierced wood in an attractive design. Outside, the sky was the bright clear blue of an Indian winter, and an earlier shower of rain had left the air smelling fresh and clean. Strange; he thought he could hear a lark.

'They don't have larks in Kotepore,' he muttered. Hurrying footsteps could be heard and Catherine rushed in. She had slept for only two hours in the last twenty four, and then had risen to greet Rose, who had taken the children for a walk with their ayah. They had been fretful and could not understand at all why they had to keep their voices hushed. Nor did they understand why Grandpa kept to his bed and not play with them as he usually did, or tell them wonderful fairy stories of princesses and giants.

Nancy had been there too, ready to attend the sickroom in case Catherine wanted more sleep. Her heart bled for her friend, but there was nothing she could do. She had been the first to spot Joe's heart attack, as he had clutched his chest and slid sideways from his chair. She could only try and be supportive as she could in the days or perhaps months that were to come.

Daniel and Robert were talking together in subdued whispers, even Robert's ebullience temporarily quelled. They had all turned sharply when the nun had run in, nearly tripping over her floor length habit,

'Mrs. Harrington, I think you had better come!' They all followed Catherine to the bedside.

'Catherine,' the blue lips moved, but no sound emerged. She knelt and took his hand; it was ice cold. She bent her head to catch the slightest sound,

'Can you hear it, a lark?' She shook her head, not sure if she had heard properly.

Joe's eyes fixed on the window. It expanded so he could only see the blue of an Irish summer sky. He could see a sheet of water at the bottom of a hill. A dark haired man had his arm around a woman. She was tall and slender, with tumbling red-gold hair and stood with proud carriage. She held two girls by the hand. One was about seven years old with a fall of straight brown hair that looked like a flowing river in the sunshine. She smiled a shy, secret smile. The other child was two, a blue eyed imp with red-gold curls and dimpled cheeks. A boy stood next to the man; a boy with dark hair and eyes. There was one person missing. He turned to Catherine,

D'you see them? Goodbye larla. I must go. I love you.' And then, though no-one in the room heard it,

'Wait for me!' for the figures were dissolving in the mist that swept down from the hill, 'Mam, Pa, wait for me.'

The only sound in the room was of women weeping.

Historical Notes and Acknowledgements

I have tried to be as historically accurate as possible in recounting events of the Irish Famine and the Indian Mutiny. Any liberties I have taken with dates and facts were purely for the sake of the story! For facts and figures of the Irish Famine, I am indebted to 'The Great Hunger' by Cecil Woodham-Smith. Likewise for details of the Indian Mutiny, I drew heavily on 'The Indian Mutiny' by John Harris.

The only significant departure from established facts was the identity of the person who carried a message from Campbell to Outram in Lucknow, thereby easing the passage of Campbell through Lucknow. This event actually occurred, but the message was not carried by the fictional Joe Harrington. It was, in fact, the same lowly clerk who had distinguished himself in the mining operations, Thomas Henry Kavanagh. He was tall and golden haired, with piercing blue eyes. Outram did not believe he could pass as an Indian, but Kavanagh stained his skin with lamp-black and oil, and dressed in shabby Indian clothes, with a turban covering his head. He succeeded in fooling Outram, who promptly agreed to his carrying the message when his identity was disclosed. The rest is history!

There are several family anecdotes used in the text, as my grandmother and mother were born and raised in India, and had many little tales to lean on. I hope they will forgive my stealing them for my tale. My great-grandfather did leave Ireland in the mid-19th Century and join the British army, and went to India as a very young man. He spent the rest of his life there. He did go to a convent to seek out an Irish girl to marry, and found one who had refused to leave India when her father did. They had many children, but the oldest of them was my grandmother, Rose. My mother was the youngest of their six children.

Indian Words
used in the text

Charpoys	bed frame strung with light rope
Doolies	covered litters for carrying pasengers with poles
Coolies	lowly workers
Munshi	language teacher
Picanninies	small children
Cha	tea
Lungi	skirt like garment made of cloth
Chota hazri	small meal taken in the morning (breakfast)
Tiffin	lunch
Chuldi	quickly
Derzees	tailors
Sepoy	Indian soldier in European service
Ghats	series of steps leading down to a river – usually sacred
Ayah	children's nurse
Sari	traditional Hindu female wear made with continuous strip of cloth
Bunnia	money lender
Bidi	small hand rolled cigarette
Dharma	what is meant to be
Karma	fate
Burra Sahib	notable figure
Syce	groom
Namaste	polite gesture made with the hands touching the forehead
Maidan	large open grassy area outside town

Khitmagars	table attendant
Kala Pani	'black water' (open sea)
Dhobi	washer of clothes
Quisqualis	Rangoon Creeper
Chota peg	small drink
Badmashes	trouble makers
Din	battle cry
Terai	marshy grasslands south of the foothills of the Himalayas
Dak-bungalow	wayside inn
Zenana	women's house (usually for mistress)
Chiks	bamboo blinds
Nautch girl	dancing girl
Chatti	water vessel
Dak-ghari	vehicle for the road
Chupattis	flat bread baked on a griddle
Suttee	the custom of a widow throwing herself on her husband's funeral pyre.
Thugs	tribe of murderers who ambushed wayfarers for their valuables, and killed them by strangulation
Rohilla Raiders	Warlike people from Rohildkhand of Northern India
Sheeshum Tree	Indian Rosewood/hardwood
Choli	midriff bearing blouse
Talkuqdars	landowners
Jemadar	Armed officials of the Zemindars (lords)
Burra-General-Anson	Major General George Anson
Rissal	private army
Ferenghi	foreigner
Nawab	Indian aristocracy
Begum	princess
Mohur trees	Fire trees/flame trees
Imambarra	imposing building
Sowars	mounted troopers
Achkan	long men's jacket, usually worn by upper class Indian

About the Author

Adèle Smith nee Forster, was born in Cawnpore, India, during the last stages of the Second World War. India was also in a state of flux at this time, and shortly after the end of the war, through the efforts of Mahatma Ghandi, became independent. Her family had first taken root in India in the mid1800's when her great-grandfather, Joseph Harrington, left County Cork in Ireland to join the British Army and travelled with them to India. His eldest child was called Rose, and her youngest daughter was the author's mother.

With Partition threatening in India, many familes of British origin decided to repatriate to the United Kingdom, and the author's mother boarded the Lusitania with her two older brothers in 1946, and settled in Chislehurst, Kent. The children were raised by their step-father, Leonard Hunt, when he married their widowed mother on February 14th 1947.

The author received a Grammar School education in Bromley, Kent, and progressed to South Bank University to study Polymer Technology, from where she graduated with honours; the first ever female Polymer Technologist. She worked in the polymer industry for four years before retiring to raise three children. During their early years, she worked part-time as a folk guitar teacher in adult education. She also qualified as a scuba diver in 1968, and became a BSAC Club Instructor and enjoyed teaching in the pool, open water or in the classroom. These activities engendered a love of teaching, and once the children were in full-time education, she studied for a Post Graduate Certificate of Education, which she achieved with Distinction, and began a career as a Further Education Lecturer in Chemistry in Kingston College. She rose 'through the ranks' and finished her career as Head of Science. During those busy years, the author started on 'Of Mists and Monsoons' based on the many anecdotes recounted by her mother from her own growing up years in India. But computers were very limited in those days, and it was difficult to save the manuscript, which languished as hard copy for many years.

After retiring from teaching, Adèle relocated to Koh Samui in Thailand with second husband Wally where she became active with the Rotary Club for the first time in her life. She also became restless to finish the job she had started so many years before, and finally completely edited and retyped the manuscript.